DAHVEED

ALSO BY TERRI L. FIVASH
Historical Biblical Fiction

Joseph: A Story
Ruth and Boaz: Strangers in the Land

THE DAHVEED SERIES

Book 1: *Yahweh's Chosen*
Book 2: *Yahweh's Warrior*
Book 3: *Yahweh's Fugitive*
Book 4: *Yahweh's Soldier*

Forthcoming in the series:

Book 5: *Yahweh's General*
Book 6: *Yahweh's King*

Devotional and Spiritual Life

Myrie's Lord's Prayer
Your Spiritual Toolbox

Visit my web site to order and learn more.
www.terrifivash.com

DAHVEED

YAHWEH'S SOLDIER

BOOK FOUR

BY

TERRI L. FIVASH

Copyright 2012 by Terri L. Fivash

All rights reserved

All rights reserved. No portion of this book may be reproduced, stored in a retrieval system, or transmitted in any form or by any means (electronic, mechanical, photocopy, recording, scanning, or other), except for brief quotations in critical reviews or articles, without the prior written permission of the author.

The author assumes full responsibility for the accuracy of all facts and quotations as cited in this book.

This book was
Edited by Gerald Wheeler
Cover Designed by Rhonda Root - Copyright 2012
Cover art by Olivia Makador
Interior Design Copyright 2012

First printing April 2012
Second printing May 1012
Third printing October 1012

DEDICATION

This book is dedicated to
Sharon
who taught me how to be a soldier for God.

ACKNOWLEDGMENTS

As always I am indebted to many people for their help in the creation of this book. Among them are:

Gerald, Myla, and Katie for their editing skills.

Again to Bethany Bolduc for her last-minute suggestions that sharpened the story.

All my advanced readers, and

Brian Strayer, for being a "minute-man" when I needed one! Thank you.

List of Maps

Maps are found at the end of the book.

The Ancient Near East

Israel

Central Israel

To Parents of Young Readers

Please remember that the audience for whom this book is written is young adult and adult. While the story of David is one of the best known in the Bible, David lived a violent life, and warfare back then was very up-close and personal. A certain amount of blood and gore is unavoidable if I am to remain faithful to the culture of biblical times and the biblical narrative itself.

And again in this book I deal with demonic activity and practices. Please keep this in mind if you choose to read this book to your children.

To the Reader

As in Dahveed 3, there are three main story lines in this book: Jonathan, Dahveed, and Akish of Gath. While there are some points of contact between Jonathan and Dahveed, the main story line involves the interplay between Dahveed and Akish. In the last section of the book, a fourth storyline emerges, that of Abigail. During this last section, PLEASE PAY CLOSE ATTENTION TO INDICATIONS OF TIME. One of the fascinating things about the biblical narrative at this point is the coincidences of time. I have done my best to highlight this in the story.

Please bear with me if you read something that seems like a rabbit trail, unconnected with the story. There are two more books to this series, remember, and many of the things which happened now build toward the next part of Dahveed's life.

And just as a reminder, I am following Dahveed's story as recorded in 1 and 2 Samuel, translations of psalms in the book are my own, and numbers in Dahveed's time were very mushy! See "A Word About . . ." on my web site for further discussion of the above.

Characters in Dahveed 4

Names in **Bold** appear in this book.
Names with an asterick (*) are biblical characters

Abiadan–Sahrah of Ammon, daughter of King Nahash, wife of Jesse, and mother of Abigail and Zeruiah. Deceased.
***Abiathar**–Son of Hakkohen Haggadol Ahimelech. A priest.
Abiaz–Trouble-maker in Heshbon when Ruth was a young woman.
***Abiezer**–Member of Hassar Jonathan's personal guard sent to Dahveed.
*Abigail–Dahveed's half sister, and full sister to Zeruiah. Daughter of Abiadan.
***Abigail of Carmel**–Former wife of Nabal. Gebirah to the Carmel Calebite clans. Dahveed's third wife.
*Abinadab–Jesse's second son by Miriam, his Israelite wife. Half-brother to Dahveed.
*Abishai–Dahveed's nephew, first born of Zeruiah, half-sister to Dahveed.
*Abner–General of Shaul's armies and his cousin.
Achsah–Maid to Michal.
*Adnah– A commander from Manasseh who deserts to Dahveed.
*Adriel–Son of Barzillai. Marries Merab.
Ahaz–Elder of Bethlehem.
***Ahiam**–Habiru sworn to Dahveed.
***Ahibaal**–A Jebusite, loyal to his adon and who first looked for Dahveed on a mule, who now keeps track of Dahveed and advises him.
*Ahimelech–High priest in Nob during Shaul's reign.
***Ahimelek**–A Hittite. One of Davheed's men.
*Ahinoam–Shaul's wife.
***Ahinoam of Jezreel**–Daughter of Ahlai. Sister of Zabad. Dahveed's second wife.
*Ahithophel–see Ahibaal and A Word About . . .
*Ahlai–Father of Zabad, Ahinoam, and Lael. Rival to Nabal.

*Ahor–Canaanite landowner near Shechem. Grandfather to Hushai the Archite.
Ahuzzath–Man who replaces Beor as Seren Manani's scribe.
*Aiah–Father of Rizpah, Shaul's concubine. Lives in Jabesh.
*Ahiezer–Commander of the unit of Shaul's kin who desert to Dahveed
*Akish–Son of Maoch of Gath, who becomes Seren of Gath when his father dies.
Ala–Zelek's sister. Taken by Manani in Ekron and tries to stop her brother from assassinating Hassar Jonathan. Half Ammonite, half Cushite, and blood cousin to Abigail and Zeruiah.
Amarel of Dibon–Man who took Moab's throne during the time of Ruth.
*Amasa–Son of Dahveed's sister Abigail.
*Amasai–Commander of a unit of Benjamites who desert to Dahveed.
*Armoni–Rizpah's first son.
*Araunah–Title for king of Jebus. Used as a name.
Areli–Man from Naphtali in the second unit. Cousin to Cheran.
*Asahel–Dahveed's nephew, third son of Zeruiah. Father of Zebadiah.
Asaiah–Boyhood friend of Dahveed in Bethlehem, son of Telah.
Atarah–Jebusite woman rescued by Dahveed and Ethan. Sister to Ornan. Concubine to Hassar Jonathan.
*Azmaveth–Former bodyguard to the hassar and father of Pelet. One of Dahveed's men.
Baalyaton–Powerful adon in Ekron who becomes Seren.
*Balak–Advisor to King Yira of Moab, four years older than Dahveed and dislikes him.
Baqqush–Envoy from the kingdom of Mari who makes a covenant with Shaul.
*Barzillai–Man from Jabesh in Gilead who buys a lamb from Ruth. Father to Adriel.
Basemath–Maid to Rizpah.
Batashima–Philistine woman dependent on Hassar Jonathan who speaks Yahweh's word to him. Peleth's mother.
Bathsheba–Daughter of Eliam. Granddaughter of Ahibaal.
Ben-Geber–Dahveed's childhood name.
Ben-Shimei–One of Dhaveed's men. Not a nice man. Companion of Hiddai. Son of Hassar Jonathan's cousin.

Characters ~ 11

Beor–Long-time scribe of Seren Manani with a phenomenal memory. Captured by Hassar Jonathan.
Beriah–Gibeonite who comes to take Ishmaiah's place.
*****Bichri**–Man of Benjamin who tries to bully a beggar and is stopped.
'Bijah–Boy in Navyoth who watches the soldiers prophesy.
*****Boaz**–Dahveed's great-grandfather. Ruth's husband.
Bodbaal–Philistine member of Ethan's band. Mute. Brother to Geresh and Peleth.
Bukki–Lahab's father. Landowner in Bethlehem.
Bunah–Scribe to Jonathan Hassar.
Bunni–Scribe to Jonathan Hassar.
Caleb–Habiru member of Ethan's band with twin daughters, Leah and Rachel. Guides Sar Ishvi to Merab's funeral.
Carmi–Homesteader north of Bethlehem. Comes to the gate for Jesse.
Casluh–Youth of Ziklag.
*****Cheran**–Personal attendant to Shaul. Cousin of Areli. Becomes Shaul's armor-bearer.
*****Dahveed**–Jesse's eighth son, anointed to be king for Yahweh. (Dahveed is also a title.)
*****Dara**–Hassar Jonathan's shield bearer.
Dathan–Nagid of the Hebron Calebite clans. Supports Abigail of Carmel.
David–See Dahveed.
Debir–Usurper in Jebus who meets his worse nightmare, the Emmanuel.
Dedan–Faithful guard in Jebus who helps the Emmanuel.
Dishon–Commander of the eighth unit.
*****Dodo**–Father of Eleazar of Benjamin.
*****Dodo**–Father of Dahveed's childhood friend Elhanan.
*****Doeg**–Edomite in Shaul's service who kills the priests.
Dumah–Kin of Ornan and Atarah, who betrays them.
*****El**–Mighty One, God.
*****El Elyon**–God Most High. Worshipped in Jebus.
*****El Shaddai**–God Almighty.
*****Eleazar**–Left-handed swordsman who becomes shield-bearer to Sar Ishvi.
*****Elhanan**–son of Bethlehem's innkeeper. Dahveed's childhood friend and member of his band.

*Eliab–Jesse's first born child, his bekor. Can be greedy. Half-brother to Dahveed.
***Eliahba**–Sar to Seren Manani. Protected and hidden by Yahweh for His use.
***Eliam**–Son to Ahibaal. Joins Dahveed's band at his father's command. Father of Bathsheba.
***Elihu**–Jesse's seventh son. Trains to be a scribe. Half-brother to Dahveed.
***Elika**–One of Dahveed's men. From En-harod. Friend of Shammah.
***Eliphelet ben Ahasbai**–Steals from Dahveed. Then joins him. From Abel Beth-Maacah.
Elyaton–Name that Dahveed uses when he goes to Jonathan's wedding.
***Eshbaal**–Shaul's fourth son, younger than Michal. Very good administrator.
Ethan–Grandson of Patah and Gaddi. Bodyguard for Ruth. Leader of the Habiru near Bethlehem and Dahveed's teacher.
***Ezer**–Commander of the Gaddite spear men who join Dahveed.
Ezra–Man from Judah whose family needs help. Deceased.
Gabri–Honest jewel merchant in Jebus.
***Gad**–Roeh Shamuel's servant.
Gaddi–Grandfather to Ethan. Life-time slave to Boaz's house.
Gadmilk–Seren of Ashdod. Likes the women and money from Tyre.
Gaham–Personal bodyguard to Hassar Jonathan who takes Abiezer's place.
Gareb–Man of Judah who joins Dahveed.
Gedor–Man of the second unit who died saving Sar Malchi.
*Gera–Benjamite whose clan does not like Dahveed.
Geresh–Philistine Habiru of Ethan's band. Brother to Bodbaal and Peleth.
*Goliath–Traditional name of the champion of the Philistines whom Dahveed kills.
Hadar–Ishmaelite merchant with Gebirah Abigail for a customer.
***Hanan**–Habiru and one of Yahweh's Arrows. Dahveed's best scout.
Hanabaal–Seren of Gaza. Principle Seren of the Five Cities Alliance.
(the) Hassarah–Title of respect given to Ruth, Dahveed's great-grandmother.
Hannah–Sister of Ira, and great-granddaughter of Shamuel.
Hazzel–Akish of Gath's sister. Ittai's mother.

Characters ~ 13

Heber–A Habiru dahveed near the ravines of Gaash.
*Hezro–Former commander in Nabal's household. Comes to Dahveed with Abigail.
*Hiddai–unsavory man who tries to use Dahveed before joining him. Shows loyalty to Dahveed when least expected.
Hod–Balak's father. A Moabite landowner in Bethlehem.
*Hushai–The Archite. Grandson of Ahor and who likes Dahveed.
*Igal–Man from Zobah who exasperates Dahveed, but joins him.
*Ira–Great-grandson of Shamuel, who asked for a song. Brother to Hannah.
*Ira–Man of Judah who joins Dahveed.
Irad ben Omar–Chief elder of Ziklag.
Iscah–Woman in Shaul's clan with a very helpful son.
*Ishmaiah–Gibeonite ark-bearer who becomes one of Dahveed's mighty men.
*Ishvi–Shaul's second son. A sar.
Ishvi ben Ezra–Only survivor of his house. Foster son to Sar Ishvi.
*Ishvi-benob–Kin to Goliath of Gath with four relatives all of whom hate Dahveed.
*Ithmah–Man of Moab who joins Dahveed.
*Ittai–Philistine/Israelite youth bound to Dahveed through circumcision.
*Jaasiel–Abner's son.
*Jaasiel–Friend to Igal, who also joins Dahveed.
Jalam–Overseer to Abigail of Carmel.
Jamin–Ethan's younger brother. A Habiru and one of Yahweh's Arrows.
Jarib–Demoted Commander of the second unit. Executed by Dahveed for his part in the Gibeonite crime.
*Jashobeam–See Josheb.
Jerioth–Sister of Asaiah, and wife of Elhanan. Deceased.
Jemima–Sister of Palti of Gallim who marries Ahiam.
*Jephthah of Tob–Habiru leader in the time of the judges who ruled in Israel.
Jeshua–Leader of the Gibeah band of Habiru.
*Jesse–Dahveed's father. Elder and rich landowner in Bethlehem.
*Jether–Abigail's husband. Ishmaelite trader.
*Jeziel–Son of Azmaveth. Comes to Dahveed in Ziklag.

***Joab**–Dahveed's nephew. Second son of Zeruiah. Wanted by the Egyptians.
***Joash**–Leader of the band of Shaul's kin who desert to Dahveed.
Joel–Habiru dahveed of the Keilah band. Supporter of Ethan. Yahweh's Arrow.
***Jonadab**–Second son of Shammah, and Dahveed's nephew.
***Jonathan**–Dahveed's uncle (brother of his mother).
***Jonathan**–Shaul's oldest son. The Hassar.
***Jonathan**–Dahveed's nephew, son of Shammah.
***Jonathan**–Son of the Habiru Shagay. Yahweh's Arrow.
Jonathan ben Ezra–Son of Ezra who died.
***Joseph ben Jacob**–favorite son of Jacob who became Tate of Egypt.
***Josheb-Basshebeth ben Zabdiel**–Former bodyguard to Hassar Jonathan. One of Dahveed's men.
***Jotbah**–Handmaid and scribe to Gebirah Abigail.
Jozabad–Commander with Adnah of the men of Manasseh who desert to Dahveed.
***Judith**–Maid to Ahinoam and abandoned wife of Balak. Becomes Meribbaal's nurse.
***Kemosh**–god of Moab.
Kemosh-dan–Overlord of Moab when Ruth was a young woman.
***Keren**–Dahveed's mother and Jesse's wife.
Keturah–Gibeonite woman dependent on Dahveed. Sister to Naharai.
***Keziah**–Wife of Dahveed's half-brother Shammah.
***Khay**–Egyptian slave found by Dahveed in the Negev.
***Kish**–Shaul's father.
Kohath–Head scribe under Eshbaal. Killed himself over the Gibeonite crime.
Lael ben Ahlai–Young man who cannot seem to control his spending.
Lahab–Vintner of Bethlehem and son of Bukki. Sets up shop with Raddai.
***Lahmi**–Kin to Goliath of Gath. Brother of Ishvi-Benob. Hates Dahveed. Commander to Akish.
Leah–One of Caleb's twins. Habiru. Loved by Sar Malchi.
Libni–Commander of the tenth unit. Supports Abner.
Lotan–Man of the second unit. A Hittite mastersmith.
***Maacah bat Talmai**–Young daughter of Geshur's king who is amused by Dahveed.

Characters ~ 15

Mahesa–Banish Egyptian officer who serves at the Tabernacle.
Malcath bat Talmai–Older sister of Maacah who is getting married.
Malchi–See Malchi-shua.
*Malchi-shua–Shaul's third son. A sar.
Manani–Seren in Ekron. A cruel man, universally hated and feared.
*Maoch–Father of Akish. Former seren of Gath.
Mari–Messenger sent to Shaul, who is murdered on the way. Also a city-state north of Israel.
*Matred–Handmaid to Gebirah Abigail.
Mattan–Meshullam's son and dahveed after him. Swore his band to Boaz and Boaz's bloodline.
*Mephibosheth–Rizpah's second son.
*Merab–Shaul's oldest child, his bekorah. Wife of Adriel.
Merab bat Ezra–daughter of Ezra of Judah. Deceased.
*Meribbaal–Son of Jonathan Hassar.
Meshullam–Habiru dahveed of Boaz's time.
*Mibhar ben Hagri–Shepherd to Nabal of Carmel who recognizes Dahveed.
*Michal–Shaul's younger daughter and Dahveed's wife.
Milcom–God of Ammon.
Minelek–Philistine Gibeonite overseer of Chephirah, whom Akish meets in Gath.
Miriam–Jesse's Israelite wife.
Mishmannah–One of the Gaddite spear man.
Muwana–Seren of Ashkelon. Ally of Akish.
*Nabal–Nagid of Carmel's Calebite clans. Husband to Abigail. Greedy for honor.
Nadab–Quartermaster of Shaul's army.
*Naharai–Gibeonite man of the second unit. Keturah's brother.
*Nahash–King of Ammon and grandfather of Abigail and Zeruiah. Saves Dahveed.
*Namea–Handmaid to Gebirah Abigail.
Nashon–Shaul's shield bearer, who vanishes.
Natan–Commander of the fifth unit.
Negbi–Treasurer of Keilah. Not necessarily honest.
Nemuel–Jonathan's boyhood friend. Killed by Philistines.
*Ner–Abner's father. Uncle to Shaul.
*Nethanel–Jesse's fourth son, Dahveed's half-brother.

Nimshi–Ethan's youngest son.
*Obed–Ruth's son, Jesse's father. Deceased.
Og of Bashan–very tall man killed in Joshua's time.
*Oholah–Handmaid and scribe to Gebirah Abigail.
***Ornan**–Jebusite youth rescued by Dahveed and Ethan. Brother to Atarah.
Orpah–Foster sister of Hassarah Ruth in Heshbon. Marries a prince.
*Ozem–Jesse's sixth son. Younger twin to Raddai, Dahveed's half brother.
Pallu–Man of the second unit. Good archer.
*Palti of Gallim–Scribe to Sar Ishvi. Brother of Jemima. Is given Michal Sahrah.
*Parai–Slave to Gebirah Abigail who runs away. A tanner. Joins Dahveed.
Pasach–Commander of the eleventh unit.
Pashur–Habiru of Boaz's time and life-time friend of Boaz.
Patah–Old dahveed of the Habiru when Ben-geber is a child. Grandson of Meshullam and grandfather of Ethan and Jamin.
Patisi–Father-in-law of Manani. Very good at persuasion. Dies inconveniently.
Pekah–Son of Zalmon.
Pelet–Son of Azmaveth. Taken by Abner.
Peleth–Former Philistine slave to Hassar Jonathan and overseer for him. Brother of Bodbaal and Geresh.
Puah–Wife of Shagay and mother to Jonathan.
Qas–One of the Amalekite gods.
Qausa–Habiru who accepted money to kill King Shaul. Deceased, but won't stay dead.
Rachel–One of Caleb's twins. Habiru.
*Raddai–Jesse's fifth son. Older twin to Ozem, Dahveed's half-brother.
Ram–Commander of the first unit in King Shaul's permanent forces.
Rapha Clan–Goliath's clan.
*Recheb–Gibeonite from Beeroth. Son of Rimmon to whom Jonathan Hassar gives hesed.
Regem–Son of Ethan. Guide to caravans.
Reu–Man of the second unit. Good engineer.
*Ribai–Israelite slave who married Akish's sister Hazzel. Father of Ittai. Deceased.

Characters ~ 17

*Rimmon–Gibeonite from Beeroth who tried to kill Jonathan Hassar.
***Rinnah**–Man of Ziph who doesn't want Dahveed around.
***Rizpah**–Concubine to King Shaul, from Jabesh in Gilead.
*Ruth–The Hassarah. Wife of Boaz and great-grandmother of Dahveed.
Sakar ben Hissil–Prince of Heshbon and husband of Orpah in Ruth's time.
Samlah–Merchant who is not too picky about where he gets his wares or how he makes his money.
*Samson–Judge in Israel who was captured by the Philistines after betrayal by Delilah.
Samuel–See Shamuel.
***Saph**–Kin to Goliath of Gath, Ishvi-benob and Lahmi. Hates Dahveed.
Saul–See Shaul.
***Shagay**–Habiru and Yahweh's Arrow. Dahveed's first retainer.
***Shammah**–Jesse's third son, Dahveed's half-brother.
***Shammah**–One of Dahveed's men. Friend of Elika. From En-harod.
***Shammah ben Agee**–See Shagay.
***Shamuel**–Roeh, seer, in Israel. Anoints Shaul and Dahveed.
***Shaul**–King of Israel, Jonathan and Michal's father.
Shemel ben Elnaam–Trusted commander to Akish. Loyal to Sahrah Hazzel.
Shepho–Alluph of the Amalekites who lies and gets killed because of Abigail's words.
Sheva–Commander of King Shaul's guard.
*Shimei–Cousin to Jonathan Hassar. Banned from appearing at court. Of Gera's clan.
Shoher–Father of Ethan. Deceased.
***Sibbecai**–Bitter man from Hushah who takes Dahveed's sword. Then joins him.
Sithri–Man of the second unit who can sharpen things well.
Steward of the House of Tahat–Man whom Jonathan Hassar finally finds.
Tahan–Man of the second unit who knows jewelry.
Tahat–Business associate of Dahveed's great-grandfather Boaz.
***Talmai**–Father of Maacah and Malcath. Tries to use Dahveed.
Tamakel–Son of Nahash, father of Ala and Zelek. Deceased.

Tanhum–Hiddeous cripple saved by Dahveed, and appreciated by Jonathan. Father of Ziba.
*Taphath–wife of Jonathan and mother of Meribbaal. From Jabesh. Cousin to Azmaveth.
Telah–Elder in Bethlehem.
Teman–Head elder of Keilah.
Tilon–Caravan master whose caravan, along with himself, is borrowed without him knowing.
Tiras–Very tall Habiru dahveed who finds the Lion of Judah. Brother to Uzzia.
*Tirzah–Plump handmaid to Gebirah Abigail.
Tokhath–Nabal's intelligent and ambitious scribe.
*Uriah the Hittite–Neighbor of Dahveed who joins him and who can teach. A lot.
*Uzzia–Tiras' taller brother who is hostage to Dahveed. From Ashterath in Bashan.
Yah–Short form of Yahweh.
Yahas–Balak's great-grandfather. Son of Abiaz.
Yahoadan–Jamin's daughter. Habiru.
*Yahweh–Israel's God. Has chosen Dahveed.
Yahweh's Arrows–Habiru who have affiliated with Ethan and his band to protect and serve Boaz's bloodline.
*Yira: King of Moab and very wary of Dahveed.
*Zabad ben Ahlai: Disowned son of Ahlai. Brother of Ahimoam. Good fighter. Given to Dahveed.
*Zalmon: Benjamite who finds Dahveed by descending on him. Joins Dahveed.
*Zelek: Unfortunate Ammonite/Cushite who is forced to assassinate Hassar Jonathan. Brother to Ala. Blood kin to Abigail and Zeruiah.
Zemirah: head elder in Bethlehem.
Zeri: Habiru from the Gibeah band. Yahweh's Arrow. Refuses to hunt Dahveed.
*Zeruiah: Jesse's oldest daughter by Abiadan. Mother of Abishai, Joab and Asahel
*Ziba: Son of Tanhum. Brother to Atarah. Unhappy with Jonathan Hassar.
Zorath: commander of the 3rd unit, and supporter of Dahveed.

Habiru lineage:
Meshullam–Mattan–Patah–Shoher–Ethan–Nimshi

Dahveed's lineage:
Salmon–Boaz–Obed–Jesse–Dahveed

Masculine title of respect in Israel–least to most
Geber–Adon/Baal–Sar–Nahsi–Nagid–Melek

Feminine titles of respect–least to most
Geberet–Baalah–Sahrah–Hassarah

Vocabulary

Pronunciations:
A pronounced "Ah." Spelled "ah;" occasionally pronounced as short "A." Spelled "a."
E pronounced as long A. Spelled "ay;" occasionally as short "e." Spelled "eh."
I pronounced as long E. Spelled "ee."
O pronounced as long O. Spelled "oh."
U pronounced as "oo." Spelled "oo."
AI pronounced as long I. Spelled "aye."

Italics indicate the stressed syllable.

Abbi–(*ah*-bee), my father, term of endearment, i.e. Daddy.
Adon–(ah-*dohn*), masculine title of respect: Lord.
Adonai–(Ah-dohn-*naye*), plural of adoni–used exclusively for Yahweh.
Adoni–(ah-dohn-*ee*), my lord.
Aijalon–(Aye-yah-*lohn*), a pass from the hills into the Shephelah about 15 miles west of Jebus.
Alluph–(ahl-*loof*), Amalek masculine title of respect.
Baalah–(bah-*ah*-lah), feminine title of respect: Lady.
Bat–(baht), daughter of, or female descendent of.
Bekor–(beh-*kohr*), first born, masculine.
Bekorah–(beh-kohr-*ah*), first born, feminine.
Ben–(bayn), son of, or male descendent of.
Chinnereth–See Sea of Chinnereth.
Couscous–(*koos*-koos), cooked cracked wheat.
Cuirass–(kwee-*rahs*), armored "shirt" for heavy infantry.
Dagon–fish god of the Philistines.
Dahveed–(dah-*veed*), probably "Beloved one." May have been used to designate an important or "beloved" leader in war. It is used in this context in this book, although there is much argument over the word's ancient usage and meaning.
Dod–(dohd), kinsman, uncle, indicates close kinsman relationship.

Dodi–(doh-*dee*), my uncle.
Geber–(*gehb*-behr), masculine title of respect: master or sir.
Geberet–(geh-*behr*-eht), feminine title of respect: mistress or ma'm.
Gebirah–(geh-*beer*-ah), the woman in whom the kingdom is embodied. She is also called the "Handmaid." Whomever the gebirah marries will have the right to rule the kingdom. The gebirah was normally of the same clan as the royal family, if not the royal family itself.
Girdle–wide wrap of cloth or soft leather wrapped around the waist to hold a robe together and provide a place to put things.
Great Sea–Ancient name for the Mediterranean Sea.
Habiru–(hah-*bee*-roo), name for bands of nomads, usually small, which roamed Israel during the time of David. They were composed of landless family units or displaced persons from the twelve tribes or any of the surrounding nations. Their main occupation was as mercenaries, but many bands simply supported themselves by robbery and murder. Habiru can refer to the entire band, or a single member of it.
Hakkohen Haggadol–(hah-koh-*hayn* hah-gah-*dohl*), the High Priest.
Hallelu–(hahl-lay-*loo*), second person plural command. "You (all of you) praise."
Hamsin–(hahm-*seen*), harsh dry east wind from the desert.
Hassar–(hah-*sahr*), *The* prince, hence first or crown prince.
Hassarah–(hah-sahr-*ah*), *The* princess/queen, hence most important princess/queen.
Henna–reddish stain from plants used to decorate nails and skin.
Hesed–(*hes*-ed), voluntary kindness on the life-saving level provided by the only one able to give it.
Jebus–ancient name for the city which became Jerusalem.
Kohen–(koh-*hayn*), priest.
Leben–(*leh*-behn), curdled milk, churned in a skin bag and used for food.
Mashiah–(mah-shee-*ah*), anointed one.
Meil–(may-*eel*), expensive, richly embroidered tunic worn only by royalty.
Melek–(*mel*-ek) King. Dahveed was anointed as melek.
Nahsi–(nah-*see*), also Nasi, masculine title of respect: high/governing lord. Carries the connotation of political/judicial authority.

Nagid–(*nah*-geed) Prince, captain or leader. Used in this book as the next step down from king. Shaul was anointed as nagid.
Pithoi–Plural of pithos
Pithos–Large pottery jars used for storage. They were wide at the top and tapered to a near point at the bottom.. A grain pithos could be six feet tall and 30 inches across at the widest point, just under the neck.
Roeh–(Roh-*eh*), seer or prophet.
Sahrah–(sah-*rah*), feminine title of respect: princess, queen.
Sar–(sahr), masculine title of respect: prince. In Philistia it means "commander".
Salt Sea–Ancient name for the Dead Sea.
Sea of Chinnereth–Ancient name for the Sea of Galilee.
Seren–(*seh*-rehn), Philistine title equivalent to Sar/Nagid.
Sereni–(Seh-rehn-*ee*), my seren.
Shephelah–the gently rolling hills between the coastal plain by the Mediterranean Sea and the central hills of Palestine west of the Jordan River.
Shobeh–(sho-*beh*), captor.
Yah's fire–Lightning. Lightning was considered fire from the god of the land.
Zammar-(zah-*mahr*), singer.

Cultural Notes

Blood guilt—The murder of a person always brought the curse of blood-guilt, which could only be cleared with blood. If a family member was murdered or killed by someone, the family would appoint a "redeemer (goel) of the blood" to track down and kill the person responsible. This was the reason for the cities of refuge. A person who caused accidental death could flee to them and be safe from the avenging Goel of the Blood. If a person was found murdered out in the forest, or on the road somewhere, the land itself had incurred blood-guilt, and there was a specific sacrifice and ritual associated with cleansing the land of the murdered person's blood, and thus removing the curse from the land and/or any nearby towns. Curses were terrible punishments and greatly feared since they were enforced by the gods or by Yahweh, and there was no protection from Yahweh's curse. There isn't any today, either.

Clothing and honor—Clothing was a social signal of status. In addition, clothing literally bestowed authority. To this day, we still have investiture ceremonies wherein the clothing (the vestments) of an office are given. We just don't continue to wear that clothing every day! The opposite of invest is divest, and if we divest someone of something, we strip away the associated vestments, and thus the authority. The possession of a high office brought with it the obligation to wear the clothing of that office, so people would know who held what place. By wearing the clothing associate with an office, a person laid claim to that authority. Because of this, simply wearing the king's clothing could be an act of treason.

Emmanuel—The term "emmanuel" during the time of Dahveed was connected with the concept of the Gebirah (see below). The institution of the Gebirah often brought with it some form of "sacred" or "divine" marriage. Here on earth the king, representing rulership, would "marry" the Gebirah, symbolizing the kingdom, thus echoing the mythic marriage of the gods in heaven. Any resulting child would be the "emmanuel," a physical symbol of the union of ruler and kingdom.

In some cases he was the heir to the throne, rather than just any son that the king might have with his queen or concubines.

En-dor—Probably only those living in Shaul's own culture could fully understand his interaction with the medium at En-dor. What is still evident to us today is that it carried extremely serious consequences. Leviticus 19:26 connects eating meat with blood in it with divination and witchcraft. The biblical description of the preparation of the meal at En-dor mentions all phases of the preparation of the (unleavened) bread. But the medium simply slaughters the calf. The word used for slaughter is the same word normally employed to describe the killing of an animal for sacrifice. Unleavened bread is normally added to such a sacrifice, and with the meat being eaten with the blood, it is a strong indication that she prepared a covenantal meal for the dead. Space limitations do not permit me to explore several other indications of such a meal

Family Relationships—Family was of primary important in the Ancient Near East. However, families were organized differently then than they are today. The closest bond a person had was with siblings, not parents. Brothers and sisters were expected to look out for each other, and be the confidants and advisors for each other. The husband-wife relationship was more of a business/contractual partnership than anything else. A wife was not expected to love her husband. She was expected to be loyal to him, but her supportive relationships would come from her family of origin, and she would not be counted part of her husbands family until she bore a son. The closest bond for a married woman was with her son, who was expected to stand up for her against all comers, even his father if necessary, and who would care for her in her old age. The function of a father as we understand it today, was not performed by the man who sired you, but by your mother's brother, your maternal uncle. He was the one responsible for emotional support, teaching and guidance.

Forever—In biblical times, forever meant "as long as one or other of the parties swearing live." Since Jonathan asked for hesed for his "house" and his family would presumably continue for generations, Dahveed must swear for as long as *he (Dahveed)* shall live, as he would not expect to outlive the generations in Jonathan's family. This is why Joab flees to the tabernacle altar when he hears that Dahveed has died. Any covenant of protection given to him "forever" ceases to be, since with Dahveed's death forever is over. This is also why the death of an overlord king demanded that all the under-kings come and renew allegiance even though they swore to be faithful forever. The other party died, so forever is over. Of course, not all the under-kings would want to renew a covenant, which usually precipitated war . . .

Gebirah—The Gebirah was the woman who owned the land, and so embodied that land. Whoever married the woman, "married" the land and became its ruler. The idea of the Gebirah had several variations in ancient times. In Egypt, any woman in the palace could be named Gebirah, so to be safe, the Pharoah married them all. In Edom, one woman was Gebirah, (and her daughter probably became the next Gebirah) and whoever married her became the next king of Edom. The Hittites had a position similar to the Gebirah which also carried religious duties, and this woman was appointed to the position, but held it for life independently of other political changes. The institution of Gebirah existed in Israel until King Asa, as attested in 1 Kings 15:13 and 2 Chronicles 15:16. The word is translated as "queen mother" in these verses.

Gibeonites—The Gibeonites lived in four cities occupying the heart of the territory of Ephraim west of Jebus/Jerusalem—Gibeon, Beeroth, Chephirah and Kiriath Jearim. See Joshua 9 for the beginning of their service to the tabernacle. The genealogies in 1 Chronicles 8: 29-34 and 9: 35-40 give clear indication that Shaul's clan descended from Gibeon.

Hesed—This word is translated "loving-kindness" in most modern translations. Sometimes it is translated "mercy," but both translations again leave out some of the important connotations of the Hebrew idea. Hesed can only come from the one person who must act in order for another's life to be preserved. This makes it the perfect word to describe what God does for us. If he didn't act, we'd all die, and he is the only one whose action will give us life. Therefore, he gives hesed.

Honor—Honor was the grease which made ancient society work, much as money does in Western societies. Honor can be thought of as the respect and approval of one's community. To understand honor, think of it as a credit rating. Without honor, the avenues open to a man to support himself and his family were severely limited, much as a bad credit rating limits a person today. Anything which would make people think less of a person or their family reduced the family honor. Keeping and maintaining honor, therefore, was of primary importance, and every action had to be measured against what people would think of it. Generally speaking for people on the same status level, older persons had more honor than younger ones. All honor belonged to someone, and gaining honor meant someone else lost it. Where honor came from was very important, and being greedy about honor brought dishonor! Also generally speaking, richer people had more honor than poorer ones, but only generally speaking. The most honorable man in town didn't have to be the one with the most possessions. To be rich without honor meant a person was greedy, and so the person was despised. To be rich with honor meant a person was wealthy, and therefore blessed and honored.

Honor Wars—Honor wars involved what we today call "disrespecting" someone. Wars could only develop between persons of the same status. Therefore, a householder could not have an honor war with a servant, only with another householder who held the same amount of honor in the eyes of the community. Servants could have honor wars with each other, but not their master/employer. Disrespect could be shown in either overt or subtle ways. Deliberately not bowing low enough to someone would slight their honor. Refusing to look at someone could do the same, as well as the order in which you spoke to people when in their presence. If an honor slight was given, the person slighted was obligated to either protest the slight or return it in some way, or else lose honor in the eyes of the community. Wars could also develop, though, over compliments and gift giving. Any gift/compliment received brought the obligation to return a gift/compliment of equal value, otherwise honor was lost to the giver. *Any* society interaction, therefore, had to be carefully viewed and calculated to take honor into account.

Cultural Notes ~ 27

Israel and Judah separate—In the time of Shaul and Dahveed, Israel and Judah were considered separate political entities, which is the reason they are named separately in so much of the Bible. This may hark back to Gen 38:1 where we are told that Judah separated himself from his brothers and lived around Adullam. What was involved in this separation, how long it lasted and how it effected his relationship with Jacob and the rest we don't know. In any case, Judah was apart from the rest, and in many of the stories in Judges, the tribe is never mentioned. Archaeology tells us that at the time of Shaul and Dahveed, Judah was very sparsely populated and people lived at subsistence level. Only around Hebron was there some measure of wealth. The separation between Israel and Judah continued during the "United Monarchy," preserved in the differing political arrangements between the two countries and the king, who simply happened to be the same person.

Power—Just like today, power in Bible times brought responsibility. Much power in the Bible was based on influence, and influence was based on honor (see above.) In other words, honor brought power. With death and/or disaster able to descend in so many ways, anything which might protect the family was much sought after, and power opened up ways to ease the family's position, and provide a small cushion between the family and death. Therefore, when an individual acquired honor/power they were compelled by social norms and sheer survival to seek ways to use that power to benefit their family first, then anyone connected with the family. Because power was connected to honor, however, it must be used very carefully to avoid anything which would detract from honor, and thus lessen the power itself.

Satan—The noun "satan" (sah-*tahn*) means in the Hebrew "adversary or opponent." The connotation is that of one who hinders, or stands in the way. In the judicial sense, it means the accuser, or the opposing party. When the Philistine commanders use this word about Dahveed, they are describing very well what he might do during the battle.

Teraphim—Teraphim were spirits or gods who protected a house. They were part of the Elohim, supernatural beings from spirits and demons up to the gods. Spirits were everywhere and were capable of action for or against humans. It was wise to remain on their good side with sacrifices and gifts. Fortunately, all spirits and gods were tied to a geographical location, and their power weakened quickly when outside the geographic area. Crossing a border meant leaving the power of one god and coming under the power of another. House gods, teraphim, could only guard a single house, a hill spirit could only operate on that single hill, etc. A god's power was directly tied to the amount of territory he could operate in. Thus, the more territory a king conquered for his god, the stronger the god became. This is why war was a sacred activity.

Titles—Hebrew has several titles of respect. I have decided to use them, somewhat arbitrarily, in the following order from least respect to greatest. Geber (sir)—adon (lord)/baal (lord)—sar (prince)—nahsi (governing lord)—nagid (ruling prince)—melek (king).

Feminine titles are as follows: Geberet (ma'am)—baalah (lady)—sahrah (princess)—Hassarah (queen.)

The Philistines also had sars, but for them, "sar" was the equivalent of the Hebrew "commander" The word they used for "sar" or "prince" was "seren" See Vocabulary

In Hebrew, as in many other languages other than English, the title normally follows the name rather than preceding it. But to make it easier for my readers, I have used the English convention, unless the title is used in its most formal sense. Also in Hebrew, it is more courteous to call someone simply by their title. Personal names of respected persons would have only been used by intimate family or very close friends. Thus, to begin with, Dahveed calls Jonathan "Hassar Jonathan," or "Hassar." For very formal introductions, or when a personage is being called on in their formal capacity, Jonathan's name would be "Jonathan ben Shaul, Hassar Israel," with the title last. It will behoove the reader to pay attention to how the titles are used in the story!

Transfer of the throne—The time of Shaul/Dahveed/Solomon was very uncertain politically for the emerging nation of Israel/Judah. Many of the same problems occurred between the tribes as occurred between the states here in the USA under the Articles of Confederation before the Constitution was adopted and George Washington became president. Each tribe was independent, indeed each town and clan were autonomous and provincial in outlook. Shaul rose to power on the need for protection from the Philistines, and "ruled" only through his alliances with the elders of towns and tribes who followed him only because he was the best one at keeping the Philistines out of the highlands. Dahveed inherited this chiefdom, and gradually moved it toward a monarchy. The old autonomous ways, however, resurfaced after Solomon died, producing the divided kingdom.

As in every political entity, the transfer of power was important, and since Shaul was the first "king" there was no precedent to follow. In the Ancient Near East, power normally transferred in one of three ways. When the old king died, the throne could pass by inheritance to his son, or return back to the Gebirah (see above) who might or might not be the king's daughter or relative. Her husband if she had one, became the next king. The throne could also pass by popular acclaim, the candidate the most people liked getting the position. This method usually disintegrated into civil war with any number of sides until one candidate slaughtered all the rest, or a foreigner with a bigger army came in and took the throne. If he married into the previous royal family, he could be accepted. Often, however, the fact of his foreign blood would produce rebellion against his son, or his house even generations later.

In the case of Shaul and Dahveed, it is clear that Dahveed rivaled Jonathan in popular acclaim, and married to Michal he became a son of the king. If Michal was named Gebirah, Dahveed would have a very strong claim to the throne no matter which way Shaul chose to pass it on. Hence Shaul's eagerness to remove Dahveed from the picture to assure that Jonathan, the son of his blood, would get to rule.

Units of measure—I decided to use modern units of measure for units of length since the flow of the story would not be interrupted while the reader tried to equate ancient units of length with modern.

A Word About . . .

Names—specifically Ahithophel and Mephibosheth. Both of these names were most likely given their present form by scribes editing Samuel's books. At the time of the editing, David was a national hero, and anyone who opposed him was obviously a bad person. Names where then altered to indicate this. We have Mephibosheth's real name, Meribbaal, which is what I use in the book. But Ahithophel's real name has not survived in the record. However, other name changes indicate that "thophel" was often substituted for "baal", which in David's time simply meant "husband" or "lord" or "owner." Only later did it become the popular name of the Canaanite god. Ahithophel's name could, therefore, have been Ahibaal, and that is what I use. In addition to being a nicer name for the man, it's also shorter. That means less to type. When it comes to typing, I'm lazy.

Now a word about . . .

The ark—the "Ark narrative" as it is called in scholarly circles is the fragmented account of the whereabouts of the Ark of the Covenant and is spread out from Exodus to Chronicles. Trying to piece the picture together is always iffy. What becomes clear is that the ark was not always contained within the tabernacle after the destruction of the tabernacle at Shiloh by the Philistines in Samuel's time. Whither and how far the ark may have wandered after that is unclear in the narrative. There are some indications that Shaul had access to the ark during his reign, which would mean it was probably within the sanctuary at Nob. What is very clear, however, is that when Dahveed brought it to Jerusalem, he didn't get it from the sanctuary, which was then at Gibeon. We know that because that's where Solomon goes after his ascension to the throne to seek God. Presumably, the ark was separated from the sanctuary at the destruction of Nob. Where was it during Dahveed's fugitive years? As mentioned in the footnote in the text of this book, there is a good chance that Dahveed had it with him. Context is clear that the word "ephod", when not motified by "linen" cannot refer to a garment, but to some kind of solid object. In addition, Solomon, when sparing Abiathar's life at the time Adonijah made a bit for the throne, specifically says he is doing so because, "you carried the ark of the Lord God before my father David, and because you shared in all the hardships my father endured." 1 Kings 2:26 (NRS version. Some other versions use the word "afflicted" instead of "hardships") The only time this could have happened was after the destruction of Nob when Abiathar fled to David, and the "ephod came down by his (Abiathar's) hand." (Literal translation 1 Samuel 23:6.) Notice that Abiathar is not the subject/active agent in the Hebrew text. The ephod itself is. Such action would never be attributed to a piece of clothing. But the culture at the time would attribute such actions to the gods through the item they dwelt in. I have, therefore, placed the ark with Dahveed during his wandering years. My apologies if this offends anyone.

Now a word about . . .

The way I wrote this book—as with my other books, one of my purposes is to tell these stories in their proper historical and cultural context. This means that I try to tell the story from the perspective of the protagonist using the mindset, attitudes, and accepted ways of the world **as they were understood back in the late Bronze Age/Early Iron Age,** when Dahveed lived. Details and comments in the Bible make it clear that Israel and Judah in Shaul and Dahveed's time were very much a part of the Bronze Age culture in the Ancient Near East, just like we are part of our culture today. Therefore, to really appreciate much of what these stories have to say, we must forget our own ideas of "the way things should be," and put ourselves in the sandals of the Biblical characters, attempting to view their lives and times using the same perspective that they had back then. And speaking of time, let's have a word about . . .

Chronology—as I've discussed in my previous books, historians argue endlessly about chronology. There is only one generally accepted date in ancient history, and that is 664 BC (or BCE of you prefer) and the end of the third intermediate period in Egypt. Every date previous to that one, and many after it, are simply educated guesses. Some guesses are more educated than others, and the further back one goes, the more "guess" enters the picture. The usual estimate for the beginning of Dahveed's reign is around 1000 BC, give or take

50 years, with Solomon taking the throne around 970 BC with the same margin of error.

The other very important aspect of chronology is that the Bible comes to us from an oral tradition. All the stories in the Bible were originally told orally, and only written down much later. This means that the stories about Bible characters are told in **thematic sequence, not necessarily in straight chronological sequence.** This is very important for our understanding of the stories. This should not be surprising. When you are telling someone about events which happened to you that occurred over several days or weeks, you don't tell them everything that happened in between the relevant events! You skip those until the entire connected sequence has been told. Then, if there is some other theme you want to discuss, you go "back in time" and begin another sequence. **The stories of Dahveed's life are told in exactly this way.** This means, of course, that **we don't know how much time may have passed between events in a sequence**, or even how the sequences actually fit together in straight chronological order. We can only guess. Note the amount of time I have put between Goliath's death, and the covenant between Dahveed and Jonathan.

English readers, however, are used to written history and stories being told in straight chronological sequence. Again, to make it easier for my readers, I have given my best "guess" at the chronological sequence of many of the events in Dahveed's life. There are times, however, when I have followed the thematic sequence, and then "gone back in time" to pick up the story in another place. (For those of you who are curious, yes, this thematic sequence is indicated in the Hebrew. This involves the use of the Hebrew letter vav, about which Hebrew scholars argue with as much verve as historians argue about chronology.) Now, let's move on to a word about . . .

Samuel or Chronicles—I have chosen to follow the plot of Dahveed's life as outlined in 1 and 2 Samuel. These books were written hundreds of years before Chronicles, and are, therefore, considered more reliable than Chronicles. By the time Chronicles was written, Dahveed was considered a national hero, and you'll notice that his life in Chronicles has been purged of any hint of wrong-doing with the exception of his affair with Bathsheba. That got him in so much trouble that it simply couldn't be ignored, even hundreds of years later! But notice that it's only mentioned in Chronicles, it isn't told. I feel that the books of Samuel reflect a truer picture of what Dahveed was like, so I have only used the account in Chronicles for additional details to the narrative if I thought they might be useful.

Next, a word about . . .

Translations of the Psalms—They are my own. Don't blame anyone else for them. Don't look for them in a Bible.

I realized when I was writing my book about Ruth that I needed to know more about Biblical Hebrew in order to really understand the story. By the time I started research for Dahveed, I realized I needed to know a lot more about Biblical Hebrew. So I sat in on Hebrew classes at the Theological Seminary at Andrews University. (And my profound thanks to the teacher for so graciously allowing my presence in the classroom!) I learned how to do my own translations.

My goal has been to reflect more of the Hebrew usage and words rather than tweaking them for a smooth English translation. Thus, if the Hebrew uses the word "voice" three times in three sentences, so do I, rather than put in a synonym as "better English usage" demands. Note Psalms 23, and the "ruts of righteousness!" "Path" is more melodic in English and flows better, but the Hebrew word is "rut" not "path." Rougher sounding in English, I know, but a much more vivid word picture! So, if the Psalm translations use repetitive words arranged rather oddly, leave out or add some words, and sound a bit skewed to your ear, blame it on the flavor of Biblical Hebrew! I hope you like the tang, as if you've had the chance to taste an exotic food for the first time. Now that my last two sentences have thoroughly mixed that metaphor, let's have a word about . . .

Numbers—this is where the cultural differences between our day and Dahveed's day rear their heads in an unmistakable way. Today, our lives are intensely entwined with extremely accurate and precise numbers. We assume that the rest of the planet is also ruled by these accurate and precise numbers. Sorry. There still exist cultures today that have two numbers. One and two. Anything else is "more."

We also assume that past cultures must also have loved very accurate and precise numbers. We received 60 seconds in a minute and sixty minutes in an hour from Babylon, after all. But, Israel isn't Babylon, and Hebrew numbers are mushy. We're dealing with a culture where the smallest amount of time that we know they used is the hour, not the split second. And the hour was defined as a certain segment of dawn to dusk, and dusk to dawn. That meant the hour stretched and shrank according to the season of the year!

Therefore, "40 years" can mean 40 years as we understand it, or "the years from adulthood to death" or "a generation." Since the scribes who wrote down the stories for us were not concerned with our passion for absolute accuracy in numbers, they neglected to indicate which meaning was meant when they used the term, leaving it up to us to guess which one seems the most logical. If more than one meaning can logically fit, take your best guess.

For instance, Dahveed reigns for 40 years. Does this mean exactly 40 years to the day, or 38 .5 years, or maybe 43 years and two months?? If we were to ask the recording scribe which one is "right", he would look at us as if we were crazy. Dahveed reigned from his adulthood until he died. What more do you need to know? The exact amount of time that covered was irrelevant and useless information, so no one bothered with it. This attitude naturally drives us western number-oriented people right up the wall, and it's one reason why historians argue so intensely about chronology!

Now, one of the favorite units of numbers in the Bible is the "elef." It's translated in one of two ways, either "family unit" or "thousand." Here's where things get very sticky. The meaning of elef in Dahveed's time is "family unit" and very well could have had a standard number assigned to it that everyone back then understood. But, by the time the Hebrew scriptures were translated into what we know as the Septuagint, the number that went with elef had long since been lost. So the scribes doing the translating assigned a number to elef. They chose "thousand." It seemed the best guess to them.

For hundreds of years, no one thought to question that assignment. However, modern scholars have much more to work with than did the scribes who created the Septuagint. We have thousands (our thousands) of clay tablets from numerous places in numerous languages, from different time periods of ancient history. We have archaeological discoveries to help us interpret what is translated. And this word elef, or it's equivalent, is quite common. There was just one problem. "Thousand" didn't fit. Scholars, therefore went back to the records, trying to understand. The essential question was, "how many is a 'family unit?'"

Well, that depends. How many people are in your family? Mushy numbers, remember? Therefore, hold onto your hats! Currently, the best scholarly guess at how many an "elef" is stands at 5-14 people. (Is it safe to come out now?? OK.) Naturally, this wreaks havoc with the general ideas of how many people were involved in the biblical battles for instance. However, it does bring the Biblical record into line with what we know about the general culture, the population, the amount of land available, and the size of towns, settlements, and kingdoms. So, maybe deciding that the guess of the Septuagint scribes was not quite correct isn't such a bad idea.

Because we really don't know how many an elef is, I've used the word "unit" as a substitute. "Unit" can be mushy, just like elef. How many a unit contains depends on who's counting and what is being counted. Elef was probably exactly the same way. (Yes, I know. If 'thousand' is 5-14, how many is a 'hundred?' Since 'hundred' can also mean 'fraction or multiple' maybe we should just leave it alone for now and turn the page and enjoy. . .

Tamar bat Dahveed

Do come in. I've been expecting all of you. Everything is ready so that we can begin right away. Make sure there are cushions for everyone, now. Did you enjoy hearing the harp this morning at the sacrifice? Good. Let's see—we ended with Dahveed marrying Gebirah Abigail didn't we?

That was quite a surprising event for Dahveed. Remember, he had grown up as a servant in his father's house, and a shepherd at that, until he was 15 years old. Then his abbi claimed him as son and Roeh Shamuel, Yahweh's seer, anointed him as Melek for Yahweh on the same day!

Before long, he began playing his harp at Gibeah to soothe the tormented mind of King Shaul, and after he drove the demon from the king and killed the Philistine champion on the battlefield, Shaul's son and heir, Hassar Jonathan, guessed what Yahweh had in mind for Dahveed, and took him under his wing, sheltering him in his new life and teaching him what he needed to know.

After the battle with Goliath, Dahveed proved himself in battle time and again, until his success roused Shaul's fears that he would usurp Jonathan's place. Of course, Balak, a childhood acquaintance and enemy of Dahveed, stirred up the king's suspicions until his own plotting and treason were discovered and he had to flee from the court.

With Balak gone, Dahveed was soon married to Sahrah Michal, Shaul's youngest daughter, but again his success against the Philistines roused the king's enmity, and this time, not even Jonathan could turn it aside. Dahveed fled to Gath, hoping to find safety as a mercenary in Seren Akish's professional army. Instead, he found Goliath's kin, who soon exposed him as Philistia's worst enemy.

He escaped with his life both by acting insane in Akish's court and because of the covenant he had made with a young Philistine named Ittai who, unbeknownst to Dahveed, was Akish's nephew. Ittai's immi, Sahrah Hazzel, secretly sent her son to live with Dahveed to keep him from the clutches of Seren Manani, ruler of Ekron, and Hassar Jonathan's worst enemy.

As Dahveed struggled to live on his own, gradually collecting men around him, Israel's beloved crown prince worked to keep his abbi and king from bringing more dishonor on their family. While Dahveed learned how to govern men, Shaul announced Jonathan's marriage, an event that Dahveed attended as a blind beggar despite General Abner's determination to capture him. After the wedding, Dahveed fled north from Abner's men, going clear up to the Sea of Chinnereth before he and Abner met head-on in the throne room of King Nahash of Ammon. There Dahveed's half-cousin, Ala, repaid the debt of hesed she owed Dahveed, saving not only his life, but his sister Abigail's also. Nahash's sheltering of Dahveed led to a treaty of peace between them before Israel's future king returned to Judah and Adullam.

Then Jonathan discovered the clue he needed to fulfill one of his heart's desires, and he located the Steward of Tahat in Dan. But he returned home to find Nob destroyed, and the blood of Yahweh's priests and their families burdening his house and family. The horror of what his abbi had done finally drove the hassar to accept the task of taking the throne and safeguarding Israel until Yahweh's chosen king would be ready to rule.

Down in Judah, meanwhile, Dahveed fled before Shaul's wrath rather than fight him until they met in the cave at En-gedi, and Dahveed spared the life of the king he loved, but who hated him. Shaul returned home, submitting to Yahweh's will at last.

Dahveed, though, faced a time of famine for his men, finding help at last from the beautiful Gebirah Carmel, Abigail, wife of Nagid Nabal. She had waged a war of her own to recover the honor of her house that her husband, Nabal, had stripped away by his greed and cruelty. It was his refusal to give the supplies Dahveed begged of him that precipitated the final break between Abigail and her husband, and she banished him from her presence.

After the nagid's death less than two weeks later, the Gebirah used all her wealth, land, and possessions to recompense the people of Carmel and Maon for the injustices he had caused. But when the news of Nabal's death reached the other nagids of the Calebite clans, the rush to take Abigail as wife nearly started a civil war. Only because Dahveed's offer of marriage reached her first was Abigail able to slip away, vanishing from sight until the New Year's new moon feast when she announced her marriage to Dahveed Israel, at the same time revealing her total lack of possessions and land.

But the people of the Calebite clans loved the beautiful Gebirah even more for the sacrifices she had made, and when the political alliances reformed, Abigail of Carmel became the most powerful political figure in the south. With her marriage to Dahveed Israel, the two of them effectively united all of Judah under one house. The wedding feast celebrating their marriage didn't occur until after the political situation calmed down, but it was worth the wait, for Ethan made sure that Hassar Jonathan attended!

Even as Dahveed finds a time of rest, Yahweh is still working. The seeds of the next lessons that Dahveed must learn, and of the final granting of Jonathan's heart's desires were sown in the days following the uniting of the south. Dahveed must find a deeper understanding of what it means to be king for Yahweh, and Jonathan Hassar must yield a final piece of his heart before Yah can avenge the wrong that has tormented the hassar for so long.

Prologue

Jonathan and I spent the day after my wedding feast catching up on everything that had happened since we'd last talked. He asked several questions about Moab when I told him what little I had gleaned from the infrequent messages from my family and the things Ithmah had let slip from his trips back and forth. The story of Sibbecai joining my band made him laugh when he heard how the man had taken my sword, but when I explained about Ahibaal, he seemed especially interested. "He's got clan in Jebus?"

I nodded.

"I'll ask Tanhum about him, then."

"How is he? And Ornan and Atarah?" I asked eagerly.

He laughed again. "Well, between that Jebusite and your brother Elihu, the kingdom nearly runs itself. Last I knew, Ornan was still working with Jamin, although he's much more than an errand boy now."

"Jamin must be doing well. Ethan now wears the richest clothing I've seen him in yet."

The hassar's eyes twinkled. "Yes, Ethan and Jamin have done a great deal, I think."

"Have you heard anything from Atarah?"

"Not really. She spends a lot of time in Gibeon now, and I think Abbi is just as glad to have her there." Jonathan shifted restlessly on the dried leaves that we sat on.

I wondered if Jonathan wished just the opposite, but decided not to ask. "What about Meribbaal?"

A grin spread across his face. "Judith can hardly keep up with him. He's nearly 2, and nobody can get anything done while he's around."

"You know, Hassar, there's been something that has puzzled me since En-gedi. Why did Abner inquire about my man, Jaasiel? He's from some city clear up north in Zobah, and it didn't make any sense that Abner would pay any attention to him. Is there some family or clan relationship that I don't know about?"

To my surprise, Jonathan burst out laughing a third time. "That's what Malchi's been looking so smug about, and why Abner's been so tame! I can't remember if I told you that Immi got upset about Abner's tampering with my personal guard, so she removed Abner's son from him. His name is Jaasiel!"

"And Abner thinks I have him?" I asked, stunned.

"Apparently. Knowing Malchi, he probably gave the general just enough information for the man to jump to that conclusion, and when you responded to the name at En-gedi, Abner would have been sure that's where he was! I'll have to send Malchi something for this one." The hassar chuckled.

"But where is Abner's son?"

"I'm not entirely certain myself. "When you think about it, do you really want to know?"

"No, I don't think I do," I decided, leading the way back to my tent.

Jonathan's visit lasted for a full three days, and by the time he left, everyone in camp was sorry to see him depart. Ishmaiah, one of the Gibeonite ark-bearers, had decided to return to Israel with the hassar, since his clan needed him. I was sorry to see him go. He had become an excellent warrior.

Abigail came to me as Ishmaiah led his donkey toward us, giving last instructions to Beriah, another Gibeonite who had come to take his place as an ark-bearer. "Dahveed, I don't know how it happened, but I must have lost the earrings the hassar brought with his wedding gift," she said, obviously upset. "I wanted to wear them for him. They are so pretty."

I sighed. It was too much to hope that the hassar's visit could have ended without some sort of trouble intruding. "Just a moment," I said to her, heading into the center of camp. "Eliphelet!" I bellowed. I had to admit, it was amusing to see the reaction to my call. The thief did not appear, of course, but nearly every other person in my sight started frantically checking their possessions. "*Now*, Eliphelet!" I yelled again.

"What's he taken this time?" Ahinoam demanded, handing me the piece of his girdle to put by my tent.

"Abigail's earrings, and who knows what else!" I explained, setting the cloth in place.

"You called for me, adoni?" Eliphelet said at last, sidling up to me as the rest of the camp gathered around.

"I believe you forgot to leave something outside my tent this morning," I replied sternly.

"Well, adoni, the—the cloth wasn't out there, and—"

I just glared at him.

"I suppose I should have returned the things anyway."

I pointed to the cloth.

Nervously, he put Abigail's earrings on it, followed by a ring I didn't recognize but which brought an annoyed exclamation from Ethan. Then he added three bracelets and a necklace which made the Gebirah's handmaids gasp, and finally a leather pouch. With a surprised expression, the hassar reached in the back of his girdle.

I stared at Eliphelet. "Is that all?"

"Yes, adoni," he said quickly, keeping his hands as far out of my reach as he could.

"Did you steal it all yesterday?"

Sweat appeared on his face. "Uh, n-no, not exactly."

"You broke your oath then. Whose things did you have the longest?"

"The earrings, adoni." He cast a glance at Abigail and backed away. "Please, adoni, perhaps we can skip this part? I'll remember this time."

"You'll remember better with a little reminder," I said remorselessly. "Abigail, since he had your things the longest, you have to do this."

Obviously puzzled, she approached us. "What do I do?"

"The bargain is that Eliphelet can keep anything he can steal overnight without reprisal. But it must be returned to the cloth outside my tent the next morning, or else he has to add a little more blood to it to help him remember the bargain."

Her face paled. "I'm supposed to cut him?"

"You don't really have to," Eliphelet suggested, trying to sound magnanimous. "I wouldn't want to trouble you, and–"

"Oh, yes she does."

Bowing to the inevitable, my personal thief retrieved the cloth, leaving the jewelry on the ground, and brought it to Abigail. Kneeling, he gave her a slightly sick smile.

The Gebirah looked at me rather helplessly.

"All you have to do is nick his finger with your belt knife," I explained.

"I don't have one, Dahveed," she reminded me.

"Please, use mine," Hassar Jonathan offered, pulling his from his girdle, eyeing Eliphelet as he handed it to her.

Abigail accepted it with a nod, holding it awkwardly and taking the hand that Eliphelet offered her. I saw her glance at Hezro, then she took a deep breath and pressed the knife down against Eliphelet's finger. It slipped, slicing into her own finger as well as his.

She jerked, giving a little cry as she held out her hand. Hezro started for her instantly, but I motioned for him to remain where he was, and Shagay restrained him. Eliphelet was still on his knees, his own cut forgotten, staring at the blood dripping from Abigail's hand with the most horrified expression I'd ever seen.

"Gebirah! No!" he cried, snatching up the cloth and squeezing it tightly around her finger. "It will stop," he said hoarsely, shaking from head to foot. "It will," he repeated. "It's got to!"

But the wound was deep enough that it bled for some time, Eliphelet moaning and crying the while. The cloth had quite a large stain on it when he finally removed it, and he stared at it in anguish while Keturah washed Abigail's finger with wine, making my wife gasp.

Once she had the finger bound up, Abigail picked up the cloth and stared at it. Then she turned to me. "It would seem this man has forgotten his oath rather frequently?"

I nodded. "And it's caused considerable trouble."

She still looked pale, and I wondered what she would do. But she seemed to be thinking of something.

"Eliphelet, look at me," she said finally, her voice calm.

He managed to meet her eyes.

"Do you know what will happen the next time you break your oath?"

"More of my blood will go on that cloth," he quavered.

"No. More of *my* blood will stain that cloth. And *you* will have to make the cut."

Everyone around me became very still as she disappeared into her tent.

"Yahweh above!" Hassar Jonathan said softly. Then he turned to me. "Dahveed, a woman like that comes once in a thousand generations!"

"And I've got two of them," I replied, smiling at Ahinoam.

Prologue ~ 43

¥ ¥ ¥ ¥ ¥ ¥

"Are you laughing or crying?" Jonathan asked two days later, gently tipping Michal's face up so that he could see her eyes.

"I don't know," his sister confessed as they stood together on the southeast battlements of Gibeah as the last of the sunlight faded. "It's so good to hear about Dahveed, but at the same time, it hurts."

"Do you still think of him?" he asked, a bit surprised.

She nodded. "I think I always will. He went deep into me, somehow, and I can't cut that part out."

"I know," he agreed softly, touching the twisted brass earring he again wore. Dahveed had made him take it back for kneeling to him when he first arrived at the wedding. The memory made him smile slightly. The surprise on Dahveed's face when he'd seen him there was worth it.

"There was something else interesting about my visit," Jonathan continued, his voice now filled with suppressed excitement. "Dahveed has shalishim! He has a Hittite in his band who knows the technique of fighting in groups of three and can teach it! By the time he's done, there won't be an army in the land that can stand up to what Dahveed will have. He won't just be king of Israel, Michal, he'll rule an empire."

"And he'll do it from Jebus," Michal added decidedly.

"Do you still think he'll conquer the most perfect fortress ever built?"

"Keep laughing if you like, Jonathan, but he will."

The hassar stood silently a moment. "You know, Michal, after what I saw down there, I don't think I am laughing anymore."

For some time, he and Michal watched the distant walls of Jebus fade into the twilight. "Is there news of Merab?" he asked. "I was considering visiting her after my stop in Shechem, but Dahveed's wedding intruded."

"A message came two days ago. She had a hard birth, but her fourth son is just fine. Adriel is rejoicing, of course, and Merab is delighted to have another boy."

Jonathan smiled into the growing darkness. "I'm glad things are going so well for her. Oh, do you know what Eshbaal is not telling me?" he ended, amusement in his voice.

Michal laughed. "And here our little brother was just telling me that he didn't think you had noticed anything! He said Abbi has been discussing a project with Abner. Something new, and it involves several squads of men. But he's been trying to find out more before reporting to you."

Jonathan stiffened. "Does it involve Dahveed?"

"Eshbaal said the squads were supposed to be going north from here, which is why he felt he could safely delay reporting to you."

"I wonder if this ties in with what Ishvi heard," the hassar mused, leaning his shoulder against the wall and staring south. "He said Abbi was talking about cleansing the land."

"Is he trying to regain Yahweh's favor in some way?" she asked, startled.

"I don't know."

¥ ¥ ¥ ¥ ¥ ¥

The courier stood in silence in the courtyard of the house in Giloh. Ahibaal let him wait while he finished his meal. The man had three or four messages, which he handed over before bowing deeply and leaving. The Jebusite adon looked up to chastise the man for leaving without permission when the seal on one of the messages caught his eye. Returning to his upper room, he set all but the one message aside for the scribe who would arrive after the noon rest.

Breaking open the document, he quickly scanned it. As usual, it contained no greeting, nothing before or after the message itself to identify anyone. "You have served well. Word has come that Dahveed Israel heeded your advice, and the south is united. Continue to report everything you can learn. We must know all that he does before we make a move. The news of your son's marriage gave us much rejoicing. El Elyon be with you."

The adon paused a moment, savoring the approval in the message. So far his Habiru link to Dahveed Israel had apparently delivered his messages accurately and swiftly. But it annoyed him that the Dahveed would not meet with him personally. Shoving the thoughts aside, Ahibaal stuck a corner of the papyrus in the flame from the lamp and then deposited the burning message in the pottery bowl on the table. After crushing the ashes to fine powder, he tossed them over the edge of his roof. "I will do as you command," he whispered.

Prologue ~ 45

¥ ¥ ¥ ¥ ¥ ¥

"What do you think of this latest development in the Calebite clans?" Gadmilk of Ashdod asked, shifting his skinny body in his chair to stare at Akish of Gath. The five serens representing the five cities in the Philistine alliance had gathered at a council hosted by Muwana in Ashkelon.

"I hadn't heard anything yet," Seren Akish said, his face impassive since, for once, the remark was true. He was always careful during such councils either to keep a low profile, or a somewhat incompetent one. As a result, Manani of Ekron had underestimated him on more than one occasion, enabling Akish to hold his own against the scheming ruler of the other inland city who wanted the primary place in the alliance.

The other three serens turned to Gadmilk. "What has happened?" Hanabaal of Gaza questioned.

"Haven't you heard either?" the ruler of Ashdod exclaimed, looking around importantly. "Nagid Carmel died, and his Gebirah ruined his house, then married again."

"Why should we care?" Hanabaal retorted. "If his house is destroyed, that's one less clan we have to worry about."

"Not when she gained more alliances than ever," Gadmilk retorted. "The pledging went heavily in Gebirah Carmel's favor, and given whom she married, we have a problem."

"Whom did she marry?" Manani asked carelessly.

The ruler of Ashdod glanced around again. "Dahveed Israel!"

For a moment, every seren froze, stunned by the news.

"Dahveed Israel?" Akish choked out.

Sitting back in his chair, Gadmilk nodded, pleased with the sensation he'd caused. "Judah is all but united, and that demon Israelite will know what to do with it!"

The other rulers began talking all at once, and for some time no one could really make himself heard.

Akish remained silent. It had been six years since his nephew, Ittai, had brought his covenant abbi, Dahveed Israel, into the palace of Gath, precipitating the Israelite's short, eventful stint as a mercenary in the city's service. The seren could still remember the scene of Dahveed's feigned insanity in his throne room, and the terrible thunderstorm afterward when Baal's fire had struck his palace. The next day, Ittai had vanished, and his sudden disappearance had thrown the succession of Gath into the forefront of everyone's mind.

For months afterward, he had braced himself for Seren Manani to seize advantage of that fact. The Ekron ruler hadn't done so, much to Akish's puzzlement. As time passed with no information about Ittai forthcoming, he had gradually given up hope that the youth still lived, and assumed that Manani had him assassinated.

"You don't seem worried, Seren Akish," Manani commented during a pause in the babble.

"Why should I be?" Akish asked absently. "Dahveed Israel is more than occupied with running from his master, Shaul."

"Perhaps it has escaped your notice that he now has a good portion of the Calebite clans at his beck and call," Gadmilk interjected sarcastically.

"But you said they pledged to the Gebirah, not Dahveed," Akish retorted. "And if my sister is any sample, women don't like war!"

Hanabaal threw up his hands in disgust, and even Muwana frowned.

"Really, Akish, you can't be that naive," Baalyaton, Manani of Ekron's principal adon, protested. "Or do you have other reasons for downplaying this event? If I recall correctly, your nephew is half Israelite."

Silence greeted the remark, and Akish carefully settled back in his chair. This could be very dangerous ground. "I assume my nephew is dead," he stated quietly.

"And what proof do you have of this?" the Ekron adon challenged.

The seren looked away. "After six years, what else can I think? Do you know for certain that he's not?"

Baalyaton reddened, and Manani gave him a deadly look.

"Why haven't you named an heir?" Muwana questioned.

Akish shrugged. "Who is there to name?" As soon as he spoke the words, he went cold. If he himself died, whoever married his sister, Hazzel, would rule Gath. Suddenly so much became clear. The seren of Ekron undoubtedly planned on assassinating him also when the time was right, then marrying Hazzel, thus becoming legitimate ruler of two of the five cities.

And the last thing Manani wanted at this moment, judging from the expression he'd given Baalyaton, was to bring the succession of

Gath to the attention of the coastal rulers, so that indicated that he wasn't ready to make his move yet.

"It seems to me Seren Akish is right in discounting Dahveed Israel at this time, if for rather different reasons," Manani commented. "The Calebite clans may have pledged to Carmel, but there are far too few people in the whole of Judah to threaten us and too little plunder to be worth our while. We can safely leave Judah and Dahveed Israel to Shaul. It is Israel that we need to penetrate. And if Shaul is distracted by Dahveed, that will make things easier for us."

Breathing a sigh of relief, Akish said nothing more, but he would need to be extremely careful from now on. If his guess was correct, his very life was in danger, not just his position as ruler of Gath. And there wasn't a sar in his professional force he would trust to be Keeper of his Head—his chief bodyguard—unless it was Shemel. And he needed Shemel out circulating among the other sars.

Jonathan and Gath

Chapter 1

Another war season had passed, and a second would soon commence. Seren Akish of Gath watched with narrowed eyes as Manani of Ekron approached the canopied chair where the Egyptian emissary sat. It was midmorning and already hot. The emissary flicked his horse-tail swatter at a fly and nodded courteously as Manani bowed. Behind the Egyptian tents, pine forest covered the hills sloping down into the huge depression of Beersheba. The exposed chalk of the road winding up into them glared in the sun.

While the emissary's scribe intoned the usual endless list of titles the official held, Akish noticed a Phoenician giving a copper piece to the crippled beggar lying by the entrance to the Egyptian camp. The man seemed to be taking a long time doing it. The seren wondered why the beggar was here. He had wounds healing on his torso, and someone had said he'd come with a caravan from Moab. Finally the Phoenician wandered off, and Akish wondered why the serens' council had been convened here, and why Manani was the one summoned forward instead of Hanabaal of Gaza. After all, it was the principal city of the five, and the Egyptians still had a presence there in the old governor's palace they had used long ago when Egyptian overlordship had been more than just words.

But then, Seren Manani had been grasping for more prestige lately. Seren Hanabaal was not pleased to be slighted in this way, although Gadmilk of Ashdod had a slight smirk on his face over it. Muwana of Ashkelon said nothing, and Akish hoped his own face was as devoid of expression as his fellow seren's.

Akish had his own ideas about how to increase Gath's prestige, based on both the fact that Gath was an inland city, and that he had a very private understanding with Dahveed Israel, who, in spite of his marriage to Gebirah Carmel a year ago, had stayed in the highlands during the past war season to guard the border from Lehi to Cabon. So while Manani had to take into consideration two fronts in his schemes—Israel at his back as well as the other four cities—Akish didn't have to worry about Israel as long as Dahveed was in Judah.

Ekron and Gath protected the back of the alliance, but Gath also defended the underbelly against raids from the southern desert tribes, a fact which the other serens forgot for the most part. He had been unable to capitalize on his position, however, since a big part of Manani's plans apparently centered around control of Gath. Increasing senility and a resulting loss of power had marked his abbi Maoch's last years, and since taking the throne, Akish had had his hands full simply retaining what little freedom remained to him. He knew the only reason he had succeeded so far was because of the death of Goliath at a very opportune time, and because his nephew had never fallen alive into the clutches of the cruel Ekron seren.

Akish pulled his thoughts back to the present as the scribe finished announcing the countless titles of the emissary and got to the point, a presentation of some kind. The serens of the three sea cities exchanged a quick glance as the Egyptian official summoned Manani forward and handed him two rolled parchments.

"Pharaoh has awarded you, the cities of Philistia, this privilege, knowing that your loyalty to him is unquestioned and that you will fulfill his wishes as he commands," the emissary announced.

"We of the Five Cities thank Pharaoh for his graciousness and confidence in us," Seren Ekron replied. "As always, we shall obey his commands and fulfill the duties given to us in return for the benefits he has brought to our land by his overlordship."

Hanabaal's face slowly turned red as Manani bowed again, backing away. Akish stirred uneasily. Manani had to know that taking Hanabaal's place in so public a manner would bring severe political repercussions, if not military ones. What could possibly have induced the wily ruler to take such a risk? Or had Manani managed to usurp Hanabaal's place without anyone noticing?

"How dare you do such a thing without consulting us?" Hanabaal snarled at Manani less than an hour later as the serens met outside Muwana of Ashkelon's tent.

Sar Shemel, the unit commander, stood beside Akish, and the seren felt the man tense a little. The heat was oppressive, making short tempers even worse. Glad that he had brought the reliable warrior with him, it had not escaped his notice that Shemel had maneuvered them into a position with the sun at their backs.

Manani had the sun blazing full in his face, but he managed to ignore it somehow. "I would have thought the advantages of authorization to collect Israelite taxes would be plain to your political astuteness, Seren," the Ekron ruler replied.

Trying to find some answer to that remark, Hanabaal squinted in the glare.

Akish shifted his weight a little, easing his hand closer to the sword Sar Shemel had suggested he wear this morning. Who knew what could explode in this heat? It wouldn't have been so bad if they could have met in a proper palace. His eyes flicked in contempt to the hill not far south upon which Beersheba sat. The settlement was nothing more than a rough triangle of houses surrounding a central open space which, from the amount of dung in it, served as a corral during the night. It had what passed for a gate, but precious little other fortifications of any kind, and it existed because of one reason: there was water here.

"Perhaps you should explain to the honored seren how the alliance is to be protected," Baalyaton, Manani's powerful adon, suggested.

"Why don't we start with actually reading the documents," Muwana put in, holding out his hand. Reluctantly, Manani handed over one of the parchments, and Muwana's scribe opened the protective cloth, unrolled the scroll, and began to read aloud.

It didn't take long for Hanabaal to explode. "This should never have been negotiated without all five cities in agreement!" he shouted. "It has made all of us responsible for payment of any deficit in the taxes stipulated. How are we supposed to bear that expense? When was the last time you actually made it into the highlands? Let alone collected taxes? You just told us you pushed harder than ever to get into the highlands last year and failed. Again!"

Gadmilk of Ashdod shifted his skinny body. "I refuse to honor this deed," he sputtered. "Don't come to me for help making up any shortage. You didn't consult with me, and I wash my hands of the whole affair!"

"Which I am more than willing for you coastal cities to do," Manani said blandly. "As these authorizations are made out to Gath and Ekron as the inland cities, Seren Akish and I can be completely responsible for any deficits if you wish."

Akish froze in amazement, staring at Manani. How dare the Ekron ruler implicate him in this! Anger rose in him. Gath was the poorest of the cities, and, as he well knew, getting into the highlands had been nearly impossible since Shaul first raised a professional force, to say nothing of what Dahveed Israel had done! "I do not see how I am involved in this, Seren," he said coldly. "I am as much in the dark about this as the others!"

"Then why is your name on this document?" Muwana's scribe asked, passing the parchment to Shemel, who handed it to Akish.

Flipping open the cloth, he glanced at the scroll, noting the alphabetic script used and quickly picking out his name. Icy calm settled over him as he unrolled it to stare at the thin, smooth, stretched skin, careful to give no hint that he could actually read the document. "I knew nothing of this," he stated again, realizing even as he spoke that the other serens would not believe him.

Gadmilk huffed in disgust, bouncing in his three-legged chair, which tipped a little under him. Hanabaal glared at him, but Muwana had a perfectly blank face.

"May I remind the serens of the benefits to this?" Manani asked mildly, but Akish still felt those cold eyes on him as he rolled the parchment in his hands.

"There are none!" the Ashdod seren huffed again.

"We must remember what this means politically," Manani continued calmly. "This authorization is an admission by Pharaoh that he can no longer collect his taxes, which means he is, practically speaking, admitting that he cannot rule Canaan any longer. He has, therefore, given rulership of Canaan to us. Surely, this should be worth a little effort for a year or two?"

"What effort did you have in mind?" Muwana, the oldest of the serens, inquired after a pause.

"We shall have to make some attempt to actually collect the taxes required in this document, of course, but so long as we send along something, Pharaoh will leave Canaan to us. And if, in say three years, the taxes begin to lessen, we will have had three years to build our strength unhindered, plus however many years it might take Pharaoh to decide if it is worth his while to protest less taxes with something besides words."

"And what if he does?" Hanabaal spat out. "Gaza is the southernmost city. He would strike at me first!"

"But would he consider it worthwhile to do so if the Way of the Sea should somehow cease to be open to him?" Manani suggested quietly.

"Cut Egypt's trade?" Gadmilk gasped, hitching himself around in his chair again, but more carefully this time. "The governor in Beth-shean would send his troops on us!"

"He might, unless he was already busy keeping the King's Highway open."

Akish eased back a little, fingering the scroll he held. "Nahash or Yira?"

Surprised, Manani glanced at him. "Nahash."

The seren of Gath silently cursed himself. The look in those cold eyes said he had just drawn too much attention to how politically astute he might really be.

"What does Nahash have to do with this?" Hanabaal growled.

"If we had an agreement with Nahash that he would cut the King's Highway at the same time we did the Way of the Sea, the Egyptian governor in Beth-shean would find himself fighting on two fronts," Muwana said thoughtfully. "And he doesn't have the troops to do that effectively. Furthermore, he would find it difficult to communicate with Pharaoh unless he used the route through the highlands, which comes out here, at Beersheba."

Silently, the serens stared at the small unfortified village that topped the hill.

"Let us be realistic," Manani resumed, smiling at them all. "Pharaoh has just given us Canaan. Let us not be backward in accepting his gift!"

"What do you see that we need to do?" the Ashkelon ruler asked, sitting back and staring at Manani again.

That evening, Akish sat in his tent fingering the parchment and studying the seal. After having had his scribe read the entire authorization to him, he had just finished reading it himself after the man left. As far as he could tell, it was the usual agreement. Philistia could collect as much as they wanted from Israel, keeping whatever Pharaoh didn't claim. The only drawback to tax collecting was the obligation to make up any shortfall.

But Seren Manani had convinced the alliance to support him for three years while he developed his plans, and Akish knew a big factor in that had been the assumption that Gath already supported them. He sighed. How could he keep himself distanced from Manani? He shifted uncomfortably, feeling as if a trap were waiting to be sprung, yet he had no indication of what it might be.

What bothered him most was Manani's willingness to bear the expense of negotiations with Nahash by himself. Everything had sounded reasonable until that. If Manani was willing to pay for the travel and gifts that the negotiations would require, he must be expecting more from the Ammonite ruler than just making trouble on the King's Highway. There had to be more to this. A lot more.

At last he rolled it again, wrapped the protective cloth around it, and stepped out of the tent, looking for Sar Shemel.

"Sereni?" someone else said instead.

"Where's Shemel?" Gath's ruler did not bother looking at Sar Lahmi. He didn't like any of Goliath's kin, the Rapha clan, and not just because they were related to Manani and in his pay as spies. All four of the giant men were quarrelsome and arrogant. Ishvi-benob, Saph, and that six-fingered brother of theirs were the worst. He'd brought Lahmi with him since he knew he'd have to take one of them, and Lahmi was the quietest. He might have been a decent unit commander if he hadn't had his three relatives involving him in trouble all the time.

"He's off duty, Sereni."

"See that this is put in the scribe's travel case, sar," Akish ordered, handing the authorization document to the giant commander.

"Yes, Sereni."

Akish settled himself for sleep, having ordered camp to be struck by first light. He needed to get back to Gath as soon as he could. A tiresome number of details always awaited him before the war season. He had just lain down when the singing began, so off-key and off-rhythm that he didn't recognize the song at first. Coming along the road to Beersheba, the noise slowly got closer.

Impatiently, Akish turned over, wishing the man responsible into Sheol. Gritting his teeth, he set himself to endure until the racket went past the encampment. But it didn't. Instead, it approached until the seren could make out most of the words and realized the singer was Philistine and giving a rousing rendition of a favorite song from the wine shops. The man must be abominably drunk, and the sounds settled themselves not far away.

"Shemel!" he roared, stalking out of the tent.

"Yes, Sereni?" the sar answered.

"That had better not be one of the men under your command!" he raged, trying to ignore the yowling.

"Er, it's not, Sereni. I believe I know who it is. I'll take care of him."

Akish retreated to his tent again, and in moments the horrendous noise ceased.

It promised to be hot again the next day, and Akish had had enough of the other serens and their disgust at his supposed collusion with Manani. When they departed Beersheba, he headed directly north into the highlands, smiling to himself as they climbed up the white chalk road into the coolness of the pine forest. Although both Shemel and Lahmi urged the men to close up ranks, the seren knew that nothing down here was strong enough to challenge the two units of professionals he had with him. Since it was obviously not a raiding party, he didn't expect any trouble from Dahveed. They could stay in Eglon tonight, 18 miles north, then head back west onto the plain in the morning and pick up one of the roads northeast to Gath. It would make a long day tomorrow—24 miles—but the coolness today was worth it, as was the time alone.

He needed to think. Manani had stepped up his efforts to control Gath, and Akish had spent nearly all his time the past year staving off the covert attacks on his position in the alliance. In addition, his unit commanders had seemed reluctant to carry out orders on more than one occasion. Not that he blamed them. Sending units into the highlands against Dahveed's men this past summer had been tantamount to suicide unless they stayed close to the land stair and sped back down it the first time a twig snapped near them.

However, with Manani's spies ever alert, he had not dared to slacken off his efforts, ordering his sars and units back into the highlands time and again. His face tightened at the thought. He'd lost several good men as a result, weakening his permanent force, which was undoubtedly just what Manani wanted.

The only good thing that had come of the past year was Shemel. The man had always been a good soldier, but after his capture by

Dahveed at Keilah, and subsequent enslavement and redemption, he had developed into an excellent tactician, and Akish was well aware that the majority of his permanent force was still intact because of Shemel's careful planning. He was grateful that the commander had done much to quell the restlessness and discontent of the sars. Briefly, he wondered what caused the trouble, but then went on to more pressing matters, such as who had attacked and wounded one of his adons not long ago. Come to think of it, there had been a similar attack near Ashkelon, and he seemed to remember that an adon down near Gaza had been killed months ago.

About mid-morning, Akish motioned Shemel to ride beside him.

The sar urged his mule forward. "Yes, Sereni?"

"Who was making that horrible noise last night?"

"Sar Eliahba of Ekron. I quieted him down and got him back to his proper tent."

"I'm surprised Manani keeps someone who gets that drunk!"

Shemel didn't say anything for some time. "I would beg a favor of you, Sereni," he said in a strained voice.

Surprised, Akish turned to look at the commander. "What would you have of me?"

"Please say nothing of what happened last night to anyone, Sereni. Sar Eliahba is a decent man, and if Seren Manani ever learns he drinks to this extent, the sar will be begging to die."

"I would not see a good man killed, sar. I will say nothing."

"Thank you, Sereni!"

A slight frown on his face, Akish faced forward again. Why did he get the idea that Shemel had questioned whether or not he would hold his tongue?

The sar continued to ride beside him, shifting a little on the mule. "Sereni, I saw something very late last night I think you should know about."

"What was it?"

"I had gone in back of camp to relieve myself, and as I was returning, I saw Sar Lahmi leave his post. When he headed toward Ekron's tents, I followed. He walked to a spot close to Manani's tent, and waited there for some time. When he finally approached it, he was trembling so badly that he could hardly walk. In fact, he looked terrified."

"How could you see his face in the dark?"

"Manani's tent was lit up, Sereni. There were two lamps burning outside it, and at least two inside. When Seren Manani emerged from the tent, Lahmi knelt and then prostrated himself."

"One of the Rapha did that?" Akish asked in amazement.

"It took me aback, Sereni," Shemel said in a subdued voice. "I've never seen one of that clan bow to anyone, let alone go down to the ground."

Trying to digest what the incident might mean, Akish rode along in silence a moment. After this past year, he had toyed with the idea of bribing the Rapha away from their contract with Manani, but obviously the Ekron seren had a much stronger hold on them than he had imagined. "What was he doing there?" he asked finally.

"He pulled something from his shirt, and gave it to Manani. I just glimpsed it, but Sereni, I'd swear Lahmi gave the Egyptian tax authorization to Ekron's ruler. I was so sure of it, I checked the scribe's box this morning, but the authorization was right where the scribe put it. I didn't know what to think after that."

"You've done well to tell me, sar." Again Akish rode on in silence, trying to fathom what it all might mean. They had travelled more than a mile before he turned to Shemel again, his eyes still unfocused in deep thought.

"Sar, did I notice a distinct lack of enthusiasm among the commanders last war season?"

"There might have been some," Shemel finally said uncomfortably. "Begging your indulgence, Sereni, we have lost a lot of good men in the highlands with nothing to show for the price we pay."

"I know," Akish said, his voice hardening. "And enforcing this tax authorization means an even greater effort this war season. That won't be welcome news, will it?"

"No, Sereni," the sar admitted in a low voice. "I would plead with you, Sereni, if you are really interested in keeping good men alive, do what you can to keep us from the land of Yahweh."

"I intend to, sar."

Two days later, Seren Gath stood in the middle of the palace records room, the lamp burning on the table beside him, his hands shaking so much that he could hardly hold the papyrus in them. The night they had stayed in Eglon he had sent for the Egyptian authorization, and then conveniently forgotten to give it back to the scribe, keeping it with him at all times. Tonight, he had personally brought it to the records room to shelve. On impulse, he had opened the cover cloth, only to find papyri rolled in it, not parchment.

In a daze, he had picked up the smaller papyrus scroll. It was a message from Seren Manani informing him that unless he aided Ekron in every way, the fact of the forged tax authorization would be made known to the rest of the Five Cities. Then Akish had unrolled the larger papyrus to find the aforementioned forgery, a copy of the tax document minus some significant clauses, the most prominent being the one stating that the holder of the authorization must make up any tax shortages. That's when his hands began to shake. Lahmi had indeed delivered the tax authorization to Manani and substituted this in its place.

Clenching his teeth, he slowly set the papyrus down, then leaned on the table, trembling, whether from anger or fear he couldn't decide. Was he never going to have that Ekron demon off his back? He read the smaller message again, noticing this time the private instructions to the scribe and the list of workers in the palace who should receive their regular bribe. Three of them he was already familiar with. The other four had escaped his notice so far. The last name was his sister Hazzel's personal handmaid, an older woman with a sour face and a disposition to match.

After thinking frantically for a long time, he admitted he could see no way out of the situation. Manani now had him under his complete control. Then Akish smiled grimly. He supposed he should take his predicament as a compliment. If he'd been enough trouble to Manani that the man had to tamper with Egyptian documents, he must have worried him considerably.

But what should he do now? As he fingered the smaller papyrus, he realized that it had never occurred to Manani that he could read. And right now, that might be the sole fingerhold he had to hang from. He would, therefore, do nothing about the names listed, other than be aware that they were in Ekron's pay.

The scribe must have had other instructions about what to do with the substituted document, but by taking it at Eglon, Akish had unknowingly thwarted that. What if this document never got back into the scribe's hands? If Manani never knew for certain if the substitution had been discovered, it might provide a tiny amount of freedom to him.

He would have to be very careful to do nothing that would annoy or threaten the Ekron ruler, so his hands would still be tied to a large extent. But if he made enough remarks like the one about Hazzel and war, perhaps the seren would resume thinking that Akish was as senile as his abbi had been.

The document tucked into his robe, he left the room.

¥ ¥ ¥ ¥ ¥ ¥

Sar Eliahba stood perfectly still, listening to the tones of the voice rising and falling in the next room. Beor, Seren Manani's personal scribe, sat at a table not far away, his hands compulsively sliding up and down his chest. One glimpse of the movement had been all it took for Eliahba to know that Manani was in a rage. He wondered who was in the other room with the seren. It couldn't be one of the household staff or slaves. There weren't any screams.

The door behind him opened, and Seren Patisi entered with his daughter, who was Manani's wife, clinging to his arm. The woman vanished immediately into the inner courtyard. The elderly Patisi had been the most influential adon in the city when Manani began his rise to power. That his daughter still lived and was treated reasonably was because Patisi had submitted completely to his son-in-law's wishes. His gaze was rather vacant now, as it always was in the presence of Ekron's ruler, but his skill as a persuasive negotiator was unparalleled.

Eliahba turned back to the other door. It seemed the rumors among the sars of the alliance with Ammon had some substance to them. Which meant the plans for a sustained invasion into the highlands were probably true also. He wished he had stayed in camp in Beersheba instead of going to town. Then he would know more. In addition, the wine hadn't been worth drinking.

The inner door opened, and Baalyaton stalked out, his face red, hands clenched with barely-suppressed anger. Eliahba stepped aside with a slight bow to let him pass, then braced himself. Baalyaton was the perfect second to Manani for the simple reason that he possessed a high temper and couldn't think outside of his own interests enough to fear the seren. The only way Manani could control him was to keep him angry at everyone but himself. Consequently, whoever had to deal with Manani after Baalyaton left would have to endure the man's irritation that, once again, the adon wasn't afraid.

"Get in here," the seren snapped, frowning at Baalyaton's retreating back. Eliahba walked into the room, followed by Patisi and Beor. "What are you doing here?" the seren lashed at Beor.

"Sereni, I am here to serve you," the scribe replied, his fingers touching each other, then brushing down his chest.

"And serve me you shall," Manani said softly. "But only when I desire it. Or have you forgotten that when I want you, I send for you?"

Eliahba instantly stiffened at the sight of the seren's expression.

"Go back to your table, Beor. I will be sending for you tonight, after the lamp is lit. And you will come, won't you?"

The scribe paled and sweat broke out on his face. "I will come at your will, Sereni." The man managed to back out of the door and close it behind him.

Manani turned to the others. "I have a rather delicate task for you, Patisi. Since it will involve a great deal of travel, I have assigned Sar Eliahba to be your escort. I will supply a scribe to accompany you, and each of you will have orders directly from me. There is much to be done, and while you will be working together for the most part, there will be some tasks given to each of you alone. Do you understand?"

"Yes," Patisi said.

"Good. Because if you please me in this, Patisi, if you really please me, I just may divorce your daughter."

"Yes, Sereni."

Not a muscle in the man's face moved, but Eliahba saw the tension that rippled across his back.

The seren glanced at Eliahba. "Sar, you will take picked men with you who can fight and pay attention on guard duty. I want a full unit of professionals only. No militia."

"Yes, Sereni. There are some good men from Ammon available. Would they be appropriate?"

"Ammonites? No. In spite of the rumors, you are not going to Rabbath Ammon. As if that fool Nahash would be useful to me! No, you are going to Jebus and Araunah Debir, and you are going there very quietly. And if I hear even the slightest whisper of your presence there, not even Dagon himself will rescue you from my hand!"

Eliahba bowed his head and touched one knee to the floor. "As you command, Sereni. I will arrange for such silence, but it may take a while, unless there is silver to spend."

"Do whatever is necessary. If you are not satisfied with anyone's performance, replace him. I require absolute obedience. There will be several trips, and you will need a core of a dozen picked men who will obey without question. Others can be hired if needed."

The seren turned to Patisi again. "You will take a southern route around Judah. I will have instructions prepared for you to study on the way. You will leave in a week. Go prepare."

"Yes, Sereni." Bowing slightly, Patisi withdrew.

Eliahba waited.

"You will attend me, sar."

"Yes, Sereni."

The sar followed him from the house and through the streets of the city to the public buildings. They passed the town treasury, a room off one side of the palace with thick, massive walls and huge timbers for the roof. Around the corner, stables faced the opposite direction. The only stableman in sight hastily bowed.

"Bring the new chariot horses bought for me to the back courtyard," Manani ordered.

The man hastened to obey.

The seren went into the stables, and the sar followed. The first stall was used to store harnesses, and Manani motioned Eliahba into it. "Take the harness from that hook," he directed, pointing to one about chest high.

His muscles tensing with apprehension, the sar obeyed.

"Push the hook up, and then pull."

Knowing he dared not hesitate, the sar complied, and a small door swung open. He stepped back after a moment of amazement.

"You will bring pack saddles and load them with what is in there. Do this as soon as you can. Then leave them in there. I will tell you when to do more."

Eliahba bowed his head to hide the fear in his eyes. "Yes, Sereni. Will you allow me at this time to assess how many saddles will be required?"

"Certainly, sar."

Trying to hide his trembling, Eliahba slipped through the door and glanced around the small space. He could barely stand upright. Four chests lined one wall, two jars of liquid leaned against them, and more than two dozen clay lamps lay stacked on a blanket. He backed out and turned to find himself less than a foot away from Manani.

The man grasped the front of his robe, and his eyes seemed to glow in the dim light of the stall. Unable to look away, Eliahba's knees melted, and he hung from Manani's hand, paralysed at the sense of evil spilling from the seren.

"Do I need to tell you to say nothing of this at any time for the rest of your life?" the man asked pleasantly.

"No, adoni seren," Eliahba heard himself whisper.

The ring of horses' hooves on the stone of the courtyard jerked Manani's head up, and he cursed softly, shoving Eliahba from him and pulling something from the front of his robe. He stepped into the space behind the door for only a moment, and then shut it, moved swiftly to the entrance of the stables, and walked calmly into the courtyard.

The sar slowly stood, lifting the harness with shaking hands. The door wasn't quite shut. Setting the harness down, Eliahba opened the door again, getting a brief glimpse of a cloth wrapped around what was probably a scroll sitting on the ground by the lamps. He closed the door, keeping the pressure on it as he pulled the hook down. It clicked into place, and he hung the harness on it again.

Then he went into the next stall and quietly lost his stomach. He was marked for death. It had been there in the seren's eyes. Unless he could find some way to escape, Manani would kill him the moment he was no longer needed to handle whatever was in that room.

As he forced himself to his feet and back to the doorway where he looked out into the sunshine, his thoughts flew to his childhood, to the woman who had nursed him when his own immi died. When she had fled from Ekron to save her children from Manani, he'd been too afraid of the god of the highlands to go with her.

By then he had served in the Ekron military force and had killed many of the people of the highland god. Who knew what vengeance he would endure if he fell under the deity's power? He had never forgotten his first raid into the hills, and the dawn attack when the Israelites had rushed the camp, screaming their war cry, calling on their god to destroy the enemy!

Eliahba tried to stop his body from trembling. The thought of facing Hassar Israel, let alone his god, haunted his dreams every war season. Nothing had ever frightened him as much as the fury blazing from the eyes of the oldest son of Shaul as he had swung his sword and taken the life of Eliahba's childhood companion. Nothing—until today. "Batashima, I should have gone with you as you asked," he whispered, shuddering again as he watched Seren Manani discussing the good and bad points of the new chariot horse.

Chapter 2

"How is he, Dara?" Sar Malchi asked.

"It's never been this bad, Sar. He kept things under control for the first month. But you told me to send for you if things got worse."

"When did it start?"

"When we moved to this camp three weeks ago. Every night here is worse than the one before. I have never seen Jonathan like this, Sar. He is utterly savage. Commander Ram has been hiding the prisoners from him lest he slaughter them. The men are afraid, and I don't blame them! He can't go on like this. The only relief we have is after a battle. He may sleep for a few hours then."

Sar Malchi glanced around the Israelite war camp located at the Aijalon pass. Dara's message had found him at Birzaith, and he had headed south immediately. General Abner was still farther north, at the land stair west from Shechem. Philistine pressure against their scattered units was constant and heavy, and the only reason they could manage up here was because Dahveed again patrolled the Shephelah south of Lehi, for which Sar Malchi thanked Yahweh every day.

He had known at the end of the previous war season that his brother was haunted again by nightmares, and Malchi had hesitated about asking Jonathan to serve this war season. But he badly needed his oldest brother's fighting ability and presence to bolster the men. However, if what Dara reported was true, he would have to do something.

"Where is he now?"

"In the tent, resting."

"Check and see if he's asleep. If he is, I won't disturb him."

¥ ¥ ¥ ¥ ¥ ¥

Nemuel's scream echoed in his mind, and Jonathan woke to the fact that he was in the clearing, lying paralysed while Manani tormented his dearest friend. Desperately he struggled to move, to break the bonds that held him. He must save Nemuel! Then the Philistine turned and looked at him, a smile of amusement on his face.

Darkness gathered around the figure that gazed mockingly at him, and hatred washed through the hassar. He welcomed it, knowing that it would set him free.

Someone else bending over him now touched him. With a savage cry, he lunged off the ground, his hands grappling with the man and bearing him back to the ground. In another instant, he was seized from behind, lifted, and thrown aside.

His head had barely cleared enough to realize that he was in the back corner of his tent when Sar Malchi threw aside the tent flap and advanced toward him, eyes blazing. His younger brother grabbed him by one arm and the back of his shirt and hauled him to his feet, giving him a hard shake.

Rage flamed through the hassar, and he gripped Malchi's wrist. "Not even Ishvi dares to touch me so!" he said savagely.

"If Ishvi were here, honored eldest brother, he'd have that dagger you hold buried in your heart by now!" Malchi said, furious. "How dare you attack Dara in such a manner and disgrace our house and name to this extent!"

Stunned, Jonathan looked down to see the red-stained battle dagger in his hand. Unable to reply, he looked back into Malchi's icy eyes, and the chill of the wrath behind them numbed him.

"As of now, you are relieved of all military duty," his brother said in a barely controlled voice. "You will return to Zelah to your private estate until such time as you can be of use to Yah, and not spread terror through our ranks!" Malchi turned on his heel and strode from the tent, yanking the door flap closed behind him.

Still too stunned to speak, Jonathan returned the dagger to its sheath and stepped to the door, pulling the flap aside. The sight of Abiezer bending over Dara, helping to stem the blood from the long cut on his shield-bearer's arm, stopped him cold. "Yahweh, what have I done?" he whispered as he let the flap fall again.

At dusk, Jonathan lay on the bed in his upper room, staring at the ceiling. Turning over on his stomach, he gripped the blankets. He had thought the nightmares were gone for good. It had been years since any had troubled him. Then, in the middle of the previous war season, he'd dreamed of Nemuel, and gradually, the nightmares had become more frequent, worsening in character.

This year he had very nearly begged Abbi to let him remain home, but when the reports came that the coastal cities had increased their support to Gath and Ekron, he had said nothing. He knew Malchi and Abner would need him. And they had.

Twisting on the bed, he pounded the blankets in frustration. Yahweh had named him Melek Israel. It was his duty to defend his people! He had been rid of this torment for so long! Why had it returned now? Had he done something? Or neglected something? Was Yahweh angered?

"Yahweh, help me," he whispered. "You promised that Your hesed would always remain with me. I must know what to do, for Your people have need of me." He straightened the blankets on the bed, his motions slowing as a thought crept into his mind.

All those years ago, Immi had soothed his nightmares with an herbal mixture a healer from Babylon had taught her. It was the last thing he could think to do. If the herbs could make him sleep, he could continue to fight during this season. Then he would be able to deal with the problem later.

Rising, he went to the door. "Gaham?"

"Yes, Hassar?"

"Send to Hassarah Ahinoam. Tell her I need the herbs."

"Yes, Hassar."

He was walking up the hillside to Nemuel's grave. Huge cypress trees crowded around, making everything dark. The little dale that held the grave, like a scoop out of the hillside, was thick with thorns and brambles. The open, gaping hole in the side of the ridge had black smoke boiling from it like burning pitch.

"Look into it," the voice commanded.

His mind screamed at him to run, but something more powerful than he compelled him to climb the path. Eyes tightly shut, he faced the grave.

"Look into it!"

Although he tried to refuse, he was held by bonds that he could not break, and then his eyes were open, and he saw.

Nemuel was there, just as he'd found him in the clearing. Only Manani stood there too, laughing, because through all those years there had never been an end to his friend's pain. His dagger was in his hand, only this time Jonathan didn't cut Nemuel's throat. He slashed his own, and then stepped down into the grave to join Nemuel at last.

Jonathan Hassar jerked upright and awake, his own cry ringing in his ears. For long moments he sat there on the bed, his head swimming with the herbs and the clinging darkness. Then he lay back, his arms wrapped around his head to keep from beating it against the floor, while tears of helplessness ran down his cheeks. What could he do now? "Yahweh, where is Your promised hesed?"

Sometime later, he woke again from the beginning of another dream. Bitterly, he stared out the small window at the clear night sky, hatred of Manani raging in him. At last he rose, threw on the first clothes he touched in the darkness, and let himself out of the upper room, shoving the battle dagger into the girdle around his waist.

The compound was dark and still, the vast expanse of stars arching overhead, ending in the thicker darkness of the forest to the west. Approaching the gate, he was startled to see a figure step from the shadow of Peleth's house into the dim starlight.

"Geberet," he greeted her shortly, recognizing his overseer's immi.

"I have something to say to you, Jonathan ben Shaul."

Annoyed, the hassar paused, wanting only to escape to the forest, where he could be alone. "Speak, then," he finally said.

"Seren Manani was angered that he did not have Hassar Israel in his power the day he took Nemuel, but he did," the old woman began. She straightened a little and reached out to touch him, but Jonathan jerked away. "He has you still, you know. He has tormented you so that you cannot bear to have a grateful and harmless old woman rest her fingers on your skin, for it brings too much pain."

Unable to look away, the hassar stared at her.

"Nemuel is dead, Hassar, but while your hatred lives, it binds you to Manani and to your pain. You must go back, and give it to Yahweh, for no man is able to bear such a burden." Again, she reached out to touch him, and the hassar shied away, nearly stumbling as he rushed out the gate, one hand on the dagger hilt.

How dare that Philistine woman touch him! Fury surged through him. How dare she even think to speak to him that way! Telling him what to do! He clenched his teeth. "Go back!" he spoke aloud, his throat tight with rage. "*Go back?* I've been back every time I dream!"

Shaking with anger, he strode away from the estate, driven by the hatred and rage boiling inside. "It was not right!" he said between clenched teeth. "Manani should pay for his deed! Nemuel must be avenged. Your own justice demands that!" he threw up at the sky, as his feet pounded the path faster and faster, until he raced through the forest, bursting out on the road and turning west.

Once again, the sight of his friend's last moments rose in his mind with stark clarity. And then he saw at his feet the overseer of Beeroth, the man he had executed for using his name to abuse the Gibeonites. For the first time, he realized he had done the same things to the overseer that Nemuel had suffered! Horror filled him, and he fled from the thoughts that pursued him like ravenous wolves.

Hours later, he stumbled to a halt, panting, legs and feet sore from the beating he had given them. Even in the faint starlight, he knew where he was. Not quite three miles ahead was the eastern overlook to Eshtaol. And in the ravine this side of it was Nemuel's grave.

"You will have Your will one way or the other, won't You, Yahweh?" he said ironically, giving a quick look upward. "What more do You want of me?"

"*No man is able to bear such a burden.*" The words sounded in his mind again.

"But, Adonai, how can I refuse to avenge?" he nearly shouted, falling to his knees on the road. "I swore to Nemuel that I would bring those who did this to justice. Would You have me break my vow? You command that vows be kept! Am I to let such evil remain in the world? You Yourself said that only by the blood of the murderer could the land itself be cleansed of the curse brought on it. How else can I cleanse the land? No matter what I do You will be displeased! How can You ask this of me?"

"*How could I ask Isaac of Abram?*"

"This is not the same!" Jonathan replied without thinking.

"*No, for Isaac was Abram's son. Nevertheless, you stand at Abram's place.*"

It took several moments before he understood. "You have given me a command that contradicts what You have already said, and I don't understand, just as Abram didn't then."

"*When did Abram find understanding?*"

"After he obeyed." After, not before. The hassar continued down the road, clinging to the thought that somehow Yahweh would give him relief if he returned to face the haunted darkness of the grave.

The sun's rays streaked the sky behind him as Jonathan turned down a ravine, picking his way across the steep hillside slippery with last year's leaves. Exactly as he remembered it, a huge stone pine soon towered over him, thrust into the sky. He started up the slope, stumbling once or twice as he climbed to the base of the tree that marked the depression in the hillside scarcely more than 50 feet across. The bare face of an outcropping of rock formed the back side, covered with dark green moss and colored lichens.

Anemones in blue and lavender waved near the rill that formed a tiny waterfall down the rock face. Opposite him, less than 20 feet above, was the small cave opening he remembered, the entrance almost entirely feathered by ferns, still green despite the heat of summer. Not far from it, a young olive tree grew, covered with olives.

The peaceful, quiet beauty of the place contrasted so sharply with the tormenting visions he had had, that a long time passed before he dared to step into the miniature garden tucked away in the hillside. As he did so, he stared around in awe. All these years—all these years— he had been afraid to return because of the frightful visions his nightmares had created. "Yahweh, what have You done?" he whispered.

"*I have honored one who is dear to My heart. You loved him as a boyhood friend, the one who taught you the depths to which loyalty must sometimes go. I loved him as My child of covenant, the one who gave to the uttermost, and thus preserved his house, and yours.*"

The hassar sank to the ground with the realization of how much greater Yahweh's regard for Nemuel was than his own. "If you would do this much for Nemuel, why haven't you avenged him?"

"*You know that vengeance is Mine. But I cannot take up what you will not give. Why haven't you offered Nemuel's honor to Me?*"

Suddenly, his efforts and determination to avenge his friend's death seemed petty indeed, compared to what Yahweh might be prepared to do. "Have I stood in Your way all this time?" he asked, amazed.

"*Your hatred has. Only as you have clung to it have you, also, blocked My way.*"

For a long time Jonathan remained silent. "I do not know that I can let go. I have held it for so long."

"*How much of your nightmare was true?*"

"None," he had to admit.

"Hatred always lies."

Gradually, complete disgust swept over him as he realized how easily the lies in his own mind had deceived and tormented and held him captive. Anger followed it as he remembered all the misery, pain, and fear he had suffered, to say nothing of what that hatred had driven him to do all those years ago in Beeroth. And what he would have done again, just days ago, to the Philistines captured in battle if he could have found them.

Suddenly Jonathan cried out in self-loathing, "El Shaddai! I am becoming what I have hated for so long! And I betrayed Dara and brought disgrace and contempt on Your name! What must I do?"

"Do you still wish to keep your hatred?"

"No!" he nearly shouted, feeling as if he had awakened to find himself in a stinking refuse heap, covered with filth. He stretched full-length on the ground. "Take it, Yahweh! Rid me of it! Do with me as You will, for I have been a fool."

A sense of calm settled on him and over the tiny clearing, the only sound the soft rippling of the tiny stream flowing over the rocks, almost as if it was washing over him in some way. New thoughts crowded his mind, bringing memory after memory to his attention. There had been so much that he had thought he had known, but now recognized that he hadn't really at all.

As the hours passed, Jonathan felt the quietness and peace of the place seep into him as he opened himself to Yah's searching, cleansing power, and yielded to his God whatever rose in his soul.

At last, he stood and faced the mouth of the cave. Shadows covered the cup in the hill, although the sun still bathed the top of the stone pine. Climbing the path to the opening, he reverently entered the cool, dim space with head bowed. The cloak he had used to cover his childhood companion had long ago rotted away, and the bones were jumbled and chewed by animals. "My hatred has not served you well, either, Nemuel," he whispered.

After collecting the bones, he stood a moment longer. "Adonai, was there more to Manani's hold on me than just my hatred?"

"I gave you both the same dream. You were willing to follow My path to it. He was not."

Amazement flashed through the hassar, and then regretful sadness. "I have not always done Your will, have I?"

Laughter seemed to shimmer around him. "*No. But you have not always been mulish, either.*"

In spite of himself, Jonathan chuckled.

Back outside, he climbed above the opening to the rock that had partially separated from the hillside all those years ago. He had planned to return with someone who could help him push it over, but never had. Now, the weather, wind, and water had eroded it free even more, and it shifted easily when he braced himself against it. As he pushed harder, the rock shifted, slowly tipping until its weight broke off the ground beneath it, letting it fall, rather than roll, into the opening below, and bringing down enough dirt, gravel, and debris to seal the grave.

When he stood again at the stone pine, Jonathan turned back one last time, then bowed to the ground. "In spite of all the ways I have strayed from You, Adonai Yahweh, You have been most gracious to me, giving me all of my heart's desires. I am grateful."

"*You gave me your heart, Jonathan ben Shaul, and that was My heart's desire.*"

When he finished his worship, the hassar stood and looked up at the now closed grave. "Rest in peace, Nemuel ben Abner."

Chapter 3

As he climbed out of the ravine, he caught the aroma of roasting meat and suddenly realized that he'd been fasting for more than 24 hours. Knowing the most likely place for someone to camp was at the overlook, he headed that way. Staying in the verge of the forest, he located the camp and crept closer, studying it cautiously, for the only weapon he carried was the battle dagger.

The young man by the fire looked up. "It took you long enough to get here, geber. I was wondering if I'd have to deliver your dinner personally."

"Nimshi, how could you possibly know it was me?" Jonathan asked, stepping into view.

With that mischievous grin, his armor-bearer jerked his chin toward the mules tethered to one side. His own light gray mount stood with head up and ears pricked, nose reaching toward him to be scratched.

"It's a good thing that mule knows you. I doubt I'd have recognized you in the kilt you're wearing. What did you do in it last, clean out a cistern?"

The hassar glanced down and winced. "It was dark when I dressed. I set this out to be sent to Immi for rags."

After he'd eaten, and then drunk from the nearby seep, the hassar settled by the fire again, watching the last of the sun's rays slanting toward him. "You trailed me here, I suppose?"

"Most of the way. Once I was certain you were going to the grave, I just came directly here to wait."

"I never told anyone where I buried Nemuel."

Nimshi glanced up at him. "All of Yahweh's Arrows know where He-Who-Remained-Silent is buried. And we honor him," he finished seriously. "Geber, there's been a lot of activity in the night on the Shephelah. Dahveed Joel sent news that every unit of Gath has moved north. The local band here also said that still others have shifted north, but there are a lot of them camped just at the base of the land stair from here to Aijalon, with more arriving. I think we should go to the other overlook. The scouts say that the Philistine units begin to move about dusk."

Jonathan glanced at the disappearing sun. "We'll have to hurry then."

Not long after, they stood surveying the terrain below the drop-off in front of them.

"Can you see if they are climbing?" Jonathan asked.

"I haven't seen any movement up the land stair, nor any fires. They are carefully keeping out of sight."

"You know what the trouble with your abbi is?" Jonathan asked unexpectedly.

"What?"

"He rubs off on you. I'm afraid I am quite curious about what all those Philistines are doing down there."

Nimshi grinned. "Shall we go see?"

Jonathan chuckled. "Lead on."

¥ ¥ ¥ ¥ ¥ ¥

Sar Eliahba checked the sentry posts around the camp again before returning to his bedroll. Beor the scribe lay just a few feet from him, an ill-fitting helmet on his head, a small leather shield and short sword beside him. Every time he looked at the man, the sar wanted to cringe. Seren Manani had made it plain that Beor was to die the day after next on the raid into Israel.

As always when he received such orders, anger seized him. He had managed to leave several of the would-be victims alive in the highlands, knowing that whatever happened to them there would be better than what they had left behind. Once back in camp after reporting to Manani that they were dead, he always gave a sacrifice to Dagon asking the god to shield them, and hoped that Israel's deity would overlook them.

Beor seemed completely apathetic about his fate during the day, but at night, Eliahba had seen the terror in the man. It caused the sar's anger to rise in his throat, giving him courage to disobey Ekron's ruler one more time.

Wondering if he would manage to save Beor, he lay down, looking at the steep cliff that loomed above them, and tried to relax enough to sleep. He would give anything to be away from this place. Who knew what could happen to them this close to the highland god? The darkness lessened around him as the moon rose. It was nearly full, and shed enough light that he could plainly see the figures of his men lying in a rough circle in the small open space under the trees.

Resisting the urge to check the sentries again, he gripped his dagger and settled a little more into the dead leaves. The moon was high in the sky when his eyes opened again, and his hand tightened around the dagger, sure that someone lurked nearby. Silently he turned his head, catching sight of one of the sentries standing not far away, studying the camp. He was about to speak when he heard Beor's breath catch in his throat as he looked at the man, wide-eyed with terror.

The "sentry" took two quick steps, yanking a dagger from his girdle, and dived for the scribe, flattening him on the ground, one hand covering his mouth, the other raised to strike. It took a moment or two for Eliahba to realize that the face of the man over Beor was Israelite, and the knowledge burst on him that they had an enemy in their camp! The intruder's back was partially toward him, and the sar expected that Beor would die even as he swung his dagger around in a useless attempt to save him.

Then the sar froze in mid-movement. The Israelite wasn't killing Beor. Never taking his eyes from his captive's face, the intruder shoved the dagger into the girdle holding up a filthy kilt, then practically lifted the man bodily from the ground and took him back into the trees the way he had come.

For long moments Eliahba debated what to do, then eased back down. Given what that Israelite had been wearing, and the fact that he'd only had a dagger, he wasn't any soldier. He was probably a Habiru, who would sell Beor the first chance he got. Which would be good for Beor. The Habiru hadn't done anything else, unless he had stolen something, and he didn't see any reason to send his unit after a thief, risking giving away their presence to the Israelites by doing so. They had been told to get here and stay put until dawn tomorrow. He would just obey orders.

¥ ¥ ¥ ¥ ¥

A somewhat heated discussion woke Hassar Jonathan in the morning. He and Nimshi slept in his war tent, still pitched at the camp above the Aijalon pass. His captive slept outside. They had arrived about four hours ago in the dark of the night after heading north with the information they had gleaned from their foray down the land stair.

About 12-15 Philistine units camped between Eshtaol and Aijalon, and they appeared to be planning a major raid into the uplands soon.

The voices moved close enough to understand, and the hassar listened with amusement.

"Then why is that man lying outside the tent? I saw the hassar!"

"Sithri, the moon was nearly down, and this tent is in the shadows as it is," Tahan replied reasonably. "Even if there is someone in there, it can't be the hassar!"

Jonathan sat up. If the second unit was here, perhaps Malchi was still around, and that would save a great deal of time. He stood and stretched, opening his clothes chest to see if he had something besides the ragged kilt to wear. The rustling sounds he made suddenly caused total silence outside the tent.

"I told you someone was in there," Sithri hissed.

"But who's going to find out who?"

"That's Sar Malchi's job, I think," Commander Ram said. "Don't you agree, Lotan?"

"Completely. Pallu, go get the sar."

By the time he heard Malchi arrive, Jonathan had a clean undergarment and kilt on, and had emptied the cruse of wine he found. Nimshi still slept peacefully.

Outside, Lotan tersely explained to the sar why he'd been summoned, and Jonathan heard his brother loosen his sword before he approached the tent, only to pause just at the entrance.

"Nimshi's still asleep, Malchi. Come in quietly," Jonathan directed in a low voice.

His brother entered quickly and glanced around, assessing the situation before turning his gaze to him.

Jonathan bowed his head slightly. "I believe I will now be of more use to Yah, and to you. Adonai drove me back to Nemuel's grave, and I repented of my stubborn foolishness there. Yahweh cleansed me of my hatred, and I found peace."

Malchi searched his eyes for a long moment, then dropped down on his knees in front of him. When Jonathan took his younger brother's hands, Malchi gripped them hard.

"I will send gold to the sanctuary for this, adoni. My life fell apart when I saw you burst from the tent with your dagger out against Dara! Thanks be to Yah for accepting you again!"

"And I must send a sin offering," Jonathan said, helping his brother stand. "I came north to tell you what Nimshi and I learned last night. After that, I need to return to Zelah for the day. Then I am free to return here or remain in Gibeah as you think best."

Malchi's eyes widened. "As *I* think best?" he echoed. "Yah's hand must have been very effective!"

The hassar flushed a little. "It was," he said softly.

His brother regarded him a moment longer. "In that case, I will expect you back for duty when Dara has recovered. What did you learn?"

Jonathan reported what he and Nimshi had gleaned.

Malchi smiled grimly. "We will have to prepare a warm welcome for them. Now, who's that outside?"

"I haven't had time to find out yet. All I know is that he's another of Manani's victims."

The two of them exited the tent, to find that nearly everyone in the two closest units was covertly watching. Ignoring them, Jonathan approached his captive.

"Hesed, shobeh," the man said, his voice faint.

The hassar stopped a few feet away from him. "How are you called?"

"Beor, shobeh."

"What do you do, Beor? I know you aren't a soldier."

"Hesed, shobeh," the man repeated, his hands stirring restlessly, the fingers picking at his clothing. "I'm a scribe."

"What city are you from?"

"Ekron."

The restless movements grew, and he rubbed his hands together a little, then slid them up and down his chest, only to brush the fingers against each other. He raised one to his face and tried to lick his lips.

"Whose household in Ekron?"

The man's eyes glazed over with fear, and Jonathan repressed his angry reaction. His question had been too direct, and from the way Beor's hands fluttered up and down his chest, it was no use continuing to interpolate him. Unable to stand the sight, Jonathan stepped forward and caught the scribe's hands in his own. His captive did not move except to tremble.

"Hesed, hesed," the man whispered repeatedly.

"Send a message to Peleth to come and get him, Malchi," Jonathan said, turning away, his stomach sick. "From the looks of this one, I'll have to leave him with Peleth for quite some time before he'll be able to stay coherent in my presence."

"All right. Ishvi sent you one he found last year, didn't he?"

Jonathan nodded. "I can't imagine what that man does to make them this way."

Malchi was silent a moment. "I always wondered that, too. When I remember how close I came to finding out there at Birzaith, it scares me. If Dahveed and the second unit hadn't been there—" Shuddering, he turned away, his face pale.

At noon, Jonathan arrived with Nimshi back at his private estate. He had dismounted before anyone there recognized him. "Where's Immi?" he asked the guard staring at him.

"In the small house, Hassar," the man managed to say.

As he started toward it, she burst from it, followed by Michal and Shaul. Ahinoam clung to him tightly, her trembling telling him how much she had feared for him. As he loosened one arm to include Michal in the embrace, the news of his return flashed around the entire compound.

"I'm fine, Immi," he said at last when her hold on him let up a little. Then he glanced at his abbi. "Yahweh helped me," he added.

"I prayed He would," Ahinoam said, her voice shaking. "When we found you gone— Then when Nimshi said he found your trail, I dared to hope you would come back!"

"Did Dahveed come?" Shaul asked, his face emotionless.

"No, Abbi."

Relief eased the lines of Shaul's face. "He has not come north, then. Yahweh will keep him away."

"I have news," Jonathan said, ignoring the reference to Dahveed. "There will probably be a hard thrust into the highlands from Eshtaol to Aijalon. Malchi is planning a warm reception, and he wished me to request that you would meet with him at Aijalon tonight. Otherwise, I—"

"You will remain here, Jonathan," Shaul interrupted. "You must rest."

"As you wish, Abbi. Malchi strongly suggested the same thing."

Calling for his mule, Shaul departed.

Ahinoam turned the hassar's face to her with her fingers as Michal hugged him again. "You seem very willing to do as Malchi suggested."

Jonathan gave her a little smile and pulled his sister closer. "Yes, Immi. I'm learning to listen to wisdom from others."

It was close to dusk when Jonathan woke to find the bath and meal he had ordered still waiting for him. After eating, he bathed out on the balcony in the gathering dusk where the water would not seep into the house or storerooms. Then, having two visits to make, he dressed carefully.

As he descended the stairs, he glanced over at the small house. Dara sat on a stool outside, leaning against the wall. The hassar hesitated. Perhaps it would be better to talk to his shield-bearer alone. He shook his head. No, he'd attacked Dara in public, and his apology must be in public also.

Nimshi lounged by the gate. Jonathan motioned to the armor-bearer, and as Nimshi strode to him, he realized the young boy had grown into a strong, sturdy warrior, shorter than his abbi, Ethan, but probably soon to be stronger.

"Yes, geber?"

"Nimshi, I am sending you to Dara. Ask him if I may speak with him."

The Habiru straightened up at the formality of the request. "I will go at once, geber."

Jonathan watched him stop in front of the shield-bearer, speaking in a low voice. Dara glanced his way once and replied to Nimshi, who returned to the hassar.

"What did he say?"

"That he was not prepared to receive you."

Jonathan's breath caught in his throat. "Ask him if he would consider sending for me when he is."

Nimshi went back to Dara. By now, the interchange had attracted attention, and the guards and servants watched from various parts of the compound. The Habiru came back again. "He said no, he would never consider sending for you, and he is angered that you would think he would."

For a long moment, Jonathan said nothing, wondering how he could go into battle without Dara at his side. But he certainly couldn't blame the man for his decision. After the years of selfless loyalty Dara had given him, attacking him had been inexcusable. He looked at Nimshi. "Was that all he said?"

"No, geber, but that was all he told me to tell you."

"Was there something more you were not to tell me?"

"He didn't say one way or the other," his armor-bearer said with a straight face.

"Then what else did he say?" Jonathan asked, curious.

"He muttered under his breath about a certain kind of sar who didn't know left from right and something about staying where he was until said sar sent for him as was proper."

Exasperation filled Jonathan. He was trying to make things right—as Dara certainly deserved—and his shield-bearer was acting like a certain southern hill man of their acquaintance. Then he glared at Nimshi. "You go tell that man that if he doesn't allow me to apologize to him as I ought, I'll—I'll kneel here in the center of this courtyard until he does!"

"Yes, geber."

By now, everyone stood around in the near darkness, intently watching.

Nimshi delivered the message, eliciting an exclamation from Dara. When Nimshi responded, Dara grabbed the warrior's hand, hauling himself up to lean against the house wall.

The armor-bearer trotted back to Jonathan. "Dara said that if you insist on seeing him in his unwashed, ill-dressed, unprepared state, he can't stop you."

At that moment the hassar saw his shield-bearer already walking toward him. "Nimshi, go help him so that he doesn't fall on his face," he commanded, striding toward the man. When they met, Jonathan took Dara's hands, steadying him.

"Hassar, there is no need—"

"Yes, Dara, there is. My hand attacked you. We cannot ignore that."

His battle companion held his gaze a long time, then looked down. "No, I guess we cannot."

Jonathan let go and stepped back, bowing formally. "Allow me to extend my apologies for the attack on you. It was inexcusable that I, Jonathan ben Shaul, Hassar Israel and your adon, would turn on you as

I did. What recompense will be sufficient to restore your honor?" As he finished, Jonathan touched his knee to the ground.

"Your apology is accepted, Jonathan, Hassar Israel. I lay this recompense on you, that you will not engage in combat until I am able to shield for you again."

Jonathan looked up. "It shall be as you wish. I shall not fight," he said, bowing before he stood. "Do you, Dara, wish to carry the shield for me?"

Leaning heavily on Nimshi, the man knelt. "I do."

"Then I shall accept you as before."

"And I shall serve you as before."

It was fully dark when Jonathan walked up to the small, one-room house by the compound gate. "Peleth?" he called.

His overseer came to the door. "You wanted something, Hassar?"

"I have come to speak with your immi. I wish to know if she will receive me."

For a moment, Peleth didn't know how to respond. The fact that the master of the estate would ask to be received by one of his dependents left him bewildered.

But the shuffle of slow, unsteady footsteps from the house made the overseer bow slightly and disappear into the house to help his immi.

"It is you, adon?" she asked when she arrived at the door.

"Yes, geberet. I have come to ask how you are."

She straightened up as much as she could. "I am as well as can be expected, adon. It is kind of you to ask."

"Are you comfortable? Do you have all you need?"

"More than enough. Your hesed has provided for us even though we are strangers in your land."

"And you have repaid that hesed. Yahweh found in you a willing messenger to me, and I am grateful. When you spoke, you would have laid your hand on me, but I rejected it. I would accept it now, if you would extend it again." Bowing his head, Jonathan Hassar knelt on the raised threshold and waited.

"You do me much honor, Hassar. Yahweh has indeed blessed you greatly. Receive now what comes from His hand."

The old woman laid her hand on his head a moment. When he rose, a deep sense of peace filled him.

80 ~ Yahweh's Soldier

"Shalom go with you," she said.
"And with you, geberet."

Tamar bat Dahveed

At last the hassar has truly given all to Yahweh, and yielded what he held close for so long, opening his mind and heart to accept whatever Yahweh will use to avenge Nemuel. In so doing, he has also opened his heart wide enough that Yahweh can grant Jonathan the greatest desire of his life: to set Israel free.

Now, however, there are other things which must be done. Yahweh has turned his attention to Philistia. The politics of the Five Cities and the serens that rule them will become our God's tools, for we must remember that the ways of Yahweh are not our ways, especially when the ground he chooses to work seems unlikely at best.

What's that you say, little one? You don't want to hear about Philistia, just about Dahveed? I know how you feel, but Yahweh works when and where he wills. So although what happens next in Philistia doesn't involve Dahveed directly at this time, it is very important for you to know, because much of what will happen later began now, with the events Yahweh set in motion through Ittai and Eliphelet. So enjoy this little digression, tuck it away in your mind, because the results from this time will affect Dahveed's life in many ways.

You see, Yah gave Eliphelet to Dahveed to accomplish two important tasks. The time for the first is here. And, as always, the Evil One has been working to hinder those who are part of Yah's will. Ittai will find himself caught between his blood clan and his covenant clan. Seren Manani, by rejecting Yah's leading, has been a thorn in Yahweh's will, tolerated for many years since his evil could still be made to serve Yah's purposes. But he has overreached himself, and Yah will not allow his power to grow greater.

Not only will Yah use this situation to clear away the hindrances to his will, but to return Ittai to his house, for the time has come for him to leave Dahveed. Yah has need of a dependable agent in Philistia, and the young half-blood has grown into exactly the man Yah intended him to be.

The First Five Weeks

Chapter 4

Week One, Day One

With the war season over, I decided to talk to Ittai the morning after I arrived back at Hachilah. The skirmishes had been constant below the Elah Valley even after Shaul and Malchi had repulsed a major thrust into the highlands north of Eshtaol. Why were they so persistent? It didn't make sense.

"You sent for me, Dahveed?"

"Yes. The Philistine push against Israel was worse this year than last. It isn't like Akish to waste men and efforts in this manner, especially down here in the south where there isn't much to reward them even if they did penetrate the highlands. Do you know any reason for what's going on?"

My covenant son rubbed his chin. "I've wondered about it myself," he said slowly. "It isn't like Dodi to do this, which means there has to be some compelling reason." His voice drifted into silence, and he stared blankly for a few moments. "No, I can't think of anything."

I sighed. "Well, I'd appreciate knowing anything you do find out about the change. At this rate, we'll have all-out war next year, and there won't be much left of Gath's fighting force if they come up here and meet us head-on. The shalishim would cut them to pieces."

Ittai became lost in thought again. "They would, Dahveed," he murmured. "I'll do what I can."

"Good!" So far I'd never sent more than one shalish against a unit of Philistines, having no need to. Uriah's training had become ingrained in the men, and they fought now like nothing I'd ever seen. I couldn't imagine the Philistine sars hadn't noticed, and why Akish would continue to send them against an obviously superior fighting force puzzled me. From the way the Philistine units acted, especially after the expedition at Eshtaol failed, they apparently wondered the same thing. Well, maybe Ittai would learn more. He usually did.

¥ ¥ ¥ ¥ ¥ ¥

"Here you are!" Sahrah Hazzel exclaimed, her hair flying behind her as she rushed through the door to the palace roof. "I've been looking all over for you. It's got to stop, before that slimy Phoenician leaves and there's nothing left but a pile of rubble with the Rapha buried beneath it! And may the gods grant us that at least! I saw him again, and I heard Shemel and Lahmi with that purse! You've got to banish him from the city, Akish, before we're all ruined!"

In spite of his somber thoughts, Akish shook his head in puzzled amusement. "Banish whom, Hazzel?"

"The slimy Phoenician, of course! Jingling his purse and never saying anything, which makes them talk all the more! It's a disgrace, Akish, and the sars won't take much more!"

The seren jerked his head around to see his sister. "Slow down, Hazzel! The sars won't take much more of what?"

"Useless slaughter! They are supposed to fight, and they know it, and I suppose they do their share of killing, which by the way, wouldn't be necessary if you would just stay out of the highlands where there isn't anything worth having anyway. But this time, with Dahveed up there, and—"

Grabbing her, he clapped his hand over her mouth. Hazzel's eyes stared at him, then turned furious. Hastily, the seren jerked his hand away. "I apologize, Hazzel, I didn't mean to, but you can't say—"

Without a word, she jerked around and started toward the door. Akish jumped after her, grabbing her arm and pulling her around to face him again. She stopped, staring at him, enraged.

Reddening, he dropped his hand. "Please, Hazzel, don't do this to me, not tonight. It's already bad enough, and—" Unable to go on, he rubbed his hand across his face and turned away. "I apologize, Sahrah. I trust I didn't hurt you."

Hazzel said nothing for a long time. "Why did you keep sending our units into the highlands, Akish? Haven't you been listening to the sars? They ran into something up there that overmatches them on every level. It has to be Dahveed Israel." Her voice was even and quiet.

Akish looked at her. "I know," he admitted, speaking as quietly as she had. "I have heard every word of every report, and I know exactly what it means. But I don't have a choice. And the only reason more of our men didn't die was because it *was* Dahveed up there. But Manani doesn't know that. He thinks we are drawing units from Israel's army down here to keep us from infiltrating from the south. And that's the only reason I can keep my units close to Gath, where they are fighting a foe who lets the militia run back to safety and where the professionals are learning from Shemel what to do to save themselves when they go up there!

"I thank Dagon every day for that sar, Hazzel. He's the only reason Gath has a viable professional force right now. If our units were being used up north, with Manani in command, we wouldn't have an army left! That Ekron devil would make absolutely certain of that. As it is, all he can do is insist that our forces climb the highlands where they only get carved up a little at a time."

"You are in charge of your units, Akish. Why should you let Manani's commands destroy them?"

Taking her hands, he pulled her to him so that he could speak even more quietly. "Manani has a stranglehold on me," he admitted, hoping that telling this to his sister wouldn't spread it all over the city the next time she opened her mouth. She seemed so empty-headed, flying from one subject to another, her spate of words incomprehensible, but at times such as tonight, when she looked him in the eye, she revealed a grasp of the situation that sometimes exceeded his own. And he wondered if maybe her tongue said only what she wished it to and not one thing more.

"What has he done?"

"You know Gath and Ekron received the authorization from Pharaoh to collect his taxes. Before we'd even left Beersheba, Manani had substituted a forgery for the document given to me. It's so badly done, it can't be mistaken for anything else, especially since the clauses about making up any tax shortage are missing."

His sister sucked in her breath. "Why would he—Oh."

"If I don't do exactly as he says from now on, he can reveal that forgery and bring Egypt's wrath down on Gath."

"It's not Egypt you need to worry about, Akish. It's the coastal cities," Hazzel said, staring east over the wall. "If they think you've tried to get out of paying your share of the deficit, they will accuse you of treason against the alliance. Particularly since this year there will be a shortfall, won't there?"

"Yes. I have nowhere to go, Hazzel. Manani owns me now."

The sahrah took his hand. "Don't give up yet, Akish. There is something building against Manani; I can feel it. The other serens can't be happy that he failed to get any plunder from Israel this year."

"They are furious, but I may be dead before they do anything," he said bitterly.

"I don't think so." She squeezed his hand. "I think Manani has forgotten one important thing—the god of the highlands."

"What would he care about us, Hazzel? We are Dagon's people."

"Not all of us. There is a very important one of us who belongs to Yah."

"Ittai must be dead, Hazzel."

"He's not," she said positively. "I'd feel it if he were."

Taking her into his arms, Akish said nothing. He'd loved his half-Israelite nephew more than anyone except Hazzel. And now he was almost glad the boy was dead. He just wondered how long he could keep Gath from Manani's clutches, and himself alive so that Hazzel wouldn't end up married to that cursed demon. Now he also looked east to the highlands, and silently made the decision that if bad came to worse, he'd send Hazzel up there with Shemel. Maybe Dahveed would protect them for Ittai's sake. And maybe the highland god would accept them for Dahveed's sake.

Week One, Day Six

"Dahveed, didn't you say the caravan the men are guarding belongs to Hadar?" Gebirah Abigail asked me five days after I'd talked to Ittai about the war season.

"Yes. Hadar has allied with Jether's caravans. Jether wants to find a good route down the Arabah and across the Negev. He's tired of the taxes on the King's Highway. They were trying out the route up to Arad, then over to Beersheba. One of Ethan's sons is guiding them."

"Could I go with Ittai? I'd like to see Hadar again."

"I'll tell him to plan on it. While you're in town, see if there are any skins available. Now that we're not hunting so much, Parai doesn't have enough to make all the leather we need."

Abigail brightened. "Maybe Hadar knows something. I'll ask!" She hurried off to get ready, and I watched. Although she never complained, I knew living here in the stronghold was hard for her. She missed being in a town and having a house. A thought occurred to me, and I looked around. We practically had a town now, and there wasn't any reason we couldn't construct a house. I'd have to ask Zalmon about that. He was the best builder among my band. Maybe we could put up two houses. Ahinoam would appreciate one also, and with the reconciliation between Shaul and me, there wasn't any reason why we couldn't just establish our own town!

With that thought in mind, I walked through the encampment, looking for Ittai and assessing the possibilities of turning the place into a town at the same time. I'd need to consult with Shagay and Josheb about defense, and whether or not we should use this hilltop or another.

My half-cousin Zelek stalked by, holding the bracelets that Eliphelet always managed to steal from him no matter where he hid them. It made me smile a little. At least Zelek had caught the thief in the act this time. Then I sighed. I should get Eliphelet out of this camp for a while. His constant thefts were grating on people here, but I hated to inflict him on our other strongholds without being there to watch him.

Ittai was at the trail head out of our stronghold, tightening up the riding cloth on the donkey, so I gathered that Abigail had found him and let him know she was going. While I was giving him some silver for their stay at the inn in Arad, Abigail arrived, her face flushed with excitement. Eliphelet followed her.

"Dahveed, Eliphelet wants to come also. Is that all right?"

Ittai frowned slightly.

"Can you handle him?" I asked. "It would be a blessing to get him out of camp."

"I'll look after him," the Gebirah added, coming up to us.

My covenant son shrugged, and I turned to Eliphelet. "You will do exactly what the Gebirah says, and *no stealing!*" I commanded.

"I promise," he said, tucking his hands under his arms as he always did when someone mentioned cutting them off.

"Good, because I will hold Gebirah Abigail responsible for you," I added sternly.

Gulping, he glanced at my wife. "Oh, well, then, uh, maybe I'd better not go," he stammered.

Abigail caught his attention. "It's only for two days, maybe three, and I know you won't steal anything for my sake."

As I watched them leave, I hoped Abigail was right. His thefts had been nearly nonstop the past few weeks, making me wonder again what drove him to do it.

"Sar Dahveed, Joab has come," Pekah, Zalmon's oldest son, called, running up. I turned to go to my tent. Joab had been with the group of people at the cave camp in Horesh where the hassar had visited. If he was here, I could leave on my fall inspection of the strongholds tomorrow. Well, at least Eliphelet was gone and Hachilah would have a little peace for a day or two!

I turned to Pekah. "Call Abishai." Usually I left my nephew in charge when I went away, and I needed to tell him what I expected from Ittai when he returned from Arad.

Week One, Day Seven

"It's so small," Abigail commented as she entered the inn's courtyard and noticed the miniature sling taking shape under Ittai's fingers. "Is that leather?"

"From deerskin. I had Parai cut it from the thinnest part as narrow as he could. It was a good way to use up his scraps."

"What's it for?"

The young man shrugged. "I made a small one for Pekah, and then I wondered just how tiny I could make them. Are you ready to go to the caravan?"

"Yes. Where's Eliphelet?"

"He's bringing the donkey."

"Do I have to ride it?" she asked ruefully.

Ittai smiled. "If you'd rather walk today, I assume the donkey won't mind. I think he was as tired as you were by the time we got here last evening."

The caravan had camped on the east side of town in a level field. Sibbecai greeted them when they arrived.

"Baalah," he said, nodding slightly.

"Is Hadar here?"

"I'll get him," the man said shortly, casting a warning glance at Eliphelet, who quickly tucked his hands under his arms.

Instantly Ittai hid his grin. The thief rarely stole from Sibbecai, being too afraid the morose man would cut off his hands first, then inform Dahveed of the event afterward.

Not long after, the merchant hurried over. "Gebirah Abigail?" he asked in astonishment. "I am delighted to see you again!"

"And I, you, Hadar."

"Please, you must take the noon meal with me. Sibbecai will take you to my tent. I will come as soon as I've finished with the donkeys. The trail up from the Arabah had washed out, and we have six animals lamed. I will have someone entertain you while you wait."

"I will need to speak to Regem, the guide," Ittai put in. "Dahveed had some questions for him."

Hadar nodded. "I will send him."

Sibbecai led them to a spacious tent and wordlessly provided some fruit and water. Ittai took his time looking around. He could see the influence of the Habiru in the arrangement of the encampment, the placing of guard posts, and the weapons each guard carried. It would be harder than it looked to overrun this place, he decided.

The merchant joined them sooner than Ittai had expected.

"Baalah, it is so pleasant to see you again," he said, bowing as he entered. "You are a bright spot in an otherwise dark day."

"I'm glad to bring what light I can. What has brought darkness?"

"We will be forced to stay here for a week while the animals recover. But that means I have plenty of time to attend you, baalah. What can I do for you, and how did you find me, if I may ask?"

"My husband's men are guarding your goods!" Abigail smiled.

"I had heard that you married Dahveed Israel," he remembered. "Good! The south needs someone who can fight now. The raiding from Edom and Amalek is worse every month, and a couple of lamed animals are a small price to pay for avoiding the southern roads. And Pharaoh's guards are useless!"

"But I thought Egyptian archers were the dream of every caravan owner," Abigail said, her eyes widening.

"Since Yahweh's Arrows have shown us what real protection is, Pharaoh's archers sit in their fortress and complain. And we are happy to let them. Not only do we keep more of our silver, but we don't have to listen to them grumble!"

"You look like you have done well," she commented, glancing around the tent. "Where all do you trade now?"

"Mostly between Damascus and Egypt. But I would like to expand a little. Maybe contact Gaza."

Ittai jerked his head around involuntarily with the idea that exploded in his mind as Hadar spoke. Stroking his chin absently, he stared out the tent. He had that sling he'd just made, and he was sure he'd seen Hanan about dusk yesterday, so he could send something. "Yah, I pray that Immi did as she promised," he silently added.

"So for now, you are only going as far as Beersheba," Abigail summarized.

"Yes, baalah. I think Gaza will have to wait for another trip."

"If I may suggest something?" Ittai put in respectfully.

A bit surprised, Hadar turned to him. "Certainly, geber."

"I may be able to serve you, if you are willing," he began. "I have a message for Sahrah Hazzel in Gath, sister to Seren Akish. Her beloved is traveling and sent a message to her. I gathered that the regular courier service cannot be used for fear of discovery by their enemies. Therefore I am sure she would be most grateful to whoever delivered the message, and could do so quietly."

Hadar's eyes lit up. "She is sister to the seren?"

"Yes. I was told it would be very easy to identify her. Apparently, she bewilders nearly everyone she speaks to, and keeps the city in a constant state of ferment. Perhaps if you could take some samples of your wares to show her, it would be an excuse to speak to her."

"I would be happy to help. Now, baalah, what can I do to serve you?"

"Have you any skins suitable for tanning? It's been so long, I've forgotten what you carry," she replied, switching her attention from Ittai to Hadar.

"Let me show you," the merchant offered immediately. He called some men away from their repair of his stall awning, and had them bring samples for Abigail to inspect. Noticing the distinctive strip used for the repair, Ittai excused himself for a moment and wandered to the edge of camp. When he returned, he paused to watch the work on the awning, collecting a piece of the patch cloth before sitting down by Abigail again. At the same time he kept an eye on Eliphelet, whose hands were practically twitching, but the thief controlled himself.

The heat of the day was nearly past when Ittai saw Hanan walking along the margin of the forest. After making sure he had the scrap of cloth and the little sling, he followed. By the time he got to the trees, the Habiru youth waited for him.

"Hanan, how soon can you get to Gath?"

"Tomorrow."

"You know Sahrah Hazzel?"

The young man thought a moment, then nodded.

Rolling up the cloth and fastening it with the sling, Ittai held it out. "Can you get this to her without anyone knowing?"

"Yes. Will there be a return message?"

"I'm sure there will, but I have no idea when, so don't worry about it."

"Tell Dahveed the Amalekites have grown," the young man said before he disappeared into the trees.

Ittai returned to the tent, noticing that Eliphelet was gone.

"Was that Hanan? Is everything all right?" Abigail asked as soon as he arrived.

"Yes."

"Do you know him?" Hadar put in. "He's been hanging around for two days looking for mischief."

"Hanan serves Dahveed, Hadar," Abigail said reassuringly. "He would never cause mischief, although he will know exactly who does!"

"Then ask him who our petty thief is," Hadar grumbled. "We've had everything from rings to one of my old seals pilfered in the past three weeks, and no indication of who is doing it. But that need not concern you, baalah. Was there anything else today besides skins for tanning?"

"Dahveed wanted me to ask about battle bows," Ittai said.

"I have only a few this trip. How soon does he need them?"

"Before the next war season. He could use about 30."

"I have 12 now. Would you like to take them with you, and I'll bring the rest on my way back?"

"Standard price?"

"Of course."

"I'll take them. If they are good quality, he might want more. You'll be here for another week, you said?"

Hadar nodded. "Just send a message."

Abigail stood to go. "Where's Eliphelet?"

"Sibbecai will know," Ittai assured her, turning to Hadar. "I will send the message for the sahrah in Gath as soon as we return to the inn," he promised as they took their leave.

They stopped by Sibbecai on their way out of camp.

"Eliphelet?" Ittai asked.

The silent man jerked his chin to indicate where Eliphelet waited by the road, another man with him, obviously trying to persuade him to do something.

"Who is that?" Abigail inquired.

"Samlah," Sibbecai said with a snort. "He's got 14 donkeys and loads, and hired three Habiru guards. They joined us down on the Arabah. The way Samlah avoids Hadar, I'd guess Hadar would turn him out if he knew he were here. He hates him."

"Who hates whom?" Abigail asked.

"Samlah hates Hadar. I've posted extra guards every night. Samlah's arrival looks deliberately planned to me. He's up to something."

"And we'd better get over there before Samlah convinces Eliphelet to get up to something," Abigail said a bit tartly. "Come on, Ittai."

That evening, Ittai sat out in the inn courtyard enjoying the coolness and watching the stars. He and Immi had used to do it nearly every night, and it was at this time that he missed her most. Eliphelet wandered over and sat on the bench beside him.

"Why don't you stop stealing?" Ittai asked casually.

The man shrugged.

"Who's Samlah?"

"An old associate."

"What did he want today?"

"Wanted me to steal, just like everyone else."

"The Gebirah doesn't."

Eliphelet didn't reply.

Ittai glanced at the man beside him. "But you like stealing. That's why you don't stop."

An odd smile spread across Eliphelet's face. "There's nothing like the feeling of succeeding in a really good heist, Ittai. I match my wits against that of others, and I win. And the more difficult it is, the better I like it. The best one I've ever done involved nothing more than a brass bracelet, but it took me three weeks to figure out how to get it, and another two to do it. I can steal anything, from anyone. I can become six different people while I do it, and walk away with the plunder, and no one will know it's gone. It's the best game I've ever found, and I love it."

"It will get you killed one day."

"I know. But I can't stop playing." The thief looked down at his hands and clenched them.

"You did today."

"I promised the Gebirah."

"What did Samlah want you to steal?" Ittai couldn't resist asking.

Eliphelet snorted. "He planned on joining the first caravan of the right size that came along, and then switch his donkeys for some of theirs. When he discovered his donkeys were too small compared to most caravan animals, he decided to exchange some packs instead. Then, when he recognized me, he got the idea we could get away with the whole caravan. Said it was the perfect time, since Hadar was so excited about opening trade with the ruling house of Gath that he was leaving early tomorrow with samples and had given orders for the caravan to join him there. Samlah even has an old seal of Hadar's we could use."

"With a seal, it shouldn't be too hard."

The thief laughed. "With a seal, it's not worth doing, it's so easy. I thought of six different ways to do it while Samlah jabbered on. But Dahveed's men are guarding the caravan, and I promised the Gebirah."

"Samlah didn't look too happy when we left."

"He was furious. But Samlah will never be successful. The man drinks too much, and he's too careless. I could tell just by looking that the chests on his donkeys have rocks in them, and the bales of cloth are nothing but rags. Although he may look prosperous, he's only got one donkey load of samples, and another loaded with supplies. He never considered that the weight difference between those chests and the real ones would tell any good caravaneer that something was wrong the first time they loaded them. One of these days he'll get himself killed."

Week Two, Day One

Late the next afternoon, Hazzel, accompanied by her maid, went to the almond grove to see how long it might be until the crop was ready for harvest. The maid carried a basket just in case they might find some nuts ready to pick. As always when she was alone now, the sahrah's thoughts turned to the problem of Manani. She clearly saw the danger, for in order to stave off the seren's immediate control of Gath, Akish must continue to go along with Ekron's wishes, and that would erode the trust between him and his sars.

And as worried as Shemel looked lately, that had probably gone further than Akish thought. It wouldn't surprise her, what with Ishvi-benob, Lahmi, Saph, and that growing brother of theirs, all talking about how careless the serens were with every life but their own. And that slimy Phoenician was still around, clinking his gold together, except when Ishvi-benob was doing the same.

All the time she wandered the grove, occasionally looking at a tree, she was in deep thought. She needed to know if other cities were having the same problems as Gath. That could be important. But maybe they had problems of their own. If she remembered correctly, Gadmilk of Ashdod had two adons who'd been attacked on the roads near there. Then she remembered the Phoenician. Why would a foreigner be around making trouble in Gath, the least important of the Five Cities? He had too much gold to be working for Manani, who never spent anything unless he was sure he would get double back.

That made her wonder how much the seren had bribed Pharaoh to get those tax authorizations, and why he would even bother paying out that much. There had to be more to this.

The sun had nearly set, so she started back to find her maid. The basket beside her, the elderly woman was sleeping under a tree.

Bending over to pick it up, Hazzel saw a piece of cloth in it that she hadn't put there. She pulled it out. The striping was different from anything she had ever seen. Unrolling it, she saw it was just a scrap tied up with something leather. When she looked at the leather in her hand, she froze. A sling? *A tiny sling!* Hastily she closed her hand over it, then stuffed both the cloth and the sling into her girdle. Only one person would send her a sling. Dahveed. And that meant Ittai! And that meant her son was either fine, or not.

Trying to still her shaking, she wakened the maid, hurrying them both back to the palace. Somewhere, she would see that striped cloth pattern again, and when she did, she was certain she would get news of Ittai.

Week Two, Day Five

Four days later, Hazzel was still looking. She had been out of the palace to the market three or four times a day, wandering around, staring at what people wore, at the stalls of the merchants, at every bale of cloth offered for sale. Next she had toured the palace, straining to see what the lowliest slave in the place had on. Finally she haunted the throne room, not saying a word, which puzzled her brother as well as relieved him, while she scrutinized every piece of clothing that anyone wore. And nothing matched the stripes she kept wrapped up in her girdle.

Discouraged, she retreated to the palace roof for the noon rest. Why hadn't she found the cloth? She hadn't missed it; she couldn't have! Finally, the late summer heat made her drowsy enough to sleep. When she woke, the market was coming to life. Standing by the parapet, she watched as a few more merchants took up places around the square. Not far from her, an awning was going up, taking up space that someone else wanted, and she watched the ensuing discussion. Must be someone new, she mused to herself, and not very prosperous considering the mismatched patch on the top of the awning.

She'd been staring at it for several moments before the striped pattern registered in her mind. Trembling, she pulled the cloth from her girdle to make certain. It was the same. Then she laughed in delight. That patch was on top of the awning, and only someone up here, on the palace roof, would be able to see it.

As Hazzel nearly flew down the stairs to her room, she called for her maid who, naturally, was never around when wanted. Impatiently, she fastened a necklace on, and then found a hair band. Paying little attention to what she was doing, she rouged one side of her face and slapped eyeliner on the opposite eye before departing for the market. Then she realized she didn't know how to recognize the stall from the ground. Racing up to the roof again, she found it and counted how many it was from the corner of the palace.

As she ran for the door again, Akish came around the corner. He gave her an odd look. "Hazzel, what are you doing with—"

"Not now, Akish," she said, rushing by. "I'm late to the market. The stalls are all open, and I have to get out there!"

"Hazzel—"

Ignoring him, she pushed open the door and darted into the square, then abruptly slowed, and casually began strolling around, working her way to the stall she had marked. They were strangers, she saw. She knew the face of nearly every trader that regularly came to Gath, and these were new to the area.

"Ah, baalah," the man in the stall said when he noticed her, "you see something you like?"

"Is this the best you have?" she asked, knowing that hinting she had a lot to spend usually brought results.

It did this time, also. "Baalah, these are only for the average woman in the market. For exceptional customers like you, we have exceptional goods."

"Hm. That's what the merchant last week said, and what he brought out to show me was worth my time, but not his. I hate that when it happens, and you had better do the same!"

"Er, baalah, I do hope, well, perhaps I should just show you what I have?"

"If you must. I have most of what I need already. And what the seren will say to that, he's already said before, so you don't worry over it. Well, bring out what you have," she ended impatiently.

"Uh, yes, baalah." Bewildered, he produced a piece of silk, then looked at her again. "Um, baalah, should I be addressing you as sahrah? Dare I think I am serving the famed sister of the Seren of Gath?"

"You are," Hazzel said, fingering the silk.

"Well, Sahrah Hazzel, I have some very special things here, which I'm sure you would be interested in."

Just then one of the palace guards hurried over. Hazzel bit her lip in frustration. If only she hadn't run into Akish on her way out. Then she brightened.

"Here you are," she said, turning to the guard. "Bring this man and his wares up to the palace roof. I don't want to stand around here when I can be uncomfortable up there. Bring him along now," she said, heading toward the palace again.

That evening, after driving away her maid in exasperation, Hazzel pulled the message that the merchant, whose name was Hadar, had slipped to her in a silk bag. She had purchased the bag along with enough of the silk to make a sash. Liking a lot of the other items he carried, she said that she would summon him again.

Now, she just held the message for a while before untying the twine that bound the folded papyrus. She prayed it was written in script, because she could read that. She had promised her son when she sent him away that she would learn to read and write so that he could send messages to her. Dark readable script unfolded before her eyes, and she hesitantly spelled out the words.

"Greetings, Sahrah. I am well and in good health. I have longed to see you since we parted. But it is not possible just yet. Perhaps soon it will be different. I reached my destination safely, and where I am there has been much to learn. I have heard of the hard fighting during the war season just past, and those with me discuss why such useless fighting should go on. Surely Gath can find a better way to conquer, they say. I say nothing, although it pains me much. But if I can see you again soon, or hear from you, all will be explained, I know. May the gods preserve you.

"The covenant son."

Dropping the papyrus, Hazzel covered her face and burst into quiet tears. She wept for some time before drying her eyes and picking up the papyrus again. Most of it was blank, she noticed. Taking the ink and pen from the depths of a box no one ever used anymore, she thought for a long time, carefully composing her reply. Since she would have to write fairly large letters, it must be short, but complete. At the same time, it couldn't be obviously from her. Then she noticed that Ittai had written in a way that the message could seem to be from one lover to another.

Slowly she printed her letter, then sat back to read it over.

"Greetings, Beloved.

"I am as well as I can be without you. I count the days until you return. I heard your dodi talking of the war. He was distressed but unable to help in any way. There are problems enough here. He has lost an important document after someone put something else in its place. There is nothing he can do for his house until this is found. I fear he is in our enemy's power now.

"The rest of the town is distressed about the war also, but everyone says the Egyptian tax authorization will fix everything, even the war. I only wish it would fix our separation. Do not delay coming back any longer than you must.

"Your Sahrah."

Folding the papyrus, she tied it again. She would give it to Hadar first thing in the morning and pay him to send it off right away.

Week Two, Day Seven

Ittai looked up in surprise as Hanan gave him the papyrus he'd sent to Immi, still tied. "Didn't Hadar go to Gath?"

"This is a return message," the youth said.

"When did you get this?"

"Yesterday morning."

"Who gave it to you?"

"Hadar."

Before Ittai could ask how that happened, the youth walked away. Hastily, Ittai untied the twine and spread out the papyrus. The somewhat awkward writing told him that his immi had indeed kept her promise. He breathed a sigh of relief. Then he read the message. When its meaning sank home, he had to sit down, ice wrapping around his heart. When had Philistia gained the right to collect Israel's taxes, and how had Manani managed to steal the document that Gath held?

The longer he assessed the situation, the worse it became. Unless something were done, Manani would slowly strangle Gath, destroy his house, and wreak havoc with the alliance of the Five Cities. Then he would turn his attention to the highlands, and the resulting war would bring slaughter to both sides. Dahveed needed to know this immediately! He had partially stood before the implications of helping Gath stopped him. As Mashiah, sworn to Yahweh, Dahveed could not send aid to help a foreign city collect taxes from Israel! It would be a betrayal of his position and vows. If there was any way this could be dealt with, he had to find it and do it himself, for Dahveed could know nothing of it. Taking his cloak, he retreated to the silence of the forest.

Chapter 5

Week Three, Day One

The next morning, he waited just outside of camp for Pekah to bring Eliphelet. The thief had retreated to his tent as he always did when he put something on the cloth. It looked like Matred's ankle bracelet, and Ittai wondered if she even knew it was gone.

Before long, Eliphelet scurried over, staying out of sight as much as possible, hands tucked under his arms. "Pekah said you wanted something?" he asked, looking around uneasily.

"I need your opinion on something. Dahveed asked me to find out anything I could about why the Philistines were so determined to raid the highlands. Hanan brought me a message last night. I told Dahveed I would do what I could with anything I found, and he was agreeable.

"You know I'm covenant son to Dahveed, and that my family is from Gath?"

Shifting his weight a little, Eliphelet nodded.

"The reason the units from Gath attacked so persistently this past war season is because the ruler of Gath is being forced to send them."

"I'm not the one to talk to about politics," the thief said, puzzled. "Josheb or the Gebirah could help you better."

"This isn't a matter of politics. Someone substituted one document for another in Gath. If the stolen document can be returned, Akish will be much more reasonable with his units next year, and that means an easier time for everyone. I want to get it back if I can, and I need to know if you think it's possible."

Eliphelet looked thoughtful. "What document is missing?"

"An authorization from Pharaoh for Gath to collect Israelite taxes."

The thief's head whipped around. "*From Egypt!?* Who was moon-touched enough to steal Egyptian documents?"

"I'm not precisely certain," Ittai replied carefully. "But someone did. Would you have any idea how I could get it back?"

"A stolen document like that wouldn't be kept in any of the usual places! Most of the time you don't even want anyone to know it's *been* stolen! How did Akish find out it was gone?"

"Again, I don't know," the younger man said with a sigh. "All I do know is that it is gone, and somehow I have to get it back. Otherwise, we may have all-out war here in the highlands!"

"Do you have any idea where it might be?"

"Seren Manani of Ekron has it."

"*Manani?* Are you telling me you want to steal something as valuable as an Egyptian tax authorization from someone like Manani of Ekron?"

"Preferably in a way so that he doesn't know it's gone."

"Ittai, that's the most idiotic thing I've ever heard!"

"So it can't be done?"

"No, it can't be done! He'd have that document tucked away somewhere absolutely safe, and being Manani, only he will know where! If he risked taking it, he must have important plans for it, and—"

"Yes, I thought that, too," Ittai interrupted. "There wouldn't be any way to find out where he might have put it?"

"Manani is not the sort of person to talk to just anyone, you know! Even getting close to him would be hard enough. Gaining his confidence would take far more time than you would have!"

"I have to do something, Eliphelet! Surely there must be some appeal that Manani can't resist."

"The only chance you would have is greed. And that means you'd have to be rich! Far richer than you're ever likely to be! You're the son of an Israelite slave! Be reasonable!"

"But does Manani have to know that?"

"Well, he, I mean, how could . . . but then . . ." The thief's voice trailed off, and a faraway look crept into his eyes. At first he stood perfectly still, then slowly began to pace.

Ittai settled down with his back against a tree to wait. He must have fallen asleep, for the sun said nearly three hours had passed when he opened his eyes again.

Arms crossed, eyes gleaming, Eliphelet stood in front of him. "I can do it. But I must have Samlah and that caravan he's with. We'll need mules and the richest clothing and jewelry in camp. That means Josheb's. He and I are nearly the same height, and he's kept some very good-quality things in his packs."

"You take whatever you need, and I'll make it all right. What else?"

"We'll need some of the wine additive Tokhath used on Nabal, and get at least three doses of the same herbs Keturah gave Sibbecai when he went to Carmel for Dahveed."

"Where can we get the wine additive?"

"The Gebirah's maid, Tirzah, has quite a lot of it in those tiny juglets. She keeps them buried under her bedroll. Ask for two of them. And we'll be gone for some time and—"

"Don't worry about that, Eliphelet. I'll take care of arranging things with Abishai. You concentrate on what we need."

"First of all, that caravan."

"Then I guess we leave tomorrow for Beersheba," Ittai concluded.

Week Three, Day Four

"But Egypt is closer," Samlah protested.

"Closer is not always better," Eliphelet said patiently, pushing the jug of wine closer to him. "We would be expected to take it to Egypt. That's why we should head north, to Aphek at least, sell some of it off there if we can, and then go on to Damascus."

"Tell me again why you're so willing now, when you weren't two weeks ago," Samlah groused, reaching for the wine.

"Because I'm tired of living in the wilderness all the time. It's been years since I wore something besides cast-offs and ate food seasoned with something besides time and salt."

"Then why did you say no two weeks ago?"

"I already explained; Gebirah Abigail was there. She would have told Dahveed first thing if I left her. But he has gone on his fall inspection tour, and that always takes at least two weeks. This was the first I could get away and catch up to you."

"Who's that young man with you? I thought only you and I were doing this."

"He's part Philistine and a guide, and since we're going through Philistia, he'll be useful. Don't worry, his share comes from mine, not yours."

"All right," Samlah said reluctantly. "Just be sure his share really does come from yours! I've still got the seal. What do we need to write?"

"Hadar is still in Gath?"

"Yes, and we've orders to meet him there."

"Tell Tilon, the caravan master, Hadar wants him to check out the route to Hebron. It may be a way to avoid Pharaoh's roads."

"Who's going to deliver the orders?"

"I will. That way you can seem uninvolved should anything go wrong."

"I'll get the seal," Samlah said, rising to leave the shop. His hand reached for the wine bottle, but Eliphelet was too quick for him, lifting it to pour some into his own cup, then looked up calmly at him. "I'll be right here," he said, watching the other man stomp out of the tiny shop. "Keeping you from drinking too much wine and opening your mouth like you always do," he added under his breath, dumping the wine from his cup. It had to be the cheapest, sourest wine he'd ever had to swallow.

¥ ¥ ¥ ¥ ¥ ¥

"Akish, I absolutely must talk to you," Hazzel said, bursting into his business chamber where the ruler of Gath was consulting with his advisors regarding the failure to penetrate the highlands again another year. "Do you know what happened today? It's a disgrace to everything crawling around on our floors! And you have to do something about it. I won't tolerate another moment of such behavior."

"Hazzel!" Akish raised his voice. "I'm meeting with my advisors, as you can see. Do restrain yourself."

"Well, I don't know but what your reception isn't worse than I could have expected, I suppose, after being accosted in the market in plain sight of the entire city! Surely your advisors can wait. All they have to say is that they don't know how to get into the highlands again, which is no surprise to anyone, and there won't be anything to do about it so all the consultations can't be useful for anything, which isn't a secret to anyone either!" She stormed out the door again, leaving Akish staring after her in exasperation.

Unfortunately, he had to acknowledge that her wordy summation of the situation was quite accurate. He just wished he had had the choice of keeping his men home instead of sending them on fruitless forays into the highlands where they died for no reason.

But as he turned back to his advisors, her first sentence and the tear in her robe penetrated his mind. "Accosted!" he exclaimed. As he jerked his head to face the door, the small smile of satisfaction briefly crossing one advisor's face caught his eye.

Lunging to his feet, the seren snarled, "Get out!" at the men.

Hastily they obeyed, hurrying down the passageway to stay ahead of him as he stormed after them.

"Where did she go?" he asked the guard at the corner.

"I think Sar Shemel escorted her to her rooms," the man replied, looking frightened.

Akish turned down the next passage, arriving at his sister's door and throwing it open without warning. As he took one step over the raised threshold he nearly ran his throat into the point of a sword.

Dodging back and to the side, he yanked up the battle dagger he always wore just as the sword point pulled away and someone dropped to their knees.

"I beg pardon, Sereni, I didn't realize it was you!"

The seren lowered the dagger hand, rubbing his neck with the other hand. Shemel knelt in front of him, his sword point down on the floor. Hazzel stood in the middle of the room, her face streaked with tears.

"And don't you even think of accusing him of everything in your mind," she burst out. "If it hadn't been for him, the market would have been a sight to see and the Rapha in your house instead of the gates! He was protecting me since no one else was less than willing to do it!"

"Did you see what happened?" he asked the kneeling man, ignoring Hazzel's outburst.

"Yes, Sereni. Sahrah Hazzel was looking at goods in the market when Ishvi-benob arrived. He spoke insolently to her, and when she reprimanded him, he put his hands on her shoulders. The dress ripped as she pulled away. I wasn't quick enough to get there to prevent that. When Ishvi-benob saw me coming, he backed off, and Sahrah Hazzel returned to the palace."

Shock held the seren absolutely still. One of the Rapha had deliberately affronted his house in such a manner? "Who else responded?"

The sar looked down.

"How many men responded with you?" Akish asked again, his voice deadly.

"It was one of the Rapha, Sereni. I'm sure the other guards would have helped had it been necessary."

In other words, no one else had. Suddenly the smirk on his advisor's face, his own anger at his bondage to Manani, and his outrage that his beloved sister had been attacked combined into utterly fearless rage. "Come," he ordered.

The commander followed him as he left the palace. Anger flaming inside him, Akish spotted Ishvi-benob on the other side of the market, tasting the wares at a wine stall, and likely not paying anything for it. He knew that happened more often than not, and the thought fueled his rage even more. A length of rope caught his eye, and he grabbed it as he went by.

Staying close to the stalls, he strode around the square, his hands twisting a noose in the rope as he did. Not many people had noticed him when he arrived at the wine stall, and without pausing an instant, he walked up behind the giant man, flipped the noose over his head, and yanked him over backward by the neck. Then he started dragging the sar straight across the market square to the palace. While Ishvi-benob choked and lunged and struggled to keep up, his hands clutching the ever-tightening rope, Akish hauled him to a hitching post with a bronze ring in it.

Feeding the rope through the ring, he yanked it tight, jamming the Rapha's head against the post as he did so. Then he cut a seven-foot length from the rope, knotted the end, and thrashed the man until the knot was soaked with blood. By the time he finished, every sar in his permanent force stood guard, swords at the ready while Saph and Lahmi watched in stunned silence.

Pulling his dagger, he sliced through the rope tied to the ring, not particularly caring what else might get nicked in the process. The Rapha landed on the ground, clawing the rope off his neck, chest heaving as he tried to suck in air. The seren turned on his heel and disappeared into the palace.

That evening, Akish went to Hazzel's chambers after everyone had eaten. His own rage had drained away, leaving him tired, and less worried about Manani's reaction to this than he probably should be, he thought wryly.

"Are you all right?" he asked his sister after her maid let him in.

"As well as can be expected." She hugged herself.

Akish wrapped his arms around her. "I punished Ishvi-benob."

"I know. He's still out at the post," she said, her voice muffled in his chest. "All the sars are still out there guarding him, too. They'll probably make him stay there all night."

"It's less than he deserves," the seren said tightly. "No one touches my big sister."

Hazzel put her arms around him and burst into tears. "Not even Ittai could have done more," she sobbed when she could get words out. "And he's gone. He's gone!"

"Don't cry so, Hazzel," Akish comforted. "You've always been sure he'll come back, and I can't help but hope so also."

"I just know he's with his abbi! I just know it!" she sobbed, raising her head.

Akish looked down. She met his gaze directly, her eyes steady, before lowering her head to weep some more.

Later, as he left the chamber, Akish considered what had happened. Surely if Hazzel knew Ittai was with his abbi, the lad must be dead. Then he almost stopped in mid-stride. *His abbi?* Could Ittai be alive? Was it possible his sister had managed to outwit Manani and place her son in Dahveed Israel's care? "Maybe the gods are more involved in this than I imagined," he muttered to himself as he entered his chambers.

Week Four, Day Two

Ittai glanced around the camp at Hereth on the east side of the Hebron highway. He remembered it from his first year with Dahveed, and it was a secure place for the caravan. Ethan's son, Regem, a man considerably older than himself, had approved of the site also.

Walking to the edge of the camp, he sat on a deadfall marking its back side. Hanan appeared beside him.

"I thought I saw you," Ittai commented. "Why are you following? Regem is a good guide."

The Habiru shrugged. "You are worried. So I am here."

"I thought it was Dahveed you kept track of," he said to hide his surprise.

Another shrug. "Dahveed is content, and you are his covenant son."

"I am worried, I must admit. We are going to Ekron, for Seren Manani has stolen a document from my dodi. We hope to get it back. But Ekron is a city, and we have no idea where Manani would likely hide what he took."

Hanan stood. "When do you go to Ekron?"

"We should be there day after tomorrow."

"I will be there," the youth said, vanishing into the trees.

¥ ¥ ¥ ¥ ¥ ¥

For the third day, Hadar scanned the road from the south in vain. Where were Tilon and the caravan? People were waiting for the goods he had promised. Coming to Gath had been quite profitable so far, and would likely continue to be, if only his caravan would arrive. It had three camels and several donkeys loaded with his personal goods, in addition to the rest of the merchandise that belonged to Jether, some of which he'd already sold. What could have delayed Tilon? He should send a messenger to find out.

Week Four, Day Four

Ekron was obviously preparing for the celebration of the New Year's new moon, and travelers were abundant. The place Ittai and Regem had found for the caravan wasn't the best, but it was reasonably close to the city and had room for all the animals, even if the space for the tents was a little cramped. The city lay southwest about a mile, and Tilon had already given orders that the caravaneers were not to enter its gates. Sibbecai didn't have to tell Dahveed's men that. They were nervous enough at their duties, knowing that as Israelites, they would be noticed by anyone who saw their faces.

Tilon had left for the market, having promised the men he would return with ample provisions for them to celebrate the New Year right in camp. While the master was gone, Ittai wanted to contact Hanan, but he had no idea how. Then, remembering that Dahveed never tried to find the young man, he decided it was easiest to just wait for Hanan to locate him. Before long he appeared in camp, jogging along, glancing to either side.

"Are you all right, Hanan?" Ittai asked.

The Habiru looked up in surprise. "Why wouldn't I be?"

"This is Seren Manani's town. We are all in danger."

"Things have changed. The people are restless. There is much anger here. It is not a good place."

"I feel that, too," Ittai said, glancing over his shoulder at the city walls. "Have you found out anything?"

"That man seems constantly irritated," the youth reported. "He lost his personal scribe two months ago, although many say he had the man killed, and he has been unable to find anyone as competent since. Lamps are always lit in the night, now. People mutter in the market because the invasion into the highlands failed. Many men were lost, especially in the militia, and taxes will be high because of it. The harvest was not as abundant as last year, and the common people in the town are fearful of not having enough this winter."

"Anything else?"

Hanan looked at him a moment. "Do not go to that man's house, geber. It is a bad place."

"I have known that for a long time. But I will not be going. Eliphelet will, and he has been to many bad places before."

"The sars talk in the wine shops. It is said that if there is anyone that man trusts, it is Eliahba the sar. He has been commander for the seren for many years. But something has changed even with him. Since returning from this year's campaign, he buys wine from a shop every night he is not on duty. No one knows what he does with it. They say he cannot drink it himself, for he never drinks in Ekron, and so is not happy here."

"What do you say he's doing?"

"He drinks it, but then he weeps. I will show you where he buys the wine, but I will not go to that man's house."

"I won't ask you to, but you will need to show me where it is."

Hanan hesitated before he nodded.

¥ ¥ ¥ ¥ ¥ ¥

Once again, the road from the south was empty. Hadar fumed over the delay. Well, maybe they would arrive tomorrow, even though it was the first day of the New Year celebration. But that also meant no one would be asking for their goods. Just as he was closing his stall his courier arrived, hot and dusty from the run in the heat. He made sure the man had something to eat and drink before taking his report.

"The caravan passed through Beersheba, geber, then turned north, apparently headed here. But I found no evidence of it on the road."

"Then where is it?" He had dismissed the courier before the horrifying thought came to his mind. When entire caravans went missing, merchants inevitably thought of Eliphelet ben Ahasbai. New Year or not, word of the possibility of the caravan thief's presence had to go out on the trade routes tonight!

Week Four, Day Five

Curse that guard, Samlah fumed to himself. Didn't Sibbecai ever let anyone take a day off? Since Tilon ordered everyone to remain in the camp, the guards were present and alert. Being Manani's town, this place would have some good wine, and he wanted to taste some of it. When he'd agreed to join Eliphelet, he'd forgotten that he'd have to go without wine.

Ittai and Eliphelet emerged from their tent, looking as if they intended to spend the day celebrating. Eliphelet certainly did. He was dressed richly, with earrings, finger rings, arm bands, and a turban that had to be made from cloth of gold, the way the sun reflected off it.

Samlah hurried over. "Who are you today?" he asked a bit sarcastically as he walked up.

Eliphelet glanced at him. "I haven't decided yet. What name would go well with this outfit?"

"Where are you supposed to be from?"

"North, I think. Maybe Hamath near the Euphrates. That would fit the turban."

"Why not use 'Yasma-addu'?"

"Yasma-addu," Eliphelet said, trying out the name. "That will do."

"Someone this rich will need an attendant. I'll come," Samlah added.

"Ittai is already prepared for that. Besides, you won't miss anything. There's plenty to celebrate with right here in camp. Tilon made sure of that."

As Samlah reluctantly left, Eliphelet adjusted his turban again and whispered, "We need to tell Sibbecai to keep an eye on him. When he gets drunk, he talks."

¥ ¥ ¥ ¥ ¥ ¥

Ittai led the way to the palace in Ekron. Since Eliphelet didn't seem to be in any hurry, he slowed his pace. The thief spent a lot of time just looking, and when they got to the square by the palace entrance, he watched for some time from the alley they had followed before stepping out into the square itself. By the time they approached the entrance and the scribe stationed there, Ittai realized that Eliphelet no longer followed him, but Yasma-addu of Hamath instead. He was sure of it when the man pushed ahead of him and paraded up to the scribe.

"You will inform Seren Manani that Yasma-addu of Hamath, Asshur, and Babylon has arrived and awaits an audience with his greatness," he said in a bored voice.

"Due to the celebrations today, the seren has no open appointments, adon. I can put you at the top of the list for tomorrow, however, if it please you."

"It does not please me," Yasma snapped, annoyed. "If the seren is too busy to attend to the Pharaoh's business properly, I shall so report to the Great House."

The scribe reddened. "Adon, please allow me to check with the scribe inside. Sometimes the schedule is revised for just such exigencies as this."

"Do not waste my time," Yasma replied, drawing himself up and staring down his nose at the official.

"I will not, adon," the scribe gulped, hurrying into the building.

Ittai fought to keep himself still and his eyes down. Realizing that he would soon be in the presence of his dodi's worst enemy frightened him more than he wished to admit. He had calmed himself, however, when the scribe returned.

"Adon, Seren Manani will see you momentarily. Please come this way." Bowing, he led the way into the palace.

The throne room was larger than the one at Gath, and more richly furnished. The dais had two steps, and the hangings behind the throne gleamed with silver and gold thread. The scribes' tables were inlaid with both dark and light wood, and each had four legs instead of the usual three. Ittai couldn't help noticing that one had a small stone under a leg to keep the table from tipping. The sight nearly made him smile, and as he struggled to control himself, his fear drained away.

"Shalom, Yasma-addu," a pleasant voice said, and Ittai glanced up. The man seated on the throne was rather tall, with dark hair and a pleasant face to go with the voice. He inclined his head graciously at Yasma, who bowed briefly, then let his glance roam around the room a moment.

"We are pleased to be here, Seren," he said, turning his gaze to the ruler of Ekron. "We bring you greetings and wish health and the blessings of your gods to your house and all that is yours."

"Your greetings and wishes are appreciated and returned, of course," Manani replied. "We are honored by your visit and wish to inquire if there is anything that can be done to extend further hospitality to you while you remain here."

"We have found sufficient for our needs, although I would inquire as to the safety of your roads. There seems to be a dearth of guards along them, and since the tax goods I carry to Pharaoh are of great value, I must be certain that they remain in the proper hands."

"We can assure you that the roads through Philistia are completely safe for all travelers, most certainly for one as honored as you. The Five Cities make certain of this."

"I am glad to hear this, Seren. We would not want to have caravans with Pharaoh's taxes arrive in Egypt with an improper amount. I'm sure the procedures for making such assessments go smoothly have been explained to you, and you are fully prepared to implement them. The Great House has been strict about this."

Ittai saw Manani stiffen. Raising one eyebrow slightly, the seren regarded Yasma for a moment. "Why would *I* have need of knowing such things?"

"News travels swiftly among small communities, Seren, and presentations of tax authorizations are public ceremonies. I see that you have not done badly with what is available to you here," he observed as he glanced around again. "But as you know, collecting Pharaoh's taxes requires special attention, and can bring exceptional rewards when recommended procedures are followed correctly. This naturally pleases the Great House."

"Naturally," Manani echoed, giving Yasma a keen glance before easing back on the throne. "I would not want to be deficient in giving Pharaoh's taxes the attention they deserve. Would you honor me by celebrating the second day of the New Year with me?"

"I can remain for such an honor. What hour?"

"The seventh. I am constrained by palace duties until then. I will send someone for you. You are at the caravansary?"

"Hardly, Seren. We are nearly a mile northwest of town. There was no other place large enough for us, a situation that will soon change under your astute rule, I'm sure." Yasma bowed slightly again. Ekron's ruler gave a dismissing nod before he left the throne room.

On the way back to the encampment, Ittai said nothing. He wouldn't have believed that anyone could arrange for an invitation to Manani's private residence in just one meeting, but Yasma had hooked Manani's greed and challenged him to prove his cunning all at the same time. For the first time, he began to believe that they just might succeed.

Chapter 6

Week Four, Day Six

Patiently Ittai held the mule while Yasma-Addu took his time getting mounted and settled. The squad of soldiers sent to escort them to the city scanned the encampment, taking in the cramped tents and counting the animals. Their sar noted the respectful way the caravan master bowed as they left.

As they rode away from the caravan, the official introduced himself. "I am Sar Eliahba, adon. My seren instructed me to ask whether you found everything you needed."

"We didn't expect much from such a limited market," Yasma replied, his voice dismissive. "But you can tell your seren that we were better served here than we usually are at the caravansaries on the Way of the Sea."

"I shall tell him, adon. I know he will be gratified."

No one said anything until they arrived at the palace square. Yasma slowed enough that the sar turned to him. "Did you wish to stop here, adon?"

"The seren expects me, does he not?"

"Yes, adon, but he is waiting to receive you close to his private residence. It is farther along."

Yasma raised his eyebrows. "A private residence? He has a private house?"

"Yes, adon," Eliahba replied without expression. "Seren Manani has a private residence in town, and an estate outside the walls in addition to his rooms in the palace and his other tenant properties in the countryside."

"I would not have thought it possible in such a small holding as this." The man from Hamath glanced around at the walls. "What is the size of his city house? Does it have more than 10 rooms?"

"You will have to come and see for yourself," the sar said diplomatically. "I have not seen much of the seren's private dwelling."

"I see. Continue on then. I do hope there will be a room there somewhere fit for me to change in."

"I'm sure there will be." Eliahba urged his mount forward.

The courtyard of the house they entered was smaller than many in Gath, Ittai saw in surprise.

"This is a private residence for a seren?" Yasma exclaimed. "It's nearly a hovel!"

"This house is only used for entertaining private individuals," the sar explained. "Seren Manani uses the houses on either side as quarters for his household staff. I will show you where you can change," he added as servants appeared to help them dismount and take care of the mules.

Ittai took the bundle of clothing with him as he followed Eliphelet into a very small one-story house in the far corner of the courtyard.

Eliahba vowed slightly at the door. "When you are ready, I will escort you to the seren, adon."

Once inside, Ittai quickly shook out the robes in the bundle while Eliphelet stripped off the ones he wore.

"Do you think it's hidden here?" the younger man asked softly while the thief dressed.

"Not with staff quartered on either side. Too much chance of someone searching the place. I'll know more later. Right now, chances are about even that it's kept either in the palace or at the country estate. Pray Yah it's in the palace," he added, pulling the robe over his head. "If it's at the country estate, we have a much bigger problem."

While Eliphelet adjusted his new, and much richer, costume, Ittai bundled up the other clothes. "What shall I do with them?"

"Keep them with you. Find a comfortable place to stay in the courtyard, and stay alert. Talk to whomever you can. The more we know about Manani, the better." Putting the turban on his head, he shrugged, then stalked out of the house ahead of Ittai. Eliahba joined him with a bow and escorted him up the stairs to the upper room of the larger house.

Barely had Ittai settled himself on a bench when he noticed another commander arrive. Eliahba spoke with him briefly, then disappeared out the gate. The newcomer went to each of the guards before checking the rooms in the compound. Ittai straightened. Eliahba must have just gone off duty. And according to Hanan, he would soon appear at the tiny wine shop to buy a jug of wine.

Making a sudden decision, he picked up the bundle and hurried to the stalls where the mules were.

"Did you need something, geber?" a servant asked.

"Yes, if you would bring my mule."

Once he was mounted, he turned to the man. "If I am asked after, remind my adon that I returned to the caravan as instructed."

"Yes, geber."

Reaching the palace square, Ittai paused a moment to remember exactly which alley Hanan had taken him down. He found the tiny wine shop with little trouble, and looped the bridle reins around a rock on the ground. The tracks in the dried mud showed its frequent use as a hitching stone. Knowing the mule would kick if anyone strange tried to take the bundle, he left it and entered the shop.

The owner glanced up, took in the quality of his clothing, and rose from his stool, curiosity in his eyes.

"I'd like some of your best," Ittai said, thickening his Philistine accent. "A friend of mine mentioned that you have decent wine, but it must be asked for."

The man hesitated, then went back to his stool, getting a jug from behind it. He poured some into a pottery cup and set it on the small counter.

Ittai put a copper piece by it and moved to an earthen bench by the wall, taking the cup with him. Sipping it slowly, he leaned back, hoping he'd made it here before the sar. One or two others arrived, day-laborers most likely, glancing at him for a moment as they bought wine and murmured among themselves. Once, after a man left, he heard the mule snort and kick. With a slight smile he took another sip of wine.

More than an hour went by, and Ittai knew he must either leave or buy another cup. He sighed. The wine wasn't that good. Rising, he pushed his way to the tiny counter and placed the cup on it, nodding to the shop owner. Outside, he patted the mule and ran his hands down each leg, checking the hoof. He'd known of more than one robbery that began with someone putting a stone in a hoof to lame the animal. Not that it was likely with this animal, but it was wise to check.

Just as he took the reins he spotted the sar approaching.

The soldier noticed the mule first, then looked at him. "Greetings, geber," he said politely.

"Greetings, sar. It looks as if we both have time to celebrate this afternoon!"

Eliahba shrugged. "Celebrations are for those with families."

"Yes, I guess they are," Ittai replied, his voice catching as he remembered how long it had been since he'd seen his immi. "If you have time then, do you mind if I speak with you? I have some questions I think you can answer."

The sar paused a moment. "All right. I'll be right back if you will wait." Quickly he returned, carrying a jug.

"It's early yet," Ittai suggested, glancing at the sun. "Would you be able to accompany me to the caravan? The master purchased festival foods yesterday, and there is plenty left for today. What we have might make the wine more palatable."

Eliahba glanced at the jug in his hand. "It might at that, geber."

Two hours later, Ittai handed the sar a fourth goblet of wine. The jug the sar had purchased sat unopened by the door of the tent, and most of the food brought to them was gone.

"This is very good wine," the man said again, taking another long drink. "I'm afraid to ask the cost of it."

"So am I," Ittai said with more truth than his guest knew. He'd asked Sibbecai to bring some of the best, and the morose man had certainly obeyed. "But it was purchased for celebration, and we are celebrating. Therefore it is serving its purpose."

"And a good purpose it is," the sar added, raising the cup before emptying it.

Promptly Ittai filled it. After the third cup, the sar had become much more talkative, a circumstance to be encouraged at all costs. He had also become much happier.

After three more cups, he leaned toward Ittai and stared at him owlishly. "Do you know, I like you. You have very good wine. Do you drink like this all the time?"

"Regrettably, no. Only on festival days, and only if business has been especially good."

"Well, I'm glad business has been especially good. I shall ask Dagon to bless you. Tell me, do you come this way often?"

"We haven't been around much previous to this, but there is always the future. We may be around more."

"When you come, you find me," Eliahba said, swaying back from Ittai and nearly falling backward. "You find me, an' you tell me you're here! We can celebrate 'gain. You 'n' me." He paused. " 'N th' wine, of course."

"Yes, definitely the wine. Would you like some more?"

"You are kind, geber, ver' kind. I would." Unsteadily he held out the cup.

Ittai filled it. "Where would I find you?"

"Well, I don't go very far. Too busy. The seren, he has lotsh of jobs. But if I'm not in my room, I'll be with the seren, at the palace, or the housh." He leaned closer to his host once more. "I guard thingsh, you know. I keep 'em safe. Wouldn't do to have anything of the seren's go misshing. Wouldn't do at all." The sar wagged his finger. "So I guard 'em. 'Speshially at the stables! Ha! Guard that the best, I do." Then he took another long draught of the wine.

"The seren likes his mules, does he?" Ittai asked absently, wondering how he could get the sar talking about the other properties Manani owned, and whether he kept things there.

"Mulesh? Don' know. Never saw him with 'em, but once. Weren't mulesh, though, horses, that' what he likes. Horses."

"So you guard the horses? What about the country estate?" Ittai dared to ask openly. He didn't know how long it would be before Eliphelet returned, and every day they stayed here increased the chances that something would go wrong.

"No, don' guard horses. What for? Thatsh not what's at the stables. Nope. Wouldn't fit, they wouldn't. I can' hardly shand in there, let 'lone horse. Nope. Not horshes."

Ittai poured another cup for the sar. "Where is the country estate?" Even knowing that would be a help.

"Country, I think," Eliahba said, frowning. "Fields 'n' orchards 'n' trees 'n' such. Itsh country, that's what it ish." He hiccupped. "Never be'n there, sho don' really know."

"So, it's just the stables, is it?" Ittai asked resignedly.

"Yep. Didn' used to be. Then one day, he took me there," the sar said, his eyes getting wide and tears welling up in them. " 'N I knew then, I knew he marked me for death. It was there, in his eyesh when he stood over me an' . . ." His voice trailed off, and Ittai stared at him. Eliahba had turned pale, and his hand shook so much that Ittai reached for the cup.

"No, don' take it," the sar protested. "Shtill wine in it." He drained it. "I should have gone when I had the chance." Tears again glistened in the man's eyes. "But I wouldn't. So now I guard the stables, 'n' check the harness in the shtall, 'n' . . ." With a sigh, Eliahba folded over into sleep.

Rescuing the wine cup, Ittai watched him thoughtfully. Had he learned anything significant or not?

It was after dark when Yasma-addu returned, escorted again by a sar and six soldiers. Ittai hurried to meet him and take the mule. The man from Hamath barely acknowledged the farewells of the escort sar, and strode into the caravan master's tent.

Ittai returned to their tent after taking care of the mule. Sar Eliahba still slept to one side, and Ittai wanted to confer with Eliphelet, not the arrogant tax collector from up north.

When he entered the tent, he said testily, "Tell me next time you're going to vanish."

"I didn't have time, and it wasn't planned. I knew you'd come up with something, and I did leave a message for you with the man at the stable."

"As if Yasma would speak with him!"

"No, but he could speak to Yasma. I followed Eliahba when he left for the afternoon."

"Did you find him?"

"Sleeping behind you as we speak. He was at the wine shop, and I brought him here. He didn't start talking until he'd drunk nearly that entire jug of wine, though."

Eliphelet picked up the cup, smelling what was in it. "Where did you get this? It's top quality wine."

"Sibbecai brought it. But you need to know what he said, I think."

The thief sipped what was left in the cup. "This is very good wine!" he exclaimed. "How much did he drink?"

"Nearly the whole jug. He said—"

"Ittai, do you know how much this must have cost?"

"No, but I'm sure Tilon will. Eliphelet, you need to hear what Eliahba was saying. I can't make much sense of it and—"

"If he drank nearly the entire jug of this, I'd be surprised if you could make sense of anything he said." Eliphelet stared at the sar in wonder. "And I hope you brought a lot of money along, because wine this good will be kept track of, and Hadar will want payment!"

"Eliphelet, why would Eliahba be guarding a stable if Manani doesn't like mules?" Ittai asked, knowing he had to get the man's attention.

"What?"

"Why would Manani want Eliahba guarding stables?"

"Did the sar say that?"

"And a lot of other things." The young Philistine explained, trying to repeat everything exactly as the sar had said it. By the time he finished, Eliphelet stared down at the sleeping man, his eyes intent.

"There's only one reason for Manani to be that concerned about stables," he mused. "There's got to be something valuable there. Which stables?"

"I don't know. He fell asleep."

"Well, we've got to find out. Wake him up. If we can get him back into the city, we may be able to convince him to take us to the stables. Let me change clothes first."

Sometime later, they approached the gate of Ekron, Eliahba held up between them. The celebrations for the New Year still continued unabated, and people passed in and out, constantly watched by the guards. A group of Ishmaelites rode out just as they entered, their accents strange as they grumbled about not finding any place to stay in the city.

Once in the palace square, Ittai got Eliahba's attention. "Which way to the stables, sar?"

"What stables?" the man replied, staring around wide-eyed.

"The ones you guard," Eliphelet said. "You should be certain they're still there before we take you home."

"Good idea! I'll do that." Trying to see in the dim light, he looked around. "Where are they?"

"You have to take us there," Ittai said patiently.

"Oh. Well, where 'm I?"

"In the palace square."

"Which waysh the palace?"

"This way," Eliphelet said, jerking the sar to the right.

"Yep, thatsh the palace," the sar said when they got closer. He swayed around to his left, and his escorts followed. At the corner where the palace ended, he continued down an alley, then swung off to his right at the first turn off. At the first gate, he stopped. "Yep, shtill here," he announced. "Time to go home."

"But I don't see the stable," Eliphelet said, trying to keep the man facing the stable gate.

"You ain' lookin', " the sar accused. "You blind er somethin'?"

"Can't you show us more of it?"

"Nope. Too dark."

"But shouldn't you check the harness?" Ittai asked desperately.

Eliahba stiffened. "Did I check it today?" he asked suspiciously.

"I don't think so," Ittai replied.

"Don' 'member. Soooo." He swayed backward, then leaned forward. "Guess I should."

Opening the gate, they stumbled through. The sar led them to the first row of stalls and paused. Farther down, a low fire burned, but no one was beside it.

"Everyone must be celebrating," Eliphelet muttered. "Is there a torch around here somewhere?"

"Nope, but there's lamps!" the sar declared. "Lotsh of 'em. Dozens."

Slipping out from under Eliahba's shoulder, Ittai went to the fire. He found more fuel for it and finally managed to get some sticks burning enough to use as a makeshift torch.

Eliphelet was already staring into the first stall. "It's that harness," he said, jerking his chin at the one opposite them. "We need to get Eliahba out of here now. Take him home. By the time he gets there, he'll be ready to sleep. I already gave him a final drink from my cruse."

"All right. Where will I meet you?"

"I'll be in the palace square opposite the gate."

¥ ¥ ¥ ¥ ¥ ¥

As soon as the young Philistine disappeared, still coaxing the sar to tell him where he slept, Eliphelet inspected the stall as well as he could in the dim light. Whatever was here wasn't used much, too much dust on it for that. But this harness had been moved much more frequently, although not for its intended use, the thief saw with interest. The spot where he had gripped the leather to take it down had much less dust than the rest of it. Once it was on the floor, he inspected the wall, passing the burning branches as close to it as he dared.

Taking hold of the hook, he jiggled it a little. It seemed to give, and he pulled down on it, then tried side to side. It gave, but . . . Tentatively, he pushed upward and heard the latch open. With nothing else on the wall to grab, he pulled on the hook, and the door swung toward him. After a quick glance outside, he took his crude torch and crept into the little space. Three pack saddles sat on the ground, a chest on either side of two of the saddles. The third had a medium-sized jar on each side with a bundle fastened between. Setting the torch where it wouldn't ignite anything, he opened the bundle. Pottery lamps. "Lots of lamps," he muttered. There was nothing else in the room that he could see. Just as he was closing up the bundle, a cloth tie in it caught his eye.

When he pulled it from the pack he saw that it was a cover cloth. That was interesting. Opening it, he took one look at the parchment and smiled. To be certain, he unrolled the scroll enough to see that it was indeed the tax authorization from Egypt, then put it back, measuring the length and thickness of the scroll as he did. After he fastened the bundle again, he picked up his torch. It was close to going out, and he held it upside down to encourage the wood to burn brighter. That's when he noticed the scuff marks in the dirt. Curious, he passed the torch along them. The tiny room extended back a few feet, ending in a pile of dirt. Except the space behind that dirt seemed emptier than it should.

Stepping carefully to avoid leaving evidence of his passing, Eliphelet found a narrow tunnel stretching before him. Still holding the makeshift torch low, he edged down it for less than 15 feet. A wooden panel pushed inward easily, and he slipped around it, finding himself in a large room. The sight that greeted his eyes made him freeze in his tracks, heart pounding. "Yahweh, preserve me!" he gasped.

¥ ¥ ¥ ¥ ¥ ¥

Out on the road, Eliphelet seemed strangely tense, and Ittai broke the silence. "What did you find?"

"What we were looking for. There's a small room behind the wall of that stall. Manani keeps several things there, including the tax authorization for Gath."

"Did you bring it with you?" the young Philistine gasped.

"No. Remember, we don't want him to realize we've taken it. But I know now what to substitute for it so he won't know it's gone unless he actually opens it."

"When can you get it?" Ittai asked, realizing he was trembling with excitement.

"It will have to be tomorrow night, I'm afraid. Yasma is invited to share the last night of the feast with Manani. I'll try to get the seren back to his house as soon as I can. It shouldn't be hard since Manani is eager to hear what I have to tell him."

"And what is that?"

"Ways to lessen the value of the tax goods sent to Egypt. Sometimes substitutions can be made, or goods can be lost or stolen, but the best way is to muddy the records. Splitting up the goods between bales starts the confusion, then reporting some stolen, 'finding' it again months later, sending some with one caravan, the rest with another caravan, mixing up the goods from different towns and regions—anything and everything so that goods listed on the master list never arrive all at once. By the time that goes on for a year or two, no one knows what's really been sent, and what hasn't. In three or four years, half of it can disappear, and no one will be able to say whether or not it's really gone."

"What if he actually tries to do as you suggest? Will it work?"

Eliphelet stared at him. "Of course it will work. I am very good at what I do, Ittai!"

¥ ¥ ¥ ¥ ¥ ¥

"The caravan should leave, the earlier the better," Eliphelet instructed once they were back in their tent. "I have to find Samlah, for we need the seal again. We can send Tilon back to Gath and Hadar now, via the highlands."

"Why not just head south?" Ittai asked, unrolling his bedroll.

"If Manani puts anything together, the caravan will be safest in the highlands. And I need parchment. Is there any around?"

"Sibbecai will know," Ittai said with a yawn.

Eliphelet continued to wander around the tent. He needed Samlah, or more importantly, the man's packs. But could he convince him to give up his grudge against Hadar? Noticing that Ittai was asleep, the thief went outside and hurried to the other side of the encampment where Samlah had his tent.

To his surprise, it was empty. Now what? After lighting a lamp, Eliphelet confirmed the absence of the caravaneer, noting that his unused bedroll in a corner. Without thought, he searched through the man's effects, finding Hadar's seal and several other things in rather obvious places. Also he found a papyrus and wrote out orders for Tilon, then tucked the seal into his girdle.

Where could Samlah be, he wondered as he returned to his tent, then stifled his impatience. He would have to find him first thing in the morning. Everything had to go smoothly tomorrow if they were to survive and succeed.

Chapter 7

Week Four, Day Seven

It was barely light enough to see when Eliphelet checked Samlah's tent. Still empty. Where was that man, he fumed to himself. He had to talk to him. This was a once-in-a-lifetime opportunity, and it was just bad luck that Samlah was the one with the donkeys and packs. The man couldn't have more than one idea in his head at a time, and once something lodged there, it could take hours to budge it. Witness how long it took to convince him that going north was better than going south. Where could he be?

A sudden chill went through the thief. Had Samlah managed to slip out of camp and get to Ekron? He should have thought of that last night! By now, his former associate in crime would be very drunk, and Yahweh alone knew what the man had said! Or who had heard him!

Eliphelet had to find him immediately, and even more importantly, determine what he might have said to anybody. That meant searching the wine shops, which he couldn't do as Yasma-Addu, and given what Samlah may have said, he shouldn't go searching as himself either! That left Ittai.

The young man was already up when Eliphelet returned to the tent. "We have a problem," the thief said grimly, striding into the tent. "Samlah is gone."

"What does that mean?" Ittai asked, alarmed.

"The only place I can imagine he'd be is in an Ekron wine shop, announcing who I am to anyone who will listen. We should be leaving right now!"

"But we can't, not without that authorization! You know where it is. Can't you just slip in and take it?"

"Probably. But in order to keep Manani from knowing it's gone, I still have to substitute something for it, and if Samlah has talked as much as I'm afraid he has, I will have to sneak into the city in order to get to the stables again."

Ittai bit his lip. "Isn't there any way at all?" he asked desperately. "You said you could become six different people! Can't you become someone else? I hate to give up when we're so close!"

Gradually, Eliphelet's gaze became distant, and then a little smile crossed his face. "I hate to give up, too," he said softly. "There are a couple of things we might do. But first, we have to know how much Samlah has spilled. If you can find him and bring him back here, we can plan more."

"I'll find him." Swiftly he threw on his cloak and sandals.

"Oh, did you find some parchment?"

The Philistine youth pointed to his bedroll as he left the tent.

Seeing the parchment, Eliphelet raised his eyes to the roof of the tent. "Thank You, Yah."

Ittai returned much sooner than expected.

"What happened?" Eliphelet asked, seeing his expression.

"The entire city is talking about you," the young man informed him. "Word from the south that Eliphelet ben Ahasbai may be in the area had already reached the palace. That, with what Samlah has said, means anyone who looks remotely like Yasma Addu is being stopped and questioned. In addition, the seren has spies watching all caravans for any indication that anyone is leaving. Seren Manani has sworn that you will not escape him!"

"Word from the south? Hadar! He must be suspicious already. Well, we should be able to bluff our way through today. Here's what needs to be done next. Go back to Ekron. When you find Samlah, keep him drunk. Then get him talking about lion-birds."

"Lion-birds?" Ittai asked carefully. "What are they?"

"Samlah will tell you," the thief said with a smile. "And by the time he's finished telling you, no one will pay any attention to what he says anymore. He's got a lot of nonsensical ideas from his travels on the eastern trade routes beyond Babylon.

"About the tenth hour, come back, and be sure to ask the gate guards how to get to the stables. Tell them that Yasma-Addu will be bringing a dozen donkeys with a trifling gift for Seren Manani."

After Ittai departed for the second time, Eliphelet went to Tilon's tent.

The caravan master greeted him respectfully. "Shalom, adon."

"Shalom, Tilon. Ittai has located Samlah. He's in Ekron, turning the seren against us. I became suspicious when he did not return last night, and I opened his packs. They are nothing but rocks and rags. Apparently he hoped to switch his for yours at some point on the trail, but Regem's guards were too watchful for him. He may be trying to convince Manani you are a thief, using his own packs as evidence."

For several moments Tilon was speechless with surprise and then outrage. "How do you know this?" he sputtered at last.

"Come look at his packs for yourself If your men don't mind a little work, I think we can put Samlah's packs back where they belong and get away ourselves."

After seeing their contents, Tilon was more than cooperative, and under the pretext of providing a gift for Manani, Samlah's donkeys were loaded with the worthless "goods," and the rest of the caravan readied for hasty departure as soon as night fell.

By the time Ittai returned in late afternoon at the tenth hour, Eliphelet paced their tent impatiently. "How did it go?" he asked as soon as the young man entered.

"I don't ever want to spend another day like this again! Just after I found Samlah, some of Manani's men came to escort him to the palace so that he could be readily available if Manani should want to interview him personally. Samlah insisted I come along since I had already mentioned those bird things, and he was determined to tell me all about them. I've never heard such nonsense in my life! Animals like lions with eagles' heads and wings! And that lay eggs and have nests! About the time Samlah was swearing those unbelievable creatures were real in just the same manner he was swearing Eliphelet ben Ahasbai was here, we got thrown out of the palace and very nearly beaten into the bargain!"

"Did you remember to ask the way to the stables?" Eliphelet asked anxiously.

"Yes, although the reply I got was barely civil."

"Where is Samlah?"

"Buried in the most obscure wineshop in Ekron, for all I care. I left him at Ekron's gate, trying to convince the guards that his impossible animals were real!"

"We've got to get moving," Eliphelet said, ignoring Ittai's disgust. "Change into something that doesn't smell of wine. You have to take those donkeys through the gates."

Not long afterward, Ittai led the string of 12 donkeys into the city. He endured the snickers and suppressed smiles with composure, and Eliphelet, bringing up the rear, passed through without anyone taking a second glance. After crossing the square to the palace, they swung down the alley to the stables.

"What is your business here?" a hoarse voice asked.

Ittai looked up in surprise, and Eliphelet edged forward, bunching the donkeys in front of him. He'd been counting on the fact that the guards would be celebrating tonight as they had been the previous night.

"Sar Eliahba!" Ittai exclaimed as the man struggled to get off a stool in the middle of the walkway between the rows of stalls.

"What is he doing here?" Eliphelet muttered under his breath in amazement. He'd put enough of Keturah's special mix into his cruse last night that the man's final drink should have laid him out flat for three days at least!

When Ittai hurried forward to help the sar, the man retched all over him.

"You're in no condition to be here!" Ittai scolded.

"I have guard duty," the sar whispered, before beginning to retch again.

"Not when you are this sick. I'll take you to your room, and alert the guards to send a replacement. Will that be all right?" he asked, turning to Eliphelet.

"It will have to be," the thief said, keeping his voice down. "You can't come with me until after you've changed clothes, and that will take too much time. Get him to his room, and then wait for me back at the caravan. I can handle the donkeys alone if I tether them together."

As soon as Ittai and the sar were out of sight, Eliphelet set to work, leading the donkeys into the stable and tying each one in a stall. He unloaded the chests and bales, stacking them neatly to one side in the first stall and leaving the pack saddles on the animals. On the other side of the stall he set out the pack containing his other clothes and the items he would need when he returned. Pulling out the parchment he'd prepared, he opened the cloth and unrolled it, admiring his own work. The thin hide was decorated with strange signs he'd made up as he worked, a couple of phrases in script with some misshapen letters, a Babylonian phrase, and some Sumerian signs he'd seen on a wall in an abandoned house when he was in Ur long ago. The whole thing was utter nonsense, but he couldn't bear simply to put in a blank parchment. He smiled as he rolled it up. Undoubtedly, it would give Manani a turn if he ever looked at it!

By now it was almost dusk, and he quickly changed to Yasma Addu's garments. As he adjusted his girdle to just the right length, he noticed his hands shaking. It had been a long time since he had flirted so closely with death. He was betting his life that Manani would want to string Yasma Addu along for as long as he could, learn all his secrets for robbing Pharaoh, and collect the bribe on those donkeys before accusing and arresting him. Everything he knew of the man suggested that he enjoyed toying with people.

"You just have to beat him at his own game," the thief muttered as he straightened his shoulders and adjusted the turban. Instantly he was Yasma Addu, without a worry in the world, and he was on his way to a most tasty feast. That was one thing which could be said for Manani; the man ate well.

"At last," Seren Manani sighed, sitting down in the upper room of the private residence. Yasma seated himself also, glancing around at the lamps keeping the room brightly lit. "We are completely private here, adon. Our discussion of the procedures to assess Pharaoh's tax goods will not be overheard."

"Is there wine?"

"Of course. And of the best." The seren reached for a jug and poured both goblets himself.

Yasma took the offered cup with a steady hand. All evening he had fenced with the man, turning aside every veiled reference or jab with thinly disguised contempt, alternately angering and soothing the seren without seeming to. Manani watched him now with reluctant respect and a tiny shade of doubt.

The thief suppressed his smile. That doubt signaled his victory in the game they had played all evening. In spite of everything, it would continue to grow and torment the seren for years to come. But victory did not bring safety, for if Manani's mind was as devious as it might be, the wine Yasma had just accepted might contain an unpleasant surprise, which might be made worse by what he was about to do.

Taking a small vial from his girdle, he opened it, carefully measuring three drops into the cup. Swirling it around to mix it, he sipped, then leaned back contentedly. "This is indeed good wine."

"What do you have there?" his host couldn't resist asking.

"Something from across the Great Sea. I ran across it not long ago, and I like it, but one must be careful with it. Would you like to try it?"

"Perhaps a little."

"One drop, then." Picking the vial up, he measured a drop into the seren's cup, shaking the cup a little to spread the mixture. "Take just a sip, and wait."

Manani did, easing back on the cushions in the three-legged chair. After a moment or two, his eyes brightened. "Yes, I see what you mean. A most unusual effect!"

"I like it, but I limit myself to two cups only on infrequent occasions. Tonight I am drinking to our success," he said, raising the cup. Then he returned the vial to his girdle.

"To begin with, you will need a very good scribe," Yasma began abruptly. "Strict records must be kept, one for your usage, and one for Pharaoh's. It is always best to check each delivery as it comes in against the master list. Once that is done, divide the goods into two or more piles, keeping strict track of what goes into which pile . . ."

Before long, Manani's eyes were gleaming as he listened. Yasma poured the second cup of wine for them both, and took a vial from his girdle, measuring it into his own cup first. Holding a second vial in his left hand, he emptied the entire thing unseen into the seren's wine while carefully measuring two drops from the first one.

"Now," he continued, handing the wine to his host, "I can see that you have grasped the essentials of the record keeping. The more often you split and divide the goods, the more often you can substitute something slightly inferior, or simply create more confusion regarding when and how delivery takes place . . ."

Half an hour later Manani leaned forward, staring at his guest. "You should work with me," he interrupted.

Yasma raised an eyebrow in irritation. "Doing what?" he asked testily.

"You and I, we could work together and control Egypt's trade routes," the seren said, still staring straight ahead. "All I need is the highlands, and they will soon be mine."

"The Israelites might object."

Leaning back, Manani snorted in disdain. "The Israelites become mine the moment I take Jebus. And that part is almost finished. You understand the caravans, I control the routes. There would be no limit to our riches!" Still staring, the seren sagged in his chair, sound sleep, upright only because his weight rested on the back of the chair where there were two legs, and not on the front which had just one.

Maintaining a tight self-control, Yasma disposed of the rest of the wine over the balcony wall and then filled the cup again to the same level. In it he added a generous dose of Keturah's special herbal blend. After the amount of poppy that had just put the seren to sleep, he would wake up extremely thirsty, and he would surely not ignore a drink so readily available.

"I take my leave of you, Seren," Yasma said, closing the door quietly behind him. Heedless of his rich clothing, he climbed to the roof of the one story house and followed the compound wall back into the deep shadows. The alley he let himself down into was just as filthy and smelly as Hanan had warned him it would be, but it allowed him to leave without any of the guards knowing he had done so.

Only then did he utter the thought uppermost in his mind. "May Yahweh and all the gods stand against you, Manani! May Jebus never be yours!" he devoutly intoned as he slipped cautiously into the next street. Hearing only the sounds of celebration, he hurried past the palace, dark and still, to the gate leading to the stables.

Once there, he closed the door and got out the lamps and pack he'd brought with the donkeys. As fast as possible, he stripped off Yasma's clothing and put on those of an itinerant entertainer. After tying up the garments, he carefully put the parchment he'd folded and rolled on top of them.

Taking down the harness, he opened the secret door and propped it. Holding one of the lamps, he crept through the tunnel and cautiously opened the panel at the end. No one was in the room. Eliphelet set the lamp in a niche in the wall and briefly contemplated the rows of chests and bales spread out before him. He had the whole of Ekron's city treasury to choose from! When had Manani realized that the city treasury backed up against the city stables? From the looks of that tunnel, long before the man became seren!

Picking up a chest, Eliphelet went back out the tunnel and set it by the first stall with a donkey in it. Working swiftly, he hauled through the tunnel another of Samlah's chests from the stack he'd made earlier, bringing back a treasury chest each time. He did the same with the bales of cloth. After the last trip, he took the lamp and closed the panel.

In the little room he opened the bundle with the lamps and extracted the tax authorization document. Then, unwrapping the cloth cover, he put in the parchment he'd prepared and folded the protective covering again before returning it to the pack of lamps. Looking around, he scattered some dirt over the scuff marks closest to the tunnel, and then shut the door, hanging the harness back on the hook.

After spreading out another cloth, he proceeded to drape and tie the tax authorization document with an assortment of fringe, tassels, and bits of fabric of various colors. The rest of the small items disappeared into the depths of his entertainer's clothing, and lastly he thrust the parchment there also. Methodically, he cleaned up everything he had disturbed, and only then did he open the stable door and start loading the chests and bales onto the donkeys, leading the animals from their stalls one by one.

It was late when he finished tying the donkeys together with a tether and led them out into the palace square. The guards at the gate stopped him. "Where are you going so late?" the sar in charge asked.

"To Seren Manani's estate with the gift from Yasma Addu," Eliphelet replied, keeping his face in the shadows. "My master sent orders that it was to be taken there immediately. He is still supposed to be with the seren at his private house here in the city."

"And may the gods preserve your master," the sar muttered as he stepped aside and helped guide the pack animals through the small pedestrian door.

Eliphelet had not gone far outside of town when Ittai stepped onto the road.

"What are you doing here?" the thief demanded.

"Tilon was worried, so the caravan left for the hills as soon as it was fully dark. I waited here to get the donkeys from you."

"You take them, then," Eliphelet said in relief.

"Did you get the document?"

"Yes. Take these donkeys to Dahveed's encampment. I'll see that they are returned to Samlah in due time."

"Yahweh go with you, Eliphelet."

"And with you, Ittai."

Week Five, Day One

Sahrah Hazzel made her way through the noisy marketplace. Saph, of Goliath's family, saw her coming, and took his time getting out of her way. But she ignored him. After Akish had beaten Ishvi-benob, there had been threats of reprisal, but apparently Manani had told the Rapha to behave themselves since nothing further had developed. Now, the four giant brothers made it clear that they only left things alone because they chose to. Hazzel frowned. So long as they continued to choose to, she was satisfied.

Laughter broke out on her left, and, curious, she headed that direction. A man dressed in colorful robes and wearing a turban was making things appear and disappear for a group of children. She wandered over to watch, and the growing crowd of adults parted to let her through.

Seeing her, the entertainer instantly removed his turban and bowed deeply. "Such beauty could only belong to a sahrah," he said, smiling. "I have heard that the palace in Gath is graced with the presence of Akish's beauteous sister. Dare I think you may be she?"

Hazzel smiled. "I am. Which merchant paid you to say such things?"

The crowd laughed, and the entertainer looked hurt. "Sahrah, I heard of your beauty from the far places of the land. The wind whispered it to me in the highlands, and the roads from Ekron sped me on my way with even more tales."

She waved her hand at him dismissively. At least he was certainly inventive.

"You honor me, Sahrah," he said, touching her hand briefly. When she looked down at it, two of her four rings were gone.

"You are impudent, rogue. Return what you took from me."

"I? I could have nothing of yours, Sahrah. I am but a poor entertainer who—"

"Who is currently holding two of my rings," she finished for him. "Come now, rogue, admit that I have caught you!"

The man sighed, his face doleful. "It was your beauty that dazzled me." When he doffed his hat, her ring—to the delight of the crowd—was on his head.

She plucked it off, giving his hair a tweak by way of punishment.

"Give up the other one," she said, laughing in spite of herself.

"You say there's more?" he asked, his hat back on his head now. "Well, perhaps I can find something." Removing the hat, he pulled from the empty air inside it a fine linen scarf. "Since you insist, Sahrah," he said, his voice humble, handing it to her.

"The scarf is indeed nice, but it's not what you took," she said sternly, draping it over her shoulder and now thoroughly caught up in the performance.

"It's not? Well, let me check again." Patting his robes, he once more took off the hat. Three bracelets were in it. "These?"

"You know perfectly well they are not," she said as two other women hastily claimed their jewelry.

"You are hard to please, baalah. Perhaps this is yours?" and he handed her a wilted flower.

Beginning to loose a little patience, Hazzel glared at him.

He fell to his knees. "Please, baalah, the flower does not please you? I have something else here," and in his hand appeared a bit of papyrus twisted to look like a flower bud which he thrust into her hand. "No? What about this?" he asked, pulling out a stone pestle. "Patience, Sahrah, I'll find it," he went on, pulling another long piece of fine linen from his pouch. "Let's see," a small box materialized as the crowd gasped and laughed, along with a little alabaster cosmetic jar and a comb with broken teeth. "Ah, no, that's mine," he said apologetically, returning the comb to the air. "A round stone perhaps?" That materialized too, being added to the collection she held. "No, that goes with this," and a second small sling dangled from his hand, much too little for the stone. "Ah, here it is," he said, pulling from his sleeve a papyrus roll decorated with the most outlandish tassels, fringe, and scraps of colored cloth. "If you don't like that, I'm sure your brother would," he said, looking directly into her eyes. "Surely now, I have returned everything," he concluded, bowing.

"Everything except the ring."

"But isn't that what you're wearing?"

Surprised, she looked down at her hand. Her other ring was, indeed, on her finger. She had to laugh again.

"Ah, I have pleased you. I will take myself away, with the picture in my memory of your wondrous face smiling upon me." Bowing again and again, he backed away, leaving her with her arms full of all the various objects he had produced from nowhere. By the time she could think to call him back, he had vanished.

"Well, I like that!" she said, annoyed. Then she noticed the rolled papyrus wasn't papyrus. It was parchment. "I like that, indeed," she said quickly. "The insolence of the man, leaving me with all this—"

"Sahrah, I can take some of it," her maid offered, trying to avoid the storm she saw building.

"Absolutely not!" Hazzel said, turning and starting back to the palace. "Entertainers are all very well, but to do something like this? No, Akish shall see just exactly what kind of spectacle that rogue made of his sister in the market! Beauteous, he called me, and then leaves me with enough pieces of junk that I look like a peddler's pack on a donkey! And my brother will see it all!" she fumed, striding faster and faster.

"Where is he?" she demanded of the door servant as she returned to the palace.

"Your pardon, Sahrah, but he is in conference with his sars. He has specifically said he is not to be interrupted and—"

"He always says that," Hazzel said, sweeping past. "And it's never what he means. If he thinks that telling me he's meeting with someone will stop me from letting him know just how bad things are out there—" As she walked to his business chamber, she juggled the items around in her hands until she could wrap the tiny sling around the parchment. It made an odd contrast with the tassels and fringe.

"Open the door," she ordered the guard outside it.

"Baalah, I—"

"Now!" The man helplessly obeyed.

"Look at me!" she said, sweeping into the chamber to the consternation of four sars and her brother. "Do you see what that man did? How can you allow such insolence in the markets? Don't you care that I could be a peddler's pack? You allow another magician into the city? After what those disgusting fools have done to our house? Can't I even go outside of my rooms without being reminded of my poor lost boy? Look at what he gave me!" Then she threw everything on the desk, the round stone thunking loudly as it landed. "And what am I supposed to do with this?" she nearly yelled, slamming the parchment roll on top of everything else. "Since you let such horrible reminders of my poor lost boy into this city, you can just keep it all!" And she whirled around, leaving as quickly as she had come.

¥ ¥ ¥ ¥ ¥ ¥

    While the sars studied the floor with perfectly straight faces, Akish stared down at the collection on his desk with irritation. You would think that after years of being a sahrah, his sister would manage to control herself once in a while. He swept the items out of his way, but the feel of the papyrus made him pause. Settling the wilted flower on the top of the pile, he turned back to the sars.
    "Anything else?" he asked drily.
    "I think we have covered everything," Sar Shemel said. "We would leave you now, Sereni."
    "You may do so."
    The commanders hastily left. Akish barred the door after them, then picked up the parchment. The sling made his heart beat faster, and he carefully removed it. Hardly daring to breathe, he divested the roll of its gaudy decorations, revealing the official Egyptian seal hidden underneath. "By Dagon! It isn't possible!" he whispered, unrolling the tax authorization. Stunned, he gazed at it for some time, then rolled it up again. Dropping into his chair, he cradled his chin in his fingers. "It would seem that more than just Dahveed will take exception to someone threatening my house," he whispered. "Yahweh, You have taken my nephew for Your own indeed."
    Late that afternoon, Gath's ruler stood at the eastern edge of his almond grove, facing the highlands. He knelt silently. "I am grateful, Yahweh. I must believe that Your servant Dahveed has taken my house to him and protected it, honoring the covenant cut before You even though it was made to an enemy of his people. And now, I am free of Manani's control because my house is tied to that of Your servant. I do not know how to honor You properly, and I dare not do so openly, but I am grateful."

Chapter 8

Week Five, Day Six

It was mid-morning when Zalmon found me at my tent. "Dahveed, Jether and three men are headed into camp."

I looked up in surprise. Why would my brother-in-law be coming here? "Tell Ahinoam to prepare to make them welcome," I directed my retainer as I reached for a suitable kilt to wear.

I was nearly ready when Abigail rushed in. "Dahveed, Jether is dressed very formally," she panted. "I don't know what has happened, but it looks as if he's here as a Master Caravaneer, and not as brother-in-law. He is accompanied by his nephew, and Hadar is with him, along with Tilon, Hadar's caravan master. Abishai is getting ready, and Shagay's son said to tell you that Jether has nearly a dozen men in a camp not far away."

I stripped off the kilt while Abigail shook out a robe for me to wear and brought a silver band for my hair. "Do I remember correctly that Eliphelet has been away?" I asked grimly.

"Yes," my wife said, unbinding my hair and grabbing a comb. "He returned yesterday and asked about Ittai first thing, but we haven't seen him yet."

"Ittai is gone? Tell me quickly what has happened!"

While the Gebirah combed out my hair she hurriedly explained that Ittai and Eliphelet had left shortly after I did, without saying anything to anyone. They had apparently consulted with Keturah and Tirzah, and Josheb was quietly furious because his best clothing and jewelry were missing.

"We didn't bother informing you since we had no idea they would be gone so long," she ended, pulling more hair out of my head with the comb. "Then when you were delayed at Horesh, we rather forgot about it. You've only been back for two days since then, and there hasn't been time to say much now that the rains have come and planting has begun."

I sighed, then yelped as Abigail gave a final tug to my hair. She settled the headband on as Abishai arrived. "Do you know anything about this?" I asked as I stepped out of the tent, and Abigail looked us over, straightening both our girdles.

"No, Dodi, but Jether can't be too upset. He and those with him accepted the food and wine we gave them. He seems to be more curious than anything else."

"Thank Yahweh for small favors," I muttered, walking down the hill to the small clearing where we received visitors. Just before we arrived, Shagay's Jonathan came panting up with the news that Ittai was arriving with about a dozen strange donkeys.

"Tell him and Eliphelet that I will need to see them both immediately," I said before turning my attention to my brother-in-law and those with him.

After the usual exchange of greetings and news, I settled down on the blanket spread for us to sit on, and caught the Ishmaelite's eye. "What brings you here on such a formal visit?"

"A rather unusual story," he replied gravely. "I don't quite know what to make of it, so I brought the men here to tell it to you themselves." He indicated Hadar and Tilon.

"What has happened, and what do you feel I can do for you?" I asked the two caravaneers.

"I am not certain myself," Hadar began hesitantly, glancing at Jether, who nodded in encouragement. "But Adon Jether seems to feel that you can help us untangle what has happened in the past month or so."

As the tale of Hadar's caravan unfolded, I grew a bit bewildered, striving to find any wrong-doing by Sibbecai and the guards with him since they were my only connection to the caravan that I knew of. It wasn't until the end of the story, when Eliphelet's name surfaced, that I began to worry that there might be more to this. But I still couldn't see why they would come to me. At last I turned to Jether.

"Please, speak plainly to me," I requested. "What is it that you want of me?"

Amusement briefly flashed in the Ishmaelite's eyes. "It would quiet the minds of my associates, Dahveed, if you would verify the whereabouts of Eliphelet ben Ahasbai for the past few weeks since he is a sworn retainer of yours."

Hadar couldn't suppress a gasp, and Tilon looked shocked.

"I am unable to do that, since I have been gone myself until two days ago," I replied. "But Eliphelet is here, and we can ask him to account for his time."

Abishai sent Zalmon's son, Pekah, to find him. In a surprisingly short time Eliphelet appeared, escorted by Josheb, I noticed, and accompanied by Ittai, who looked quite composed even though he'd had little time to prepare.

Watching the two of them, I briefly recounted what I'd just been told, the grim looks of Hadar and Tilon confirming that they recognized both of my men. By the time I finished, Eliphelet looked worried and had his hands tucked under his arms, and Ittai was chewing his lower lip.

Turning to my covenant son, I said, "Perhaps you would care to tell me why these associates of our house have cause to suspect wrong-doing."

He reddened slightly. "We didn't steal anything, adoni. We just diverted Hadar's caravan for a few days."

Sensing that this was only going to get worse, I momentarily clenched my teeth, remembering that I needed to hear everything before deciding anything. "You diverted it, did you? Where to?"

"Ekron."

"Ekron?"

That calm, composed expression settled on my covenant son's face, the look I was beginning to associate with things I wouldn't be told about until it was much too late to do anything. "Start at the beginning, Ittai, and don't leave anything out!" I admonished. The exasperation in my own voice reminded me of the way Jonathan Hassar had sounded on too many occasions when I had reported to him. "Yahweh, preserve me," I muttered.

"Well, you wanted to know why the Philistines were so persistent this year, and you said it was all right for me to do what I could if I found out anything." He paused.

Closing my eyes, I tried to remember exactly what I had said to him. After all, I hadn't thought much about it at the time.

"I discovered that Seren Manani was forcing Seren Akish to go along with his wishes because Akish had, er, lost something to him."

"Lost it?" I looked over at Eliphelet, and closed my eyes again. "Don't tell me you took Eliphelet to Ekron to steal it back," I almost groaned.

"Yes, adoni."

"Where does the caravan come in?" I continued with a sigh.

"Well, in order to get close to Manani, I needed to be rich," Eliphelet said reasonably, picking up the story.

"So you borrowed a caravan?"

"We just diverted it for a few days using Hadar's seal."

"You stole the caravan master's seal?" I sputtered.

"Of course not, adoni!" he replied, indignantly. "Stealing caravans if you have a seal makes things too easy to bother with. But we were in a hurry, and Samlah already had it, so we used it."

I just stared at him. Too *easy?* Someone coughed a little, and I glanced up suspiciously. But all of my men had perfectly straight faces. I did not want to hear the rest of this tale, but knew that I had to. "Go on," I finally directed.

By the time Eliphelet finished explaining everything that had happened and how and to whom, I could only sit there and seethe with exasperation. "What were the two of you thinking?"

"We were thinking of next war season, adoni," Ittai answered quietly. "You said you didn't want war in the highlands. With Gath out of Ekron's control, there will be much less fighting this coming year."

Just from the look in Ittai's eyes, I knew I'd only been told about a quarter of the story, but there was not a single stray end anywhere that I could question.

"What about the donkeys you returned with?"

"They belonged to Samlah," Eliphelet said.

I turned to my visitors. "We will return the donkeys and packs immediately."

Hadar looked up in disgust. "Don't bother. If I had known it was Samlah who had joined my caravan, I'd have had him beaten and confiscated his donkeys myself! He's been a thorn in my side for years, dealing in stolen goods from that cursed thief, Eliph–" Abruptly he stopped, suddenly remembering that the man stood before him and was a sworn retainer to me.

"But there are the packs," I said, keeping my face composed.

"Which are filled with nothing but rocks and rags, as I saw for myself," Tilon said. He turned to Hadar. "I haven't had time to tell you this, but we discovered that Samlah planned on switching some of our packs for his on the trail. But he could not because of the watchfulness of Sibeccai and the guards. For which we are grateful," the man added, bowing to me.

I acknowledged his bow, then sat in perplexity. Even though no apparent harm had been done, I still felt that I owed recompense to Jether for what had happened, but I had no idea how much.

"You took nothing from the caravan?" I asked Ittai.

"We did use a jug of wine, and some parchments."

"How many parchments?"

"Four," Eliphelet replied.

"And the wine?"

"It was very good wine," Ittai said. He described the mark on the jug.

As he talked, Jether looked annoyed. "The wine was mine. Some of the best, and very expensive!"

Again I lapsed into thought. At the very least, I would have to pay for the wine and the parchment, but should I do more than that? From the way Jether eyed Eliphelet, I knew he would like to demand the thief be given him, but hadn't made up his mind to do that yet. If he did, I would have to refuse since—. Suddenly, I knew what to do.

"Jether, you have come to me for recompense since Ittai and Eliphelet have troubled you and yours. But in truth, both of them belong to another more than me. Ittai is covenant son to me by Yahweh's express wish, and Eliphelet ben Ahasbai has been taken personally by Yahweh as an ark bearer. Because of this, we must present this case to Yahweh and let him decide what should be done.

"I will pledge myself now to submit to whatever Yahweh may determine. Are you willing to do the same?"

After a time, the Ishmaelite nodded. "I am willing."

"Then let us go to the ark." As I rose, the others did also.

"The rumors are true, then? You do have the sacred ark?" Jether asked.

"Yes. Abiathar brought it when he fled from Shaul and the destruction of Nob."

When Ittai, Eliphelet, Jether, and I gathered in front of the tent where the ark rested, light shone under the ark covering, and Abiathar waited for us, his face blank and gaze distant. Apparently Yahweh awaited our arrival and His Spirit had fallen upon His priest.

"Why have you come, Dahveed ben Boaz?"

"I have come because of the manner in which two of my retainers used the goods and servants of others for purposes of their own and without the knowledge of the owners of those goods and servants. I do not see that much harm was done, but I am perplexed about what recompense may be owed. Ittai of Gath and Eliphelet ben Ahasbai are both bound to You as well as myself, and I bring this case before You now for judgment."

Abiathar turned to Ittai. "Ittai of Gath, did you not take Me, Yahweh, for your God?"

The young Philistine bowed to the ground. "I did."

"Then why did you not come to Me in your trouble? Am I not able to help in any need?"

"I did not remember to do so," Ittai admitted, his face flushing. "I have not done well in this matter."

"No, you have not. While you have accomplished My will, you have brought trouble to those around you. You will personally pay for the wine and parchments which you used."

"It will be as you command."

The priest turned next to my brother-in-law. "Jether ben Ishmael, the thoughts of your heart have not been good toward the servant I have chosen to serve Me. He became Mine, and I will repay. Do you now claim recompense from Me because of the deeds of my servant, Eliphelet ben Ahasbai?"

"Adonai, I would not trouble you about such a small thing," Jether said, stepping forward and bowing toward the ark.

"So small a thing? If it is so small a thing, why do you yet wish to spill the blood of My servant? Is it just for you to demand blood for theft? Would you refuse just recompense from Me in order to rob Me of the service I chose Eliphelet ben Ahasbai to perform? Are you the one to decide who serves Me and for how long?"

His face white, Jether bowed from his knees. "Yahweh, forgive me, for I have sinned in my heart! You heard my vow, that I would accept your judgment. I honor that vow!"

Abiathar turned to my personal thief. "Eliphelet ben Ahasbai, before I called you to serve Me, you brought much trouble and wrong to Jether the Ishmaelite. This is displeasing to Me."

"Yes, Adonai," he said, kneeling beside me.

"Recompense must be paid for these wrongs. What do you have to repay him?"

"Adonai, he can take the donkeys and the loads on them."

"You would offer that which does not belong to you for recompense?"

"Adonai, you know to whom the donkeys belong. You also know to whom the loads belong and the purpose for which they would have been used. Is this not acceptable recompense—for everyone?"

I got the distinct impression that Adonai was laughing for some reason, and I cast a quick glance at Eliphelet. The thief had amusement in his eyes also and seemed surprisingly relaxed in Yahweh's presence.

Abiathar moved to Jether again. "You have heard the offer for recompense from my servant. Is this acceptable to you?"

"Whatever You choose to grant to me will be acceptable, Adonai," the Ishmaelite replied, his voice unsteady.

"Even though it be but rocks and rags?"

Sweat breaking out on his face, Jether swallowed. "Even then, Adonai, for I have sinned against You, and You are a merciful God."

"You think little of My honor. Go. See for yourself the recompense brought to you."

Jether rose hesitantly. The donkeys waited patiently not far away, for no one had had time to unload them, and everyone in camp had clustered around us. Jether and his nephew went to them, and the older man opened a chest. Motionless, he stared into it, for a long moment, then fastened it again, his face completely blank. Then he went to another, and another, and another. He checked two of the cloth bales, and stood for some time before he approached the ark again, kneeling before the priest, the strangest expression on his face.

"Is My recompense sufficient for you, though it be rocks and rags?"

The Ishmaelite again bowed to the ground. "I could not have expected what You gave me," he said in an odd voice.

"Then you have no further claims against My servant?"

"Before You, I swear that Your servant has repaid me amply for any injury, now or in the past, which he has done."

"Go in peace, Jether ben Ishmael."

"You are gracious to me and my house, Yahweh," the Ishmaelite responded.

Yah's presence lifted, and the four of us stood.

As Jether took his leave, he kept glancing at those donkeys as if he couldn't believe what he saw, making me greatly wonder what was in those chests. From the wistful look on Eliphelet's face as the animals plodded out of camp, I got the distinct impression that despite what Tilon had seen, those packs were not filled with rocks and rags!

Once the visitors were out of sight, everyone quickly returned to their tasks. Josheb collared Eliphelet, intent on the return of his property, and Gad was already interviewing Ittai to add his story to his chronicle.

As I turned to go, Abiathar spoke again. "Dahveed ben Jesse, Adonai has somewhat to say to you."

I turned back, kneeling at the entrance to the tent. "What does my God wish to say?"

The priest's eyes became distant again, as did his voice. "Mashiah Israel, you, also, have not done well in this matter. I am Yahweh, God of all flesh. Is there anything unknown to Me? Am I an idol, that My eyes are blind and My ears are deaf? Is anything hidden from Me that is revealed to men? Why did you inquire of man, and not of me?"

Abruptly, Yah's presence left. I knelt there, realization pouring over me. I had indeed forgotten my God when I should have gone to Him first, trusting Him to know what should be done about next war season, rather than trusting human knowledge and opinions. In addition, I had not guarded my tongue, for my careless words to Ittai, spoken without thought, had led to this entire situation. I had been careless with my power, and both Ittai and Eliphelet could have lost their lives because of it. As Hassar Jonathan had said, I was dealing with people's lives now, and I must never, ever forget that—not for one moment.

"Forgive me, Yahweh, for I have sinned. I forgot my responsibilities and my place, bringing disgrace on Your name by my neglect of You, who are my God." Rising from my knees, I left the ark to obtain a sin offering.

¥ ¥ ¥ ¥ ¥

Hassar Jonathan strolled outside the courtyard, leaning on a wall surrounding one of his grain fields. The plowed and planted ground was dark in the dusk, and here and there only one or two shoots of grain showed against the soil.

"Adoni?"

"Yes, Peleth?" he replied, turning around.

"I know this is an odd time, but if you wish to speak with Beor, now is the time of day when he is most relaxed. He has gained some confidence that he will not be treated as Manani handled him, but he is the worst I've seen. Since he has been under Manani's hand for years, I doubt he will ever fully recover."

"Where would it be best for me to talk to him?"

"Probably your business chamber. I will take him there."

A bit later, Jonathan looked up as Peleth led Beor into the room.

The scribe looked frightened. "You sent for me, shobeh?" he asked, bowing.

"Yes, Beor. I would be pleased if you would answer a few questions if you can. And I would also be pleased if you would address me as 'adoni.' You said you are a scribe from Ekron?"

"Yes, adoni."

"Very good, Beor. You have pleased me already by addressing me as I requested. Where did you work?"

"In an adon's household," Beor managed to whisper.

"Would that be the seren of Ekron?"

"Yes, adoni. He—he made us serve him," he added fearfully.

"So I understand." Jonathan's voice was quiet and nonthreatening. "You are pleasing me well. What did your duties entail?"

"I was the chief household scribe, adoni. I had charge of the houses and lands, and the private correspondence. He communicated with many people, and I had an underscribe who helped with that. Sometimes I sat with him when he talked with people, and I took notes if he required it."

Jonathan sat motionless. "Can you remember some of the people he corresponded with?"

Beor started to list names.

"Just the important ones," the hassar interrupted softly. "Tell me about adons in Ekron, or another of the Five Cities, emissaries from Hamath, Mari, or Egypt. People like that."

His eyes unfocused, Beor paused. "One from Mari. Two from Hamath, and occasionally an adon from around Ur. There were five, no, six from Egypt, two of them of the Pharaoh's household." The scribe steadied his voice. "In Philistia, there were three from—"

"Enough," Jonathan said quietly. "Beor, how much olive oil did Manani sell two years ago?"

Again a pause. "Fourteen large jars, adoni. The price was low, and he was not pleased," he added, shivering.

The hassar sat back. "Did Manani ever send a gift to Maoch of Gath?"

The pause was longer. "Yes, adoni. Three of them. The first was a dagger made of bronze with an ivory hilt. On the hilt was carved a—"

"That's enough, Beor."

"I can tell you more, adoni," the scribe said, his hands beginning to move up and down his chest, the fingers touching and withdrawing, a slow spider's dance.

"I know you can, Beor, but you have pleased me very much with what you have said already."

The scribe's hands slowed a little, and he looked at Peleth, who nodded encouragingly. "If you are pleased, adoni, then—then—" His words stumbled to a halt, and his hands fluttered over his chest.

Slowly, Jonathan rose and came around the table, gently capturing Beor's hands in his own. "I will not harm you for asking me something, Beor."

"You—you won't send me back?" the man managed to whisper.

"The last thing I intend to do is send you back, Beor," the hassar replied fervently, letting go. "You are dismissed." He watched as Peleth led the man out into the darkness, and then eased down in the three-legged chair again, trying to comprehend the magnitude of what had landed in his lap. He'd have to go cautiously at first, until Beor gained a bit more confidence. With a memory like this man had, he couldn't understand why Manani had let him out of his house, let alone sent him to the battlefield! He must have been very certain the man would be killed. Then he smiled. He'd bet that any report Manani received would say the man had indeed died!

"Yahweh, I'm not entirely sure why You sent this man to me," Jonathan said aloud as he stepped outside his business chamber and gazed up at the stars, "but if I will need someone like him, Manani must be doing more against Israel than I've suspected."

Tamar bat Dahveed

Yes, Manani has been doing much against Israel, and Yah is about to expose it all, now that the agents of His will are free to act. But trouble is building again in Israel. Death begins to overshadow Shaul's house, for the king has chosen to tolerate those working against Adonai's stated will. In so doing, he has laid the foundation for his next sin against Israel's God, once again turning away from the blessings he could have enjoyed. Instead, his house will fragment and splinter, bringing death to much that should not have perished.

But Yah is never at a loss, and He will work out His will despite whatever anyone does, whatever decisions they may make.

Shaul and Gath

Chapter 9

"Anything else, Eshbaal?" Hassar Jonathan asked as the courier left the throne room in Gibeah.

"No, Hassar. That was the last item for the day."

"Then court is dismissed," he said, motioning for his youngest brother to remain as the rest of the scribes and courtiers bowed and departed.

When everyone had gone, Jonathan stood and stretched. "Is Abbi satisfied with the reports from the purge of the land?"

"It's mostly over," Eshbaal replied, giving him a startled look.

"How many died?"

"Nearly 200."

"That many!"

"It surprised me, also," the youngest sar admitted. "I never would have dreamed there were that many diviners and necromancers in Israel. But the farther north the purge went, the more they found. Nearly half were located from the Jezreel valley to the Sea of Chinnereth. But there were a significant number in Ephraim."

"I suspected such," Jonathan said softly. "Where's Abbi?"

"In the upper room, I think."

"I'll go see if he's ready to leave." The hassar left the throne room and headed through the gate to the former residence, climbing the stairs to the balcony. The door opened suddenly, and Abner stalked out, his face thunderous. He strode past Jonathan without acknowledging him, and the hassar's face tightened a little. His abbi's cousin never missed an opportunity to slight him in small ways, which of themselves were not worth his notice, but their cumulative effect was making itself evident to others.

Malchi followed the general. His eyebrows raised in a query, he nodded to Jonathan.

"Tomorrow, here," the hassar said quietly.

Shaul appeared in the doorway, ducking his head as he exited, his face hard as he watched Abner leave the private courtyard.

"Has the general been difficult again?" Jonathan asked.

His abbi glanced at him. "Abner has always been difficult, but he's getting worse. Come in."

Entering, the hassar saw that Cheran, the man from Naphtali who was his abbi's personal attendant, had already replenished the bowl of apricots on the small three-legged side table. It was a good crop this year, and Jonathan helped himself to several as he sat down.

"Anything to report from court today?" Shaul asked.

"No. It was strictly routine, and Eshbaal could have done it without me. We may not even convene it tomorrow. Everyone is resting after the New Year celebrations and waiting for the rains so that planting can begin."

"Good. You need to rest."

"I've recovered well from the war season, Abbi." Since learning how Dara got wounded, Shaul worried about his son's health, and his solicitude could be annoying at times.

"And we will keep you well. There is much here for you to do, and nothing will interfere with it. You can easily handle Abner, and with Yahweh so pleased with the purge I have done in the land, He will keep Dahveed down in the south away from you. You can rule in peace." Shaul reached for the apricots, a satisfied smile on his face.

Jonathan looked away. Did Abbi really think that he could bribe Yahweh out of fulfilling His will?

The next morning, the four sars met in the upper room. Jonathan reported on recent judicial decisions and diplomatic affairs, then listened while Ishvi discussed the administration of the king's lands and the private estates. Once the second sar finished, they all turned to Malchi.

"What's happening between Abbi and Abner?" the hassar asked.

"Nothing good," Malchi replied grimly. "They are still arguing about the squads used in the purge. Neither of them expected the number of mediums we found. Abner thinks we've purified the land sufficiently, and he wants to retain the men in the army. Abbi desires to keep the squads active to ensure that you continue to rule in peace," he explained, glancing at his oldest brother.

"Why does Abner want to keep the men in the army?" Ishvi inquired.

"That, I don't know," Malchi admitted. "A few of them are excellent fighters, but most are average, although they will improve with training. Some of them are the dregs from the wine shops who will hire out to do anything. I think we caught more than one medium because these men had consulted with them, and so knew right where to find them."

"Maybe we should find out why Abner wants to fill the army with men who betray that easily," Ishvi observed.

"We don't know that he does, yet," Malchi sighed. "He may simply dismiss them and keep the rest."

"Does Abbi have an opinion on this?" Jonathan put in.

"If he does, he's keeping it to himself. He doesn't say much other than direct discussion of military strategy, and the occasional jab at his cousin. He lets me do the deciding on what actually happens. Is he any different with you?"

"No. Any decision arrived at, I either make it, or Abbi consults me about it, and then leaves it up to me. Ishvi?"

"He hasn't shown a bit of interest in administration for months. He's left the kingdom up to you, Hassar."

"Then why does he always meet with Abner?" Eshbaal questioned.

"I guess we will have to wait and see," the oldest sar replied. "Is there any other news?"

"Merab sent a message. She and the child she carries are fine now," Ishvi announced.

Malchi smiled. "This will be her fourth, right?"

"No, her fifth. Don't you remember, she had her fourth almost two years ago."

"Is Immi satisfied with things?" Eshbaal asked.

"Yes. She sent a message that she'll be returning here in a couple days."

"Good. Abbi is always restless when Ahinoam is gone," Jonathan said.

¥ ¥ ¥ ¥ ¥ ¥

Ahibaal paused, glancing out the window of his house in Jebus. The rains had begun some time ago, and the sky was clouding over as he watched. The sound of the wind suggested it would be a bad storm, delaying the arrival of his message. But there wasn't much of import in it, so that wouldn't matter. Setting the brush pen on the table, he read what he had already written.

"Greetings.

"I write from my house, after receiving a message from one of my people here. The list of names you requested was compiled more than a week ago. However, when our man was ready to send it, he could not find it. He searched for two days before notifying me, for which I have chastised him. He did, however, conduct the search very quietly, showing some wisdom at least.

"Upon my arrival, I inspected his arrangements for us. During it, the list was found where it should have been, but underneath some other items. Our man was most relieved, believing that he had simply not seen it during his search. I allowed him to think I accepted his explanation.

"I do not, however, believe it. The list was missing for two days at the least, four at the most. It is my opinion that it was taken and copied, then returned. I do not think our man was involved in this. However, I will be restricting the interactions I have with him until we know more.

"Reports from the south are routine. Our primary interest, Dahveed Israel, lives in quiet and peace. The alliances in the Calebite clans have shifted as you expected they would, and Gebirah Carmel now holds the majority of the nagids. Hebron remains independent, but probably not for much longer—a year, maybe two at most.

"There have been developments here, however, that you should know about. While I was in the upper fortress outside the palace, I observed a rather disturbing event. A well-dressed adon, a scribe, and a man leading a donkey turned down the side alley, the one with the outside door closest to the private rooms. The man with the donkey was Philistine. I slipped to the entrance of the alley as quickly as I could without drawing attention. The guard at the door was helping unload the animal. Only the scribe, and the third man, a soldier, exited the alley with the unloaded animal.

"On the far side of the square, three other escorts waited, and the group left. I sent out discreet inquiries, and learned just today that no one knows who this adon is, but he has been visiting for at least two years. I have identified six separate times when he was here, and there may be more. What worries me most is that no one can tell me anything about him, or even whom he contacts. Such complete silence may indicate Debir.

"El Elyon guard you."

Picking up the brush pen, Ahibaal hesitated over whether he should add how shamed he was at the loss of the list. At last, he set the pen down and sealed the message, after folding in the list of names his adon had required of him. Tucking it into his girdle, he donned his cloak and left the room.

A week later the return message arrived. Severe storms had swept the area, confining everyone indoors. When couriers could do their runs they were overloaded with messages. As always, Ahibaal read it in complete privacy.

"Greetings.

"That the list was copied seems the most reasonable assumption to make. We must identify who did this, for the timing indicates someone who knew exactly when to strike. It is unsettling to learn that someone has kept this close watch upon us without our knowledge. Let each quietly look to his own household first. We must discover for whom the list was copied as soon as we can. Until we know, we may have to assume that all our plans are known to an outsider.

"As to the adon you saw, keep watch on him at all times. Perhaps some of your people can find a reliable Habiru to follow them when they leave and report where they are from. Let us know immediately what you find out.

"The conflict between Hassar Jonathan and General Abner is now in the open. The king's cousin shows little restraint and much bitterness. Shaul's son is cognizant of the effects of clan war, and acts accordingly, leaving most direct interaction with the man to his brother, Sar Malchi. This seems to his detriment now, but will, in the long run, prove beneficial in ways the general cannot appreciate. Hassar Jonathan does, however, demand complete respect whenever he sits on the throne as the king's direct representative. The general has learned this the hard way on occasion.

"What this will mean for us is unclear at this time, for how much power Abner will try to wield before his fall will directly affect our primary interest in the south. Keep contact with him if at all possible. We must be careful not to cross his fortunes for the time being."

With a frown, Ahibaal set the missive on the table. He had remained in Jebus waiting for this message, certain that it would contain directions about what he was to do. Only now he could not carry them out. The mysterious adon had left the city despite the weather, leaving no indication which way he had traveled. Well, the man would return at some point, and Ahibaal would have people ready to keep watch when that happened. And it might take time to find a reliable Habiru. While he'd been told they did exist, he was dubious. Again, he burned the papyrus, disposing of the ashes.

Straightening up, he clasped his hands behind his back and stared out the window. The sun shone weakly over the city roofs. His adon was correct. The conflicts in Israel would be important for the south. But how vital, and in what ways, he could not be certain of yet. Should he take another trip south? He thought for a long time before deciding to compromise by going as far as Giloh, and remaining there. His son, Eliam, would like that, and there was always his little granddaughter, Bathsheba. She adored him, and he often blushed at the way she could make him play with her, completely without dignity, but he somehow couldn't refuse that endearing face. At last he called a servant to bring his cloak. Outside, another servant held the bridle of his mule, the animal restless from waiting.

Not long after, the Jebusite entered a large room at the Brass Lion, making no apology to the men there who had waited nearly as long as the mule. He seated himself in the chair facing the others. They bowed deeply, murmuring their greetings, and he nodded shortly, looking at them sternly.

"We have been remiss in our service," he said grimly. "We have been watched, and must find out by whom and why."

The others in the room stilled as he explained what must be done.

¥ ¥ ¥ ¥ ¥

After young Ishvi, the sar's foster son, had cleared the table, he added fuel to the braziers in the upper room of the house in Gibeah. Once the heavy storms had passed, winter's chill had arrived in late fall. The sars had gathered for another conference, and the warmth was welcome.

"Anything new?" Jonathan asked, spreading his hands over the brazier nearest him.

"Just the usual speculations about how long you'll tolerate Abner's attitude," Ishvi said with a shrug. Then he smiled, his mouth tight, though. "What I find interesting is that everyone assumes you are tolerating him, not that you cannot defend your honor to him!"

"Just so long as Abner doesn't figure that out, I'll let him dig as deep a hole as he chooses," the hassar replied with a slightly malicious smile. "How much trouble is he giving you, Malchi?"

"He hasn't been, and that's what bothers me. He's been quite involved with the training of the men he brought into the units from the purge expedition, and he's been altering some of his training practices. He discussed that with Abbi before he began, saying the shift in the Philistine's war strategy required a shift in ours."

"Do you believe it?" the hassar asked.

"I don't know. I'll have to wait and see."

Restless, Ishvi stood. "We may not have time to wait and see. There by the gate, we hear a lot, Jonathan. Elihu has mentioned to me more than once that the people in Gibeah are uncertain about the king's mind. He seems distant from Abner, yet has not dismissed him. Tanhum has reported that attitudes across the Jordan in Gad and Reuben, especially to the south of Jericho, favor Dahveed rather than Shaul, especially now with the south all but united and the obvious conflict in Benjamin. In addition, for the past two war seasons, Dahveed has been the one patrolling the Shephelah in the south."

"Some of the commanders think the same," Malchi added bluntly. "I've left the question of Abner's authority strictly alone."

"Probably wise of you," Jonathan mused. "Has Abbi asked anything about what Dahveed does during the war seasons?"

"No. I've never mentioned how he's aided us. I didn't want to give him another reason to assume Dahveed is working toward taking the throne. But I get down on my knees every morning and thank Yahweh that Dahveed is down there."

"What about Abner?"

"He's got to know that Dahveed is doing something, otherwise we'd have Philistines swarming in from the south. But he never mentions it. Is that a mule?" Malchi asked, turning his head as he heard hoofbeats.

"It's a courier, coming here," Ishvi replied, turning from the window.

"Keep him walking," the sars heard a stranger order someone.

"My abbi is upstairs," they heard young Ishvi say, and footsteps hurried up the outside stairs.

Sar Ishvi opened the door, and the messenger stepped inside, glancing around the room in surprise. He saw the second sar and knelt, his rough kilt and weapons making a sharp contrast to the others in the room.

"You are not a regular courier," Ishvi commented, studying the man. "But I know you, don't I?"

"Yes, Sar. I am Caleb, of Ethan's band, and I arrive with news from Jabesh."

Ishvi smiled. "I thought someone should be coming. Merab had her fifth child?"

"Yes, adon. A boy," the man said without lifting his head.

"A fifth son for Adriel! He must be rejoicing," Jonathan exclaimed, as Malchi and Eshbaal expressed their pleasure also.

But Ishvi said nothing, studying the messenger. "And Merab?" he asked when the room quieted again.

Caleb didn't reply.

"What happened?"

"The birth went well, up to the last part. Then something went wrong."

"How wrong?" Ishvi clutched the doorframe.

The Habiru looked up, tears on his face. "I am sorry, adon. Bekorah Merab is dead."

"She can't be!" the sar said, staring at him.

"They did all they could, but nothing helped."

"No! Not Merab!" Ishvi swayed and nearly fell. Jonathan leaped to his feet in time to help Caleb catch his brother.

Once in a chair, Shaul's second son stared at the tabletop, then raised blank eyes to his brothers. "I wasn't there. She needed me, and I wasn't there! I should have gone when they called for Immi to come!"

Jonathan grabbed Ishvi's hands. "There was no way you could have known. It was just a regular summons for Immi because it was nearly time for the birth. You know she'd been pleased with the reports from Jabesh during the past couple months."

"But I should have been there! Maybe I could have done something, or at least been with her! I—Oh, Yahweh, why?" he burst out, yanking his fists from his older brother's hands and pounding them on the table. "She had so many years of sadness! Why couldn't she be happy like she deserves? I should have been there for her!"

Ishvi looked at Jonathan. The hassar saw something break behind his brother's eyes, and when he bowed his head again, his body looked as old as Shaul's.

"Hassar?"

Jonathan turned to Caleb.

"I left Jabesh this morning. Hassarah Ahinoam said they would delay burial 12 hours beyond the normal. If we leave now, I think we can get Ishvi there in time. Ethan is arranging for mules."

"Take him," Jonathan said instantly. He threw open the door. "Ishvi!" he called.

The sar's foster son appeared, his face white. "Yes?"

"Get together a change of clothing for your abbi and food for a day, as fast as you can. Get his mule ready, also."

The young man turned and ran.

Jonathan came back into the house. "Malchi, he can't go alone. You've got to ride with him. I know how you feel about mules, but a word of advice about riding Ethan's. Just hang on; the animal will do the rest."

Nodding shortly, Malchi made no protest as he squeezed his next-older brother's trembling shoulder.

"Ishvi, get up," Jonathan ordered. "You couldn't be there for Merab when she died, but you can be there when she is buried. She would want that. You must leave now, however."

"Buried? She's probably already buried!" the sar said slowly.

"No, she's not. Immi said they would wait for you as long as they could. But you've got to go now! Get up!" he repeated.

The sar rose. "I'll never get there in time. Not even my mule could go that far that quickly."

"You won't be riding your mule for long," Jonathan said, leading the sar toward the door. "Since Ethan is arranging for you to change mules, you'll make it!" Then he shoved his brother out the door, followed by Malchi fastening on his cloak and bringing Ishvi's along with him. A servant led Ishvi's mule toward the stairs, where Malchi's already waited. Young Ishvi handed a bundle to the third sar, and Caleb mounted the mule he'd ridden into the courtyard. Jonathan noticed the animal had its ears pricked and looked ready to go again.

The three left the courtyard, and not long after, Jonathan heard the faint sound of hoofbeats on the Jebus highway, headed north. His hand on his own light gray mule, his head bowed, he stood in the courtyard. "We die, Yahweh," he said softly. "Grant us hesed, as you promised." Then he mounted to take the news to his abbi.

The next day, he closed court at noon after transacting essential business. Rising from the throne, he dismissed the scribes. Eshbaal was attending to the packing and to Shaul, who had taken the news hard and remained in the upper room of the large house, until they could leave for Jabesh themselves.

Now with court business done, the hassar could let himself think about his own grief for the Bekorah, the gentle older sister who had always been a part of his life. Tears stung his eyes, and he wiped them with his hand as he descended the stairs into the anteroom. Eshbaal had everything ready, and was bringing Shaul down the stairs when the cry of another messenger reached their ears from the road outside the fortress gates.

Sweat streamed from the courier's face as he raced into the fortress. "Adoni Shaul, Hassar," he panted, dropping down in front of them. "Overseer Peleth in Zelah sends to you. Adon Ner is dead."

Jonathan hunched his shoulders under another blow, and Shaul froze in his tracks, staring at the messenger.

"Dodi Ner?" the king said. "When?"

"Not more than two hours ago, adoni. It was sudden."

The king and the hassar looked at each other, then mounted the mules.

"Very good, geber," Jonathan said quietly. "You are dismissed."

They rode from the town in silence, but once outside the gates, Jonathan urged his mule alongside the king's. "Which way?" he asked as they approached the Jebus highway.

Shaul's face was grim. "With Ner dead, everything changes," he said, turning to his son. "We dare not leave for Jabesh." Riding abreast and followed by Sar Eshbaal and the escort, they headed south and west toward Ner's burial.

¥ ¥ ¥ ¥ ¥

"I expected you before this, Ithmah," I said to the Moabite who had finally returned from his regular trip across the Jordan. "How is your family?"

The descendant of Orpah, Hassarah Ruth's foster sister, looked down as he always did when I interviewed him upon his return. "They are well, adoni. I was able to hear news of your family also. King Yira's wings continue to cover them, and they send greetings to you. Geber Ahiam's wife, Jemima, sent word that Ahiam's visit was, um, successful. She is carrying a child!"

"Is she?" I exclaimed. "You will have to tell him as soon as you are done here. What caused your delay?"

"I had to head north to the Jericho fords to cross the Jordan, adoni. Some of the smaller fords are not yet open after those heavy storms last month. On my way through Gad I travelled for a while with a band of men. I hesitate to call them Habiru, but maybe they are. They were mercenaries, that was plain, but I rather got the feeling of regular training, if you know what I mean. They acted more like Josheb than Shagay.

"There are 11 of them. A man called Ezer leads them. They asked point blank if I knew anything about you. I hardly knew what to say." The man rubbed a hand over his head. "I told them I'd heard of you just like everyone else, but I think they guessed I knew more. I'm sure they followed me. I tried to be as careful as I could coming, but . . ." He shrugged.

"We'll soon know. Shagay's son is patrolling down there, and if a group that large is around, he'll find it."

Jonathan ben Shagay reported in by midafternoon. "There are 11 of them. And they would have followed Ithmah's trail right to your tent, so I confused it a bit," he said, eyes twinkling. "They'll probably be three miles east of here by dark."

"I'll have Hanan check them out tonight," I decided. I had learned to trust his judgment of men implicitly.

Dawn had not yet arrived when Hanan woke me. "Come, adoni."

I dressed as quietly as I could, and once I was outside of camp, Hanan handed me my cuirass, helping me tie it on. Mist had gathered in the lower hills during the night, making a light gray background to the trees that appeared out of it then disappeared into it as we walked swiftly down the path descending into the Arabah.

As always, Hanan moved as if he was part of the forest itself. During the past few years he had grown into a lean young man of medium height with an odd cast to his features that left me wondering who his abbi could have been. During the summers, after he'd been in the sun for a week or two, his skin turned brown. The rest of us tanned, but not as he did.

"Wait here, adoni," he said as we crossed a small clearing. "I will bring the man to you." Then he vanished under the trees, as silent and immaterial as the mist itself.

Flipping both sides of my cloak over my shoulders and out of my way, I waited, listening for any change in the sounds of the forest around me, hearing the occasional drip of water as the mist collected on the leaves and then spilled to the ground. I heard the man approaching just before Hanan appeared, standing at right angles to me just in front of the sycamores and elms lining the open glade.

The trotting footsteps didn't hesitate as he emerged from the trees, carrying a spear ready to throw.

"Are you real, or some sort of spirit?" he asked, seeing Hanan, his voice uncertain.

"He's quite real," I said, making the man whirl to face me, the spear coming off his shoulder. Throwing another glance in Hanan's direction, he then stared around since the youth had vanished already.

I walked forward a little. "Not to seem inhospitable, but we like our lives as quiet as possible, so when a group of 11 armed men appear, we usually investigate. Are you passing through to somewhere else?"

After taking another look around, the man approached. "Not to seem rude, but I don't see the need to answer that question, geber. I will say, however, that we are not in the habit of making trouble."

Watching him carefully, I advanced to just outside of striking distance of the spear, my arms folded, but my sword hilt in my hand. He held the weapon like the hassar did, and I knew well how skillful Jonathan was.

"Can you fight with that?" I asked, nodding at the spear.

Instead of replying, he lunged forward, thrusting the spear ahead of him. I'd expected something like that, and also stepped forward, my left arm forcing the shaft up and away as I grasped it, yanking the man toward the sword now in my right hand.

Seeing the point nearly touching the cloth of his shirt, he stared in shock at it.

"We will get along much better if you will remember one or two things," I said pleasantly. "First and most important, I hate spears and prefer not to deal with them. Second and equally important, I am very good at taking them away from people who insist on using them."

Twisting the shaft of the spear out of his hand, I thrust the sharp point of the counterweight on the butt end into the ground, then stepped back. "Get your men up. Hanan will bring you to us."

As I spoke, the Habiru materialized from the mist and I walked away.

Back in the stronghold, I ate my first meal of the day, and then went to Uriah's tent, telling the Hittite about the group of men and that he would need to evaluate them as fighters.

Uriah had the regular warriors performing standard drills and the shalishim doing their exercises when Hanan led Ezer and his men from the trees. The Hittite walked over, inspecting them openly, and they straightened, recognizing a knowing eye when they saw one. "Josheb!" he called.

"Yes?" my third retainer responded, leaving the line.

"Test out their best man for me."

"With pleasure," the elegant man smiled, rotating the long spear he held in his hand to use the butt end.

The man I'd spoken to earlier came forward, rotating his weapon also, and they circled each other warily. I'd never really had the chance to watch Josheb fight, since I was usually involved with the sparring myself. But this time I could appreciate the grace of his dance. Thrust and parry seemed to flow as one, and he moved around his opponent smoothly, striking from different directions, closing in one moment, then swaying away the next.

Ezer, for I assumed it was he, soon began to pant, sweat beading his face, and he struggled to meet Josheb's thrusts. But he was quick enough to keep the butt from getting too close, and more than once I recognized Josheb's retreats as exactly that.

Just as desperation appeared in the Gaddite's eyes, my retainer shifted backwards and flipped his spear up to drive the butt into the ground. He turned to Uriah. "He's good, and can become better. If the rest are close to his standard, they will be a valuable addition to us."

"I will have to think how to use them, then," Uriah said, turning back to the shalishim.

"Geber, who are you?" Ezer asked. "I did not think there was a man alive who could do what you have done to me."

The Benjamite smiled. "I am called Josheb ben Zabdiel, retainer to Sar Dahveed Israel."

"The demon spear!" Ezer gasped, dropping to his knees. "Adon, had I known! I have wished often that I might see you, but to actually spar with you!" He bowed from his knees, and the rest of his men copied him, murmuring Josheb's name.

I smiled to myself. It looked as if I had a band of spearmen with me now.

"Adon, did you mean what you said, that Sar Dahveed would have use for us?" Ezer asked as Josheb gave him a hand to help him up.

"Yes, although I should warn you he hates spears, and can't use one anymore than a first-year recruit, which is why he has more ways to take one away than a thief has to snatch a purse."

"He already knows that," I said a bit sourly.

"Adoni, I didn't know you were near." Josheb looked abashed.

"I guessed as much when you compared me to a thief. Which reminds me: be sure you do tell them about Eliphelet. I'm placing these men under your command, and I expect to see significant improvement. See if they can make me invent some new ways to seize their spears!"

"Yes, adoni," Josheb said soberly, his eyes twinkling.

Turning away in disgust, I reminded myself to speak with Gad, who would want to add this to his chronicle.

Chapter 10

The winter sun was cold as Jonathan Hassar entered the upper room of Malchi's house in Gibeah, followed by Sar Eshbaal. "My apologies for being late," he said, removing his cloak and hanging it on a peg. "The clan representative from one of the towns near Chinnereth lingered around. I think he was hoping for an invitation to the evening meal."

"Waiting gave us time to eat," his brother Malchi said, gesturing to the table which still held the remains of a meal. "There's more if you want it."

The hassar cast a quick glance at Ishvi's back by the window, then raised an eyebrow inquiringly at Malchi, who nodded. Jonathan relaxed a little. Ishvi had eaten.

Eshbaal sat down and scooped up some lentils with the unleavened bread. The youngest sar had worked through the noon meal.

"What did Abbi do this afternoon?" Malchi asked, watching his younger brother chew.

"He had Abner in the upper room of the fortress residence again," Jonathan replied, selecting an apple from the bowl.

"Any idea what they were discussing?"

"No, but if it's important, Abbi will ask me about it."

"No, he won't," Ishvi said from the window where he stared out at the deepening dusk.

Jonathan didn't reply. Since Merab's death, something was missing from the second sar, and he was quieter than before, often seeming to be in a world of his own. Although the man still supervised the royal and private estates as well as he always had, Jonathan wondered if that was due to Elihu's efforts rather than Ishvi's.

"Why wouldn't Abbi talk to Jonathan?" Malchi would not let go of the subject.

"Because he and Abner are planning on going after Dahveed again." Ishvi turned from the window to face the room.

"Abbi might, but Abner still has Jaasiel to think of," Jonathan said softly.

"Abner doesn't care about Jaasiel," Ishvi stated flatly. "He's changed recently, and I've been trying to figure out why."

"Jaasiel is the only son he has left. He's not going to jeopardize him," the hassar retorted.

"He already has. Just ask Malchi."

Jonathan glanced at Malchi, puzzled.

The third sar shrugged. "Something is going on. Abner has been reviewing the units, as he calls it. He's dismissed a lot of the men, and when I've asked why, he always has a plausible reason. But some of those reasons have been around for years now, and he never did anything about it before. I've been unable to find any connection among the men he's dismissed, either, and I've hated to do much about it. The clan is fragmented enough as it is."

"All of those men supported Dahveed," Ishvi said, turning back to the window. "He'll go for the commanders next. And you know what the army will be like then. Have you sparred with any of the replacements he's brought in?"

Jonathan looked up from the half-eaten apple, the mention of Dahveed catching his attention. "He's been replacing professionals, not militia?"

"Yes, Jonathan," Ishvi said a bit sarcastically. "You need to pay more attention to what other people tell you. Especially me!" He faced his brother. "I know what you think, and it's true. I'll grieve for Merab the rest of my life, but that doesn't mean I've become blind and deaf or acquired the mind of a coney. And I'm telling you, Jonathan, Abner has turned dangerous!" He drove his fist into the table.

The hassar stared at him, noticing from the corner of his eye that Eshbaal's hand had frozen in place halfway back to the table. Silently, Jonathan pushed the sar's arm down, and glanced back at Ishvi. "My apologies, brother," he said with a wry smile. "I'm listening now."

The tension drained from Ishvi's body and he wilted into a chair, putting his head in his hands. "No, my apologies, Jonathan. I had no right to speak as I did. I don't know how my son stands me some days."

"The same way we do," Malchi grunted. "You're still raw from Merab's death, and temper can ease the pain sometimes. I'm just glad we made it to the burial in time. If you hadn't been there for that, you really would be unlivable."

Ishvi rubbed a hand across his face. "I don't think I've ever said how much it meant to me that you rode with me."

His younger brother leaned back in the three-legged chair. "It was the least I could do. I know how much Merab meant to you. Me, too. And if I had mules like those we rode that night, I might get to like riding."

"And then I'd know the world was coming to an end," Jonathan said, bringing a smile to everyone's lips. "Is there anything specific you've noticed about Abner?" he continued, turning to Ishvi.

"It feels as if he's been holding himself back for years, and now for some reason has finally let go."

Malchi grimaced. "He can. Ner died."

Glancing sharply at Malchi, Jonathan wondered if his brother knew of the things he'd learned from Shaul since Ner's death.

"Why would that make such a difference?" Ishvi asked.

"Because now, if Abbi executes the death sentence which has been hanging over Abner's head most of his life, Ner is not around to convince the clan that the punishment was justified," Malchi stated bluntly.

The hassar turned to him. "How long have you known about that?"

"Since I was a child. I overheard some conversations. I didn't put it all together until years later. By then, Abner was my dodi, and I didn't believe what I knew until Abner attacked Dahveed. When did you learn of it?"

"Just since Ner died. Abbi told me about it."

"Is anyone going to tell us?" Eshbaal put in.

"It happened at the battle for Jabesh in Gilead, so Abner was young and inexperienced," Malchi explained. "He was convinced the Ammonites would defeat Israel, and he thought out a plan to save Ner's house by bringing four Ammonite warriors into the camp the night before the battle to kill Shaul. He believed Nahash would let his family live if he helped him this way. Am I right so far?" he asked, glancing at the hassar.

Jonathan nodded.

"He'd led the men to the edge of camp, then ran into Ner and Abbi, who were walking together discussing plans for the next day. They attacked Ner, thinking he was Shaul, severely wounding him. Abbi saved him. He was carrying his spear and managed to kill two and wound another. Rather than raising the camp to follow the fourth man, and revealing what had happened, they let him go, even though Shaul wanted the weapons the men carried. The swords from the two he killed were the ones he and Jonathan used after that."

"But Abner betrayed Abbi?" Eshbaal gasped.

"It took a while for me to get used to thinking that way, given how closely Shaul and Abner have worked since then and what we've grown up thinking," Jonathan admitted. "I still have difficulty with it."

"I don't," Ishvi spat out. "I'd believe anything of him right now."

"Why?" Malchi asked curiously.

"Immi, I guess. She's never had any use for Abner, even before Abbi was anointed. I'll bet the Jabesh side of the family learned something of what happened that night, and Immi heard it from them. There's been a look in her eyes sometimes when she watched Abner that always puzzled me."

"Then why was she so worried when Dahveed became general?" Malchi questioned. "Seems as if she'd be relieved by it."

"She trusted Ner," Ishvi explained. "She's told me more than once that Dodi Ner was an upright man, and because of it, Abner would serve Shaul."

"Why?" Eshbaal demanded.

"Because Abbi passed a judgment that night," Jonathan said. "To give him credit, Abner was horrified at the way things had turned out. He told them everything that he'd done, and begged for pardon. But all three of them knew that Abner should die, and Ner didn't hold back. He gave his son's life to Shaul, and Abbi condemned him to death, then refused to carry out the sentence. Ner told Abner that he was to serve Shaul the rest of his life, and that if anything happened to the king, he himself would kill Abner, son or not."

"Abner must have believed him," Eshbaal said thoughtfully. "I can't think of a single time I've ever questioned Abner's loyalty to Abbi."

"You know what Ner was like. Wouldn't you believe him?" Malchi commented wryly.

Eshbaal swallowed. "I see what you mean. But where does this leave us?"

Jonathan frowned. "Now that Ner is dead, we have a very big problem. Since so many years have passed, it would seem unworthy of Shaul to execute Abner now, given the kind of service he has done since then. And after the destruction of Nob, people no longer trust the king."

Ishvi looked at Jonathan. "Do you want to argue now with my assessment that Abner is dangerous?"

"No, brother."

"Or that he doesn't care about Jaasiel?"

The hassar hesitated. "I can't believe he would sacrifice his son."

"The only thing Abner cares for is Abner," Ishvi said quietly. "At least take precautions as if I'm right."

"I think that's wise," Malchi put in.

"It can't hurt anything," Jonathan decided. "Malchi, put a stop to the replacement of professional troops. And don't let any of the commanders be dismissed. If there are any recruits you are dissatisfied with, get rid of them. And keep an eye on what Abner is doing as much as you can.

"Ishvi, contact the king's attendant again. Cheran may be able to tell us a lot. Alert him that we need to know what is happening between Shaul and Abner.

"Eshbaal, ask the scribes to keep their ears open also. We need all the information we can get about this."

Leaning against the wall, Ishvi studied his oldest brother. "What about you?"

The hassar smiled. "I'm going to go on ruling the land while I wait to find out what Abbi is doing. He knows just where he stands with Abner, and I find it very interesting that he's pulled him close again. I think Abbi intends to use the general. I just don't know what for yet." He paused. "You know," he added thoughtfully, "maybe we can use him just as Shaul does."

The others looked startled, then interested. They conferred for some time.

Shaking the rain from his hair, the hassar stepped into his business chamber at the estate at Zelah. The morning's sun had given way to more rain and a chill wind. He'd eaten and seen Meribbaal to bed. Now he wanted to speak with Beor before retiring.

Manani's former scribe had proved to be exactly what the hassar suspected him to be: an apparently bottomless fount of information about the Ekron seren, what he had done, whom he had spoken to, and anything else Jonathan cared to ask about. Peleth used the man as his assistant, reporting that Beor was painfully eager to do anything requested of him, but that every once in a while he asked some odd questions. When Peleth investigated the questions, he found they were directly connected to Manani, and he had decided that it was the way the scribe signaled that there might be something about Manani that Jonathan would want to know. It seemed to be his way of getting around his lingering terror of the seren.

Jonathan lit a lamp while he waited. Late evenings were the times Beor was most relaxed, although the hassar still had to be careful how he asked about some things, for the man could quickly disintegrate into incoherence if too many memories of his time with Manani crowded his mind.

The scribe's terrified voice reached his ears before he could see him coming.

"Please, Overseer, what have I done?" Beor pled. "Why am I called to him? I have done everything you asked. I didn't forget anything! I know I didn't. Please, why is he angry with me?"

As Jonathan stepped out the door, he heard Peleth reply, "He is not angry with you. He knows you have done everything. There is no need to fear."

"He is angry! He is angry, and I don't know why!" Beor insisted, nearly hysterical.

"Why do you think I am angry?" Jonathan inquired.

His rich voice seemed to penetrate the man's fear. "Because he called me there! I have done everything just as I was told. I didn't make any mistakes!"

"I know you haven't," Jonathan soothed. "Where is there?"

In the darkness, he could barely see Beor lift his arm and point to the business chamber. "There, the room with the light! It's always the room with the light! He is angry, and I don't know why!"

"What is wrong with the lamp? You use one every night, don't you?"

Not replying, Beor just knelt in the wet courtyard, hugging himself.

"Do you know, adoni, I don't think he does," Peleth said thoughtfully. "I can't remember there being a light in the room he stays in."

Lightening flickered briefly, and a soft rumble of thunder followed.

"Well, I'm not going to talk to him out here in the rain," Jonathan announced. He re-entered the chamber, blew out the lamp, and went back to the door. "Bring him in."

Peleth finally got the scribe off his knees, then had to lead him into the room since his eyes were tightly shut.

The hassar sat behind his table. "There is no light now, Beor. You have pleased me very much with the work you have done for Peleth. He reports that anything he asks of you is done immediately and well."

"I don't forget anything. I wouldn't, adoni!"

"Peleth has told me that, also. You have done well, Beor, and I am pleased with you," Jonathan repeated. "I am so pleased that I have called you to ask you to do something else for me."

"Yes, adoni."

"Beor, why did you ask Peleth if three of the precious stones should be taken away?"

"They were the best ones. That's what happens to the best ones. They are taken away."

"Where are they taken?"

The scribe shifted uneasily. "I don't know, adoni."

"You don't know?" Jonathan echoed, startled.

The scribe's voice rose. "He never told me, adoni. He never said! They just went away, the good things—"

"That's all right, Beor," Jonathan said, raising his own voice to be heard. "You don't have to know."

"Forgive me, adoni, but he never said!"

"Forget about it, Beor. There is something else for you to think of now. When did the good things begin to disappear?"

The familiar pause was short. "A few things were taken away five years ago, after the battle when the spearman frightened the militia. Then more the year after that. Things were not as busy, and that's when many things were taken. Always the best, and put somewhere I do not know."

"What kinds of things?" the hassar asked, curious.

"Precious stones, worked rings both gold and silver, carved ivory pieces the size of amulets, gold chains, and such."

"Any arm bands, jeweled daggers, head bands?"

"No, adoni," Beor said from the darkness. "Only small things. There was much which was missing from the treasure room just before

I was sent away. He sent me to be killed by Israelites, to die unburied away from my gods. I hate him!" Beor's voice had grown louder and harsher. "But I didn't die," the scribe went on, retreating back into his timidity again. "And if he finds out, he will rage!"

"We will do our best to see that he doesn't find out. You have pleased me well again. Go to your rest now."

Peleth took the man's arm and helped him out the door.

"I did please him, didn't I?" Beor asked his fellow Philistine. "He said so."

"You did very well."

Suddenly remembering something, Jonathan hurried out after them.

"Beor, one more thing," he said, walking up to the man in the dim light.

The scribe's hands fluttered over his chest again, fingers touching, then pulling apart, and the hassar stopped their spider's dance.

"This will be a hard question for you, Beor," he said softly. "But do your best for me, all right?"

"Yes, adoni."

"Beor, what chamber always had a light?" He felt the man trembling.

"The seren's. Manani!" the man finally gasped, then pulled away and fled across the courtyard to his room.

The hassar slowly walked back to his upper room and, shrugging off his robe, eased into bed so as not to waken his son. Little things of great value. It sounded very much as if Manani had been secreting away a very private treasure trove for several years now. Why?

¥ ¥ ¥ ¥ ¥

Cheran opened the door to the upper room in the fortress residence and stood back for Rinnah the Ziphite to go through. Shaul sat at the table, glancing up as the man entered. General Abner stepped from the shadows where he'd been waiting.

"And what news do you bring to me this time?" the king asked.

Rinnah bowed. "Another chance to rid yourself of worry, adoni. With every passing month, Dahveed becomes stronger and more settled. The new moon feast in Hebron was well attended, and the balance of power shifted again in the Calebite clans. It is clear that within another year—two at most—every clan will be loyal to Gebirah Abigail. And the Gebirah is married to Dahveed Israel."

Shaul frowned as Cheran poured wine into his cup.

"A united south, giving strength to Dahveed, is not something that favors Israel, adoni," Abner muttered.

"Why? A united south would provide a buffer that would favor us indeed. I've heard rumors that the Amalekites have forgotten the lesson I taught them, and grow restive again. And the Philistines seem much more willing to raid down there. If Judah were united, Jonathan would not have to waste resources doing what they could do for themselves."

"True, adoni, but only if someone trustworthy guides the clans. Who knows when Dahveed will decide to attack you?"

"He would not. He said so. And Yahweh honors our purging of the land. Dahveed will not come." The king took a sip of the wine.

"And you believed that?" Abner asked skeptically. "Adoni, Dahveed but waits for the right moment. And once he has the entire south behind him, that moment cannot be long in coming. Yahweh will not stop him, for Yahweh has said he will be the next king."

Cheran edged to where he could see all three faces. Rinnah appeared bored and a little impatient. Abner was intent, and the king's face was completely bland.

"With Dahveed married to the Gebirah, I don't see that we can avoid the circumstance, Abner," Shaul commented.

"We might. The key is Gebirah Abigail. The clans are swearing to her, not Dahveed. So if Dahveed was removed from the picture, and Sar Malchi, say, substituted in his place, the south would still be united, but you would not have to worry over what the nagid down there was planning. And Malchi is very capable of defending the land."

"A neat arrangement," Shaul said thoughtfully. "Unless Abigail has objections."

"How could she?" Abner replied. "She would be assuring peace and safety for her people, and Sar Malchi is hardly a repulsive man."

The king's lips twitched. "And I suppose you would propose this to her with our army standing around watching?"

"If necessary," Abner said with a composed expression.

"You assume Dahveed will be so easy to displace from the wilderness down there? Or didn't you listen to that report Malchi gave you the last time he went looking for the Dahveed?"

Abner's face reddened, and Cheran withdrew slightly. He'd noticed the barbed comments that the king often threw at Abner. He should mention them when he reported.

"If you recall, we are no longer wandering around blind, trying to stumble over him, adoni," the general continued. "Rinnah has located him again. We can go right to him, as we did last time, and if we take only professionals, we may not have to wait until the war season. We have a good chance of catching him, as we nearly did at Maon."

His face expressionless, Shaul said nothing. But Cheran noticed one finger stroking the king's beard, signaling that he was considering something seriously.

"Where is he?" he asked, addressing Rinnah.

"Back at Hachilah, adoni."

"Surely he's not at the same place."

"Not exactly."

"Have you seen his camp personally?" the king pressed, watching the man.

The Ziphite shifted his feet. "Not this time. But the report reached me through reliable sources."

"Don't come back until you've found his exact location and enough guides to get a large group of men down there," Shaul said icily. "I'll consider this further."

Rinnah bowed, and Cheran opened the door for him, noticing the worried look that crossed the man's face as soon as he was away from the king.

"Abner, I wish to be alone," Shaul said as Cheran stepped in again.

"As you wish, adoni," the general replied, his tone neutral, but Cheran felt the coiled tension of the man as he went past and out the door.

"Are there more of the dried figs?" Shaul asked when the general had gone.

"Yes, adoni. Let me get some." The servant went to the north ell of the room and put some into a bowl from the storage jar. After placing it in front of the king, he retreated into the background.

"It is difficult, Cheran," Shaul said, biting into a fig.

Lately, the king often talked to him, and the servant had quickly discovered that he need not reply.

"Yes, difficult. I will not always live. Jonathan has proved himself an excellent ruler, and the people in Israel are content with him. Surely, it cannot be good to upset things as would happen if Dahveed were to come north and try to take over."

The king remained silent for a while, enjoying the wine and another fig. "It always comes back to Dahveed or Jonathan," he mused, staring over the top of the cup in his hands. "The roeh says Dahveed. And Dahveed has sworn to give hesed to my seed." He paused again. "But people so easily forget, as Abner has that I spared his life when it should have been forfeit. And if Dahveed forgets, Jonathan will face two enemies."

Hefting the wine pitcher, Cheran refilled the king's cup. Shaul looked up at him. "You are restful, Cheran. You know how to be silent."

The servant bowed.

"And two enemies, one within and one without, are too much. I have warned him against Abner, and he listened. But Dahveed?"

Much later, Shaul looked at Cheran, still standing patiently against the wall. "I must protect Jonathan from himself when it comes to Dahveed."

¥ ¥ ¥ ¥ ¥ ¥

The next day, Sar Malchi shook the rain off his cloak as he stepped over the threshold at the top of the stair to the throne room. "Why did it have to be me out in the wet?" he grumbled.

"Because the rest of us were already here," Jonathan said, smiling. "Besides, you're used to it, working out there on the training ground every day."

The third sar sneezed. "What's happened?"

"Cheran reported that Abbi and Abner are planning to go south after Dahveed again," Jonathan said, indicating the tall servant standing to one side.

"I thought that might be it," Malchi replied. "Abner's been picking men, enough to make up about four units, I'd guess. When do they plan to go?"

"The beginning of harvest."

Malchi cursed under his breath. "And I'll bet Dahveed can't afford to lose the time harvesting, or the grain," he said bitterly.

Cheran bowed his head. "Correct, Sar. Rinnah has had spies out and inquiries made."

"At least we know in time to warn him," the youngest sar put in.

"Whom can we send?" Ishvi asked. "Abner is having the couriers watched again."

"That explains Nimshi's comment," the hassar said glumly. "He mentioned to me the other day that he was being watched, so it shouldn't be he. But we have time to think about that yet. What's been happening in the army, Malchi? You mentioned there was something important you needed to say today."

His brother nodded. "Abner's found another way to influence things. After I put a stop to his dismissing those he didn't trust, he didn't do anything for a while. Now, though, he's busy rebuilding the units' strength, something I can't argue with. It's how he's doing it that angers me!" The third sar began to pace. "He's recruiting from our tribe. I noticed that immediately, but it was Ishvi who recognized that all the new men are from families that support you over Abner, and that not all of them wanted to join the army!" he said, nodding at his oldest brother.

"And I suppose they have a very hard time of it unless their families decide to support the general," Jonathan groaned. "That's why you dismissed Eleazar as shield-bearer, isn't it, Ishvi?"

His next-younger brother bowed his head. "Once I realized what Abner was up to, I sent him away the first opportunity I had. He's been too faithful to me to suffer because of what Abner's doing!"

"I wish I could do the same," Malchi sighed. "Many of the newcomers have been quite severely injured, what with practice on the training ground, or "fun" in the barracks. I've dismissed two of the men most willing to hurt them. Both, by the way, came from the purge squads, but I can't catch them all."

"Is that why your knuckles were bruised a few days ago?" Ishvi asked.

Malchi nodded. "They didn't want to go, so I gave them a taste of what they'd been handing out. They may recover," he added, icy wrath filling his voice.

Eshbaal shivered. "This will weaken our position, won't it?"

"Yes, but possibly not permanently," Jonathan suggested. "People who are forced to change allegiances usually are more than ready to switch back at the first opportunity, and some of them may outwardly conform, while still being willing to help us if we are careful what we ask."

"Abner must be working toward a short-term goal, then," Ishvi said thoughtfully. "Probably the removal of Dahveed. If he can keep you busy enough here in Benjamin, he can attack Dahveed that much more safely."

"I just wish he'd figure out that *I* don't protect Dahveed!" the hassar exploded. "He's fighting Yahweh when he goes down there! And so is Abbi!"

"What about Jaasiel? Can we reach Abner through him?" Eshbaal asked.

"If I may speak, Hassar?" Shaul's servant interrupted, reminding the brothers that he was there.

"Certainly, Cheran."

"I have occasion to speak with other servants, and I've found more than one who is willing to tell me whatever I ask. If you will pardon the impertinence, I've inquired regarding Abner several times. His household staff report that as of a month ago, his plans for the future no longer revolve around Jaasiel, but Sar Eshbaal."

The four brothers said nothing for several moments, absorbing that news. Then Jonathan looked at Ishvi. "You are right, brother. Abner no longer cares for anything but himself."

"But why me?" Eshbaal demanded, bewildered.

Malchi started to answer, but Jonathan silenced him with his hand. "Probably because he knows Malchi, Ishvi, and I wouldn't go along with removing Dahveed. I don't think you've stated your opinion one way or the other in his hearing."

"I guess not. I just never saw the use in fighting Yahweh."

"Remember that, if anything should happen," Jonathan said carefully. "If you feel that way, you can always go to Dahveed. Abbi made Dahveed swear at En-gedi to show hesed to our family."

"All right."

Just then someone knocked at the door to the stairs. Eshbaal opened it, and a guard entered. "Your pardon, sars, but a courier has arrived who insists he must see Sar Malchi."

"Send him up," the sar directed.

The man appeared shortly, water dripping off him as he handed a papyrus to Malchi, then bowed. "I'll wait in the anteroom for a reply, if I may."

Malchi waved his hand in assent. Breaking the seal, he read the message, his face clouding over. When he was done, he tossed it onto the long table where he sat. "There have been two more injuries, serious ones, in the fifteenth unit under Amasai. Something has to be done, Jonathan."

"Abner has recruited enough to make another unit?" The hassar raised his eyebrows.

"In a manner of speaking. This unit is consists solely of men whose families still support you no matter what pressure Abner brings against them. Amasai is afraid his men are targeted for death, and he could be right." Malchi put his head in his hands.

Jonathan glanced at Shaul's personal servant. "Cheran, would you get some more papyri?"

"As you wish, Hassar," the tall man said, leaving the room.

"We can't let them be slaughtered, Jonathan," Ishvi insisted.

"And if they stay here, they will be," Malchi added bitterly. "I never thought Abner would go this far."

Silence filled the room for some time.

"We've got to provide some way for those supporting us to preserve their families," Jonathan said. "And the same thing that will work for us will work for them. Send them to Dahveed, Malchi." He looked at Ishvi and Eshbaal. "Is this agreeable, that any time someone is in danger, we send them south?"

"Once down there, they don't come back," Ishvi observed, studying his brother.

"But they live."

Malchi sat back, watching the hassar. "We will have less to work with."

"But Dahveed will have more."

"If we have to do this a lot, Abner may get the upper hand," Eshbaal murmured.

"Then we go help Dahveed."

No one said anything.

Cheran returned, handing the papyri to Eshbaal who wrote up a message for the courier to take back with him, ordering the unit to patrol south and west of En-gedi.

"I think that's all for the day," Jonathan announced when the servant had taken the message down to the waiting courier. Eshbaal gathered his things and left.

Malchi shifted his shoulders uncomfortably in the damp cloak as he put it on. "Whom are you going to send south with that earring?"

"When the time comes, I'll send Abiezer," Jonathan answered.

"He's your closest bodyguard," Malchi gasped.

"Yes, and he owes Dahveed his life, something Abner has no idea of."

Shaul's third son stared at his oldest brother for a moment. "And you know the real reason Abner wants Eshbaal?"

"Of course. Abner can control Eshbaal. But sooner or later, Eshbaal will figure out what is going on, and if I know him, he will leave if he has somewhere to go."

"We won't, though," Ishvi said, his face calm. "You know that, too."

The hassar sighed. "Not for certain. But I do think that when the contest comes, it will be between Abner and Dahveed, not Abbi and Dahveed. I don't know what part we will play."

"Whatever it is, we'll be in it together," Malchi assured him.

"I'm counting on that," Jonathan Melek Israel replied.

A short time later, as he and Ishvi stood on the wall looking south, Jonathan spoke. "Ishvi, if Malchi's house is on the west side of town, and his estate is west of here, why is he riding south again?"

Ishvi shifted a little so that he could see the mule just disappearing over a rise on the Jebus-Hebron highway. "It must be something important to get him on a mule when it's this chilly and damp."

¥ ¥ ¥ ¥ ¥

"Dahveed, Abiezer is in Maon with the twisted brass earring. He looks worried," Azmaveth called, hurrying toward me.

I walked to the edge of the barley field that we were harvesting. "You're sure it's the brass earring?"

"Yes, Sar."

"I'd better go, then." We had just begun harvest that morning. I hoped Abiezer's news wouldn't interrupt us. This would be the best harvest we had had yet.

Once in Maon, Azmaveth and I went to the town cistern. I recognized Abiezer when I saw him. He'd been on duty when Zelek tried to assassinate the hassar, and when Jonathan had accused the guards of negligence, I'd reminded him that he'd taken both of them with him to interrogate prisoners, giving Zelek the chance to loosen the tent peg.

"Azmaveth!" Abiezer called, seeing his former companion, "can you tell me where the Dahveed is? The hassar's message is urgent."

"I'm here," I said.

The bodyguard turned to me. "Sar," he said, touching his knee to the ground. "I am to give you this, and remain with you if you permit." He held out a folded and sealed papyrus.

The message was brief. "Shaul goes out against you, guided by Rinnah. Abner no longer recognizes any restraint."

Shaking my head a little, I read it again. Shaul was coming? That didn't make any sense. Bewildered, I looked at Abiezer. "Did the hassar say anything else?"

"No, Sar, but things are difficult in Gibeah. I was only able to leave because Sar Malchi rode with me to Jebus. But he stayed with me for another five miles. Please, may I remain with you? I dare not go back."

Something about his tone made me pause, and I could see trouble in his eyes. "Azmaveth?" I asked.

"The hassar would not send Abiezer unless forced to, adoni."

"Come with us," I decided. "You can tell me the situation while we travel."

"Thank you, adoni," the man said, quickly touching his forehead to the ground.

"What has been happening?" I asked as soon as we were out of town.

"You know that Ner died shortly after Bekorah Merab?"

"We'd heard."

"The quarrel between the hassar and the general has worsened since then. It hasn't helped that the king has not restrained Abner."

"Shaul has turned against Jonathan?" I gasped.

"No," Abiezer said slowly. "It's more as if Shaul is letting this happen. I don't think he agrees with Abner, but he's tolerating him for some reason."

By the time we got back to the stronghold, Abiezer had told me a great deal about the situation in Gibeah. The split in Shaul's house was open now and had spread to the clan. If Shaul had dismissed Abner, the clan would have thrown their support to the king, but since he did nothing, doubt remained in many minds over which side he really supported.

Once at my tent, I sent for Shagay's son.

He came quickly, still carrying the sickle he'd been using.

"Jonathan, I just got word that Shaul is headed this way. Take three or four men and see if the report is true."

After giving the earring hanging on my chest a wide-eyed stare, the young Habiru bowed and left.

I glanced down at the earring myself. Even after hearing Abiezer's description of the events in Gibeah, I still couldn't believe that Shaul was seeking me again after leaving me in peace for three years! Frustration rose inside me. I'd done all I could to keep away from him. What more did Shaul want of me?

"You have not died, Dahveed." Mahesa's words again rang in my mind.

Late the next afternoon, Jonathan reported in. "He's on his way with at least four units and Abner, adoni. Rinnah is the only guide."

With that many men, only one guide seemed inadequate. Seeing the hard, closed expression on my retainer's face, I asked, "Were there more?"

"Not now," he said shortly. "They were all from the southern clans of Ziphites, and hadn't gotten the word yet to leave you alone."

"How did Rinnah escape?"

"He knows better than to stray very far from the king's side."

"And where is Shaul?"

"North of Hebron. He'll be here tomorrow before noon."

I went back to harvesting barley, but discouragement clouded my thoughts. My parting with Shaul at En-gedi had been such that I'd been convinced the king would never come after me again. Yet he was here. And what did Hassar Jonathan mean that Abner no longer recognized any restraint?

The sun had almost touched the western horizon when Hanan appeared. "Adoni, there is a group of men coming up from the Arabah."

"How many?" Suddenly worried, I started jogging toward the stronghold. If Shaul was trying a pincer movement again, we had to be ready. With half my men over in Horesh, reaping the fields there, I dared not be caught unaware by anything the king might do.

"Enough to make more than a professional unit. But I don't think they have fought together much," he added.

"They are warriors?"

"Soldiers."

"Any guides?"

"No. Once they neared the higher hills, they began to wander."

That was odd, I thought.

Ahinoam and Abigail were in camp getting the evening meal started with the help of the younger children. Everyone else was reaping or binding in the fields. "Shaul is coming against us again," I said to them quietly. "He'll be at Carmel and Maon by noon tomorrow."

"Should we pack?" Ahinoam asked.

I hesitated. My band had grown still larger, the encampment widening beyond the confines of the stronghold. Besides the fields, we had a cistern, an olive and a wine press for the young trees and vineyard, and several sites picked out for houses, some of which already had foundations. "I want to see more of what Shaul is doing," I said slowly. "Just be ready to pack the most essential items if we must move to Horesh."

"You will fight him?" Abigail asked, her dark eyes on mine.

"Only if I'm forced to. But we have too much here to abandon, and we can't afford to lose the grain."

News of Shaul's approach spread through camp during the evening meal. I said nothing of the second group of men, but once the meal was finished, I sent Pekah to summon Shagay, Ahiam, Josheb, and Abishai. When they gathered, I told them Hanan's news and expressed my fears that Shaul was trying to surround us again.

Shagay shook his head. "I don't think so, Dahveed. There isn't anyone west of us. Mibhar was over that way early this afternoon, and he said the scouts at Horesh reported no one around."

"Then this group could be unrelated to Shaul's advance," Ahiam put in. "Why don't we go ask?"

"I was thinking of it," I admitted. "I don't want to worry about what is happening on our flank if we must face Shaul tomorrow."

"And we need to be harvesting, not fighting!" Abishai said, irritated. "What's Shaul doing here at this time of year in the first place?"

"Making it difficult for us to survive," Josheb observed drily. "If we're going visiting, Dahveed, the Gaddites would like to prove themselves."

"I only want to find out who the men are," I told him.

"That doesn't mean they may not want to kill you," he reminded me. "I've been talking to Ezer quite a lot. His men are the ones that forded the Jordan a couple years ago at flood stage, and barred the way into the valleys that lead to the uplands."

"Ethan told me about that," Shagay smiled. "It was quite a feat, although he said he always wondered why they did it."

"Can they fight as shalishim?" I asked.

"Not all of them yet, but they are excellent as a group of spearmen. The shalishim training has improved their performance already, and I'm expecting they will get even better."

"All right, they can come. "Shagay, you and Ahiam pick two men each to form shalishim around you. Abishai, find someone to side you and me."

The men left, and Abishai lingered behind. "Dodi, would you allow Joab to go along? We may need a messenger. He is burdened by his disgrace, and you know he has served under your sentence for years now. Please, Dodi, give him some encouragement for your favor."

I sighed. I hadn't thought much about Joab, for I was still only willing to tolerate him if he stayed out of trouble. But I had to admit Abishai was correct. Even Abigail had mentioned something to me recently about Joab's behavior. Truth to tell, Asahel had been more of a worry than Joab. "All right, he can come."

"Thank you, Dodi!" Abishai hurried away.

Chapter 11

Shagay led us into the darkness under the trees as we descended the trail into the Arabah hills. Hanan emerged from the scrubby foliage to lead us the last mile. Once we sighted the camp, the Gaddites split up, drifting off to either side. The intruders lay around three campfires, and a slight chill went down my spine, making me flex my hands. Something wasn't right about the camp. Although I studied it intently, everything seemed normal. One of the men by the third fire turned over and settled himself more comfortably. At the first fire, another man rose from the shadows and added fuel. I noted automatically that he carried no weapons. The flames flickered up, revealing the face of Eleazar ben Dodar, Sar Ishvi's shield-bearer. What was he doing here without weapons?

Flexing my hands again, I shifted my weight, glancing at the sleeping forms of the others. There didn't appear to be any sentries, or if there were, they must be very close to the fires or my men would have found them by now. If Eleazar was here, Sar Ishvi should be. But I couldn't imagine the sar not posting sentries. Restlessly, I stirred again. I needed answers, and Eleazar would have them. Finally, I stepped from the deep gloom of the trees into the half-light of the fire.

The shield-bearer glanced up, and his left hand automatically went to his waist before he remembered he was unarmed. "Sar Dahveed?" he asked, peering into the dim light.

"Shalom, Eleazar. Why are you here? Is Sar Ishvi here as well?"

"No, the sar isn't with us," he replied, walking forward.

We clasped forearms tightly.

"Is he well?"

"As well as he can be, Dahveed. The death of Merab took something from him that will never return. It was troubling to watch," the Benjamite said heavily. "For a while, he even distanced himself from Merab's sons. Sar Malchi stepped into his place for several months. Ishvi sees them now, but I know it is painful for him."

"It would be. Ishvi was very close to Merab. But how is it that you are here and he is not, this close to war season?"

"I no longer shield for him, Dahveed. After Merab and Ner died, Ishvi spent most of his time either on the king's business, or on the training ground. He watched the changes Abner made, and I am certain he was the one who alerted Jonathan about them. Then news came that my abbi was ill, and Sar Ishvi urged me to go home. When I returned—" he stopped, biting his lip. "He would not have me back, Dahveed," he finally admitted, tears in his eyes. "He had already begun to train his foster son in my place. He dismissed me from the army, and said I was to return to my family.

"I begged to know what I had done, Dahveed, and he said, 'Nothing.' But I must have done something for him to turn from me this way." A tear found its way down his face.

"Did the sar say anything else?" I asked, something about Ishvi's actions disturbing me more than anything else I'd learned so far.

"He said he knew you would take me for his sake. Why would he say that, Dahveed?"

"Perhaps he saw what was happening in Shaul's clan, and he wanted you away from it, with a place to go if the need arose. The split in Shaul's clan is an open one now, isn't it?"

"Yes. It's divided between Hassar Jonathan and General Abner. And Abner has ways of influencing many people. When Amasai came to me and told me how many were in danger—"

"Danger?" I interrupted.

"Yes, Sar. Abner has conscripted sons from families and clans which lean toward the hassar. They are watched constantly, and many have suffered 'accidents' in training or in the barracks. Those whose families begin to support Abner are soon safe enough. But those whose families were not swayed were formed into a unit under Amasai. After two more of his men were seriously wounded, he came to me hoping I knew where you were. I sent a message to Sar Malchi, not knowing what to make of Amasai's story. It's not like Sar Malchi to ignore something like this, and I wanted to be sure it was safe to talk to Amasai if I did learn anything of you."

"I will remember that, Eleazar."

The shield-bearer continued. "The sar's reply said he gave his permission for the unit to patrol south and west of En-gedi as proposed. I told Amasai what Malchi had sent, and since Abbi had been urging me to leave until clan politics settled down, I decided to come with them. We left secretly that night."

My heart sank. Not only was my existence tearing Shaul's clan apart, but the rest of the tribe was becoming involved as well. Maybe

Shaul had decided to come against me to stop the fracturing of his tribe.

"The men are all of Benjamin, then?" I asked, wincing at the thought of what the king would think if he knew an entire army unit had deserted to me.

"No, Dahveed. There are a few from Judah whom we met at En-gedi."

I looked again at the sleeping forms by the fires, trying to think this through. Eleazar appeared to be sincere and telling the truth. But what if Amasai had orders from Abner which Eleazar knew nothing of? Or was Shaul himself part of this? Was this an elaborate way to get assassins close to me? I rubbed the back of my neck, feeling as though something out in the night watched me. For once, I was glad Ahiam had insisted I wear my cuirass.

"Get Amasai up," I ordered.

Eleazar bowed, and went to the second fire, wakening a man there. He had weapons, his hand bringing his sword up while he rose.

I stepped farther back into the shadows of the trees, and the commander kept his distance when he approached me, although he had sheathed his sword. He touched his knee to the ground briefly, and rose. "You wished to speak to me, Sar?"

Instead of answering, I edged to the side a little, watching the forms around the fires beyond him, unable to shake the feeling that something was not right. But everything was extremely still and silent.

"Eleazar has told me your plight, but I find it odd that men of Benjamin would come to me looking for help. King Shaul will not be pleased with what you have done."

"Maybe. Maybe not, Sar. No one knows the king's mind these days, not even his oldest son. But all men know the hassar's mind. And he loves you as he loves his blood son. If we are under Abner's hand, our families will be hampered in their support of Jonathan Hassar. We can help best by coming here to you."

My gift continued to keep me wary, even though it had not yet signaled actual danger. The words were peaceful enough, but I noticed that Amasai didn't say exactly how he could assist or whom he would aid by joining me. Resting my hand on my sword, I checked the area around me again while I thought out my reply. I needed to know whether these men had come to me for protection, or to carry out orders to harm me.

"If you really have come in peace, and all you want is to serve me, I'm willing to accept you," I said, eyeing the commander.

His shoulders relaxed a little, and as he looked down, Hanan's swift signal for danger caught my eye, reaching me the same instant the reason for my uneasiness about the men around the fires hit my mind.

"On the other hand, Amasai, if you've come to betray me to my enemies even though I've done no wrong, Yahweh will know your heart and judge you. For you have been deceitful, commander," I ended softly, every sense alert.

The man met my gaze, the fire light gleaming off the sweat that appeared on his face. "Sar, why would you accuse me so?"

"Those around your fires do not sleep. There is no movement or breath from most of those men of yours, and the ones who do breathe do not stir, or snore, or shift around in their sleep. They lie tense and ready as men do before they spring a trap!" Taking my sword from the sheath, I turned to Eleazar. "Where are the men?" I asked in a hard voice.

Amasai cast a quick glance at Ishvi's shield-bearer and knelt. Eleazar bowed and came closer. "Forgive us, Dahveed Israel," he pleaded. "We are of Benjamin, and we feared the Lion of Judah now that Shaul comes for you again. I knew you would not turn us away, but the others do not know you, and were afraid." He knelt in front of me. "I offered to become hostage for them when you came, and so I stripped myself of weapons. They have done nothing against you, Dahveed. Do not be angry when they try to preserve their lives. Men of their own tribe have threatened them, and they could not imagine you doing any less! We only wish to live, Dahveed."

I hesitated a moment, feeling my gift, understanding now that whether danger and bloodshed would threaten me tonight depended on my actions in the next few minutes. "How many are by the fires?"

"Six, adoni, all from Judah," Eleazar replied.

"Have them go to the second fire," I pointed with my left hand, my right waving the sword point in a little circle.

Without waiting for an order, the six men carefully left their blankets and grouped around the fire, watching me uneasily.

I glanced at Amasai. "Call your men."

"You will not harm them, Sar?" the commander asked. "We have no wish to threaten you. If you do not want us, grant us leave to go.

We will cross the Jordan, or go wherever you command." He bowed again.

For the first time, I understood why Balak had been able to influence Shaul as he had. Threatening me might indeed be the last thing on Amasai's mind, but there was no way I could be certain of that. I had no previous knowledge of the man, having only his words and Eleazar's assurances to go on. I didn't like the feeling that I might be dealing with treachery.

"I have no wish to shed blood, Amasai," I replied. "Summon them."

The commander looked to Eleazar, who nodded.

"Unit, to me," he called out. Several figures rose from the ground, or stepped from beside trees, warily gathering behind their leader.

"Is this all?" I asked when no one else approached.

"All but this one," Shagay said, manhandling someone into the firelight. "He decided to draw a bow against you."

Amasai went pale, bowing to the ground. "Hesed, Sar!" he begged. "Please believe me, I did not order him to do such a thing! My orders were to touch no weapons, to flee before fighting!"

"Who is he?" I asked.

Eleazar looked at the man, and his face stiffened. "A fool from Shimei's clan," he announced, bitterly, turning back to me. "Please, you must believe Amasai, Dahveed. I heard him give the orders myself."

Having had experience already with Shimei's clan, none of whom seemed to possess any sense, I didn't doubt Eleazar's word. Yet I still hesitated. "Yah," I said silently, "help me know what to do. I do not wish to antagonize Shaul, but I know what Abner is capable of, and without Jaasiel to advise him, he can be ruthless in his actions."

The wind stirred the tree leaves and whispered through the pines, bringing with it Yah's familiar presence which settled on the commander. He looked up at me. "We belong to you, Dahveed, to Jesse's son. Peace, please. And let there be peace to you and all who help you, because Yahweh is on your side."

In the quiet following Amasai's words, I bowed my head. "Stand up, commander," I said. "It's not often that Yahweh personally vouches for someone. Welcome to the band."

Lying on the ground hidden by the brush, I and 10 of my men watched from the top of Hachilah as Shaul's units set up camp on the south slopes. Somehow, until I'd seen him with my own eyes, I had still wanted to deny that he would hunt me down again. As dusk settled around us, I watched Cheran, Shaul's personal attendant, pick a spot for his fire, the rest of the units fanning out around it. The night was warm, and Shaul bedded down by the fire, as did most of the men. It was fully dark before I finally turned away, bitterness welling up inside.

This was a raid, with the warriors carrying only bare essentials. He'd brought most of his force, probably leaving the others back near Maon with the baggage. Rinnah had selected the camping spot fairly well, for the north side of Hachilah dropped off much more steeply than the south, protecting their backs enough that they had posted only two sentries up here, both of whom had passed by us more than once.

But the Ziphite didn't know the country as well as he thought he did, for there should have been at least six sentries to adequately guard the two ways up the north side. A steep slope protected the east flank of the camp, so the only way at them from the bottom of the hill was up the narrow smooth slope on the west, or directly up the uncertain terrain in front.

When it was fully dark, I looked up at the stars. "Yah, I do not want to fight," I said silently. "But I can no longer run." My fists clenched as I looked down on the camp once more, the bitter truth forcing itself into my mind. King Shaul would never let me live in peace. Balak had done his work too well, and no one could ever reverse it.

I wished I could at least strike back at the man who had poisoned Shaul's mind, but my family still lived under Balak's hand. At the same time, I was glad they were safely out of Shaul's reach. My mind went back to my first years with the king, when he had taken me into his house as if I were a son, and the yearning to be in his favor rose in me again. I had given all I could to Shaul—my love, my service, and my skills—withholding only my loyalty, for that belonged to Yahweh. And it had not been enough. It would never be. If he would come now, after the reunion at En-gedi, he would always continue to pursue me.

I don't know how long I lay there, trying to sort out the tangle of thoughts and feelings that passed through my mind. I couldn't bear the idea of a final break from the king who had first given me honor and done so much for me. But I could not live with the constant threat of Israel's army chasing me around the land as one did the calling birds in the hills until they were too exhausted to run any longer.

Looking up at the stars again, I sighed. "Why, Yahweh?" Turning my gaze back to the campfire where Shaul lay, the desire to be close to the king one last time seized me. I had no business risking myself down there, but the urge was too strong. Both sentries were west of me, and I quietly lowered myself into the hollow paralleling the hilltop and concealing my men. Abishai and Ahimelek were still awake. The second man was a newcomer, a Hittite like Uriah.

"I'm going to Shaul's camp," I said softly. "Do either of you want to come with me?"

Ahimelek looked as if I were insane, but Abishai rose smoothly to his feet. "I'll come, Dodi."

Moving warily although we knew there were no sentries between us and the camp, and careful to keep ourselves from the sight of the men on the hilltop, I led the way down the south slope. Once within the camp itself, the only sounds we heard were the deep breathing and snores of sound sleep.

I saw enough in the dim light to identify Libni's unit, and possibly the ninth unit also. But many men were unfamiliar to me. Pine needles crunched softly under my feet when I stopped beside Shaul's sleeping form. Wrapped in his cloak, he lay half on his back, half on his side, his feet toward the small fire. Three other forms surrounded the same fire, but none of them looked like Abner. Slowly I circled the place, finding the general at another nearby fire with some unit officers.

Stroking my beard, I thought back to all the times I'd seen the general in encampment. His place was *always* beside the king's, and I would have assumed that he would share the king's fire on a raid such as this. So why wasn't he? If Shaul didn't trust Abner enough to have him sleep at the same fire, why was the man still general—or even here? I shook my head a little. Nothing about this made any kind of sense.

Glancing back to the king, I saw Abishai there, staring down at him, my nephew's body as still and straight as the spear thrust into the ground butt-end first by Shaul's head. A shiver went up my spine, and I returned silently to the king's side.

"God has given him to you again, Dodi," he whispered. "Let me kill him! He wants you dead, and this is another chance to stop him for good."

"You would murder a sleeping man? We've talked about this before, Abishai. One murderer in the family is enough. Don't follow in Joab's footsteps."

"But he's hunted you everywhere, Dodi! Our family had to leave Bethlehem and live over in Moab, watched constantly by Balak ben Hod! Please, Dodi! All it will take is one stroke of his own spear to pin him to the ground, like he wanted to pin you to the wall!"

Abishai was shaking, and I put my hand on his shoulder to restrain him. "Don't kill him, Abishai. It looks easy now, but do you wish to wake up every morning with the blood of Yahweh's Mashiah on your hands, and the guilt of that deed riding on you?"

He turned to me. "So because Yahweh anointed him, he can murder, and steal, and treat people unjustly, and no one can touch him?"

"No, Abishai. As surely as Yahweh lives, because he *is* Yahweh's Mashiah, Yahweh Himself will strike him down. Or his day to die will come, or he will be snatched away in a battle."

"When?" my nephew challenged. "After he's killed you and us? Is that justice? You're anointed, too. Why can't you kill him?"

"Remember Nabal?" I asked. "I started to do what you want to do right now. Did that seem the right thing for me to do then?"

Although he didn't reply, his stiff posture softened a little.

"It's Yahweh's job to punish those who flaunt His will. As I said at En-gedi, if Shaul attacks you in a battle, you can kill him. But until then, Yahweh forbid that I should stretch out my hand against him when he is helpless before us."

Abishai still stood there, his fists convulsive clenching and unclenching. "He should be stopped, Dodi," he whispered fiercely.

"Yes. And there's nothing that says that we can't let him know that he is in the wrong. Take his spear and that water cruse, and we'll go."

"I don't think I dare," Abishai said, turning abruptly and stalking away, although I noticed he was careful to make no noise.

I stayed a moment longer by the king. Even though his hair was heavily streaked with gray now, the repose of sleep had smoothed out his face, and he looked much as I remembered him that first time I'd seen him in the upper room when his charismatic smile had drawn me to him. For the last time there in the dim light of the fire, I knelt to the king, and touched my forehead to the ground. "Shalom, Abbi," I said. "If only I could have been to you all that I wished to be. May Yahweh stand now between us."

Rising, I picked up the water cruse, tying it to my girdle, then pulled the spear of office from the ground, and followed my nephew out of the camp.

The sky was just gray with dawn when I walked out on the outcropping of rock on top of a hill across a shallow valley from the southern slope of Hachilah. The morning mist made it nearly impossible to see the faint smoke of the fires in the camp opposite me. The men who'd come with me spread out behind me, staying in the trees. We had already decided what to do if Shaul's men attacked after I woke them up.

"Adoni melek!" I shouted.

No one moved.

"Adoni! Adon Abner! Men of Israel! Who will answer me?"

Soldiers began to stir, and a sentry appeared, looking around.

"Adoni melek, over here!" I called. I had my eye on the place where Shaul had lain, and someone was moving around. "Will you not answer me, Abner?" I yelled.

"Who is this who shouts to the king at this hour?" the general's voice roared back at me.

"Are you not a man, Abner?" I taunted, ignoring his question. "Is there anyone as great as you in Israel? Why didn't you guard your adon, the king, when someone came to destroy him?"

A flurry of activity resulted from my words, and Abner stepped into the cleared space that marked the king's fire.

"Your neglect of duty is not good, Abner. By Yahweh's life, all of you are condemned as sons of death because you neglected to protect the Mashiah, your adon!"

"*My* adon, the king, has not been threatened," Abner roared back, looking around to find me.

Stepping into view, I raised the king's spear and water cruse over my head. "Then why am I holding the king's spear, and the cruse of water that was by his head?" Everything across the valley became intensely still.

Shaul stepped forward to where I could see him. "Is that your voice, Dahveed, my son?"

"Yes, adoni melek," I replied, lowering the things I held, since my arms began to shake when he called me son again.

"Have you again spared my life?" Shaul's familiar voice came across to me.

I bowed. "I have, adoni. So why are you chasing me? What evil have I done?"

No one replied.

"I am your servant, adoni melek. Listen now to what I say. If Yahweh is the one who urged you to come against me, tell me, and I will offer Him a sacrifice so that He will accept me again," I paused, bitterness filling my mouth at what I was being forced into. "But if men have done this, I curse them before Yahweh for banishing me today from Yahweh's land and forcing me to go where I must serve other gods!

"See now, adoni, my blood must fall on ground separated from Yahweh because Israel's king came to hunt a single flea, like one chases the calling birds in the hills!"

Shaul stepped forward, as though to come to me. "No, do not leave me," he pleaded. "I have sinned, Dahveed. Return to me, my son! I will not harm you again, for my life was precious in your eyes today. I have been a fool, and have done a very great wrong!"

I didn't know what to say. Perhaps if I had been there by him, as I was at En-gedi, I could not have resisted his appeal. But he had said almost exactly the same thing to me then, calling me son, but had come after me just the same. Now, however, he had openly and publicly acknowledged my innocence and his sin. Didn't that make a difference? It should, but I remembered he had done this before, also, after Balak's treachery was revealed. And less than a year later, he had plotted to kill me.

I held up the king's spear. "See here the king's spear! Send one of your retainers to get it." The first rays of the sun tipped over the eastern heights of Moab, finding their way to me and partially illuminating Shaul's camp. I turned to them briefly. How long would my life be precious to Shaul this time? Months? Weeks? Years? I had no way of knowing. But I did know that my life was precious to Yah. And as the rays of the sun grew stronger, so did the feeling within me of His presence.

As I faced the king's camp I knew that I must carry through my farewell of last night. "Hear me now, Shaul. Yahweh will return to every man his righteousness and his faithfulness. He will give me mine because I refused to stretch out my hand against His mashiah when He delivered you to me. May my life be as precious in His eyes as your life was in mine today, and may *He* rescue me from all distress."

Across the valley, the king bowed his head, acknowledging the complete break between us.

Seeing someone coming up from the valley through the trees, I stepped off the outcropping. Two figures approached, and I signaled Mishmannah, one of the Gaddite spearmen, to let only one through. The shorter one approached, kneeling quickly when he saw me.

I held out the spear, and he looked up at me as he took it. It was young Ishvi, the second sar's foster son. Giving him the weapon, I followed him down the hill to where the second man waited.

"Go bring Eleazar, Mishmannah, then leave us," I said.

My man reluctantly withdrew, and I edged even farther back beneath the trees, concealing us from watching eyes. "Sar," I said, bowing slightly to the second of the two figures.

Sar Ishvi smiled and knelt. "Do not bow to me, Nahsi."

"Nahsi?" I asked, startled.

"You passed a rightful judgment on us, Dahveed, for we have indeed neglected to protect you, the one who is Yahweh's Mashiah, and our adon." He touched his forehead to the ground.

"Maybe others there have, but not you, Sar," I said holding out my hand to help him up. "I am in your debt for so many things, not the least of which are the items you returned to me in that donkey's pack when I first fled from Shaul. What can I do to repay you?"

He searched my eyes as he stood, and I met his gaze, gripping his forearm. "There is one thing you could do that would set my heart at ease, Nahsi."

"Name it, Ishvi."

"Let Eleazar find refuge with you. I dismissed him before Abner could."

I smiled. "He already has. But he is burdened, thinking that he has done something to offend you."

"Nothing of the kind, Dahveed!" Ishvi exclaimed. "He was faithfulness itself!"

"Then perhaps you should tell him that," I suggested, indicating the shield-bearer who had appeared from the trees.

"Sar, please forgive my fault," my retainer said, kneeling to the man.

"There is no fault on your part, Eleazar," Shaul's son assured him. "I could not bear the thought of having you with me when Yahweh's curse found our house, so I took the opportunity to send you from me. Stay with Dahveed. The Mashiah will keep you safe."

When Eleazar tried to protest, Ishvi touched his lips with a finger, silencing him. "Obey me this one last time, Eleazar, that I might have peace regarding you at least."

They embraced briefly, and the shield-bearer stumbled away, wiping tears from his eyes.

"You have someone to replace him?" I asked softly.

The sar put his arm around his foster son. "Ishvi would not hear of anyone else taking the position. He will be ready when the time comes. Our names are the same, as are our fates, I think. We will share whatever Yahweh sends from His hand." Shaul's son glanced at the spear and then back at me, a wry smile on his lips. "So you return the rulership to my abbi once again," he said, indicating the spear.

"That is for Yah to take away," I said seriously.

"Do you also return his life?" he asked, gesturing to the water cruse.

I hesitated. "In a manner of speaking, yes," I replied at last. "I will keep the cruse, for I wish Shaul to know that I hold his life in my hands. But I will not take it unless forced to do so."

"Fair enough, Dahveed. I will acquaint my abbi with your will." Sar Ishvi knelt and bowed again, then rose, and the two of them walked swiftly away.

When I returned to the outcropping, I noted the stir among the men across the valley when they saw I did not hold the spear. Sar Ishvi returned it to his abbi, touching his knee to the ground briefly before he did, then speaking to him.

The king remained still for several moments, then faced me across the valley. The sun had fully risen now, shining on the outcropping. "Yahweh has blessed you, Dahveed my son," he called out. "You will do great things, and you will surely conquer."

Silently I turned and left the rock.

"You did not bow before you left, Dahveed," Shagay said to me as we hurried through the trees away from the hill.

"Shaul no longer deserves my respect."

"Not to mention that you outrank him?" Shagay added, a small smile playing on his lips.

"That, too," I agreed.

¥ ¥ ¥ ¥ ¥ ¥

Hearing Peleth's footsteps on the stairs, Jonathan went to the long table in the south ell. He'd asked his overseer to bring Beor to Gibeah since he was too busy to go to Zelah. Shaul had left for Hachilah days ago, harvest had arrived, and most of the military decisions for the next war season had to be decided now before reaping the fields and gardens occupied everyone's attention.

Beor looked around timidly when he followed Peleth into the throne room. His hands started weaving up and down his chest again, but he stopped them himself this time, and Jonathan smiled with approval. "You have pleased me by coming, Beor," he greeted the man.

"Thank you, adoni," he replied, bowing a little.

Peleth had a pleased smile, and Jonathan nodded his approval to the Philistine. His overseer had worked long and hard with Manani's former scribe, and the man could now be in the hassar's presence without freezing into immobility

"What did you wish, adoni?" Beor asked, surprising both Peleth and Jonathan.

"I remembered something you told me a while ago, and I wanted to ask you some more about it," Jonathan began. "When you told me that small valuable things had been taken away from Manani's house, you mentioned that most of them vanished after 'things were not as busy.' What did you mean by that?"

"There was much less for me to do, adoni."

"Much less of what?"

"Letters arriving or to be written and sent. Many fewer people came, so I was not needed to take notes or assist. He did not go away as much," he added with a shiver.

"What people no longer wrote to him?"

Beor paused, his eyes blank, then he began citing names.

"That sounds like most of the people he corresponded with," the hassar commented.

"No, adoni, but it was more than half. It was nearly all of the important people that you asked about the first time that you talked to me, though."

Jonathan' eyebrows rose at the contradiction, then he glanced at Peleth. "You've done very well with him these past few weeks, Peleth," he said softly.

The overseer's smile broadened. "Thank you, adoni."

"Much of the correspondence which did come demanded payment," Beor added. "Even some tradesmen in the town sent requests for payment. They never did before."

"What kind of payment?"

"He had convinced the serens that his plans would bring riches to the Five Cities, but they didn't, and they wanted payment."

"Which plans?" Jonathan said patiently.

"Like using only mercenaries, not militia, in the push east to Gibeah, employing more units in the highlands after the authorization, making up the deficit for two years, hiring Habiru as guides, diplomatic trips. Hiring assassins."

"And when none of his plans ended as expected, the adons never got their investment back, and demanded that Manani make up the loss?"

"Yes, adoni."

After a couple more questions, the hassar dismissed the two men, then paced the throne room for a while, thinking. If what Beor remembered was correct, during the past three years every major connection that Manani had, with the exception of contacts from beyond Hamath in the north, Gath, and one in Ashdod, had either broken off contact, or distanced themselves drastically because of Manani's failure to make them rich. The hassar smiled. Manani was losing his grip.

"Hassar, Shaul is here!" Gaham said the next day after quietly entering the upper room of Jonathan's private estate so as not to waken Meribbaal. The 4-year-old insisted on sleeping with his abbi during the noon rest whenever the hassar was at his private estate.

"Is something wrong?"

"I don't know, adoni," the guard replied. "He looks troubled."

"Did Immi come?" The hassar pulled on a cleaner robe and tried to run a hand through his graying hair.

"No, he's alone, adoni. Here, let me get that for you." Expertly, the guard pulled the hassar's long hair back and tied it with the piece of rawhide lying on the table. "He's waiting on the balcony," he said, opening the door.

Jonathan stepped out to find his abbi sitting under the awning.

"Sit down, my son."

"What's the matter?" the hassar asked, easing down on a large chaff-filled cushion.

"I wanted to talk to you about what happened down south."

The hassar leaned back against the low parapet around the roof. "You found Dahveed?"

"He found us."

As Shaul described everything that had happened, Jonathan listened with a sad heart. It was the same story, repeated again.

"He will never come to take your throne, Abbi," the hassar said as he always did.

"I know," Shaul agreed, as he always did. "But he might come to take yours."

"He won't."

"You are so certain?"

"Yes, Abbi."

"But he would not return! He would not reconcile with me! What does that mean?"

It means he can no longer trust you, Jonathan wanted to say, recognizing that the break between the king and the Dahveed was irrevocable now. "It may mean that Yahweh is leading him elsewhere," he said instead. "And you know Dahveed will go wherever Yah says to."

"You think he is gone entirely? That he will never come back?"

"I'm afraid so, Abbi. Did you want him to?"

"After what Abner did, how can I not? Dahveed entered our camp, stood over me in my sleep, and Abner did nothing, knew nothing! He no longer cares for my life. Who is there to protect me?"

Shaul's voice trembled, and Jonathan looked at him, surprised. Sweat beaded on his abbi's face, and his hands shook slightly. The hassar reached over and took them, about to ask what was wrong, when he realized Shaul was afraid. The thought wrenched his heart. His abbi had always been so strong, so capable in battle. He'd only known Shaul to show fear once before, at Elah when he could not face the thought of fighting the Philistine champion without the aid of Yahweh. But this was different somehow.

"Abner doesn't care about me, Dahveed has turned away from me, and Yahweh has abandoned me. What am I to do, Jonathan?" Shaul pleaded, his voice shaking.

"Yahweh hasn't left our family completely, Abbi. He still watches over us."

"Yes, I still have my sons. Four strong sons who will never fail me. And Abner will pay for his neglect. Dahveed sentenced him there. Said he was to die for what he had done. That's the second death sentence passed on him."

"Yes, Abbi, Yahweh will hold Abner to account," Jonathan said soothingly. "And all your sons are still here for you." He held his abbi's hands until the king relaxed against the low wall and fell asleep.

Chapter 12

I was restless all through harvest. The fields in Horesh produced as well as the ones here near Hachilah, and Ahinoam and Abigail reported that we had enough grain to sustain us for the year, even with the additions to our band. But the fact that Shaul had hunted me down again would not leave my mind, reinforcing the conviction that something must change.

Threshing had begun the night I took Grandmother Ruth's harp and wandered up to the plateau toward the sheep pastures west of Maon. Finding a comfortable spot under a sycamore, I tuned the harp. The new pegs looked different, but worked well. I played the goat kid song, following it with several others from my Bethlehem days, singing just for the stars and myself. Then I set the harp aside and crossed my arms on my knees. I faced the same dilemma as I had at the Ezel stone. The fact that I wore the earring testified that, once again, the hassar couldn't prevent his abbi from trying to kill me. Only I no longer had just myself to consider, but a full band of men, some of them with families.

"Which means I can't go fleeing around the country like I did at first," I said in the darkness. "And that means one of these days Shaul will succeed in tracking me down and killing me, or else I'll have to kill him. And either outcome could very well start a war, to say nothing of what it would do to Jonathan Hassar," I finished despondently.

And that was the crux of the matter that would not let me rest easy at night. The price of remaining in Gibeah all those years ago had been either my life or the king's. And now the cost of remaining in Judah was the same. And if, as Roeh Shamuel had told me, I would know when Yah wanted me to do something because nothing would stand in my way, it could not yet be time for me to rule Israel.

"As I told Shaul, Yah, I must leave," I whispered, and that left the question of where I would go. Certainly not to Moab. King Yira might tolerate having me in Moab if I came alone and he could keep me in chains every day, but I'd be asking for death if I showed up with the band of warriors I had now, and wherever I went, I'd have to take them with me. They were my responsibility.

I could go to Ammon and King Nahash. He might be inclined to accept me, if he could settle me along his eastern border as a defense against the desert raiders. "That's a possibility, Yah," I said, getting up and starting to pace under the tree. "Nahash would appreciate the security. It would give him less to worry over."

And what would he do then? The thought entered my mind.

"He could turn his attention to other things, I guess, things he couldn't do before."

Such as?

"Such as attacking Moab," I said slowly. "He and Yira are always pushing at the border between them, and I'd get sucked into the war whether I wanted to or not. And with my family under Yira's hand, I can't attack him, and that would be a betrayal of Nahash, who was protecting me. So I can't go to Ammon, either."

I sat down again. Perhaps I could try Geshur, east of the Sea of Chinnereth. But remembering King Talmai, I doubted I could ever trust him, not if his daughter Maacah was any sample of his family. I smiled a little, remembering the look on her face when I'd snatched her up and run into the house to keep her from the rain. She was probably very beautiful now, and most likely even more thoughtless and self-absorbed.

Edom? I sighed. If I went there, I'd spend every moment of my time defending myself from attacks by the clans who were always looking for ways to gain experience at warfare, and thus increase the chance that the next nagid to marry the Gebirah would come from their clan. Besides, every time I thought of Edom, I remembered Doeg and what that man had done to Nob, and it made me burn with anger.

"That only leaves one more possibility," I finally admitted. Philistia. Which meant Gath and Goliath's family. Again. If I went there now, though, things would be a little different. I wasn't alone, and I had Ittai with me, embodying a treaty between Akish and me. And Akish would probably do the same with me as Nahash, send me to guard his borders. I sat up as my mind began to explore the thought.

"Most likely the southern one. The Amalekites are getting troublesome again," I said aloud, rolling to my feet and startling some little animal near me which scurried away. "He'd have a good reason to accept me, I could fulfill Yah's will against Amalek, and going outside of any territory connected with Israel is the one chance I have that Shaul will stop hounding me and let me live in peace."

The stars had circled past midnight before I made my decision. "We will go to Gath, Yahweh," I whispered, looking up. As I picked up the harp, my fingers touched a rough spot on the chest piece. Turning it to the moonlight, I found raw wood exposed. That little animal I'd frightened had been nibbling on my harp! I should have put it back in the case when I was done. Strapping on the instrument, I turned back east toward the stronghold. The first thing I needed to do was talk to Ittai.

I watched as he fingered his dark-brown beard. In the past seven years Ittai had grown into a slender but solid young man, taller than I, tireless on the trail, and with an archer's eye that would soon rival Hassar Jonathan's, if I was any judge. Now that he had contact with Sahrah Hazzel, and considering how he had out-thought me when I first met him, I knew he would have a very shrewd idea of what the situation was in Gath.

His eyes unfocused, he stared at the inside of my tent. "It would be possible, yes. Dodi Akish could use us in several ways, but there will be difficulties, perhaps trouble, when we arrive."

"Political trouble or military trouble?"

"Political for certain. You know how it is with the Five Cities! What I've gleaned from Immi's messages and talking to the merchant, Hadar, indicates that politics are even more unsettled than usual, and there is much animosity against Gath for some reason."

"We could be walking into a boiling cauldron, then," I said in disgust.

Ittai smiled. "You would be anyway, for no matter when you showed up in Philistia, things would boil!"

"Hence the possibility of military trouble?" I asked wryly.

My covenant son shrugged his shoulders. "I think for Dodi, the advantages of having you around would outweigh the disadvantages. I would recommend that we go."

"I appreciate your insights, Ittai," I said, getting up and following him out of the tent.

A few minutes later I found Ahinoam and Abigail discussing something with Keturah and Zalmon's wife which they quickly stopped when they saw me. "Gebirah, I need to consult with you," I said formally.

Abigail turned to me immediately.

"Ahinoam, I will also need your ideas," I added.

The three of us went to Abigail's tent, and I posted Josheb as a guard. Zalmon's wife quickly placed some dried apples and figs in a bowl on the reed mat along with a small cruse of water.

"What did you wish to know?" the Gebirah asked, bowing her head slightly.

"I am thinking of leaving Judah. But before I make a decision, I want to know how your leaving would affect the Calebite clans," I added quietly.

Neither woman said anything for some time. "Without holding land, I am not tied to any particular place, so I don't see that much will change," Abigail finally said.

"Only so long as you are still close," Ahinoam put in. "Removing you to someplace like Damascus would open a power struggle between the nagids again."

"True," Abigail responded. She looked at me. "Where would you go?"

"Gath."

Ahinoam's eyes widened, and she stared at me.

"You have some reason for believing we will be welcome there, then," the Gebirah suggested.

"Yes."

"That would be close enough," my second wife said to Abigail after a pause. "You could still attend important meetings and be at the new moon feast this year. Most of the alliances should pledge to you this time."

"The only one holding back is Dathan," the Gebirah commented. "He told me he's doing it to give those nagids who haven't made up their minds a place to go for another year."

"Then he'll probably ally with you the year after this one, regardless of what the nagids with him may want."

"In that case, there is no obstacle to our leaving," I summarized. "Aside from the political aspects, how would you feel about it?"

"Does it have to be Philistines?" Ahinoam asked, her mouth set tight.

"I don't see any other choice. If I stay, Shaul will make war here in the south, and the people here can ill afford that."

Reluctantly she nodded.

"Abigail?"

"Why not Moab? Your family is there."

"Since I have more Moabite royal blood in my veins than Yira, and the men to displace him, he will not welcome me."

"Hassarah Ruth was Moabite royalty?"

"Yes."

A quick smile crossed Abigail's face, and her eyes sparkled with laughter.

Quickly I left the tent. Abigail rarely laughed out loud, but more and more often, I saw the joy inside her. The nights she spent with me meant more to me than I dared to admit. Watching her open up, not just to me, but to everyone around her, had been a revelation. The sparkle in her eyes, matched with her dignity of carriage and demeanor, reminded me often of Grandmother Ruth. There was a depth to my feeling for Abigail that I'd never known for either Michal or Ahinoam. It had grown so slowly that I hadn't noticed it until recently.

I knew much of Abigail's new freedom stemmed from the harmony between her and Ahinoam, and I had enough sense to recognize that I could destroy that by favoring one over the other. I did my best to treat them with equal respect, and welcomed whichever one showed up at my tent. But there was something about the beautiful Gebirah that touched me in a way no other had.

After the evening meal that night, I summoned the men. They gathered quietly, tired from the labor of harvest. Once everyone had arrived, I stood on a stump so that they could see me.

"As you know, King Shaul sent an expedition against us again," I began, "and although he left us in peace, I do not believe it will be for long. We have done much here and at Horesh, but if we stay, we will have to fight."

I paused a moment while the murmurs died down. This would not be news to the men who had been with me the longest, the ones who had followed the ark for weeks on end as we marched back and forth across the forests and wilderness of the south, dodging Shaul and his men. But my retainers had nearly tripled since then, not counting the families and women who now gathered around Ahinoam and Abigail, listening silently.

Remembering the way that Roeh Shamuel had laughed when I'd complained about having 10 retainers, I suspected that my band would grow still larger since I was no longer acquiring men singly, but in groups. I couldn't help but glance at Ezer and the Gaddite spearmen grouped behind Josheb, and the Benjamites who had arrayed themselves behind Abiezer and Azmaveth, the hassar's former bodyguards.

"I am not willing to contend with Shaul," I went on. "There would be needless bloodshed which would not only weaken us, but cause disruption in Israel and bring further suffering on the people of Judah and Caleb. We will leave, going west across the plateau and out of the highlands."

"You've decided to take us into Philistia?" Hiddai called out from his place to one side. The unpleasant man had pledged to me every year, and had remained in camp since last fall.

"We may end up there, yes. But, as before, I will be following the ark just as the rest of you will. We will go where it leads, and if that is into Philistia, so be it. I plan to move as soon as threshing is over," I added. That settled the matter for the men here. They knew I would go only where I believed that Yahweh led.

"I wanted each of you to have time to notify your families and clans," I continued, "and I do not know when we will be returning. Therefore, if any of you wish to bring along wives and children, tell Abishai. They must be here before the war season begins.

"Some of you are from the north, in Israel. The same applies to your wives and clans. Just be certain they understand that we are going into exile. You are dismissed," I finished.

"Shalom, Dahveed," said a voice I hadn't heard in years.

I whirled around on the threshing floor to see my brother grinning at me. "Shammah!" I exclaimed, rushing to meet his embrace. "This is a surprise! How are you? Is everyone all right in Moab? What made you come? And who is this?" I finished, staring at the young man nearly as tall as Shammah and grinning at me with the same smile. "Jonathan?"

He laughed. "No, Dodi! I'm Jonadab! Jonathan is over there with Immi."

When I glanced to where he pointed, I saw Shammah's oldest son greeting his cousin Asahel while Keziah hugged Abishai and held out her hand to Joab, who had hung back a little.

"That's Joab?" Shammah asked in a low voice, turning his head away.

"Yes. At least five years back, he was presented to me as a slave for sale. I had to buy him, of course, and he wouldn't leave after that. He's settled down some."

Jonadab cocked his head. "He's afraid of you," he observed.

I shot a startled look at him and noticed the little smile playing around Shammah's lips before answering. "He should be. Yahweh Himself had to hold me back from killing him."

"You'll have to tell me all about that," Shammah said. "Everything is fine in Moab. Abbi sends his regards, and Keren wanted to be certain her hug got delivered." He proceeded to do exactly that until I gasped for breath. "You're as bad as Abinadab!" I finally managed to say. "Let me breathe!"

With a laugh he released me.

Jonadab left us to greet his cousins, and I looked Shammah over. He hadn't changed much, except for the occasional gray hair. "Why have you come?"

"I'm returning to Bethlehem. Eliab thinks it is safe if I show up as a laborer while I begin raising mules again. I've got several with me down at our camp."

"King Yira gave his permission?"

My brother nodded. "In spite of all that you and Abbi did, I think he still worries for his throne. The fact that I'm returning has given him one more reason to believe we have no wish to rule Moab! I've been thinking of it for a year now, and when your man Ithmah came with the message that you were leaving Judah, I decided now was a good time. Besides, Jonathan has been itching to join you. He and Jonadab have both trained as warriors, and the last time Ethan was through, he said Jonathan was ready to join you."

"What about Jonadab?"

Shammah chuckled. "He can fight; he just doesn't want to. He'd rather talk his way out of the exertion." My brother turned serious, looking at his youngest son. "He's very quick, Dahveed," he said softly. "He notices things, and he has a knack for coming up with ideas that work. I first noticed it when he started helping me train the mules. Now he's my assistant, so he'll be staying in Bethlehem with us. You can take Jonathan, can't you?"

"I don't see why not. But you do understand that I'm leaving Judah, and don't know when I'll be able to return?"

"Yes, Keziah wasn't happy about that part, but she knows she can't hang on to Jonathan any longer. He's too eager to join you."

"He'll soon learn how hard our life is."

Shammah nodded. "Ethan talked to him some. I don't know what he said, but Jonathan looked serious for nearly two days, so the Habiru made quite an impression."

Seeing the way that even Joab was smiling as he listened to whatever my nephew was saying, I could imagine that Jonathan looking serious must be a change.

"I also have a message for Asahel," Shammah continued, watching the young man, a frown on his face. "There were a few things he neglected to tell Abbi before he left, and I need to remind him of them."

I raised my eyebrows, but called Zeruiah's youngest son over.

"Shalom, Dodi Shammah," he greeted. "It's good to see you again! How are things in Moab?"

"Going well," Shammah replied. "Geber Jesse wanted you to know particularly that your son is fine, now that he's living with us."

"My son?" Asahel echoed, looking blank. Then his face reddened, and he looked down, shifting his feet.

"Are you interested in his name?" Shammah asked sternly.

"Well, I—of course—I mean, why wouldn't I be?"

"I just wondered, given that you didn't bother to tell anyone about him when you left us."

Asahel flushed again. "I didn't know about it—not really, that is."

"How could you not? You were there with his immi, weren't you?"

"Well, yes, I mean I knew about that part, but I—" His words stumbled to a halt, and he studied the ground around his sandals.

"Zebadiah is doing fine. He's fully recovered from his illness and—"

"He was sick?" Asahel asked, his head snapping up, concern in his eyes. "Why?"

Shammah studied him for a moment before making up his mind. "He'd had a hard time," he said quietly. "His immi didn't mind his coming, but it seemed most everyone else in the clan objected to having an Israelite half-blood running around the house. Her clan found someone who would marry her since her connections are fairly high up in the palace."

My nephew nodded.

"Her husband had little use for the boy, and when he became ill, the man refused to get any care for him. His immi brought him to us in desperation. She was very relieved with the welcome Keren and Jesse gave him."

"Abbi Jesse doesn't blame him for being half-Moabite?" Asahel asked anxiously, then looked at me. "If that's a problem, he can come here, can't he, Dodi? Would we have time to bring him before we leave?"

Apparently satisfied, Shammah seemed to relax. "It wouldn't be good to take him now, Asahel. He's just gotten used to us, and is learning to love Keren and Abinadab's wife. Leave him with us for a while. It eases Keren's heart. She misses Dahveed so. And your Dodah Abigail dotes on him whenever she and Jether visit."

"I'll send a message to him," Asahel said, a new light in his eyes. "Do you think he'd like that?"

"Probably, and so would Geber Jesse. An abject apology might be appropriate."

Asahel flushed again. "Yes, Dodi," he said, trotting off.

"How's he been with you?" Shammah asked, watching him leave.

"He has a roving eye, which I should probably settle with a wife sometime soon. And he's had a couple of sharp lessons when his eye roved a little too far."

"Good," Shammah grunted. "Zeruiah's tribe always did need a heavy hand."

Ahinoam had just joined me, and I'd introduced her to my brother when she suddenly laughed quietly and pointed to the group of cousins not far away. Eliphelet was edging toward them, that far-away, intent expression on his face. Abishai noticed him first and recognized the look. He nearly put out a restraining arm, then laughter flashed across his face before he gravely invited my personal thief forward. The northerner was his usual charming self with Keziah, and bowed politely to my nephews when their names were given to him.

"Who is he?" Shammah asked, noticing the suppressed laughter on both Ahinoam's and my face.

"Just watch." If I was correct, Eliphelet had already taken more than one item from Shammah's family, but Jonathan wore two rings, one a gaudy gold one. He said something, and everyone laughed.

"There it goes," Ahinoam announced, her intent gaze on Eliphelet as the gold ring vanished from Jonathan's hand while the thief bowed over it. "I've never seen how he does it before. He's amazingly fast."

As the laughter died down, Eliphelet bowed again, taking his leave.

Just as he stepped away, Jonathan casually reached out and clamped down on Eliphelet's wrist, jerking his arm upward and twisting it.

The thief, caught completely by surprise, cried out in pain and spun in a circle, trying to relieve the pressure on his arm.

"Jonathan! What are you doing?" Keziah gasped, horrified.

"Getting this man's attention," he said cheerfully. "Ethan said I might have to be firm with him."

"You have it! You have it," Eliphelet groaned.

"Good. I thought before you left us you might want to return all the things you took. I'd like my gold ring back, Immi will want her bracelet, and Jonadab really doesn't want to be without the amulet Abbi Jesse gave him. I believe you also have whatever Joab had in the back of his girdle, and Abishai might be missing something too, although I didn't have a good enough view to really tell."

"Geber, how can you—"

Jonathan twisted a little harder, and Eliphelet yelped. "Hesed, geber!" he begged. "Please, you'll break it!"

Keziah had checked her wrist and stared at my thief with bewildered eyes. Joab's face was red with disgust, and Abishai couldn't stop laughing.

"Ease up on him, Jonathan," I said, walking over. "He does have his uses. You got properly caught, didn't you?" I added to Eliphelet.

"I'm out of practice," he complained, nursing the arm my nephew released, then pulling the missing jewelry from somewhere in his clothes.

"Is that everything?" I demanded.

"I gave back everything he told me to," Eliphelet said, rubbing his arm again. "He must have eyes everywhere! No one's ever seen me do it before."

"Eliphelet, do I need to get my belt knife?" Abigail asked soberly, studying the man.

"No, Gebirah!" he replied, dropping to his knees. "Here it is! I hadn't left yet, so you don't need to do that!" His hand trembling, he handed me one more item and fled from the group.

"You might also want this," I said to Jonathan, handing him his other ring.

Not long after Shammah, Keziah, and Jonadab departed, families began arriving. Most of my men were married, and most of them wanted their wives and children with them. Abishai did an excellent job of keeping everything organized. He'd told the men that their families should bring only what they could pack on donkeys as well as what food supplies they could.

¥ ¥ ¥ ¥ ¥ ¥

"Go to Gath with Dahveed Israel?" Eliam said, staring at Ahibaal in amazement. "Abbi, why? I've always admired him, that's true, but to become one of his men? And what about my wife and child?"

"They would remain here, of course," the Jebusite said. "Gath is not that far, and you will be back here often. I will send a request to Dahveed Israel that you be taken into his service and trained as a soldier. I doubt he will refuse."

"I don't understand, Abbi. Why must I go now?"

"Because we only learned of his move this morning from Nagid Hebron, who received word from Gebirah Carmel. Threshing is over, and it is said the Dahveed will leave any day. There is no time to send someone else."

Ahibaal's son remained silent while in frustration he clenched and unclenched his hands. "Perhaps you should explain more fully," he finally said, holding his abbi's gaze.

The adon started to refuse, then saw the slight lift to his son's chin and paused. Eliam's immi had had that same look and direct gaze, and he had always been unwise when he ignored it.

"Because it is our adon's wish that we keep close track of Dahveed Israel," he replied levelly. "This is more important than you know. I haven't got the three days it would take to explain everything," he added with a slight smile. "And most of it wouldn't make sense until I'd explained more than a dozen other things that would take just as long. Suffice it to say that the adon wants to know all he does."

"I would be a spy?"

"You will not have to search around or ask questions or try to find out anything. When you come here to see your wife and child, however, I will be interested in whatever has happened since you were here last. It's also possible that the Dahveed will have a message or two for you to bring, and I may have you carry some to him as well."

Eliam still hesitated. "I may not be good enough as a fighter."

"Uriah will take care of that quickly enough." Ahibaal stood. "We are adons to the house of Jebus, Eliam. We serve as needed whether it is easy or not. You know this."

"Yes, Abbi, but—"

"Think of it as your compulsory military service. You would be sent to Jebus for that in a month or two anyway, and as much as you practice with that javelin, you may find you like learning even more about how to use it. What Uriah will teach you is not something you can pick up anywhere else."

"What's that?" his son asked curiously.

"Go and see."

Eliam smiled a little. "Yes, Abbi."

¥ ¥ ¥ ¥ ¥ ¥

The morning chill was still with us the day we left the stronghold below Maon. Because of the number of people I had following me, I'd sent Shagay, his son Jonathan, Ahiam, Hanan, and Sibbecai out as scouts. I'd told them my intention was to go to the town of Debir, on the west side of the plateau. It was less than 10 miles, but by the time we followed the Habiru trails across the rough terrain, I knew everyone would be exhausted, especially the families who had just joined us.

The camp was quiet as Abiathar offered a morning sacrifice for the last time on the altar we'd built, and everyone stared wide-eyed at the covered ark as Naharai, Beriah, Gad and Eliphelet picked it up and settled it on their shoulders. The fact that my personal thief was also an ark-bearer clearly astounded almost everyone. Those who had complained the most about retrieving their belongings from outside my tent hardly knew what to do.

Abiathar and Keturah took their places behind the ark, and the rest of us fell into line. "Yah, lead us, please, in the way we have chosen," I requested. After several moments, the ark-bearers headed west down the ridge toward the watercourse that led up to Maon. That night, we camped just north of Debir.

The next day we followed the twisting watercourse west of the town, going north a little, before turning west again and descending into the Shephelah hills and Eglon. It took us nearly all day to cover the distance, even though it was less than the previous day's travel, for today the ark often stopped or turned, twisting around and puzzling everyone, until I realized that both yesterday and today, no one had seen us pass. We camped on the north side of the highway that passed through the town on its way to the coast.

I had planned on stopping the third night outside of Lachish, which was just nine miles straight south of Gath, but the ark-bearers didn't pause until we had passed Lachish by nearly five miles. Fortunately, the walking was easier on the plains, and only the smallest children needed to be carried or placed on donkeys. The ark stopped in a hollow, surrounded by low hills covered with elm, pine, and cypress, and we set up camp.

As soon as the evening meal was over, I sent for Ittai and Hanan. It was time to let someone in Gath know that I had arrived.

Chapter 13

Sahrah Hazzel cautiously checked the street to be sure that annoying six-fingered scion of Goliath wasn't around before leaving the palace. She had gone out without even her maid, for the political situation had become nearly intolerable, and she was certain the woman was in the pay of someone, probably Gaza, since her family was from there. And she knew for a fact that the servant who attended Akish reported to Ashdod.

The peremptory summons that had come to Akish along with the usual notification of how many units he was to supply for the current war season greatly worried her. It had said all the adons of the Five Cities had been called to Ekron, but she had serious doubts about that, and from the look in Akish's eye, so did he. He had no choice but to go, along with his principal serens and adons, but he had also taken his entire personal bodyguard.

The seren had expected that Goliath's kin, Ishvi-benob, would insist that his brothers accompany him, and Hazzel had seen how angry he was when the Rapha arranged it so that the youngest brother—what was his name? she fumed—would remain behind, in charge of the one unit left to guard the town. She might welcome a small invasion about now, Hazzel decided as she emerged from the palace and hurried down the alley. It would keep that giant nuisance occupied enough to leave her in peace. The way he looked at her, and the thought of his six-fingered hands touching her, made her shudder. With Akish gone, she wasn't sure what that man might take into his head to do.

Covered by her lightest cloak, she threaded her way to the north gate. Hadar would be leaving his stall to join his caravan outside the gates, and he would help her get outside of town. Arriving just as he was ready to go, she followed him through the gate, carrying a bundle like the rest of his servants, while helping the crippled man riding a low push cart. Hadar and several other merchants allowed him to beg by their stalls and helped him travel to other cities when he needed to.

Once the trees hid her from sight, she slipped away, smiling at what Akish would say if he knew she was going to the almond grove alone again in war season, especially with the roads as frequented by robbers and brigands as they had been lately. But she felt safer out here than in her own room, even knowing that two more adons had been attacked, and the descriptions all said the attacker had been of unusual size, and very tall. That made everyone look to Gath, and Ishvi-benob's family, who were in Akish's employ.

It didn't make sense, Hazzel thought as she walked swiftly toward the grove. Surely the other adons knew that if Akish wanted to kill them, he knew better than to hire someone as unmistakable as a member of Goliath's family! If only her brother would listen to her! She had seen his personal attendant talking to a slimy-looking Phoenician—at least she thought he was slimy—and then later watched the attendant hand Ishvi-benob a sack that could only hold silver or gold. And if someone outside the Five Cities was involved in the attacks, it made more sense. But no, Akish wouldn't consider the idea, she thought grumpily. It had never happened before. Why should it now?

"Well, why shouldn't it?" she said out loud. "What's so hard to imagine about someone wanting to break up the alliance among the Five Cities? What does it matter if I can't tell him why? And Gath is the perfect first target. We're the weakest of the cities, thanks to Manani, even if my stubborn brother doesn't want to admit it!"

As she entered the rows of almond trees, the late afternoon light slanting between them in the way she loved to watch, she felt herself relax a little. She was glad she had come today. Yesterday her maid wouldn't leave her alone even a moment, but this afternoon she had firmly sent the woman away.

Hearing a sound, she quickly glanced in the direction it had come from, barely catching sight of something before it vanished. Warily she stopped, listening. But nothing moved. It had probably been a deer, she thought, continuing on her way. Then a being rose soundlessly before her, standing taller than Akish, the slender body still, brown hair tied back with rawhide, one hand casually resting on his girdle and a bow across his shoulders.

Hazzel's hands flew to her heart. "Ribbai!" she gasped, swaying a little with shock. Her dead husband had stood just like that the first time she'd seen him outside Gibeah's fortress in Israel before everything had happened, before he'd been captured in a battle and enslaved and—she backed up a step, wondering wildly why he had come back from Sheol. What would she tell him about Ittai? He'd known she was pregnant and—

"Don't you know me, Immi?" the specter said, stepping toward her. Realization crashed into her senses as she saw the shape of Akish's chin and eyes in its face. "Ittai?" she breathed, then drew in a huge breath.

"Immi, no!" he said, jumping toward her to wrap his arms around her and hide her face in his cloak, cutting off her shriek of joy.

Sobbing hysterically, she clung to him, then pulled back to reach up and touch his face, before holding him fiercely again. "Ittai, Ittai, it's you!" she kept saying.

"All of me, alive and well, Immi," he repeated again and again.

The sun had nearly set by the time she collected herself enough to think. Then she abruptly released him and stepped back. "But what are you doing here? I hope nothing has happened. You haven't gone and made Dahveed angry with you, have you, and gotten yourself thrown out of his band? Because things aren't any better here, you know. What with all the adons getting killed, and Lahmi strutting around like a cock pheasant while the roads grow more dangerous every day, to say nothing of how angry your dodi is about Ziklag defying him and probably in rebellion and in the pay of that slimy Phoenician I saw in the market. You can't stay, you know. You'll have to go back and beg Dahveed's pardon so that I don't have to threaten to stay with him myself if he doesn't treat you right!"

Finally she paused for breath and saw the tears on her son's face in spite of the smile. "Whatever is the matter with you?" she said, wiping at them as she used to. "What is there to laugh about?"

"I can't help it, Immi," Ittai said, taking her hands. "I didn't realize how much I missed the mixed-up way you talk until I heard you again. You don't need to worry. Dahveed hasn't thrown me out of his band. I'm here as a messenger to Dodi Akish. What's going on at the palace tonight? Will I be able to see him without anyone knowing?"

"Of course you could. Do you think he'd refuse to see his own nephew? But you can't tonight."

"Immi, I must. I've already stayed a day longer than I was planning, because you didn't come to the grove until now."

"Well, you'll just have to wait longer since Akish isn't here, and you can't shout your news to him all the way to Ekron, where he's probably already in chains, given what the serens all think of him, as if he'd be that stupid!" she finished in disgust.

"Does this have anything to do with the slimy Phoenician?" Ittai asked after a moment of thought.

"Of course it does. Who else would want your dodi dead? Certainly any Philistine seren with a head knows that giving Gath to Ishvi-benob would give too many other sars ideas that no one wants them to have, seeing as how they have ideas enough now, probably due to that slimy Phoenician. It's gotten so that you can't walk into the market without being muttered at by some commander who thinks you've come to have him beaten or to accuse him of deserting his post for a week while he traveled to Ashdod to make trouble there even though you've seen him just yesterday when he was standing outside the palace doors like he's supposed to. And nobody listens anymore, no thanks to Dagon, Baal, and the gods of the Five Cities!"

"I can see this will take some time, Immi," her son sighed. "Hanan," he spoke to the air.

Hazzel was about to ask what he was doing when another young man appeared from what seemed nowhere.

"Go tell Dahveed that I have to stay in Gath since it seems the cauldron is already boiling over."

With a nod to Ittai, the man turned to Hazzel. "Shalom, Sahrah," he said, disappearing as eerily as he had come.

"Who is that?" she asked. "Have I seen him before? How did he know me?"

"You probably have seen him," Ittai said. "He seems to have been everywhere, and he told me a way to get into Gath without using the gates. Can you get back to the palace all right?"

"Yes. Shemel is at the south gate this evening. He always lets me in. He was demoted by Lahmi, and your dodi hasn't figured out a way to help him yet."

"Do you trust him, Immi?"

"He's the only one left in the city I do trust."

"Then bring him to the palace with you. I'll be in your outer chamber by the time you get there."

Before she could say anything, he vanished nearly as fast as his companion had. Hazzel stood there staring at the place where he'd been. Had she just talked to her son, or not? Yes, she decided, she had, and now that he was back, things were going to be all right. Saph or no Saph. She hurried through the deepening dusk to the gates of Gath.

"I won't bite you, sar," Hazzel said, walking away from the open door to her outer chamber. "Come in."

"Please, Sahrah, I'm not a commander any longer, and I'd rather not leave the hall. It isn't seemly for me to be in the same room with you alone."

"I'm not alone," she said, catching sight of Ittai quietly waiting in a dark corner of the room. She hugged herself again. Halfway back to the palace, she'd nearly convinced herself she had dreamed the entire encounter. The sar still hung back.

Impatiently, she turned to him. "Shemel, come into this chamber," she commanded, her voice suddenly hard.

White-faced, looking trapped, he obeyed. "Please, Sahrah, what have I done to you to deserve this?"

"Nothing, Shemel," Ittai replied quietly. "In fact, my immi told me that you are the one person left in this city that she does trust. Now, shut the door."

Moving as if in a dream, the soldier did, then faced the room, looking for whoever had spoken.

Ittai stepped into full view.

"Seren!" Shemel said, dropping to his knees. "How is this possible? We understood that you had been killed!"

"No, Manani wasn't intelligent enough to understand how deeply my immi loved me. Immi says my dodi is in Ekron, and probably in considerable danger there. Tell me the situation."

Two hours later, Shemel finished. Hazzel approved of the way Ittai listened without saying a word, intent on what the guard said and the comments she had interjected every so often. And she could hardly take her eyes off the man her son had grown into, seeing a curious mixture of Akish and Ribbai in his every move and expression. She smiled in satisfaction. Yes, she had done the right thing in sending him to his covenant abbi. He had come back now, grown up and able to help in ways he never could have done otherwise.

"Shemel, I want you to take a message to Seren Akish," Ittai said, after staring at the opposite wall for a few minutes. "Tell him the adon of his sister's house is taking an interest in his troubles, and that he should remember Og of Bashan."

"I would go if I dared, seren. I am forbidden to leave the city. But I know of someone trustworthy who could go in my place."

"Send him, then. Can you be here in the morning?"

"Yes, seren. I do not have guard duty then."

"Good. I've got a feeling a great deal is going to boil over tomorrow morning."

Hazzel was headed for the palace roof early the next morning when she heard the commotion outside. "What is it?" she questioned the soldier racing past.

"Sahrah," he gasped. "We went to open the gates this morning, and there is an army camped outside! We could see the warriors! What shall we do?"

"What do you mean, an army?"

"Armed men! All over. Sahrah, what can we do? Akish is gone with all of our units! They will seize the city and destroy us all!"

"Only if they can get through the gates," Hazzel said drily, wanting to slap him. "They are still closed, aren't they?"

"Yes, Sahrah," the man stammered.

"Then we are not likely to be slaughtered for some time yet. Has this army surrounded us completely?"

An expression of surprise swept over him. "I don't know, Sahrah."

"Then perhaps I should look for myself."

"You, Sahrah?"

"Am I talking about anyone else?" she snapped. "Akish is not here, is he? That pretty much leaves it up to me, and before I can decide anything, I need to know whether or not we've been completely engulfed by invaders, or if you just saw the units from Ziklag finally reporting! Take me to the gate, will you?"

"Yes, Sahrah. Right away, Sahrah." The man backed away, then hurried ahead of her to the stairs by the south gate.

Out on a hillside in full view of the town, a cluster of tents had appeared, and the warriors that she could see didn't look anything like Philistines. The commander of the guard saw her and hurried over.

"Are there more on the other sides of town?" she asked before he could speak.

"Uh, no Sahrah, I don't think so."

"Well, go make sure, and then report."

He quickly returned. "No, Sahrah."

"Good. Send a messenger immediately to Seren Akish. Tell him we have armed men camped outside the city, and I will direct the defense until they return. Is that clear?"

"Uh, I guess so, Sahrah," the commander replied, hurrying off to find a courier.

Hazzel stared at those tents. If they were trying to surprise the city, pitching camp in plain view wasn't very intelligent of them. Unless they simply wanted Gath to know they were there. She paused.

Yesterday she had assumed that her son had had a long journey to get to Gath. But what if he hadn't? What if that was Dahveed Israel out there?

Deep in thought, she went down the stairs and crossed the market, which was strangely silent this morning. She had to find Ittai right away. If it was Dahveed, much might be done. When she had entered the palace she suddenly found her way blocked by a large form. Startled, she looked up into the grinning face of Goliath's youngest kinsman.

For a moment she froze. "Well, it's about time you got here," she heard herself say tartly. "Come along, there's work for you to do." Hiding her trembling, she turned and marched back the way she had come, heading for the throne room. To her relief, the man followed, his grin a bit uncertain now.

Good; he was off balance. She had to keep him that way. But what could she do with him? She knew what he wanted from her, and there was no one in town that could stop him, not even if Ittai and Shemel appeared in front of her right now.

The idea that presented itself stunned her at first. Then she grabbed onto it with her whole mind, thinking frantically. With only minutes to put it into effect, she had to be convincing. Once in the deserted throne room, she turned to face the huge man, a dazzling smile on her face.

"You're just the man I need," she said, gazing up at him. "You've heard the news, of course, about the armed men threatening the city?"

"Uh, well, yes," he said, trying to look important.

"Good. Because you are about to save Gath! Akish is gone, and I've been waiting for years for this opportunity. I'm not about to let it slip by me now! Do you understand?" She batted her eyelashes at him.

His eyes glazed over, and he nodded eagerly. "Yes, Sahrah. I've been waiting, too."

"I'm sure you have. We have to put up a show of strength for these invaders. And who better to do it than you? And all of those brave, tough warriors you have for friends," she added on the spur of the moment. "There are very many warriors out there yet, so you need to get ready immediately and go out now so more arrive. Take all your friends so that you can really overwhelm them! They are probably just Habiru. And once they've driven you away, the people of Gath will finally realize how much better a ruler you would make than Akish, who never does anything worthwhile, as you know. And, of course, I'll be waiting for you, too. Can you do that for me?"

The big man gulped, swelling up with pride. "Of course, Sahrah. I'll have the city safe before the morning is over! And tonight we can celebrate!"

"Yes, keep that thought in mind," she said, leaning toward him a little. "Now, you'd better go." Smiling, she touched his hand.

He staggered a little as he left the throne room, then she heard him bellowing for his armor.

"And once you and they are outside those gates, may I be struck speechless and dumb by Dagon, Baal, Yahweh, and El Elyon before Dahveed Israel dares to open them to you again," Hazzel declared, her eyes blazing.

Where were Ittai and Shemel? Well, she'd just have to continue without them and hope they showed up sooner or later. And she prayed to Dagon that it was Dahveed Israel out there, because, if by some misbegotten chance or cruel joke of the gods it wasn't, and those men actually were successful in driving away whoever was out there, she hadn't the least idea in the world what she could do. The thought made her a bit dizzy.

But she shoved it aside and hurried to her room. Opening her jewelry box, she took out the first things in it. Her hands were shaking so badly that she could hardly hold onto anything, let alone fasten it on. "Oh, where is that maid when I need her," she fumed, stopping and taking some deep breaths to steady herself.

At last she had an earring in each ear, a necklace around her throat, three bracelets on, and some rings. Smoothing her hair back, she whirled from the room and raced to the palace door, emerging into the square by the south gate.

Attendants were just finishing arming Ishvi-benob's brother, and she stopped a moment to look. Just the sheer size of him was admirable, and she sighed a little. Too bad he was such an arrogant, foul, six-fingered dog along with the size. Then she noted with approval that his worst cronies were also milling around, putting on some armor and seeing to their weapons. If she could get all these nuisances outside the gates, crime in Gath would drop to nothing in an hour. Akish should be pleased. He'd better be pleased. She'd make sure he was pleased, she vowed.

Finally, the unit formed up in the market, their commander standing tall in front of them.

"We are ready, Sahrah, to defend the city," he said grandly.

Hazzel swallowed the retort on her lips. She didn't know that much about fighting men, but she realized that if whoever was out there was half-way trained, they shouldn't have any problem with these "soldiers."

"I see that. You've done well to be ready so, er, promptly. I'm sure Dagon will look down with approval also, and lend you his aid that you will undoubtedly need. We in Gath are faithful to him, after all."

"Thank you, Sahrah. Open the gates," the giant commanded.

The guards glanced at her and Hazzel nodded encouragingly.

As the gates creaked open, Shemel and Ittai came racing across the square toward her. "What are they doing?" the older man asked before Hazzel had the time to wonder why her son, who outranked the soldier, was following like a servant instead of leading like a seren. The soldier started to yell for the gates to close, but Hazzel put her hand on his arm.

"Don't stop them. They are going out to save Gath," she said brightly. "Don't you think that's wonderful of them? Can you imagine how brave they must be, to go out there to fight for us when we have no one else to save us? The city will be delirious with joy at their victory! And they'll deserve it!"

"Sahrah, they don't know who is out there!" Shemel said, aghast. "That isn't just any band of Habiru! Dahveed Israel is here!"

"Hush, Shemel, I'm sure a small detail like that won't matter to someone as brave and resourceful as someone from Goliath's family, do you? What could that matter? We still need someone to defend the city, and there go just the men to do it!"

"But, Sahrah, Dahveed hasn't attacked the city," Shemel said desperately as the men marched out of the gate. "You must stop them!"

"Oh, I couldn't possibly do that! I've heard that Dahveed is very dangerous, and we must have someone out there who can keep him away from us. If we do that, he won't have the time to get in here! It's just the most marvelous plan to defend the city, don't you think? Akish should be very pleased with this idea!"

Shemel stared at her, open-mouthed. "Sahrah, you will succeed only in angering the man!" he said in a strangled voice. "Then he really will come against us!"

"Oh, that's unlikely, I think. After all, Ittai is with us. But if he does, I'll think of something else to do to keep everything nice and safe. Oh, I must go up to the wall to encourage them."

Once on the wall, she saw that the hillside was empty now but for the tents. Then she glanced down in time to see the savior of Gath just finishing his war speech and looking up to her for approval. She smiled dazzlingly again, waving her hand enthusiastically.

He bowed, really quite dignified, and started off, his friends following raggedly after.

Shemel appeared beside her and started to say something, but Ittai laid a hand on his arm, regarding his immi closely, his eyebrows raised in wonder. "Um, Immi, may I ask what this is all about?" he said softly.

"Is that really Dahveed Israel out there?" she asked just as quietly.

"Yes, Immi. The men you have sent out there won't stand a chance if they try to fight."

"I'm counting on that," she said, turning to her son. "And Ittai, if anyone opens those gates before every one of those men is dead, I'll not call you mine!"

Ittai's eyes went thoughtful for a moment.

Shemel's jaw dropped. "By Dagon, Sahrah, what have you—" He broke off to glance at the men spread out along the wall, watching. Then he stared at those below.

"That's not the army unit!" he gasped.

"Of course not! I certainly couldn't send them out there. They are all we have to fight with."

"Then who—"

"Some of the worst riffraff in town, I'd guess," Ittai said, his voice somewhat odd since he was trying not to laugh. "Shemel, since our one unit is now without a commander, I believe I will promote you to the post. Do you think you can handle it?"

"The men, yes," Shemel replied. "It's the sahrah I'm worried about!"

"I think you'd best leave her to me."

Chapter 14

"The gates haven't opened, adoni. There's been some activity on the walls, but nothing that looks like a courier or messenger of any sort," Shagay reported.

I nodded, sending him back to watch, and wishing that Ittai had elaborated a little more in his report, but Hanan had said Sahrah Hazzel was the one he met with. Knowing Akish's sister, it would take hours to untangle all the facts she had probably poured out. I hoped her son would soon contact me again with more information.

"Ready, Dahveed," Uriah said, approaching.

I smiled at his curt address. Usually he spoke respectfully to me, but when his mind set itself on a battle, he had little time and less patience for anything else. I had enough men now to divide the fighting force into small units, commanded by men who'd been with me the longest or were competent to handle them. The ones with the most training under Uriah, however, formed my shalishim and were composed almost entirely of my personal retainers. Some of them now had retainers of their own, such as Josheb, who held Ezer's loyalty, who in turn commanded the loyalty of the Gaddite spearmen. The Benjamites had organized themselves similarly under Abiezer and Azmaveth, who had sworn to me.

Abishai had suggested this arrangement, a familiar one that mimicked the structure of family, clan, and tribe, and which kept administrative duties for me down to a manageable level, since I need only deal with my personal men, although I was the final arbiter for any disputes that couldn't be settled any other way.

By the second day of travel from Maon, Ahinoam and Abigail had become the natural focus for the women and children now in the band, and I suspected they had already decided how they wanted to organize their own areas of authority. I was curious to see how that would work out.

"Adoni, the gates of Gath are opening," Joab reported, interrupting my thoughts.

"Tell Uriah to have the men form up in the trees as we planned," I said, fastening on my sword.

Once down among the trees, I watched as a group of about 20 men emerged from the town, led by a huge man who could only be from Goliath's family.

"They don't look much like messengers, adoni," Shagay said, a slight smile on his face as he watched. He'd been restless lately, and I knew he needed a good fight to settle him down again.

"No, they don't look entirely peaceable," I agreed, watching the way they formed up.

The leader gave a short speech, then looked up to the town walls. I saw someone wave at him, and he bowed. I studied him as he came closer. It looked like the youngest one. He wasn't big enough to be Ishvi-benob or Saph, and I didn't remember Lahmi being that stocky. But he marched toward us confidently, the men behind him straggling out in a ragged line.

"Those aren't professionals," Uriah commented beside me.

"Didn't Hanan say that only one unit was left in town?" I asked.

"Yes," Shagay replied, "and if that's the unit, I don't think much of Gath's army."

Behind me in the trees I heard the murmur of the men as the size of the approaching commander became more evident.

"Ahiam, pass the word that the regular units are to concentrate on stopping the Philistine soldiers and leave that commander to the shalishim."

Uriah looked annoyed when the murmurs and uneasiness in the trees died down as the message reached everyone.

"Don't be angry with them, Uriah," I said. "They've never seen anyone like him before."

"That's no excuse," he growled.

"Well, take comfort in the fact that none of the shalishim seem affected," I said with approval. The only change I saw in them was sharpened attention and a taut readiness.

The line behind the commander got more ragged the farther they walked, stringing out carelessly.

"At this rate, half of them will still be within fleeing distance of Gath by the time the first one gets here," Shagay snorted. "Doesn't Akish train his men?"

"Constantly," I said absently. "He's got some good commanders, or at least he did. I don't think those are soldiers, though. If I had to guess, I'd say we've got the town riffraff heading our way."

"Why do you think that?" Uriah asked.

"I recognize at least one, and he never in his life had an acquaintance worth speaking to."

My military trainer cast a glance at me, but he didn't say anything else.

I frowned in puzzlement. What was going on in that city? I couldn't imagine any circumstances under which Akish would send out such a force. And since I hadn't yet heard anything from Ittai, I was reduced to guessing. I could understand a military unit advancing toward me, either as protection for an emissary, or to drive us away, but that motley collection of ne'er-do-wells could have no useful purpose. So why was it here, with the commander looking as if he wanted trouble?

Then I cursed myself. "Uriah, send two thirds of the units out on our flanks. Shagay, I want Hanan and Sibbecai scouting on each side. Get everyone in position now!"

Who knew what might have left the city by the other gate, I thought in irritation. I should have had someone watching long before this.

When Uriah returned, I gave him further orders. "Have two units on each side ready to attack from the trees. And only two shalishim in loose formation are to concentrate on the Rapha. Everyone else hold back. I don't want to reveal our strength until I know why something as crazy as that is headed for me."

"Do we attack when they get here?"

"No," I decided. "I'll try to talk first. Given who's leading them, I doubt it will do any good. But I might be able to stall things enough so that most of them will be present for the fight," I ended as the approaching men straggled out even more.

The Philistines had nearly reached us, so I left my vantage point on the little hillock and walked toward the edge of the trees. To my right, I noticed Joab standing ready with one of the units, Naharai beside him. The Gibeonite and my nephew had taken a liking to each other, and were often together.

Everything looked as ready as it could be, and I faced the giant who stopped in the field and stared into the forest.

"Habiru, show yourselves," he roared.

I sighed. Seven years hadn't given this particular man any more tact than he used to have. I stepped into view. "Shalom, sar."

"There will be no shalom for you this day," he retorted. "You have come against Gath, the greatest of the Five Cities!"

"Your pardon, sar, but I hadn't thought we had threatened the city." I watched as a couple more of his men halted beside him.

"You bring armed men against us, and you say you do not threaten us?" he said sarcastically, and those around him laughed.

"Truthfully, sar, the only armed men I see that might threaten Gath are yours, for we haven't marched against you. You sought us out."

"We have no use for you, and want none of your trouble in our country. Do you leave now, or must we drive you away?" he asked, raising his spear a little.

"Is hospitality lacking in Gath that travelers cannot rest themselves near the city?" I asked, stalling as a few more of his men gathered.

"Travelers arrive in caravans; Habiru in packs like dogs. And I see no caravan. Therefore, you are dogs!"

"Dogs bite," I said, barely controlling my temper as I stepped back into the trees.

"After them, men," the giant roared. "Drive them from our gates!" He charged toward the trees, not even bothering to lift his shield, his men giving a half-hearted yell and running after him.

Shagay's shalishim appeared from the trees, quickly engaging the giant.

"Forward," Uriah roared, and the flanking units charged, ignoring the commander and going straight for the Philistine men. The combined war cry stopped them instantly, and two of them fell before the others realized they would have to fight.

"Dahveed, help the right," Uriah said, gesturing to the men on that side, even though his eyes were fastened on the giant holding off the shalishim. I ran to add my sword to the skirmish there, stepping in where three of the Philistines had cornered Joab and Naharai. Slicing through the thigh of one attacker, I shoved him screaming to the ground.

"Archer!" I heard Uriah roar.

Too far away for me to reach, Abinadab the Hittite was trying to protect a fallen comrade. Whipping the sling pan off the back of my hand, I reached for a stone from my pouch. Someone blocked the man hurtling toward me, and I loosed the stone, knocking over the Philistine threatening Abinadab.

"Dahveed, turn him! Strike low down!" Uriah roared at me.

Jumping back from the skirmish, I glanced at my commander. He pointed straight at the giant. I snatched up a field stone, then had to twist away from a sword thrust. Ezer was suddenly beside me, his spear holding off the attacker. "Now, Dahveed," he yelled. I whipped the sling around, aiming for the giant's lower leg, trusting that Uriah knew why he wanted it there.

The whumping sound of the irregularly shaped stone made the Philistine start to turn, and when it struck with a solid thud, he screamed, automatically looking down. Instantly, an arrow appeared in his neck, exposed when he had bent his head. He staggered and collapsed sideways.

"He's down!" Shagay roared. "After them!"

"Run," someone yelled. "They've killed him!"

In moments the Philistines fled the battle with much more speed than they had joined it, and it suddenly occurred to me that if they could be persuaded to talk, they might have a lot of information about what had been going on in Gath lately.

"Take them!" I yelled. "I want them! Alive!"

My men gave instant chase.

"Asahel!" I roared.

"Dodi!" he replied, appearing from the trees.

"Go! I want those men alive!"

"I'll try!" he said, sensibly taking the time to settle into his stride before he turned on the speed. Satisfied that he would catch up, I stopped to watch.

"That's interesting," Uriah said, beside me again. "There doesn't seem to be any activity around the city gates."

I looked up to the walls. He was right. Normally, archers would line the walls to protect the men fleeing to the city, keeping the attackers back while someone opened the gates. But I could see no indication that that was happening.

¥ ¥ ¥ ¥ ¥ ¥

"We've been defeated! The men have failed," a guard on the wall shouted. "They are fleeing! Open the gates! Open the gates!"

"No! Leave them closed," Hazzel shouted, striding forward from her place in the market square. "Are the attackers close to them?"

"Yes, Sahrah," the guard said, glancing back. "Some of our men have been overtaken."

"Then we dare not open the gates, or we will have them in the city!"

"But, Sahrah, we can't have them slaughtered at our doors!" the assistant commander said, striding toward the gate. "Akish would never condone such an act! We must help them! Unit, form up!" he shouted.

"Don't you dare!" Hazzel countermanded, turning on the assistant commander. "There are too many out there! We'll have slaughter in the market if you don't obey!"

The soldiers, who had started to assemble as commanded, halted, not knowing what to do.

"Begging your pardon, Sahrah, but I don't think you understand what you are ordering, so I must overrule," the assistant commander said. "Unit, form up!"

Hazzel pushed herself around the man and stood directly in front of the gates. There was no way in the world that she was going to let her plan be sabotaged now. "You will go through this gate over my dead body!" she raged.

As she stared at the uncertain men she heard metal sliding out of a sheath. "I believe I will stand with the sahrah," Shemel said, taking his place beside her.

"Shemel!" the assistant commander gasped, staring at him. "We can't let them be killed!"

"Did you particularly want them back in town? You saw who went out there. I don't know about you, but I am one sar who is going to stand by my baalah, no matter how crazy she is!"

"Shemel, please," the other man said. "Don't make me fight you!"

"You don't have to," Ittai said, stepping forward.

The man whirled around, staring at the man who had spoken. "Do you know me?"

Hazzel raised her chin with pride at the iron in her son's voice.

"Seren?" the assistant gasped. "Seren Ittai?"

"Correct. Are you still so willing to flaunt the chain of command? If I recall, with Akish gone, the highest ranking person in this city is Sahrah Hazzel. Am I to understand that you were threatening her?"

Sweat appeared on the man's brow. "No, seren! I would never do that!"

"Then I guess the gates remain closed, don't they?"

"Yes, seren," the soldier said, bowing.

"I also expect you to remember that, from now on, Shemel is your commander, and you will do whatever he directs. I trust you will have no objections to that?"

"None, seren! None at all."

"Unit, form up in the square," Shemel shouted.

The assistant commander immediately stood straight in front of Shemel, and the men from the walls quickly gathered in ranks behind him.

"Open the gates," a voice said frantically, pounding on the wood and bronze.

Hazzel flinched, then straightened again, holding herself erect.

"Please, open the gates! They are after us! Let us in!"

The assistant commander twitched, and Shemel raised his sword.

"He's dead, he's dead," another voice said hysterically. "There were many of them! Units and units. Let us in!"

The silent crowd watching the drama pulled back a little, staring in alarm at the sahrah.

"We can't take the chance of letting them in here!" she said firmly. "Ittai, go up on the wall. Maybe you can offer the men out there as slaves. The Habiru might go away content with that, and spare their lives."

At mention of Habiru, the crowd looked more worried than ever. "Sahrah, we could offer gold, too," someone suggested as women drew their children closer to them.

"One thing at a time," Hazzel replied as the frantic shouts and pounding outside the gates continued.

¥ ¥ ¥ ¥ ¥ ¥

I looked the situation over from beyond bowshot of the gates. Not that there seemed to be much danger. I couldn't see a single man on the walls. The Philistines trapped outside the gates finally stopped yelling and pleading long enough to realize that they weren't being slaughtered, for my men had prudently refused to approach too close to the city walls. But neither could they leave, for I had two men with compound bows, and their arrows kept the men huddled against the wooden gate.

Just then a figure appeared on the wall. "That's Ittai," I said, walking closer.

Shagay was the one who approached and exchanged some words, then retreated back to me.

"It's Ittai," he confirmed. "He gave the sign for all being well, so I went to talk. I don't know what's going on in there, but he's offering the men outside the gates as slaves."

I considered refusing. Since I already had five captives, I didn't particularly want more, but if Ittai was saying this, he had to have a reason. And it might be as simple as cleaning up the town. I didn't like the thought that I'd been used this way, but knowing Akish, it was very possible. On the other hand, my best way of learning what was happening was through Ittai, and the fastest way of getting to see him was probably going along with what he suggested.

"Take them," I ordered. "But tell Ittai that he has to come out to negotiate for them. I want to talk to the young man, now!"

"Yes, adoni," Shagay said, hiding his smile as he jogged off.

I watched while my men bound the Philistines and dragged them off to one side. Then I went out onto the road, approaching closer to the walls than Uriah was comfortable with. The little door by the gates swung open, and Ittai ducked out, accompanied by one man.

He bowed slightly as he halted in front of me. His companion was Shemel, my unit commander the last time I had been here. I wondered who had freed him from Keilah. Last I'd seen of him, I'd left him there as a slave.

"Shalom, adoni," Ittai said.

"Shalom, Ittai. Tell me what's happening."

"Akish is in Ekron, along with all but one unit, which was under the command of that giant you just killed. I've since placed the unit under Shemel's command. Things do not look good for my dodi, Dahveed. Someone is sowing discord among the Five Cities, augmenting the bad feeling between the sars and the serens. They are trying to blame it all on Gath." Then he gave a very brief but comprehensive outline of what he knew.

"Akish is vulnerable on several fronts then," I said. "When can I see him?"

"A courier went to him this morning. It's less than seven miles to Ekron, so I expect him to show up anytime. Whether he will bring all the units, I can't say."

"All right. We'll wait in camp until Akish gets here. And what about the captives you saddled me with?"

"They are outcasts from Gath."

"Then perhaps you'd better pronounce sentence on them," I said, annoyed. "I do not like being used this way."

Ittai smiled. "Please, tell my immi that when you see her!"

I winced. "It might be easier to just go along," I said ruefully.

"Yes, I thought that myself," he agreed solemnly.

He and Shemel left after he'd officially condemned all the men I'd captured to enslavement for crimes against the city of Gath.

¥ ¥ ¥ ¥ ¥ ¥

Hazzel started forward as soon as Ittai and Shemel returned to the market square. "Well, what did they say? Who are they?" she demanded.

"They are Habiru from the highlands," her son replied, "and their dahveed wants to talk to Seren Akish. I did not see any indications that they want to attack the town," he added, knowing he was speaking to the people gathered around as much as to his immi. "I assured them that as soon as Seren Akish returned, he would speak to the dahveed. They were content with that. While I was there, I interviewed the men we gave them, and all of them are undesirable citizens, so I condemned them to enslavement and left them there."

His immi nodded. "I knew it was a good thing to give them to the Habiru. And good riddance! Now all we must do is wait for Akish."

As she walked back into the palace, she noticed the somewhat odd glances she got as the people bowed, but put it down to her defense of the city in Akish's absence. Ittai and Shemel escorted her.

Once inside, Shemel turned to Ittai. "Seren, why would you tell Dahveed Israel everything about Gath and Akish? It borders on treason, does it not?"

Her son smiled. "Don't worry, Shemel. Akish is well aware of my connection to Dahveed Israel."

"I believe I deserve to know what that is," the sar said.

"Yes, you do. Dahveed is my covenant abbi, and as such is adon to my house," Ittai explained. "He has sheltered me and kept me safe since I disappeared from this city seven years ago."

The young seren turned and left them, Shemel staring after him in amazement.

"Come along, Shemel," Hazzel said. "I don't know about you, but all the fighting I've done today has made me quite tired and hungry. I'll need you to come with me to the roof so that you can refresh me before Akish comes, and we have to fight with him all over again!"

"Yes, Sahrah," he said, looking completely bewildered as he followed her.

¥ ¥ ¥ ¥ ¥ ¥

The morning was well along when Akish and two of his serens stood at the edge of the market with his sars while the other principal adons and serens of the Five Cities seated themselves and began discussing the recent troubles everyone was having. Somehow, seats for him had not been prepared, and he wondered how long he'd have to stand before any finally appeared. It did not bode well.

Several comments loud enough to be heard were made about unreliable sars, and a murmur of unrest flowed around the square. Akish clenched his teeth. How could any one of the adons have said something like that with the sars standing right here listening? It was ridiculous, and simply asking for more trouble.

It didn't help that the message he'd gotten last night from Shemel made no sense whatsoever. The courier hadn't been any help, simply repeating it word for word. But why would Dahveed Israel be involved in anything going on at Gath right now, and why on earth should he be thinking of Og of Bashan? The man had been dead for centuries!

Hanabaal, ruler of Gaza, finally raised his hands to silence the conversations going on around him. The square gradually quieted. "Is Seren Akish of Gath here?"

"I am, Seren," Akish replied, stepping forward.

"Stand forth, then, Akish. It is required that you provide answer for complaints brought against you by the Serens of the Five Cities."

Akish felt the blood drain from his face. It was an official court of inquiry! His heart began to pound, and he took a quiet breath to steady himself. The temper that had been rising in him faded away, replaced by an icy calm. He must be very careful how he handled this. Could this be how Manani planned on removing him and gaining Hazzel and Gath? Had he discovered that the Egyptian tax document had been removed, and this was his response? He forced himself to step forward again. "I stand ready to answer, and to ask a few questions of my own."

"You will answer as we demand, Akish," Hanabaal said sternly.

"I will answer as ruler of one of the Five Cities," he replied, noting the flicker of surprise in Manani's eyes. Akish knew that if he survived until the end of this meeting, Manani would have a revised opinion of him, but it couldn't be helped. He was going to have to reveal himself.

"Then I hope you see fit to answer why sars from Gath nearly killed me less than two weeks ago," Gadmilk of Ashdod said, his voice flinty. "They were seen, Seren. And no one can mistake that size."

Akish's face tightened. Every city in the alliance had been troubled for two years by the elusive assassin who struck without warning, and whose only recognizable feature was his unusual height. Then the ridiculousness of the charge roused his temper. "Are you seriously suggesting that I would use as assassins the most recognizable sars in the land? The ones who can even be identified in the dark of night?" he asked sarcastically.

Ashdod's ruler flushed a little at the subdued smiles that spread among the sars as everyone turned to see Ishvi-benob, Saph, and Lahmi, standing not far from Akish.

"You may accuse me of insanity, but do not accuse me of stupidity of that order," Akish added, his voice icy.

Manani wasn't quick enough to hide his surprise.

Yes, I am much different than you think, Akish thought to himself.

"They are under your command! It is up to you to control them," Hanabaal retorted.

"That is an entirely different question," Akish responded, knowing he had scored an important point. "Controlling them is a far different matter from sending them out as assassins. It would appear that I can control them enough to have them here, Seren, yet I notice that once again you have not brought your full complement of units to the war this season. You are three units short, I believe. One unit more than last year. Don't your sars come when you summon them?"

Gaza's ruler turned red, clenching his fists. "I must leave some defense along my south and east borders. The Amalekites are raiding again."

"And if Gaza must leave units behind to guard the borders, perhaps it might be a good idea to be certain that Gath is equipped to do the same," Akish suggested. "It would be a shame to have the desert raiders plundering in the heart of Philistia, would it not?"

An uneasy silence settled over the square. Akish smiled to himself. They'd forgotten that. If Gath was not kept strong, the soft underbelly of the Five Cities remained open to the desert tribes. For the first time, Akish blessed the circumstances that made the raiders especially active this year.

"I've had all the same troubles as everyone else, including having one of my adons killed, and another severely wounded," he said into the silence. "And from what I can find out, the only thing definitely known about the assassin is that he is very tall and is never seen entering or leaving a city." Suddenly he paused, nearly gasping. Og of Bashan! He was still the measure for tall men, hundreds of years after his death. For a moment, Akish felt dizzy as the bits of information whirled around in his mind, arranging themselves in an entirely new way. Hazzel and her slimy Phoenician! He'd have to beg her forgiveness when he got back.

"That being said," he continued, barely speaking before someone else did, "perhaps the Serens should remember that the Rapha and their kind are not the only men known for height. And perhaps the Serens would want to consider the way we have all been induced to cast suspicions on each other, with the inevitable result of weakening our alliance. Let me ask this. Which of you adons spoke out against the sars before this meeting began? Was any one of you eager enough for trouble that you would accuse them of unreliability in this assembly?"

"I heard no such accusation," Gadmilk retorted. "Did anyone else?"

None of the serens or adons responded.

"We are not stupid, Akish," Manani said, watching him as if he'd never seen him before.

"Which of you sars heard the accusations?" Akish asked, turning to the crowd.

Hands and voices were raised instantly.

Gath's seren turned back. "Perhaps we should be spending our time trying to discover who is wreaking havoc with our alliance rather than sitting around assuming that every other seren in the league is an incompetent wretch, and the sars are the same!"

Again, the silence stretched out. Hanabaal of Gaza looked angry, and from the corner of his eye, Akish noted the thoughtful expression on the face of Muwana of Ashkelon. But Manani's face was still and stiff. Obviously, things hadn't gone as the Ekron ruler had wished. Akish dared to relax a little. He'd turned this assembly completely around and probably saved his own neck, but from the look in Manani's eye, he'd have to be very cautious from now on.

Someone touched his arm, and he looked around. One of his commanders motioned his head toward the Ekron gate, where a panting courier stood.

"Bring him here," Akish said, as the adons began to discuss the situation with each other, and he strained to hear as much as he could.

"Seren, please attend," the messenger said beside him just as he was trying to make out what Muwana was saying.

Impatiently, he turned. "What is it?" he hissed.

"Seren, please, Gath is under attack. Armed men were waiting outside the city at dawn. Sahrah Hazzel sends for you to come back immediately, and wants to assure you that she will order the defense of the city until you arrive."

"Hazzel said she is defending the city?" Akish asked, loudly enough for those around him to hear. The commanders behind him turned their entire attention to him.

"Yes, Seren! Please, come quickly. Anything could happen."

"That's truer than you know." Akish again faced the assembly.

"Serens, I must ask to be excused. News has just come that Gath is under attack." He turned to the men behind him. "Ishvi-benob, bring the units along as fast as possible. I'll be leaving instantly, and—"

"No, Akish, I think not," Manani said evenly. "It occurs to me that this message has arrived a little too conveniently for you."

Akish looked around in amazement. "You would have me ignore it, then? There is only one unit left to defend the entire city! And with Hazzel in charge of it, who knows what will happen!"

A suppressed ripple of amazement, then amusement, ran through the square since most of the adons had met Hazzel, and the commanders knew innumerable stories about her.

"Yes, I'm sure you must return before your sister reduces your city to rubble, but I question whether we can spare the units you have brought. They should remain."

The other serens nodded in agreement.

"How can I defend Gath without my men?" Akish asked, astonished that they would go along with the absurd suggestion.

"Given how much danger the city may actually be in, I don't think you will find it hard," the Ekronite replied, his voice flinty.

The man thought it was a bluff, Akish realized in the short moment before six of his nine sars broke into protests, demanding to be allowed to return with their seren. Only the Rapha were silent, and Saph had that satisfied look on his face that always signaled a successful end to some plan of the three brothers.

Akish clenched his teeth. He'd been unable to find out which Seren had been contributing to the Rapha so lavishly, but now that he was looking at things right-side up, he realized that Hazzel had been right all along. Someone outside the alliance was responsible. But did Manani realize his agents were accepting foreign pay? There was no way he could know, and he had other worries right now, such as defending his city and keeping his head on his shoulders for a day or two longer.

The shouting around him became louder, and Akish realized that fights could easily break out. "Sars, silence!" he roared.

The men obeyed unwillingly. "All right, Serens," Akish said coldly, bowing to the inevitable. "Since you require my units, they will stay until I can assess the situation in Gath. But if I send for them, and they do not promptly appear, I will invite whatever raiders are at my gates to help themselves to whatever they can find north of my city, since I will not have the units to stop them.

"And after enduring the insults that have been handed out to me this day, do not assume that this threat is an empty one."

"We will not, Seren," Muwana of Ashkelon replied, bowing his head respectfully. "Please assess the situation, and let us know if we need to march south instead of east this season."

Akish left the square.

Chapter 15

"Sahrah! Sahrah, someone comes!" a guard called up to her place on the palace roof as he ran toward her.

"Is it Akish?" she asked, jumping up.

"It could be, Sahrah. They come from the north, riding fast."

Akish. Hazzel took a deep breath. Somehow she had to make her brother see that she'd done everything for the best.

"Do I look all right?" she asked Shemel distractedly.

The newly reappointed commander looked flustered. "I am hardly the one to say, Sahrah," he said, giving her a quick glance, then looking away, his face flushed. "It might be best for Seren Akish to see you just as you are, however."

"Yes, that way he can see the strain we've been under. Come along, Shemel, I feel the need of an attendant, and that maid of mine has vanished as she always does whenever I need her. I wish I could discover a way of making her vanish when she's a nuisance and I send her away and can't figure out where to go myself."

"Yes, Sahrah," Shemel said, hopelessly confused.

After leading the way to the north gate, she watched the approaching men, the mules racing at full speed. She did notice that Akish pulled up at a discreet distance from the city and sent out scouts before making a dash toward the gates. He didn't have very many men with him, she noticed. Was that good or bad? Well, it was too late to wonder about it now.

"Open the gates," she called down to the guard. "Seren Akish is coming."

The single sentry struggled with the heavy mechanism for lifting the bar, and Shemel went to help him, the sahrah following him down the stairs.

She stood to one side as the gates creaked open, and Akish and his bodyguard swept into the open square, reining in their mules. He looked around at the emptiness of the market.

"Where is everyone?" he asked, catching sight of her.

"Waiting on the south side of town, where the danger is, of course," she snapped, impatient with his question. "Come on, you've taken so long to get here that we could have been overwhelmed three times by now. I just hope that boy of mine has managed to keep things under control so that we have panic in the streets and make it harder for however many are out there to see that we're helpless in here once they get past the walls!

"Well, are you coming?" she ended, glancing back as she started up the stairs to the walls again.

For once, her brother didn't say anything but just strode toward her, walking so fast that she soon had to trot to keep up with him as they circled the walls toward the south side of town.

"You did mention your son, didn't you?" he asked halfway there.

"Ittai did a marvelous job of handling things," Hazzel replied proudly. "All he needed was a little help with the riffraff of the town."

"And just what has that idiot of Goliath's done?" Akish demanded savagely, halting.

"I killed him, of course! You didn't think I'd let this end any other way, did you? After the way I had to talk to him when he found me," Hazzel panted.

Akish halted abruptly. "*You* killed him?"

"Akish, that's not important now," she said impatiently. "You've got to get out there and talk to the man. He's been waiting for days now, Ittai says, and he might be annoyed. After all he's done, you want him annoyed. At least, you'd better not," she ended. "Can we go now?"

Akish opened his mouth, then shut it again, and hurried toward the south wall once more. He had just rounded the corner at the southeast tower, when Ittai heard them coming and turned to see them.

Akish stopped in his tracks, and Hazzel nearly ran him down. "Ribbai!" he gasped, wiping a hand across his eyes.

"Yes, he does look like him, doesn't he?" his sister said with satisfaction.

Stunned, Akish watched as the well-knit warrior walked gracefully forward and stopped in front of him.

"Shalom, Dodi. It's been a very long time."

"Ittai?" Akish said, reaching out to touch him. "You're tall," he murmured, realizing that he had to look up to see his nephew's face.

"Benjamites can be that way," Ittai said with a smile.

Without a word, Akish embraced his nephew, hanging on tightly, until he had to wipe the tears from his eyes. "When did you come?"

"I met Immi in the almond grove yesterday in the late afternoon. Things have been busy since then. How many men came with you?"

"Just my personal bodyguard. The serens in Ekron wouldn't let the military units leave."

"It's as bad as that?"

"It was nearly worse. Who is out there on the hillside?"

"Dahveed Israel."

Akish froze. "Is he attacking us?"

"No, but unfortunately some assumptions were made on that score which resulted in a battle this morning."

"Who was responsible for that?" Akish said between clenched teeth.

"Well, it was the only way I could do it, you see," Hazzel said. "You didn't expect me to pass up an opportunity like this, did you?"

In despair, Akish looked at Ittai. "Do you know what she's talking about?"

"About half of it," his nephew replied, telling him what he knew.

"That six-toed idiot is dead?" Akish sputtered.

"Killed during the battle. And since he had nearly all his cronies with him out there, they are either dead or captive to Dahveed. I've already passed sentence of slavery on them. Dahveed should gain considerably from their sale."

Akish looked relieved. "So he's not in a complete rage."

"He's not in a rage at all. Once he understood that the skirmish this morning involved Sahrah Hazzel, he decided it would be impossible to understand and dropped the subject. All he wants is to talk to you, which is why he sent me here in the first place."

"Is that Dahveed coming now?" Akish asked, seeing the party of three men approaching a midpoint between the trees and the walls.

"Yes."

"How does he know Akish is here?" Hazzel asked curiously.

"Hanan told him. He reported to me today, and left the market as soon as I greeted you."

"He was inside the walls?" Akish asked sharply.

"Yes. It really is true, Dodi, that there is a back door into every city, and the Habiru know them all."

"See, I knew it was best to keep him busy outside the walls!" Hazzel said triumphantly.

Akish swore.

As Seren Akish headed out the city gates accompanied by Ittai and Shemel, he tried to control his savage mood. Nearly everything that had happened today had left him in ever deeper trouble. And the events at Gath were no exception. If the city had truly been under attack, the situation would have been different, but now his position with the other serens would sink like a millstone in the Great Sea. He was going to have to discipline everyone involved, and the fact that one victim had been related to Ishvi-benob meant he'd have to be severe and public.

"Shalom, Sar," Akish greeted the Dahveed, who bowed slightly when he arrived. "That is the correct title, is it not?"

"It is," he replied, smiling. "Shalom to you, Seren. I trust your family is well?"

"And very pleased with themselves," Akish said sourly. "And yours?"

"Relieved that the small altercation this morning did not escalate into something more. I trust their feelings are warranted."

"They are," the seren replied, relaxing a little. "My nephew has said you came here to speak with me."

"My covenant son is correct," Dahveed replied, glancing at Ittai, amusement in his eyes. "I wished to present my petition to you in person, Seren, so I would request an audience with you at your convenience."

As Akish stroked his chin he wondered how much he should tell this man. But then, he probably knew everything already, given how close he and Ittai seemed to be. "I find myself enmeshed in difficulties, Sar. I'm sure you know something of the political situation in the Five Cities these days."

"Yes. Those slaves Ittai gave me are free with information. From what they have said, you may find yourself under attack by the other four cities by dawn."

"Or else in chains," Akish added grimly, "so I've had enough surprises to last me for some time. I wish to know, then, what you will request at the audience tomorrow morning at the third hour."

"I want to shelter under your wings, both myself and my people, for I dare not remain within Judah. The people there do not deserve what Shaul would bring upon them because of me."

The simple directness of the request took Akish aback. It had been a long time since anyone had been this forthright with him. Since the last time this man had come to him with a request, in fact.

"You ask a great deal," Akish sighed.

"No more than last time. I am still bound to you by my oath of military service, given when I joined your professional force. Although you drove me from your throne room, you did not release me from my oath."

For a moment, Akish didn't know what to say. Then possibilities began to present themselves to his thoughts. "How many tents are on that hill?"

"Twelve, on the hill," Dahveed replied, looking at him steadily.

That meant anywhere from 10 to 15 warriors, Akish estimated. And if that many men had brought down that insufferable giant and 20 of his friends, they were good fighters. He could use such a force.

"Come tomorrow," he said, snapping out of his reverie. "Present your petition, and I will grant it. I will have to think of where I will want you to serve."

The Dahveed bowed again, a little deeper than before. "You are gracious to me, Sereni."

Akish acknowledged the homage and left, his mind already busy with a thousand things. He needed to think, for the situation had altered again. But Hazzel waited on the walls, and he knew he wouldn't get the time he wanted.

She met him in the market square. "Well? What did he say? He must have wanted something!"

"He wants to present a petition." Then he turned to the unit's assistant commander. "Let the Habiru dahveed in when he comes in the morning."

"Yes, adon." The officer bowed.

"You're going to let him in? Do you think that's wise?" Hazzel began.

"Yes, I'm going to let him in," Akish said, his temper rising again. "But right now, I need to talk to you." Shaking his head, he looked her over. "And you need to make yourself presentable, at least." Then taking her arm, he hurried her toward the nearest palace door.

"Presentable?" Hazzel said indignantly. "I'll have you know, Akish, I didn't have much time to comb my hair this morning, what with invasions, and armed men causing panic in the streets, and being left with nothing but my wits to defend myself and the town! After the way I've cleaned your city for you, I can't believe that you'd fuss about whether all the tangles are out of my hair!"

"I wish all I was concerned about was your hair," Akish said savagely, hurrying her down the passage. "Do you know what you've done?"

"I got rid of another one of Goliath's nasty relatives, and didn't lose a single man doing it," she flared at him. "So don't you dare mention my hair! I've been handling a lot of trouble today!"

Akish opened the door to his sister's outer chamber and went in, Hazzel slamming it behind them. He turned on her. "I'm well aware you've been handling a lot of trouble, sister mine! You've got three bracelets on top of each other on your left arm, four rings crammed onto one finger on your left hand, and nothing whatever matching them on your right. Your necklace is on backwards with two more tangled in it and hanging down past your waist, and your earrings are as different as night and day! As soon as I saw you, I knew you'd been doing things again!

"But do you have any idea what the death of that sar is going to mean? He's got three brothers bigger than he was whom I can barely command now! They will be completely unmanageable after this! And dragging me from that meeting with the news that Gath was under attack, when it wasn't, just may be the final nail in my coffin! The Serens were planning on accusing me of treason as it was!"

Defiantly she folded her arms. "And if you had left adequate guards here instead of leaving me to the tender mercies of that huge dog, his precious life would probably still be his! Or would you rather he had raped me in your own house? And if that *had* happened, tell me, just what would you have done? Caved in to those disgusting bullies once again? You might as well bring them back here, seat them on your throne, and crawl to their feet begging to be allowed to leave the city!" she finished, tears streaming down her face.

Akish stiffened. "He tried to rape you?" he asked in a deadly voice.

"He cornered me in a passage in the palace. I've told you before how he looks at me! But you never listen, Akish! I had to get him thinking about something else, and there were those armed men outside the city! I told him all kinds of things, and promised him more if he would just s-save the city, and—and—" She was sobbing too hard to continue.

"Hazzel, Hazzel, don't cry," Akish said, holding her close. "I didn't know."

"You would if you listened!" she choked out, crying harder.

"I know," he admitted. "But you say things back to front and forget that not everyone knows what you do, so most of what you say doesn't make sense."

"I make perfect sense!" she raged.

"Only after you've explained what's going on in your own head!" he replied, hugging her tighter. "And now that you've done that, I agree, you had to get rid of that man, and you did a brilliant job."

"And I c-cleaned up the t-town while I did," she stammered.

"Yes, and did something I couldn't have done for myself the way things are now. Calm down a little and tell me everything."

Wiping her face on the ends of her girdle, his sister finally gave him the complete story of what had happened.

"It looks as if I need to talk to Ittai, also," Akish decided, going to the door to summon a servant.

But Ittai waited in the hall. "I thought you might need to see me," he said soberly when his uncle invited him inside. Once he'd heard Ittai's side of things, Akish sat down on the nearest three-legged stool. "The only good thing about this is that you pronounced a formal sentence. The rest of it is a disaster; nothing else!"

"But we—" Hazzel began.

Akish raised his hand. "I know. There wasn't anything else either of you could have done. That's not the point. The point is that one of my sars was knowingly sent to his death by a sahrah, another sar defied my orders, and explaining all that by making an accusation against a dead man will only make things worse. If I return to Ekron without an acceptable response to what happened today, we die."

"What can we do?" she asked, subdued for once.

"Shemel must be executed," Akish replied.

"Shemel?" Hazzel gasped. "But he's the only trustworthy man left in this town! You can't possibly do that!"

"I dare not do anything else!" Akish said savagely. "His defiance of me has to be punished! The other sars have to know that I will not tolerate the unnecessary death of their fellows! They are close to mutiny now over how often Manani wasted their lives in the highlands.

In addition, the other four cities have to know that I can rule my own house. So I will have to discipline you as well, Hazzel."

"You can't betray Shemel like this!" Hazzel shouted, her eyes blazing. "If he hadn't helped me, those criminals would be in this city ready to do anything those three vultures left by Goliath told them to!"

"Dodi," Ittai interrupted.

"He defied me, Hazzel," Akish replied, his face wan. "I don't like it any better than you do."

"Then don't do it!"

"Hazzel, if I don't, we die!"

"Dodi," Ittai said again.

"Then we die!" she said defiantly. "He stood there and would have fought that entire unit for me. I won't leave him hanging now! If you kill him, you're going to have to kill me, because I won't live if our house is this devoid of honor!"

"Hazzel, don't do this to me," her brother pleaded. "You don't know what you're saying!"

"Dodi, if you would—"

"I know exactly what I'm saying," she blazed. "I always thought you were different from our abbi! I thought you would never betray a man like Abbi did Ribbai! If you do this, if you betray the one man that means anything at all to me, I'll rot in Sheol beside him, if that's the only way I can stand with him!"

Akish stared at her. "Hazzel, I've got too much to handle now. Don't be this unreasonable. Don't tell me he means something to you!"

"He means a great deal to me," she snapped, then stopped, a surprised look on her face. "He really does!" she said in wonder. "I'd never noticed it before, until just recently with everything so upset. He's always been the one to attend me when I went out, and— Don't you *dare* touch him! I'll not lose him like I lost Ribbai!"

The ruler of Gath groaned. "You won't have—" Then as a waving sword appeared between him and his sister, he stepped back in astonishment.

"Ittai, what are you doing?" Hazzel asked, irritated.

"Getting your attention. I know some other ways, but I doubt you'd like them."

"I'm not sure I like this one," Akish replied, eyeing the sword as his nephew returned it to its sheath.

"We may be able to solve this problem, if I may offer a suggestion," Ittai said and proceeded to tell his dodi just what was on his mind.

"I don't like it," Hazzel commented.

"Immi, think for a moment," her son said softly. "What will happen to everyone in Gath if the other four cities turn against us?"

Hugging herself, Hazzel turned away. "All right," she agreed at last.

¥ ¥ ¥ ¥ ¥ ¥

Even after my meeting with Akish, the gates of Gath remained closed. I wondered if he was keeping us out, or the spies of the other four cities in. But the small door by the gate opened when I arrived, and Ittai waited to take me to the throne room.

"Any advice?" I asked as we proceeded to the palace.

"Go along with whatever happens and maybe we can all keep from being scalded," he said under his breath.

Akish was in the throne room when I arrived, and Ittai left me with several others waiting their turn to be called. He gave my name to the scribe as he returned to his dodi's side.

To my surprise, the scribe immediately called out, "The Habiru dahveed to present a petition before Seren Akish, ruler of Gath."

I walked forward and touched one knee to the ground.

"What is your petition?" Akish asked

"I would request permission to shelter myself and my band under your wings, Seren. We have been driven from the highlands, and the women and little ones with us cannot bear the harshness of the Negev to the south."

"What can you give in return for my protection?" he continued formally.

"Seren, I would serve you as warrior and command my men after me," I replied, and bowed my head, waiting.

The seren thought a moment, leaving me kneeling in front of him.

"I would not have women and children suffer when I can shelter them," he said at last. "You may remain within my borders. But in return, I shall expect you to control your people so that there is no trouble from them."

"It shall be as you wish, Sereni. You are gracious to us."

"Stand to the side. I may have need of you in a moment."

Bowing again, I stood, then backing a few steps before moving off to the side, wondering what would happen next.

"Seren, a messenger from Ziklag," a scribe announced, and a man came forward, obviously just in from the roads. "The elders of Ziklag send to you again, Sereni," he began, bowing. "They beg for your indulgence and plead with you to send to them—"

"The elders of Ziklag presume a great deal in sending to me after their past actions! I will deal with you later!" Akish said, his voice hard. He motioned to one of the guards, who took the man into custody and escorted him from the room. As the courier went by, I saw the surprise on the man's face change to bitterness, and his posture slumped in defeat.

"Sar Shemel ben Elnaam, Seren Akish calls you before him," the scribe intoned.

The unit commander went forward and knelt. "I am here, Sereni."

"I have heard of all that you did yesterday, sar," Akish began, his face wooden. "Hazzel bat Maoch Sahrah Gath reported to me, Seren Ittai also spoke, and you gave me your report last evening as well."

"Yes, Sereni," Shemel said, a wary look in his eyes.

"I have found little to commend in these reports, and much to condemn," Gath's ruler went on. "I cannot pass over your actions in ordering your unit to disobey what you knew were my express wishes, endangering citizens of the town left outside the gates when under attack."

Shemel's head jerked up, and he stared a moment in astonishment at his adon's hard face before his own drained of all color. "Yes, Sereni," he said in a toneless voice.

"For this, you are worthy of death. However, as I said, Seren Ittai has also spoken to me, reminding me that Sahrah Hazzel, the highest authority in Gath at the time, commanded her son, Seren Ittai, and he commanded you. For this, you will keep your life. But you are stripped of command, dismissed from the army, and sentenced to become a slave."

I jerked my head up, staring at Ittai. His fingers formed themselves into the sign that all was well, although he didn't look at me.

"Guard, bind him."

The soldier obeyed, the former commander too numb from the blow to resist as he was stripped of his weapons and clothing down to his loincloth and then bound.

"Habiru?" Akish said.

I stepped forward, "Yes, Sereni?"

"This slave will be in your hand until such time as I deem it otherwise."

"Yes, Sereni," I replied, my jaw clenching.

Shemel raised his head. "Seren, I have served you faithfully for years. Such 'hesed' as you give me today is beyond belief!" he said bitterly.

"You know nothing of my hesed," Gath's ruler said impassively. "Had not Seren Ittai spoken for you, you would be dead."

"I will try to be grateful," Shemel said in a low voice. "I also hope that all my years of service to you will garner me one thing at least. Does Sahrah Hazzel know of this sentence?"

"Sahrah Hazzel has been banished from Gath," Akish answered coldly. He turned to me. "Take him, and get yourself gone from my presence!"

"Yes, Sereni," I said, keeping myself tightly under control.

The noon rest was nearly over when Ahiam came to my tent. "Dahveed, I think you need to talk to Jonathan ben Shammah."

I found my nephew just beyond the camp, sitting alone under an elm, staring down at his hands. I sat down beside him and leaned against the tree without saying anything.

"I've never killed anyone before. It wasn't like I expected," he said at last.

"Whom did you kill?"

"The commander. The big one. Uriah shouted for an archer, and I'm good with a bow. He sent me up a tree right at the edge of the field and told me just what to do. The shalish kept the commander in my line of shot, and then he yelled and looked down, and I shot. He fell."

"When someone comes at you, you have to fight."

"I know, but it shouldn't be that easy. It's harder to kill a deer for the table than it was to strike down that man."

"Do you think the men in the shalish battling him would agree that it was easy?"

"No," Jonathan said, stirring a little beside me. "They were fighting as hard as they could."

"And it still wasn't enough. It took six of us to bring him down. Uriah, the shalish, the man who slung the stone that distracted him, and you with your bow. Whatever it was, it wasn't easy."

"Do you like fighting, Dodi?" he asked in a low voice.

"No, Jonathan, but I am good at it, and right now, it is the way we survive. Someday, when I no longer have to go out and face another battle, I want to have a house with a grape arbor in the courtyard, enough Tekoa figs so that I can eat them every day if I want to, and a flock of two breeds of sheep so I can mix them up and see what comes of it."

The young man grinned a little. "It sounds good except for the sheep. And there should be an almond tree in the courtyard, and some mules to ride."

We sat a while longer in silence, then I stood. "You have a decision to make, Jonathan. You have had a taste of our life. You have to decide whether or not you wish to share it. Your abbi can certainly use you at home, so returning to him will be a good thing, and I will be as pleased to have you return as I will be to have you stay."

He looked at me. "Thank you, Dodi."

Chapter 16

Back at camp, I'd barely reached my tent on the hillside when Pekah appeared. "Adoni, the ruler of Gath is on his way here. "Geber Ira is on sentry duty, and he says he's approaching the hill."

"Tell Shagay and Abishai that I will need them to side me."

While Pekah ran off, I stripped off my kilt and shirt, wondering if I should put on clean ones or a robe.

"A shirt and kilt again, I think," Ahinoam said from the entrance. "He's not dressed formally."

"That's good to know." She unbound my hair and combed it quickly, making me grimace, then settled on the silver headband that I'd worn to court that morning. Buckling on the sword and giving her a hasty kiss, I hurried down to the cleared area below the tents. Abishai appeared, but instead of Shagay, Ahinoam accompanied him.

We stood together as the Philistine ruler rode up with his escort of three men and Ittai.

Seeing us, he dismounted and came forward with just his nephew.

We went to meet him. "Welcome to our camp, Seren," Ahinoam said graciously, bowing.

Looking surprised, Akish nodded in reply.

"Sereni, may I present my wife, Ahinoam bat Ahlai," I said.

"Your welcome to me is very warm, baalah," he greeted her.

While Ahinoam replied, Ittai spoke quietly. "Where is Shemel?"

"Still bound in one of the other tents. He wasn't in any mood to be reasonable."

"Dodi is actually here to see him."

"Tell him to be careful."

My covenant son nodded.

"Dahveed, I am here to review your men," Akish said, turning to me. "I wanted to assess what you have to offer me."

"All of them?" I asked, keeping my voice even. "It might take a little for them to gather. They are somewhat scattered now."

Akish glanced around at the dozen tents in sight. "Yes, I think all of them."

"Abishai, please tell Uriah to assemble the men for review," I told him, then turned back to Akish. "May we offer you hospitality while we wait?" I stepped aside for him to precede us up to my tent, which was in plain view of his escort.

Keturah and Pekah waited on us, providing some bread, raisins, and a little wine.

Before long, Abishai returned. "The men are ready, adoni. Uriah assembled them up in the clearing behind the hill. Seren Akish can see them from the crest there," he pointed above us.

"Very good, Abishai." I stood. "Sereni? If you will come? I hope they are all here," I said while we walked to the top. "Some may be out hunting."

"I'm sure the ones here will give me a good idea of your warriors."

"There they are, Sereni," I announced, as we got to the top.

He looked down into the sizeable clearing and gasped, leaning on the sycamore next to him to stay standing. The clearing was filled with unit after unit of my men, and line after ragged line of tents crowded the area surrounding them.

"I apologize," I said, noticing the empty spaces in about five units. "I see that not all of them have been able to gather in time."

"Dahveed! That's an army down there!" he gasped.

"Yes, Sereni. What would you like me to do with it?"

"Do with it?" he echoed, turning his astounded gaze on me.

I kept my amusement off my face. I'd rather thought Akish hadn't the least idea what he had acquired when he accepted my service.

The seren turned to his nephew. "Ittai, why didn't you tell me?" he hissed between clenched teeth.

"We have had several other things taking our attention, Dodi. And Dahveed can be discreet."

"If I may speak, Sereni?" I asked, knowing full well that he dared not have so many warriors remain in Gath for any number of political reasons, as well as the fact that the city would strain its resources to feed and support all the families that went with them.

"Please do," Akish said, facing me.

"It would be easier if we did not have to stay in Gath. We would not want to cause unnecessary trouble here. Surely there is some town within your borders where we can settle. If you would favor us to the extent of granting us such a place, we will be grateful."

Akish looked from Ittai to me and back. "I suppose you both planned this entire situation."

"No, Sereni. But we both had a fairly good idea that this many people could not remain long in Gath," I explained.

The Philistine ruler glanced at his nephew. "And you had an idea about it?"

"Since this morning, the thought of Ziklag did cross my mind."

"I don't even want to think of them! If they had sent the men required of them, I could have left more than one unit here, and probably avoided this entire mess!" Akish growled. "And I won't be able to attend to them until—" He stopped, seeing the expectant look on Ittai's face.

Then he looked thoughtful for a moment and one hand went to his chin, before he turned to me. "Ziklag it is. Since the people there failed in their duties to me, I am giving you the town as a military grant for your service. The documents will be delivered to you by this evening."

"You have favored me, indeed," I managed to say. A military grant, by its very nature, was irrevocable. I now personally owned an entire town in the middle of Philistia that would remain in my family as long as someone of my blood lived. What an entry this would make in Gad's chronicle!

"You may not think so for long," the seren commented. "I will expect the taxes to be brought up to date and paid promptly thereafter."

"I will do what I can, Sereni."

"Shall we go, Ittai?"

"There is still the matter of Shemel, Dodi."

"Yes, and I dare not forget that!" his uncle sighed.

"Shall I have him brought?" I offered.

"No, I will go to him. Ittai, bring the things from the mules, and try to be certain those escorts of mine don't get curious. The last thing I need is for this to become public!" he said, gesturing to my men, still assembled below.

"I will send someone to take them food and remain with them. If you will follow me, Sereni." I started down the hill toward the waiting military units.

"Who is that?" Akish asked as we wandered through my men.

"Uzzia," I replied, after seeing Akish staring at the tall northerner. "He's from around Geshur."

"That would be Bashan?"

"Yes, Sereni."

"Has he left your band for any reason lately?"

"No."

Akish considered. "Keep him in Ziklag and points south. If he is seen around here, he will probably be killed. He's too tall."

"As you wish, Sereni," I said, puzzled.

By the time we arrived at the tent where I'd left Shemel, Gath's seren was looking even more thoughtful, and I wished I had an idea of what was brewing in his mind. Something certainly was. But he brought himself back to the present, however, as Shammah and Elika, my men from the springs near Gilboa, brought the Philistine captive outside.

Shemel saw Akish, and his face blanked out instantly as he stared off into nothing.

Without a word, Ittai knelt to the commander and bowed to the ground, remaining there in the silence. Shemel stood it as long as he could, then cast a wary, questioning glance at Akish.

"My house bows to you, Shemel ben Elnaam," Akish said. "I would do it myself, but I am forbidden by protocol from such an act. I am here because you saved my sister, Sahrah Hazzel, from more than you know yesterday morning. She made certain I understood that. I am here to tell you why I have acted as I did, if you are inclined to listen." Bowing his head, he waited.

Shemel let the silence drag. "Stand up, Seren," he said at last.

Ittai rose, and the sar turned to Akish. "I don't think you need to tell me much. I understand the political implications of the commander's death. But your position with the other four cities must be worse than I thought."

"It is. I am fighting to keep the alliance from destroying Gath itself. If it matters to you, it was only that reality that made my sister agree to treat you like this."

The bound man lowered his eyes. "It matters," he said roughly as Ittai cut the bonds with his belt knife. The bundle Ittai had brought contained two changes of clothing, one a warrior's dress, and the other an adon's robe. Gath's ruler watched while Ittai dressed Shemel and returned his weapons, then stepped back.

"Dahveed, I gave this man to you until such time as I deemed it right to withdraw him. I am doing so now. He is no longer a slave."

"As you wish, Sereni," I said, bowing.

"Am I restored to my command?" Shemel inquired.

"Unfortunately, that I cannot do. But since you have served me honorably and well, I wish to reward you before you leave. I'm sure you will find this useful," he said as Ittai opened up a bundle of glittering jewelry and placed it on the ground by the freed man.

"And I hope you will accept this," Akish continued, holding out a document. "I also hope that Hazzel remembered the name of the town correctly. It is Bethel-yad, isn't it?"

"Yes, Sereni. That's my hometown. My family is there." He accepted the document. "I don't read. What exactly is this?"

"Title to an estate which has just come to me through the death of the owner with no heirs. It's a large one, on the northwest side of the town."

Surprise swept across Shemel's face. "That's the largest estate in the area! The local adon lives there."

"Which would now be you."

"Sereni, I don't need something like that!"

"That depends, adon. There was something else my sister made quite clear to me yesterday. She told me she would never return to Gath again if I carried through this part of the bargain. I believe she meant she wouldn't return if I *didn't* carry it through."

"She really is banished, then?"

"Yes. And it will have to be for a considerable length of time." Akish looked down. "I love my sister a great deal, Shemel, and I would not have her remain alone. She made it very plain that the only man she would accept was you. I need to know if you are willing to take my sister as your wife. If not, I will have to arrange something else."

Shemel's jaw had dropped, but Akish didn't see it. The seren was fighting not to shed tears at the moment.

"Marry her? I mean—I never thought—well, I did, but there was no point, and—she wants me?"

"Yes," Gath's ruler said roughly, able to raise his head again.

"Well, I—I, Sereni, do you know what you are doing? As husband to Sahrah Hazzel, I become heir to Gath's throne!"

"You do," Ittai agreed, smiling. "And when you have children, they will come after you."

"But what about you?"

"Adon, the rulers of the Five Cities would never consent to have an Israelite half-blood governing Gath. They will, however, accept you or your sons," he pointed out calmly.

"Just where is Sahrah Hazzel?"

"On her way to Gerar, where she will wait until she hears from you. I'm not certain what state you will find her in. She may be wearing her jewelry back-to-front again," Akish replied, his voice filled with both laughter and frustration.

Shemel shrugged. "I rather thought that necklace looked better that way anyway."

"It did," Ittai agreed. "But the mismatched earrings were definitely lopsided."

"Seren?" Shemel said, looking beseechingly at him.

"Marry my immi, Shemel. She will be happy with you, and it might be interesting to have three abbis."

The Philistine hesitantly reached down and picked up the adon's robe, holding it out. "Do you think it will fit?"

"I'm sure it will, adon," Akish replied.

As Akish promised, the documents irrevocably granting me Ziklag arrived by mid-afternoon. Ittai brought them and told me that his dodi wanted to see me privately that night.

"How privately?" I inquired.

"He'd prefer if no one at all knew. Especially no one in Gath. As you may have guessed, the place is riddled with spies."

"Tell him I'll come to the same chamber I first met him in."

"That will be perfect."

Just before sunset, I entered the north gate of Gath, dressed as a poor laborer carrying a heavy load on my back, and disappeared into the maze of streets and alleys that made up the poorer section of town. During the evening meal, I made my way to the palace square where Ittai waited to open the same alley door. Since it contained all his things, he took the pack, having decided to remain here.

I settled myself in the small chamber where I'd first met Akish all those years ago. When I heard him coming, I stepped into the shadows to one side. I was glad I had, for a servant followed him into the room, fussing around in a way that said he was determined not to leave if he could help it.

"I said that would be all," the seren announced in a cold voice. When the man still hesitated, he added, "I trust I don't have to beat out of you which particular party is paying you to report, do I?"

"No, Seren," the man stammered, edging toward the door.

"Good. Since you have already noticed that there is no one in this room, and if you station yourself at the end of the passage, you will also be able to determine that no one could get in here to speak with me, your masters should be satisfied, correct?"

"Yes, I mean no, I mean, I—"

"Get out!"

The man hastily fled, and Akish made sure the door was securely closed. When he turned back to the table, I was sitting on a stool beside it. His dagger appeared in his hand nearly too fast for me to see his hand move.

"You're as quick as Shaul is with that," I commented.

He shoved the dagger back where it belonged. "You are not an easy person to deal with, do you know that?" he said irritably.

"I'm also still here to be dealt with. What did you want to discuss, Sereni?"

"I want you to know the other reason I've sent you to Ziklag. You know where it is?"

"Just east of Gerar, I believe, about 25 miles south of here, and therefore close to your southern border.

"It is the southern border. And once you are in the town, I don't want any more raids into Gath's territory from those pestilential desert tribes. But there's a hitch. Ittai said one of the escorts I took with me recognized you. Sooner or later, it will come out who you are, and the only thing that will convince the other Serens that you have come over to us is if you raid in Judah."

I just looked at him.

He raised his hand placatingly. "I know, Dahveed. You won't fight Yahweh. But somehow we have to convince the others that you are. That's another reason I sent you so far away. It will be easier for the others to tolerate your presence, and the number of spies hanging around will be greatly reduced."

"Just how badly are you surrounded with spies?"

"Let's just say that I doubt there's a single person in this palace who doesn't report to someone."

"And you have your sources in the other cities also?"

A smile briefly touched his lips.

"Maybe we shouldn't waste all that effort, then. If I show up with spoils and report to you where I got them, is it likely that any of them will trot along after me to check out my truthfulness?"

Akish's eyes gleamed. "Highly unlikely." Once again his gaze turned inward for a moment and he stroked his beard. "They already think I'm a dolt, and when I have to return tomorrow and report, they will be surer of it. But if, by some twist of favor from the gods, I manage to reduce the number of raids, they will let me remain, and possibly will even stop watching me so closely."

"How much of the spoils do you claim?"

"A tenth. You, personally, get to keep two tenths. The rest is yours to distribute or keep as you see fit."

"Do you prefer animals or valuables?"

The seren shrugged. "Valuables are easier to transport, but animals are fine if that's all there was worth sending."

"I'll remember. What's wrong in Ziklag?"

"Dagon only knows!" Akish said bitterly. "That courier who arrived yesterday can no longer be found. I charged the town with guarding the southern border two years ago, and I've heard nothing from them since. Messages go unanswered, they send none, and the raids only get worse. This year and last, they have failed to send their conscription quota for the war season. I wouldn't mind if they would at least guard the roads, but they aren't."

"I'll look into the situation, Sereni."

I arrived back at camp to be greeted by Abishai and Eliam, Ahibaal's son, whom I had accepted into my band as requested. "What is it?"

"I just received this message from my abbi," the young man said, holding it out. "He said it was urgent."

Taking it over by the fire, I added some smaller sticks so that the flames increased enough to see. I'd only read a line or two when I looked up at Eliam. "You're dismissed."

A slight bow and he left.

I finished reading the entire message, then stared into the fire. This could be trouble. On the other hand, it could be nothing at all. *What shall I do, Yah?* I asked silently. "Abishai, has there been any news of Philistines traveling into the highlands?"

"Not that I've heard, Dodi."

Then what was a Philistine emissary doing talking to the nagids of Caleb? "Abishai, I've got to go to Hebron. I may be gone three or four days." From the back of my girdle, I pulled the pouch that contained the band's treasury. "Here, use whatever you need of this to stock up on supplies. Tomorrow, send the families camped over the hill a day's journey south. These tents here need to stay in sight of Gath. As soon as I return, we'll be heading south also. Send Hanan after me if you see him."

"Yes, Dodi."

I dropped the papyrus into the fire and watched it burn before I headed east into the highlands again.

¥ ¥ ¥ ¥ ¥ ¥

As he rode into the gates of Ekron the next morning, Akish certainly hoped the Dahveed would look into things. He needed something good to happen, because once he reported to the other serens today, he'd be lucky to keep his head, let alone his throne. He just needed a little time, and he'd likely have to beg for that.

His arrival in the square where the serens had gathered caused a stir. Gadmilk of Ashdod looked annoyed, but Muwana of Ashkelon studied him carefully. Briefly, Akish wondered which of the spies in Gath's palace had reported to him.

As before, Hanabaal raised his hands to quiet the crowd, the hush quickly spreading to the sars standing around the outside of the square. The ruler of Gaza turned to Akish. "Since you have returned safely, I assume that nothing has happened at Gath since you left us day before yesterday."

"Quite a lot has happened, Seren," Akish replied with a tired smile. "It took considerable effort to sort everything out." He noticed the subdued smiles that crossed most faces at his veiled reference to Hazzel. "To be brief, the assumption was made that the armed company of Habiru who appeared outside the walls threatened the city. Before it could be determined what they wanted, a battle did occur outside the gates, resulting, I regret to say, in the death of the sar I had left in charge of the unit protecting the city."

The three Rapha brothers looked stunned. "Dead?" Lahmi gasped.

Akish bowed his head slightly. "Regretfully. I have dealt with the situation, of course. Since Sahrah Hazzel ordered the attack, I have sent her from my house. The sar who aided her was enslaved. I did not execute him since it was plain he was obeying the commands of the highest authority left in Gath, Hazzel bat Maoch." The fact that he did not give Hazzel a title was not lost on the group in the square, and a little murmur arose.

Then Gadmilk snorted. "This situation could have been avoided," he growled.

"Barring leaving more units in the city, and thus shorting my duty here, I don't see how it could have," Akish replied coolly. "The Habiru did not consult me before they arrived."

Muwana covered his smile with a hand, and Manani settled back in his seat, watching Akish closely. "Where are these Habiru now?" he asked.

"I have removed them as far south as possible from the Five Cities. They had been driven to my lands from the east, and they properly requested leave to stay, offering service as warriors in exchange."

"And you let them, after they killed my brother?" Ishvi-benob shouted.

All the adons turned to stare at him, and he flushed in spite of his size, subsiding a little.

"I thought I would take a lesson from King Nahash of Ammon and put them to work guarding travelers," Akish continued. "If you recall, he has had much success doing that, and if it works as well on this side of Jordan, I will have more men available for war season needs."

"How many are there?" Muwana questioned.

"There were a dozen tents on the hill in sight of the town."

"Maybe twelve warriors then?"

"That's what I estimated. I believe there are enough to make a difference. They have the skills necessary to track down the robbers who have troubled travelers so much lately."

"Provided they actually do that, and don't rob people themselves!" Gadmilk put in sourly.

"And if that happens, the problem becomes worse than before! I can't see that your decision was wise, Akish," Hanabaal fumed. "You've settled more trouble in my back courtyard with your misplaced generosity."

"Hardly that, Seren." An icy calm settled over him. The next few minutes would be crucial, and he had no idea what Manani might be planning on throwing at him. "They will be operating from Ziklag, miles to the east of you. If they are inclined to go raiding, I would expect them to head east before anywhere else. They were not pleased to leave the highlands."

"But you don't know that," Hanabaal complained.

Manani interrupted. "I'm sure that the good ruler of Gath is ready to accept full responsibility for those he has hired."

"Of course," Akish responded, bowing to the Seren. "I hereby pledge myself to keep them as hired, or I will destroy them myself."

"I want more than just promises, Akish," Hanabaal fussed. "We'll be the ones to suffer if these Habiru get out of hand."

"Then I'm sure the good ruler of Gath will be willing to give hostages," Manani put in smoothly, his eyes glittering.

Akish stiffened. Hostages? Hazzel! His mouth went dry. Manani undoubtedly had plans to make certain the sahrah would fall under his control. And what if someone here knew of Ittai's sudden return? His thoughts churned while the ruler of Ashkelon raised his voice over the ripple of discussion.

"Are you not being a little unreasonable, Manani? Such a thing has never been done before in the Five Cities! Gath has done nothing to warrant such a contingency," Muwana said, angered at the demand.

Akish watched the seren from Ashkelon. It looked as if the man had thrown him a lifeline, if he could just figure out how to use it. He'd owe Muwana for this, but given the level-headedness of the ruler, that might not be a bad thing. Hanabaal of Gaza was afraid of anything that came from the desert, but was one of the best when it came to sea trading. Gadmilk constantly stuck his nose where it didn't belong, stirring up more trouble among the serens than anyone else. Something ticked in his mind at that thought, but he didn't have time to pull it back and examine it.

"And where would such hostages stay?" Muwana added.

"In Gaza," Hanabaal said instantly.

"It should be neutral ground," Gadmilk asserted. "Ashdod is furthest from both Gaza and Gath, and would be the safest place."

"I don't agree," Manani said pleasantly. "Muwana has a point. This would be something quite harsh, and as the ruler of Ashdod has pointed out, it would be paramount to keep the hostages safe and make the situation as lenient as possible. Ekron is less than seven miles from Gath and thus is neutral ground in this situation. I'm sure the seren would agree that it is the best place for any hostages."

Akish felt the chill of those eyes on him as the Ekronite faced him. He'd been right; Manani wanted charge of whomever he had to send, and if everything he guessed about the man was correct, he planned on having Hazzel. And the way that gaze was boring into him, he knew Manani expected that he would have no choice but to agree. Sweat broke out on his forehead. Did that mean the seren was gambling on the tax authorization to control him? Was now the time to defy his enemy? What if he tried and failed? What would happen to Hazzel then? Before he let Manani have her, he would send her to Dahveed.

"Yahweh, protect her," he barely whispered, looking down. The unspoken plea had barely left his lips when the answer to his dilemma flashed through his mind. Although he trembled inside at the risk, he had no choice. If Manani had held anything back, if Muwana was not as upset as he seemed, or if his men had talked about Ittai's return despite his orders, Gath would die. He realized the square had subsided into silence, every eye in the place fastened on him. Trying to seem calm, he bowed to the assembly.

"I can see that sacrifices must be made to preserve the unity of the alliance for the war season," he said, keeping his eyes down. "Since further reassurance to my brother rulers is demanded, I will give it. A matter such as this, easily solved, should not interfere with the more pressing business before the serens this year."

Gadmilk nodded his head emphatically, and Hanabaal huffed in his seat, but looked Akish's way inquiringly. Manani had begun to smile a little.

"I will offer the best I have in Gath."

"I'm sure that will suffice," Muwana agreed, watching intently as everyone in the square wondered whom Akish would name.

"I will be greatly handicapped, and consequently may have to depend on your hesed, Manani, should anything happen," Akish continued, bowing deeply to the ruler of Ekron, whose eyes glowed with triumph at his words.

"My hesed is always available, if properly asked for."

"That is well known," Akish said as humbly as he could. "Since Hazzel bat Maoch is no longer in my house, I know Hanabaal will not accept her as proper surety for the security of his city." Then he glanced to the men standing behind him. "Ishvi-benob, Lahmi, and Saph, you are now to remain in Ekron as hostages to Manani." He turned back to the square. "I trust you will treat them well, Seren," he said, bowing to Manani again. "I know they will serve you as well as they have served me, and I am sure the alliance will see to it that no occasion will arise when I will have to beg for their return to fight for Gath."

For several moments the square was completely silent. Akish remained still, head bowed and his heart in his mouth, waiting to hear what would happen. If he had misjudged the Ashkelon seren, he didn't know what he would do. He nearly fainted when he heard Muwana speak.

"As you said, an affair easily settled," the man declared. "Your willingness to weaken yourself for the benefit of the other four rulers is commendable, and I'm sure it will be long remembered. Do let me know how those Habiru you hired work out. I, for one, am tired of paying ridiculous amounts of silver to the Egyptian governor in Beth-shean for the guards he supplies for the Way of the Sea. They are hardly worth the trouble of hiring, from what I've heard."

Hanabaal huffed in his seat again. "And the ones coming up from Egypt itself are hardly better. I've heard the caravans going up to Beersheba don't even bother with them anymore."

"They don't. They hire Habiru," Akish managed to say in a steady voice, refusing to look at Manani.

"Sereni," Ishvi-benob growled, looking at Gath's ruler.

"If you have something to discuss about your situation, sar, you will have to speak with your new seren, Manani," Akish said, keeping his face and voice carefully impassive while he struggled to believe that he had actually survived this situation.

Tamar bat Dahveed

The next part of unraveling the plans that the Evil One has laid will demand that Dahveed send to Jonathan Hassar one last gift, which Jonathan will accept with his usual exasperation! But Yahweh has a special reason for sending it to Israel, having carefully hidden this man from harm, guarding him all his life for just this purpose. Yah will pay His agent well, giving him more than he could ever dream that he would receive, for Yahweh is ever honorable and pays every worker for Him, whether or not he realizes for whom he is working!

It was for this man that Yah sent Israel's Hassar back to Nemuel's grave, for Jonathan could not have been trusted with him otherwise. Much hangs on human decisions, for what happens now will determine the future and fate of not just Dahveed and Israel, but of Jebus and its people as well.

Jonathan and Jebus

Chapter 17

Hanan caught up to me in the highlands. We had both traveled most of the night, and we slept for several hours at the top of the land stair. Consequently, it was late in the afternoon when we arrived at Hebron. While I checked the three inns for the mule that Ahibaal rode, Hanan went to the town well. The mule was nowhere to be found, but all the inns were full, which let me know that something unusual was happening here. When I rejoined my best scout, he informed me that the nagids were meeting at Dathan's house for the second night in a row.

Once again, the two of us attended the feast, acting as servers just as last time. Ahibaal was at the first table with Dathan and a richly dressed Philistine, older than I, who was attended by a scribe. The Jebusite recognized me as soon as he saw me carrying the huge wooden platter of dried fruit while Hanan asked the guests what they would like to have. As Hanan handed him the apricots he had chosen, Ahibaal's chin pointed quickly to the Philistine. "Remain after the feast," he said softly.

"As you wish, adon," I replied before moving on to the next table. Once the meal was over, the Philistine circulated among the tables while Dathan presented several of the principal nagids. I stayed within earshot as much as possible, and it didn't take long for me to glean that the Philistine was an envoy of some sort, and he was sounding out the nagids regarding a possible treaty with the Five Cities, one of the benefits of which would be mutual protection from the desert raiders to the south.

The situation seemed a little odd to me, since Gebirah Abigail held the vast majority of the alliances, which meant that any treaty would have to have her approval. And while the nagids might conceivably arrange for a treaty without her, the adons and householders under them would erupt at such an act.

In addition, I'd listened to enough envoys during my time in Gibeah to know that they rarely said anything definite, no matter what the subject. The fact that I had learned as much as I had just from overhearing comments as I passed by was highly unusual. I studied the envoy, whose name was Seren Patisi of Gaza. He was probably 10 to 12 years older than I, and while his clothes fit his station, he seemed to wear them oddly. A couple of his mannerisms didn't fit my picture of diplomatic behavior, but I'd never met anyone from Gaza before, so had nothing to compare them with.

It was late when Seren Patisi and his scribe left the compound, the seren stepping along carefully, for he'd had several cups of Dathan's best wine. Hanan and I helped to clear away the remains of the feast while the rest of the guests took their leave. Once they had gone, Hanan produced the food he'd acquired for us, and we ate while we waited by the gate as Ahibaal had requested.

The adon came to us at last. "I had hoped that because of the seriousness of the situation, Dahveed Israel would have come himself," he commented, nodding his head slightly in greeting. "I didn't realize you were part of his band."

I shrugged in reply. "How did the seren call the nagids together?"

"I joined him on the road from En-gedi five days ago. He was pleased that I could introduce him to Nagid Hebron, and Dathan took it from there. Now, it's important that Dahveed understand what Gaza is trying to do. This would be a pact of mutual aid and support against the desert tribes. One of the terms in the agreement would be the establishment of a permanent military outpost in Hebron."

"Why Hebron?" I interrupted. "If any real effort is made to repel the raids, that outpost needs to be much farther south."

"Of course it does," Ahibaal said impatiently. "The purpose of the treaty can't have anything to do with protection against raiders, not if Hebron is targeted. What Gaza wants is a legitimate reason to put some Philistine units in the highlands."

I caught my breath. And eventually rule Judah and then threaten Israel. A year ago, the nagids wouldn't have given this offer the time of day, since they would have counted on me to protect them. But with my self-exile to Philistia, an entirely different situation arose.

"What has the response been?"

"Several of them are listening," Ahibaal replied grimly. "Dahveed's absence leaves the south open to raiding. Have you any idea as to why he left?"

I decided to answer him. "Sooner or later, Shaul would have come to destroy him, and the south would be plunged into war. Dahveed wished to avoid that."

"But if he is to rule Israel, why wouldn't he fight?"

"When the time comes, the throne will be given to him. He will not have to take it."

"He expects the throne to be *given*?" the Jebusite asked in disbelief.

"It will be. Have you never heard the story of Jephthah of Tob? He was driven out by his brothers and became a Habiru dahveed. Then when war ravaged his people, his brothers came to him and begged him to fight for them in exchange for ruling over them. He fought against the Ammonites and won and received the rulership over his people."

Ahibaal didn't know what to say, but even in the dark I could sense his disdain. "I suppose we shall have to wait and see what actually happens," he finally commented, his voice carefully neutral. "Are you free to come with me now?"

"Yes."

"Patisi's scribe informed me that the seren would like to speak with a Habiru. You will do, so I will take you to him. He is waiting at the Corner Vintner. Do you know where that is?"

"Hanan?" I asked.

The young man started out the gate, and I followed, taking the torch by the gate with me, Ahibaal hastily following.

"Why would Gaza talk to the clans without Gebirah Carmel there?" I asked, curious.

Ahibaal snorted. "The envoy wasn't aware of the number of alliances she holds, and seemed to be expecting her to give them the pact if enough nagids wish for it."

"Have they considered Dahveed Israel's opinion of Philistines in the highlands?"

"Since he has left the highlands, he can be ignored."

It was on the tip of my tongue to remind him that Gaza couldn't have known that fact when Seren Patisi was sent out, but I decided to refrain. "Yes, I should not forget that. Seren Patisi has spoken extensively with you," I observed as we turned another corner.

"He is not very experienced, which is likely why he was sent just to the highlands. I learned whatever I wanted from him."

I didn't reply, too busy thinking about geography. Gaza was far west of us. What was Patisi doing east of the highlands on the road up from En-gedi? Every which way I looked at this, nothing made sense.

"You do see why I am concerned, and why Dahveed Israel needs to know of these developments?" Ahibaal asked, as Hanan led us along a larger street.

"Yes, adon. If the Calebite nagids are willing to consider a pact with Philistia which involves the military in any way, Dahveed Israel needs to keep close track of the situation so he can be ready to counter it if necessary."

"Very good. Be certain he understands the problems that could develop."

"I will do my best, adon," I promised as Hanan turned down a small alley and stopped before a small, dingy door.

"This cannot be the place!" Ahibaal exclaimed looking around. "We want to go to the Corner Vintner, not a soldier's dive, Habiru," he said harshly.

I bit my tongue. "Hanan is usually reliable," I commented mildly. "It will only take a moment to check inside." Before the Jebusite could say anything else, I handed the torch to my retainer and opened the door. The place was empty except for two men on a bench in a corner. Both of them appeared drunk. Then I looked again. Only one was quite drunk, our Philistine friend Patisi. The other wasn't as inebriated as he seemed.

"He is here, adon," I said, opening the door and stepping back. Reluctantly, Ahibaal entered the room, staring around in disgust. I had to smile. He was probably used to doing business at the Brass Lion in Jebus, not a dirty hole-in-the-wall such as Hebron offered.

"I believe the scribe said this place was for our exclusive use," he said to the shopkeeper. "Why is there someone else here?"

The man hurried from the counter, going to Patisi's seat-mate. "Geber, the adon I told you of has come. You will have to leave now."

"But I don' want to," the man slurred, leaning toward Patisi. "Tell th' adon to come back later."

"We can't do that," the shopkeeper said. "Let me help you, Tokhath." He expertly gripped the man's arm and pulled.

Tokhath vacated the seat with a gasp. "Careful, careful," he pleaded, still pretending to be soused. "Lemme get my legs." He let himself be escorted out the door, and the shopkeeper closed it, then disappeared into the back room, returning with two more lamps that gave better light. With a bow, he left again.

Ahibaal seated himself beside the seren, and I pulled up a stool. "Geber Patisi, I've found a Habiru as you requested."

Patisi looked up, blinking a little. "Seren. It's Seren Patisi," he said, turning his head carefully to look at me. "Are you the Habiru?"

"I think so. What did you need a Habiru for?" The smell of the man's breath said he really was drunk. Odd. Why would an envoy on a mission be so careless as to get this drunk, and in this sort of wine shop?

"To be a guide in this cursed land, because you can't see farther than the end of your arm, and only then if you're lucky!" he said petulantly.

"That's what makes it a good place to hide in," I said. "Whom did you want me to guide?"

"Eh, eh, eh!" he said, leaning toward me, wine fumes spilling from his breath. "I'm not suppose' to tell that until I know if you'll be the guide across this miserable dark forest."

"I understand that. But Patisi—"

"Seren Patisi," he interrupted. "I like my title."

"Then I will certainly use it. Seren Patisi, I am certain that I could guide you wherever you wish to go, but I need to know a few things. Just little unimportant ones that won't matter to you."

"Why?" he asked, swaying the other way, his eyes open wide.

"So that I can properly prepare. If I am to guide you safely, I must plan ahead. And that means I need to know a few things."

"Oh. Soundsh reasonable. What little things did you need me to tell?"

"How many men will I be guiding? I have to be certain we can find enough water. If it's just going to be you, there are several ways we could go. But if there will be five or six, I'll have to plan a different route. And if there will be whole units of soldiers, I need to know that, also."

Patisi considered. "There will be more than just me. There won't be me at all, if I can help it!" He hiccupped. "Let's shee," he moved his fingers, eyes wide, counting. "Theresh that many. 'N' then the adon. Very important he is! Got lotsh of special req—requi—requi'ments."

"You need me to guide one group across Judah?"

"Yesh. Maybe more. Don' know 'bout scribe. Maybe one of them. My, this ish good wine," he said, looking in his cup. "More?"

"I think you've had enough," Ahibaal announced. "Will this Habiru be satisfactory?"

Patisi regarded me owlishly. "Why wouldn't he be? As long as he can guide me to more of this good wine, he'll be very satisfactory indeed!"

"I think we can do that," I said, helping him up. "Where is he lodging?" I asked Ahibaal.

"At the inn we passed just before the corner."

I had my arm around Patisi's waist supporting him, and I felt how hard his body was. "There's no need for both of us to handle him," I said, making a sudden decision. "I'll take him to his room and see that he gets put to bed."

The adon gave me an approving glance. "Very well. I have much to do."

"Come along, Patisi," I said, guiding him away from the three-legged table.

"I'm coming. Oop, just a moment," he added, swinging around. "Theresh more of that wine," and he latched onto a jug sitting by the table.

"I'll take care of it," Ahibaal said. "Here," he added, holding out three silver pieces. "Take them for your trouble."

"Thank you, adon," I made myself say, accepting the silver.

I got my drunken companion out of the door, and we weaved down the street, the Philistine trying to sing and succeeding only in abusing my ears. Hearing us coming, the inn guard opened the gate.

"He is lodging here?" I asked.

"Yes, geber. He asked for a place to himself, so we emptied out a storeroom." The guard pointed to it.

Patisi draped himself over me. "Do we still have the wine?"

"Yes, Seren. You're holding it."

"Good. You will join me, of coursh."

"Of course," I agreed, managing to get him into the room with the guard's help. Then he gave me a crooked grin as he shut the door after himself.

Once I deposited Patisi on the bedroll, I lit a lamp.

"Come, Seren, we must get you into bed," I said.

"Oh, but why? We haven't finish the wine."

"You don't have to stop drinking to get ready for bed. You drink, and I'll do the rest."

"I like you. You have good ideash." He raised the jar to his mouth and took several gulps.

"Now tell me again, how many men are in this group I'm to guide?"

Trying to focus his eyes, he regarded me seriously. "You should lishen th' first time."

"I will try. But please tell me again."

"Sishteen, unless th' scribe comes. Then theresh one more. But not me!" He waved the wine jug enthusiastically and broke out into song again.

"Do you drink like this a lot?" I asked, untying his girdle.

"Only when I'm far 'way from, from Ek—" he hiccupped, "—Ekron! Then I get to fin' a wine shop, 'n' taste the wares, 'n' forget! This one was a s'prise!" Hefting the jug again, he started to fall back.

"No, not yet," I told him, finding it interesting that he would mention Ekron, not Gaza. Perhaps Ahibaal hadn't found out as much as he assumed. "Let me get the robe off you. Now, what about those special requirements for the important adon."

"Very strict, he wash. Must have the re—req—the whatevers."

"Requirements. What are they?"

As he held out his arms so that I could pull the robe off, I noted the scars on him.

"What will the important adon want?"

"Extra donkey," he hiccupped. "One with just oil 'n' lamps. Lotsh of lamps. Dozens!"

"Did he say dozens?" I asked, startled.

"Nooo, don't think so." Patisi thought for a moment. "He said four, 'n' some extry onesh in case one broke. Or two broke. Or they all broke. Don' know why. Maybe the scribe needsh 'em."

"Now you're settled," I said, helping him lie down. "You keep the jug, and I'll take care of everything else."

"Such nicsh ideas you have. Can you be my servant all the time?"

"I don't think that would work out well. Just enjoy it tonight."

"Good idea! You tell my scribe to pay you in the morning," he managed to say before he fell asleep.

As soon as he started snoring, I began a thorough search of the bundles and bags and loose items strewn around. I found a dispatch case first, then a pouch with clay tablets. There were two dispatches, a letter, and a list. The first was a formal introduction from Akish, ruler of Gath, for Seren Patisi to Araunah Debir of Jebus. I shook my head. Just which city was this man from, anyway?

The second dispatch was a recommendation to Debir's official for trade, stating that one Qausa the Habiru was a reliable, knowledgeable guide for caravans into the south. That gave me pause. Strange how that man refused to stay dead after Ethan had killed him years ago.

The letter was terse and looked as if it had been wrapped around something. It said to keep the brooch and deliver the letter of recommendation while Patisi was in Jebus, and since Beor had died during the war season, communications should no longer be directed to him. The list was just names. Merchants for trade, most likely.

It took me a little longer to grasp the essence of the clay tablets. It had been a long time since I'd read cuneiform, and these were not business documents, but instructions of some kind. When I spelled out that Patisi was to find a reliable guide who could be ready to take the envoy across the south to En-gedi, then Jebus, my hands began to tremble.

I looked at the drunken man sleeping on the bedroll. Not one single thing I knew so far matched with anything else. As tangled as this seemed to be, it would take someone like my brother Elihu to figure it out. But the person who really needed this man and his dispatches was Hassar Jonathan, and as soon as I could get him there, for any sort of cooperation between Jebus and the Five Cities meant death for Israel! A possible military post in Hebron didn't even compare with what I had just found. Thinking as furiously as I could, I stood.

Dawn was barely lightening the sky when Hanan and I returned to the inn. The sleepy guard just going off duty let us in, and the donkey pulled the little cart into the courtyard. We swiftly loaded Patisi's belongings into it, then wrapped the Philistine seren warmly and tucked him into the middle. As we left the gate, I turned to the guard. "Was the seren paid up for his room?"

"Yes, geber."

"Tell the innkeeper that he's been invited to stay with another adon and will not be returning."

"I will, geber."

"Invited to stay with another adon?" Hanan said as we headed swiftly down the street toward the town gates.

"I'm sure the hassar will invite him to stay indefinitely after he gets acquainted," I said, my face sober. "Where did you say the nearest army unit was?"

"Up near the head of the Elah valley, adoni."

We had an all-day trip then, 10 miles along the road, before we had to locate their camp. I wondered how long Patisi would sleep. Then I saw the jug of wine by his hand, and I smiled. It had worked for the Gebirah! It probably would for me, also.

Late afternoon had come when Hanan returned to the cart with news that the second unit was camped just half a mile away on the bench of land underneath the cave where Malchi had unknowingly trapped me when I first fled from Shaul.

"Is the sar with them?" I asked, silently thanking Yah for His help.

"Yes."

"Then I'm going to go calling."

Hanan settled by the fire while Patisi snored from his place in the cart. He'd wakened about noon and had soon nearly emptied the entire jug of wine, happily singing song after song while praising my ideas every chance he got since I had provided such a comfortable way for him to travel. I wondered what he would do when he realized I'd handed him over to Philistia's worst enemy.

Since I'd trained these men personally, I approached the second unit with caution, but managed to locate all the sentries without being seen. They were so alert, however, that I settled down to wait for darkness.

Once the camp had nearly quieted for the night, I watched until I saw one of the men leave the camp perimeter to relieve himself. Silently I followed after him. Waiting an appropriate interval, I wandered away from the place where he'd disappeared, coming into sight of another sentry and casually entering camp. Then I made my way to the sar's tent. He'd pitched it in exactly the same spot. Someone was approaching, so I eased down on my side by the sar's fire, and crossed my legs like he usually did, making sure my face was well hidden in the shadows.

"Don't move," Pallu commanded, stepping where I could see him. I just turned my head a little.

"Uh, your pardon, Sar," he said, backing away.

Nodding, I relaxed my shoulders.

When Pallu had moved on, a chuckle reached my ears. "If I didn't know that I'm here in my tent, I'd swear I was out there," Sar Malchi said quietly. "Where did you learn to mimic me so well?"

"You forget, Sar, I had plenty of time to study you from up there," I said, indicating the ledge above us.

"To what do I owe the honor of this visit?"

I smiled. "I have something I think the hassar will want, and it needs to get to him as quickly as it can. It would be much easier if you delivered it, rather than me."

"You caught me at the right time, then. I'm headed back north tomorrow. Where is it?"

"You'll have to come and get it." My smile broadened. "It's a little bigger than something you can put in your girdle."

I rolled to my feet as the sar emerged from the tent.

"Sar! Sar!" Sithri called, running up. "The sentries say there might be an intruder in the camp!" He bowed.

Malchi looked at me. "You're slipping, Dahveed,"

Sithri's head jerked up, and he stared, his mouth open.

"No, I just did a very good job training this unit. Who figured it out?" I asked Sithri.

"Pallu and Reu," he stammered. "Sar Dahveed, I—" Tears in his eyes, he dropped to his knees.

"I think our departure will be delayed a little," Malchi said. "Sithri, call the men."

I looked away. "Thank you, Sar," I said softly.

"I am honored by your trust, Dahveed, especially after what my abbi has done."

The men were, indeed, overjoyed to see me, and I spoke personally to each one. We hadn't much time, and they knew it, but we made the most of what we had.

"You might as well choose three to come with us," I told Malchi as we prepared to go.

Pallu, Reu, and Tahan were soon ready to accompany us, and I led the way. While we walked, I told Sar Malchi everything I could remember about my conversations with Patisi. The sound of his singing impinged on my ears long before we reached the cart.

Malchi looked at me, his eyebrows raised.

"He's had a very enjoyable day," I commented.

"So I hear," Malchi replied.

"Just get him and his belongings to Jonathan as quickly as you can. There is danger for Israel in what he carries. Nothing about him makes sense to me, but if I had to guess, I'd say he comes from Ekron, and that may mean Manani's involvement."

Malchi's face tightened, all the humor leaving it instantly. "In that case, we'll leave with him tonight."

When we arrived at the cart, I introduced Patisi to his new servants.

"Don't leave me," he moaned when I said I had to go.

"I must, Patisi. But don't worry. I've given all my good ideas to these men, and they will be sure to follow them."

"Are you sure?" he asked, peering at Reu.

"Very sure, adon," Reu replied solemnly.

"It's 'seren,' " Patisi corrected solemnly. "I like my title. Can I shtill sing?"

"You can do whatever you like, seren, so long as you stay in the cart," Sar Malchi assured him.

"Good. I like thish cart."

Hanan had it ready to go, and Tahan led the donkey on down the path as Patisi began to sing again.

"What can I say to Jonathan for you?" Malchi asked after they had gone.

"Tell him this," I said, kneeling. Taking his hand, I kissed the back of it. At the same time, I pressed the twisted brass earring into it.

Malchi burst out laughing. "I'll do it! If only to see the expression on his face!"

Hanan and I left immediately for Hebron once the sar had taken Patisi away. We took to the road again, bedding down in the hills surrounding the town just before daylight. I woke in late afternoon, made myself as presentable as I could, and walked into town hoping Ahibaal was still there.

"Habiru!" a guard called as I entered Hebron.

My hand automatically went to the hilt of my belt knife as I halted and swung around to face him.

"Geber, the adon from Jebus wants to see you," the man said, hurrying over. "He asked us to watch for you, and send you to him if we saw you."

"Where is he?" I asked, relaxing.

"At Nagid Hebron's house, geber."

I bowed. "I'll go at once."

I went to Dathan's compound and had the guard take the message that I had arrived. The Jebusite glanced up when the guard spoke to him, saw me at the gate, and nodded curtly before going back to his conversation with Dathan.

Obviously he expected me to wait, and I debated whether or not I would. I needed to get back to Gath and move my band to Ziklag. Who knew what sort of trouble awaited me there? In addition, Ahibaal's assumption that I had nothing better to do irked me. "Yah, should I stay?" I muttered to myself. Just then a servant arrived with some bread, wine, and a couple of apricots, and provided me with a place to sit. "Looks as if I stay," I whispered again, answering my own question. I nodded my thanks to Dathan as I sat down.

Full darkness had fallen before Ahibaal motioned me to join him. "Where have you been?" he demanded.

"Attending to my business, adon," I replied, keeping a tight grip on my temper.

"I told you the information I had for Dahveed Israel was urgent! Have you sent the message yet?"

"He received it in good time. Was there anything else?"

"Yes. I've just learned more which he will need to know. I'll try to make it clear enough for you to understand. The Philistines have permission from Pharaoh to collect his taxes from the highlands."

"When did that happen?" I gasped, so many things becoming clearer in just an instant, such as why the Philistines had been so persistent the past war season! Then I smiled. I couldn't imagine the serens of the Five Cities were very happy with the lack of plunder.

"They have had it for a year now at least," he replied. "I would imagine this will mean even harder fighting for Israel in the future, and it makes it even more imperative that no Philistine military be allowed into the highlands for any reason. That would include guiding Seren Patisi and his guards. Perhaps they could be taken around through

Beersheba instead. Did you speak with him any further about that? I tried to contact him today, but he's gone from the inn, visiting some adon. Do you have any idea where he went? We must keep track of him."

"He's in good hands by now, I'm sure," I answered. "The adon he is visiting will likely keep him for some time. As far as guiding him is concerned, I made no commitment. If there is nothing else, adon, I will take my leave. The information about the tax authorization must be passed on immediately. Shalom." I left before he could say anything more.

¥ ¥ ¥ ¥ ¥ ¥

Ahibaal adhered strictly to the truth in his message to his adon regarding what had happened with Patisi. He had been sent to meet the man after it was determined in Jebus that Patisi was the adon he himself had seen entering the palace. The adon had been followed to Jericho, and a Habiru had been hired there to watch the inn and then track the man when he left. The hireling had sent word that the party would stop at En-gedi, and Ahibaal had been on his way to meet them there when they appeared in the highlands.

At first he was suspicious, for there were only the two men, Patisi and the scribe. But further thought made him admire the subtlety of the ploy. Who would ever expect an important adon to be traveling with only one companion and no guards? No wonder the man had slipped unnoticed across to the Arabah so often!

Then, after joining the adon and gaining his confidence, he had allowed the Dahveed's Habiru to take the man away to who knew where! What his adon would think of that, he dared not consider. Such a spectacular error regarding something so important would demand a severe punishment. Before adding his acknowledgment of his culpability to the end of the message, he bowed his head briefly. He had made too many assumptions about too much, and could now only pray to El Elyon that his adon would not have to pay a heavy price for it.

¥ ¥ ¥ ¥ ¥ ¥

"Hassar?"

Jonathan looked up from the table.

"Sar Malchi is coming, with a, um, singing cart."

Puzzled, Jonathan left the room and headed to the gate of the courtyard at his estate in Zelah. Again this year, Shaul had absolutely refused to allow him to serve on the front lines. When Malchi had confided to him that not having to worry about the honor battle between the hassar and the general would make commanding the army much easier, Jonathan bowed to the king's wishes. With administrative work so light now, he had begun coming here every evening to spend the night with Meribbaal, who clearly delighted in the arrangement.

Sar Malchi was indeed arriving, accompanied by three soldiers and a donkey pulling a cart from which issued some of the strangest sounds he had ever heard.

Malchi's mule trotted up to the gate. "Shalom, brother."

"Shalom." The hassar eyed the cart. "What is that?"

"It's a present for you. From a friend of yours."

Bewilderment crossed Jonathan's face as the donkey, ears flattened against its head, pulled the cart through the gate and stopped in the courtyard.

He went around to stare at the man gesturing widely with a wine jug and reclining in the middle of the cart, the most horrendous squalls issuing from his mouth. Then he looked back at Malchi, who regarded him straight-faced.

"What is he doing?"

"Singing. He used to be better at it, before the last jug of wine, and before his voice got hoarse."

"Can you make him be silent?"

"Haven't found a way yet."

"What am I supposed to do with him?"

"Talk to him, I think. Although you might want to wait until he's sober. That could be a while though."

"How did you get saddled with him?"

"He was by our campsite. Singing."

"Just he and the donkey?"

"No. Someone brought him. But they had to leave. The seren in the cart was quite sad to see them go."

Jonathan backed up at the new burst of sound from the cart. "Who did you say sent him?"

"A friend." Malchi paused a moment. "From down south."

Slowly Jonathan faced his brother, that exasperated expression dawning on his face. "Did this *friend* have anything else to say?"

"He did," the sar replied. Sliding off the mule, he came around it to face his brother. "He said this." Kneeling, Malchi kissed the back of the hassar's hand, put the brass earring into it, then raised his eyes to his brother's face, waiting.

Jonathan's hand closed over the earring. "Why, that undeserving, worthless wretch of a Habiru! How dare that hill man even *think* to do this to me?" he burst out in that strangled voice that was half whisper and half shout.

Malchi stood up, grinning, while Jonathan glared at him.

"Didn't he say anything about this—this— *abominable noise* he sent me?"

"I believe he mentioned something about this being a most puzzling seren, and that there was danger to Israel, probably involving Manani," Malchi stated before mounting his mule and riding after his men.

The hassar watched his brother's back retreating down the road before turning to regard the newest trouble the Dahveed had sent him. The man smiled on him beatifically, what could only be described as howls coming from his mouth now. The donkey put its head down, ears as flat as it could make them.

Gaham approached, trying to suppress his laughter. "Should I unhitch that poor donkey?"

"Only after it has taken this detestable sound out of my hearing!"

The guard looked around. "Where shall we put it?"

"Bury it under the back grain field, or smother it in the nearest cave. Just get it out of here!" Jerking about, he nearly slammed into a mule standing beside him. He looked up into Immi's smiling face.

"Has the Dahveed sent you a new zammar?" she asked.

"Immi, I shall—I shall take that man and—and—"

"—and send a thank offering to Yahweh, like you always do," she finished. "Gaham, take the new zammar into the granary and settle him on some sacks. Keep it dark. I imagine when he wakes up, he'll be quite sick."

"Yes, Hassarah," Gaham said, leading the donkey away.

Immi cocked her head at her son. "I'd guess you'll be busy for a while. I'll take Meribbaal back to Gibeah with me."

"That would be a help," Jonathan admitted. "If this is anything like the chaos Dahveed has handed to me before, it will take a while to untangle."

Once Immi had left and his newest acquisition had apparently fallen asleep, Jonathan took the time to go through the dispatch case left on his table. The clay tablets he set aside. He'd have to get a scribe to read the cuneiform. The dispatches were unsettling. Any hint of cooperation between Philistia and Jebus meant problems for Israel. As he carefully went over them, he decided that he definitely wanted to talk to this man. He wondered how long it would be before he sobered up.

Chapter 18

"A message for you, Hassar," Sar Eshbaal said two days later, and Jonathan motioned the courier forward.

The man touched his knee to the floor of the throne room. "Gaham sends to you, Hassar. He says the new zammar at your estate is ready for you to interview."

"Very good," the hassar replied, dismissing the man. He turned to Eshbaal. "Notify Ishvi that the meeting we normally have at my estate tonight will be put off one day."

His youngest brother nodded and signaled the scribe to bring in the next clan representative, one from En-harod, the springs not far from Mount Gilboa and Beth-shean. The hassar expected to spend some time with this man, gleaning as much information as he could about what the Philistines and the Egyptian governor in the Jezreel Valley were doing.

It was near dusk, and he hadn't eaten yet, when he rode out of town. He still hadn't had time to have those clay tablets read to him, and he wondered how he should approach Patisi. The man was genial enough when he was drunk and singing, but what would he be like sober?

Angry, very angry. Jonathan stood in the upper room of his private estate and regarded the bound man who was dressing him down in fine style. The effect was somewhat marred by the way his voice kept cracking, since he was still hoarse from his previous vocal exertions. And now that he was standing in his loincloth, Jonathan noticed the scars on the man. He didn't think he'd ever imagined the possibility of a seren having that many.

Gaham had informed him when he arrived that Patisi had been kept isolated from everyone, and from the way the seren was addressing him now, Patisi must have assumed that he was in Philistia and was on the estate of a Philistine adon, not that of Hassar Israel.

The seren had begun his harangue the moment Jonathan entered the room. Since he was learning more with every word, he stayed back in the shadows and let the man yell. So far he'd picked up that Seren Patisi was an important man, known among all the adons of the Five

Cities, that he was on a credentialed journey on behalf of the Five Cities, that the serens would not be pleased with any delay in his report, and most importantly, Seren Manani of Ekron, who was his son-in-law, would take personal exception for his delay since he must report directly— At that point, the man swallowed his words, coughing hoarsely.

Jonathan winced just thinking about how the man's throat must be feeling. He waited to see if anything more was forthcoming, but Patisi simply glared at him. "May I assume, then, that you have found our hospitality wanting and wish to leave?"

"You may so assume," Patisi replied haughtily, then winced even though his voice was barely above a whisper.

"What hurts more, your head or your throat?" the hassar asked, curious. "I would guess your throat since I believe you had been singing for several days when you arrived."

"Singing?" Patisi squeaked, his voice cracking again. "For days?" His eyes widened in dismay. He looked around. "What estate is this?"

"It's mine," Jonathan said reasonably.

The seren looked down at himself and groaned a little. "That Habiru must have stolen my clothes," he grimaced, automatically trying to reach for his head, and not succeeding. "Geber, please accept my apologies for the trouble you've been put to. If I can return to the Inn of the Stars in Hebron, I will be able to repay you well."

"That might be a bit difficult. My estate is quite far from Hebron."

The dismay in the seren's eyes turned to worry. He looked around with more purpose this time, glancing out the small windows, but seeing only the darkness of night outside. He did note Jonathan's rich robe, however.

"Then it would seem I have been more trouble to you than I thought, adon. Please excuse my former speech. I am understandably upset," he ended, smiling wryly.

"Since your former speech was quite enlightening, think nothing more of it. You seem eager to return, so your mission must have been successful. How many times did you wish you could strangle Debir before he decided to cooperate?"

"At least three, adon," Patisi sighed, not realizing that he had never actually said where he had gone. "He is the most suspicious man I've ever met. But, adon, may we continue this conversation in the morning? I would like to clean up and sleep off the rest of this headache."

"I don't think I can allow that," the hassar replied, sitting down at the table where his face was more visible. "Given what I read in the dispatches, I need to know everything you can tell me as soon as you can."

"You read official correspondence?" Patisi gasped.

"Of course. And since I know that Seren Manani's position with the Five Cities is eroding underneath him, and that dealing with Qausa the Habiru would be difficult, even for him, I am very curious about the reasons he is recommending the man to Debir."

"I think I will refuse to answer anything more until I know with whom I am dealing," Patisi said, his eyes hard now, even if his voice still cracked.

A shrug. "I'm called Jonathan ben Shaul."

"Hassar Israel?" Patisi whispered, turning pale.

"Correct."

The Philistine seren stiffened into absolute stillness. "I have nothing to say."

"You have a great deal to say," Jonathan replied, his voice smooth. "Say it, and you will live."

"You expect me to believe you? I am not a fool, Israelite."

The hassar gritted his teeth, wondering how to convince the man he could be trusted. Then something about the total immobility in his prisoner, coupled with the acute awareness he could sense from the man, made him wait in silence. The feeling of this man's fear had a familiar taste. "You are of Manani," he said softly.

For an instant, stark terror crossed the Philistine's features. Then he stiffened again. Silently, Jonathan cursed Manani. It might be days before he could talk to this man. Then a knock sounded on the door. His captive crumpled into a heap on the floor. Make that weeks, the hassar thought savagely. He glanced over his shoulder. "Enter."

Gaham stepped over the raised threshold and handed him a large cloth-wrapped pottery shard, giving a curious look at the man on the floor.

Unwrapping it, the hassar angled it toward the flame of the lamp to read the message. It was from Dahveed! He got halfway through it before he looked at his personal guard with unseeing eyes. "Gaham, arrange for Patisi to be sent tonight to my estate near Bethel." Then he went back to reading the message as the soldier hauled his captive off the floor and out of the room. Once he was finished, he placed it carefully on the table, his mind whirling. No wonder the Philistines had pressed them so hard last year. They were trying to collect Pharaoh's taxes! Malchi needed to know this instantly!

"What did he say?" Jonathan asked Nimshi as the young man mounted his mule again.

"Sar Malchi went north to Birzaith. He's meeting with King Shaul there."

The hassar hesitated. Abbi wouldn't be happy to see him anywhere near the units. But this news had to be delivered, and he wanted to do it personally. "Let's go," he decided.

Nimshi led the way back to the road, and they put the mules into a slow canter that the animals could keep up for miles.

Malchi waited outside his tent when they arrived just before noon. "I didn't know if I should believe the sentry or not when he said you were coming," the younger sar greeted them. "What brought you here?"

"Disturbing news. Is Abbi around?"

"In the tent. Come in."

"Jonathan, why have you come?" Shaul asked anxiously as the hassar entered the tent and bowed in greeting.

"I received news that explains why the Philistines have been so determined lately. They now have authorization to collect taxes from Israel for Pharaoh."

"Where did you hear this?" Malchi demanded.

"Sources down south."

"How long have they had it?" their abbi questioned.

"This will be the second year," the hassar replied.

"Then they will press us harder than ever, for they got little last year," Shaul said, his face hard. "We must send a message to Abner immediately. Jonathan, you will take one of my units back with you when you leave. Also fill out the unit you have with you in Gibeah with half the usual number of militia. We will depend on you to keep the Philistines from penetrating into Ephraim from the south."

"They would have to break through Dahveed first, and he doesn't want them in Judah any more than we want them in Israel," Jonathan replied.

"Dahveed has gone to the Negev west of the land stair," Malchi said quietly. "Word came to me day before yesterday," he added, turning to his abbi.

Shaul was silent for a while before speaking. "Then he is outside of Yahweh's lands and will not be a concern any longer." A satisfied smile on his face, he looked at the hassar. "You will not have to worry about him now, and can concentrate on Philistines."

"As you say, Abbi," Jonathan replied, his heart sad at how little his abbi understood. "I will keep scouts on watch to the south. Shalom, Abbi." As he stepped outside the tent, Malchi followed him.

"I'm sorry, Jonathan. I should have remembered to tell you yesterday."

"Do you know specifically where he went?"

"Ziklag, a few miles east of Gerar. What I can't understand is why Seren Akish would allow Dahveed anywhere in his territory, unless Dahveed has turned against Israel. Would he do that?"

"No. Dahveed has a covenant son, half Benjamite, half Philistine, named Ittai ben Ribbai. I would guess the young man's clan is well-connected enough in Gath to allow Dahveed to stay in Akish's territory. But you'll notice the seren sent him as far south as he could, which makes me doubt very much that the other four cities know whom Akish is sheltering."

"Hassar!" someone called.

Jonathan glanced around, and a panting courier approached. "Geber Elihu sends to you, Hassar," the man said, holding out the papyrus.

Breaking the seal and unfolding the message, the hassar read it swiftly. "Malchi, get that unit down to me as soon as you can. According to this, a Philistine envoy met with the Calebite nagids just days ago, suggesting a mutual protection pact against the Amalekites. For some reason, the nagids are considering the possibility."

Malchi swore under his breath. "With Dahveed gone, whom do they have to help them?" he asked savagely. "I wish there was some way I could make Abbi *see* what he's done by driving Dahveed away! If the nagids agree to this, the time of the judges will be upon us again! We can't hold both the west and south borders."

His brother sighed. "You heard him just now. The only thing Abbi can think of is preserving the throne for me."

"If that's what he wants, he needs to worry more about Abner than Dahveed," Malchi growled. "The general has lots of plans, and they don't involve you. The only reason he still fights for Shaul is because those plans don't involve the Philistines, either!"

"Keep an eye on him, then," Jonathan said, mounting his mule. "I'll watch what's happening south of Jebus!"

¥ ¥ ¥ ¥ ¥ ¥

The courier arrived just as Ahibaal was carrying little Bathsheba up the stairs on his back, lumbering from side to side as a camel would, with the child shrieking in delight with every step. His overseer prudently ushered the man into the business chamber to wait. Knowing the man had come from his adon, Ahibaal shortened his time with his granddaughter a little, too apprehensive about what might be in that message to really enjoy his time with her.

When the Jebusite adon entered the chamber, the courier touched his knee to the floor and handed him the message. Seeing that he had already been served with fruit and wine, Ahibaal dismissed him with a curt nod. Once alone, he sat down and read the missive carefully.

"Greetings.

"The disappearance of Patisi is of grave concern. Cooperation between Philistia and Jebus at this time would be disastrous for everyone concerned, especially our particular interest in the south.

"It is unfortunate that you do not have direct contact with him. Our experience with Habiru suggests that, although they will ally together, they will still act independently. Perhaps your contact has done so in this case, even though he is obviously closely connected to our primary concern. Try to learn whatever you can about Patisi and your contact. Keep your sources alert for anything that could be related to this matter. It is of vital importance that we determine to whom Patisi reports."

His brow furrowed, Ahibaal stared unseeingly at the flame of the lamp. The message contained not one word of condemnation or disappointment about the way he had mishandled the situation. Just encouragement to do whatever he could to compensate for it. He would kiss the ground before his adon the rest of his life for this. And he would make certain he never made such a mistake again.

¥ ¥ ¥ ¥ ¥ ¥

"Seren, the scribe has returned," the sar at the gate informed him.
"I will interview him in the business chamber," Manani replied.
The man bowed. "He is waiting for you there."
"Send Sar Eliahba also."
"He is not here, Sereni. The scribe arrived alone."
Manani paused. Alone? What had happened? Instead of eating, he went immediately to the business chamber. The scribe waited for him outside of it, bowing silently when he arrived. Manani preceded the man into the room and sat down. "Were you successful?"
"Yes, Sereni. All has been arranged as you wished it."
"Where is the sar?"
"He is dead, Sereni."
Manani leaned back. Eliahba dead? Did it matter? Not really, he decided. The man had done everything necessary, and if he was dead now, that just saved the trouble of killing him. He glanced up at the scribe. "Tell me what happened," he ordered.
When the man finished his report, Manani dismissed him. Things couldn't have worked out better if he had planned them this way.

¥ ¥ ¥ ¥ ¥ ¥

Ten days after I left Hebron, I rested in the noonday heat on the slight rise and stared south across the 200-foot-wide 40-foot-deep ravine between me and Ziklag. The little town sat on a raised island in the middle of a 1,000-foot-wide watercourse valley, and from what I could see, they didn't want any visitors. The raised ground was barely wide enough for a town, and four times as long as wide. Makeshift defenses between the houses blocked all entrances into the place. Although the gates on the south of town would probably crash down at the least push, the question of whether they would collapse inward on the defenders or outward on the attackers wasn't something I wanted to find out by trying it.

Silence had met our hails, and since my messengers would be fools to contend with barred gates, they returned with the news that Ziklag wasn't receiving visitors. Frankly, it didn't look like it had done so for quite some time.

"Do we even know there's someone in there?" Shagay grunted beside me, wiping the sweat from his forehead.

"Hanan said he saw some movement," Abishai replied. "What shall we do, Dodi?"

"Wait until dark. Then maybe we can get someone close enough to find out more. Akish warned me there had been trouble with the town."

After dark, Shagay's Jonathan, Hanan, and Sibbecai descended into the valley. I went to the overlook again and watched silently as Sibbecai drifted by below me. He disappeared in the shadows as he climbed the steep incline toward the town. Suddenly, the sound of a dog barking shattered the silence. Within moments, figures appeared at the walls, and good-sized rocks began crashing randomly down, making Sibbecai hug the ground, scrambling for what cover he could find. There wasn't much. More dogs barked, and then all was still.

An hour later, the three scouts reported back. Sibbecai was limping. He'd twisted an ankle trying to get away, and Jonathan had a long graze down his back where a rock had barely been deflected by a protruding tree branch, thus just missing his head. Hanan didn't look much worse for wear other than scrapes and scratches.

"What happened?" I asked.

"I got close to one barrier before the dog barked," Hanan reported. "It felt flimsy, and things shifted when I pushed a little, but there's no good footing to stand on to take it apart. I wouldn't want to climb it in the dark."

Coming from Hanan, that meant there was no way in.

"I'll think about this," I said.

It was still dark when I woke, but the night felt nearly done. When I went outside I felt a slight mist that must be rising from the dampness of the watercourse below. Knowing it couldn't last long, I walked among the widely spaced trees and enjoyed the coolness while I could.

Hanan found me. "The gates are barely held together, adoni. They could easily be forced."

"How did you learn that?"

"I got right up to them in the mist. But it is too quiet in that town."

"Did you see any sentries?"

"One. And the tops of the walls are above the mist."

After another day of studying on the problem, I developed a plan.

The next morning we went down into the watercourse just before dawn. As the sun crept above the eastern highlands, eight of my units headed silently up the gentle eastern slope to the town. To our surprise, they actually got to a barrier and began to dismantle it before someone sounded an alarm.

"They're attacking!" a voice shouted. "Defend the barriers!" and then a battle horn blared. As planned, my men pulled back, shields up to protect themselves. Also as planned, the slanting rays of the sun made it nearly impossible for the town's warriors to see, and most of the missiles hurtling from the walls hit nothing. While my men made as much noise and commotion as they could, keeping the pressure up, I ran through the trees to the road that led to the gate.

"Now's our chance!" I panted, and the seven of us made a dash toward the gates, expecting to hear another alarm at any moment. I could see at least one sentry, but he wasn't moving, nor did he turn our way.

We reached the gate, and it swayed when we pushed on it. Still no alarm from the town, and the faint sounds of battle continued north of us.

"Try pushing it in," I suggested.

"No, Dodi, look," Joab said. He kicked the wood on the bottom, and it splintered easily.

Shagay smashed the back of his ax into it, and an entire panel broke off. Two more swings, and Hanan squirmed under. I looked up anxiously. I couldn't believe we hadn't been heard. That sentry was in plain view.

Sibbecai, Shagay, and I waited, shoulders against the gate.

"Now," Hanan gasped, and we shoved. The gate swung open three feet before the big bar crashed to the ground, blocking any farther movement. Elika and Shammah rushed through, bows ready. The rest of us quickly followed, and the Benjamite archers jumped up from their hiding place just west of the approach to the gate and shoved their way in.

We all stopped in amazement.

"Yahweh save us! What happened here?" Abiezer exclaimed.

My eyes left the destruction around me and fastened on the rooftops. "Joab," I snapped. "Tell the men to stop their attack, and pull back."

He bolted out of the gate instantly. The rest of us advanced down the narrow street that twisted down the long axis of the town, watching the rooftops. When we got close to the noise, we climbed to a rooftop, jumping from one to the next.

The town's defenders were lined up along two house parapets, flinging things on my men below

"Immi!" A child screamed. "Immi! Look!"

A woman whirled around and snatched her child to her, screaming. At her cry, the rest of the defenders swung around also, to stand frozen at the sight of my archers, bows at ready. The noise from below soon ceased. We faced one elderly man, two more even older, a dozen women (some with helmets on their heads), perhaps eight teenaged young people, and 10 or so children.

"Yahweh, have hesed!" Sibbecai muttered.

"Shagay, bring them to the south market," I said quietly. "Abiezer, you and the archers make sure we don't lose any on the way. Sibbecai, you and Hanan take down a barrier on the north side, and get the units in here. I want a house-to-house search, then bring everyone to the market square. Be as reasonable as you can."

"Yes, adoni."

I toured the rooftops, finding what was left of rock piles and seeing the "sentries," padded robes attached to propped up staves. Most of the robes they had used had tears and bloodstains on them. I felt my face harden.

When I returned to the market, I surveyed the motley collection of people. Three more women had joined us, along with six very young children who clung to them, too frightened to cry. There were two more teenage boys, one of them nursing an injured arm.

When he saw me raise my eyebrows, Shagay said, "He tried to fight. Nearly got me, too."

There was also another elderly man, obviously sick, and two old women who sat beside him.

Just then, Hiddai and Ben-Shimei, the Benjamite archer who had tried to shoot me when Amasai joined us, appeared from an alley, roughly handling two women as they came. One woman already had a torn robe and was crying, her eyes fastened on the baby Ben-Shimei carelessly held in one arm.

Squinting against the sudden brightness of the sun, I started toward them, flexing my hands. Ben-Shimei wasn't expecting any interference with his desires, and I managed to get quite close before he realized I was there.

His eyes widened when he saw my face, and I took the baby, returning it to the woman. Without a word I smashed my fist into his face, and he tripped, falling backward. When he jumped up, reaching for his sword, I seized his hand, driving my knee into his groin. He screamed, and I yanked his arm upright with my left hand while I pounded him with my right fist, adding another blow low down that practically lifted him off the ground before I let him fall. Once he sprawled limply on the ground, I turned on Hiddai.

Releasing the woman he held, he tried to back away, but I lunged at him. He wasn't fast enough in dropping to his knees to protect himself, and he doubled over from my blow, moaning, but had sense enough not to resist while I beat him, too.

The terrible anger left me as he fell, and I swayed a little, looking around.

Ahiam handed me a cruse, and the tingle left my hands while I drained it. When I found that I could speak, I faced the people now bunched together. "Who is your spokesman?" I asked a little hoarsely.

All eyes turned to the elderly man from the rooftop, and he stepped forward. "Who are you, and what do you want with us?"

"I come from Seren Akish, who sent me to investigate his concerns about Ziklag."

"Seren Gath abandoned us last year," the elder said, his eyes steady.

"He is of the opinion that you abandoned him the year before. From the looks of this market, a great deal has been happening in Ziklag. Since the town has been given to me as a military grant, I would appreciate knowing just exactly what has happened."

The elder studied me for some time. His people kept their attention on him. Obviously, whatever he decided would dictate how they viewed me.

He looked at the two men lying in the dust of the square, and then back at me. "Whence are you?"

"The highlands of Judah."

"You do not fight like Habiru. There is discipline in your force."

"Akish noticed, and I serve him."

Again he stared at Hiddai and Ben-Shimei.

"I think you and I have much to discuss," he said at last.

That evening, after the first good meal the people in the town had had in weeks, Irad, the head elder of Ziklag, and I sat outside my tent where he had shared the meal with my wives and me. In the quietness he told me what had happened during the past two years. To begin with, the town had supported two units, one of which had been designated to protect the road from Ziklag north 10 miles to the next guard station. But after the first month, that station was abandoned, and the men from Ziklag had to travel the additional 10 miles to the next town. It kept them away from Ziklag overnight, and when the second unit left to protect people coming up from the south, or to respond to the news of another raid, Ziklag was without protection.

"At first it was just thievery, or trouble in the wine shop," Irad explained. "Then one of our warriors was severely wounded in a fight with a stranger. After that, a gang of men terrorized the town at night. Then the town itself was attacked, and not by Amalekites either, Seren Dahveed," the old man said bitterly. "It was Philistines, or mercenaries in Philistine pay. We sent message after message to Seren Gath requesting help, and never heard a reply from him."

"In the meantime, your men were gradually killed off," I guessed.

The elder nodded. "By the middle of the second year, we had only one unit left, and the only things we had heard from Gath were demands for more troops during the war season and more protection for travelers and towns from raids."

"If it helps, he never got your messages."

"I began to suspect as much. But by then, we hesitated to send anyone for fear of what might happen to them. Finally, we had no choice, and when two of our men left to escort some travelers north, the second one just kept going.

"A week later, the sar arrived. The commander said he was from Seren Akish and had two units under his command. We were so grateful, seren," Irad continued, his lips trembling. "We thought our message had gotten through, and he had been generous enough to send us one of his best sars, one of Goliath's kin."

"Oh?" I asked, suddenly alert. "What did he look like?"

"Taller than anyone we'd ever seen, and very good with a sword."

"Was he big all over, like my man Shagay grown another foot or more?"

"No," the elder said hesitantly. "He was more slender, like that nephew you have with the long legs. Just taller."

"How was he called?" I asked, trying to decide which of Goliath's kin it had been. "Did he have six fingers on his hands?"

"We never heard his name, and he had five fingers like everyone else. He didn't talk much," Irad added. "The assistant sar with him did that."

I frowned a little. Not talking certainly didn't sound like Ishvi-benob or Lahmi. Saph maybe. I'd have to ask Akish when Saph had been sent south. Then my thoughts stopped dead. Akish had never gotten that message! So who had "responded" to it?

"What happened next?" I asked, my stomach tight with apprehension.

"The sar said he had information about a large group of raiders from Amalek who were camped about 15 miles south of us. We sent our unit with him as he requested." Irad stopped.

"They never came back, did they?"

"No. But a young servant managed it and told us how the sar and his men had turned on our unit during the evening meal and slaughtered them all. I knew then, we were all in danger, and we fled the town. The destruction you saw in Ziklag happened when the sar and his men returned and found no one here."

"I'm surprised they didn't burn the place."

"They started to. But then some actual Amalekites arrived, and the sar and his men ran, leaving the town to be looted. When we got back, there wasn't much left. We've survived on the food in the one storehouse that they didn't find."

"I didn't see any gardens. Surely you could have planted something in the spring."

"We did. They were all destroyed by 'Amalekites' just before harvest. The sar's men have kept track of us, and attack every so often. We have lost eight more people to sickness, starvation, and injuries."

His face somber, Irad fell silent. I watched the fire. "Given what happened the last time someone announced he'd come from Seren Gath, I'm surprised you trusted me."

That even gaze fastened on me again. "You nearly killed two of your own men for abusing two of our women, and not one of the men with you so much as looked as if he thought it was unwarranted. That kind of discipline and loyalty shows, seren. We had given up petitioning Dagon for aid, and we must shelter somewhere if we are to live. Now you have come and spread your wings over us, giving us food and hope. Since our gods have abandoned us, if we learn the correct rites to please your god, will he accept us?"

At first, I wasn't certain what to say. Would Yahweh accept Dagon worshippers as His own? Then I remembered Roeh Shamuel's words that I was to teach Yah's ways to those who came under my command, and I remembered Grandmother Ruth and Mahesa, the Egyptian army officer who served still at Gibeon.

"He will," I said confidently. "Yahweh seems to have a special regard for those who are outcast or have nothing. He will be your God."

"How often will we have to go to the highlands to worship?" Irad asked. "We live in Dagon's land and will have to continue sacrifices to him in order to keep his anger from us, but we will serve your Yahweh if He will have us. In return, we can teach you how to keep Dagon satisfied, so that he will not harm you as a stranger in our land."

I pursed my lips. Although I might have been forced to give my service to Dagon, through his servant Akish, I would never worship the deity. I ignored that part of his comment. "You won't have to go to the highlands. You can worship Yah right here."

Irad looked bewildered. "How can we? He cannot come here. He is god in the highlands. We want to be sure He knows us, so we will go to Him. Some of us can stay in the hills if necessary."

Looking at the man's expression, I knew that he would not understand anything that I said. "Follow me, Irad."

He rose stiffly.

"Pekah, please tell Abiathar that we are coming," I said to the lad who'd been waiting nearby.

As Irad and I approached the huge oak under which the ark rested in its tent, I felt the gradually growing presence of Yahweh. Abiathar met us at the boundary of the area for the ark.

"Why have you come, Dahveed?"

"Irad and his people have been cast off by Dagon, and they wish to worship Yahweh. But Irad does not understand how he and his people can worship Yahweh here." I knelt to the priest. "I have come to see if Yahweh will reveal Himself to those who have nowhere else to go."

Hardly had I finished speaking when I felt my hair stand on end, and I bowed my head as Irad gasped.

Abiathar's voice became distant. "Irad ben Omar, come forward."

Hearing his full name, the elder trembled, barely able to allow Abiathar to lead him onto sacred ground to the entrance to the tent. There he knelt, still clutching the hakkohen's hand. The darkness inside the tent lessened, getting brighter and brighter until the light spilled around the curtain in front of the ark and out onto the ground. The Philistine tried to edge away, but Abiathar held him firmly until the man's face was bathed in the Shekinah.

"My people," Irad gasped. "Please, Great One, my people must know this blessing! Please, they must come!"

The hakkohen turned to me. "Dahveed ben Jesse, send for Irad's people that they may have the comfort of My acceptance."

"As you command, Adonai." Rising from my knees, I backed away. By now, many of my own band were gathering, drawn by the warm, golden glow of the Shekinah radiating from the ark.

I looked around for some men to send. "Abishai," I began.

"No, Dahveed, we will go," Keturah said, hurrying toward me, followed by Ahinoam, Abigail, Zalmon's wife, and several other women. "If warriors come at this time of night, the people will be terrified. We will bring them."

"Namea, bring Dahveed his harp," the Gebirah directed. "You must be playing a song of peace when we come," she added to me.

When the women returned with the townspeople, I knelt off to one side in the darkness, singing the song I'd written as a shepherd for Patah, to comfort him. Irad was standing now, and the smile on his face glowed as he turned to the group of bedraggled, worn-down people who had come. "Yahweh has accepted us! He has come here to be with us! All of you must receive His blessing." When he held out his hand, one of the elderly men who'd been on the wall took it and came forward, kneeling in the light for a moment. Tears streamed down his face when he backed away, bowing as he went. The others pressed toward the tent, and Irad and Abiathar brought them forward individually to kneel in the light of the Shekinah.

The young woman Ben-Shimei had mistreated clutched her baby and sobbed as if her heart would break when she knelt. Abiathar put his hand on her head. "Take comfort, daughter," he said in that distant voice. "Your husband is not dead. He will return to you and give you three more fine sons and a daughter as well."

"Oh, if that were only true!" she said, turning to Irad, fresh tears spilling down her face.

Abiathar's voice was still distant, but there was a distinct tone of amusement in it when he said, "My word always comes to pass, daughter!"

Irad helped her up and held her close. "There, niece, you don't have to fret any longer. He'll come back."

Abiathar had a word for three or four others, and last Naharai and Eliphelet came forward, the sick old man from the town carried on a stretcher between them, his harsh, labored breathing easily heard above my soft song. They placed the stretcher in the light, and the man opened his eyes, turning his head toward the ark. "Irad?" he said.

The elder knelt beside him. "I'm here, Abbi."

"Where is this place you have brought me?"

"Yahweh, the Israelite God, has taken us under His wings since our own gods have abandoned us."

"This is a good place," Omar said slowly. "You will be cared for here, with Him. You all will. He just promised." His face turned to the ark again and he sighed deeply. "I can rest now." A look of peace settled over his face, and his hand reached upward a moment before his life left him.

Abiathar gently placed Omar's hand down by his side and then closed the man's eyes.

Irad looked up at the hakkohen, wonder on his face in spite of the tears of grief in his eyes. "Your God cares!" he exclaimed. "How can this be? You must tell us about Him—everything! Everything, so that we can stay His!"

I ceased my song, and the Shekinah faded until only a small glow remained. None of us left, however, until the first rays of the daystar touched us, and the last of the Shekinah disappeared.

Chapter 19

After that night we spent three weeks rebuilding and repairing the town. Then I sent a complete report to Akish by Eliam ben Ahibaal, since he was headed north to see his family. I cautioned the young man to go into the highlands via Keilah and Gedor, and to avoid the military units on both sides. Ithmah sent a message to his family in Moab at the same time. Akish's return message arrived shortly, with badly needed supplies. Not long after that, Eliam returned with news of home and a richly embroidered cloth to be used to cover the ark.

Once we had cleared the worst of the mess away, Abishai split my band into groups responsible for repairs in various parts of town. I couldn't help noticing that Hiddai and Ben-Shimei were assigned opposite ends of the town, and the few men who tended to follow them were split between groups and kept so hard at work that I heard no complaints about them.

Eliphelet, however, was another matter, which came to my attention when Irad arrived one morning, hardly knowing how to tell me what one of the townspeople had seen.

"How long have things been disappearing?" I asked.

"At least a week, sereni," he confessed.

"You should have come to me sooner," I said, a bit sternly.

He flushed. "Sereni, you have done so much, and—"

"Come to me immediately next time," I said before sending for Eliphelet and Abigail. My personal thief was so distressed when he had to nick Abigail's finger again, that he couldn't eat for the rest of that day or the next. The piece of his girdle now sat on a small stool outside the door of the house I stayed in, but nothing appeared on it for more than two weeks.

One reason Abishai divided the men into groups was to alternate them between working on the town and going out as guards on the roads. The first time robbers attacked a group we were guarding, none of them got away, and after my men had nearly wiped out four other gangs, the raids stopped. I reported the news to Akish, along with the fact that all the robbers we'd killed so far were Philistines carrying more silver than could be expected.

The day that two strangers arrived, watching all that we did between stops at the wine shop—opened especially for their benefit—I knew trouble was on the way. After consulting with Irad, I detained them both. It took almost a week before seven of their friends showed up to collect them, carelessly entering the square in a group. They were not pleased with the welcome we gave them, and even less so when I packed them off to Akish. Their leader got away, slipping back through the gate and vanishing, although I did get a brief look at him. He was as Irad had described him, and I didn't think it was Saph. All the same, that glimpse nagged at my mind.

And while we kept busy in Ziklag, Shagay, his son Jonathan, Hanan, and Sibbecai went on extended scouting trips into the Negev.

¥ ¥ ¥ ¥ ¥ ¥

Jonathan Hassar glanced up as the overseer from his Bethel estate entered the throne room in Gibeah. Up to now, the Philistine seren had still refused to say anything. How could he convince the man he wasn't going to be slaughtered and get him to talk? He had the feeling that he needed to be certain he got not just the truth, but everything the man knew. And he still hadn't had those clay tablets read to him!

"Shalom," he greeted the man.

"Shalom, adoni. I am sorry to report there has been no change in the Philistine's attitude."

"Has he caused any trouble?"

"No, Hassar. He's always done what he was told though he still never speaks to anyone. What has surprised me is the way he has acted sometimes."

"How was that?"

His overseer paused. "I really can't say. It just seemed odd for a seren to do as he has."

With a silent sigh, the hassar dismissed the man. At times like this, he sorely missed Dahveed's ability to notice things. Come to think of it, Malchi had said Dahveed told him the seren seemed different. Well, maybe a few more weeks would change the man's mind. There was always hope anyway.

¥ ¥ ¥ ¥ ¥ ¥

Just before dawn, two of my units and I crept up on the huddle of Geshurite tents more than 20 miles south of Ziklag. There were three more such groups scattered within a two-square mile area. Shagay, Josheb, and Eleazar commanded my other raiding parties that would attack them.

It was our first serious raid into the south, and the war season was at its height. My scouts had located five such regions in the half-desert of the Negev where the Geshurites and Girzites liked to gather in loose bands before combining to send men on a raid.

A baby wailed and then quieted.

I gritted my teeth, glad I hadn't eaten anything. Yahweh had placed these people under His ban, and we had passed two towns on our way here where the raiders had come and gone. Even so, I didn't look forward to what we must do. When it was light enough, I gave the signal, and we advanced into the encampment, entered the tents, and began to kill.

I'd given strict orders, and I knew most of my men would follow them. The killing was to be done as quickly and cleanly as possible. None of the people—man, woman, child, or baby—could be left alive, but I certainly didn't intend to leave behind grisly evidence of torture and slow death such as what we had passed on our way here.

By the time enough of the Geshurites realized what was happening and began to fight back, the job was more than half done. Igal and Jaasiel fought on either side of me, and we plunged into the knot of warriors who had gathered in a cleared space. My gift roused, and I knocked the sword from the first man's hands, spinning him to Igal, who tripped him and stabbed him as he fell.

The next man tried to run, and an arrow appeared in his back as he fled. He tumbled to the ground, and a young girl ran toward him from a tent, screaming. As she bent over him, I brought my sword hilt down on her head, ending her cries and her life with the quickest blow I could before advancing again. We entered the tent she had come from, finding two women there with another child. Leaving them dead behind us, we cut our way into another tent.

Within minutes, it was over, and we stood in the silence.

"What do we do now, Dahveed?" Igal asked, his face pale.

"Go through the tents. Make sure absolutely everyone is dead." Besides the need to be sure the ban had been carried out, I also couldn't afford to have anyone get away who could identify me or my men. Not if I was to conceal what I was really doing from the Philistine serens.

"What about the animals?"

I looked around. The camp had some sheep and goats, donkeys of course, and four camels. "Save them."

"But the ban," Elhanan said, his face tight.

"We have honored Yahweh by bringing His judgment on the people. But we must also honor Seren Akish, who has sheltered us. Once we know everyone is dead, take spoils from the tents, but leave the people and what they are wearing for Yah."

After we had gone through the entire place, we packed everything we took on the donkeys. It would have been easier if we could have used the camels, but none of us knew how to pack or harness them, so we simply herded them along with the sheep and goats. We could sell them.

"Do we just leave them?" Igal asked when we were ready to go.

"No. Wrap the dead in their tents. Collect them in a pile and burn them."

The heavy, rough goat-hair tents caught fire quickly and burned hot. We left a column of smoke behind us, and I soon saw three others just like it rising in the distance.

We attacked two more gathering places of these tribes and one belonging to the Amalekites in the next week before we headed back north to Ziklag. All of us were tired, but not from the fighting. These tribes depended mostly on their bows for warfare in the open country. They were not skilled in close-in fighting, other than killing people with less training than they had, or those with no weapons at all. Consequently when we entered an encampment, nothing could stand against us. But the burden of such slaughter weighed heavily, and I quickly realized that I would have to rotate this duty among the men, otherwise it would be too much to bear.

The morning after we returned from that first raid, Shammah's Jonathan waited for me when I left outside the house in Ziklag. His face was strained. He had been in Josheb's units.

I put my hand on his shoulder as soon as I saw his face. "Have you decided that your abbi needs you more than I do?"

"Yes, Dodi," he whispered.

"Good. Our lives are hard, in ways you could not have anticipated until you lived with us. Shammah and Keziah will be overjoyed that you have chosen to remain with them. And I will count on you to keep a house with a grape arbor, so that I can sit under it someday."

He straightened up a little. "I will, Dodi. And I might even manage to have some sheep!"

"You are a good man, Jonathan. Never forget that Yahweh does not call everyone to be a warrior. Some of us have to raise mules! Shall I have Hanan take you home?"

"Please, Dodi. I like Hanan. He's restful."

"He knows how to be silent," I said, squeezing his shoulder. "Go get ready."

I watched him leave, then looked around. What was I doing here in Philistia? Should I, too, be packing my things and returning to Bethlehem and home? When I had held Atarah against the wall in the niche there in Jebus the day of Debir's purge, I had never wanted to hear again the cries of defenseless people as they died. What was I doing now, but causing those same cries as we put the ban on the Amalekites? Was I so certain that *I* was the one who must enforce Yah's decree? If I died tomorrow, someone else would take up the task, so was it really mine? But it was the shepherd's job to protect the sheep.

The sun burst over the hills and shone in my eyes, breaking into my thoughts. I sent Pekah to look for Hanan, but it took a while before the youth found him.

"Hanan, Jonathan ben Shammah must return to Bethlehem. His abbi needs him. I want you to take him there," I directed when my guide appeared.

"Yes, adoni."

"Hurry back. I'll need you as scout the next time we raid."

"No, adoni. I will not scout in the south."

I turned in amazement. Where had this come from? "Why not, Hanan?"

A shrug. "I need the highlands, and maybe it is too hot in the south."

Having seen the way he worked when we were down there, I knew I hadn't gotten the truth.

"And maybe you should tell me what is on your mind," I said sternly. Then I put my hand on his shoulder as I had my nephew's. "Give me the truth, Hanan," I commanded softly. "Does the ban bother you?"

He nodded.

"You know it was decreed by Yahweh, for you've seen the kinds of things these tribes do, haven't you?"

"Yes, but something in me says it is not for me to guide you to the places where children are so that they can be killed."

Annoyed, I frowned. Did everyone but me get to avoid this task? He was my best scout, and I depended on him. But looking into his eyes, I knew I could not demand that he continue. His gaze was as direct and clear as a child's, and I knew how simply he thought. If there was something inside that said he was not to do something or go somewhere, he wouldn't, and that was final.

Given how many times those same warnings had saved me and my band, I knew I would be a fool to throw that away. "All right, Hanan. I will not ask you to go again. You go where you think you should. Jonathan is probably ready. See him safely home."

"I will, adoni."

That night I spent a long time outside the town at the altar we'd built. Had I made the right choice coming to Philistia? We had followed the ark here, but was Yah simply making the best of my wrong decision? "Yah, am I in Your will?" I asked aloud. But the stars remained silent, and no reply came to my mind. At last I woke Abiathar. In the darkness next to the tent which covered the ark, I knelt to the priest.

"What do you wish, Dahveed?"

"Hakkohen, I would know whether or not I am to remain here in Philistia."

Abiathar remained silent. At last he touched my shoulder. "Adonai did not come," he stated.

I froze. He had not come? What did that mean? Was He rejecting me for something I had done? I know my shoulder trembled under the hakkohen's hand. "Is He displeased?" I barely whispered.

"No," the priest replied after a pause. "There was no condemnation. Just silence."

"What should I do?" I asked, bewildered.

"Wait. Go to your rest, now, Dahveed. Yahweh will speak when He is ready."

¥ ¥ ¥ ¥ ¥ ¥

"I tell you, it was your sars, Muwana," Gadmilk accused the seren of Ashkelon. "They were seen in the square, and the gold was actually found on one before they fought their way from the market and fled the city! And just the evening before I was attacked again! Would have been killed, too, if I hadn't chanced to drop back in the line to speak to my—to someone."

Akish raised his eyebrows at the hesitation. Gadmilk had another paramour? How many did that make this year, anyway? Likely another one from Tyre—his thoughts stopped. Feeling Manani's eyes on him, he looked down, feigning disinterest. Hazzel's suspicion of a slimy Phoenician had been right on the mark, and he'd bet his treasury Gadmilk was party to the plot, teased on by his exotic bed-mates who were probably as hard and shrewd as they were beautiful. Ashdod was the city closest to Tyre, and he wondered what the Phoenicians had promised the skinny seren for his aid.

"All my sars are either with their units on the Shephelah, or in my city, Gadmilk," Muwana said, his voice angry.

"Don't pay attention to him, Muwana," Hanabaal said. "I'd bet one of his own sars planted that gold on your man and at his own orders. And don't look so outraged," the Gaza seren added to Gadmilk, "judging from their performance this last month, your sars aren't any more skillful at trapping innocent men than they are at fighting!"

"My units fight just as well as yours, Hanabaal," Gadmilk retorted. "And *all* the units required of me are fighting as we speak, even though you shorted your duty for the third year! That being the case, you should have to pay more of the tax deficit than the rest of us!"

"That seems fair," Seren Manani put in evenly. "There have been several raids that would have succeeded if the requisite number of units had been available. That means little or no plunder for taxes."

"The problem isn't the lack of my units! I need every one I've held back to protect trade from the desert tribes," Hanabaal nearly shouted. "Why haven't those giant commanders of yours managed to get themselves into the highlands and stay there? This is the second year, Manani, and your promise of plunder from the Israelites has come to nothing, like all the other plans and plots you've wasted our gold on! Now we're saddled with paying the taxes again."

"I warned you it might be so," Manani replied coldly. "Once we have complete control, though, we can regain everything we have paid out."

"But how long will that take?" Muwana demanded. "From the reports I receive, any attempt to get into those hills meets great resistance. How have you found things, Akish?"

The seren of Gath glanced up. "My sars report that the moment they appear at the top of the land stair, they encounter warriors. It makes no difference when or where they go. I lose men every time."

Manani didn't try to hide the pleased look on his face, and Akish strictly controlled his own expression. He *was* losing men this year. Whoever was up there fighting his units now had no reason to allow Philistines to get away. And with Shemel gone, the raids were often ill-planned and ill-executed, losing even more men. All he could do was refrain from pushing the units into the hills and say nothing when the professionals in his force voiced their opinions.

"It would seem our efforts are coming to nothing," Muwana grumbled. "Perhaps we need to change tactics."

"What do you suggest?" Manani asked drily.

"Let each of us consult with the priests of our gods, asking what needs to be done to gain victory against the hill people," Muwana proposed. "We will then know what to do. I suggest we meet in another two weeks. In the meantime, we will encourage our men to do their best for Philistia and the gods."

Akish left with the rest. On his way back to Gath he debated how much good it would do to ask the gods to give advice. They weren't the deities of the highlands and couldn't do anything up there anyway. How would they know what would conquer Yahweh? But he would have to inquire, and waste gold in doing so. After he'd talked to the priests, he'd ask Ittai's opinion. And then he'd do what Ittai said. Hazzel's son was a better counselor than any of the priests.

¥ ¥ ¥ ¥ ¥

Seren Manani arrived at his private estate outside of Ekron, well pleased with the way the meeting had turned out. Dissension among the cities was getting stronger with each passing week. The more trouble that resulted, the better for his plans. And Muwana's suggestion at the meeting this afternoon simply provided the excuse he needed to leave. Before he retired, he called the sar at the gate to him.

"You sent for me, Sereni?" the man asked, entering the chamber.

"Yes. See that the lamps are lit in my bed chamber. I will be leaving the day after tomorrow to consult with an oracle regarding the war in the highlands. Prepare what I will need for a trip of a week. I will need two extra donkeys also. One for the gift for the oracle, and one for my own use."

"Yes, Sereni," the sar said, bowing.

"You are dismissed."

As the man left, Manani stood in the doorway looking east. He smiled. Soon, very soon, he'd be looking west again, only then he would be untouchable and absolute adon over the entire land. First he would subdue those pestilential hill people. After that, he would return to Philistia, and every one of the serens of the Five Cities would crawl to his feet. And then—then riches beyond belief!

¥ ¥ ¥ ¥ ¥

"Sar Malchi has just arrived, Hassar," the scribe at the door announced.

Both Jonathan and Eshbaal looked up as their brother strode through the throne room door.

"Shalom. Is all well?" Jonathan asked.

"As far as I know, Hassar. I came to ask if you had received any information about Philistines in the south."

Jonathan regarded his second brother a moment. "Eshbaal, what else do we have on schedule for today?"

"Routine reports," the youngest sar answered.

"Then court session is dismissed for the day," the hassar said, nodding to the scribes. Murmuring their shaloms, they and the courtiers exited, leaving the brothers alone.

"What's happening?" Jonathan asked.

"Nothing. And that's precisely why I'm here. Instead of more trouble with the Philistines, we are having less. Fewer units are attempting to enter the highlands, and those that do put up hardly any resistance before scurrying back down the land stair. Some of the Habiru have reported units leaving the area. I want to know if you've heard of any gathering south of Gath. The only reason I could think of for this to happen is an attempt to come up through Judah. Especially if news that Dahveed has left there has reached them."

"I haven't heard anything, but Ishvi had some interesting news during the noon meal. Elihu and Tanhum's network reported that dissension among the serens has worsened. The sars and professionals from all the cities are dissatisfied with the way the war seasons have gone for the past three years. I'd say that has affected their enthusiasm for fighting."

Malchi relaxed a little. "I hope that's the case. I wasn't coming up with any good ways of defending Israel on two fronts, not with Abbi and Abner battling each other as hard as they fight the Philistines."

"How bad is it?"

"It's affecting the men, of course, but it's what will happen when the recruits go home that worries me," Malchi explained. "We have militia from Dan to Beersheba, and they are all aware of the rift between Shaul and the general. All the tribes will know of the split in our house when this war season is over. It makes me wonder if a call to arms next year will even bring any response."

The brothers remained silent for some time. "Well," Jonathan said, "there's nothing we can do about it now. Go talk to Ishvi about what Elihu has heard. I'm going to Zelah tonight. I have to see if I can make a man talk about a seren, or a seren talk about a man; I don't know which," he ended in disgust.

And may Yahweh take a hand, Jonathan thought as he rode the light-gray mule down the road. He'd been unable to get Patisi off his mind the past couple days, and finally yesterday had sent a message to Bethel, requesting that the man be moved to Zelah again. And sometime, he had to have those clay tablets read to him!

Nimshi waited to take his mule when he dismounted. "Did our guest give you any trouble on the way here?" the hassar asked.

Ethan's youngest son glanced up at him. "No, geber. And I expected that he would. He is very afraid of you. He seems, well, so certain of death."

Jonathan frowned. He had hoped that by now the man would have lost some of that fear at least. After climbing the stairs to his upper room, he paused a moment to appreciate the blaze of colors in the western sky, highlighting the dark trees of the forests and hills. "You have given us a good land," he whispered. "Preserve it for us, Adonai, for I fear there is much trouble ahead. This man You gave to me knows that which I must know. But he fears me. Show me what I must do to learn what You wish me to know."

Peleth emerged from the house. "Shalom, Hassar," he greeted, bowing.

"Shalom, Peleth. Where is Meribbaal?"

"Sahrah Michal came earlier this afternoon and took him to Gallim. Merab's sons are there visiting."

"Good. He will enjoy being with his cousins. Did she say anything about Sar Ishvi?"

"She said to tell you that Ishvi is there also."

"Good. Those boys need to see him."

"Yes, Hassar."

As Jonathan put his hand on the door, Peleth turned back to him. "Adoni, is that man from Ekron?" he asked hesitantly.

"I believe so. He is supposed to be a seren named Patisi."

A puzzled look crossed the Philistine's face. "Forgive my forwardness, but why is he here?"

Jonathan looked toward the door and sighed. "Because I think he knows quite a lot that I need to know, and I haven't yet found a way to get that information out of him and be sure it's going to be the truth."

"Adoni, are you certain his name is Patisi?"

"I'm not certain of anything about him." Exasperation surged through Jonathan again. "If I didn't know better, I'd say he was another southern hill man sent to plague me for my sins!"

"It is important that he speak with you?"

"I suspect so, yes," the hassar replied, eyeing Peleth. The man had never pushed to know this much about anything before. "Dahveed seemed to feel that what he knows affects the safety of Israel, and I agree, even though I have nothing to go on."

"Then, if you would be patient a little, I know someone who might help," his overseer said.

Jonathan shrugged. "All right."

Peleth hurried down the stairs and into the room by the gate where he lived with his immi.

Wondering, Jonathan went inside and sat down, leaving his prisoner standing in the middle of the room. As Jonathan neither spoke nor moved, the man gradually stilled into perfect immobility again, and his fear permeated the room. At last, slow footsteps approached the door, and Peleth opened it, carefully helping his immi step over the threshold.

Keeping the surprise from his face, Jonathan stood. Since this woman had been Yahweh's voice to him, he treated her with the same respect that he gave his own immi. He picked up a chair and placed it close by her, where she could sit and observe all that went on. The hassar steadied it as she sat down.

Patisi watched closely, barely turning his head to see who had entered.

Peleth's immi studied the man in the light of the lamps in the wall niches of the room. Then she spoke. "It has been long since I saw you last, Eliahba. I could scarcely believe it when my son told me that you were here, but I see with my own eyes that it is true."

The man's head jerked around, and he stared at the old woman.

"Dodah?!" he gasped. "Dodah Batashima, you live? We knew you had fled Ekron, then heard that Manani's hirelings struck you down! How can you be here?"

"I and my two youngest sons fled Ekron and found shelter with a Habiru band. Even though I had Geresh and Bodbaal to comfort me, I mourned for Peleth. And then after years of grief, Geresh brought the news that Peleth lived, saved by the hesed of Israel's Hassar."

"Israel's Hassar has no hesed! I myself saw Peleth's death!"

"He struck me with the flat of the blade," Peleth said quietly. "And even though I was slave to him, he treated me better than Manani did his adons, let alone his slaves."

The captive stared at Peleth. "He treats you well, though you are Philistine slaves?"

"We are not slaves at all. I am overseer of this estate, and my immi lives with me free of labor and hardship. If you would know the sort of treatment you can expect from Hassar Israel's hand, I will bring Beor, Manani's chief scribe, and he will tell you."

"Thank Dagon, Beor lives!" Eliahba exclaimed, then cast a frightened glance at Jonathan.

"Better you should thank Yahweh," Batashima put in tartly. "What has Dagon ever done for us? We have found shelter under Yahweh's wings, and we are grateful. You must honor Yahweh with us."

"He will never accept me, for I have made war upon His lands and killed His people. There is only death for me here," the man said, his voice shaking. "But you have done nothing against Him. I say it before Him now. You have done nothing."

Well, that was one reason the man was so afraid, Jonathan thought. Maybe he could set that one to rest. "Death need not await you here," he said quietly. "If you are part of my household, Yahweh will not harm you."

"I am not a fool, Israelite! You have no reason to grant me hesed," Eliahba said shortly.

Batashima spoke sternly, gesturing to Jonathan. "How is it that you do not show him proper respect, Eliahba? I live in a comfortable room with all three of my sons alive because of this man's hesed. He had no reason to grant it to me or to Peleth! But he has."

Slowly the hassar sat down, watching his prisoner carefully.

Eliahba flushed. "Would you have me aid the one who troubles our land?"

"And do you think he would trouble us if Seren Manani did not send raiders into his land?"

"It is ordered by the Pharaoh to collect his taxes," the man replied defensively.

Batashima snorted. "Then let Pharaoh come and collect his taxes! This man has been gracious to us, preserved our house, given me back my son, and promised that my bones can stay in the land of Yah, who has sheltered us all. And you would lie to him about who you are and refuse him when he asks you a question? Eliahba, you shame us!"

His hands twisted in their bonds, and he looked at Peleth's immi in indecision, then cast another tentative glance at the hassar.

The knock at the door boomed in the room, and Jonathan nearly cursed with frustration. Why did he have to be interrupted now, when this man had nearly given in to him?

Silently, he jerked his chin at the door, and Peleth opened it.

Beor stepped over the threshold, his eyes fastened on Jonathan. "Adoni, adoni, forgive me for coming unsummoned, forgive me! I heard that Eliahba has come into your hand. Is this true?"

"It is true."

The scribe approached, his attention still fastened on Jonathan. "Adoni, you will show him hesed? He is a good man. He served as we all did, but he did many things the seren knew nothing of. He helped many of us. He helped me, adoni! He allowed you to take me from the camp that night. He was awake and would have stabbed you, but he saw that you did not harm me, and he let you take me away so that I would not die the next day, and he said nothing to his men. Please, adoni, he is a good man! Do not let harm come to him," the scribe finished, kneeling in appeal.

Jonathan stared at Beor in amazement. He had been seen the night he took the scribe? As the silence stretched, the scribe seemed to realize how bold he had been, and his hands twitched, then began their soft brushing up and down his chest.

Saying nothing, Jonathan rose and again captured the scribe's hands in his own. Then he looked over the man's head to Peleth. "You have indeed done well with this man."

His overseer smiled.

The hassar switched his gaze to the bound man. "Is what he said true? You were awake the night I took Beor from a Philistine unit?"

"I saw it happen and did nothing about it, but a Habiru seized him."

Jonathan smiled sourly. "A mistake I can't fault you for making. I certainly wasn't dressed in my best that night. It would appear, then, that I do have cause to show you hesed."

He turned back to the scribe. "Look at me, Beor."

Trembling, the man complied.

"Is it your wish that I grant Eliahba hesed?"

"Yes, adoni," the scribe managed to whisper, realizing now that there were other people in the room, and that he had interrupted a private meeting.

"Then I certainly shall," the hassar said, letting go of the scribe's hands and stepping back. He faced his captive. "Do you want my hesed?"

Once again the man twisted his bound hands in indecision. "But you are our enemy," he said, briefly meeting Jonathan's eyes.

Batashima snorted. "He is Manani's enemy, Eliahba! Or have you forgotten how much that rabid dog has done to our house? When the gods place you in the hands of the one who will cause Manani's fall, do not refuse them! Or I will no longer call you son, even though my milk sustained you when your own immi died."

Her voice sent a shiver down Jonathan's spine.

The bound man looked down. "Yes, Dodah." Taking a deep breath, he turned to Jonathan. "Swear by the death of Nemuel that you will protect me from Seren Manani and all that are his."

Jonathan pulled the twisted brass earring out of his robe and closed his hand around it. "As surely as I buried Nemuel, I will protect you."

Eliahba knelt, but when he raised his eyes, they were hard. "Ask whatever you want. I'll tell you anything you want to know."

Jonathan bowed his head briefly, amazed again at how much Yahweh had drawn from his spur-of-the-moment decision not to kill Peleth.

"What is your clan and how are you called?"

"As Batashima has named me, I am called Eliahba from the town of Shaalbim on the coastal plain just opposite the Aijalon pass. Dodah was from my immi's clan. I was 'recruited' into Seren Manani's service when I was a young man. I could fight better than most, so my life was useful to the seren. I rose to become one of his sars, commanding a unit. He used my men mostly for fighting in the highlands during the war season, but I saw enough of his cruelties to hate him. We all did. As Beor said, I used to do what I could at times to aid some of the seren's victims."

Jonathan leaned forward a little. "How?"

"Whenever he sent his slaves to the highlands in my unit, I would give them leave to run if they could, or try to see that they were captured instead of killed. Then I would report to Manani that they had died. Once I was escorting a young Ammonitess to his estate after he took a fancy to her and killed her family to have her. I let her go, and Manani never caught her, although what he did with her brother, I never did find out."

The hassar stilled. This was the man who'd let Dahveed's half-cousin, Ala, go! He wondered how it was that Manani hadn't discovered what this man was doing. Then he considered the man's name. Eliahba—my God hides. Truly, God had hidden him. Suddenly he smiled to himself. The problem of what to do with Eliahba had just been solved. "How did you end up in Hebron?"

"Seren Manani sent me to guard his emissary, Seren Patisi, on a trip to Jebus."

"Why was Manani dealing with Jebus?"

"That will take some time to tell, Hassar. I'm not sure how long ago he started asking me to do things for him, and—"

Jonathan held up his hand for silence. "Baalah Batashima, you do not need to remain here longer if you do not wish to. I see this will take a great deal of time."

The old woman pushed herself to her feet. "You are thoughtful of my old age, Hassar. Eliahba will tell you truth now."

The hassar bowed slightly. "I am grateful for your assistance, baalah."

Peleth helped his immi from the room. Half an hour after that, Nimshi was riding a mule down the road to Gibeah as fast as he could with instructions to have all three sars go to Tanhum's house, and make sure that Elihu ben Obed did also. Beor could read cuneiform. The hassar followed, at a scarcely saner pace, bringing Eliahba with him. What little he'd heard had made his blood run cold, and he prayed Yahweh they weren't too late, that there was still time!

Chapter 20

The courtyard of the house Tanhum occupied was dark, and straw had been piled in one corner for the escorts to sleep on. Jonathan's two guards joined the others, while he climbed the stairs to the balcony, taking his bound Philistine prisoner inside the upper room with him.

Everyone he'd sent for waited, and he noticed that Tanhum sat behind a curtain. The sword scars on the Jebusite's face had left him looking so hideous that he frightened most everyone, and Jonathan had to admit that he hadn't gotten used to it himself.

"I must ask everyone's pardon for summoning you like this," he said, taking off his cloak. "But once you hear what Eliahba has to say, I think you will all agree that it was necessary."

"I'm sure we will," Sar Ishvi said wryly, glancing at Elihu. "That's what's always so troubling about your summons."

Tanhum chuckled behind the curtain, letting Eliahba know that someone was there. Sar Eshbaal and Elihu shared a table with their scribal materials spread out ready to use, and bread, apricots, pomegranates, figs and wine were close at hand for everyone.

"Since time may be short, unless anyone has something to say, I'll begin now." The hassar waited a moment. No one spoke.

"Just as war season began, Sar Malchi found Eliahba and brought him to me. I fault myself for not discovering what he had to say until now, and I pray Yahweh will cover my mistake. Eliahba is a commander in Seren Manani's employ."

"A commander, not a seren?" Malchi interrupted.

"Yes, Sar," Eliahba replied.

Malchi smiled a little. "I wondered. The songs you sang seemed more fitted for soldiers than adons!"

Flushing, the Philistine looked down.

"During the past two years," Jonathan continued, "he and his men were sent as guards for Seren Patisi on diplomatic missions for Manani to Araunah Debir in Jebus. They crossed the Negev and came up the Arabah each time, changing guards along the way, since Manani wanted to be certain no one knew who they were, where they came from, or where they were going."

The men listened intently as the hassar's rich voice went on.

"At the end of threshing, they came to Jebus again, and Patisi met with Debir, sealing an agreement with him. However, the trip up the Arabah in the heat had been hard on the seren, who was an elderly man. He became ill in Jebus after his meeting with Debir. Rather than risk having healers in the city know of his presence, the attending scribe directed that he be taken to Jericho for treatment. He died within three days. The four guards deserted, deciding that with the seren dead their chance of payment was questionable, and left the scribe and the commander to deal with the situation alone."

Jonathan paused, taking a sip of wine. "The scribe realized the one thing which might save them from Manani's anger was that they could report a successful mission, even though Patisi had died. It was at that point that the scribe read all the documents sent with Patisi, as well as the clay tablets found when they prepared the man for burial. After I had heard that much, I decided all of you needed to know Eliahba's story. I have the documents the scribe read here. You should all look them over before Eliahba continues." The hassar handed the diplomatic pouch he carried to Ishvi. His brother passed it immediately to Elihu without even looking at what was inside.

Dahveed's brother emptied the pouch, glancing at each document as he did so, and the hassar noted with a smile that the man read the clay tablets first, something he would never forgive himself for not having done sooner. Elihu summarized them aloud.

"The first cuneiform tablet contains instructions for Patisi to travel through Judah on his way back to Philistia and stop in Hebron to speak with the Calebite nagids. He was to sound them out regarding a treaty to cooperate in protecting the southern lands from raids by the desert tribes.

"The offer seems to be an excuse for Patisi to stop in Hebron. The second tablet is the important one, I believe. It directs Patisi to find a trustworthy guide across the south for a party of 15 men. Both tablets are signed with Seren Manani's seal."

"Who were the men to be?" Tanhum asked from behind his curtain.

"An envoy with a scribe, myself with 11 picked men, and the guide, adon," Eliahba replied.

Elihu glanced at the other documents. "These in the pouch include a diplomatic letter of introduction for Seren Patisi from Akish of Gath to the Araunah, a recommendation for Qausa the Habiru as a reliable guide for trade caravans, and a personal letter to Patisi directing him to keep the brooch which had been sent to him, and to direct all correspondence to Manani, personally, since Beor had died." Elihu passed the documents to Sar Ishvi, who looked them over in silence, then offered them to Malchi, who waved them away. Finally Eshbaal handed everything through the curtain to Tanhum.

When no one spoke, the hassar turned to Eliahba. "What did you and the scribe decide to do?"

"We decided to keep the seren alive a little longer," the Philistine said wryly. "Since his clothes fit me, I would be Patisi. Although we knew we couldn't keep up the pretense for long, we also knew we didn't have to. We planned to travel to Hebron immediately, where I would meet with the nagids and hire a Habiru guide. We would stay at an inn, and I would disappear after talking to the guide. The scribe would report to Manani that I'd failed to return from the meeting with the Habiru, and that he assumed I, as Patisi, had been killed. He would say he didn't know if the guards had been killed, or fled, since they had become unreliable after their sar, Eliahba, had died of fever in Jericho."

Ishvi chuckled. "Ingenious."

"And Manani's suspicions of everyone would lead him to believe it," Jonathan added. "Was the scribe going to report in person?"

Eliahba shrugged. "I don't know. He hadn't decided yet when we started for Hebron. On the road south of Jebus, we met a man named Ahibaal. He's of some local importance around Hebron, and he took us to Nagid Dathan's house. He is friendly with the nagid, and Dathan agreed to call the clans to a meeting.

"Everything went according to plan, and I asked Ahibaal if he knew of any reliable guides across Judah. He said he'd bring one to me. I picked a wine shop to wait in, and by the time the adon returned, I'd had more to drink than I should have. I would guess the Habiru took the opportunity to help himself to my clothing, and who knows what else, for the next thing I remember, I found myself bound in a storeroom."

"Actually, he didn't take your possessions," Jonathan said gravely. "He packed everything from your room onto a donkey cart and sent it north along with you. The loaded cart is still at my estate."

"That's good to know, Hassar. I'd like to think that I could buy my weapons back some day."

"I'll think about it," Jonathan smiled. "If I understand you correctly, the scribe would not be surprised to find you gone and would then report as planned to Manani."

"Yes, Hassar. He could also say that Patisi had been successful with Debir. Because of that, I would assume he reported in person. He has a wife and children."

"Commander, do you have any idea what the agreement with Debir is about?" Ishvi asked.

"I only know that Debir was to receive some type of document, and I assumed that's what the envoy would be bringing to him. The men I was to pick for escort duty were to be the best fighters I could find."

"Why would he chance crossing Judah when it would be much safer going the Negev-Arabah route again?" Elihu inquired.

"I don't know," the sar replied. "There was another odd thing about the trip, however. Manani said it would take three or four days, since the envoy could only travel a short distance each day."

"Didn't you tell the Da—the Habiru guide something about lamps?" Malchi asked.

Eliahba thought a moment. "I might have," he admitted. "Manani has been planning what the envoy would take on this trip for months at least. He showed me the packs already made up. There was one donkey load that had oil with several lamps."

"Why is there mention of this Qausa?" Jonathan asked, curious.

"All I know about him is that he will be in Jebus, and that he will take the blame for something."

"And it's the fact that we've heard nothing of Qausa which gives me hope that we are still in time to untangle this," Jonathan said.

Once no one had any more questions, he sent the Philistine out to the balcony, leaving him in Nimshi's care, and marveling again at how Yah had, indeed, protected and hidden this man. As Jonathan returned to the room, Sar Malchi was just finishing telling everyone that Dahveed was the one Eliahba hired as a guide, but for 16 men, and to En-gedi and Jebus. "Given how drunk the man was when I saw him, I'd expect some of the details to be mixed up. Do you know anything more about this, Jonathan?" he ended.

"I know that Beor isn't dead. He's at my estate." Jonathan outlined what the scribe had told him of the seren's activities up to the time he was sent away. "What else do we know of Manani?" he asked. "I can't shake the feeling that we must figure out what that man is doing."

"Especially since it involves Jebus," Tanhum added thoughtfully.

"I had Jether the Ishmaelite check up on some things," Elihu spoke up. "Manani is heavily in debt. His creditors, who all seem to be serens of the Five Cities, have been pressing him during the past winter. And for the first time, there have been messages traced from him to someone in Israel."

"Who could that be?" Jonathan asked sharply.

"Someone near Chephirah," Tanhum interjected. "I have been unable to determine anything more. The Gibeonites are exceptionally close-mouthed. But I just got word that a message was delivered again today. Knowing Manani, his contact would be Philistine. But it would be unusual to find a Philistine there."

"Well, there's one there at least, and by all accounts he's an unusual man," Malchi said.

The hassar whirled around. "What Philistine?"

His brother looked at him in surprise. "The Gibeonite overseer. The one Dahveed appointed years ago when he uncovered the incompetence of the former one, and the corruption of the head scribe. Don't tell me you've forgotten that!"

"I haven't forgotten; I guess I just forgot Minelek was a Philistine," Jonathan admitted sheepishly.

"His name is *Minelek?*" Tanhum asked, startled. "What city is he from?"

"I don't know," Jonathan replied. "Eshbaal, did we ever check on him?"

"There was no reason to," the youngest sar replied. "He's done an exemplary job as Gibeonite overseer."

"Anyone else know?" the hassar asked.

"I met him once," Elihu spoke up. "He didn't have much of an accent left, but the ends of some words had that twist that made me think he came from Ekron."

"Would he be Manani's contact?" Jonathan asked, facing the curtain.

"It's possible," Tanhum replied. "But if Minelek has been there for years, it's odd that Manani would wait until now to make overtures." The Jebusite sighed. "We don't have enough information to really tell."

Jonathan started to pace in the limited space of the room. "We don't have enough information about anything!" he fumed in frustration.

"Was there anything else in Eliahba's possessions?" Elihu asked.

"Not that I can think of," Jonathan said. "But I didn't go through everything personally."

"I did," Malchi said. "The only documents were the ones here, and that list."

"What list?" Tanhum asked instantly.

"A list of names, merchants or something. It was in the pouch."

"It's not here now," the Jebusite said.

Sar Eshbaal checked the pouch still on the table, and then shifted things around. "Here it is," he said, pulling it out from under a papyrus. "It got covered up." He passed it through the curtain.

Tanhum sucked in his breath, and Jonathan swung around to face the curtain. "Is that list important?"

"I'm not sure, Hassar. It could be. But it just doesn't fit now."

"Nothing fits," Ishvi sighed.

The door opened. "Geber?"

Jonathan turned to Nimshi, annoyed at the interruption. "Yes?"

"Eliahba said something about Qausa, and that reminded me that I got a message from my abbi yesterday saying I should tell you that Qausa is in Jebus expecting to be rich soon."

"But that's impossible!" the hassar sputtered.

"Why?" Tanhum asked.

"Qausa has been dead for years," Malchi put in. "Didn't you always suspect the silver he had came from Manani?"

"I could never prove it," Jonathan said, "but I'm personally convinced of it. Manani has to know he's dead, too."

"What happened that you are so sure?" Tanhum asked

"He was hired to assassinate King Shaul. Ethan got to him first, and brought his body to the king. Abbi left it unburied in the forest."

"That changes things, Hassar," Tanhum said. "This list contains the names of Debir's key supporters, all of them Kassites. Debir went to them when he couldn't convince the Hurrian conclave to betray the old Araunah. The list, the supposed presence of an unsavory Habiru, and the necessity for 11 guards could fit together."

"How?" Ishvi asked.

"The list is probably a death list," Elihu explained. "Eleven men, if used correctly, would be an effective killing squad. Manani may be planning to assassinate Debir. Assume he knows a way to get someone close to Debir in private so the Araunah dies quietly. His signet can then be used to order the admittance of a party of travelers, diplomats, petitioners, or some such who are actually Eliahba's men. Then an emergency summons goes out to all of Debir's key supporters, probably saying that he has been attacked and severely wounded by Qausa. Once they are all there, the squad kills them. It's a simple beheading of the government."

Eshbaal looked thoughtful. "Would it work?"

"That's the way I'd do it," Tanhum commented softly. "But there would have to be a compelling reason for Debir to meet alone with anyone."

"But Patisi is already a trusted envoy," Jonathan observed.

"True. So provided the document was indeed very important, it would probably work," the Jebusite agreed.

"And it would have to be profitable," Malchi added. "Debir's no adon, just a robber who got rich instead of getting caught."

"We're forgetting, though, that Patisi is dead, and Manani knows this," Elihu interrupted. "If we've figured out what his plan was, what will he do now?"

"Maybe nothing," Tanhum mused. "The message pouch this evening said that the Philistine serens are consulting their gods regarding the war in the highlands. Manani left early this morning with gifts, a scribe, and a unit of 13 men."

Elihu put down his quill and stared hard at one of the lamps. "Adoni, when was the delivery of the document to Debir supposed to occur?"

Jonathan stopped pacing long enough to open the door and summon Nimshi and Eliahba back into the room. "What was the delivery date for the document?"

"Eight days from now," the Philistine replied. "The scribe said Debir was impatient for it. That limited our time in Hebron since the scribe had to report to Manani soon enough to allow travel time for the delivery. If it is to be delivered as agreed, the envoy must have left today."

"Somehow, I don't think Manani is planning on consulting the gods," Elihu said evenly. "He's headed for Jebus as his own envoy with everything in place for him to become the next Araunah."

"Yahweh, save us!" Jonathan groaned.

Tanhum stirred restlessly behind the curtain. "Is there any direct evidence that Manani is coming personally?"

Jonathan stopped pacing. "The lamps!" he exclaimed. "Beor told me that Manani is never without light at night."

"Which might also explain the short travel periods," Malchi suggested. "He'd start long after dawn, and would probably want to be camped well before dusk."

"I knew I'd be up all night with this," Ishvi sighed, looking wryly at his older brother. "How is Manani going to convince Debir to see him alone if he's not the expected envoy?"

Silence settled on the room, then the Jebusite's hoarse voice spoke from behind the curtain. "The only way is if the document he is carrying is valuable enough for Debir to take that risk."

Malchi pursed his lips a moment. "But what kind of document could Ekron have that would tempt Debir that much? I can't imagine anything enticing that disgusting liar to risk his neck unless it would make him very rich."

"What about an authorization from Pharaoh to collect Israelite taxes?" Jonathan nearly whispered. "With Debir in an impregnable fortress right in our midst, he could plunder to his heart's content."

A second silence filled the room. "That would do it," Tanhum agreed.

"Well, how do we stop this?" Ishvi asked.

"Kill Manani as he's crossing the south," Malchi said immediately.

"That might bring retribution from the Five Cities on us."

"It would be cleanest to have the Philistine serens take him down," Elihu sighed. "If we could leak the information that Manani plans on becoming Araunah, every other seren in the alliance will be after him. They know him well enough to know what would happen if he became ruler of Jebus."

"Who is the best one to leak it to?" Ishvi asked.

"Akish," Jonathan and Elihu said at the same time. "And it has to be in such a way as to protect Beor and Eliahba," the hassar added. He turned to his young armor-bearer. "Could you get word to Akish?"

Nimshi thought for a moment. "No. But I could get word to Ittai."

"That's good enough," Jonathan said with a smile. "We're in a hurry, so take my mule."

Nimshi flashed a smile. "With pleasure, geber!"

¥ ¥ ¥ ¥ ¥ ¥

Ahibaal paused for his servant to remove his cloak, then sat at the table, waiting until he'd been served some food before dismissing the man and taking the message from his girdle, his face impassive. He opened it. The writing was hurried.

"Agent who copied list reports to Seren Ekron who has established contact with Minelek, now Gibeonite overseer in Chephirah."

The Jebusite nearly dropped the message. *Minelek?* After all these years? Everyone had assumed the man was dead after his sudden disappearance from Ekron. Was it possible Minelek would aid Manani now? If so, the political situation had just taken a sudden, dark twist that could lead to anything.

Resolutely, Ahibaal picked up the message and continued reading.

"Imperative to watch Minelek's movements. Report anything instantly. In addition, locate Qausa the Habiru now in Jebus. Be ready to pay him to disappear when I give the word. A hint that his employer is Seren Ekron who does not plan for him to survive his assignment should prove helpful. El Elyon has favored us at last."

Ahibaal frowned slightly. Minelek must not be heavily involved at this time, or the message would not have ended so positively. The adon's shoulders relaxed as he burned the papyrus, dumping the crushed ashes in the large, covered pot provided for personal relief during the night. "As you command, adoni," he whispered again.

¥ ¥ ¥ ¥ ¥ ¥

Seren Akish looked up in surprise as his nephew entered his private chamber with an expression on his face that said something important had happened.

"What is it?" he asked sleepily, stretching and rising from his bedroll where he had lain down for the noon rest.

"You know Seren Manani left Ekron?"

"Yes. The morning report said he departed yesterday with gifts for an oracle to consult about the war effort."

"He's not going to an oracle. He's on his way to Jebus, and he entered the highlands this morning, using the watercourse just south of the Elah valley."

"What's he going to Jebus for?" his dodi asked in amazement.

"If all goes as he has planned, he will be the Araunah in little more than a week."

Akish snapped alert instantly. "The Araunah? How? And how do you know this?"

"Nimshi ben Ethan brought word. I've already ordered two units to assemble. We've got to stop him, Dodi."

"If he went up to the highlands, whoever is up there this year will stop him."

"He didn't go alone. He's got a dozen of the best professionals with him. Besides, Nimshi said he crossed Manani's trail west of the Hebron highway and followed it down the land stair. Manani has already slipped through. He had a guide with him."

"Where did this information come from?" Akish asked, reaching for his girdle which he had removed while he slept.

Ittai hesitated. "You don't want to know that, Dodi."

Akish swore. "We can't just drag Seren Ekron back here and accuse him of something without being able to produce evidence, Ittai!"

"I know. But if this information is accurate, Manani has dangled Gath's copy of the Egyptian tax authorization in front of Debir, and will use it to get into his presence. At that point, Debir dies, and Manani rules."

"He doesn't have Gath's copy. I do."

"Which means we may have a difficult time convincing the seaside cities we aren't conspiring with Manani in this plot also! Our only chance is to expose him ourselves."

"Even then, Gath may go down with Ekron," Akish said bitterly.

"I know. But let's work with what we have now. Maybe after we get our hands on Manani, something else will turn up."

Just then a knock sounded on the door.

"Enter," Akish called, wondering who else would have something important enough to interrupt the noon rest.

One of the guards bowed himself into the room. "Sereni, there is a strange scribe insisting that he must see you immediately. He's from Ekron."

"Did he say that?" Akish asked.

"No, Sereni, but he has the accent."

Ittai and Akish exchanged a glance. "Bring him to this chamber," the seren ordered.

Before long, hurried footsteps in the passage presaged the arrival of the strange scribe. Once the guard had ushered him into the room, Akish studied the man kneeling before him.

"What is your city and how are you called?" he asked.

"I am from Ekron, Sereni, and I am called Ahuzzath. I have been Seren Manani's principal scribe for more than a year now. When the seren left to consult an oracle, I became suspicious of what he was doing. With the help of his wife, I searched his house, and the house of his father-in-law. What we found in Seren Patisi's records is frightening, Sereni! You were the closest city, so I have come to you. You must stop him! He is not consulting an oracle. He is on his way to Jebus!"

Akish grabbed the man's shoulders. "You have records of where Manani is going and why?"

"I have all the records and evidence that Seren Patisi collected, as well as a copy of the agreement already sealed between Seren Ekron and Araunah Debir! He copied it out before he went that last time—"

"Where is Patisi?" Akish demanded.

"He is dead, Sereni. He died shortly after he concluded the sealing of the agreement with Debir, and—"

"How do you know this?" Akish interrupted again.

"I was there, Sereni."

Akish looked up at Ittai. "Go!"

Without a word, his nephew nearly ran from the room.

¥ ¥ ¥ ¥ ¥ ¥

It was nearly dusk when the messenger arrived at Jonathan's camp east of the Elah valley. "What news?" the hassar asked immediately.

"Hassar, two more units of Philistines have entered the highlands. They are tracking the first unit, and Dahveed Joel says to tell you the units are led by Nimshi ben Ethan on your mule."

"Very good. Eat and tend to your animal. Then tell Dahveed Joel to keep watch, but not to interfere. If I mistake not, the units will be headed back down to the lowlands by tomorrow night."

"Yes, Hassar," the man said, bowing.

¥ ¥ ¥ ¥ ¥ ¥

Seren Akish of Gath entered his throne room, accepted the greetings of the scribes and courtiers, and sat down on the throne, setting the parchments he carried on the small three-legged table beside him. He glanced briefly at the blackened spot to the right on the floor where Baal's fire had struck years ago. Only now, he wasn't certain it had been Baal's fire. Given everything that had happened since then, he was beginning to think it had been Yahweh's.

Ittai had reported in late last night with the news that Manani would be brought before him this morning, and he was curious about how the Ekronite would react to the current situation. He dealt with the routine reports and one or two minor disputes before signaling to the scribe that he was ready for the interview.

When the doors opened, and a servant ushered Manani in, Akish noted with approval that the seren was not bound, but that he came in alone. Ittai, wearing his sword, escorted him, with five of the palace guard following.

"What is the meaning of this, Akish?" Manani demanded as soon as he was close enough to the throne. "How dare you bring me before you like this! The serens of the alliance will hear of your effrontery against them!"

"*My* effrontery?" Akish asked, raising an eyebrow. "I do not know that I have affronted the alliance. You, however, have betrayed it."

For a moment, Manani stood totally motionless. "I have done no such thing," he said finally, his voice soft. "It is not a betrayal of the alliance to seek the advice of an oracle regarding the war, as Seren Muwana suggested."

Akish felt a chill run down his spine. Something about the tone of the man's voice made him feel cold. "I have never heard of an oracle in the highlands," Akish said neutrally.

"There is one in the Arabah, near Jericho, and I was on my way there when this Habiru took me captive in your name," the Ekronite said, casting a glance at Ittai.

"And you were going to give that oracle this, I suppose?" Akish asked, picking up the top parchment and unrolling it, turning it so that Manani could see the written side. "That is your seal at the bottom, and my scribe tells me this is an agreement between you and Araunah Debir in which you promised him genuine authorization from Pharaoh to collect Israelite taxes now and half the profit from the coastal cities later, in return for safe haven in the highlands, should you ever need it. I fail to see how you can possibly fulfill this agreement unless you have control of the profit from the coastal cities."

Manani looked at the agreement in contempt. "I don't know where you got that, but it is utter nonsense," he scoffed.

Akish laid the agreement down. "Of course it is utter nonsense. I recognize that, but will the other serens? The ones whom you've promised to impoverish for the benefit of Jebus?"

"Then perhaps it would be better for us both if the other serens never saw that agreement." Manani said, stepping closer to the throne. "Perhaps a private discussion could resolve this."

"I don't think we need to discuss anything privately, Manani. Given how often you have insinuated that I was party to your plotting, I feel that this entire interview should take place before my courtiers, most of whom report to one seren or the other. What has already been said is enough to incite the alliance against you as it is."

"Then lock your city gates until you know that every spy in your palace is dead," Manani said savagely.

Akish arched his eyebrow again. "I have never found that wholesale slaughter of my citizens served any useful purpose."

"Perhaps you will see the use of it after we talk," Manani replied, holding himself stiffly.

"Then speak, and we will see."

"Keeping the agreement from the other serens will save your life, Akish," the Ekron ruler declared, his voice soft again. "Once they realize that you gave me your copy of the Egyptian tax authorization to give to Jebus, and kept a document that said you did not need to pay your share of the tax deficit, you will be the one who has betrayed the alliance!"

"To quote your own words, that is utter nonsense."

"Bring the authorization, and we will see," Manani challenged.

"As it happens, I have it here," Akish said, reaching for the second parchment he'd brought, knowing that he must break free of Manani's control now, or forever be the man's slave. He handed the document to his chief scribe, whom he knew reported to Manani.

The man took it with an expressionless face and opened the cover cloth. Unrolling the document, he stared it at for a long moment.

"Is that the tax authorization?" Akish asked in a hard voice, glaring at Manani.

"Well, Sereni, I—I, that is, it certainly, well, it is written on parchment and—"

"And does it have the official Egyptian seal at the end?"

"Yes, Sereni," the man said in a low voice. "It is the authorization, without doubt." As the scribe said those last two words, he glanced at Seren Manani.

"That's impossible!" the prisoner gasped, pulling a cover cloth from the front of his robe. "You have a forgery!" he declared, holding up the scroll he held. "This is the genuine document. You gave this to me! See for yourself!" He started forward, holding the document out to the seren of Gath. Instantly Ittai drew his sword and barred the way.

Akish motioned to his scribe. "Go look."

The man reluctantly approached Ekron's ruler, holding out a hand that shook slightly. Ripping the cover cloth off, Manani thrust the rolled parchment into the scribe's grasp. "Read it," he snarled.

Unrolling it, the scribe scanned it, then looked again, slowly perusing what was in front of him. Then, with a cry of horror, he dropped the parchment and scrambled away.

"What does it say?" Akish asked, hiding his surprise at the scribe's actions.

"It is a curse, Sereni," the man gasped. "I dare not read it aloud. It is written in mixed script with powerful signs in it and twisted letters. Some of the words are Babylonian, I believe, in the old speech.

It talks of feeding the earth, and dying in darkness and torments by the dead." The scribe continued to back away as he spoke, looking at his hands in horror. "It had the sign for clinging and carrying. The curse must cling to the one who carried it! I held it, Sereni! I beg you, let me go to the temple to wash!" The man started to brush his hands against his robe.

"No!" a priest said. "Don't touch your clothing! Sereni, let me take him to the temple."

"Go," Akish said, his face hard. He turned back to Manani. "Shall we also add an attempt to attack me to the list of your other crimes," he suggested, staring at his fellow ruler. But he didn't think Seren Ekron heard him. Manani was staring at the fallen parchment as if it were a snake that had come to life and bitten him.

Chapter 21

The regular messenger pouch sat beside Ahibaal's hand at the table on the balcony of the main house in Giloh, and he opened it. It contained the usual business correspondence, a complaint from his overseer at the Jebus residence, and a small sealed papyrus. The seal made his breath stop. Blinking, he looked again. Then, his hands shaking, he broke open the message.

"I require your presence."

Ahibaal stood, carefully placing the message in his girdle. Calling a servant, he descended the stairs. "Put the message pouch inside the upper room," he ordered. "Tell Eliam's wife I have decided to go to Jebus for a few days." Shortly thereafter, he rode from his gate, keeping the mule at a relaxed trot. The time for speed would come later, when he was out of sight.

It was dusk when he rode into his estate outside of Jebus. He had been careful when approaching the place to remain as unnoticed as possible and planned on washing and changing his clothes here. Entering the upper room, he had thrown his cloak aside before he noticed the other figure that rose from beside his table.

The Jebus adon gasped and fell to his knees, stretching himself out flat on the floor.

"Rise, adon," the man said in his quiet voice.

Ahibaal obeyed, staying on his knees, and bowed over the hand the man gave him. "I hardly dared to hope when I saw the message," he said. "What use would you make of me?"

"We already owe you much, adon. If not for you, my wife and son would not have survived. I will not forget this."

"It was the least I could do," Ahibaal said, his voice trembling. "It is a blessing of El Elyon to have you with us again, Emmanuel."

The hand touched his lips. "There. You have done your obeisance, and given me my title. Do not do so again until all is finished. If Debir hears that the Emmanuel, the heir to Jebus' throne, did not die in his purge, all we have worked for will be lost. Stand now. We have much to do, for word has come that Gath holds Ekron in his hands."

"How are things on the Shephelah, Malchi?" Hassar Jonathan asked, reaching for another dried Tekoa fig.

"Quieter than before. I assume you know why," his brother replied, moving the fig bowl out of his reach.

"Elihu knows that. He's coming with Ishvi."

Not long afterward, Sars Ishvi and Eshbaal climbed the stairs to the large house on Malchi's estate in Zelah, trailed by Elihu.

After the usual greetings, the brothers reported any news, and then they all turned to Dahveed's brother.

"What is happening in the lowlands?" Jonathan asked.

"As you know, Nimshi was successful in contacting Ittai ben Ribbai in Gath, and two units went into the highlands, catching Seren Manani and his men on the central plateau," Elihu explained. "Reports since then indicate that from the moment Manani was brought before him, Akish established control, and has kept it. Messages have gone out to the alliance, and the serens will be convening a trial for treason in a week in Ekron."

"Then it seems Manani is no longer a problem for us," Ishvi said with satisfaction.

"What is Tanhum doing?" the hassar inquired.

"He has been concerned about Debir," Elihu replied. "You know that the Araunah is expecting a meeting with an envoy in another two days, and if, as we suspect, he's also expecting to have permission to collect Israelite taxes, he may decide to do any number of unpleasant things if he's disappointed. Tanhum is concerned that Debir may decide to collect taxes whether or not he has permission. He's working on a way to find out what the man may be planning. Also he asked if you would be willing to loan him Eliahba. Since the Araunah assumes he will be meeting a man named Qausa, Tanhum thought Eliahba could be that man. Then we would have an agent in Jebus."

"I think that can be arranged," Jonathan said. "Come back to my estate when we are finished here. You can take Eliahba with you. And just in case he runs into trouble in Jebus, I'll give him a letter to Dahveed. Your brother can always use a good man, and this particular commander is the one who allowed Ala to escape years ago."

"Thank you, Hassar," Elihu said.

¥ ¥ ¥ ¥ ¥ ¥

"You received word, and the Habiru is gone?"

"Yes, adoni," Ahibaal said, restraining his urge to bow to the Emmanuel. "He was not inclined to leave at first, but after our substitute Qausa took him aside and explained a few things to him, he left rather hurriedly."

"Good. And the appointment?"

"That is set for tonight, after the evening meal. Our Qausa will accompany you. I will be in the background as your servant."

"Everything is ready then. Leave me now, adon."

Ahibaal did bow a little this time, and backed several steps before exiting the room. As he walked out into his courtyard, he wondered again if the Emmanuel would be able to play his part. He certainly didn't look it, and yet— Ahibaal paused. Every once in a while he got a glimpse of something harder than bronze under the quiet exterior of the heir to the throne.

Although he tried to distract himself with business affairs while he waited for evening, finally he gave up and sat down to write a letter to Eliam's wife and daughter in Giloh. He added a couple of lines about where to find the most important business correspondence just in case he didn't return from tonight's appointment. Then he burned the papyrus and started again, sending only the usual news this time.

The evening meal was nearly over when Ahibaal accompanied the newest Qausa the Habiru and the Emmanuel into the palace complex on the Jebus heights. Dressed in plain clothing—a lower grade than he normally wore—he tried to still his nervousness. He and the "envoy" were searched at the outside doors, and he tried to pattern his behavior after the meek acceptance of the necessity that the Emmanuel displayed. When the soldier turned to Qausa, the Emmanuel spoke.

"This man is our guard, geber. He will, of course, remain outside the audience room in the presence of Debir's guards during our meeting. As you see, he carries only a short sword."

The soldier hesitated a moment, then let them pass.

At the reception room door, the "envoy" told the guard whom to announce.

"I'll see him in the private audience room," Debir said. "Is this Qausa with them?"

"They have an armed escort, adoni," the guard replied.

"He is to wait outside the chamber with the door guard, and you will remain in the chamber during the interview."

"Yes, adoni," the soldier replied, bowing.

Ahibaal and the Emmanuel exchanged a quick glance. They needed Debir *alone* in that room.

Returning to them, the man escorted them around the corner to the smaller audience room. Once there, he spoke to the guard at the door. "Return to the throne room and take my place at the entrance," he directed. "I will stay here with these men."

Looking relieved, the other soldier hurried off.

When he vanished around the corner, the escort opened the door to the chamber. "If you would all enter," he said softly.

Ahibaal tensed. What was happening? The three of them preceded the guard into the room.

The soldier closed the door after them, then barred it with his spear. Facing the "envoy," he sank to his knees, then prostrated himself on the floor.

Ahibaal started to speak, but stopped at the hand signal from his adon.

"What is the meaning of this?" the "envoy" asked.

The guard looked up, tears on his face. "We have waited so long, Emmanuel," he replied simply. "How can I best serve you in whatever you plan to do here?"

"Weren't you a palace guard to the Araunah?"

"Yes, adoni. But I had gone to visit my family the day the usurper took the throne. I joined the squads who buried the dead and realized that you were not among the bodies. After a suitable time, I returned and applied again for a position as a palace guard. I knew you would return, and I hoped I might be of some use when you did."

"How are you called?"

"Dedan, adoni."

"Rise, Dedan. Perhaps you can be of help today."

The Emmanuel stroked his chin in thought while the guard stood.

"If I may speak, adoni?" the guard said. "The usurper always goes armed. He carries a belt knife hidden in his girdle."

"You have been helpful indeed, Dedan. The light is dim in here. Give Qausa your spear. He will be guarding this hall door. When Debir enters, you stand guard at the door to the large audience chamber. Only I will approach Debir to begin with. He will suspect nothing that way."

After questioning Dedan closely regarding where Debir kept the knife, the Emmanuel took the prepared parchment from Ahibaal and placed it on the table with the Egyptian royal seal clearly in view.

Before long, Debir entered from the side door, and the two men knelt, the Emmanuel gracefully bowing to the floor. "I am the envoy from our mutual friend in the west, adoni. He sends you greetings."

Debir stopped, peering at him in the dim light.

"I had thought Seren Patisi would come again," he said, motioning to the guard.

Dedan stationed himself at the side door, murmuring to the attendant who had accompanied Debir to stand guard outside. Once the soldier had complied, he quietly barred the door.

"Our friend thought it would be better not so," the Emmanuel was saying. "The seren is old and became ill. The journey was rigorous due to the war season. Thanks to Qausa, we slipped away from the coast and through the fighting units without anyone the wiser. He is an exceptional man, one who is faithful to his duty."

"There are few such these days," Debir said with a snort, walking to the table. "You have the delivery?"

Rising, the Emmanuel stepped aside as Debir approached the table. Ahibaal bowed again and remained still.

While Debir seated himself, the "envoy" remained a respectful distance away. The Araunah picked up the document and examined it, struggling with the seal.

"May I help?" the envoy asked, stepping forward. "The heat must have made the seal sticky again."

As he spoke, "Qausa" silently moved forward, seizing Debir's left wrist and twisting the arm around the back of the chair while covering the man's mouth with his other hand. The Emmanuel quickly pinned Debir's right arm to the table.

Debir's chest heaved, and he stared at them with wide eyes.

"There are a few things you should know, Debir," the "envoy" said. "First, Qausa the Habiru has been dead for years, something Seren Manani well knew. Second, even if I had not come as Manani's envoy, this meeting would have had the same ending, for Manani had plans which you did not fit into. Third, allow me to make myself known to you. I am the Emmanuel." Then he pulled the hidden knife from Debir's girdle and drove it into the man's heart.

When Debir slumped over, the new ruler of Jebus twisted the signet from Debir's finger. Ahibaal came forward with the order to admit the party waiting at the palace gates and the messages to be sent to the list of Debir's key supporters. In less than a quarter of an hour the squad of soldiers had arrived, each of them bowing to the Emmanuel, and the messages were spreading throughout Jebus.

The new Araunah looked at Qausa, handing him several gold coins. "Go now. Let yourself and the gold be seen, then leave the city. Do you have a place to stay?"

"You are kind to ask, Araunah," Eliahba said. "Yes, I have a chance for life within my home country. May your rule be longer than the usurper's."

"That is in the hands of El Elyon."

When the Shaalbonite had gone, the Araunah turned to Ahibaal. "The room is prepared for the Kassites?"

"Yes, adoni."

"Once it has been used, it is to be destroyed, for the thing which we do now is shameful, no matter how necessary. And may El Elyon pardon me for this night's work!"

¥ ¥ ¥ ¥ ¥ ¥

The four sars sat in the upper room of Ishvi's house in Gibeah. The news of the coup in Jebus, and Manani's impending trial for treason had effectively distracted everyone from the war season, and fighting had completely stopped along the border.

"I still think Tanhum had a lot of nerve using us like that," Malchi said irritably.

Jonathan smiled a little. "He didn't use us; he used the opportunity we brought. And you have to admire the way he stepped into Manani's sandals."

The third sar snorted. "I just hope this is the last we'll ever hear of Qausa the Habiru! Every time he resurrects himself, there's more trouble for us!"

"This time it was trouble for Debir, and Tanhum's connections have made our lives easier by removing that disgusting man from the picture," Ishvi said, tossing aside a piece of dried apple that looked more fit for the rats than himself. He got up restlessly, staring out the window into the darkness.

"And with Manani also in trouble, maybe politics will settle down into something resembling predictability," Malchi added.

The hassar stroked his beard. "That may depend on what the new Araunah thinks about Israel and Shaul. Do we have any information at all about the Emmanuel who now rules Jebus?"

"Very little," Sar Eshbaal said. "Apparently he was always quiet and content to stay out of the public view unless required to be present during a ritual or ceremony. Then, when Debir usurped the throne, anyone who knew anything about him was either killed or stopped talking in order to stay alive. Ethan's latest report said that no one is speaking even now, and the Emmanuel is just as retiring as Araunah as he was before."

"Which means we know nothing of what he may be thinking, or whether he will leave us in peace," Jonathan sighed.

"I don't think we need to worry, brother," Ishvi said from the window. "Somehow I don't think Tanhum would appreciate anything that threatened his livelihood."

"And as capable as that man is, we should be safe enough," Malchi grunted.

"I hope so," Jonathan muttered.

¥ ¥ ¥ ¥ ¥ ¥

Ahibaal listened to the panting messenger in disbelief. "You're certain?" he asked.

"Yes, adoni. We don't know how. The man is simply gone."

"When?"

"He was last seen yesterday early afternoon."

Controlling his wish to curse the messenger and his news, the Jebusite turned on his heel and strode up the stairs to his upper room in Jebus.

Grabbing a papyrus, he hastily wrote his message. "Minelek vanished from Chephirah. He was last seen yesterday afternoon. No indication how he left or where he went."

Back in his courtyard, he handed the sealed message to the runner. "Get this to Tanhum of Gibeah as soon as you can," he ordered.

¥ ¥ ¥ ¥ ¥ ¥

"Is Manani of Ekron here?" Hanabaal asked formally after the crowd in the square by Ekron's gate had quieted.

When the man refused to answer, Akish spoke up. "He is here," he said as Ittai took the prisoner forward to stand before the other four serens and Baalyaton, who represented Ekron as the city's principal seren. Baalyaton nodded to Ittai, then motioned him aside, and Ishvi-benob came forward to act as guard. As Ittai returned to him, Akish noted the puzzled glances cast at his nephew from the crowd. It made him smile. So far his adons and sars had been very closed-mouthed about his nephew's return, and Akish knew it still wasn't commonly known.

It was too bad that Patisi had died, Akish thought, turning his attention to Baalyaton. This man was just as ambitious as Manani, but not nearly as cunning and on occasion couldn't seem to see more than two moments ahead. Still, having been busy while Manani was gone, he had garnered the backing of all the leading clans and adons in the city. He ruled it now, and Akish knew that recognition of him as Seren Ekron would only be a formality.

As was this trial.

The serens had met last night, examining all the evidence Akish had provided. At Gadmilk's insistence, they had even questioned Manani's wife before deciding that the man was guilty of treason. All that remained for today was a declaration of the charges and the evidence, then the formal condemnation.

From the looks of the square, nearly all the sars and adons from every city were here. Most of the local merchants were in their stalls, and as many of the residents as possible had packed into the square behind the sars. A familiar-looking beggar lay in a cart of straw by one stall. Akish frowned. Where had he seen the man before?

As Hanabaal's scribe read the charges, and then the documents Akish had provided, the ruler of Gath studied the people in the square closely. Two more adons had been attacked in the past month, one from Gaza, and one just last night here in Ekron. In spite of the close attention they paid to the scribe, Akish still felt the unrest and tension from the adons and sars. It was at times like this he missed Shemel the most.

"What reply do you give to these charges and evidence?" Hanabaal asked sternly, turning to Manani.

The Ekronite still refused to answer, simply glancing in contempt at the pile of papyri on the low three-legged table.

"Given the evidence before us, what is your decision regarding Manani of Ekron?" Hanabaal asked the other serens.

"Ashdod declares him guilty of treason and worthy of death," Gadmilk announced, shifting on his chair.

"Ashkelon declares him guilty of treason and worthy of death," Muwana said next, turning to Akish.

"Gath declares him guilty of treason and worthy of death," Akish added.

"Ekron serens, adons and sars agree," Baalyaton declared.

"Gaza concurs. Manani of Ekron is guilty of treason against the alliance and shall be put to death," Hanabaal finished. At the declaration, Ishvi-benob removed the golden circlet from Manani's head, handing it to a scribe, who took it to Hanabaal.

The ruler of Gaza stood. "Serens, the city of Ekron stands in need of a ruler. Who shall take the place of the traitor in the alliance?"

"I, Baalyaton, am worthy to do so," the seren said. "I have established order in the city, giving justice in the courts, and stand ready to fulfill Ekron's contribution to the strength of the alliance whether by military units or tribute in kind. I hold the support of the serens, adons, and sars."

As he finished, the sars, led by Saph and Lahmi, Akish noticed, all shouted their support, and the crowd joined in.

"Let the crown of Ekron be given to Baalyaton," Hanabaal stated.

The man stood and walked to the ruler of Gaza, taking the circlet from him and placing it on his own head. Then he faced the crowd. "I am Baalyaton, Seren Ekron."

Once he was seated again, the serens, adons, and sars from Ekron all came forward one by one and swore allegiance to their new ruler.

By now, the heat of the day approached, and Akish leaned back a little, wishing for a drink. He glanced at Manani, then looked a second time. Instead of just Ishvi-benob guarding him, all three of the Rapha were there.

"Ittai?" he said softly, jerking his chin toward the prisoner.

"I noticed," his nephew said, fingering his sword hilt.

Hanabaal spoke again. "Seren Baalyaton, one of your people stands before the alliance guilty of treason against it. He has been judged worthy of death. What is your will concerning him?"

"Treason against the alliance will not be tolerated in Ekron," Baalyaton said, staring at his former superior. "Manani shall be put to death. It shall be done to him as he has done to so many others. He will be sent without weapons into battle in the highlands, to be killed there."

The growl from the sars around the assembly made the hair on Akish's neck rise.

"Execute him now!" one of the townspeople shouted. "Run him through," another voice added before the general outcry against the former seren filled the square.

Baalyaton stood, holding up his hands for silence. "As your ruler, I have spoken," he said coldly. "There are weeks yet left in the war season, and Ekron will not shirk her part in supplying plunder for taxes. Sars, prepare your units. You will return to the front in two days. That is all you need concern yourselves with. Guards, disperse the crowd," he ended.

Akish looked at Manani. The man stood with an expressionless face, but he had relaxed, and he exchanged a glance with Ishvi-benob.

As the people spilled out of the square, the seren of Gath joined the serens who were giving Baalyaton their congratulations. While he waited, he saw Ishvi-benob and Saph escorting Manani from the square. Lahmi paused by the crippled beggar, and Akish watched as the beggar swiftly passed something to the huge commander. It clinked slightly as Lahmi shoved it into his girdle.

Absently, Akish turned back to Baalyaton to find the man obviously waiting for him.

"Congratulations, Seren," he said, bowing slightly. "The alliance is fortunate to have you as part of it."

"I appreciate your support," Baalyaton responded a bit frostily.

"A word to you if I may," Akish added. "You are aware that the Rapha still serve Manani, but did—"

"I think that I am more than able to rule my city without hints and advice from you," Baalyaton interrupted. "Of course the Rapha still serve Manani, but the Rapha will be busy elsewhere very soon, not that it is any of your concern!"

Akish stepped back. "Certainly, it is not. You are undoubtedly a worthy successor to the former ruler," he added drily. Nodding, he too departed the square.

"Dodi, we should leave," Ittai said as they walked down the narrow street toward the compound they were staying in.

"We will, in the morning. I want to consult with Muwana."

"No, Dodi. We should leave *now*," Ittai emphasized. "This compound belongs to Manani. We should be quit of it."

Akish cast a glance at his nephew. The young man looked around uneasily. "Hanan was right; this is a bad place," he murmured. They paused at the gate, which had no guard, Akish noticed, and angry shouts rose from the direction of the palace.

They soon quieted, and before long, the rest of the unit Akish had brought with him hurried into view, led by their sar.

"Sereni," the man said, "if it is possible for you to leave, I would recommend that you do so immediately. The people are angered that Baalyaton is not executing Manani publically, and the sars are raging because their lives are endangered with the decision to have Israel serve as executioner. The Rapha guard the room where Manani is housed, but no other men will join them."

Akish felt a chill go through him. The situation could turn ugly in moments, with anything tipping the balance, including something like his own departure. The fact that not a single Ekron guard was here added to the danger of remaining.

"Pack up," he decided. "We will leave before the heat of the day is over."

It did not escape Akish's notice that his nephew was ready to leave long before anyone else, or that his pack was organized and neat in sharp contrast to those of the men. Ittai and the sar checked for anything left behind as soon as everyone had gathered in the courtyard.

They left the compound just in time. As they turned into a side alley, Akish caught a glimpse of men armed with clubs and knives heading toward the compound.

Another group passed ahead of them as they waited in another dark alley, and by the time they arrived in the square by the gate, not a soldier or sentry could be seen. The silence was nerve-wracking, and the hoof beats of the three donkeys with packs now crossing the empty space almost echoed from the surrounding buildings. The well-dressed, older man leading them glanced around in bewilderment.

Something about the man's face briefly stirred Akish's memory as he rode out of the alley, followed by his men.

"May we be of service, adon?" Ittai spoke up as they neared the stranger.

"Perhaps you can. I have a message for Seren Manani of Ekron. Where might I find him?"

Why was someone who looked like a Philistine asking for Manani in an Israelite accent? Noting the intentness with which his nephew studied the man, Akish also gave him careful attention.

"Perhaps you have not heard, adon, that Manani is no longer ruler of Ekron. He has been condemned of treason against the alliance. Baalyaton is Seren Ekron now. Do you need to speak with him?" Ittai asked.

The man hesitated. "I am not certain," he admitted at last. "Has the execution taken place yet?"

"Not yet, adon."

"Then perhaps I might speak with the sar that Seren Ekron left in charge. Can you direct me where to go?"

"This is not a good time to be going anywhere in this city, friend," Akish commented wryly, trying to calm his increasingly jittery mule.

"I gathered that." The stranger bowed slightly. "I am afraid, however, that my message is urgent enough to take the risk."

"In that case, you can go around the palace here and down the main street toward the south. I believe you will find the man you are looking for in the second compound on the left, and—"

"—and perhaps he should not go anywhere at all," Saph sneered, stepping into the square from another alley, followed by several armed men.

The stranger's eyes widened a little as he glanced at the man who'd spoken, but other than that, he didn't react.

The giant Rapha turned to Akish. "Surely you weren't planning on leaving us?" he asked. "Seren Ekron would find that most insulting. He will also want to know why you and all your armed men were conferring with this stranger about a condemned man. Shall we notify him?"

Barely controlling his anger, Akish looked around. More soldiers had already entered the square, but he knew that his own unit would fight if he told them to. His gaze passed over Ittai, and the young man shook his head once.

Without a word, Akish reined the mule around and started in the direction of Baalyaton's house, his animal nearly running Saph down, before lashing a hoof at the giant man for good measure. The stranger in the square followed, keeping tight hold of the tether on the donkeys.

They encountered Ishvi-benob in the street before reaching Baalyaton's residence. The giant trouble-maker watched them approach with a malicious grin on his face. "And why would you be bringing Seren Gath here, Saph?" he demanded.

At the mention of his title, Akish saw the stranger's head bob up to stare at him briefly. It caught Ishvi-benob's attention. He studied the man for several moments, and then a deep chuckle rumbled from him as he strode past Akish and grabbed the older man's arm, jerking him around. "By Dagon, if it isn't Seren Minelek! What might you be doing here?"

Akish couldn't suppress a gasp of surprise. *Minelek?*

"I see your manners haven't changed much, ben Goliath," Minelek said coolly, staring up into the sar's face.

"A lot of other things have changed," the Rapha replied. "Now, why would Seren Gath be keeping company with Seren Minelek, unless they were plotting the best way to rescue Ekron's dearly beloved former ruler?"

"You can't possibly believe that!" Akish exclaimed.

Ishvi-benob looked back at him. "Of course not, seren," he said, his eyes hard. "But it is just the sort of nonsense that Baalyaton would, particularly if these donkeys are carrying what I think they are. How much did you bring?" the giant asked, turning to Minelek again. "As if there would be enough ransom in the whole of Philistia to buy that demon's freedom!"

"Maybe not from you, ben Goliath, but perhaps enough to sway Baalyaton," Minelek retorted.

Ishvi-benob's hand came up to strike the seren, but then he hesitated, and his eyes shifted away from Minelek's steady gaze.

"We will have to wait to find out," he said instead. "Seren Ekron is taking his noon rest and stated he was not to be disturbed. Saph, take the serens and all with them to the courtyard outside Manani's room. They can wait Seren Ekron's pleasure there. And rest assured, serens, Baalyaton will be fully informed by the time he gets to you!"

"Lies will only rebound on you, Ishvi-benob," Minelek said softly.

"Lies?" the giant man replied, his eyes flashing with rage. "I won't have to lie about you, seren. Baalyaton will come up with enough to condemn you all on his own. As for Seren Gath, I owe him a very public beating, and given the way Baalyaton hates him, neither of us is likely to pass up this opportunity!"

Akish went cold. The look in the Rapha's eyes said plainly that he would not survive any beating. Before he could think further, his mule unexpectedly bunched under him and crow-hopped, nearly unseating the seren. Ittai quickly grabbed the bridle and turned the animal around, leading them back down the narrow street, his unit following them.

He didn't have time to pay a lot of attention to where he was going, for his own mule was also nearly uncontrollable, and it took all of his concentration to keep the animal from charging into the men surrounding them and trampling them. He was relieved when he entered the courtyard and could swing the mule around without worrying about what was behind him.

But what he then saw made his hair stand on end. Most of Ekron's sars and many of the professionals filled the street or had filed into the courtyard, all of them fully armed, and all of them silent and intent.

Minelek appeared, still in control of his donkeys, but surrounded by Saph's men. Akish's face tightened as Saph entered right behind the seren.

"Seren Minelek!" Lahmi exclaimed, rising from the stool outside one of the storerooms, staring in amazement.

"Get off the mule," Ittai said quietly, distracting Akish from the scene before him.

Akish looked down to see that his unit had assembled in a rough ring around him, backing slightly as more professionals entered the courtyard.

"*Now*, Dodi!"

Instantly, his uncle obeyed, even as his mind told him that, up there on the mule, he was an inviting target.

"Look who showed up to rescue Manani!" Saph said, shoving Seren Minelek forward.

"Rescue?" Lahmi said, his voice puzzled, then his eyes widened, and he yanked his sword from the scabbard and lunged forward even as the men behind his brother silently attacked, knocking the back of Saph's knees in and clubbing him into unconsciousness.

As the huge man fell, the soldiers closest to Lahmi drew their swords.

Faced with the chilling silence and the circle of weapons pointed at him, the giant halted. Then he smiled, and lowered the sword. "All right," he said. "You get Manani, and I'll bring the other one!" He strode over to stand beside Seren Minelek.

Two of the sars pulled down the crude bar fastened across the door and shoved it open, disappearing inside.

They reappeared moments later, roughly hauling Manani between them. The wave of hatred that greeted the sight of the former ruler sent a shiver down Akish's spine. "How dare you do this!" Manani blustered, straining against the men, then somehow pulling them to a stop when he saw Minelek.

"Minelek! Get–"

Another sar walked over and smashed his fist into Manani's face, silencing whatever he had been going to say.

The blow dazed the former ruler enough that he could be dragged out of the compound and into the street before he recovered enough to begin struggling again.

Akish and his men stood completely motionless, watching as the silent Ekronite soldiers followed Manani away from the house.

"Whatever you do, don't let go of the mule," Ittai instructed in an undertone, keeping his eyes on the soldiers remaining in the courtyard. "If anyone crowds too close, bump it twice with your fist. That will make it kick."

One of the Ekronite sars pulled his sword and gestured toward the gate with it. "We wouldn't want you to miss the excitement."

One look at the murderous rage in the man's eyes, and Akish turned toward the gate, leading the mule, his unit somehow staying around him. As he walked, he noticed that his legs were shaking. The hatred and bloodlust lingering in the air made him sick to his stomach. The last thing he wanted was to see what he knew was about to happen.

As they went along, Akish noticed the city's inhabitants running through the alleys toward the gate. News of the sars' actions must have spread rapidly.

As Ittai predicted, they were led out through the gates and down a path to the east side of the city. As soon as they were out in the open, Ittai hissed, "Make the mule kick, Dodi."

Akish balled his fist and bumped the animal twice. It erupted, lashing out with its hind legs and bucking, Akish clinging to the reins, trying to stay out of the mule's way. By the time he had the animal back under control, they were off to one side of the procession, and Lahmi, still escorting Minelek, had passed them.

Most of the men escorting them were becoming distracted by the crowd gathered on the Ekron training ground up ahead, with Manani, stripped of all clothing, on display in the middle of them. Blood dripped from several wounds and bruises had begun to swell all over his body.

As they approached the circle, Akish heard one of the sars sneer, "Nothing will save you, Manani. You're not dealing with scheming serens and greedy adons. You're dealing with us, the people you've despised and tormented and robbed and murdered. And we have decided for ourselves that you will die."

"Do you think there is anything you can do that will matter?" Manani taunted.

"No, we don't," the man said, his voice steady. "That's why we decided not to torment you to death as you've done with so many of us. We decided to let the dead to that."

"The dead?"

Wordlessly, the sar gripped Manani's arm and shoved him across the field further south toward a rise of ground. In spite of the crowd that had gathered, the procession was mostly silent, even when several of the townspeople availed themselves of the opportunity to avenge themselves for past injuries. The sars yanked Manani back to his feet once more, everyone ignoring the steady stream of curses that poured from his mouth.

"Should we try to break away," Akish asked Ittai, noticing that their guards no longer paid much attention to them.

"Not yet."

A hole, shaded by cypress trees and surrounded by thorn bushes, opened into the hillock.

"What is this place?" Manani sneered, jerking himself away from someone intent on striking him.

Akish riveted his attention on the former ruler. The man's tone was uneasy.

"I'm surprised you don't recognize it," the sar said softly. "Those of us who have been forced to do your will are well acquainted with it.

This is the place where you ordered all your problems buried, and it's where we decided to bury our problem also."

Manani grew pale.

As Minelek was shoved into the space at the mouth of the cave with him, Manani turned to him. "Why haven't you done something?" he snarled, blood dripping from his face.

"I did everything I could years ago. There is nothing I can do now."

The prisoner glared at him. "Then why did you even bother to come?"

The seren remained silent.

Gripping Manani's arm again, the sar shoved him into the black opening, another man following him with a single lamp brim full of oil, already burning steadily.

Chains clanked, then several sars emerged.

Moments of silence passed, then a terrified shriek issued from the cave. "A grave! You have put me into a grave!"

Minelek dropped to the ground, his whole body shaking.

Ignoring him, the sars began to block up the cave entrance.

"No! *No!* What are you doing?" Manani's voice shrilled. "You're dead! You're all dead!"

Akish could hear the man thrashing around wildly, scream after terrified scream coming from the mouth of the cave.

"Nemuel!" Manani's voice cracked into a last shriek of horror before the last stone was hoisted into place, muffling the sounds from within.

By now the crowd made not a single sound, completely silenced by Manani's shrieks and pleas.

"Now, Dodi," Ittai said.

"What about Minelek?" Akish asked, gathering the reins.

"Even if we stayed, there is nothing we could do for him."

Akish mounted the mule and turned the animal toward home, his unit forming around him.

The Ekron sars barred their way.

Ittai stepped forward. "Step aside. Do not join Manani on this day."

"Who are you to tell us what to do?" one of them demanded.

"I am Ittai ben Ribbai, seren of Gath, and I have returned to see justice done."

"Akish's nephew died years ago!" the same sar scoffed.

"A thought which should give you pause," Ittai said evenly.

Faintly, from inside the grave, they could hear Manani's voice repeating name after name of his victims.

"If you wish to see *them* again, I can arrange it," Ittai added, nodding toward the sealed cave.

The men in front of him paled, then began to shift away, their retreat becoming more and more frantic.

Akish nudged the mule into a walk. Ittai remained where he was as the unit passed him. By then, the Ekron sars had started hurrying after the subdued crowd that made its way back into the city.

The unit nearly ran the entire seven miles to Gath.

The next morning, Akish's chief scribe found him still in his rooms. The seren had slept hardly at all during the night, and when he did doze off, he dreamed of countless silent men surrounding him, driving him forward while the wind smashed huge thorny bushes into his face until a black yawning pit opened in front of him. Finally, he'd wakened, covered with sweat and shaking.

"What is it?" he acknowledged the knock at the door.

"Sereni, an adon has asked for a private audience with you."

"Who is he?"

"He will not say, sereni." The man hesitated. "He speaks as a man from the hills, but he looks Philistine, and his clothes are rich, although old."

Gath's ruler raised an eyebrow. It was unusual for the scribe to be so puzzled about anyone. Normally, he could quickly pinpoint a petitioner's city of origin as well as what status they held.

"Have Ittai bring him to the private audience chamber. I'll be there shortly."

"Yes, sereni."

Akish entered the private audience chamber not long after, and the man waiting there bowed politely, his face averted.

"What would you have of me?" Akish asked, approaching him.

The man raised his face.

"Minelek!" Akish gasped. "Thank Dagon you were not killed!"

His visitor smiled sadly. "Your greeting gives me hope that you still call me friend today, as you did yesterday."

"Today, and any time. You do not know what your kindness meant to me all those years ago." His eyes filled with the memory. Maoch had just died, and Gath's throne had become his. He had still been reeling from the shock of his abbi's death and the sudden responsibility of ruling a city. Minelek had unexpectedly attended the convening of the alliance after so many years of absence that many thought him dead. He had been the only one who had thought to comfort his sorrow. Before he left, he had given some advice. "Do not be afraid," he'd said. "Do not cross the serens, but only give in to them when you must. Just wait. Your day will come."

"That was a long time ago, Akish," the man replied.

"And my debt to you and your words has grown with each passing year. Had you not advised me as you did, I doubt I would still rule. What can I do for you?"

"Perhaps you should hear why I am here before you decide anything."

"Then come to a more private chamber." Akish led the way to the room where he normally met with Dahveed.

Once they were seated, and Ittai had brought some fruit and wine, the seren leaned back in his chair. "What happened after I left?"

"It was your leaving that saved my life, I think. Who was the young man fronting you? The sars looked as though they had seen a ghost!"

"Many of them thought they had," Akish chuckled. "That is Hazzel's son, Ittai," he explained, telling his guest of his nephew's first encounter with Dahveed Israel, and the young man's subsequent disappearance. "I underestimated my sister, as did Manani. She had sent Ittai back to Dahveed for safety. He returned to us again only weeks ago," he ended. "Since general knowledge had it that Ittai died years ago, probably at Manani's hand, the sars would not have known what to believe about Ittai's reappearance!"

"Well, however it happened, I am thankful that it did." He stared at the floor. "The sars were so shaken that they took me back to the compound, and left Lahmi as my guard. Saph was still lying there, by the way."

"How did you escape?"

"Lahmi let me go." Minelek turned away a little. "Not many know this, but Lahmi was one of Manani's first victims. Their clans are related, you know. I helped him more than once. And he remembered." The older man glanced up. "I have been blessed indeed with more friends who remember, than ones who choose to forget. When I heard, in the hills, how you had turned the Rapha over to Manani, I thought you were unwise.

"But I am alive now because you did. When Baalyaton heard that I had come, he turned against me, and now seeks my life."

"He is a fool, then."

"Yes, but he is a dangerous fool, and as long as the Rapha support him, he will rule."

"Why are you here?"

"Manani located me again after years of peace, and demanded my help one more time."

"After all these years, after all he did to you, why did you respond?" Akish asked gently.

"Because in spite of everything, he was still my little brother." Tears fell from his eyes, and he covered his face with his hands.

Akish sat in silence as heart-broken sobs racked the other man in the room.

¥ ¥ ¥ ¥ ¥ ¥

"Dodi, there's a man asking for you," Asahel announced.

I looked up from the terrace I was building down in the watercourse below Ziklag. "Where is he?"

"Zelek challenged him east of here before he could see the town."

Brushing my hands off, I stepped over the two courses of the terrace wall. Then, donning my cuirass, sword, and sling, I followed my nephew up the road. When we caught up to the newcomer, Zelek was questioning him.

"I was told to give this to the Dahveed and no one else," the fellow insisted, clutching a spot in his girdle. He appeared frightened, but I wondered. The way he was standing said he was ready for any move Zelek might make, and with his hand on his girdle that way, it was very close to his sword hilt.

"Give the man some peace, Zelek," I interrupted, walking into view. "I'm the Dahveed. What do you have for me?"

For a moment he looked me over carefully. "Turn around."

I smiled tolerantly. "And place my back to a stranger?"

He flushed. "Your pardon, Seren, but I need to know what you look like from the back."

My eyebrows shot up in surprise, then I laughed. "You've met Elihu!"

The stranger relaxed. "Yes. I guess that's good enough to identify you. I was instructed to give you this." He pulled a folded papyrus from his girdle, and Zelek took it from him, handing it to me.

I unfolded it, finding it a little difficult to read because it was creased in so many places. "What did the Ammonitess look like?" I asked him when I finished.

"Small, unusual dark skin, delicate features, and small hands and feet. Black hair. She was," he paused, "well, lovely. I could see why Manani wanted her."

I glanced at Zelek. "Be nice to him, cousin. He's the commander who let Ala go after Manani took her. He's called Eliahba from Shaalbim, and he can probably fight as well as you can."

"We'll have to see about that. Shalom, Eliahba. I am Ala's brother, and we are kin to the Dahveed."

"I am grateful I could serve you, Seren, even unknowingly."

"Come into town, and we will find you a place to stay." I led the way down the road. Zalmon's children greeted us as we returned, the youngest crowing with delight when I picked him up and gave him a ride on my shoulders. The two oldest raced Asahel up the hill, and the third studied Eliahba for a moment before demanding a ride also.

Looking bemused, the man complied. "These rascals belong to Zalmon, one of my men," I explained, noting the careful way the Philistine carried the child. "Do you have children?"

"I've always wanted them," he confessed. "But I'm a professional sar, and I've had to take the news to too many widows to want to put someone through that grief on my behalf."

"What news do you bring?"

"Had you heard of the events in Jebus?"

"No."

"It seems the Emmanuel was not killed in Debir's purge, and he returned. With the help of one of the palace guards, he was able to kill Debir quietly, then summon all his key Kassite supporters to the palace. They were killed that night. He showed remarkable restraint, however. He did not touch the families of the men, nor did he rob them. Instead, he returned their dead, let them bury them, and allowed them to pack some possessions before sending them into exile south of Edom, where they are to remain on pain of death. The city is wild with rejoicing, not only because the Emmanuel has returned and is now Araunah, but because he showed such hesed to begin his reign."

"That is news," I exclaimed. "What is his feeling toward Israel?"

"I don't know, of course, but I believe he will stay out of Israel's politics."

I hoped so, for Jonathan's sake. That night, I considered what the Araunah had done. His actions reminded me of what Jonathan taught me. "If there is any way for hesed to be given, it should be." I wondered if Atarah would return to Jebus now. She had seemed to miss it the most, and with her skill as a healer, she could make a good living for herself there. But I doubted Ornan would. The news I heard said he was doing very well working for the House of Tahat, and he'd always been interested in hearing about faraway places. "Yahweh, guide them," I whispered to myself.

The news of Manani's downfall and death arrived some days after the events occurred. I immediately shared it with Eliahba.

"That is a relief to me, Seren," he said. "I would never rest easy so long as Manani lived."

"And you would have been wise not to. Do you wish to return to Ekron?"

Eliahba glanced around just in time to brace himself as Zalmon's third child hurled himself at the sturdy man. After catching the reckless boy, and setting him on his feet, the Philistine turned to me.

"Would you allow me to stay, Seren?"

"Yes."

"Even though I am an enemy?"

"Anyone who saves my kin is not an enemy."

"Then I would like to remain. I have found something here that I never dreamed I could have."

"Then perhaps you won't have to drink anymore in order to be happy enough to sing," I commented.

"How do you know I sing when I drink?" he gasped.

"You demonstrated your talent the night you hired me to be the guide you needed across Judah," I told him, walking away.

Tamar bat Dahveed

Time is running out for Shaul's house also. Death draws ever nearer, hastened by the king's refusal to submit to Adonai's will. And because this is so, events in Philistia must move rapidly also. But all is prepared. Yah's agent is ready to act his part to ensure that the Mashiah will be in place to take his final steps to kingship. And then, the Mashiah himself nearly ruined everything that Yah had taken years to arrange! This was, perhaps, the hardest lesson my abbi ever had to learn—to wait without seeing, to trust without knowing what the next hour would bring, to believe that Yahweh is working for good when every evidence screams otherwise.

Akish and Gath

Chapter 22

The war season was over as I left the gate of Ziklag on my way north to Gath with a caravan of back taxes for Akish. The town looked very different now. We had repaired everything. The barriers between the houses were now sturdy permanent ones, and the gates were strong once more. A couple merchants from Gerar had opened stalls in our market, and a small caravan had stopped a few days ago, the caravan master willing to make us a regular stop on his route between Beersheba and the coast. He bought all the camels we had accumulated, and I was taking his payment to Akish, since that would account for his tenth of the spoils so far.

I had not kept my share of any of these first raids, distributing everything we brought back to the townspeople and the poorer of my men. While I would feel better when we had a good harvest behind us, at least now no one looked as if they were starving any more, and the men had created more shallow terraced fields in the valley in preparation for planting during the fall rains.

We also brought back any food supplies we captured, and found that one wheat silo we'd emptied was contaminated with scabious seeds. I was ready to throw it out when Ahinoam decided to have the children and the recovering wounded sort through it, picking out the bitter scabious and leaving the wheat for seed for planting in the fall. I was dubious, but after a week, they had cleaned more than enough to plant two fields, and when I sifted the kernels through my fingers, I couldn't find a single one that wasn't wheat.

Halfway to Gath, Hanan joined me, approaching from the west. I'd been grateful that I'd made the decision I had when he refused to scout in the south. The first time I reported to Akish, Hanan had met me as now, and told me of three raids on the Jerahmeel Negev, giving me enough detail that I had convinced the listening courtiers that I had been there, and not farther south ravaging the Amalekites. Even Akish had questions about it for me when I met him privately later.

"Where did I raid this time?" I asked Hanan as soon as we were alone.

"The Kenites. They were hit twice." He told me everything he had learned from scouting the battle sites and overhearing people discussing what had happened. I listened closely, repeating anything I didn't think I understood or didn't have clearly in mind.

Once we arrived at Gath late in the afternoon, the men with me set up camp on the same hillside within sight of the wall of the city. Ittai arrived shortly after we did.

"Shalom, adoni," he said, touching his knee to the ground.

"Shalom, Ittai," I replied, giving him a hand up. "Your family is well?"

"Yes. I heard from Immi just last week. She and Shemel are very happy, although I gather that the town is either on its ear or a bit dazed, depending on what happened during Immi's latest visit there!"

"Well, at least Akish has some peace now."

Ittai smiled. "He won't admit how much he misses her. Hazzel stirred things up in Gath, and now that she's gone, he's bored and can't find out half the things he wants to know!

"And he said to tell you to come to the morning audience."

"I'll be there."

The next morning I appeared in the throne room well before the third hour, giving my name as usual to the scribe at the door and slipping inside the throne room itself when he was distracted. Up near the throne I found the spot I'd heard of more than once. The rumors were true. This was where the advisor to Akish who had wanted me sent to Manani had stood the day the seren drove me from his presence as a crazy man. The floor was, indeed, blackened and pitted, and above it I could see where the ceiling had been repaired.

Rubbing the burn mark on my arm, I retreated to a place next to the wall in the back of the room and watched as courtiers drifted in, paying attention to who was talking to whom.

Akish arrived and the audience began.

"The Habiru dahveed to report to Seren Akish," the scribe announced, and I came forward, touching my knee to the floor briefly and rising again.

"My scribes tell me you have brought payment for Ziklag's back taxes," he said approvingly.

"I have, Sereni, and your share of the spoils besides." I produced the pouch that held the gold paid for the camels, and Ittai took it, handing it to his uncle.

He hefted it in his hands. "You have done well."

I bowed, noticing the strict attention of three of the courtiers. The same ones as the last time I had reported to the seren.

"Who did you raid this time?"

"The Kenites, Sereni. We hit two settlements in the Negev." I nodded toward the pouch he held. "They lost a lot."

"Very good, Dahveed. I must also commend you for the improved safety of our roads up from Egypt."

I bowed again. "You have given us shelter, Sereni. I will serve you as best I can."

He dismissed me, and the scribe called another name as I left the throne room, returning to my tent on the hill until after the noon rest, when I would reappear in the market to make purchases as I did every time I came.

Today when I returned, I spotted a merchant whose stall matched the description my wife, Abigail, had given me. I wandered over. "Would you, by chance, be the merchant Hadar?"

Looking a little startled that I would know his name, he nodded. "Was there something special you wished to purchase from me?"

"According to my wife, I wouldn't be able to afford anything you have for some time, geber," I said smiling. "She does miss seeing you, though. She said your news was always as welcome as your merchandise."

Puzzled, Hadar looked me over carefully. At the same time I noticed that the beggar by his stall seemed inordinately interested in our conversation. He sat hunched over, a ragged blanket covering his legs. Something about him made me scrutinize him, and I decided not to tell Hadar who I was so long as the beggar was listening.

"Give my greetings to your wife, then," Hadar said courteously, raising the tone of his voice slightly in a subtle question.

"I will," I said, bowing and moving on.

Once I'd made my purchases, I circulated around the wine shops and an inn or two, listening, making a comment here or there to elicit some more information. The atmosphere of the city had changed considerably since I was here the first time. The citizens were confident that Akish would remain as seren, that his response to the events of my arrival had satisfied the other rulers, and that they need not fear attack. They were also very relieved that the Rapha no longer resided here. And from the tales circulating in the shops, Baalyaton of Ekron was having troubles with them now.

Later that night, I met with Akish in the same room we always used.

"Shalom, Dahveed."

"Shalom, Sereni."

"Rumors that you are Dahveed Israel have begun circulating since the end of the war season."

"How has that affected things?"

"I've been able to identify three more spies by watching who is asking what about you," he chuckled. "Two I suspected already. The third one was a surprise. Ittai was right. You are discreet, so it will take awhile before anyone gets confirmation of who you are.

"Now, who attacked the Kenites?"

"Probably Girzites. Although my scouts reported that at least one raiding party consisted of two tribes."

"Sounds as if you are cutting down on their activities significantly."

"Frankly, there were more of them than we expected, Sereni. I have enough men without families now that I'm considering continuing the raids during the winter. Probably not a lot, but enough to keep them from feeling secure. And we could conduct more extended expeditions if necessary."

"Just keep doing it," Akish said shortly. "I know such warfare is not agreeable, but I saw a settlement they had raided once. It was enough."

I rose and turned away. "Every time I think I can't go on another raid, we find another place they have destroyed, and what they leave behind hardens my resolve."

"Your men are willing to continue as well?"

"Yes. Most of them feel as I do, and I rotate the duty because of it. I have a few, though, who would go on every raid if they could."

"Those kinds of men make uncomfortable bedfellows, Dahveed."

"I know. Most of them are unmarried, and currently they stay outside of town in tents while the barracks are being built, which may take longer than I expect."

"How many like that are there?"

"Probably around 15 to 20. We keep them scattered among the other units. There are only two or three that really worry me." I shuddered a little and turned back. "The city seems much more secure now than previously."

"Thanks in a large part to you, Dahveed. Raids into southern Philistia have diminished, and travelers no longer fear to use our roads. But another adon, in Ashkelon this time, was attacked just last week. Two of Hanabaal's sars were there visiting relatives, and Muwana has detained them even though the giant attacker was seen fleeing from the scene.

"Baalyaton promptly accused me of still controlling the Rapha. But he's not getting much hearing from the other rulers because all three of the brothers can account for their presence in Ekron when the attack occurred.

"Then there was the riot in Gaza, centered around sars from Ekron, who claimed they were there in response to a message from Hanabaal. He and Baalyaton are now snarling at each other, and the only reason the sars are still alive is because they actually produced the message, which no one claims to know anything about, and that fuels the bad feeling between the sars and the adons."

"How are things between you and your sars?"

"They could be better," Akish admitted. "Getting rid of the Rapha helped, but with Shemel's sentencing, I am viewed warily. Given how things are going, that could change any time. But again, because of the difference you are making, no one wants to upset the situation. For once I'm thankful we're the weakest politically of the cities. I know of six agents withdrawn by their masters now that the Rapha are in Ekron, and none of those six have been replaced. On the other hand, Baalyaton has increased his contingent of spies. Speaking of which, one of them will be along soon to assure himself that I am alone. Where's your report?"

I handed it to him.

"Is there anything you need?" he asked as I started to leave.

"More grain, if you have it. We've been hoarding every kernel we can for seed. Barley is just as useful as wheat."

"Good. I've got plenty of barley. I'll send it."

A quick bow, then I slipped into an alcove in the passage where I always waited until the way was clear for me to exit the palace unseen.

Chapter 23

After Dahveed departed, Akish tapped the report against his palm, debating whether or not he would open it. Then he heard the scribe coming, the one who worked for Baalyaton, and Akish stared in thought at the wall for a moment. Maybe now was the time to feed Ekron some more misinformation. He didn't have to worry about his eastern border, Dahveed would soon have the southern border controlled, he'd gotten rid of all of Goliath's kin, and Hazzel had cleaned out the worst of the riffraff in the city. While his hold on the throne was a bit tenuous, the other serens were turning their attention someplace other than Gath, leaving him much more room to maneuver. And with the obvious cutbacks in raids and the improved safety of the roads, Dahveed had done enough to give the other serens a favorable opinion of him.

The scribe arrived at the door. Yes, now was the time to make Ekron think he was somewhat of a simpleton and possibly not worth watching so closely.

"Enter," he called when the scribe knocked. Picking up Dahveed's report from the stack on the table, he handed it to the man.

He opened it and began to read, the intent expression on his face telling Akish that the details of this report would reach Ekron soon, and that someone might even be sent to see if they were true. The seren smiled to himself. They were. He'd checked up on Dahveed's reports the first couple times himself.

By the time the scribe finished, his personal attendant had arrived, the one who worked for Gadmilk, and Akish stared again at the wall, his hand on his chin.

"Yes," he said softly, "he's made himself into such a stink in Israel, he can never go back. He's mine, now. Mine forever."

"Who is?" the attendant asked in a low voice.

"The Habiru dahveed." Akish replied absently.

¥ ¥ ¥ ¥ ¥

I left Gath that night with a couple assistants to merchants who had had a little too much to drink and could barely keep themselves upright as they stumbled toward the north gate. With me between them, the two men approached the gate guards and halted, listing a little to one side.

Since the fumes coming from the other two were nearly overpowering, the guards had no reason to suspect that I wasn't as drunk as they were. The little door by the gate opened, and they helpfully guided us through it.

"Than' you, geber," one said with dignity as we wove away.

Once out of sight, I got the two of them holding onto each other, then melted into the night, taking the way west around the city.

I'd already told the men with me to return to Ziklag in the morning, for I would start back tonight. I followed the roads since I wasn't well acquainted with the trails here, and the quiet, cool night air felt soothing as it washed across my face. Putting everything else from my mind, I increased my pace, relaxing into the stride as I used to do when I ran with Ethan and Jamin in the hills. The flat country enabled me to keep the pace for mile after mile as I felt the blood rushing through me and heard the sound of my own breath in my chest.

At last I noticed the figure pacing me off to one side. A brief glimpse in the moonlight let me recognize Hanan. When he turned east, I tagged after him, the rougher ground of the trails and forest slowing us a little. It was close to dawn when we finally stopped, having run halfway back to Ziklag and then up into the Shephelah country just south of Lachish.

I kept moving, walking for some time to be certain my leg didn't cramp up. "What is it?" I asked.

"Men looking for you. They are afraid."

Knowing I would get no more than that, I followed him farther into the hills and soon smelled the smoke from a fire. Hanan circled the place, giving me a chance to study the five fires and the 23 figures lying around them. We also located the sentries, and soon took the opportunity to slip by them to the fifth fire which had only three people by it.

I was thirsty and built up the fire while Hanan brought water from a nearby spring. While the water heated, I added some wine, and Hanan threw in a handful of mint leaves that he'd just picked. I drank the last of the water Hanan brought and stretched out, resting my legs and keeping my feet warm. By the time the first man by our fire stirred, it was light enough to see well, and Hanan and I were sipping our drink. He raised a tousled head and blinked at the flames.

"Smells good," he muttered. "What is it?"

"Hot wine with mint. Help yourself."

"I will, in a minute."

Crawling out from his blankets, he went into the trees, soon returning, looking slightly more awake. After pouring some of the wine into a cup, he sipped it gingerly to keep from burning his mouth. Then he closed his eyes and leaned back against a tree. "This is good! Why haven't you made this every morning?" He cracked an eye at me.

I shrugged. "Didn't have the mint."

After another sip, he rubbed his eyes and idly watched the other two sleeping figures.

I knew the instant it dawned on him that there were too many men at this fire. He didn't move a muscle, but his body became rigid anyway.

I stretched and put my cup on the ground, lying back. "What did you want with the Dahveed?" I asked, yawning, the all-night run combined with the hot wine making me sleepy.

The man looked from me to Hanan. "We would join him," he said cautiously, relaxing a little.

"What clans are you from?" I asked, closing my eyes.

"Shaul ben Kish."

My eyes popped open, and I jerked up on my elbows to stare at him. "King Shaul's clan?" I gasped.

"Yes. The hassar said—well, he didn't actually say but he implied—that Dahveed would welcome us."

I eased back again. I'd been too busy lately to give much thought to what was happening in Israel. "Abner has grown powerful enough to drive you out?"

"Maybe. No one knows for sure."

"Shaul has done nothing?"

The man rose, gripping his cup tightly. "If he would just say one way or the other," he burst out in frustration. "But he says nothing, sitting in the throne room day after day while the hassar rules the land." Then he stopped, snapping his mouth shut.

I sat up. "That has always been Shaul's wish, you know."

"Yes, but not like this," the man sputtered. "Not with General Abner watching every move Hassar Jonathan makes, hampering him everywhere he turns, eating away at his influence as every day goes by. And the king does nothing!"

"Who are you spouting off to now, Joash?" a sleepy voice asked. "Don't yell so."

Joash flushed and sat down again.

I picked up my cup and drank. "How did you, and these with you, end up here?"

"Abner 'recruited' most of us, and Sar Malchi weeded us from the rest of the units. Then at Feast of Weeks we were warned to guard ourselves and wait for orders to move."

"Warned? How?"

Joash paused. "Message, I guess."

"To whom?"

"I don't really know."

"Immi told me," a young voice said, and a short figure walked over from another fire. "It surprised me because usually she's against the hassar."

One of the two men still lying down at our fire yawned. "I asked Commander Zorath, and he told me."

"Why did you ask?" Joash questioned.

The man blinked at the fire. "My wife suggested it. What smells so good?"

"Minted wine," I replied. "There's probably enough for one more cup if you get it now."

Quickly he rolled out of his blankets and drained the last of the drink into his cup.

As a couple others woke, questioning produced the same answers. While the newcomers discussed it, I sank into thought. The pattern was the same. If a commander was mentioned, it was Zorath or Ram. But always the initial warnings or suggestions came from women.

If I was any judge, Hassarah Ahinoam had a hand in this. And as smoothly as it had been done, all four of the sars were in on it. But why?

I went back over the conversations. "Joash, you said Sar Malchi weeded the units. What did you mean?"

"Well, he picked us. We're all from different units. The sar and the general are changing things around, shifting men and trying different combinations of fighters. By the beginning of last war season, we had all ended up together, and somehow stayed together,"

Joash said grimly. "Abner spends most of his time recruiting. He shows up a couple times a week and consults with Sar Malchi. As soon as he's gone, the units are scrambled again because Abner wanted something new. Nobody likes it. They can't settle into a team and learn how to fight together. I don't know how we managed to survive this past war season, although the sar didn't shuffle the men around as much, just the units."

I lapsed into silence. Something lurked just at the edge of my thoughts, something that made sense of all this, but I couldn't quite bring it into my mind. What were the sars doing?

I turned to Hanan. "Why these men?" I asked him privately. "Is there anything special about them, other than their connection to Shaul?"

Hanan looked at me with a slight smile on his face. "They are the best archers and slingers the army had."

I froze, staring into the fire while everything took its proper place in my mind. To be sure, I asked one more question. "Do your families support Abner, or the hassar?"

"The hassar, of course. That's what worries us so much about being sent away. When the orders came, they said we were to take the boys south of Gath on the Shephelah, and stay there until we heard word of Azmaveth. It makes no sense to send us all."

"It makes perfect sense," I said, not knowing whether to laugh or to cry. I wanted to pound on something, raging over the covert war the hassar had to fight within his own family, and the way he had found to continue to serve me while he did. He must feel that the conflict would come down to a fight between me and Abner. And while Abner was weakening the families and clans that supported the hassar by taking away their fighting men, Jonathan and Malchi were skimming off the best of them, removing them from Abner's grasp and sending them to me, saving their families and clans from coercion by the general, and making sure that when the contest came, I would have all the best that Israel could offer.

And when that time arrived, I prayed they had sense enough to take advantage of all the talents and skills they had snatched from Abner's hand. They would come, then, I told myself. They had to, after doing all this. Jonathan and I were going to see this through together.

The silence finally penetrated my thoughts, and I looked up to see a man approaching with his sword drawn. "Just who are you?" he asked sternly.

I smiled in recognition. "You should know, Ishmaiah," I replied, surprised to see the Gibeonite here with Shaul's kin. "Put up your sword," I added. "If anything happens to Azmaveth's sons, he'll never forgive you, let alone what Jonathan Hassar will feel after all the trouble he's taken to get these men down here to me."

"Dahveed?" the ark-bearer gasped.

I raised my cup to him. "Welcome back." After draining the last of the wine, I rose. "We'll leave tonight, Hanan. I don't dare parade 23 of Shaul's kin through the middle of Gath's territory. Akish will overlook a lot, but not something like that." I turned to the men, all of whom were now awake and watching. "And once we get to Ziklag, the less you say about your clan, the better."

"Yes, Sar," Joash whispered.

Needing a place to sleep for the day, I walked into a grove of trees.

After I returned to Ziklag with Shaul's kin, I turned them over to Azmaveth to command. The shock on his face when he saw his sons brought smiles to everyone, especially to those of us who knew how much his wife disliked the hassar. From the comments we heard, Abner's strong-arm tactics had disgusted her thoroughly, and she sent her sons out of his reach.

Azmaveth appointed his older son, Jeziel, as his second-in-command, a decision I wondered about until I watched the young man work with the newest additions to my band. His easy manner and respect for the men soon reassured them, and at the same time, his quiet commands were always obeyed. Zalmon, the first retainer I had from Benjamin, became Abiezer's second-in-command, and the men were very loyal to him in spite of his penchant for saying or doing the wrong thing at the wrong time except during a fight.

We had barely found places for, and adjusted to, Shaul's kin when the New Year's new moon was upon us. While Ahinoam, Abigail, and I made the trip up the Shephelah to Lachish and then east to Hebron, Eleazar had charge of the town. Nearly 40 of us made the pilgrimage, for I had said that anyone who wanted to come to Judah with me could do so. Out of consideration for Eleazar, I also took Eliphelet with me.

Only five of us actually went to the feasts, the rest going about their own ways. I knew Ahiam and Shagay would check in with Ethan's band near Bethlehem, and while I longed to go with them, I knew I should not. Word had come from Jonathan that Shaul was finally satisfied to leave me in peace now that I had left Judah. I didn't want to upset things and put the burden of watching his abbi on Jonathan Hassar again. He had enough on his mind dealing with General Abner.

As Ahinoam had predicted, by the end of the third day, Gebirah Abigail held all the alliances except two consisting of small interior clans, many of whom had been loyal to the nagid of Jezreel, Ahinoam's home town. Nagid Dathan of Hebron held those.

I met with Ahibaal while I was in Hebron. The Jebusite adon had much to say about what was happening in Israel, gave me his opinion on the current state of politics in Philistia, and reluctantly answered my questions about events in Jebus. The Emmanuel had firmly settled in as Araunah and had made it plain that he saw no reason to interfere with Israel so long as it did not meddle with Jebus. I knew that would be a load off the hassar's mind. He also mentioned that anything I could do to woo the elders of Judah to the Dahveed's favor would be worth my while.

With the coming of the fall rains, we planted the fields spreading out around the raised island of the town. All of the repaired houses were occupied, and work had begun on smaller ones around the bottom of the slope. But, as in every town, many of my people lived in tents scattered on all sides.

Once the crops were in, Abishai suggested that reliable commanders be sent to Beersheba with men to guard caravans between there and Egypt. We could charge less than the Egyptians did, and with the reputation of Yahweh's Arrows, he thought we would find plenty to do. He was correct. It wasn't long before Gerar west of us demanded some of our guards, and I sent men there. Abishai continued to refine the organization of my band, and since those men who were part of the shalishim were the most respected, they became the natural commanders for the units I sent out.

And during the winter months, we occasionally raided deep into the Negev, striking far to the south, from the border of Egypt to the Arabah valley. By spring, the three tribes were grouping together into larger encampments, making it harder for us to successfully attack them. I knew that during the next war season I would have to send many more men on each raid, and that increased the chances that what I was really doing would become known. Although I claimed my share of the spoils from the raids, following Ahibaal's advice, I sent it to the elders in various towns in Judah, beginning with the ones who had accepted us from the first year I left Shaul. Ahinoam and Abigail helped me choose what to send from the clothing, jewelry, and animals that we captured.

I only reported to Akish twice, bringing gold each time. Raids against the Judah Negev had virtually ceased, leaving me without an excuse to be bringing spoils.

One other thing worried me that winter. Uzzia. The stories of the tall assassin had gone from one end of the land to the other by now, and Uzzia had quickly discovered that anyone who saw him immediately connected him with either the Rapha or the assassin, and he wasn't certain which designation was worse. He spent considerable time alone, brooding. Abigail came up with the solution. She reminded me that Uzzia had been raised as a Habiru, and so would make a good scout.

I tried him out, sending him south alone, and he soon equaled Hanan in skill, and because of his size, he could cover even more territory in the same amount of time. He was content until nearly harvest when he returned from his last scouting trip greatly upset. But he wouldn't talk of what had happened, not even to Sibbecai, his closest friend.

Sibbecai's bitterness had lessened somewhat, due in a large part, I am sure, to the Gebirah's maid Namea, who simply packed her things and moved into his tent one afternoon about midwinter. The astonished man came to me, wondering what to do. I told him the accepted response was to take her for his wife, since she was determined to be that anyway. As if that was a trigger of some kind, we were soon celebrating wedding after wedding, among them the marriage of Asahel and Matred, another of Abigail's handmaids. Since both of them had a tendency toward roving eyes, the match was a relief to everyone.

By the time harvest came, not an unmarried woman remained among those in Ziklag when we arrived, and all of Abigail's handmaids, except Jotbah, had husbands also.

Harvest was over when Abigail came to me. "Did Akish summon you?" she asked.

"He sent for me to come at the quarter moon."

"You have a day or two yet, then."

"Yes. Is there something happening?"

"Irad approached me yesterday about the ark. The townspeople want to bring it into the town."

"They would be willing?" Remembering the trouble the ark had caused in Philistia the last time it was here, I'd been hesitant to take it from the tent on the raised ground across the north ravine. I wasn't certain how the people of Ziklag would feel about it.

"They have already prepared a special place for it, the two-story house at the northeast corner of town. Irad said the ark would be high enough there that Yahweh could look to the east to the highlands and not be lonely for them, and He could look to the north and see the sacrifices to Him," she ended soberly.

I scratched the back of my head in perplexity. I would feel better myself if the ark was in a more secure place, but Irad's request clearly showed me that the people here had not yet grasped the idea that Yahweh was much bigger than the ark that represented Him.

"Let me think about this," I said.

"It might be easier just to ask Abiathar what Yahweh says," my wife reminded me.

I had to smile. "Yes, Abigail, it would." Giving her a kiss, I started for our high place.

Once there, I stopped at the boundary, and Beriah the Gibeonite came from the tent. "What do you wish, Sar Dahveed?"

"I would inquire of Yahweh. Is Abiathar available?"

"Yes, adoni," the man said, going to the hakkohen's tent.

Abiathar soon appeared, wearing his plain white priest's clothing. He took me to the entrance to the tent, and I knelt.

In a moment, his hand touched my head. "What do you want, Dahveed ben Jesse?" his distant voice asked.

"Adonai, Irad and his people have prepared a house for You in Ziklag, thinking that You need a place to dwell to be happy here. What shall I tell them of Your will?"

"They have done this to show Me gratitude and honor. Let the ark be taken to the place they have prepared. You shall tell Irad ben Omar that the work of his hands down below is acceptable to Me also, and this town shall have My blessing in return."

"I will tell him, Adonai."

Abiathar took his hand away, and I stood.

"Abiathar, the people of—"

The Hakkohen held up his hand. "Yahweh allowed me to hear your request, and His reply," he interrupted. "I will have the ark ready to move on Shabbat, day after tomorrow."

We made quite a celebration of the transfer, with Abiathar performing peace and fellowship offerings. Only the ark bearers, Keturah, her husband Josheb, and Abiathar remained at the high place after the offerings. The rest of us went back to Ziklag, lining the road up the slope to the gates, women on one side, men on the other.

As soon as the ark, covered by Ahibaal's cloth, appeared, the music started, and we all linked arms, beginning our dance with three steps to the right, our left feet ducking behind our right. I'd always loved the two forward kicks that came next, left and right, remembering the contests in Bethlehem to see who could kick the highest! Then the quick hora step, right-left-right, before the steps began again to the left.

Those too small or elderly to dance, sang and clapped in time as the ark proceeded up the road. When the women of Ziklag gave the high ululating shout for joy, they introduced a variation in the dance. Instead of taking the sequence of steps back and forth, they surged forward and backward! Shouts of laughter rang around me as the men took up the song, and we all joined in, dancing right, left, forward and back, only to begin again. The rejoicing continued on into the square, and everyone crowded in.

Since the streets of Ziklag were so narrow, only Irad, the ark attendants and I continued to the house itself, leaving the rest singing and dancing behind us. Abiathar had approved the arrangements made, with the balcony as an outer court, so to speak, and the upper room divided into two parts by a curtain behind which the ark would rest.

Once the ark was in place, we left the house. As we stood in the street, I turned to Irad.

"Yahweh has a word for you," I said. "He wanted you to know that not only is He pleased with the place you have made for Him, and will bless the town, but that the work you have done down below is acceptable also."

The elder's eyes opened wide, and he gasped. "Sereni, I have said nothing about that! I was going to tell you tonight."

"Nothing is hidden from Yah. What is it that you have done?"

"There is a place below this house prepared for Yahweh in case of attack, Sereni. It was originally dug out under the floor of this house to hold weapons and valuables. I enlarged it. The trap door is bigger also, so the ark can be lowered into the space." He showed me what he had done. "We have placed food and water in there so that Yahweh will not go hungry or thirsty while He is there."

I opened my mouth to say that Yahweh most certainly did not need provisions such as that, then closed it again. Yah had said He was pleased with what this man had done. Who was I to say otherwise?

"You have done well, Irad. Let us go join the feasting."

We ate and rejoiced long into the night, and I played the harp until my fingers were sore and my voice hoarse. As I returned it to its case, I noticed that a small piece of inlay had loosened in the dry desert air. I'd need to seal that back in and oil the harp more.

The next morning I left for Gath.

It didn't take long to discover that I wasn't the only one summoned. Representatives of the various towns filled the roads as they traveled toward the city. Listening to the conversation around me soon elicited the information that this was the regular summons before the war season when each town representative would find out their duties to the overlord for the year.

I chewed at the inside of my lip as I waited with the others in the square for Akish to appear. I'd given considerable thought to what we would do this war season, and I'd come to Gath with a proposal to set before Akish for keeping us busy—and away from Israel—for the year. But from what I was hearing, I might not have a choice as to what I was required to do.

I didn't. Akish appeared in the square, sitting on the throne on the dais set up for him while the scribes read off the towns and listed what each was to do. Ziklag, being near the southern border, was one of the last.

"From Ziklag, no supplies. But all the armed men shall report in their units on the day of the summons."

The scribe droned on, and I drifted away, deep in thought. It sounded as if we would have to report as soldiers for the Philistines this year. I wasn't certain how my men would respond to that. Some of them, such as the ones who had attached themselves to Hiddai and Ben-Shimei, wouldn't care one way or the other. I knew my personal retainers would do whatever I requested of them, but did I really want to ask them to fight their own people? What about Shaul's kin, and the Gaddites and those like them? Did I dare send them away?

Ittai passed me as I stood at the gate, staring down the road. "Meet Akish tonight," he said as he walked by. He continued on, and I leaned against the wall a little longer before drifting outside the city and heading toward the orchards and hills to the east.

"Yah, what am I do to?" I asked once the coolness of the forest had closed around me. "I have followed You as best I know how. Akish has sheltered us, saving Judah from Shaul's wrath. But now he is asking us to fight against Israel and You. How can we do this? Should I refuse? I have waited for Your voice, but I have heard nothing, Adonai. Have I missed Your word?"

All afternoon, I wandered amid the cypress, pine, and oaks of the hillside, listening to the stillness, waiting for direction from Yah. But again, there was only silence. The time neared when I must return to Gath. "Yah, I do not see how obeying Akish can be Your will," I pleaded. "I am bound to him by an oath of service, one that may have been a mistake on my part. But I also know that You wish such oaths to be kept, just as Joshua was obligated to keep the oath made to the Gibeonites. It is my duty to serve as he wishes, but how can I when it means breaking my loyalty to You?"

I glanced at the sun. I had to go. "Yahweh, please, I beg of You, make the path before my feet plain."

I returned just at dusk, barely making it into the city before the gates closed for the night.

As I crossed the square, I noticed Hadar's stall. He must be back in town. Akish was already in the room when I entered.

He looked up. "Did you see anyone watching?"

"No, Sereni."

"Good. Maybe I've finally convinced Baalyaton's spies that it's not worth their time to watch me when I come here." He sat up in the chair. "I have much to discuss with you, Dahveed, about the approaching war season." The seren gestured to the stool by the wall.

I sat down and leaned back. "I have a few questions myself."

"I'm sure you do. But I am ready to take the next step, and that means I need you and your men."

"Going after Ekron?"

"Yes, and Gadmilk of Ashdod. I finally found the right information source. Gadmilk's penchant for stirring up trouble is quite lucrative for him. And I should have believed Sahrah Hazzel from the very first. The Phoenicians are paying."

"Why would they be making trouble down here?"

"I would guess someone wants Ashdod as another port, probably Tyre," he said drily. "Splitting the alliance would make taking Ashdod much easier."

"Which means that tall troublemaker is probably paid by them also."

"Troublemaker?" the seren growled. "He's an assassin out to kill us!"

"Then he's the most inept one I've ever heard of," I commented. "Out of nearly a dozen attacks in two years, only two, maybe three died. That kind of record would get him laughed at."

Akish's eyes went thoughtful a moment. "I hadn't thought of it that way. He's just been feeding the distrust between the sars and the serens."

"Which would be very useful if an outsider decided to take over a city," I finished for him. "How am I involved in your move against Ekron?"

"I want to make a show of strength at Aphek this year. With your men, I will have the largest contingent of warriors in the Five Cities. I'd like them to know that."

"Wouldn't we be more useful in the long run if we kept up our campaign in the south? We've got the Amalekites worried, and the Geshurites and Girzites have combined forces. I'd like to keep them on the run if we can."

"I need you with me."

"What if I left half of the men in Ziklag to keep the pressure up against the desert tribes?" I offered, trying to find some way I could avoid fighting Israel. "Even half my band will still give you a show of strength."

Akish looked at me, his face hard with anger. "*You will be going with me, Dahveed.* Both you and your men."

I had overstepped my bounds. Ziklag might be mine, but it would be useless surrounded by hostile territory. Hastily, I knelt. "I beg pardon for my tongue, Sereni. It shall be as you wish."

The muscles in his jaw clenching and unclenching, he looked away. "I know what I am doing, Israelite!"

"Yes, Sereni. I was wrong to suggest otherwise." I bowed to the floor.

"Get up," he said at last.

I stood, keeping my gaze down.

"There is more I want you to do," he said, his voice still hard. "This year, the serens will be going out to battle along with their units."

I couldn't help but look up.

"Yes, Israelite, I have arranged for that, too."

"Yes, Sereni."

"Since Gath is the least of the cities at this time, we will be the last to advance. By that time the fighting will be well started, and battles can be very confusing. Baalyaton of Ekron and Gadmilk of Ashdod will unfortunately be killed. Do you think you can manage to arrange that?"

My own anger rose, and I clamped down on it. The only saving aspect of this proposal was that it would benefit Israel as much as Akish. But if Gath's seren intended to turn me into his personal assassin, we would part company soon. I tried to keep my voice even when I answered him. "Very well, Sereni, you will soon see what I can do."

"If you succeed, I will promote you to commander of my bodyguard. We can discuss more later," he said shortly. Rising, he yanked the door open hard enough to slam it against the wall as he stalked down the passage. I followed silently, fuming over his use of me and not at all sure I wanted to become the "Keeper of Akish's Head"! Consequently, he had his hand on the door to the alley before my gift finally broke through into my mind.

"Sereni, no!" I gasped, lunging forward.

Ignoring me, he pulled open the door, his body outlined in the door frame by the passage lamp.

There was only one thing I could do. Crashing into his back, I hurled us both out the door and into the opposite wall of the alley. The arrow sliced through the skin of my left shoulder, thudding into the wall of the passage, as my mind told me the slight movement at the end of the alley was an archer's hand flashing back for another arrow.

Sweeping Akish's feet from under him, I shoved him down, then threw myself back into the doorway, my hand swiping the sling against my leg just as the second arrow whistled past. The alley was so narrow that my sling shot was weak and off center, but still effective enough to make the attacker scramble back. As I charged toward him, grasping another stone, I heard Akish's voice bellowing for torches and guards.

I stopped short in the square, turning swiftly right, the only way the attacker could have gone without me seeing him. The night seemed strangely light to me, and I spotted the man instantly, standing motionless beside the closed awning of a market stall. The sling circled my head twice, but the tall man ducked just before my stone smacked into the wall where he'd been, spraying bits of plaster in his face.

One hand up to wipe his eyes, he stumbled away from the stall.

"There he is!" someone shouted, and torches and guards appeared, spears at ready, and the man scrambled into the open.

Yahweh's gift flooded through me, and I pulled my sword, a battle cry issuing from my lips, stopping the guards in their tracks. The man I faced topped my height by a foot. As I walked toward him, his sword was out, inviting me forward.

"Do not interfere," someone commanded.

We crossed swords briefly, enough for me to know he was very good with it. I pulled my belt knife with my left hand, and we engaged again, the dull ring of bronze on bronze reaching my hearing, the smells of the market filling my nose.

The man blocked a blow, but instead of thrusting again, he retreated.

Driving him back with every strike, I pressed forward.

He blocked easily, giving ground every time. The market was silent except for the sounds of our feet shuffling on the ground, the sputter of a torch almost out, and the ring of our weapons. Then the man no longer evaded or gave ground, and his blows became more powerful. I shed them to one side or the other, refusing to retreat as we fought. He brought his sword down on me from above, and I stopped it, ducking under and around, my belt knife grazing his side as I turned.

He gasped and jumped away.

The power of that blow had nearly numbed my arm. I dared not stop another as I had that one. When he attacked again, I spun out of his way, hearing his sword scrape on the bronze plates of my cuirass. For endless minutes we fought, the pace of our thrusts and counter thrusts, parries and strikes gradually increasing. Then he gave ground, but not because he wanted to.

Hearing the way he gasped for breath, I realized that he was nearly winded and wouldn't be able to fight much longer. He recognized it also, and tried the overhead blow again. I avoided it altogether, and he tilted forward, off balance from the unexpected lack of resistance. Giving another battle cry, I lunged in, slamming my knuckles wrapped around the knife hilt into his sword arm just below the shoulder.

The sword fell from his numbed hand and arm as he groaned in pain and threw himself backward, smashing against the small wooden door by the gates. The torch burning beside it cast light on my face. "What are you doing here?" he gasped as the latch of the door rattled.

"Take him alive!" someone commanded.

He shied away from my sword, and with sudden understanding, I drove my belt knife into the wood just above the latch, preventing it from lifting to open the door. We faced each other, the point of my blade pricking the skin over his heart, frozen in time for a moment. "Kill me," he said. "You owe me that. Don't give me to Akish."

I couldn't reply.

"I want him alive!"

"No," the man under my sword said. "You owe me. You take my life."

Whether it was his plea, or my anger at Akish, or that the seren had ignored my first warning, I never knew. But I shoved.

His hands automatically pressed against the blade and the wound. A half smile on his face, he looked down at me. "Thank you, adoni. Tell Uzzia he was right."

As he slumped forward, I withdrew my blade, stepping back.

"I said alive, you—" someone started to say.

My gaze burned into the face of the man striding forward.

He halted abruptly, never finishing his sentence.

I swayed a little, waiting to see if anyone else attacked, never taking my gaze from the face before me.

Sweat appeared on it, and he backed away a little.

"His God has entered into him, Dodi," a quiet voice said. "And when a god commands a man's death, it is not for us to refuse."

"Far be it from me to do so. I do not go against the gods," the man agreed, bowing slightly.

It was getting darker, and my arm felt tired.

"Adoni, here is water. Will you drink?" that soft voice inquired.

I backed a step. Ittai held a cruse out toward me. Where was I? I looked at the sword in my hand, then back at my covenant son.

"Answer me, adoni. Are you thirsty?"

"Yes," I managed to say.

He walked up to me, and I reached for the cruse.

"Give me the belt knife," Ittai said, and I let him take it. Putting the cruse in my hand, he helped me to drink.

The world returned to normal, and I bent over, gasping for breath, driving my sword into the ground so that I wouldn't fall flat on my face. Then I drank the entire cruse, a second one, and wolfed down the two pieces of bread Ittai fed me a piece at a time.

Once the worst of the aftermath was over, memory returned. Leaning on Ittai, I faced Seren Akish. "Are you all right?" I asked. "He intended to kill this time."

"I'll be sore from hitting that wall, but if you hadn't shoved me, I'd be dead." He smiled wryly. "Well, you've shown me what you can do, and I'd be a fool not to make you 'Keeper of My Head.' " He walked over to the dead man.

Ittai and I followed. I took a look at the assassin and gasped.

Akish turned to me. "You know him?"

"Yes," I said, pain stabbing at my heart. "I hold his pledge."

"Who is he?"

"Tiras, of Bashan," I replied, looking down at the proud man I had killed. I tightened my hold on Ittai. How was I going to tell Uzzia that his brother was dead? And that I had killed him?

Chapter 24

I stayed the night in the palace in Ittai's chamber. Before I left the next day, Akish and I had another discussion, and I told him I wasn't certain how some of my men would react to fighting against Israel.

"As far as the serens and sars will be concerned," he said, "all your men are just Habiru, right?"

"As far as I know, Sereni."

"Then why don't we say that they will all come to the camp. Whether or not they fight will have to be decided once we know how the others receive them."

I agreed.

On the trip back to Ziklag, doubts and uncertainty hounded me. I had killed the brother of a retainer in order to save the life of an enemy whom I was sworn to serve. How could this be Yah's will? Again I questioned how I came to be in such a situation, reviewing every decision, every turning on the way, every possibility I hadn't chosen. If Yah would only speak! Then I would know whether or not I had done as He willed! But His silence continued.

My pace increased, my feet pounding on the road as I slipped into a run, trying to leave behind the tormenting thoughts. Everything developing around me seemed to be driving me further and further down a path with disaster looming at the end. If I served Akish, I would betray Israel. But if I served Israel, I would betray Akish. Either betrayal meant a sin before Yah. So why didn't He tell me what to do? Surely His silence meant I had strayed from Him in some manner!

Leaving Philistia would solve the problem before me, but where would I go? The same situation that had brought me here still existed. I slowed on the road in the early evening darkness, my doubts dragging at me. At last I landed on my knees in the dust. "Yahweh, *what am I to do?* You know my desire is to fulfill Your will!"

I panted for breath on my hands and knees in the road. My leg started to cramp, and I hurriedly rose, walking and stretching it. How could I continue in this path, leading those with me to disaster? "I cannot see the road I am to follow!" I said. "I see only the waters of chaos and destruction."

"The Reed Sea, perhaps?"

The thought gave me pause. Was this what Moses felt when he faced the sea with the children of Israel behind him and Pharaoh behind them? "Yahweh, have hesed, and deliver me as You delivered them," I prayed. I clung to that thought the rest of the way home.

I didn't get back to Ziklag until late that night, so it was the next day before I called everyone together in the square and broke the news of our responsibility to Akish for the current war season. "We will all have to report to Aphek with Akish," I said at the end. "That isn't something either he or I can do anything about."

"Who stays to defend the town?" Elhanan asked.

"Akish has summoned all the units," I replied.

"Surely he doesn't expect us to leave no one here!" Zelek exclaimed.

"I would assume he thinks enough men are left in Gerar to cover Ziklag," I said with a shrug. "But all of us must report. It is not yet decided whether or not we will have to go into battle. We will have to trust to Yahweh for a solution to that problem, and to protect the town while we are gone."

"Lot of good that will do," I heard Hiddai mutter to Ben-Shimei as he turned away.

As I headed toward my house, my own thoughts echoed those of Hiddai. What possible solution could there be to this situation? How could I tell my men so glibly that we must trust Yah when my own heart churned with doubts? If I had led my men outside of Yah's will, how could I expect that He would care for us?

With a sigh, I shoved the thoughts away and sent Pekah after Abishai, Shagay, Josheb, and Eleazar, the four men who had become my closest advisors and assistants, and then told him to bring Uzzia also. Ahiezer and Joash, the two brothers who commanded the unit made up of Shaul's kin, waited for me at my door.

"Adoni, how can we fight against him?" Ahiezer asked, distressed.

"I can't tell you what will happen," I replied honestly. "But if all else fails, I will ask you to guard our baggage."

"I think we can do that," Joash agreed, after exchanging a glance with his brother.

As they left, I glimpsed Eliphelet off to the side, and called him over. "You will have to report also, I'm afraid," I said.

He paled. "But Dahveed, I can't go to war! Surely I'm needed here for the ark!"

"Akish was insistent that I bring every single man," I sighed. "Only Abiathar and Gad will remain, since they are priest and seer. Everyone else must go."

"But I can't fight! Not in a battle with all the blood . . ." his voice trailed off, horror filling his eyes.

"I know, Eliphelet," I said. "You can stay with Joash and Ahiezer's men, but you will have to report."

Before he could protest more, I dismissed him, seeing Uzzia arriving.

"You sent for me, adoni?"

"Yes. Come into the house. Joab, guard the door," I said, catching sight of my nephew. "I am not to be interrupted."

"Yes, adoni." He gave me a startled look, then stationed himself a little way in front of the entrance.

"Sit down, Uzzia," I said when we were inside. I ran my hand through my hair, not knowing how to say what I must tell him. "I have some bad news," I finally began.

His face paled a little. "Did something happen to Tiras?" he asked.

"Yes."

He looked at my strained face. "He's dead, isn't he?"

"Yes, Uzzia. You have seen him lately?"

The man looked away. "He was waiting for me on the trail when I returned from the last scouting trip. I tried to tell him not to do it, but he wouldn't listen!"

"Did he mention how he came to be here?"

Uzzia put his head in his hands. "You know how dissatisfied he was in Geshur. But after you took me, things went along all right for a couple years. Then King Talmai started hounding him again. He swore he hadn't done anything, and I believe him, adoni."

"I'm sure he didn't. He would never have jeopardized your life."

"Talmai finally succeeded in driving him out, and he roamed around Tob and northern Ammon before deciding to head south and find me. He was coming through Moab when he met a man who offered him work in Philistia. All he had to do was show up at a certain city at a certain time, and attack or frighten men pointed out to him."

"And he didn't want to turn down silver made that easily."

"Correct, adoni. He found us at Maon, and met me there, telling me where he was going. He entered Philistia as a crippled beggar with—"

"Hadar!" I exclaimed. "That was Tiras sitting there that day! But I never saw his face!"

"Not just Hadar," my retainer went on. "Several merchants would let him beg by their stalls and help transport him from place to place. He soon realized he was being used to make trouble between the sars and the serens, and the blame was falling on the Rapha. But he was perfectly safe, for no one saw him as anything other than the beggar in the market.

"He knew when we came to Ziklag, but he couldn't get away to see me until a couple weeks ago. He gave me his silver to keep. He'd collected a good amount by now. He said he had one last job in Gath, and then he would join me, and swear to you. I told him that Gath protected you, so if he did anything there, he was going against the pledge which I was surety for. But he wouldn't listen! What did he do?"

"He was to assassinate Seren Akish."

"How did he happen to miss?"

"I was with Akish at the time," I said softly.

"He got caught then," Uzzia said dully. "I don't suppose Akish showed much hesed."

"He wasn't tortured, Uzzia. He died from a sword thrust to the heart."

My retainer's face relaxed. "It was quick then."

"And before he died, he said to tell you that you were right."

"I wish he would have listened." Raising his head, he held my gaze. "It was your sword, wasn't it?"

"Yes."

¥ ¥ ¥ ¥ ¥ ¥

The four sars of Israel met in the upper room of Malchi's private estate. Ishvi looked around at the clutter scattered here and there, covered with a thin film of dust. "Don't your servants ever clean?"

"When I tell them to," Malchi replied. "That's the side of the room I don't use. If it matters to you, the table and the bedroll are up to Immi's standards."

Ishvi just shook his head and sat down on one of the stools.

Eshbaal had his scribal materials laid out ready, as the hassar cleared his throat. "What's the news, Ishvi?"

"Elihu and Tanhum both have reported that the Philistine call to arms this year has extended to all units of all five cities."

No one spoke for some time.

"That seren from Ekron finally got everyone's attention, did he?" Malchi asked. "I keep forgetting his name."

"Baalyaton," Eshbaal reminded him.

"It's going to be a rough season, then," Jonathan sighed.

"Maybe not as bad as it could be," Ishvi commented. "Tanhum also said that the divisions among the Five Cities are even worse, and there is much distrust between the rulers and the commanders."

"Isn't there a rumor going around that they caught the man attacking the serens, one of the Rapha?" Malchi inquired.

"Tanhum said the man was killed, and it wasn't one of the Rapha, although one of them is dead now also, the one that had six fingers and toes," Eshbaal answered.

"Where did they find someone as tall as the Rapha?" Jonathan asked.

"Bashan, where else?" Ishvi replied. "He tried to kill Akish of Gath. Tanhum said his name was Tiras."

"Tiras!" Jonathan gasped. "What was he doing in Gath?"

"You know him?" Malchi asked, curious.

"I met up with him on my way to Dan. He wouldn't be easily killed, and I can't imagine he'd miss what he aimed at."

Ishvi averted his face. "He wouldn't have this time, but Dahveed was with Akish, and saved him. Then he fought Tiras. Tanhum's source reported Dahveed was so caught up in his gift that even Akish was afraid of him, and not much frightens the seren of Gath. It's also said that Akish made Dahveed commander of his bodyguard."

Eshbaal looked worried. "If Dahveed is Keeper of Akish's Head, does that mean we'll be fighting him this year?"

During the silence that followed his remark everyone heard a guard outside open the gate for the man who banged on it.

"Pray Yahweh that catastrophe doesn't descend on either Dahveed or ourselves," Jonathan Hassar said fervently as footsteps pounded up the stairs.

The door opened, and the guard announced, "Sar Malchi, there is an urgent message for you."

Puzzled, Malchi left the table, absently taking his cloak with him as he followed the guard out the door, leaving the other three waiting to hear what had happened.

Within moments, the sars heard the hoofbeats of a mule racing down the road, and not long after that, a second mule left the compound.

Jonathan went to the door and called the guard. "What happened?" he asked as the man entered.

"We don't know, Hassar. The messenger spoke to Sar Malchi, who raced off immediately on the mule the man rode. He followed the sar on the sar's mule. He looked like a Habiru."

After the guard left, the three sars stared at each other. "I guess we won't know until he gets back," Jonathan sighed, sitting down again to resume the meeting. "Eshbaal, get a full call to arms ready for distribution. We will need all the men we can muster this year."

Eshbaal made notes as the sars turned their attention to immediate concerns again.

¥ ¥ ¥ ¥ ¥ ¥

The summons for my units to report to Gath didn't arrive until well after threshing. Knowing that we might have to do battle, I told Abishai and Uriah to be sure that the men took only essentials, and added that I didn't want any carts used. Only donkey packs.

The next day after the noon meal, I walked up the narrow central street of the town to the house in the northeast corner. I felt the need to be out in the hills in the god places, but knew that I couldn't leave the town. Beriah was on duty and met me on the balcony. "What do you wish, adoni?"

"I would present myself before Yah."

He let me into the upper room and left me alone. I knelt briefly before the curtain that shielded the ark, and then sat on a stool, my chin on my hands, waiting to see if Yah would speak to me, and tell me how to avoid fighting against Israel. But all that came to mind was my agreement to kill the serens of Ashdod and Ekron.

Having lived here nearly a year now, I had a much better feeling for the politics of the country. If Akish wanted to be the foremost seren in the alliance, it would require the removal of both Baalyaton and Gadmilk. And since Baalyaton was nearly as much against Israel as Manani had been, his death would benefit Israel. On the other hand, a quarreling, divided Philistia would benefit Israel just as much, if not more, and Gadmilk was the principal instigator of much of the dissent.

Once again, I couldn't see how to follow my first loyalty to Yahweh and Israel without betraying my secondary duty to Akish, or the other way around. I nearly groaned aloud. Was there anything about my life now that didn't lead to betrayal? The thought gave me an even greater understanding of what I owed Jonathan Hassar, who had faced this same dilemma for years. How had he borne the burden for so long?

I left at the end of the noon rest, no wiser than before. "All I can see to do, Yah, is to go forward," I said, looking up to the sky. "I haven't any idea what will happen, but I will obey Akish as best I can. If You don't want me to do so, keep me from it somehow."

The next morning, the town was awake before dawn, and the men quietly gathered in the square. Wives and families crowded around, and I sent up a silent prayer that all of us would return in safety. I'd said my farewell to Ahinoam and Abigail last night, so the three of us just stood together, watching the others arrive. Abigail kept Eliphelet right beside her, the man looking sick enough already that I wondered if he'd be able to stand the trip to Aphek.

Irad, who would be in charge while I was gone, walked up to me. "Sereni, you do not take Yah with you?"

"We do not need to take the ark to have Yah with us," I explained. "Yah is a great enough God that He can go where He wills. The ark will remain here in the care of Abiathar and Beriah."

"The people are glad of that, sereni, but are you saying that Yahweh can stay with us and yet go with you?"

"Yes. His presence is not tied to the ark in the house."

The town elder looked puzzled. "But He is not in His own land. How can He go about here? Dagon will become angered if He does."

I was saved from finding an answer to that when Abishai arrived. "Everyone is here, adoni."

Once everyone crowded into the square, we knelt. Abiathar raised his hands over us in a blessing, petitioning Yahweh to preserve us while we were away. We stood, and I gave Ahinoam a long hug, then turned to Abigail.

The Gebirah had a smile on her face, but the look in her eyes troubled me. "What is it?" I asked softly as we embraced.

"There is danger ahead, I think. Yah go with you."

"And you," I said, letting her go and giving the command to leave.

Chapter 25

"It's been a while since I found you out here," Sahrah Michal said, walking along the wall to the southeast corner of Gibeah's battlements.

Jonathan turned to her. "That's because you aren't here much anymore, sister mine. Merab's boys are keeping you busy?"

"Yes. I'm just glad I can bring them here to visit Immi and Abbi so often. Adriel came also," she added, speaking of her nephews' abbi. "Barzillai sends his greetings, by the way, and says the next time he sees you, he's got a story you'll never believe, but which he swears is true."

Her brother grinned. "If Immi's cousin is swearing, I know there's a catch somewhere! I'll find it. And I've got one to tell him in return!"

"What brings you out here?"

"The Philistines are gathering at Aphek, so chances are they will head north. Abbi plans on going out again with the army."

"What about you?" she said slowly.

"I can't decide if I should accompany Abbi, or stay here and take care of the kingdom."

"Eshbaal can handle that."

"Yes, but Abner has convinced Abbi that Eshbaal should go with him."

Michal turned to Jonathan. "Eshbaal? He's never been out on a campaign in his life!"

"Which was precisely Abner's point. He said the sar needed some military experience."

"He's talking of giving Eshbaal battle experience when we may be facing the worst Philistine threat since Abbi drove them out? What's Abner thinking?"

"I wish I knew," Jonathan sighed. "I've got the feeling that if I did, I'd know what I should do this year. And that makes me think I should be around to keep an eye on Abbi's cousin. And maybe on Abbi, too," he added quietly.

The sahrah turned to him. "Do you think Abner would endanger the king?" she breathed.

"After the way he's savaged the professional forces, coerced his own clan and tribe, and thrown away his son Jaasiel's life, I don't think I'd put much of anything past that man."

"Why haven't you stopped him?"

"What could I do, unless Abbi makes his support of me plain?"

"Don't expect me to believe that, Hassar!" Michal said fiercely, glaring at him. "You could have stopped Abner any time you wanted to!"

A little smile touched his face. "You always did see things clearly, little sister. We've been using him."

"How?"

"He forgot a couple things. Immi did more than she knew when she took Jaasiel away from him. There have been some long-range consequences we've taken advantage of."

"I think Immi knew just exactly what she took from Abner," Michal said. "She told me one time that Jaasiel was the one who could think as far ahead as you could, and who would face the truth even if it hurt."

The hassar put his arm across Michal's shoulders and drew her close. "There are times when I'm profoundly thankful that Hassarah Ahinoam is on my side."

"It doesn't make sense for Abner to do all this. He's just turned people against him."

"He wants to rule Israel."

His sister caught her breath.

"Until I started looking at things from that angle, a lot of what he's done for years didn't make sense," the hassar went on. "Why be so antagonistic toward Dahveed, for instance. Why not use him as he could have been used? If Dahveed had been fighting for us these past eight years instead of dodging around down south avoiding Shaul, we could have controlled the Jezreel long ago, and would probably have conquered Edom as well. Shaul would have become the most powerful ruler in this land, and Abner had to have known that. He's too canny not to!

"Instead, he said nothing while Balak poisoned the king's mind. Then he fed Shaul's distrust of Dahveed and started to undermine me, using the ideas he gleaned from Jaasiel, while beginning to coerce his fellow clan members."

"And then Immi took Jaasiel."

"Yes. He must have been nearly insane with frustration that night I told him we had Jaasiel, and he realized he had to stop his plans or face Ner. That's the night he decided I had to die."

Michal shivered, and Jonathan hugged her closer. "And the rest of us with you, I suppose," she said.

"No, probably just Malchi and me, once he figured out he'd lost Malchi. He knows he can manipulate Abbi and Eshbaal, and with Malchi gone, he could woo the army's loyalty back to himself."

"What about Ishvi?"

"That's one of the things he's forgotten, but which his son well knows," Jonathan smiled. "Abner can't see the danger in scribes. He never fully understood the power of that information network Jaasiel set up for him, beyond its use for his immediate needs. With Malchi and me gone, Abner would be the power behind the throne, ruling Israel through either Abbi or Eshbaal, and he'd sit there complacently while Ishvi, Tanhum, and Elihu calmly whisked the kingdom out from under him. That's how we've been able to use him now. He never did grasp exactly how I took Abbi's power, and the only way he can see to take mine is to kill me for it."

Michal frowned in thought. "So he thinks he's gaining power because he is taking control of the clans, or at least preventing them from supporting you, so that when he kills you, no one can call him to account."

"Yes. And because I haven't answered in kind, he assumes I've done nothing. But Tanhum knows exactly who Abner has approached or coerced nearly as soon as it happens, and Ishvi and Elihu send them our help and support and tell them how best to protect themselves and their loved ones if it becomes necessary. And while Abner shuffles the men around the army, making sure his supporters are in every unit, Malchi is bleeding off the best and most loyal and getting them safely away."

The sahrah wrapped her arm around Jonathan's waist. "But that must weaken you."

"In the short term, yes. We've lost some invaluable men. Malchi nearly destroyed everything within his reach the day Abner ravaged the second unit. He managed to keep them all in the professional forces at least, but he had to sacrifice one of them to do it. Sithri, I think his name was. But with every passing day, the foundation we're building gets stronger."

"So you're thinking years and years ahead."

"It's the only way I can win, Michal, without beginning a civil war that would tear us apart and leave us to the hesed of the Philistines. You see, the other thing Abner forgot, and Jaasiel could remind him of, is that Yahweh said Dahveed will be the next king."

Sahrah Michal turned to him. "I can see that what you're doing is undermining Abner before he even gets set, but what does Dahveed have to do with this?"

"Because everything we are doing also strengthens Dahveed, Michal. The people know and like him, and his refusal to fight Shaul has done him more good than he can understand right now. This has thrown Abner's actions into sharp contrast, and the northern tribes at Jezreel and above already look with disfavor on what Abner is doing. They say nothing now, out of loyalty to Shaul, but if the king's cousin were on his own, he would come to the end of their loyalty very soon."

"That's what Immi and Rizpah have been doing!" she exclaimed. "I wondered why they spent so much time talking about happenings down here the last time we visited in Jabesh!"

"Yes, Michal. It takes a long time for people's loyalties to change, and Jabesh owes the house of Shaul a great deal. Immi and Rizpah are planting the idea that loyalty to Shaul does not necessarily mean loyalty to Abner."

"That will mean Barzillai will support the idea. He and Immi think a lot alike."

Jonathan leaned against the wall and folded his arms. "Let me bring you in on a little secret, Michal. Barzillai is Dahveed's. To begin with, he knew Dahveed's grandmother, Hassarah Ruth. Then when Dahveed stepped aside when Merab married Adriel, Barzillai was very impressed. He watched things closely after that and soon figured out where I stood. But when Roeh Shamuel announced that Dahveed was to be king, he made his decision and notified me of it. When the time comes, he will throw his considerable weight on the side of the Mashiah."

"The rest of Jabesh will go with him, and that means Gilead, too," Michal said, smiling.

The hassar nodded. "Leaving Abner that much weaker, just in case this does disintegrate into a civil war."

"It won't, not so long as you live."

"But what if I don't, Michal? I have to be sure that if there is a war, it is as short and as bloodless as I can possibly make it."

"Why does that have to involve risking defeat by Abner now?"

"Because I am Melek Israel, Michal. Yahweh gave His people into my hands, and I must do the best I can for them, before I do anything for myself. Otherwise, I'm just like Abner."

"Yahweh, grant us hesed," Michal said, putting her arm around her brother again.

Two days later, Jonathan stood beside his mule in the fortress courtyard, listening to Abbi's usual address to the commanders. He had decided to go with the army, leaving the kingdom in the hands of Elihu and Tanhum. In the end, he had made his decision on the need to keep an eye on Abner, the wish to support Shaul as much as he could, and the hope that this time Yahweh would grant them the victory that would give them control of the Jezreel. And, if he was very honest, there was a tiny fear buried in his heart that Dahveed Israel might be waiting out there. He knew if anyone had a chance of keeping Dahveed from fighting against Israel, it was he. But only if he were up there.

Once Abbi finished and the commanders left, Jonathan turned to Immi, feeling her tremble as she hugged him. Michal took her place, clinging to him tightly. He mounted the mule while she went on to Ishvi. Once the good-byes were all said, Immi came back to him, holding up her hand for him to take.

"Don't worry, Immi. No matter what happens, you, and all my house, will be protected."

"May Yahweh keep you, my son," she said, stepping back for him to go.

¥ ¥ ¥ ¥ ¥ ¥

Aphek, twenty-eight miles north of Gath, was the cross-roads of five major trade routes, two of which led into the highlands of Israel. Eighteen and a half miles east on the northern route was Tappuah, the place where Sar Ishvi had been wounded in our ambush of the Philistines. I wondered if I'd be marching up that road soon, but turned away from the thought. From what I could see of the gathering here, Akish had neglected to tell me several things. I sighed. And if I had kept to my place, he wouldn't have gotten angry, and I'd probably know a lot more.

Apparently all five cities had sent full units. Hanan and Shagay's Jonathan had roamed around the nearby country, and the estimate of the number of men gathered here chilled me. Shaul had never faced anything like this army before. Baalyaton had apparently convinced all the cities that Israel must be subdued, and Philistia had mustered its full strength in response.

Seeing the number of units the coastal cities had supplied, I wondered at Akish's claim that with my men he would have the largest contingent of warriors. That night, I talked it over with Uriah.

"You're counting men, he's counting professionals," the Hittite observed. "I've wandered around myself. The units from the coastal cities have one, at most two, professionals commanding militia. Akish has three professionals for every unit of militia, and with our band of nothing but professionals, his army is the most to be feared."

"Abner did say that a good professional is worth five militia," I acknowledged.

"And one of our shalishim could easily defeat three to four entire units, Dahveed," Uriah said coolly. "Give me the right battlefield, and I can defeat everything the Five Cities can bring against us."

"May Yahweh grant Shaul the right battlefield," I muttered, staring out over the tents and campfires.

The next day, the final muster was called, and each city paraded their troops before the assembly of serens. Gath was last in the line-up, and we were last in Gath. I had the men arranged in units, each commanded by one of the shalishim. But my assistant commanders were fully competent to command the units without the shalishim, and with nearly 40 trained in that style of fighting, I could field more than a dozen of the three-man units. Something Akish still didn't know.

As we marched past, I heard the murmur among those watching grow louder and louder. My men took their places, and I stood at their head, sided by Abishai with Shagay, Eleazar, and Josheb just behind us. The parade had given me a chance to look over the entire army, including the chariots, and by the time I took my place, I would have assassinated every seren there if Akish had asked me to.

Unless Yahweh took a hand, there was little chance that Shaul could defeat this force. There were simply too many. And knowing that Yahweh had rejected the king would mean that Israel would face the Philistines alone, unless Yahweh had hesed on Jonathan Hassar once again, and worked through him. For the first time, I was afraid of what might happen this war season. I vowed that if I went to war, every seren or sar I encountered would die.

¥ ¥ ¥ ¥ ¥ ¥

Seren Akish and his principal serens took their seats at the head of the parade ground, Akish careful to keep any expression from his face as he listened to the comments and murmurs swelling around him as Dahveed's band took their place.

Baalyaton was clearly furious, Hanabaal and Gadmilk definitely annoyed, but Muwana gave careful study to the Habiru before turning thoughtful eyes toward Akish.

"Those Habiru you hired seem to have multiplied," Baalyaton commented.

"The fault is mine," Akish said, bowing slightly in the man's direction. "When I agreed to shelter the band, I myself didn't know how many there were. An oversight I will not commit again, I assure you. However, as evidenced by the safe roads and drastic lessening of raids from the desert tribes, they have served well."

"I can vouch for that," Hanabaal said unexpectedly. "Complaints about raiding from my people in Gaza have stopped."

"They are good warriors, then," Muwana decided.

Gadmilk looked sour, but said nothing.

To Akish's satisfaction, Baalyaton had to let the review continue. When it was over and the units dismissed, Akish settled himself, waiting for the storm he knew would come. It began with the angry crowd of sars that quickly gathered, led by the Rapha. "What are Habiru doing here?" Ishvi-benob raged. "We have enough trouble without those treacherous dogs among us! Or have the serens forgotten the battle of Michmash? Do we have to remind you that we lost the highlands because the Habiru you hired turned against us? Why take the chance that it will happen again? Or was that the point?"

A growl of agreement rose from the men gathered in front of the serens. "How are we supposed to fight if we have to worry about our backs?" someone shouted.

"To say nothing of what's behind the trees in those cursed hills!" another added.

Baalyaton raised his hands. "Sars, as you well know, we are not going into the hills this year, but into the Jezreel valley where Yahweh is weak, our gods are strong, and we can use our chariots."

"And you're so sure the Israelites will meekly venture down in to the valley to fight? They'll stay in the hills by day and attack and kill us in the night!"

"Provided those Habiru haven't already killed us for them!" Ishvi-benob added. "But then, a mere sar's life doesn't mean much to you, does it? How many of us died because of Seren Manani? Just go to Sheol and ask Sar Eliahba! But you did nothing until Manani tried to sneak off without paying his debts to you! And even after you condemned him, you still wanted us to take him into the highlands, risking our lives in a battle, just so he could be killed, rather than executing him yourselves!"

Akish hid his private amusement.

Baalyaton's flushed face grew even redder at the mention of Manani's sentence. The Ekron seren's stubborn attitude and harsh reprisals over what happened had come home to roost.

"And now you want us to fight with Habiru!" another sar spoke up. "I didn't want to believe that my seren would care nothing for me, but what else can I think now?"

"First you accuse us of treachery, and then you try to kill us off with Habiru," Lahmi roared. "We won't have it!"

The lesser serens sat silently, while Baalyaton sputtered some incoherent replies, Gadmilk couldn't quite hide the smile on his face, and Hanabaal huddled down in his seat.

Akish let the wrangling continue until he saw Muwana watching him. Then he stood, raising his hands again. "Sars! Sars!" he yelled. "Let me speak!"

Gradually the angry shouts of the commanders died down.

"First, I know there has been trouble between the serens and you," he said, waiting for the muttering of agreement to stop. "But I had a hard time thinking my sars would do some of the things they were accused of, so I did some investigating, as I suggested should be done last year. The death of the assassin in Gath enabled us to learn that he was hired by a Phoenician power."

Out of the corner of his eye, Akish saw the smile vanish from Gadmilk's face. He had everyone's attention now. "The seren of every city needs to look into this carefully. I know I am, and I have already identified two agents in Gath in the pay of Phoenicia." He paused. That should give Gadmilk even more to keep him awake at night.

"Second, the men you are calling Habiru are just as disciplined as the rest of the professional soldiers serving Philistia. The man I have brought to fight for us is Dahveed Israel, who deserted to me more than a year ago, and has served me without fault since then. All of you have entrusted your goods, your families and your lives to him whenever you traveled the roads in Gath and farther south, for he is the one guarding them and protecting you from the desert raiders."

"Dahveed Israel?" Muwana gasped, automatically glancing to where the Habiru band had stood in the parade.

"Yes. Shaul has driven him out. Let us not waste him."

"If he fights for us, we will surely win," Hanabaal commented.

"He will fight as I command," Akish replied smugly.

"How can you even consider this?" a voice from the sars roared, and Saph stepped forward. "You want us to go to war with *Dahveed Israel* at our backs? If you command him, the only thing you should tell him is to go back to wherever you put him! The only thing he will do in the battle is become our adversary, a satan right in the middle of our ranks, and with the perfect opportunity to buy Shaul's favor again with our heads!"

"And he's the one who inspired that song of victory!" Lahmi added. "Or have the serens forgotten that 'Shaul has slain thousands, but Dahveed his ten thousands?' I don't think any foreigners are paying anyone anything. The serens have done enough to us already. They are the ones who want us dead!"

Akish listened without showing any trepidation. He had known from the beginning that he wouldn't be able to use Dahveed in battle, but the uproar the man's presence had created produced the exact situation he wanted. He caught the eye of one of his own sars and barely nodded his head.

"We do all the fighting and the serens stay safely within walls, and get all the rewards," the man shouted. "Since you serens are so certain the gods will be with us and give us victory, you should lead us into the battle! Every one of you!" He pointed an accusing finger at the group.

"Good idea," someone else yelled, causing the sars to erupt in uproar again.

Hanabaal huddled even further down in his chair, and Gadmilk looked queasy. Baalyaton's face was white now, as he tried to shout down the demands for the serens to go to battle.

Akish stood again, holding out his hands as before. It took some time for the commanders to quiet enough so that he could be heard. "Given the situation, and since my own sars have joined in the request, I, as Seren of Gath, will accompany my men into the battle, and yes," he turned to the other serens who stared at him in shock, "I am willing to go first and risk that danger."

Another growl came from the assembled sars as they turned to look at the other rulers. Muwana stood also. "I am against this, since it breaks with the usual practice which has served us well. However, if my sars also demand that I accompany them, I will do so." He turned to face the commanders.

After a short silence, one of the men stepped forward, and knelt. "It would reassure us, Sereni. And after all that has happened in the past couple years, we need reassurance."

"Then I will surely go," Muwana replied, taking his seat.

"I've fought before, I can again," Hanabaal growled, casting a baleful glance at his sars.

"Well, yes, I suppose it should be done," Gadmilk stammered. "I do have armor, you know."

"And I bet you've never worn it," someone muttered in Akish's hearing.

"What about you, Baalyaton?" the seren of Gath asked after a long silence.

The Ekron seren glared at him, knowing full well that with that question, he had just lost any chance at the primacy of the alliance.

"Don't worry about Ekron, Sereni," Ishvi-benob said grimly. "Seren Baalyaton will be more than glad to lead us into the fray!"

"Of course I will lead," the seren snapped. "And I mean lead! As always, Ekron will fulfill its duty to withstand the attacks of the hill tribes!"

"We are reassured to hear it, Seren," Akish said wryly, sitting down again. He listened to what discussion remained with only half an ear. He could already feel the beginning of the subtle shift of power from Ekron to Gath.

Only one thing remained. Dahveed. He had to send him home, for his own safety if nothing else. And he had to do it without unduly angering him. After feeling what had emanated from the Dahveed when he fought Tiras, he did not want to lose his service. Ittai had told him about the gift, but he hadn't believed it until that night. Shaul must indeed have been insane to drive such a man from him, instead of heaping him with rewards and sending him against his enemies.

Nothing in Philistia could stand up to what he'd seen that night, not even the Rapha. Previous war seasons had provided ample indications that Dahveed's band was much more than it seemed as well. He'd watched Ittai sparring with the professionals a time or two, and just the way his nephew handled himself hinted at a disciplined training far beyond what the best of his professionals had. He very much wondered what had gone on in the hills during his nephew's seven-year absence.

¥ ¥ ¥ ¥ ¥ ¥

I waited restlessly in our encampment. Akish had sent a messenger with orders for me and my men to keep within the bounds of our camp. Feelings against us must be very high.

It was dark when Ittai appeared outside my tent. "Adoni, Seren Akish commands your presence."

Wordlessly, I threw my cloak over my cuirass and followed him, wondering at the formality of the summons. I half expected to find all the serens with Akish when I arrived, but he was alone.

"Shalom, Dahveed," he greeted me as I entered his tent.

I bowed. "Shalom, Sereni."

"Sit down," he directed, indicating a stool across the little three-legged table from him. "As you may have guessed already, things did not go well once the units were dismissed. Strenuous objections were raised to having Habiru go into battle with us."

"The battle of Michmash is still in everyone's memory?" I asked.

"Yes."

"All right, I'll send the men home. Most of them will be glad to go. And there is plenty of raiding we can do, to say nothing of the howls of protest we can quiet by returning to guard duty on the caravan routes."

"Not just your men, Dahveed. You must go also."

I stilled. I had to leave? I couldn't. Getting into that battle was the way I could serve both Akish and Israel. Shaul would need all the help he could get to save his kingdom, and leaderless men are easy to rout. "Sereni, if my men are gone, no one will notice me."

"They'll notice. The Rapha will if no one else."

This couldn't be happening. I couldn't leave, not with all the might of the Five Cities about to descend on Jonathan Hassar and Israel!

"Sereni, don't send me away. I don't even have to be with you. I can join you in the battle any time after it begins! Surely you can trust me that much!"

Akish sighed. "As Yahweh lives, Dahveed, I know you've been upright with me. I've been more than pleased with the way you have fought, and you have served me faithfully from the day you arrived until this very moment. But that doesn't mean the other serens are willing to accept you. They aren't.

"Take your men and go back to Ziklag in peace. Your service for the year is done. Don't upset the serens now, or I'll lose everything that I gained today."

I stood facing him. Yahweh had to have placed me here where I could help save Israel and still honor Akish! I must stay, somehow. Maybe the seren was still angry over my impertinence there in Gath. "Have I done something wrong?" I asked desperately, dropping to my knees. "If I've served you so faithfully, why can't your servant stay and kill the enemies of adoni melek?"

Akish looked puzzled a moment, since I'd reverted to Israelite usage, but at the same time everything was so confused in my own mind, that I myself couldn't have said whether those last words referred to Seren Akish, King Shaul, or Hassar Jonathan! I couldn't get this close to helping Israel and then be sent away. It couldn't happen!

Akish stood and reached for my hands. "Dahveed, you are as good in my eyes as an angel of the Elohim. But the sars have absolutely refused to have you go into battle with them. They are very worked up now, and with the Rapha talking against you as they are, you cannot stay! You and your men must be gone by daylight tomorrow."

I very nearly rebelled, and Akish saw it. "Dahveed," he said softly. "If the sars and serens attack you, I will be obligated to defend you, and that will bring the wrath of all four cities on Gath. Would you destroy the lives of my people?"

His comment brought me up short. I had been so focused on one thing that I had forgotten what the consequences might be for others. With all my men involved, we probably could have made sure that Baalyaton and Gadmilk died, but even then the risk seemed greater than this man would normally accept.

Akish pulled me to my feet, and I stepped back a little, able for the first time to think without worrying about a conflict in my loyalties. If Akish wanted another seren dead, he surely knew a dozen safer ways to do it.

"You never expected me to get to battle, did you?" I asked softly. "Your request was an excuse to get me here. It was simply my presence that you needed."

A little smile quirked his mouth. "Ittai said you would figure it out sooner than I thought you would. But there is a bit more to it, Dahveed. I have now been *commanded* by the serens to return you to the south, where you can, indeed, do the most good, and where, according to comments made to me, you will not be tempted to do anything beyond what I hired you for."

"Hired?" I asked. If the other serens believed Akish had hired me, then no one knew that I had sworn service to Akish as Ben-geber years ago. No wonder those sars had demanded that I be sent away if they thought I was only a mercenary!

Akish smiled. "Yes. Now, go down there and carry out your God's will on those desert tribes."

"I will, Sereni," I promised. As I was leaving the tent, I paused. There might be more to this than even the seren knew. It occurred to me that Yahweh might have a purpose in this and be working on Akish's behalf. I turned back.

"Sereni?"

He looked up.

"A word to open your ear. When you go into battle against Israel, don't be too forward. Yahweh works in odd ways."

Tamar bat Dahveed

Yes, Dahveed has seen more than once the odd ways that Yahweh works. Now, though, the path he must travel will be dark and completely obscure, for the final days have come. He will be tested to the limit of his endurance, and bitter grief will overwhelm his life.

And Jonathan Hassar, as Melek Israel, faces his last bitter choice, and yet will find his heart's desire in the hands of his God.

The Last Ten Days

Chapter 26

Day One

By the time the first rays of the sun touched the plain, my men and I were well away from Aphek, heading toward home. Behind us, the Philistines broke camp and started north to the Jezreel valley. We traveled as fast as we could make the donkeys go. I was eager to get back south now that I had, at last, a clear path before my feet. And I had plenty of time to think as we hurried along the road. For days, I had needlessly fretted and worried and agonized.

The disaster that had loomed so huge before me had been nothing but a mirage. Akish had never expected me to fight, and had I not angered him by trying to get my own way, he probably would have explained enough for me to understand that from the first. Yahweh had also known all along that I would not be fighting Israel, that there was, in reality, no danger of betrayal ahead of me.

"Forgive me, Yah," I whispered to myself, watching Eliphelet nearly dancing down the road ahead of me, the most relieved man in Philistia at the moment, barring myself. "I should not have doubted You. I will not do so again."

¥ ¥ ¥ ¥ ¥ ¥

"What do you think, Adnah?" Jozabad asked, squinting as the early morning rays of the sun streamed over their backs. The two men crowded together on the rickety platform of the ruined watchtower on the hill overlooking the coastal plain toward Aphek.

"There's definitely dust, and whoever is making it is headed south," the commander replied.

The assistant commander sighed. "I suppose that means we go south, too?"

"That's our job," Adnah said shortly. "Here comes the courier," he added, carefully descending the ruined stairs on the inside of the tower.

"Commander," the youth gasped, running up to them. "The Philistines are headed north to the Jezreel. All of them. My abbi says to tell General Abner that there was trouble yesterday between the sars and the serens over the Habiru forces Akish had with him. He thinks they will not be allowed to fight."

"That's good news, considering how many we have to deal with as it is," Jozabad said sourly as he emerged from watchtower.

"You'd best get back home," Adnah said, waving the boy away. "And stay out of sight of any soldiers," he called after the lad.

"They won't pay any attention to him. He's just a shepherd," the assistant said.

Adnah grunted. "They should. The last I knew, the Dahveed was a shepherd at that age."

"True," Jozabad agreed as they walked back to the three waiting units. "Any idea why Abner is so sure the Philistines are going to send raiders into the hills down here?"

"I don't know that he thinks that. He wasn't talking to me. Barely noticed me enough to give me his instructions."

"Seems a waste," Jozabad continued. "That's not a bunch of raiders out there. That's an invading army, and if they plan on using those chariots, Jezreel is the only place."

"So why the dust cloud going south?" Adnah asked, exasperated, as they approached the rest of their men. "In spite of what that lad said, not all the Philistines are going to Jezreel."

Adnah sent a courier off to General Abner waiting at Tappuah, and then the units started south using the local roads and paths on the Shephelah hills, paralleling the cloud of dust off on their right.

"How many do you think there are?" Jozabad asked after a while.

"A lot more than we have, even filled out with our militia," Adnah replied shortly. "And if we have to fight them, we better hope Yahweh fights for us. What we've got behind us are barely trained farmers."

"They aren't even of our tribe," Jozabad said softly. "I wonder what Abner was thinking when he mixed up the militia leaders and the units like he did. Always before, the leaders of the militia units stayed with the unit to help the professionals command the men."

The commander didn't reply.

Late that afternoon, the seven officers from the units watched as the dust settled on the road. "They've camped," Jozabad said. The others stared west silently. They were all from around Shechem, the heartland of western Manasseh.

"The men are restless," Zillethai, whom everyone called Zill, said. "They want to be where the fighting is, not running off on a partridge chase around the hills."

"Let's send them back, then," Jozabad said suddenly. "They can report to Abner that the units of Philistines going south seem to be headed home, and that we're staying behind to make sure."

Adnah started to protest, but Jozabad gestured slightly, and the commander quieted. "I think it's also important that the hassar knows there will be no Habiru at the battle."

"What makes you so sure of that?" Zill questioned.

"Because that's who we've been following," Jozabad explained. "And I think we should keep following, all the way to wherever they go."

Adnah eyed him, puzzled. "Mind telling us why?"

"I think it's the best place for us, that's why. You remember what you told me, Zill? When did Abner switch you from the unit you came with?"

"Right after I overheard someone telling him that our clan favored the hassar," the man replied.

"Same with Adnah and me."

The others thought about that for a little while. "Given the other things I've heard about Abner and the hassar lately, I agree with Jozabad," one of them said quietly. "We should go south."

"I think so, too," Zill decided. "You know what's whispered of the hassar's wishes regarding the Dahveed, and Roeh Shamuel did call him the Mashiah."

"And somehow, as mixed up as the army units are now, I doubt Abner will notice that we've gone," Adnah said. "How far into Judah should we go?"

"I don't think we should go to Judah." Jozabad pointed. "I think we should head out to that highway."

"Why?" the others asked.

"Remember the lad said that the Habiru came from Gath. Who's the only Habiru leader likely to have that many men and be south of Gath?"

"Dahveed Israel," Adnah said with a smile. "Send the units back," he decided. "If they start now, they can make a few miles north before it's dark."

Day Two

"Dahveed, someone is following us," Hezro, Abigail's former commander, reported.

"More? Hanan told me he spotted someone yesterday, about two hours after we left Aphek."

"Then it may be the same ones. It was Hanan who told me to come to you. He said something about looking them over."

"Good. He'll be around soon then."

Bowing, Hezro returned to his place in the line of marching men. We were tired of the dust we raised, advertising our presence to anyone who cared to look. With this many men, however, taking the Habiru trails would be more trouble than it was worth, and I wanted to be certain everyone knew I had done as Akish commanded me.

My elation at knowing Yah's will at last had left me already. The heavy heat and my worry over Israel's chances with the Philistines gnawed at my thoughts. I kept thinking that I should take my personal retainers, the shalishim, and head for the hills. We could beat the Philistines to the Jezreel valley and help with the battle. Hide ourselves and attack from the rear or something. But that would be a deliberate breaking of my oath to Akish, and he was trusting me to serve him faithfully. In addition, most of my men were glad to guard the southern borders, where we aided Judah as much as the Philistines. Silently, I prayed that, once again, the embrace of the hills would prove deadly for the Philistines and be the saving of Shaul. Yet, even as I did, I wondered what would become of us if Akish happened to perish in the battle. If Ittai also died, our position would be untenable at best.

We halted just before noon, breaking out food that we could eat quickly. The men were eager to return home, and they talked and laughed with each other, relieved that we would not be fighting Israelites.

"Hanan is leading some men in, Dahveed," Elhanan said, coming in from his sentry post.

"Tell him to bring them here," I said, reluctant to leave the shade of the cypress I lay under.

Before very long, I saw Hanan bringing them into our group, my men watching, curious. All seven looked Israelite. I glanced at the sun again. It was just noon.

Suddenly Hanan gasped, jerking around to face south. Then he took off at a dead run with such a look on his face as I had never seen before. A chill went over me, and I rolled quickly to my feet, watching the young man disappear into the shimmering heat waves.

"What was that about?" Abishai asked.

"I don't know. But I don't like it," I replied, turning to the seven men who looked around them warily now that their guide had vanished.

"Shalom," I greeted. "You are seeking someone?"

"Shalom," the first one replied, bowing a little. "The young man who just left said he could take us to the dahveed of the Habiru band in the south of Philistia."

"In other words, you want to see Dahveed Israel," I said, smiling.

"Yes, geber, but we didn't think we should ask using that name."

"It would be quite a shock to most people here, although not for much longer," I agreed. "I am Dahveed. What did you wish?"

"We would stay with you, adoni. Yahweh's spirit has left Shaul, and has come to you, and we would follow you."

"Yahweh's spirit still rests on the hassar," I retorted softly.

"True, adoni. But the hassar has let it be known that those who help you, help him."

"What is your clan and how are you called?"

"We are from Manasseh on this side of Jordan, adoni. Our clans are close together near Shechem, and our families support the hassar. I am called Adnah."

"What weapons do you use?"

"We are archers, adoni."

"Elika?" I called.

He trotted over.

"I am giving these seven archers from Manasseh to you to command. Get them something to eat and drink before we leave."

"Thank you, adoni," Adnah said. "We were out on scout duty and didn't have time to bring provisions with us."

"Go and eat now. I will take your report later, on the road."

The men bowed and followed Elika away.

More troubled than I cared to admit, I sat down again. This seemed to indicate that Abner was branching out from his own tribe. And that could cause nothing but trouble.

¥ ¥ ¥ ¥ ¥ ¥

Abigail had just returned to the house from the high place after the morning sacrifice when a commotion in the square drew her back outside. "What is it?" she asked Ahinoam, who was already in the street.

"Sounds like someone shouting," the other woman replied.

"Immi! Immi!" Zalmon's youngest child called from the rooftop on the next house. "Everyone's running toward the town! Immi, come see!"

Abigail exchanged a swift glance with Ahinoam and hurried toward the market. Her heart pounded as the troubled feeling that had plagued her since Dahveed left again rose in her mind.

"Raiders, Irad!" Casluh, one of the three young men left in town, shouted. "Amalekites, coming in from the southwest. At least five units or more!"

Behind her, Zalmon's youngest shrilled, "Immi! There's smoke!"

Breaking into a run, Abigail reached the square in time to see Irad shouting orders, women and children racing inside the gates, and more hurtling along behind them. As Abigail watched, Irad went to the gate while the other two elders and Casluh stationed themselves at the other three sides of the market, all of them giving orders.

Even in the confusion, she noticed that the people of Ziklag living outside the town had come in carrying what weapons they had, mostly hunting bows and arrows. The people of Judah carried nothing, or else clothing or valuables. She closed her eyes briefly, knowing that none of the families who had joined Dahveed when he left Judah were prepared to face anything like this.

Keturah raced into the square from the narrow central street. "Ahinoam," she panted, "there are armed men closing in around the town from the north!"

"Tell Casluh," Ahinoam said, pointing to the youth directing activities not far away. "That seems to be his side of town."

When Keturah reported, Casluh immediately sent her back for more information.

"Abigail," Ahinoam said, turning to her. "We have to get our people out of the way. We are hampering Irad. Have the women quiet their children, and get everyone seated either in houses close to the north side of the market or just outside them."

Seeing the wisdom in the order as soon as she heard it, Abigail obeyed instantly, plunging into the middle of the milling crowd of women and children.

"Come now," she commanded, raising her voice. "Listen now, everyone! Quiet your children. We must have order." She stopped a child running around two women and attached the young one's hand firmly to the mother's skirt. "Calm yourselves," she added, picking up another child and placing him in his immi's arms. "Collect your children, go into these houses," she pointed. "Quickly now! We must be out of the way!" She shoved one or two women toward the doors, repeating her orders in as firm a voice as she could manage. Soon Jemima, Ahiam's wife, echoed her commands, helping to sort everyone out and get them into houses while she carried her 9-month-old boy in her arms.

"No questions, now!" Abigail said as some stopped to ask something. "Get out of the way first! Then we can settle ourselves and see what has happened. Inside now!"

Gradually the crowd calmed, and the women took their children into the houses. Abigail quickly visited each house, silencing the occupants and checking to be sure that every woman had her own children. Then she collected the women who had no children yet and took them back outside with her, leaving Jemima, who was the calmest of the group, in charge behind her. Ahinoam was standing at the gates with Irad as a last straggling family rushed inside before the gates slammed shut. The woman stopped to report to the elder before taking her children farther into the square and out of the way.

The Gebirah waited as Irad and Ahinoam walked up to her.

"Good, everyone is together and quiet," he said approvingly. "Ahinoam says you are a Gebirah and used to leading the people."

"I will do my best, Irad," Abigail replied. "I have never been under attack before, however, and most of the others here have not either, except for your people. The women waiting with me do not have children. What can we do to help?"

Casluh rushed up. "Irad, the town is surrounded. We have warriors on every side."

"What defenses do we have?"

"There are five bows for each side of town, but very few rock piles were ever restocked. We didn't think we would need them again," he said, his face white. "But we can repel them at least once, I would say."

"Then we will have to see how determined they are," Irad replied. "We will do what we can."

But the look on his face told Abigail that the raiders would capture the town. It was only a matter of when. As Casluh took the single women to its east side, she and Ahinoam went back into the houses lining the square and informed everyone of the steps taken so far for defense.

"Well, at least there is plenty of food," one woman said. "We've just had harvest."

Abigail bit her tongue. She doubted they would have the chance to prepare even one more meal, for already column after column of smoke was rising outside the walls as the Amalekites looted and then burned the tents and houses surrounding the raised island of the town.

Back in the square, Ahinoam approached Irad again. "Where will Abigail and I be the most useful?"

"The Gebirah will be useful here, keeping the people calm and orderly," the elder replied. "Ahinoam, you can go to the rooftops on the east side of town. That is where the band's women have been stationed. They will need your support."

"As you wish, Irad."

Once Ahinoam had left, Abigail organized three people in each house to bring water and some food to the children. She circulated almost constantly, trying to answer questions as best she could, and keep hope alive. "We don't know if they will attack the town or not," she said again and again. "They may be satisfied with what they have captured outside, and if we resist, they may decide not to continue and leave. We will have to see."

Keturah arrived, her calm demeanor giving Abigail's spirits a lift. "Here, you need a drink, too," the Gibeonite woman said, holding out a cruse.

Just then shouts arose from the west side of town, and Abigail heard the crash of rocks thrown down from the rooftops.

Irad hurried over. "Keturah, it must be done now. They are coming toward us on all sides." As he spoke, the young boys by the gate began shooting arrows and yelling. "Do not let the men come!" he added over his shoulder as he hurried back to the gate.

"I will need you, Abigail," Keturah said, pulling her arm. "Come on."

"What is it?" she asked as they ran.

"Irad has ordered the ark hidden. The town will be taken. But the ark must remain safe for the Mashiah. We can't let Abiathar and Gad come with us. They'll be killed. Here is what we will do," she said, explaining breathlessly while they ran down the street.

The curtain was down, and the ark had already been covered, when she and Keturah arrived in the upper room. Abiathar and Gad already stood between the carrying poles, ready to lift.

"Irad says the town will fall," Keturah gasped.

The two men lifted, easing the ark from the table, and walking heavily out the door and across the balcony. Keturah gestured to some bundles on the floor, and Abigail grabbed two of them, following the hakkohen.

Casluh turned from the parapet, "Hurry," he implored. "They are almost close enough to see you!" Turning back he loosed an arrow, and three of the women also hurled some stones over the side.

"Now!" Abigail heard Ahinoam yell, and she cast a hurried glance down the east side as she walked down the stairs to the tiny courtyard. The women from Dahveed's band were heaving rocks down, and one shrieked as an arrow nearly struck her.

"Again!" Ahinoam called, looking toward the ark, worry on her face.

The trap door was open already, and the hakkohen started down the steps. They were steeper than the ones from the balcony, and Gad struggled to keep the ark from tilting too far forward.

At a glance from Keturah, Abigail put her bundles down and got a lamp, hardly able to make her shaking hands light it. The Gibeonite woman followed on Gad's heels, setting the bundles down on the stairs, and retreating back up them while the men shifted around in the dark space below.

"Now, Abigail," Keturah said, softly.

The Gebirah quickly set the lamp on the steps, while Keturah raised the trap door. The men were still setting the ark down when they closed it over them.

"Wait," Gad called.

"They're getting into the houses!" Casluh yelled.

As he spoke, Abigail saw the shutters on the wall across from her begin to shake. Frantically, she shoved the rug over the door, and they tipped the heavy wooden table onto it. The shutter splintered, and a hand reached in. Casluh loosed an arrow that struck the side of the wall, making the hand disappear.

"Come on," he yelled. "They're in the town! Don't show yourselves!"

The pounding from the trap door stopped, and Keturah and Abigail raced outside, hearing Casluh slam the door behind them. As she sped down the narrow street, she saw Ahinoam and three other women racing down an alley on the left. They arrived at the market at the same time, to be greeted by the sound of the gates splintering as the Amalekite axes bit into them.

"It is done?" Irad asked anxiously, seeing them.

"Yes," Keturah replied.

Irad nodded to the women holding bows and rocks. "We can go in peace, now," the elder said. "Yahweh will not be disturbed." The people of Ziklag put down the weapons and joined the others.

"Yahweh will go with us," the Gebirah heard herself say. "Remember, we are His."

She, Ahinoam, and Jemima stood close together as the first ax broke through the gate. The bar seemed to lift itself, and then crashed to the ground. Amalekites rushed in, meeting the ones who poured in from the alleys of the town. Fear seizing her heart, Abigail glanced up at the sun. It was just noon.

¥ ¥ ¥ ¥ ¥ ¥

The courier found them just as they stopped for the noon rest. Hassar Jonathan noticed that he had someone start walking his sweat-covered mule to cool it down. The messenger walked up and bowed to Shaul. "Adoni, the scouts report that the Philistines have taken the northern route through the Ara gorge to Megiddo."

"Then it was fortunate we decided not to keep the Philistines from entering the Jezreel," Shaul said calmly. "We never would have made the northern gorges in time, and would have exhausted the men for nothing."

The hassar's face tightened a little, but he remained silent. Once they had learned the Philistines were likely on their way to the Jezreel valley, he had argued strenuously for the army to go immediately to Dothan, where they were within striking distance of the passes through the hills southeast of Mount Carmel that led into the Jezreel plain. It was their best chance of stopping the Philistines, negating the chariots they had, and potentially inflicting a serious defeat.

Abner had argued against it, because the move to Jezreel might be a feint, and the Philistines would strike into the hills farther south. The hassar had responded that an Israelite army descending on Philistia from the north would draw their army back. The general's attempts to discount that hadn't been very convincing, and Jonathan had nearly persuaded Shaul of the wisdom of the plan, with barely enough time to implement it. Then the report of the column of men leaving Aphek for the south arrived, and Shaul hesitated over that news too long.

"Any news about the Philistines that went south?" Abner asked.

"Yes, General. The three units that had been watching them are returning, and they report that there is no attempt to enter the hills south of here. They left a few men behind to continue to observe."

"Good," Abner grunted. "We can go directly to the springs at En-harod just east of the town of Jezreel. I'd like to be sitting on that water before the Philistines decide they want it."

"And we'll have the ridge coming west off Mount Gilboa at our backs," Shaul said with satisfaction as he and the general drifted to where Cheran, the king's personal attendant, had some food spread out for them to eat.

The hassar turned to the courier. "Any other messages?"

"Yes, Hassar," the man said, meeting his eyes. "The commanders of the units which are returning wanted you specifically to know that there will be no Habiru fighting with the Philistines. They are tracking those Habiru south even as we speak."

Something deep inside the hassar slowly relaxed, and he closed his eyes a moment. "Thank Yahweh for that," he said. "Did the commanders say what men they kept, and when they would be turning back north?"

"The commanders sent everyone in the units north, Hassar. They said they would be tracking the Habiru wherever they went."

"Very well," the hassar said crisply. "Get something to eat and drink, and take care of that mule. It's a fine animal."

"It is, adoni," the man replied, bowing.

Instead of joining his abbi and Abner, Jonathan checked in with his brothers.

"There's news you might be interested in," he said, repeating what the courier had reported. "Who were the commanders of the units Abner sent south?" he asked when he finished.

"Supporters of ours from Manasseh, all of them good, competent men. Abner shifted them to units of farmers from Asher. Any ideas on where Abbi plans on fighting?" Malchi replied roughly.

Jonathan turned to him. The third sar rarely spoke any other way since the night he had ridden off. He had returned riding his own animal late the following day, and taken up his duties the next morning without a word to anyone. But Ishvi had drawn Jonathan's attention to their brother's frequently red eyes and the fact that Malchi had plunged into the final days of training for the professionals with an unusual intensity. The coiled tightness inside him made even his brothers wary of him.

"I don't think he's decided yet," Jonathan replied. "Camped there at En-harod, he's got several options."

"I hope he makes up his mind soon," Malchi snarled.

Jonathan hoped so, too. He didn't want to be anywhere around when his brother let loose whatever was chained up inside him.

¥ ¥ ¥ ¥ ¥ ¥

You must think, Abigail, the Gebirah said to herself as she hurried along in the line of women and children driven by the warriors on either side. They had been traveling for hours now, and the children were nearly dropping with fatigue and thirst. Even though the sun was losing some of its heat, they desperately needed water.

She cast a glance at the man riding the mule just to one side. Called Shepho, he was the alluph left in charge of them. She repeated the word a couple of times, guessing it was the Amalekite equivalent for adon. They had stopped at a small oasis a couple hours back, but Shepho had deliberately let the animals drink first. By the time they were done, the water was so muddy and foul that no one else could drink, and, of course, the man had not been willing to wait for it to clear.

She caught sight of the young slave bent under a bundle of spoils on the other side of the mule. In spite of his dusky skin, he was pale, and staggered more than he walked. He'd badly needed that water and hadn't gotten any either.

Up ahead, another man was approaching. Abigail stared a moment. From the looks of his clothes and mule, he was of higher status than Alluph Shepho. There might be possibilities here, Abigail thought.

Behind her, Gareb's wife stilled the cries of her toddler. Elika's wife had three children, one a babe in arms, the other two hanging onto her skirts. Shepho kept an eye on them. He had threatened to kill the first child who fell, and Abigail knew he would.

His own slave fell first, though. The alluph reined his mule up and slid off, kicking the bundle of spoils away and roughly hauling the young man off the ground before cuffing him across the face. There was no response. With a scowl of disgust, Shepho dragged the slave off the trail and dropped him. He re-mounted the mule, ordered Casluh to pick up the bundle, and rode on.

No one paid any attention to the abandoned slave. Abigail risked a glance backward just as the approaching rider arrived, and saw the slave pushing himself up from the ground. She hoped he'd be able to follow now that he had no burden to carry.

Elika's middle child, a girl, stumbled against her immi's legs and the woman slowed.

We have to carry the children, the Gebirah said to herself, looking around quickly to see how many adults could take a child. There weren't as many as she had hoped, for the Amalekites had packed the spoils too hurriedly to get everything loaded on the animals.

As the newcomer rode toward her down the line, looking everyone over, a slight frown appeared on his face, and the greeting he gave Shepho expressed more dislike than anything else. Elika's girl stumbled again and fell.

Grinning, the alluph pulled his sword and turned the mule, making Elika's wife cry out and bend down to pull her girl away, halting the line.

"Don't kill her!" Abigail said sharply, stepping forward.

Shepho stared at her in surprise, then anger. "You dare to speak?" he growled.

Abigail had to listen closely to understand his thick accent. "Would you kill for nothing?" she asked, then realized the futility of that question.

"I kill the weak," the man retorted, urging his mule forward again.

Abigail put herself between Elika's wife and the mule as the woman scrambled away, her children crying now. "What did you expect? The child has had no rest or water for hours!"

His face furious, Shepho raised his sword to strike her, and Abigail braced herself, but a sharp word from the newcomer restrained him.

"Didn't you stop at the oasis?" he said, turning to her, his words easier to understand than Shepho's.

Abigail looked at him. He was well-made and strong, sitting on the mule easily, with a good-looking face that seemed vaguely familiar.

"They refused to drink there," Shepho said sullenly.

The other man frowned, and suddenly Abigail realized the shape of his face, the set of his eyes and the point to his chin were the same as her late husband, Nabal's. Only there was none of his weakness in this man. Even so, his look was the same as the nagid's had been when he was calculating how much he would make from a deal.

Without thinking, Abigail spoke as she would have to Nabal, using the same cool voice. "Yes, we stopped. But Alluph Shepho was careless enough to let the less valuable half of the spoils drink first, thus depriving the more valuable part of much needed refreshment and strength. Now he threatens to rob you of even more profit by outright killing one of the more valuable pieces of booty. Who knows how much he might have lightened your purse if you hadn't come just now?" She bent down, picked up Elika's girl, and walked down the trail, expecting to feel a sword in her back at any moment.

Instead she heard the man forbid Alluph Shepho to strike her or anyone else. A little sliver of hope struck Abigail's heart. She was dealing with Nabal again, and she knew just how to do it. Only this time, "Nabal" was much more intelligent.

The sun had touched the western horizon when they came to a shallow 300-foot-wide watercourse. All the women carried children, and Abigail was almost too tired to move another step. Slowly, the line plodded across, barely able to make the gentle climb onto the narrow finger of land that rose between it and another watercourse.

"Besor," she heard one of the guards mutter. Exhausted, Abigail looked up. Besor marked the boundary between her land and that of the nomads. Tears stung her eyes. "Yahweh, don't leave us now," she whispered. Any hope of rescue lay with their husbands, who wouldn't be home again until the war season ended. By then, weeds would be growing in the market square, and there would be no trace left of where or how they had gone.

Chapter 27

Full darkness had settled. Abigail had eaten the unleavened bread and water given to them, and watched as another group of raiders arrived with a few captives and animals loaded with spoils. The guards crowded an obviously well-to-do man and his wife, both nearly dropping from fatigue, next to her.

She moved aside to give them more room, then handed them the still half full cruse. The couple thanked her gratefully.

"What is your clan and where are you from?" she asked softly.

"We are of Gaza," the man said. "My wife and I were traveling to Gerar to visit her sister, and we were taken on the road. We had gifts for everyone, and they took those."

Before they had time to speak further, another guard came and pointed at Abigail and the woman from Gaza. "Both of you, come," he said, then turning and walking away.

Abigail got up, helping the other woman, and saying nothing when her husband followed. They were taken down the long finger of land a little way to where the larger tents of the alluphs were set up.

The Gebirah clenched her fists. In the back of her mind she'd known this would happen, and wishing it away wouldn't help any.

"Here they are, Alluph Zaavan," the guard said, leaving without a backward glance.

From the looks of the tent, Zaavan was the highest-ranking alluph here, and when he turned around, she saw the face of the man who had restrained Shepho. Then Shepho himself appeared, looking at her enviously before grabbing the arm of the other woman.

"Please, adoni," her husband said, stepping forward. "Do not take her! I can pay much gold."

Shepho turned to the man. "I have your gold already," he said coldly, "and now I will have your wife!" He grabbed the shoulder of her robe and jerked toward him. She resisted, and the dress tore.

"Adoni, please!" the man said, as Shepho pulled a dagger from his girdle.

"And now you have even less gold," Abigail put in tartly.

Zaavan turned his head toward her, his hand gesturing Shepho to stop. "Oh?"

"The dress alone would have been worth three gold pieces, had it not been so carelessly torn. As for the woman, she's highborn Philistine, unmarked, good skin and hair, worth twice as much as the dress, but only if she's untouched. The man is in good health, still strong, hasn't lost any front teeth yet, and would be worth nearly as much as the woman. Unless, of course, he's dead. And if you plan on killing him, you should at least set a ransom for the woman and let him pay that before you take his life."

"We have his gold!" Shepho said furiously, glaring at her.

"Come now," she said reasonably. "Look at the two of them! Do you really think they had all their valuables packed on that donkey? Those were but gifts. Imagine what more he must have."

The couple stared at her in bewildered betrayal, and Abigail resolutely kept her eyes away from them. Alluph Zaavan's eyes glittered as he took a good look at the couple, then stared again at Shepho.

He smiled a little. "It seems to me, Shepho, that once again you are thinking only of what is immediately at hand, and not what might be available over the horizon. This is also the second time today you have attempted to 'lighten my purse,' I believe the phrase is. And after I generously allowed you to use some of my spoils for your reward."

Zaavan stepped toward Abigail, and then without a flicker of emotion crossing his face, his hand flashed to his girdle, then drove his dagger into Shepho's heart. "Thief," he said as the man fell.

"Now, my beautiful one," he went on as Abigail struggled to keep from screaming and to avoid looking at the man dying on the ground, "you have interested me considerably. Tell me exactly how I can reap the most profit from my spoils."

"As you wish, alluph," she managed to say.

Zaavan called one of the guards and gestured to Shepho and the stunned couple staring at him. "Clean up," he said. The guard shoved the travelers toward the cluster of captives again while another arrived to pick up the body, and the alluph ushered Abigail into his tent.

Not long after, Abigail left the Amalekite's tent, still dazed by the casualness of Shepho's death. She found Ahinoam waiting for her when she reached the circle of captives.

"Are you all right?"

Abigail nodded, and in whispers told what had happened.

"What's Zaavan like?" the other woman asked, her voice thoughtful.

"Cross Nabal's greed and Ahlai's shrewdness with a great deal of intelligence."

"Can we trust him?"

"Not for a moment. But we might be able to gain a little from him. Call Jemima and Keturah. We must plan."

Once the others had arrived, the four women talked softly in whispers. "We have to be up early tomorrow," Abigail said. "The thing Zaavan wants most now is speed. He has to get well away before anyone realizes what has happened. We have leave to pack the spoils. That way, we can get them all onto the animals, leaving the people free to carry the children so that we can travel faster. If we can pack well enough, we may even have a couple of spare donkeys for the older men from Ziklag, or some of the children."

"We're cooperating, then?" Jemima asked, cuddling her son as he suckled.

"We must," Keturah responded. "We are buying time this way, and keeping ourselves from being abused in the process. As long as we are useful, they will let us live, and we're worth more on the slave market if we aren't injured."

"Correct," Abigail said. "Now, they took a lot of food supplies along with everything else. I convinced Zaavan it was a waste to have all that food, and all these women, and not have the women cook it for him and his men."

"We'll be cooking for them?" Jemima gasped.

"Good, Abigail," Keturah said. "Jemima, you be sure that everyone does a very good job of cooking, even if they don't want to. This is the best thing yet!"

Abigail looked up in the dim light. She could hardly see the Gibeonite woman's face, but the expression on it sent a chill through her. Before they bedded down, she followed Keturah to the edge of camp to relieve themselves.

"Why is cooking so good?" Abigail asked quietly as they returned to the circle.

"I've noticed some useful herbs along the way," Keturah said. "I've also been talking to some of the other captives. The Amalekites hit Gerar, and also one of the eastern settlements between there and Ziklag. The alluph in charge of that raiding party was to meet up with the ones attacking us. They were nearly to Ziklag when the captives rebelled and fought. He killed them all, and burned the bodies in vengeance. It apparently happened just after we'd left the town."

Abigail stopped. "Why is that important?" she asked, too tired to think.

"That close to Ziklag, what will our men think when they return?"

"Oh, Yahweh," Abigail whispered. "They'll think it was us!"

Keturah nodded grimly.

Day Three

Seren Akish, followed by Ittai, entered the courtyard in Megiddo where the Philistine serens were conferring.

"Thank Dagon we made it through those passes yesterday without incident," Muwana said as Hanabaal from Gaza clanked in, wearing full battle dress.

"I'll bet he hasn't taken it off since we left," Akish heard someone comment. "You should have seen him yesterday. His neck has to be sore from craning it all around, afraid some Israelite would take a shot at him!"

"Well, I don't blame him," another replied. "I can't say I was comfortable in those gorges myself. Why didn't the Israelites try to stop us there? Seemed like the perfect place to me."

Akish and Muwana exchanged a glance. Dahveed's departure had served more than one purpose. It had been the saving of Akish, and as Muwana had hoped, it apparently distracted the Israelites long enough for the Philistines to get to the passes and traverse them unmolested.

Baalyaton stood up. "Now that we are all here, let us decide where we will camp. Our scouts tell us that the Israelites have taken the En-harod springs east of Jezreel.

"That's the best water in the valley!" Gadmilk complained.

"But it's not the only source," Baalyaton retorted. "There's plenty for all of us."

"And not far away, either," Muwana added. "We should go to Shunem. It's just four miles north, with the hill of Moreh to guard our backs, and we can force Shaul to fight on the plain."

"If he's at En-harod, he's got the flanks of Gilboa at his back," Akish spoke up. "Should he retreat up there, we have to go after him on foot. The chariots will be useless."

"And he undoubtedly will retreat up there!" Gadmilk said. "Whatever else he is, he's never been a fool, and those cursed hills swallow up any number of men who never come out again!"

"Then we will just have to roust him out of them," Baalyaton insisted. "And now that we have all the troops and militia from all five cities, we should be able to do just that. If he stays by En-harod, we can drive him directly back into the ridge of hills and keep him busy enough that he can't move very far, while we use the chariots to take men around the end of the ridge and send archers up in back of him."

"Unless he's got some of those Habiru or something waiting for us to try just that," Hanabaal protested. "Can't we draw him out into the plain?"

"We've already established that he's not a fool," Baalyaton said coldly. "I didn't say this would be easy. But it must be done."

Akish listened while the other serens argued the plan and finally concluded that it was the best one to accomplish their purpose. The seren smiled. The plan was his, refined in a talk last night with Muwana, who had then presented it to Baalyaton in such a way that the Ekron ruler thought he'd come up with it himself.

"The plan depends on pressing the Israelites very hard into the hills, and on the speed of the chariot transport of the archers," Muwana said. "Who will be responsible for the chariots?"

"That's just the job for Seren Akish," Baalyaton said casually. "He contributed several chariots, and I believe he has extra commanders in his militia units who can be useful in that area."

Akish went rigid. His plans for those extra commanders didn't include directing chariots. Then he stifled his reaction. Had Baalyaton gotten wind of his plans somehow? If so, he'd bet it was just a suspicion. He'd have to be very careful how he handled this! "That's true, Seren," he said, bowing slightly to the ruler of Ekron. "But the chariots are a critical part of the plan. Perhaps someone with more experience should lead them. I believe Hanabaal has directed chariots much more than I."

"I have," the Gaza ruler spoke up. "I would be very willing to lead them."

"And keep yourself well away from the fighting while you do," the same man muttered behind Akish.

"I'm sure you would be," Baalyaton said, "but your professionals and militia are badly needed, and they will fight all the better for your presence with them. We couldn't possibly have you anywhere else. No, Akish is the one to lead the chariots. He will do nicely in the rear."

Feeling his face flush, Akish had started to speak when he felt a light brush on his arm. Without seeming to have moved, Ittai had shifted to touch him, then nearly imperceptibly shook his head. The ruler of Gath gritted his teeth, clamping down on his anger.

"I do not agree," he said, "but I will serve wherever the serens think it is best."

"Something I'm sure we all will do," Muwana put in quickly. "So then, shall we move to Shunem and meet again this evening after we have surveyed the land a little?"

"An excellent plan," Baalyaton agreed, satisfaction spreading across his face. "Serens, you are dismissed."

Akish mingled with the others as they left, more to prove that he was not angry with the part assigned to him than anything else, even though he could hardly contain his frustration. Well, he had some time at least to see if he could salvage anything of his own plans for this battle before it happened.

"Why did you not want me to protest the slur to my honor?" Akish stormed quietly as he walked with his nephew back to the house where they were staying.

"You found out what you needed to know," Ittai said, unperturbed. "Baalyaton has an agent somewhere that you haven't identified yet. And that agent can't be very close to you either, since he didn't know for certain of your plans. Also, Dodi, you should keep in mind the last thing Dahveed Israel said to you before he left. Don't be too forward in this battle."

Akish cast a sidewise glance at his nephew. "Oh?"

"Yahweh has His hand in this. The battle will be won by the side He wills to win, but the manner of that victory may not be what either side is expecting. You felt what entered into Dahveed. Do not be found fighting the gods, Dodi. Especially Dahveed's God—and mine."

¥ ¥ ¥ ¥ ¥ ¥

We were almost home, and so eager to get there that we had traveled through the heat of the day after a quick meal at noon. It still surprised me how much the heat drained us. In the highlands, I could have made the 53-mile trip from Aphek to Ziklag in a day and a half. But down here in the heat, 20 miles a day was nearly our limit.

Shagay's Jonathan approached. "I found Hanan's trail again, adoni. He was still running, taking the straightest paths. I found one place he stopped to drink, but he didn't stay."

"At that rate, he must have gotten to Ziklag yesterday about dusk," I estimated. "I'm surprised he hasn't reported in. We're nearly there, now."

I hurried forward on the track we followed from the last crossroad, which took us straight south to Ziklag. Then Ahiam appeared. "Dahveed!" he shouted, running to me. "The altar at the high place has been torn down!"

I ran forward, the look I'd seen on Abigail's face just before I'd left flashing in my mind. We burst through the trees and stopped. The altar had been torn apart, the stones scattered. Just then, the breeze shifted a little, bringing the smell of charred wood and burned goat's hair.

"The town!" Elhanan gasped, and we raced on, finding the first burned tents before we could even see Ziklag.

"Yahweh, no!" I cried, but every dwelling we passed was destroyed, and by the time we slid to the bottom of the watercourse, we were staring ahead with dread at what we would find. Silently, we approached, finding a few scattered possessions here and there on the road up to the burned gates. I could hardly breathe as I stepped over the remains of one gate, and crossed the square to the blackened walls that marked the house I'd lived in.

Behind me, the men who dwelled in town spread out, the others who had lived outside it running toward the houses or tents they had left behind. But everything was gone.

Shagay picked up an arrow. "Amalekites!" he said bitterly, throwing it down.

"Where are my wife and my children?" Zalmon asked dazedly as he stumbled over the threshold of his home. "Dahveed, what happened?"

As Ahiam stared around, hand clenched around his sword hilt, I knew he was thinking of Jemima and their 9-month-old son.

I looked at the burned pile of debris in the center of the square.

Zalmon's face went white, and he ran toward it, several others following.

"Yahweh, save us!" I said, turning toward it myself, but all we found there were bits of clothing, charred pottery, and burned wood from the gates. The ashes were still warm.

"Yesterday," Shagay said.

Tears streaming down it, Zalmon's face appeared in front of me. "They're gone! All of them! Who took them? What happened?"

"Shagay says Amalekites," I heard myself say, still too shocked to take everything in.

Just then the wind from the sea brushed by our faces, bringing with it the faint, unmistakable stench of charred human flesh. All of us turned toward the west.

Shagay and Jonathan set off at a run, the rest of us too shaken to follow. It seemed like hours passed before Shagay appeared again, coming in what should have been our gates. My heart in my mouth, I went to meet him. "Abigail? Ahinoam?" I asked.

The look on his face gave me my reply.

"No," I said. "Shagay, you're mistaken! You didn't see right." When I started past him, my retainer pulled me back.

"Don't go, Dahveed."

"I have to see!" I said, edging around him.

He grabbed me, shaking me roughly. "Dahveed, don't go!" he commanded. "Not now. Wait until tomorrow. None of you go!"

Jonathan appeared beside him. The men stared from me to them.

"But our families?" someone said.

"Don't go now," Shagay said again, his face pale and tight.

Ahiam landed on his knees.

Jonathan had his sword out, barring the way, and deep inside I knew what they had found. The same thing we had found in too many settlements of the Negev, the same thing we had left behind us time and time again during the past months.

Eliphelet shoved by me to the edge of the square, and I heard him vomiting.

I choked on the bile rising in my own stomach. "El Shaddai, nooooo!" I cried, feeling my own knees give way. My hands closed over the dust on the ground as sobs shook my body, and all around me the wails and cries of my men weeping for their dead loved ones rose as the smoke of the town had only hours before.

It was nearly dark when I pushed myself from the ground, my eyes at last dry of tears, and my entire body sore from weeping. Pekah held a cruse to me, and I drank, staring around at the other men who sat in the dusk, as drained as I was. The entire band had gathered here, drawn together by the ruins around us and the devastation that had touched us all.

"We should have been here!" Zalmon said, hoarsely. "We could have defended the town!"

"Yes, we should have been here," Ben-Shimei said, his voice harsh. "And some of us would have, if Dahveed had listened to reason!"

"That's right," Ahimelek the Hittite added. "We questioned making everyone go to Gath, but he said everyone must!"

"It's irresponsible and unreasonable," Ben-Shimei continued. "What kind of a dahveed is he, to leave our homes and families unprotected while we go running up to Aphek for a Philistine! We're Israelites, not Philistines, and we never should have gone up there anyway!"

"He's right!" someone else shouted. "It was a useless trip! After all that traveling, we get kicked out and sent back here! Only it's too late when we get back! And now my family is dead, and we all know how Amalekites kill!"

"Pekah, leave the square," I said to the young man. The atmosphere was turning ugly, and I didn't want him to get caught in what might happen. Ignoring the men who watched as I walked to the ruins of my house, I stood in the doorway, staring into the blackened room. A shudder went through me as the memory of Abigail's twinkling eyes crossed my mind.

My stomach turned over, and I thought I would be sick. Yes, we all knew too well how the Amalekites killed, and that thought of searching through the remains for the bodies of my wives, and seeing what had happened to them, made me land on my knees again. I didn't think I could bear what I'd have to do tomorrow.

"He should have known better," Ben-Shimei said behind me. "It's because of him that our families are dead! He should pay."

I looked over to the niche in the wall where I'd left Grandmother Ruth's harp. The wooden door over it was ripped away, lying on the floor partially burned. I wouldn't know what to do if the harp had been destroyed, too.

"Stone him! That's what needs to happen."

"Yes, take him out and stone him. What are we doing over here in Philistia, anyway? We should have stayed in the highlands."

"Now we've lost everything, and obviously Yahweh couldn't protect us, or our possessions!" someone else added. "We have to go back to Judah, and we don't need Dahveed for that! He should be stoned."

Keeping my back turned, I tried not to recognize any of the voices reaching my ears. I didn't want to know who was suggesting my death, as more men joined in with their opinions, and the talk of stoning spread with more and more approval.

Feeling sick, I finally turned back and stepped outside the house. Uriah stood on one side of the door, arms folded, watching the knot of men not far away.

"Take him down in the valley. It's what he deserves. He left our families defenseless!"

"Well, how was he to know?" another voice rose above the rest. "You talk as if he planned it! If Akish ordered all of us to go north, we all have to go, that's all! And we all know that there were units left in Gerar. Why didn't they do anything?"

As I turned in the direction of the speaker, I could hardly believe my ears.

"I don't see what you should have to say about it, Hiddai!" Ben-Shimei shouted. "You haven't lost any wives or children."

"Neither have you!" Hiddai retorted. "And are you going to be the one to tell Dahveed he's going to be stoned?"

The uproar lessened a little.

"Go now, Dahveed," Uriah said without moving.

"Maybe I should—"

"No, you shouldn't," he interrupted. "Stay in the shadows. Go!"

"Well, what's he going to do, resist us all?" Ben-Shimei sputtered. "He shouldn't be dahveed any longer! Not when he does crazy things such as leaving our homes defenseless against attack!"

"And who's going to take his place? You?" Hiddai sneered.

Heading down the narrow central street of the town, I climbed over the piles of debris, exiting the cluster of houses where the barrier between two of them had been torn down. The darkness wrapped itself around me like a familiar cloak, and I soon found myself at the high place, staring down at the ruined altar.

There was still some water in my cruse, and I drank, then sat down, devoid of any feeling but emptiness, able only to sit and stare at the ground in front of me. The waning moon had come up, shedding pale light on the altar, before I started moving the stones. One by one, I picked them up, piling them together again, not trying to make an altar, just putting them into one place. Some of them were heavy, but I wrestled with them anyway until the mound was complete. Then I knelt in the grass.

"Why has this happened, Yah? We have lost everything. My men are ready to take my life, and I cannot blame them."

Guilt and discouragement pressed on me. My men were right. We had had no business leaving the town. Nor any reason for being in Philistia, the land of our enemies. And because I had gone against Yah's will, our women and children were dead, slaughtered and burned as sacrifices to a cruel god. I had made a mess of things again, as Eliab, my oldest brother, had always predicted I would. Only it wasn't one that anyone could ever clean up.

I didn't deserve to live. I had been deceived into spurning Yahweh's will, substituting loyalty to Akish for loyalty to my own people and Yahweh. I had gone north because Akish commanded it. Once there, I had refused to stay where I might have done some good for Yah and Israel, because the seren had pleaded the lives of his people. Destined to become king of Israel, not Philistia, I should have been more concerned about my people than about those in Gath. And according to the report Adnah and Jozabad gave me, seeing me leave Aphek had drawn away from Shaul badly needed units, weakening him even more for the coming battle. Everything I had done had aided Israel's enemies and harmed the ones I was anointed to protect.

The blade of Boaz's knife gleamed silver in the faint light of the moon. "Do you want my blood, Yah?" I asked, turning the knife to see the light flash. "I have failed every way I could fail, and my people have paid the price. Israel will pay the price, and so will Jonathan Hassar, who rules them. What do You want of me, Adonai Yahweh?"

"*Your trust. You said you would not doubt Me again. Remember?*"

"But that was before, when I thought I had taken the path You laid out for me. I am outside Your will now."

"*Who told you that?*"

"Look at what has happened! All we have and love is gone! How could You do this? I asked for Your leading, I inquired of You, I told You every move I planned to make and asked You to stop me and direct me and keep me in the path You placed before my feet. I trusted You to lead me in the right way, and You didn't!" I nearly yelled. "My wives are dead! The families of my men were slaughtered. We have nothing left! Why didn't You answer me, and lead me where I should have been?"

"*You didn't ask.*"

"What?!" my voice cracked in stunned amaze. "I just told you I've asked time and again, but you didn't answer!"

"*Did you consult Me when you sat in the pasture at Hachilah and decided to leave Judah?*"

Slowly, I bowed my head as shame swept through me. I hadn't asked. I had assumed I knew what was best, and I had decided my course on my own. A course, I realized now, I had set myself on with my own words of parting to Shaul. I had spoken then of leaving Israel and serving other gods, and I had spoken it as Mashiah. All the rest had only been fulfillment of the words I had spoken in that moment.

"Yahweh, forgive me!" I groaned, digging my fingers into the grass. "I have sinned and led my people into destruction because of it! Why did you not correct me sooner, and bring me back to your will?"

"*How do you know I haven't?*"

"It cannot possibly be Your will for me to be here, stripped of everything I love, about to be executed by my own men and aiding in the destruction of Your people Israel!"

"*How do you know it's not?*"

The question flabbergasted me. "You do not bring pain and death to your people! This is both! It is of evil!"

"*Yes, it hurts. But have I really stripped you of all you love? There is no one at all?*"

I opened my mouth to reply, then shut it again. "My family in Moab still lives," I admitted.

"And how do you know the plans I have for My people Israel? Must they surely be destroyed because you think they will be?"

"But, Yah, I cannot see how they can win against the army going against them!"

"And I must have you there to save them? I am Yahweh, God of all flesh. Is anything too hard for me?"

Ashamed again, I looked down. "No, Adonai. You can save by many or by few. Truly I spoke whereof I knew not."

"And how do you know that you are about to be executed by your men?"

"I know there are some who wish it, but that is all."

"Then, if nothing you said was true, how do you know it is of evil and not My will?"

"I do not know," I said, bowing my head.

The presence of Yah drew very close. *"So then, my Mashiah, even though you strayed, who told you that I have not brought you back into My will?"*

I had thought that I was emptied of tears. But I stretched out on the ground, clinging to it as hard as I clung to Yahweh, while all the hurt and worry, bewilderment and anger and pain, gushed from me as I opened my heart to my God and let Him see everything that was in it.

The moon had marched a long way across the sky before I lifted myself from the ground. I was exhausted, but my mind was clear. I had, as usual, forgotten a few things. In every difficulty in my life, Yah had provided for me, usually in ways that I didn't expect. I had not expected His fire to protect me from the Rapha when I fled Gath the first time. I had not expected Ittai to be there when I nearly died of starvation in the cave by Elah. I had not expected that Hanan would bring word of a Philistine invasion when Shaul had surrounded us at Maon. I had not expected Shaul to be given into my hand at En-gedi, or Abigail to bring food at Horesh or Akish to send me away from Aphek. Surely Yah had provided answers enough times that I could trust Him for the answers now, that despite the hard path I had chosen, Yah in His faithfulness had still guided me, working His will in all that happened.

As yet I didn't understand. Nor could I see the path. But I didn't need to, anymore than my sheep needed to understand my plans, or see the entire path when I took them to a pasture they had never been in before. They knew I was leading them, and that was enough. So now, all I needed to do was go where He led me, and give to Him my highest and best loyalty.

"Yah," I whispered, "I will follow You, for I cannot know the way I should go. I cannot save Israel. I cannot save Jonathan Hassar, I cannot save myself from what may be in store today. You are the shepherd, and the sheep are in Your hand, not mine. You must work things out in my life. You must help us bear the pain of this day, and all the days to come, for Your ways are Your own. I must trust that they are the good ways for me, no matter what the beginning of it may look like."

Chapter 28

Day Four

As dawn approached, I watched the black of the night change to grey, and then the pinks and yellows of the coming dawn painted the sky. The first rays of the sun spilled over the hills, hitting the top of the one house in the northeast corner of the town which still stood, for all the others had collapsed from the fires.

Rising, I bowed my head in worship, not knowing how Yahweh would get us through the burial of our loved ones, but trusting now that He would somehow, that He had some answer to the disaster visited on us, that He would work things out.

Slowly, I raised my head and stared at that house. Every other structure in the town was wrecked. Why not that one? Turning, I started to run.

I burst through the hole where the gates had been. "Josheb! Shagay!"

"Adoni?" Shagay replied, coming quickly from what had been my house.

"Shagay, get Josheb and Naharai! The house in the northeast corner of town is intact. The ark has to be there!"

Without waiting for him, I started down the central road, clambering over the piles of debris for the second time. The wall to the tiny courtyard was burned and had tumbled down, but the blackening of the fire stopped well before the walls of the house. I ran up the stairs to the balcony and pushed open the door, ducking out almost immediately. The room was empty.

That meant the ark had to be down below.

"Is it there, adoni?" Shagay called as he made his way to the courtyard, followed by his son, Naharai, all three of my nephews, and Josheb.

"No. It must be down below."

We entered, finding that raiders had at least made it into the house, for the window shutter was broken, the table overturned, and a huge grain pithos smashed on top of the table, the grain spilling everywhere.

"I'll get some sacks," Joab said, leaving the house, while the rest of us began to clear away the broken pottery.

"Abishai, go get some men, and start to clear out the street," I directed.

"Dodi, I don't know if anyone will help."

"Go find out. I'm not ordering anyone, I'm asking."

"Yes, adoni."

He vanished. Joab returned with sacks, and Josheb began to shovel the grain with an intentness that was nearly frightening. I knew he was hoping that if we found the ark, we'd find Keturah. Finally, we could remove the last of the huge pottery pieces and then slide the table out of the way, using our hands and arms to sweep more grain to the side, where Joab and Asahel continued to fill the sacks. Uncovering one edge of the rug, we rolled it up to expose the trap door.

Pulling it up, Josheb looked down the stairs and called, "Keturah?"

"Josheb?" Abiathar's voice answered.

"Yes, hakkohen! Is Keturah there?"

"No. She and Gebirah Abigail were the ones who shut us in here just before the Amalekites broke into the room."

The hassar's former bodyguard swayed a little, tears filling his eyes again. "We rejoice that you are safe, hakkohen," he said huskily. "Please come up. Is the ark there as well?"

"Yes. Help Gad first. He strained his shoulder trying to open the trapdoor once we thought everyone was gone."

Aside from Gad's shoulder, he and Abiathar were fine. The food and water Irad had provided for Yahweh had served them well, and I saw the tunnel they had started to dig under the wall of the house. I estimated they would have broken through to the outside very soon.

Beriah, Ishmaiah, and Naharai arrived, and with their help, the ark was wrestled back up the stairs and carried into the courtyard. "It's good to see the daylight again," Abiathar said. Then he turned to me. "Dahveed, is anyone still here?"

"No," I said, my voice shaking. "Everyone was taken outside of town and killed."

"Everyone?" the hakkohen choked, his face white.

"Yes." From the look on his face, I knew that memories of Nob were haunting him. "Please, Abiathar, what can you tell us of what happened?" Pulling himself together, he recounted all that he knew.

By the time I finished questioning him, the sounds out in the street indicated that Abishai had found some men willing to clear things up.

I went out, to find all of my personal retainers, the Gaddites, Shaul's kin, and several others busy removing debris. They greeted Abiathar with what gladness they could muster as he and I went by on our way to the market.

Uriah still stood by the door to my house, and I wondered if he had been there all night. Off to one side, a group of men sat around, the seven commanders from Manasseh standing near them. Hiddai and Ben-Shimei looked as if they had been in a fight, with Ben-Shimei getting the worse end of the dispute. Ignoring them, I went into what was left of my house and cleared enough away that I could pace a little.

The first thing to do was to go outside of town and bury our dead. I knew that would take the rest of the day. And by the time we were finished, the men just might decide to bury me along with their loved ones.

I paused to lean against the wall. If our loved ones had been treated as some of the other Amalekite victims we'd found, I would let them kill me and count it the hesed of Yahweh.

"Adoni Dahveed! Hanan approaches!" Pekah said from the doorway.

Hanan? I'd forgotten all about him. I strode toward the gap for the gates, followed by several of my men. One look at the staggering figure weaving toward us, and I ran down the slope. "Bring some water!" I shouted, and Pekah turned back. I got to Hanan before he fell, catching his shoulders.

He tried to speak, but couldn't.

"Wait for the water," I said, turning to look impatiently for Pekah. Once the lad arrived with the cruse, I poured some into my retainer's mouth, and he swallowed painfully.

"Amalekites," he gasped.

I gave him more to drink.

"They broke in the town at noon," he said, panting, his legs trembling.

I eased him to the ground, and he drank again.

"They took everyone. Tracked them to the Besor. They crossed it."

"Yahweh above, Hanan! You haven't been all the way to Besor and back? That's 30 miles! After your run to Ziklag?"

"Go after them, Dahveed," he gasped.

"We have to bury our families, first, Hanan," I said quietly. "Shagay and Jonathan found the burned bodies west of town."

Hanan shook his head. "People from closer to Gerar; another raid there." He grabbed my shirt. "You have to go after them. I tracked them! They are still alive!"

I didn't know what to say.

"Come and rest, Hanan," I finally managed. "We must plan." His eyes closed. "Get him into town," I commanded.

As we strode through the gates, I stood by the remains of the bonfire in the market. What should I believe? Hanan was my best tracker, but both Shagay and Jonathan had announced that the people of Ziklag were dead. As the news of what Hanan had said spread among the men, they talked excitedly among themselves and began to gather, all of them looking at me. What should I do? If I led them into a false hope, they would kill me when it collapsed, for already the possibility that all wasn't lost had revived in them, and in myself as well.

I couldn't afford to make a mistake about this. "Abiathar?" I called.

"Here, adoni," he responded, getting up from some shade by the side of the square.

"Bring the ark. I must inquire of Yahweh." And I knew I must do it as publicly as possible.

The street had been cleared enough that the four bearers could walk down it without too much trouble. Everyone grew silent when the ark appeared.

Visible to all the men, I knelt by the hakkohen, and he stilled beside me.

"What do you wish, Dahveed ben Jesse?" he asked after a moment.

"Adonai, Amalekites have destroyed our homes and taken our loved ones. We do not know if they are dead or alive. Shall I go after them? Will I overtake them?"

"*Pursue them, for you will overtake them. Moreover, you will rescue them all.*"

I could hear the reactions from the men gathered a little way away, for Abiathar's distant-sounding voice had been loud enough to carry to them.

"Thank You, Adonai. Your servant hears and will obey," I replied, my voice shaking with relief. Standing, I turned to the men waiting behind me. "I'm going south. Who is coming with me?"

My personal thief stepped forward instantly, such a look on his face as I had never seen before.

In the end, everyone but Hanan, Gad, Abiathar, and Beriah accompanied me. Hanan was simply too exhausted, and I ordered him to stay in Ziklag. We left before noon, pushing ourselves recklessly along the trail that Hanan had described.

¥ ¥ ¥ ¥ ¥ ¥

The noon rest was nearly over when Dara entered Hassar Jonathan's tent. "Cheran is here," his shield-bearer said.

"Has Abbi sent for me?" he asked, getting up to put on his meil again.

"He didn't say so. But he seems worried."

Leaving the meil on the bedroll, Jonathan stepped hurriedly out of the tent. "What has happened, Cheran?"

"Since returning from the scouting trip on the hill of Moreh, the king is very distressed, Hassar," Shaul's personal attendant explained. "He is finally resting, and I came to you, hoping you might be able to calm him."

"Is he agitated, or watching the sky? Has he complained of shadows?" Jonathan asked quickly.

"He is very agitated, adoni. I could hardly get him to lie down to rest. He has said nothing of shadows, though."

Dara brought out the meil, and Jonathan hastily donned it, Cheran following him as they hurried to Shaul's tent not far away.

"Please, if he is asleep, do not waken him," the attendant said as they walked up to the fire outside the tent. "He needs to rest."

The hassar stopped and turned to him, noticing the tears in the man's eyes. "What are you worried over, Cheran?"

"Go in and see, adoni," the man from Naphtali replied.

Quietly pulling the tent flap aside, Jonathan entered. His abbi lay on the bedroll, breathing heavily in the way he hadn't done in years. Without moving, the hassar glanced around. Then his gaze riveted to the piece of white cloth with brown stains on it in the corner. Silently, he moved across the tent, bending down to pick it up. The cloth was stiff in his hands, and he trembled as the Hakkohen Haggadol's breastplate emerged as he pulled the cloth out from under the small three-legged table.

Dropping the cloth, Jonathan sank to his knees. The only reason for this to be here was if his abbi was trying to use the Urim and Thummim stones to inquire of Yahweh. And if he was so agitated as to worry Cheran, he had not received an answer. How could he possibly expect to, Jonathan wondered, staring at the gems on the breastplate. Yahweh had pronounced sentence on Shaul, and the king had responded by slaughtering the priests and people at Nob, piling bloodguilt on top of rebellion and treason. The pain and darkness of that time pressed on Jonathan's mind again, and he bowed his head.

The Urim and Thummim gleamed from the table, and with shaking hands, the hassar picked them up to return them to the pocket made for them in the breastplate. To his surprise, the stones seemed warm to his touch, and he hesitated. What would happen if he tried to use them? Yahweh had said he was Melek Israel, after all. And Israel desperately needed Yahweh's guidance and protection now.

His hands tightened around the stones, and they nearly burned his palms. Then his eyes riveted on the dried blood of Ahimelech on the cloth of the breastplate. Yahweh had been very explicit that it was the duty of the Hakkohen Haggadol to use these stones, not his, or Shaul's. He managed to get the stones into the pockets, and then forced himself to pick up the breastplate, finding the cloth his abbi had wrapped it in underneath it. After folding it around the breastplate again, he stood. His abbi's breathing never altered as he left the tent.

Cheran waited for him.

"He's still sleeping," the hassar said. "Let him sleep as long as he can. How long has he been trying to inquire of Yahweh?"

"Since he returned from seeing the Philistine camp from Moreh this morning, Hassar. He would pick up the stones and ask his question, then drop them on the table, but they never changed appearance. There was no light or shadow over either of them. He would pick them up and try again, asking the question differently this time. And all the time, that breastplate was right there, the Hakkohen Haggadol's blood on it, and he never even looked at it. I couldn't stand it, Hassar," Cheran added. "I left the tent. When I came back, he was so agitated, his whole body shook, and he just kept trying and trying. Finally he threw the stones down. I got him to drink some wine and eat a little before he finally agreed to rest. I can't stand to see him abandoned this way, adoni. He is Yahweh's Mashiah! Why won't Yahweh answer him?"

"Because he turned away from Yahweh. You know this, Cheran. You've had the evidence of it in front of you all day. How can Yah answer Shaul when the blood of Yah's priests drips from his hands?"

"But it's tearing him apart, Hassar," Cheran protested. "He is afraid."

"I know," Jonathan said, the familiar pain stabbing at his heart.

Returning to his own tent, the hassar wrapped the breastplate in a larger bundle and summoned a courier, telling him to deliver it immediately to Mahesa the Egyptian at Gibeon. He stood with his hands clenched as the messenger jogged away. He did not dare keep the breastplate himself, afraid the temptation to try to use the Urim and Thummim might be too much for him to resist. And if Israel was to have any chance in the coming battle at all, he needed to remain as close to Yahweh's will as he could, in order to be used however His God saw best.

As he turned back to his tent, a quiet sense of peace settled over him. "Yahweh, grant us hesed!" he murmured.

When evening approached, Jonathan returned to his abbi's tent for the evening meal. The war council that afternoon had not gone well, for Shaul refused to finalize on any plans. The only thing decided was that the army should not try to face the chariots, something that was a foregone conclusion already.

No one else had arrived yet, and the hassar found the king standing beside the tent, staring toward Shunem.

"Shalom, Abbi."

Shaul turned. "You are here, my son." Then he resumed staring toward the north. "What do you think they are doing?" he asked, his face lined and old.

"Probably getting ready for the evening meal as we are, and worrying about what we will hit them with this season."

A brief smile crossed Shaul's face. "We have certainly surprised them often enough. But Yahweh has left me alone now. I tried to inquire of Him today, and He would not answer." An undertone of anger vibrated in his voice.

"Cheran hinted as much," Jonathan said carefully, not wanting the man to suffer the king's anger for talking. "But there is time yet for

Yahweh to make His will plain. He speaks in many ways, and the Philistines do not seem to be in a hurry to engage us."

Shaul was silent for a while. "That's true," he said at last. "He does speak in different ways. And night is coming on. Roeh Shamuel said He often sends dreams. He will tell me what to do, Jonathan. I am the anointed king of Israel, and after all I have done for Him, He must come to our aid now! He has seen how well you have ruled Israel, how the people love you. He knows you must reign after me."

"Abbi—" Jonathan started, then closed his mouth, clenching his teeth. As long as the king set his own will against that of Yah, nothing could be done. And every time it seemed his abbi had bowed to Yahweh's will, the king soon returned to his own ways again.

"Ishvi and Malchi have come," the hassar said. "Let us eat."

His face no longer worried, Shaul turned to him. "Yes, we must have strength for the coming battles. And Yahweh will surely tell me how to fight tonight, and tomorrow we can please Abner by telling him exactly what he is to do with the militia!"

¥ ¥ ¥ ¥ ¥ ¥

"How much do you have, Keturah?" Jemima asked in a low voice.

"Almost enough," the Gibeonite woman replied, stirring stew for the evening meal over the fire.

Jemima slipped something from under the cloth she had tied around herself to make it easier to carry her son. "Here, Ahinoam found this."

"Good," Keturah said, swiftly setting the bundle of herbs aside.

Abigail listened to the exchange while she pounded grain into flour. The heavy pestle made her arms ache, but at least her legs were getting a rest. Travel both yesterday and today had been difficult. It had been nearly noon yesterday before she realized that their numbers had dwindled by nearly half. And by evening, less than 20 of them remained. She knew that the ideas she gave Zaavan had made the split-up possible, and she had blamed herself for a lot of things last night, fearing that she had caused the separation of the people of Ziklag, making any hope of rescue just that much more unlikely.

But today, little groups had been drifting in every hour or so, until more than half of them were together again.

"Are you going to do it tonight?" Abigail asked Keturah in a low voice.

"I thought I might, but did you notice the last two groups to arrive are strangers?"

"No," Abigail said, careful to keep her eyes down so that the guards wouldn't think they were talking.

"I think tomorrow even more will come, probably everyone from our group will be here again, and others as well. Three groups today, and these last two just now aren't Amalekites. We must be headed for a gathering of all the tribes somewhere."

"Any idea where we are?"

"South of Beersheba. We turned west again. We may be headed more toward Egypt now."

She bent over the pot, adding salt. They said nothing more, for a guard roamed by, stopping to sniff the pot.

After the meal, Zaavan sent for her. She walked into his tent looking calm, but her palms were sweaty, and she hoped she looked as unappealing as she felt. As far as she knew, the women had been left alone so far. But the look in Zaavan's eyes as he lounged on some cushions said that he intended to have her tonight.

"You have been very useful," the alluph said. "I'll have to remember your recommendations the next time we raid. Things have gone much smoother, and we've been able to travel a good deal farther."

"You are pleased, then, alluph," she said impassively.

"Very. And I expect that you will please me even more. If I find you acceptable, I may keep you myself and treat you reasonably well."

"I am a married woman. And my husband will pay for my return."

Zaavan smiled. "Your husband is dead, as we both know. Shepho's assistant informed me of the pile of bodies burned by the road as a warning to anyone else who tries to resist us."

Abigail caught her breath. Was it possible Zaavan didn't know there had been no warriors in Ziklag when Shepho had taken the town, that those bodies were from a different town? She tried to still her trembling at the hope that suddenly pierced her heart. As soon as she could, she would have to talk this over with Ahinoam.

"Come now, it is time," Zaavan said brusquely. "There will be no rescue. Your future depends on me. Why do you hesitate?"

Her thoughts scrambled frantically. "I hesitate because I would not see more harm come to you, alluph," she heard herself say.

"Harm?" he said, eyebrows raised in amusement, and the first real smile she'd ever seen from him flashing across his face. "Not only are you beautiful, but you are amusing also!"

Abigail looked away, an unexpected pang running through her heart. For just an instant that smile had shown her the kind of man Nabal might have been, and she realized she could have loved him.

"You like my smile," the alluph said, flashing it at her again. "I am easily amused, beautiful one, but do not keep me waiting overlong, for I am easily angered as well."

"You have shown us hesed, alluph," Abigail said, without moving. "Allow me to show you hesed as well. Leave us in peace. If you don't, you will die. You already have Yahweh's curse on you, and what you wish to do tonight will only make it worse."

"A curse now, is it?" the man said, putting his hands behind his head and watching her. "Why?"

"You took from Ziklag a sacred woman," she blurted out. "One dedicated to the service of Yahweh for generations before her birth. Yahweh is not pleased that His maidservant has been taken from Him."

"And I suppose you are this woman?" he asked, his lips quirked into a smile.

"No, alluph," she said in surprise. "It isn't me. Why would you think it was?"

His smile faded as he studied her. "Yahweh cannot touch us here," he said shortly. "He is god in the highlands to the north."

"If I may remind you, alluph," Abigail said softly, "Yahweh came from the desert generations ago. He is as much at home here as anywhere else. I say again, Alluph Zaavan, do not anger Him more. Your life stands in the balance."

The tent sides billowed as a dry wind passed over the tent, making the lamps inside flicker. Zaavan glanced around uneasily. "How are you called?"

"Abigail, alluph."

"Where is your clan from?"

"Maon and Carmel in the highlands."

"The Calebite Gebirah!" Zaavan exclaimed, rolling to his feet, and staring at her. "That's who you are! Nabal from an Edomite clan married you! His clan is related to mine."

"I guessed as much, alluph. There are certain similarities in your looks. Another reason why I urge you to caution."

Zaavan chuckled. "And I have the famous Gebirah of the Calebites in my tent as a war prize! How fortunate! But Nabal died some years ago, if I recall."

Abigail looked him directly in the eyes. "Yes, he displeased Yahweh, alluph, and Yahweh struck him."

The lamps flickered again as the wind hit the sides of the tent. He glanced around once more. But when he smiled at her this time, his eyes were wary. "You married again."

"Yes."

"To whom?" Before she could answer, Zaavan's eyes grew dark. "Dahveed Israel! That's who you married! What are you doing in Philistia?" Abruptly he lapsed into silence, and Abigail could almost see the thoughts spinning through his mind.

"By Qas," he breathed. "It's been Dahveed Israel wiping out our people! We pieced together that it was someone in south Philistia close to Gerar, but Dahveed Israel? And to think that Shepho took him so easily, and left his body burning by the road without even knowing it!" He laughed. "By Qas, I hope he hears this in Sheol and knows how stupid he was!"

Abigail held herself tight, praying that her face wouldn't give anything away.

But Zaavan stared past her as if she wasn't there. "This changes everything," he said in a soft voice. "For now we have the women and families of our enemy among us!" He flashed that smile at her again, only this time it chilled her. "Go back to your place, Gebirah. If I recall, Dahveed Israel has two wives, and I will take you both. And the rest of the women and children of Ziklag will go to the families of those whom Dahveed has slaughtered, to be used however they see fit to avenge themselves for their dead. Tomorrow night will be the perfect time. Until then, Gebirah," he said, dismissing her with a wave of his hand.

Shaking, Abigail hurried from the tent. "Yahweh, protect us!" she whispered softly as she nearly ran back to the other captives.

Chapter 29

Day Five

Two-thirds of my men waited with me by the trail, now that the approaching dawn had washed out the light of the waning moon. Traveling through the heat of the day yesterday had brought us to the Besor while it was still afternoon, but once there, we had to pay for our haste. One third of my men had been unable to go on.

Those of us who could continue had stripped down to the barest essentials, leaving everything else with the men who had stayed on the narrow finger of land between the watercourses. After a few hours of rest, we had left in the night, taking advantage of the late waning moon.

I glanced up again. It was light enough to continue, and I rose, nodding to Shagay, who started off. The edge of the sun soon appeared red over the horizon. In the shadows it cast across the thin grass of the semi-desert, I could see the faint signs of others passing this way before us. Then I noticed another trace that seemed to come in from the southwest. Not long after, I thought I glimpsed another before the sun climbed too high. An hour later, Shagay stopped, casting around, studying the ground intently. He checked the sun and sighted a couple of landmarks.

Jonathan returned, and they conferred. My men took advantage of the halt to drink a little and eat some of the provisions we'd brought with us.

I walked to Shagay. "What is it?"

"They split up," he said sourly. "I wasn't expecting this, and I didn't notice until now. The trail ends here. Little groups have left the main one all along the line, but in the dark, we didn't notice. We have nothing to follow now."

My heart sank. "What do you suggest?"

"We'll have to go back, try to find where various groups left, and then track them to see if they head in any particular direction."

I closed my eyes in frustration. "How long will that take?"

Shagay sighed. "I'm sorry, Dahveed. It could take days, and even then, we can't be sure we'd be going in the right direction. This doesn't usually happen with such a large group. Too many women and children."

I thought back. "When was the last time you actually saw a child's track?" I asked. I hadn't paid much attention, and the moonlight had been faint at best, but I couldn't remember seeing small footprints after the campsite between the watercourses.

Shagay began to curse. "Not since the camp," he said finally. "We should have noticed that right away! If they've put the children on donkeys or some of those camels, they could have gone anywhere, and much faster than we've counted on! Forgive me, adoni," he said, his face strained. "I've failed you just when you need me most."

"Maybe not yet, Shagay. Take us back to where we were just as the sun was rising. I think I might have noticed one or two things that may help."

My men looked confused when we turned around, and it didn't take long for the news that we had lost the trail to pass down the line. Faces grew strained, but no one spoke a word of reproof, for which I was grateful.

Once back at that stretch of trail, I managed to tell Shagay and Jonathan about where I'd noticed the traces. Jonathan quickly found the first one, but it took Shagay much longer to locate the second. Both angled more toward the southwest. We headed that way, advancing slowly now, everyone hunting for any sign of anything passing along our way.

The sun climbed steadily higher. Why had we lost the trail now? I fought the frustration and worry, grimly reminding myself that I knew, now, why Akish wanted us at Aphek, and that our families hadn't been killed in spite of the evidence back at the town. I would know the reason for this also, in Yah's time.

While I struggled with my thoughts, Uzzia, Sibbecai, Shagay, and Jonathan drove themselves as hard as they could, searching for any clue that might help us. But the land stretched out around us, rolling out under the hot sun, dotted by the occasional tamarisk or acacia tree, the thin grass growing dryer under our feet as we walked. Just before noon, we split up into smaller groups, trying to cover more territory, even while we knew it was more and more hopeless. The land was simply too vast, and our band too small. But we had to try. Our wives and families were out there. And Yah had said we should pursue.

"You will not eat, Abbi?" Hassar Jonathan asked, entering the king's tent at noon.

His abbi's fear-filled face turned toward him from where he sat on a stool. "You saw that camp yesterday! How many have come against us! And the number of chariots! Yahweh must tell me what to do. He would not send me a dream, so I shall fast until He answers me!" Real desperation trembled in his voice.

The hassar studied Shaul a moment, then he went back and closed the tent flap. Kneeling by the stool, he took his abbi's hands. "Abbi, please listen! There is only one way that Yahweh can answer you. You must turn from your rebellion against Him! Accept the judgments He has passed on our house. Give up your determination that I will be king after you, for Yahweh has said that is not to be."

Shaul stared at him.

"Do not let this thing bring disaster upon Israel and your own house!" the hassar continued. "Think of Immi, and Merab's little ones! Remember Rizpah and your sons by her. They must live, Abbi! And you can assure that they will if you will only return to Israel's God and beg His hesed and His forgiveness.

"Remember how Yahweh has saved His people in the past? All the times while the judges lived when Israel repented, and how He delivered them? He will do it for us! But we must turn away from our own will and place ourselves in His hands."

"But He has rejected me. He rejected you, and you must rule after me!"

"Why, Abbi?" Jonathan asked, his rich voice trembling. "Why must *I* be the one to rule after you? You called the Dahveed son many times, and he loved you as one. Why cannot Dahveed be the son who rules after you? Yahweh sent the zammar to bring us the light! You can still accept His gift! Please, Abbi! Place yourself under Yahweh's will again, and the Philistines' chariots will not stand up to the power of our God anymore than Pharaoh's did in Moses' time!"

The hassar felt the king trembling against him. "He would save us?" Shaul whispered.

"His hesed is always there, waiting for us, if we will but give ourselves to Him. We cannot bribe Him, Abbi! We must obey His will!"

Shaul remained silent for some time. "I must think on this, my son. You are right, Yahweh has forgiven much in the past and saved His people. But I have strayed very far, and you are the first son of my blood."

"And I can be with you until you die, if you will but give up the idea that I must rule."

The king said nothing more, and Jonathan finally left.

¥ ¥ ¥ ¥ ¥ ¥

The sun beat down on us as we walked. As my eyes scanned the ground and the terrain around me, I had come to the point where I repeated, "I will trust Yah. I will trust Yah" endlessly. He had promised that we would catch up to the raiders who had taken our loved ones and would rescue them. Another hour went by, and my eyes were tired from the strain of studying every little bit of ground, and the words "Trust Yah, trust Yah," pounded through me with every heart beat. Suddenly I heard a shout.

Igal jogged toward me. "Adoni, we found someone!" he gasped as he arrived. "He's nearly dead. The others are bringing him."

"How did you find him?"

Igal pointed upward to the three or four vultures still circling.

"There's an acacia," I pointed. "He'll need shade."

The others followed as soon as they saw where I was headed. We all arrived at the tree about the same time, and Uzzia carefully lowered the young man he carried to the ground.

While Jaasiel started a signal fire to alert the rest of my men, I looked the youth over. Uzzia held his head and wet his lips with some water. He wore Amalekite clothing, nearly in rags, so he must be a slave. Probably Egyptian, I guessed. A bit unusual. Most Egyptians who were slaves remained in Egypt.

As Uzzia gave him more water, he opened his eyes, staring upward unseeingly, but he drank more. I took some bread from my girdle, and we wet it to make it easier to eat. Once he got that down, he drank more, then closed his eyes again.

By now, the others were arriving, eager to know what we'd found.

Asahel immediately took over the care of the youth, checking him carefully. "He's very weak, Dodi," he said quietly to me. "I'd say he's been without food or water for two days at least, maybe more. As pale as he is, he's probably been sick, too. Maybe that's why they abandoned him."

"Will he be able to talk to us?"

"If we keep giving him water, he should."

Every little bit, someone would get more water down the youth, and gradually he started stirring around more. I looked at the sun anxiously, for we were losing time, then reminded myself that Yah was guiding us, and that His word would come to pass. He had led us to this youth, another step closer to our families. So we waited. I ate a little and encouraged the men to do the same.

At last, when the young man opened his eyes, he seemed to see us. Asahel held the cruse for him, and he hesitantly drank. When he realized he could drink as much as he wanted, my nephew nearly emptied the cruse into him before he stopped.

We had some figs and raisins, and he ate them, staring at us the entire time. Then he drank the rest of the cruse and tried to sit up.

"You stay resting," I said, kneeling beside him. "Who is your master, and where are you from?"

"I'm an Egyptian, a slave to an Amalekite. He left me on the trail three days ago when I became ill," he whispered.

"Where was that?"

"North of here. I've traveled some." He ate some more raisins and took another drink.

"What were your masters doing north of here?"

"Raiding. They hit Judah and Caleb in the east, and more went to the Cherethites in Philistia, going north as far as Gerar and Ziklag. They burned Ziklag," he said, his voice stronger.

I fought back my excitement, even as my mind told me that we weren't looking for just one small band of raiders. It sounded like a major attack by the desert tribes.

"Do you know where they are going?" I asked.

"Yes."

"Will you take me there?"

He looked around at us, his eyes blank.

"They took our wives and children. You must help us."

His gaze settled on me again. "If you will swear by the Elohim not to kill me, or to give me back to my master, I'll take you to them."

I took his hand. "As the Elohim live, may they slay me if I kill you or give you back to your master."

"May the gods of Egypt send the soul-devourer to your judgment if you betray me," he added.

"Amen. So be it."

Glancing at the sun, he struggled to stand. It was nearly the ninth hour. "There is a place hidden by the rise of the desert where the water comes up in several places. Water does not always come abundantly there, but this year it has. They agreed to meet there after the raiding. Alluph Zaavan is leading them. He is the primary alluph of the Amalekites since his brother was killed last year by the destroyers."

I smiled grimly. "Which way do we go?"

"That way." He pointed southwest.

"Bring him along, Uzzia," I said, taking the big man's weapons so that he could carry the Egyptian on his back. "By the way, how are you called?"

"I am called Khay, adoni."

¥ ¥ ¥ ¥ ¥ ¥

It was the ninth hour before Shaul summoned the war council. The four sars and Abner gathered by the king's tent, and Jonathan prayed that, somehow, his abbi had found the wisdom to bend himself to Yah's will.

"What reports have come in?" Shaul asked as they seated themselves around the fire.

"The Philistines are preparing to march. They will probably advance against us tomorrow," Abner replied.

"Then we must be ready," the king stated. "If we form up the units with the ridge at our backs, we can retreat as they attack, and draw them up into the hills. Once we get them to chase us up the watercourses and over the top of the ridge, we can ambush them there and on the other side. The Benjamite archers can provide cover while the units move into position."

"That sounds workable," General Abner said, his voice bland. "What will the line of battle be?"

"I thought Sar Ishvi could take the east flank on my right, Sar Malchi the west flank, with the hassar and me commanding the center. We need all the strength we can get in that line, since we will have to hold it with the majority of the professionals while you and Sar

Eshbaal take the militia over the ridge with enough officers to prepare for the Philistines to pursue us."

"They might swing around the end of the ridge and approach us from the south," Ishvi said. "The slopes on that side are less steep."

"But there are a lot more places where we can attack them from cover," Abner replied. "Why don't we send a few of the professionals with units to watch for that and set ambushes if they do try it."

The king agreed.

"And, I think you should keep as many of the commanders with you as possible," Abner went on. "There are several professional soldiers with enough experience to command militia. I think the usual leaders in the militia are experienced enough now that we can do this."

Shaul hesitated. "But the professionals are the ones who know best how to set ambushes," he protested.

"How about one commander over every three militia units?"

Reluctantly the king again agreed.

Jonathan said nothing, knowing Abner would simply override him if he did offer any suggestions, but he would speak to Ishvi and Malchi afterward. He had a feeling they would need to be on the other side of that ridge as soon as they could get there.

The council lasted only a little longer while they worked out the details. Abner took Eshbaal with him when he left, and the other three sars gathered at Jonathan's tent.

"What do you feel about this?" Malchi asked, pacing back and forth, his hands clenched.

"I think it's the best we can do. You and Ishvi will need to get over the ridge quickly to help with the militia," the hassar replied.

"We should have attacked them in the gorges leading up to the Jezreel," Malchi said bitterly. "I thought you'd finally convinced Abbi to try that. Why didn't he?"

Jonathan sighed. "That column of units headed south worried him."

"Was it that, or Abner's constant fretting that we'd be attacked in the south?"

"Both, I think," Ishvi said. "Is Abbi all right?" he asked, turning to Jonathan. "He seemed preoccupied during the council."

"He was. I had the chance to talk to him alone, and I told him how I felt about everything, asking him to remember Yahweh."

"It's a little late for that," Malchi snarled. "He should have done that before he killed the priests!"

"Maybe, maybe not, brother," Ishvi said quietly. "Yahweh has more hesed for us than we give Him credit for, I think. It may be too late for our house, but it may not be too late for Israel."

¥ ¥ ¥ ¥ ¥ ¥

Cheran paced restlessly while the king remained in his tent, refusing food or water, his eyes growing more and more troubled. What could he do, the attendant asked himself again and again. Shaul was not just troubled, but afraid.

Since asked to become the king's attendant, he had served faithfully, doing his part while the hassar gradually assumed power in the kingdom. He had been glad to do it, knowing that it was the only way his family and clan could be covered from the king's sin. But as the months had become years, and Cheran had seen the king in those private moments when no one else was around, first his compassion and then his love had been stirred by the man sitting on Israel's throne.

It had been difficult at first, while the king did his utmost to capture and kill the Dahveed, the man to whom Cheran owed the life of a beloved younger brother. Dahveed had stepped in front of him on the hillside at Birzaith, protecting him when he was down and wounded, and never knowing he had done it, so deep had he been in Yahweh's gift.

But after the king had reconciled with Dahveed at En-gedi, and Cheran had more time to see the king with Merab's sons and Jonathan's Meribbaal, he had begun to understand more about the complex man he served. He knew now why Dahveed refused to kill the king, for he felt the same charisma that still clung to the man, the remnant of Yah's Spirit placed on him at his anointing.

And now, to see Shaul so distressed, so fearful, tore at his heart. The king didn't show it in public or in the war councils, but Cheran had noticed the haunted look in his eyes when the ruler was alone. He had seen the way his hands shook as he had tried to use the Urim and Thummim, and the way he huddled down in the bedroll, hunched over in the darkness of night.

Now he longed for some way that he could bring his master comfort.

"Cheran," Shaul called.

He went immediately. "Yes, adoni?"

"Is my armor ready for tomorrow?"

"Yes, adoni. Nahshon looked it over very carefully. He then returned it to the chest. All is ready."

"That is well, then," Shaul said, wandering restlessly about the tent.

But Cheran could still see the worry in his eyes. It had always been General Abner's job to tend the king's armor, but now Shaul didn't even trust his cousin enough to have him close to him in battle. The shield-bearer was from Benjamin, of course, but he was a silent man who did his job well enough but without any real enthusiasm. Cheran kept his eye on the man whenever he was around, not certain if he trusted him or not.

"You have served me well, Cheran," Shaul said, turning to him with a tired smile. "I should reward you."

"You don't need to do that. I am happy to serve my king."

"And just so the zammar spoke to me," Shaul said, his eyes gazing back into the past. "Would you like to be my armor-bearer?"

"I will be whatever you wish, adoni. Will I go into battle with you?"

"If you want." Another smile touched Shaul's lips. "I am troubled," he added.

"I've have seen it, adoni, and wished I could do something to ease you."

"Yahweh has not yet answered me, and it grows late, for time marches on and the Philistines will move against us in the morning. The hassar has told me how to approach Yahweh, but—" Shaul stopped and sighed. "The price is high," he added to himself. "But where else can I go? If I turn to Him, I may find rest."

The attendant averted his face. "You would find rest if you could touch the realm of the Elohim?" he asked softly.

"Yes, for then I could approach Yahweh that way. If only Shamuel were still alive! I could go to him and beg him to intercede with Yahweh for me. Shamuel was bound to me by my anointing. But now he is dead."

"He is in Sheol," Cheran replied. Dare he speak what was on his mind? Up north in Naphtali, his family occasionally consulted the Elohim.

"It is the same thing," Shaul said absently.

Cheran took a deep breath. "Not necessarily, adoni."

Shaul turned to him, eyes flashing. "What do you mean?" he demanded.

The personal attendant slipped to his knees. "I beg your indulgence, adoni. But sometimes there are those in the north who are troubled, and who have found a way to ease their minds and speak with our ancestor spirits who know the mind of the Elohim."

"Through a medium?" Shaul snapped. "I have purged them from the land, as commanded by Yahweh."

"Yes, adoni, but now Yahweh will not reply to *you*. But if Shamuel were to come to your aid, you might learn what you wish to know."

The king didn't reply for several minutes. "I would be consulting with Shamuel then."

"Yes, adoni," Cheran said, glancing up. Some of the fear had left the king's face, replaced by a tentative thoughtfulness.

"Please, adoni, it will ease your mind. That is a good thing. It is just another way of seeking Yahweh's will."

"One that might have a chance, with Shamuel to speak for me," Shaul said slowly. He looked at his attendant. "Seek out a medium for me, Cheran, so that I can inquire of her."

"Yes, adoni," the servant said, relieved at how much fear had left the king's face, now replaced by hope.

¥ ¥ ¥ ¥ ¥ ¥

"It's done," Abigail said to Keturah, bending over the fire to tend the stew.

"Good. The women know exactly which kettles are to go to the alluphs, and which to the other warriors?"

"Yes."

Her heart pounding, Abigail watched as the sun neared the horizon. They'd arrived here two hours ago, the dip in the land dropping away suddenly before them, and the scent of water and the sight of palm trees welcoming them with the promise of coolness. Several bands of warriors were already here, and more had arrived until tents, men, and fires filled the depression.

Keturah had been worried that they might not have enough of the herbs, but with the bundles five more of the women had picked during the day, she decided that they did.

Ahinoam had taken charge of the dazed captives coming in with the other bands, most of whom had not been treated well, or had seen the death of their loved ones and were now mourning them. Soon the familiar task of cooking had calmed the captives somewhat, and Irad had taken charge of the few men and boys still alive, spreading them out to carry the heavy kettles, bring food from the packs, or help watch the children.

During the day Abigail had passed the word of what would happen tonight, and she noticed the tension among the women as they prepared the meal. Everyone watched the sun, knowing that with darkness came the feasting, and the celebrating after it.

Jemima made sure that the cooked food tasted good, so that the men would be sure to eat it, and all four of them checked that the correct amount of herbs went into the correct pots.

Irad and Casluh reported that the animals they planned to use were readily available. Abigail went from fire to fire, encouraging everyone. "We just have to wait a few more hours. Do what you have to do to stay alive. Remember, we'll be heading west, trying to reach the caravan routes up from Egypt. Once we get started, we dare not stop, so be sure you and your children eat."

"Gebirah, what if some warrior takes us?" Elika's wife asked.

"Someone probably will," Abigail replied. "Don't fight him. Remember our instructions. Do whatever you can to get him to take you somewhere alone, whether it's in his tent, or off into the darkness. It shouldn't be very long before you'll be able to get away. Come directly back here."

"What about our daughters?" another woman asked, looking at her nearly grown child huddled beside her.

"I doubt they will be touched tonight," Abigail surmised. "Zaavan knows that they are worth much more as virgins on the slave market."

"Slavery?" the woman cried.

"Hush, now. Remember, we are working toward one thing at a time, and that means we do what we can to protect ourselves tonight. We will worry about tomorrow when it arrives."

When she returned to the cooking fires where the food was nearly done, Ahinoam awaited her. "Irad says there is a tremendous amount of spoils," she said. "They must have raided from the sea to the Arabah, and half of them are already drunk. Have you seen how many captives are now here? Do you think we should try and take them with us?"

"I can't stand the thought of leaving them. You know what will happen to them if we get away."

"Then we'll manage somehow. How are those orphans doing?" Ahinoam inquired.

"That Philistine woman and her husband have taken all three of them to heart," Abigail said. "When I think of what those poor children must have seen to shock them like that, I wish we had hemlock to put into this food!"

"I wouldn't be surprised if something like that is already in it," Ahinoam said. "I haven't dared to ask Keturah just what it is we are using."

The sun had started to slip below the horizon, and the guards arrived to escort the women carrying the food for the feast.

Abigail took a deep breath as she and Ahinoam picked up a kettle between them and headed for Zaavan's tent.

Chapter 30

Night of Day Five

The sun was halfway below the horizon when Seren Akish and Ittai arrived at the compound where Seren Baalyaton was staying for the evening meal.

"And how is our seren-of-the-rear?" the Ekron ruler asked as Akish approached to pay his respects.

"Planning the most efficient way to get those chariots where they should be," Akish replied without blinking an eye. Ittai's calm acceptance of their place in the battle had made it much easier for the ruler of Gath to regain his equilibrium from the insult of being relegated to the rear.

Seeing the disgusted look Gadmilk and Muwana gave Baalyaton also soothed his feelings, and he took his place at the table provided for him with something close to cheerfulness. He and Ittai had driven a chariot out today, finding a place where they could see the ground they would need to traverse in order to get the archers around the west end of the spur of hills.

It had sounded simple in the war council, but after actually driving the chariot, and surveying the terrain, Akish privately wondered if any of the archers would ever make it across that rough country in time to be of any use at all. Still, he had noticed several places where they might be able to bring the chariots close to the watercourses spreading down from the hills. The ground seemed to be fairly open on that side of the spur, with not too much brush or dense forest of the kind Ittai had described growing in Judah.

They had decided Ittai would go with the very first chariots to direct them around the spur and up the first of the watercourses. Akish would stay on the battle site until it was clear how many chariots would be needed there. Then he would send the rest ahead with archers.

After the meal ended, discussion started again over battle plans.

"I don't like the idea of taking away our best archers," Gadmilk complained. "We should have them in the battle line, pressing the Israelites back."

"We have enough numbers to do that without our best," Muwana said for the third time. "We won't be able to get a lot of archers around the spur of hills that quickly, so the ones we do send must be our most skilled."

"What about swordsmen?" Hanabaal wanted to know. "Are we sending any of them to attack from the Israelite rear?"

"Yes, but not a great many," Baalyaton answered. "Remember, the forest on Gilboa isn't as thick with brush as the forests farther south. Our archers will be more effective, and will not need as much support from swordsmen for up-close warfare."

"Well, since you're taking my best archers, I want the best swordsmen to back them up," Gadmilk announced.

"I agree," Akish spoke for the first time. "I want as many of my archers back as possible. They're the backbone of my army."

"As they are of everyone else's," Muwana reminded him. "It's settled then? The best archers and swordsmen will go first?"

"We'll plan that way," Baalyaton conceded. "If we assemble by the second hour, we should be over to Jezreel and En-harod by the fourth hour."

"What if the Israelites won't fight?" Hanabaal asked, looking as if he wished that would be the case.

"Then we chase them until they do fight, or we kill them," Baalyaton said shortly, while the servants brought torches to light the courtyard now that dusk had faded.

¥ ¥ ¥ ¥ ¥ ¥

In the near-darkness I almost fell into the depression that dropped away under my feet. Quickly backing up, I motioned for my men to go to their knees and crawl forward. Spread out below us, scattered among several large pools, a collection of tents, palms, and fires dotted the depression.

Abishai gasped beside me. "Dodi, how many are there?"

"At least three or four times as many as we are," I said grimly. "I had no idea the desert tribes had grown to this extent. Look at that herd of animals!"

Sibbecai crept up beside me as shouts and the noise of celebration rose from the tents below.

"Sounds like some of them have been celebrating for some time," Elhanan said drily.

"They have reason to," I said. "This must have been the largest, most successful raid in their history. Look at all those packs over there. Sibbecai, where are the sentries?"

"There aren't any."

"There must be!"

"Not anymore."

I looked at him.

He shrugged.

As I scanned the camp below me again, the volume of celebration increasing rapidly, an idea stirred around in my mind. Thanks to Yahweh's timing, we had below us the majority of the warriors of the three desert tribes, giving us our chance to execute Yahweh's justice on them in a single stroke.

"Uriah, do we have enough men to bottle up everybody down there?"

"Barely. But it could be done, adoni."

"From the sounds of things, by midnight a lot of these raiders will be too drunk to be aware of much of anything. How many do you think we can eliminate before they even know what's happening?"

"Quite a few. The more we reduce their number, the easier it will be to keep the others in a trap. And if we can get the captives to barricade themselves on their side of camp, we can guard them there."

"Shouldn't we get them out of there as soon as we can?" I asked, worried about my wives.

"If we did that, Dahveed, we'd turn this into a running skirmish with all the advantage and mobility on their side. Right now, we can move; they can't. With their superior numbers, we dare not give up a single advantage, certainly not one as big as that."

My desire to get our families out of there nearly overpowering, I had to fight the temptation to attempt to rescue them first. But I knew Uriah was correct. If we didn't take this chance to strike, we might be combating these tribes for years, with all the destruction and unending blood feud that would entail. I gritted my teeth. "All right."

Backing away from the rim, I hurriedly assembled the men. "Divide up into your units. We are going to take up positions ourselves all around this oasis. As soon as you get into place, keep alert. If an opportunity comes to eliminate anyone without raising an alarm, do so, but remember, there must be no alarm! That is paramount! We must wipe out as many as we can tonight."

I went on to explain what we were doing and why. None of them liked the thought of leaving our families down there, but there was no help for it unless we wanted to pay a much greater price later.

As the men moved swiftly away, Sibbecai, Zalmon, and I made our way carefully down the slope until we reached the edge of the camp, then we settled down in the darkness to watch.

¥ ¥ ¥ ¥ ¥ ¥

"We have found one, adoni!" Cheran announced, entering Shaul's tent shortly after dark. "We must go to En-dor, just seven miles north of here."

"That's on the far side of the Philistine camp."

"En-dor is beyond Shunem, yes, but it is also east of it. We can easily avoid the Philistines," the attendant assured him.

The king looked vexed. "I don't like that way. The risk is great. Perhaps we shouldn't go."

Cheran saw the king's hands start to tremble again, and the fear rushed back into his face. "Adoni, please. You must find comfort! We can disguise ourselves so that even if anyone sees us, they will not know who we are. And with Shamuel to help you, all your worries will be over."

"But a medium? Yahweh has forbidden it."

"But if Yahweh has rejected any direct communication, then you must seek Him however you can," the servant persisted. "Please, adoni. Come and be at peace!"

The king paced the tent, wringing his hands. "I don't know what to do. And they will attack tomorrow, and Yahweh has not said how to fight them."

"Come, and we will find out," Cheran urged, stifling his own distress at how the king's voice trembled.

"Who will go? I must have someone with me, and I dare not ask Jonathan!"

"Your shield-bearer, Nahshon, and I will accompany you, adoni. I have already asked him, and he is willing. He knows of some who have consulted mediums and received answers. We will take weapons.

There is a house just outside of the town close to where the medium works, and we can leave them there with the mules."

"She may not conjure for me," he said, pacing again. "What if she curses me instead?"

"You will be in disguise, adoni. She won't know who you are and cannot hurt you."

"But Jonathan won't like it. He says we must trust Yahweh and bow to Him."

"We are trying to, adoni. Shamuel will tell you Yahweh's will, and you will have peace!"

"And I must know! The roeh can tell me, and I won't be afraid anymore. We'll go. Have the mules brought!" the king commanded, taking off his meil and dropping it on the ground. Cheran helped him out of his girdle and robe.

"What will I wear?" Shaul asked.

"Nahshon is nearly as tall as you. We can borrow some of his clothes."

The attendant hurried to the shield-bearer's tent and the two servants found some clothes for the king. It was fully dark when Cheran led the three mules to the entrance of the king's tent and they mounted, riding away with cloaks fully fastened and hoods pulled up.

₩ ₩ ₩ ₩ ₩ ₩

"The king is gone," the guard reported to General Abner.

"Where?" Sar Eshbaal asked, glancing up.

The guard raised his hands a little. "He didn't say, Sar."

"That will be all," Abner said.

When the guard departed, the general stood. "Will you come with me, Sar? I must go encourage the men, particularly the militia. It will do them good to see you, also."

"I can, if you really think it will help."

"It will, Sar," the general replied, leading the way from the tent. It had been ridiculously easy to take Eshbaal under his wing, he thought as they walked toward the tents of the militia. And the hassar had done nothing. He smiled a bit grimly to himself. Perhaps he should have challenged Jonathan much sooner, but with both Shaul and Ner united, he might not have gotten very far.

No, he'd been wise to wait until Ner was dead. And with Shaul so apathetic, with eyes only for his grandchildren, it had been far easier than he'd expected to push the hassar aside. Of course, Dahveed had helped with that, weaning the people away from the king's oldest son.

For a while, he'd been worried about that. Dahveed was too popular and had somehow kept his hold on the people's hearts even after he was outlawed. When the roeh had declared he would be king, things had gotten even more difficult. But then Shaul's determination that Jonathan should rule after him had come to his aid, and now with Dahveed in exile, things should go as planned. He had Eshbaal to sit on the throne for him, and after tomorrow, everything should fall neatly into his hands. As he approached the first of the fires, he greeted the men.

"General Abner!" those around it gasped, scrambling up to stand as he stopped. "Why have you come?" someone asked.

"To make sure that everyone knows what will happen tomorrow. You've had your instructions from the professionals commanding you?" he asked, knowing they hadn't, since he had not yet informed the professional soldiers commanding the militia of their part.

"No, adoni," the same man answered. "But we've heard we're supposed to go over the ridge and prepare ambushes when the Philistines come."

"Partly right. The professional commanders will tell you when to retreat up the slopes. But keep your eye on the battle line. In order for us to effectively win this battle, that line must hold. If it breaks once you are over the ridge, keep going! We must move as fast as we can to the south side of the Jezreel plain ahead of those chariots. The king will reform there, and we must be ready to support him. That's vital."

"Yes, adoni. We'll remember," the men said.

Eshbaal had a slight frown on his face as he listened, but he said nothing as they went to the next group of tents. "You noticed the slight change in plans," Abner said while they walked. "Good. I should have told you about this modification, just in case the chariots overwhelm our front line."

The worry eased from Eshbaal's face, and by the time they were done visiting the militia, and the professionals assigned as commanders over them, Eshbaal was giving the same orders without any second thoughts. It was so late when they got back that Abner convinced the sar to spend the night in his tent.

¥ ¥ ¥ ¥ ¥ ¥

The food had all been served and eaten and the women silently gathered again, those from Ziklag crowded around Abigail and Ahinoam, the others in their own little clusters. A warrior strode over, wiping his mouth on the back of his hand and eyeing the women in the next group.

"You," he said, hauling one of them to her feet.

She cast a desperate glance at Ahinoam, who nodded a little.

"Yes, adoni," the woman said, her voice shaking. "C-can you come over here? It's better to lie down on." She edged toward the darkness.

Looking surprised, the man followed.

"I was hoping you'd pick me," the woman went on. "Shall we go a little farther? Under that palm maybe?"

"You wanted me, eh?" the man said, taking her arm roughly, but accompanying her into the darkness.

Abigail watched, her heart pounding. They would just have to survive this and get away as soon as they could.

Then a strangled cry barely reached them, and the sound of something falling. Abigail jerked her head around, staring. Shortly thereafter, the white face of the woman appeared out of the darkness, and she gestured to Abigail.

Checking to be sure no one was looking, the Gebirah went to her. "What happened?"

"I don't know, but he's dead!"

"What?"

"Something happened, and he fell, and he's dead!"

She thought swiftly. Another warrior had started their way. "Does he have a cloak?" she hissed quickly.

"Y-yes."

"You'll have to stay with him a bit. Get down beside him, and cover up the two of you with the cloak. Stay as long as you can stand, then get back here."

"Yes, Gebirah," the woman whispered, creeping back to the palm tree.

Abigail quickly spread the news, and the women watched closely as the second warrior simply walked up and took the first woman to hand, hauling her after him in the opposite direction from the first.

"Adoni, please let me get to my feet," the woman said, then tripped and fell. Instantly an arrow appeared in the man's chest, and he toppled over. The woman had the presence of mind to throw herself forward, clapping her hand over the man's mouth, pressing her other hand into his throat for good measure.

The guard from Zaavan's tent approached, and Abigail stood, turning to Jemima. "Tell the others that someone is out there helping us," she said swiftly. Gesturing toward the raiders milling around in the camp, she whispered, "If at all possible, get the men to go outside the camp!" Then she and Ahinoam followed the guard away.

¥ ¥ ¥ ¥ ¥ ¥

Silently raging, I watched my wives taken to the center of camp. "Whose tent is that?" I asked.

"Adoni, that is Alluph Zaavan," the Egyptian slave said from beside me. I jumped, having not heard him arrive. We watched as the alluph made a speech of some kind, gesturing to my wives as he did. Shouts of anger from the warriors gathered around made me tense, and then came the words I'd prayed that I wouldn't hear.

"Dahveed Israel! Dahveed Israel is the one who has ravaged our families and destroyed our clans! But Qas has defeated him and given him to us!" Zaavan shouted above the noise.

Sibbecai raised his bow, but I put my hand out. "Wait!" I commanded, puzzled by the alluph's words.

"Alluph Shepho destroyed him and his band at Ziklag!" Zaavan continued. "He burned the town and the bodies, sending them up to serve Qas for eternity."

Zalmon and I looked at each other.

"What's he talking about?" Sibbecai asked.

"Apparently he thinks we're dead."

The alluph finished his speech, gesturing toward the largest group of women captives. His men cheered while Zaavan shoved my two wives into his tent.

Gritting my teeth, I jerked forward. Sibbecai put his hand on my shoulder. "Save your vengeance, Dahveed, for when it will be complete," he said softly.

Taking a deep breath, I tried to calm myself. More warriors began to head our way.

"That's my wife!" Zalmon said in a choked voice as someone led a woman back into the camp.

"What's she doing?" I said.

He watched as his wife spoke to the warrior. The man hesitated, and she said something more, then they started toward the edge of camp.

"Josheb's over there," I said with an effort, "Leave it to him. We have someone to take care of here. That's Elika's wife, and she's headed our way." But before we could do anything, the warrior suddenly doubled over, retching, his arms wrapped around his stomach.

The woman instantly vanished.

"Take him!" I commanded Zalmon. "Hide him as best you can after he's dead!"

"Look, there goes another one!" Sibbecai exclaimed as another man bent over. The woman with him helped him to the edge of camp before shoving him to the ground and hurrying away. "What's happening?"

I turned to Khay. "Can you get into camp? See what you can find out for us."

Without a word, the Egyptian slipped away. Suddenly two more men stumbled toward us, and Sibbecai and I went to greet them.

¥ ¥ ¥ ¥ ¥ ¥

Abigail tried to keep her hand from trembling as she held out the cup of wine for the alluph to drink. He had insisted that she and Ahinoam serve him some food, giving her the perfect chance to add the crushed herbs Keturah had provided to his drink. Catching her hand, he pulled her to him as he accepted the wine, drinking half of it down immediately.

"This is a night which will be long remembered," he said, and then his eyes glazed over.

"Have some more wine, alluph," Ahinoam said, holding a different cup to his lips with the second mix of herbs Keturah had given to her. Obediently, he drank. He stared at nothing for a long time, then his eyes closed.

Hastily, the two women removed most of Zaavan's clothing, leaving him partially covered with his robe before searching through his tent.

Ahinoam stood at the door, peeking out. "Make more noise," she said.

Abigail clattered some cups around and overturned a little table. The guards outside laughed, gesturing toward the tent. "Is there anything that looks like it would help us?" Ahinoam asked.

"Not that I found. You look," the Gebirah said, taking her place by the door.

Ahinoam kicked a few things around, crying out once. The guards laughed again.

"I found some papyri. Dahveed likes them better than pottery shards for messages," she said. "Do you think we can leave?"

"The guards aren't sick yet," Abigail warned. "Do you think they will notice we took those papyri?"

"Probably." Ahinoam looked around. "Can we make it appear as if someone stole them?"

"It's right by the tent wall," Abigail said, pointing. "What if we cut a slit next to it?"

"Good idea." Ahinoam slipped Zaavan's battle dagger from the sheath. They managed to slice through the tough goat's hair of the tent wall, then replaced the dagger. A groan caught their attention.

Abigail checked outside. "Both guards are down. It's time."

Quickly, they roughed up their hair, removed their girdles, disarrayed their clothes, then fled the tent. Clutching their girdles and the skin sack with the papyri, they hurried back to the place where the captives were.

"How many women are back?" Ahinoam asked Irad while she tied on her girdle again.

"Only half, but it doesn't matter," the elder said. "Dahveed Israel is here!"

"How can that be?" Abigail gasped, finishing the knot on her girdle.

"I don't know, but Casluh said all the captives are to gather together at this end of the camp and barricade ourselves with the spoils."

"Then let's get started before the moon rises and they can see what we're doing," Ahinoam directed.

Chapter 31

There was no moon when the dark hill of Moreh loomed from the Jezreel plain, obscuring the horizon, and Cheran saw by starlight the house they were told to watch for, a single light burning in a window. While Nahshon tied the mules in the courtyard, Cheran knocked on the door. The householder emerged, putting on his cloak as he did.

"This way, gebers," he said, leading them outside the courtyard and around behind the house to a path leading up into the hills. Cheran had to hurry to keep up with him. They came to a saddle between two hills, climbed it, and turned south to the higher hill. The man abruptly left the path, pushing his way through the brush to a small hidden clearing with a little house and an enclosure with some goats, sheep, and a calf in it. Across the little dale a path led off into deeper darkness.

"Wait here," the man said, going to the door and knocking on it.

It opened almost immediately, and a woman stepped out. The man spoke briefly, and she handed him something. Their guide left without a word.

The woman approached them. "Shalom, gebers."

"We have come seeking guidance," Cheran said, stepping up beside the king and bowing a little.

"May I direct you anywhere?" she asked.

"We need guidance for our decisions, not our feet. It is said that you can provide that."

"How could I?" the woman retorted, turning away.

"Wait!" Shaul commanded, stepping forward.

The woman turned back. "Why should I?" she asked stiffly.

"Please," the king said, softening his tone. "I want you to divine with the spirits of the dead for me, to bring up—well, to bring up the one I will name for you."

"Divine?" the woman said, outraged. "Do you think I am a fool? You know what King Shaul has done, rooting out and destroying both the ancestors and those who divine and are possessed by them! This is nothing but a trap! I have done nothing to you, and you want to cause my death!" She started back to the house.

"Wait, please! No harm will come to you."
"And I am supposed to believe that?"
"I will swear," the king said, stepping forward.
The woman approached slightly. "By what?"
"By the life of Yahweh."
Silence settled around them in the darkness as the woman considered. "Swear," she said at last.
"It will be Yahweh's life if any punishment comes on you for this thing," Shaul vowed.
A little chill went through Cheran, but he shook it off. His master sounded confident again, and that was the important thing. In order for him to fight tomorrow, he must be confident.
The woman went into the house, then returned almost immediately to lead the way to the path across the clearing.
The three men followed her back through some more trees and brush to where the rocks of the hill broke through the soil. Close to where the path ended, a hole opened down into the rock, cold air flowing from it.
Nahshon and Cheran stepped back under the sycamore that shaded the spot.
"Whom shall I bring up for you?" the woman asked, facing Shaul.
"Bring up Roeh Shamuel."
The woman turned to the hole, pulling some items from her girdle and laying them on the ground. A chant issued from her lips, and she stepped back, watching the hole. Suddenly, she stiffened, throwing her head back and screaming.
Cheran shivered as the presence of "another" enveloped them.
The woman turned to Shaul. "Why have you betrayed me? You are Shaul himself!"
The king jerked back, and the hood of the cloak fell from his head. "Don't be afraid," he said hastily. "I swore, did I not? You will not die. You are safe. Tell me, what do you see?"
The woman didn't move for a moment, then she turned back to the hole. "I see elohim coming up from the ground."
"In what form?"
Again the woman paused. "It is an old man, wrapped up in a meil."
"Shamuel!" the king whispered. He dropped to his knees, then bowed to the ground, stretching himself flat on it.

"Why have you roused me and brought me up here?" Cheran heard a dry voice whisper. He started to shake, edging closer to Nahshon. What had he done by suggesting this? Then he reassured himself. The roeh had come. The king would get his answer, and that's why they were here.

Shaul stood, his head bowed. "Roeh, I am very hard pressed! The Philistines have come against me, and Yahweh has deserted me! He will not answer me either with prophets or dreams. I have called you, so that you can let me know what I should do!"

The air stirred a little and Cheran held his breath. Surely now Yahweh's seer would instruct the king and soothe his mind.

"Since Yahweh has deserted you and become your foe, why do you ask me? Yahweh has only done as He promised in my word to you. He has torn the kingdom away from you and given it to your friend, Dahveed. Since you did not execute Yahweh's wrath on the Amalekites, He has done this to you today."

"But, adoni—"

"Also," that dry whisper went on, "Yahweh will give Israel, along with you, to the Philistines. Tomorrow, you and your sons will be with me. Oh, yes," the whisper chuckled faintly, "Yahweh will give the army of Israel into the hands of the Philistines!" The air stirred again as the whisper faded away, taking the presence with it.

Shaul landed full-length on the ground, clinging to it, his body twisting in fear. "No," he moaned, then went limp.

Frozen with horror, Cheran couldn't take his eyes from the king. How could the roeh have passed a death sentence on Shaul? Shamuel was supposed to help them! He looked around for the medium, but she had disappeared.

Nahshon stepped forward. "Adoni?" he said, going to the king.

Shaul didn't reply; he simply lay there without moving.

Cheran started for the path to the house when the woman appeared on it.

She hurried over to Shaul. "What is it?" she asked, bending over him. "Ah, the message was not to his liking. I've seen this before. You go on now. Leave him to me," she said, standing up and shooing the two men away. "I know just what to do. This happens every now and then. Go on," she urged.

"He will be all right?" Cheran asked anxiously.

"He'll be fine. Just give me some time."

Reluctantly, the two men withdrew from the spot. Cheran glanced over his shoulder and saw the medium drop her girdle to the ground and pull off her robe. He nearly went back, but Nahshon pulled him along. "She said she knew what to do," he said. "We'd best let her."

"But—" The night suddenly seemed cold, and Cheran shivered. Nothing had gone as it was supposed to. Shamuel was supposed to reassure the king, explain to him what he needed to do, give him confidence for tomorrow. How could the Elohim have told the king that he and his sons would die tomorrow?

Time seemed to pass so slowly as they waited. Finally, they made their way back down the path to the rock on the hillside. The medium was kneeling beside Shaul, talking to him. "Adoni, do not speak so. Come now, I obeyed you. I listened to you and did what you asked, even though it could have meant my life. Now it's your turn to listen to me, your maidservant, even though you're the king. Let me give you at least a piece of bread for you to eat. It will provide strength for you on your way."

Shaul shook his head. "No, I will not eat."

"What is wrong with eating, adoni?" the woman persisted.

"Yahweh may yet have hesed on me. I will fast."

"Yahweh has no hesed. He wants you to die. But all may not be lost. Come, you must have strength. Eat what I will give you."

"Please, adoni," Cheran urged, also kneeling by the king. "You have had nothing from before dawn until now. You must eat!"

"And if you do, I know a way that may help you yet," the medium said. "Come, adoni, and accept what I have to offer."

"There is no hope," Shaul moaned, tears welling from his eyes. "Yahweh has condemned me."

"Yahweh is not all there is," the woman said somewhat tartly. "Come."

With Nahshon's help, Cheran supported the king as he stood, leaning heavily on them while they walked the short distance to the little house and eased Shaul down on the bed in the corner.

"Where is that bread?" Nahshon asked tersely.

"There can be more than bread," the woman said hurriedly. "Bread may not be enough." She turned to the king. "Adoni, will you let me prepare what I think is best? I know what may help you even though your god has rejected you."

"What help can there be?" Shaul asked, still dazed.

"As I said, Yahweh is not all there is. The spirits have much power and can be convinced to use it if approached in the right way."

"How can they?" Shaul whimpered.

"How did they know who you were, and tell me? I couldn't even see your face, but they knew. They can help you."

"No. We should go," Shaul protested. "I will go back to Jonathan, and he will ask Yah to give me hesed!"

"But, adoni, Jonathan is condemned, too," Cheran interrupted. "How can he help?"

"The sons also?" the woman said. "This is indeed a terrible thing, adoni. You must accept help where you can find it. Place yourself in my hands as I placed myself in yours. Let me bring you peace."

"I want to rest," Shaul sighed.

"You will have rest," the woman promised.

"Do your will, geberet," Shaul finally said, closing his eyes and leaning back against the wall.

Going outside, the woman started a fire in her oven, then took a knife from a shelf, and hurried to the animal pen. Soon the sounds of a calf being butchered drifted into the room. Cheran found some water in a cruse, and the king drank a little, his gaze empty in the dim light of the lamp on the table. "It will work out all right," the attendant assured the king. "You will be able to rest and be ready to conquer the Philistines tomorrow."

The medium returned, spilled some flour on the table, and added oil, salt, and water. She hastily kneaded the dough, then put it to bake in the oven. By the time the bread was done, she had brought in some of the raw meat in a bowl.

"All is ready," she said, and Nahshon and Cheran helped Shaul to the table. "Now you must eat, and I will tell you what will be done for you," she said, gesturing to the dishes on the table.

"This is a covenantal meal," Shaul said, looking over the food, his eyes tormented. "Jonathan will be distressed. He says Yahweh is our God."

"But Yahweh is not *your* god," the woman reminded him. "He rejected you, and has condemned you. If you want to live, you must take shelter under another's wings. The spirits of the ancestors will not fail you."

"Please, adoni, do what you must to find comfort," Cheran said, seeing one more chance for the king he loved to be at peace.

"You must all eat," the medium said. "You will be stronger that way."

Nahshon took some of the bread and ate it, then reached for a piece of the raw meat. Shaul closed his eyes and accepted some of the food also, followed by Cheran. While they ate, the medium explained the power of the spirits residing in the realm of the Elohim, and how they could intercede and protect those who turned to them.

When they rose to go, Shaul stood without any help.

"See, adoni, you are better already," the woman announced.

"Yes, I do feel stronger," Shaul admitted.

"Go now, then, for all will be well."

Day Six

Hassar Jonathan jerked awake on the bedroll, Nemuel's name on his lips. He stared around at the darkness a moment, then eased back down with a sigh. It had been years since the nightmare had been this vivid. He turned over, trying to sleep, but too many thoughts intruded. Before he had gone to bed, he had stopped by Shaul's tent, hoping to speak with him one more time and bring him to his senses before it was too late.

But the guards had said that the king had left some time ago with Nahshon and Cheran, and had not returned yet. Hoping to find some indication where his abbi might have gone, he had looked in the tent. The first thing he saw was the king's meil, crumpled on the ground, his robe beside it. Where could Shaul have gone that he wouldn't want the symbol of his kingship on him? Why had he thrown it off so carelessly?

Giving up on trying to sleep, the hassar went outside. The stars seemed especially close this night, and he sat down, staring up at them. Dahveed had a song about the stars, about the wisdom they gave, and the glories of Yah that they proclaimed.

Where had Abbi gone with just two attendants, and on the eve of battle? He was still sitting there when he heard hurried footsteps. Silently he rose, stepping into the shadow of the tent. Cheran appeared, and the guard started to intercept him.

"Let him pass," Jonathan spoke softly.

The guard withdrew, and the king's personal attendant came forward eagerly. "Adoni, I'm glad you are awake. I had to tell you. The king's fear is gone, and he will be confident and ready for battle tomorrow."

The man's voice was shaky and his words spoken too quickly. Jonathan gestured him inside the tent. Cheran seemed a bit reluctant, but he obeyed, waiting restlessly while the hassar lit a lamp from the fire and set it on the three-legged table in the tent.

"The king is no longer afraid?" Jonathan asked.

"Yes, adoni! He is confident again, and will be able to lead the army well tomorrow."

"How did this happen?" The hassar did not like the odd shine he saw in Cheran's eyes. He knew the lamp was dim, but there seemed to be darker shadows than there should be around the attendant.

"He found someone to help him, adoni. I wanted you to know so that you wouldn't worry."

"Did he finally bow to Yahweh?"

"Well, I don't know, Hassar. I—I don't think so."

"Where have you been with the king?"

"We went to En-dor."

"En-dor? That's north of the Philistines! Why would you take that risk?" Jonathan said sharply.

"We had mules, adoni, and rode in plain clothes so that no one would recognize us," Cheran said hastily. "We saw no one on the way."

"What was at En-dor?"

"Help for the king, Hassar. He was so distressed, I had to find something to soothe him."

Shaul's son reached over, gripping the man's shoulder. "Where did you take the king, Cheran?"

"To a medium, adoni," the man replied in a low voice. "But it's not what you think," he said, looking up. "We went there to consult with Shamuel, that's all."

"That's all?" the hassar echoed in disbelief. "Cheran, what have you done?"

"The king is at ease now! Don't you see? That's all we did."

At the pleading look in the man's eyes, Jonathan eased back, biting back his temper. "Tell me everything. *Everything*, Cheran!"

Half an hour later, as the attendant finished the tale, Jonathan could only grip his hands together in despair at what the king had done. "Did you leave anything out?" he asked tonelessly.

"No, adoni. It has helped the king, don't you see?" the man pleaded.

"Yes, I see. I see that you have taken every bit of hope away from the king, and Israel," Jonathan said in defeat.

"But the king is no longer distressed, adoni. He will be confident before the army tomorrow."

"What good will that do, Cheran? His distress was the one thing that might have driven him to finally give himself over to Yah's will, and that would have allowed Yahweh to grant His hesed again. We are doomed now. Go."

The attendant left, looking subdued.

For some time, Jonathan just sat, trying to take in what he had learned. Then he picked up the bow case for the composite bow Dahveed had given him, grabbed his cloak, and left the tent.

Seeing the cloak, one of the guards stepped forward.

"No," the hassar said. "I'll take Nimshi."

His armor-bearer woke quickly, and the two of them climbed the slopes of Gilboa. As usual, Nimshi had sensed his mood, and they traveled in silence. A break in the trees gave onto a view of the plain below, bathed now in the weak light of the waning moon that had risen not long before.

When Jonathan stopped and leaned against a pine, staring out across the plain, Nimshi moved off a little way and settled himself down to sleep some more. After a time, the hassar slowly sat down, his hands smoothing the wood of the case, his fingers touching each of the inlaid symbols, one at a time, ending with the royal scepter. A scepter that would never be his.

He closed his eyes again. His abbi had committed the final act of treason. There was no hope of going back now. Shaul's anointing by Yahweh had begun with a meal with Shamuel, and now it had irrevocably ended when Shaul had eaten meat with the blood in a covenantal meal to honor the spirits of the dead. How could he have, Jonathan wondered. The hassar well remembered Shaul's anger at the people for eating raw meat after the battle of Michmash, and that hadn't had covenantal significance. The soldiers then had been simply too hungry to properly prepare and cook the food after obeying Shaul's command to fast until the Philistines had been driven out.

But Yahweh had been angered, refusing to communicate with Shaul until the king had set up a stone as an altar where the soldiers could properly slaughter the animals. And now the king himself had not only eaten raw meat, but done so in an act of homage to the dead.

Jonathan stripped a piece of pine bark from the tree, throwing it from him, Cheran's tale running through his mind again. The irony of Abbi swearing protection for the medium by the very God he was repudiating bit into his soul. And when the king enumerated his troubles, he had mentioned only Yahweh's failure to support him, not his own to follow Yahweh's commands. Nor had he mentioned the Urim and Thummim either, probably afraid he would then have had to admit his own sin about how he had obtained them. The hassar rested his arms on his knees. The reply had stabbed straight to the point: the king's disobedience.

As he leaned back against the tree trunk, the hassar let the tears spill from his eyes. In the end, the trip had been completely futile, for Shaul had not learned a single thing that he did not already know. Only this time, Jonathan thought, his abbi had finally believed it. Even after that medium had offered herself to Shaul, and then convinced him to eat with her, Yahweh had still struggled to get the king to turn to Him.

Reaching down, the hassar stroked the smooth wood of the bow case again, wishing he could send his arrows into the heart of every one of the people who had led his abbi into this final, irrevocable sin. But the medium had looked after herself too well. He smiled wryly into the darkness. Since all three of the men had eaten with her, none of them could condemn her for what she had done without revealing their own complicity. After that meal, each held the life of the others in their hand.

"And so I die," he sighed out loud, looking up to the stars. "Do you have any wisdom for me now?" he asked.

Open the bow case.

The thought popped into his mind so clearly that he blinked. After a moment of hesitation, he opened the case, taking out the bow, which arched backward into nearly a full circle.

String the bow.

Getting up and bracing himself to use his knee, Jonathan forced the arc right-side out, slipping the bowstring into place.

Aim the bow.

Puzzled, he held the bow in his right hand, as though sighting down an arrow, and suddenly he felt again those large, strong hands on his, sending reassurance through his defeated thoughts.

You are My bowman. I will be with you always. You have been faithful to all My will, and your name will ever be before Me.

Setting the bow down, Jonathan knelt on the sparse grass peeking through the dead pine needles. "After what my house has done, how can You still be with me, Adonai?" he whispered. "Can Your hesed truly extend this far?" Above him, the stars shimmered and seemed to encircle him closely. "Yahweh's hesed will be found with you always," the roeh's words rang again in his mind.

When his worship was done, the hassar sat down again, holding the bow. He had a choice to make. He knew that he had been condemned to death that night, but if Yah's hesed remained with him, the possibility also remained that the sentence might not be carried out today if he was not at the battle. The same might apply to his brothers. If they lived, they could benefit Dahveed in so many ways, dealing with Abner and passing the kingdom on with as little upset as possible.

But as much as he loved the Dahveed and longed to see him as Yahweh's king, he knew he would not leave. Dahveed had the help and support of many people, including the roeh's successor Gad, the hakkohen Abiathar, even the ark itself. He also suspected someone very astute was advising Dahveed, and with both Tanhum and Elihu in Gibeah, the kingdom would become Dahveed's eventually.

But there was no one for Abbi. Cheran was not the only one who knew of the king's fears, and the thought of what Abbi would go through if his sons left him shredded Jonathan's heart. Staying now, even though it meant his death, was the final way he could show his love and loyalty to his abbi and king. He had to be there in case his abbi needed one final act of service. If capture seemed imminent, he must kill Shaul himself rather than let him suffer his fate at the hands of his enemies.

His decision made, he rose, noticing the night had begun to fade. He must talk with Ishvi, Malchi, and Eshbaal, telling them that they should leave if they wished. Eshbaal particularly, since he was Immi's comfort. The thought of Immi and Michal brought tears to his eyes, and he nearly reversed his decision to remain. But Abbi was the one who needed him most now. His beloved immi and sister were covered by the covenant he had made with Dahveed, so he did not need to worry over them.

Stepping from under the trees, he looked upward and raised the bow to the sky with both hands. "You have named me Your Bowman, Adonai. Grant me the hesed to fulfill all Your will on the Philistines. And You have made me Melek Israel. Let me safeguard Israel before I die."

I have heard your prayer and granted your request. The words formed in Jonathan's mind, and he lowered the bow, turning to face the day.

Back in the camp, he sent Nimshi around to his brothers, asking them to come to his tent. As his armor-bearer jogged away, the hassar watched, thinking how much Nimshi had changed since he'd first met the little 9-year-old boy who had blandly led him into an ambush in order to protect Dahveed. He was a warrior to be reckoned with now, no matter what weapon he had in his hands.

"Yahweh, do not let him die," Jonathan murmured. "Dahveed needs him."

It didn't take long for the older sars to arrive, both of them carefully dressed, he noticed. They waited in silence for Eshbaal, but Nimshi came instead.

"Geber, Sar Eshbaal is not in his tent. The guards there said that General Abner has him."

"Very good, Nimshi," Jonathan said slowly. "I think that's all I need now." Maybe it was best that Eshbaal not know what he was going to say, he thought. Besides, Abner's plans for the youngest sar did not include getting him killed.

Malchi had built up the fire a little, and the sars sat around it as Jonathan quietly told them what Shaul had done during the night.

"How can he turn from Yahweh?" Ishvi demanded. "To abandon his God for this?"

Jonathan was silent a long time. "You know, I don't think I've ever heard Abbi call Yahweh his God," he said finally. "Yahweh has always been the roeh's God, or Israel's God, but never his God."

"We are doomed then," Ishvi said, putting his head in his hands.

Malchi said nothing, just stared into the fire.

"You don't have to stay," the hassar said. "That's what I called you here for. Yahweh has made it plain that hesed still remains for us. You do not have to die here today unless you choose to. If you leave, I would ask you to take the best of the men you can get with you to Dahveed."

Ishvi jerked his head up. "I didn't mean that I minded for me, Jonathan, and Abbi needs us now, more than ever. What bothers me is the men who will die with us. What have they done?"

"As the king, so the people," Jonathan said softly. "When Israel asked for a king, they accepted all that went with it, as Roeh Shamuel warned them would happen. But if you stay, Ishvi, what of your son?"

"Now that Merab is gone, I don't particularly care one way or the other," the second sar replied. "And I know that if I die, young Ishvi would prefer to die with me. He has said as much more than once."

"Malchi?" Jonathan said, turning to his next brother.

"I was wondering if I could beat Samson's record," Malchi said, still staring at the fire. "Three units is a lot for one man to bring down at his death. It would be interesting to know what I could do." His fingers flexed as he spoke, his voice flat and emotionless.

"What happened below Jebus?" Ishvi asked softly.

Malchi didn't reply for some time. "Leah died," he said at last.

"Leah?" Jonathan asked.

"Caleb's daughter, one of the twins, you remember." Malchi stood and turned his back to the fire. "I saw her again at Feast of Weeks two years ago. She–she had grown up all of a sudden," he said, his voice full of wonder. "I couldn't forget her, so one day I rode down there. She was glad to see me, and we—"

Malchi paused to steady his voice. "Caleb wasn't sure how he felt, though. He didn't welcome me even though Leah did. He softened a little when I told him I wanted to take her for my wife, but in the end, he refused to let me marry her. Said she was bred to the hills, and not to walls. But he gave me permission to see her whenever I wished."

"And you went often," Jonathan put in, staring at Malchi's back.

"As often as I could get away. There was peace down there, and so much pain and trouble in Gibeah. I could go down there and forget."

"Is there a child?" Ishvi asked.

"No. But we didn't mind. It seemed so hard at first, when Caleb refused to let us marry, but now I can see the wisdom of his decision. If I had brought her to Gibeah, she might have been poisoned somehow by everything going on there. As it is, I can remember her down there in the hills, laughing at something I told her and calling me 'Dodi Sar.'

"Then that message came. She had a fever of some kind. But I got to be there and hold her one last time. We were all there when she died. There's been a hard knot inside me since we buried her. I'd like to let it loose," he added, turning back to them, his eyes burning. "So, yes, Jonathan, I'm going to stay. Besides, you've been my adon for a long time now, and I don't see any reason to leave you now."

"Then you will be more than welcome, brother. You both will," Jonathan said.

After they left, the hassar stayed out by the fire while the sky turned gray, taking a little time to wonder what this day might have been like if Shaul had obeyed Yahweh and executed the divine wrath on the Amalekites.

Chapter 32

I watched the sky gradually turn to gray. During the night I'd made two circuits around the camp, checking in with my men, getting estimates of how many of the warriors from the camp they had executed during the night, and telling them what to do at daylight. The young Egyptian slave, Khay, had proved his worth, and I vowed I'd give Yahweh a thank offering for him as soon as I got back to Ziklag. He had slipped into camp twice, talking to Casluh each time, and brought back word that Keturah had added her own personal choice of seasoning to the food served for the feast, telling us that anyone who ate it would be very ill for several more hours and severely weakened for three days after that.

Sibbecai had chuckled grimly when he heard Khay's report. "She must have given them the same thing she gave me when I went to Carmel," he had said. "Dahveed, they'll be weak as newborns."

Unfortunately, Keturah only had enough of the herbs she'd given Sibbecai to fully dose the stew pots for the alluphs and high-status warriors. The rest she loaded with beans from the castor—or gourd—plant, and senna, some of which she found in the food spoils, the rest collected by the women as they traveled.

The first wave of warriors had become violently ill within an hour or two of eating. The rest were due to feel the effects of her cooking skills any time. Uriah and I had figured we had killed nearly our own number of men during the night, many of them the better warriors and the alluphs from all three tribes.

But with the need to safeguard the captives, now barricaded as securely as we could manage at one end of camp, the number of men I had available to fight was also reduced, and we had agreed that so long as the enemy came to us, we should continue to ambush them. At some point, our presence would become known, and the time for an outright battle would be then.

The edge of the sun tipped the horizon, the first beams finding the tents below us. Those of us still stationed around the camp waited patiently. The lower-status warriors, who hadn't rated a woman, had been rewarded with wine, and they had taken full advantage, so they would be ill from the drink as well as Keturah's additions to their diet.

The sun had fully come up before the first man appeared from his tent, stumbling as quickly as he could to the edge of camp. Now that the darkness no longer covered us, we had to be doubly careful when and how we killed. The first few were easy, since no one else was up to see us, but before long, enough men had emerged that we had to pick and choose.

The Geshurites had pitched at the eastern end of camp, and I finally noticed that no one was stirring down there. Using extreme care, I circled the edge of camp, the moans and groans of the sick warriors plainly audible. Eleazar and Abiezer met me.

"No one has come from these tents yet?" I asked.

"We'd hardly expect anyone to, except from that one," Eleazar replied, pointing to the one in the very middle.

"What did you do?" I asked, noticing that the Benjamites were cleaning their weapons.

"They were very drunk last night, and Eliphelet suggested we visit them this morning. They were all still asleep," he explained. "They are now, too," he added, his eyes hard. "Some of the men's families came with them to escape Abner, you know. The men didn't take too well to having the desert raiders bothering them, not after all the trouble they'd already had with the general."

Studying a few faces, I decided not to protest. "All right, clean out that last tent, and then position yourselves throughout this area. Just make sure you can retreat if you need to with as little danger as possible."

"Yes, adoni," Eleazar said.

By mid-morning the stream of warriors racing to the edge of camp had thinned down to a mere trickle, and I consulted again with Uriah. What remained was the central core of the camp, with probably twice the number of my men still showing signs of activity.

"If we attacked, could we wipe them out?" I asked Uriah.

"We'd have to plan carefully. There's still too many of them."

"All right, I'll call the men in, and we can decide what to do."

Since we had to be careful not to be seen, it took nearly an hour for everyone to gather. I had sent Khay down into the camp again to check with Irad. Casluh reported that there was little stirring in the camp that they could see. Then my division commanders—Shagay, Eleazar, and Josheb—with Uriah, Sibbecai, and I all sat down to prepare a plan that would give us the best chance of sweeping up everyone in the camp.

¥ ¥ ¥ ¥ ¥ ¥

Once Casluh had gone to report, Khay drifted back into the camp. The price of his survival with the Amalekites had been the ability to blend so well with the background that no one noticed him. While he moved through the captives toward the barricade of spoils, he stole two pieces of bread and some dates without conscious thought. He would have starved to death on what Alluph Shepho actually gave him to eat, so taking any food available was second nature to him.

Finding a place to sit, the Egyptian began to eat, gradually aware that he could hear a low-voiced conversation near him.

"We've got time now. Tell us what happened that second time Zaavan sent for you," a woman's voice said.

At the mention of the alluph's name, Khay stilled, alert. He listened closely as a second woman described how she had convinced Zaavan to leave her alone by telling him he was under the curse of Yahweh.

"You told him I was a sacred woman?" a third voice asked incredulously.

"It was all I could think of, and it's true—sort of!"

There was silence for a time, and then someone started to giggle. "Oh, Gebirah! Just the thought of you standing there telling that alluph that I'm sacred to Yah, and having him *believe* you! It's too much!"

"Well, it worked," the Gebirah said. "He got all uneasy, especially when the wind blew against the tent."

"Zaavan, uneasy? No wonder he tried to be so masterful with us last night!" the first woman said, then she started to laugh, too.

Within moments all three women were giggling half hysterically, muffling the sounds they made with their robes or girdles, he guessed. He crept away, leaving them trying to control themselves.

Easing away from the barricade, he slipped among the tents, hardly knowing why he did so and realizing that it was foolish, but unable to turn back. He listened carefully outside of several before he went in. Most were empty, the former occupants lying outside the camp somewhere, dead. In one the two men inside were still sleeping, both looking pale. Then in another the man lying inside was dead.

Khay saw no visible wounds, so he decided the man had probably died from whatever had been in the food. Having spent years of his life cringing before these people, to find them gone and dead was almost more than he could grasp.

He was near the center of camp when a hand reached out and clamped down on his arm, dragging him into a tent. The alluph twisted his arm painfully and out of long established habit, Khay endured it silently.

"What has happened?" the man demanded, his voice hoarse, sweat beading on his white face. "It's too quiet!"

"I don't know, alluph," Khay gasped. "There are many empty tents."

"Empty!" the man said, twisting tighter.

The slave gasped again. "Please, alluph! I am telling you what I saw. Another tent had a dead man in it, and in another the men were alive, but ill."

"Come with me," the Amalekite ordered, pushing Khay in front of him and stumbling after to Alluph Zaavan's tent.

It had no guards outside, and they went in. Khay stared at the sight of the half-clothed man lying on the bedroll.

"Alluph!" his captor said, shaking the adon. "Zaavan, wake up!"

Zaavan groaned, tossing his head.

Khay stood trembling, knowing he would tell them of their danger because he was too afraid to do anything else, and that they would kill him. Part of himself told him to run, but he'd seen too many slaves killed for trying to escape, and he remained.

"Alluph!"

At last, Zaavan opened his eyes, staring around, then groaning again and twisting into a ball on the bedroll.

"Alluph, this slave says there are empty tents, that men are dead and ill!"

"Dead?" Zaavan asked, gritting his teeth while he tried to sit up. "What are you talking about?" He looked up at the Egyptian. "You dare to stand before me?"

The fury in his eyes made Khay drop instantly, gasping for hesed. But the alluph's hands were on him, seeking his throat.

"Alluph! Zaavan, no! He's the only one who knows what has happened!" the other man said, prying the chief's hands away. "Let him live! He must tell us what has happened."

Terrified, Khay blurted out what he had seen in the camp, while Zaavan struggled to get himself dressed.

"He must be lying," he said when the slave finished.

"I don't see how he could be," the other man protested. "The camp is too quiet. My companion went out last night and has not returned. The guards are gone."

"And the captives?" Zaavan asked, turning to Khay.

"They are still here, alluph," Khay said, and into his frantic fear crept the memory of what the Gebirah had said and the memory of the concern on the face that had bent over him, giving him food and water, asking for his help. He could feel the body of the giant man who had carried him when he was too weak to walk, and somewhere down in his mind, the determination grew that while he lived, he would do what he could to help those who had been kind to him.

"They are still here?" Zaavan asked, amazement breaking through the pain showing on his face.

"Yes, alluph," Khay answered. "They are waiting for something," he added, his voice shaking.

"What are they waiting for?" the alluph demanded, grabbing him and shaking him.

"They mentioned Dahveed Israel! Don't kill me!" he pleaded.

"Dahveed Israel is dead!"

"Maybe the sacred woman called him back," Khay managed to whisper.

Zaavan froze. "What do you know of that?" he asked, his hands shaking, and he curled them into fists to stop the trembling.

Hope pierced Khay's heart, and he took a deep breath. "She serves the same god as Dahveed Israel, alluph. The dead man I saw had no wounds on him. He was just dead. He must have been cursed by a god. The gods are angry with us," Khay babbled on. "We took what was His, and killed His servants! He is taking vengeance on us!"

The other alluph slapped him across the face, and Khay covered his head.

"This is nonsense, Zaavan," the man said.

"Is it? How did we all get so ill? She warned me," he added.

"Who?"

"The Gebirah, Dahveed's wife. She told me how Nabal died, struck by Yahweh for displeasing Him, and she warned me not to do the same, and I felt the passing of the Elohim when she spoke, but I didn't want to believe." His face was white, and he suppressed another groan, bending forward.

The other man looked uneasy, and sweat beaded on his face.

Just then another man staggered into the tent. "Alluph Zaavan," he said, "there are dead men lying outside the camp, and the tents around the edge are deserted. I checked when I saw men slipping away up the hillside."

"It is the curse," Khay moaned. "We will all die! She has called Dahveed Israel back to the desert, and he will wreak his God's vengeance on us!"

"Silence!" Zaavan growled. "You're sure of what you saw?" he asked the second man.

"Yes, Zaavan, but I don't know how many men are dead." Just then he clutched his stomach and bent over. "What is this which has struck us?"

"The curse, the curse," Khay whispered.

Zaavan didn't say anything. "We've got to get out of here," he said finally. "I don't like it that those captives are just sitting there, waiting. And if you saw men, then we will be attacked soon."

Staggering to his feet, he checked the sun. "It's nearly the fourth hour. We won't have much time. Find out how many are still alive. We can fight the men off, but at any cost we must be gone before the Elohim come. They probably strike in the dark, and that's why the captives are waiting. If they catch us after the curse we're suffering now, we have no chance at all. We'll need the camels and—"

With that finely honed instinct that had saved his life often before, Khay realized no one was paying him any attention, and he slipped from the tent, fleeing as fast as he dared to the edge of camp, thanking his god for preserving his life. Returning to the captives, he drifted in among them and huddled down. If he avoided the Dahveed, maybe the man would never learn who had betrayed him!

¥ ¥ ¥ ¥ ¥ ¥

It was before the fourth hour and Hassar Jonathan scanned the battle line stretching off to both sides, waiting for the approaching Philistines to reach them. Beside him, Shaul sat tall on his mule in a cuirass and kilt, Nahshon on another mule beside him. The king's eyes shone with a strange light, and the hassar kept his gaze away, for whenever he looked at his abbi, the dark shadows began to gather at the edges of his eyes.

Off to the right, Ishvi was behind the line on his mule, his foster son on another beside him. To the left, Malchi rode back and forth, his mule as restless as the man on it. Shaul had formed the battle line much farther out on the plain than anyone had expected, and all three older sars were uneasy about it. When Jonathan had asked why, Shaul had replied that Yahweh was God of the hills. The hassar had said nothing more, realizing that the king expected better help from the spirits here on the plain.

On the other side of Shaul, Abner waited on his mule, Sar Eshbaal with him, the two of them ready to lead the militia off when the time came. The professionals in the line had all been briefed early this morning and knew that they would then need to get over the ridge quickly to help organize the ambushes planned there.

But looking at his abbi now, Jonathan wasn't certain Shaul would retreat as planned. He seemed almost eager for this battle.

"Don't worry so, my son," Shaul said, turning to him. "All will be well. I have seen to that!"

"Yes, Abbi," the hassar replied, keeping his eyes ahead of him as the first units of Philistines arrived—and kept on arriving. They matched the Israelite line, and then doubled their own. His attention sharpened. Why were most of the chariots on the west flank? Sunlight flashed off the armor and helmets of the advancing Philistines, and Jonathan noticed far more officers riding mules than normal. He squinted. The light coming from the armor on those men was subtly different. Was it gold, he wondered. Had the serens themselves decided to lead their forces?

As the numbers of the Philistines became apparent, Jonathan felt the nervousness of the men. "Steady," he heard several commanders saying. After a moment of breathless silence, the Philistines' battle horns sounded, echoed almost instantly by the Israelite ones. A flight of arrows arched toward them, answered by the Israelite archers, and the men raised their shields. Before the arrows had even arrived, the Philistines gave a tremendous war cry and charged, a single line of chariots leading the way.

"The horses! Shoot the chariot horses," all three sars roared, and then the confusion and cries of battle erupted all down the line. Almost immediately, the Israelite line wavered, but then chariot horses began to fall, and the commanders steadied the line. Another flight of arrows rained down, and more men fell as the Philistine swordsmen hit the line. As agreed, the commanders began a slow retreat while they fought.

"No," Shaul shouted. "Hold the line! Hold the line!"

"Adoni, we cannot!" Jonathan countermanded, waving the men back. "Look out there! They've only sent out their first line! There are as many waiting as we're fighting now! We can't hold them!"

"But we must fight on the plain today!" Shaul protested.

"Here come the chariots!" Jonathan pointed, yelling in his abbi's ear.

Shaul watched as both of their mules retreated, staying behind the fighting men. "Signal the men back to the hills," Jonathan shouted. The horns sounded, passing the signal down the line, and the retreat sped up.

Take up your bow, My Bowman. Without thinking, the hassar obeyed the order as Shaul reluctantly fell back, Abner and Eshbaal already hurrying away. He whipped an arrow from the quiver on his back and drew the bow. The strong hands guided his, and he saw that different shine of sunlight, his fingers releasing the bowstring. The arrow sang through the air, flashing as it struck his target, the helmet disappearing. Dara's mule crowded close as his shield-bearer raised the shield, then his mule turned and rode the other way.

Quickly!

"Hassar!" Dara shouted, but Jonathan had drawn another arrow, sending it into the line of men close in front of him, transfixing a Philistine commander just as he was about to shout an order. The man screamed as he fell, a strained, high-pitched sound. Jonathan's mule turned again, and he drew a third time, sending the arrow low over the line toward the east, and another man gave the same scream, while another helmet decorated with that shine tumbled across the ground. He shot twice more before his mule suddenly bunched under him, and he grabbed the mane as the animal charged west down the line, Dara barely keeping up with him.

Jonathan had time to glance back and see that they were finally approaching the rise of the hills. All around, units of militia were disengaging and disappearing into the trees. Ishvi and Malchi were expertly shortening the battle line in response, pulling in the wings to form a shallow semicircle.

Now, My Bowman. The mule sat down, sliding to a halt, and Jonathan whipped another arrow to the bow, the hands guiding his as his eye caught that glimmer from another officer on a mule. The arrow flashed brilliantly as it flew, knocking the man off his mule, the scream drowned out by the clash of arms around him.

The king shouted behind him, and battle horns sounded again, but whether Philistine or Israelite, the hassar couldn't tell, his whole mind being taken up with the commands he heard, watching the arrows streak through the air, man after man tumbling to the ground while his mule raced back and forth without visible guidance.

He could hear Ishvi and Malchi shouting orders, and then Dara grabbed the reins of his mule, whipping the animal around. His mount rose under him, and Jonathan barely had enough time to grab the mane, clinging to the animal's back. There!

The mule came down facing the Philistines, and Jonathan sighted again, loosing the arrow when the hands told him to. Flashing like lightning, the arrow sang away, piercing the armor of a battle dress at hip level. The hassar didn't hear the man scream but was already under the trees on the slope, Dara swearing at the mules, which raced upward, but soon slowed.

All around, other professionals were scrambling upward, and Jonathan slid off the mule, giving it a slap. Dara landed beside him. "Adoni, if you die, it will be your own fault," the shield-bearer snapped. "How can you expect me to stay with you if you run all over the Jezreel plain?"

"Blame the mule," Jonathan panted in reply. "I wasn't guiding him." Suddenly he jerked around, and by the time his eye found the brilliance he looked for, he had the arrow drawn back.

Steady.

He waited, feeling the hands tracking the gleam through the trees. Then he released, and the arrow whipped down the hill, knocking another man off his feet with that same death cry.

When he glanced out on the plain, there didn't seem to be as many Philistines out there as he had expected there to be. Above him on the crest, he heard Malchi and Ishvi shouting orders, and more men, both militia and professionals, ran past, the unit commanders lagging behind to encourage the stragglers.

As he topped the ridge he saw the Philistines down below already advancing upward, but slowly and cautiously. They had time, then, to prepare a warm welcome for them. Hearing a strange silence behind him, he turned to the south. Everywhere he looked, he could see men running, and none of them paused.

"What is it?" he asked, puzzled.

"Betrayal," Shaul said bitterly. "Look!"

Less than a mile away, and more than 400 feet below, two mules raced south across the round valley encircled by the spur of Gilboa.

"Adoni," a man shouted, racing up. "Commander Ram sends to you. He says there is no militia for him to work with!"

"Adoni," a second courier called, throwing himself down in front of the king. "Commander Natan says he found some militia running and ordered them to stop. They refused. They said their orders were to flee to the hills south of Jezreel if the battle line collapsed!"

"We gave no such orders!" Commander Pasach said, arriving in time to hear the report.

"I'm sure you didn't," Jonathan said, staring at General Abner and Sar Eshbaal as they disappeared into the distance. "I'd say General Abner gave those orders himself." Smiling grimly to himself, he remembered Abner's promise to regain his honor.

"Then the rumors I heard were true," Pasach said softly. "I also heard that Eshbaal joined him in giving them."

"Eshbaal betrayed me?" Shaul said.

"I doubt it, adoni," Jonathan answered. "If you think back, Abner has kept him with him constantly since the last war council. Eshbaal gave those orders under the impression that they were yours."

"We have no one to fight with," Shaul said, looking around blankly.

"Where's Nahshon?" the hassar asked, seeing that only Cheran now attended the king.

"He wasn't here when I got to the top, though Cheran was," the king replied. "What shall we do?"

Jonathan turned quickly. "Commanders, gather as many men as you can. Bring them here. We've got to know who remains and who has gone before we can decide anything!"

"You haven't got time," a familiar voice called, and Jonathan turned to see Ethan running toward him. "The Philistines have sent chariots around the spur! There are six units of archers and swordsmen advancing up these slopes. My men are bringing any commanders and professionals they find up this way. You must move, Hassar! Go east to the higher slopes closer to the summit."

"Run!" Jonathan ordered. "All of us, as fast as we can. We've got enemy advancing up the north slopes, too, so keep an eye that way."

The men scrambled east along the crest of the slope, spurred on by the sight of more chariots on the north side emptying men to climb the slope farther east.

"You won't have to worry overmuch about that side," Ethan said, amusement in his voice even as he ran beside Jonathan. "That bow of yours has been very effective. They've lost too many serens and commanders to mount much of an offensive from there."

"Sars and serens!" Jonathan gasped, suddenly seeing how Yahweh's hand was leading.

Stop, My Bowman. The hassar halted immediately, reaching back for an arrow. Jumping toward the crest, he scanned the north slope below.

"Hassar?" Ethan asked, pausing with him.

"There," Jonathan said, pointing down the slope.

Beside him, Ethan barked like a fox, and instantly every Habiru warrior in hearing darted over.

"Your bows, I think," Ethan said to his men, taking his own. "Down the slope."

More of the professionals and some militia passed them, Malchi hesitating, but Jonathan absently waved him on, his attention below, eyes searching for the shine of his target. He caught a glimpse, and raised the bow.

"Shoot," he ordered Ethan.

All the Habiru warriors responded, and arrows rained down the slope, sending more than one Philistine tumbling, and many more leaping downward to get out of range. Those strong hands guided his a little more to the left, while the Habiru warriors shot again. There! The hassar released, the arrow finding its mark nearly as soon as it left the bow. Giving a death cry, the Philistine fell down the slope, and the entire unit below them fled.

"Come," Jonathan commanded, turning back a little, and running south. The Habiru followed, Libni's unit joining with them.

"They'll come there," Jonathan said quietly, pointing to a watercourse below them. "Wait for my word."

In moments Philistine archers appeared in the watercourse until two units were below them, cautiously making their way upward.

Jonathan drew his arrow again. "Shoot when I release," he ordered.

He let fly, and instantly a hail of arrows flashed after his own. The units below melted. "Again!" he shouted, and another volley instantly followed. When they left moments later, not a man remained standing below them.

They raced back east toward the higher ground, stopping twice to fire on archers scrambling up the slopes after them, and collecting another Israelite army unit on the way.

"Here you are," Ishvi said as they raced up. "Abbi refused to go on without you."

"What's on the north side?" Jonathan asked, trying to catch his breath.

"Nothing. We seem to be beyond their archers."

"You're out of the circle, then," Ethan said. "What's that?" he asked, pointing south.

"Looks like Philistines," Caleb replied.

Go down to them, My Bowman. "We should introduce ourselves," Jonathan said drily, advancing down the slope. "Malchi, take some units and get on that side of the watercourse," he called, pointing. "Ishvi, stay on this side."

Once again the Habiru waited with him while Philistines filed up the watercourse, hurrying along. Three units this time, the hassar estimated, an arrow ready to draw the bowstring. His target came last, and he waited until the man was nearly even with him, then drew and let fly all in one motion. As if the man's scream was a signal, arrows rained down from both sides of the watercourse, and after two more volleys, dead and dying filled the streambed.

As they scrambled back up the ridge, Jonathan glanced at the sun. The fifth hour. It seemed like more time than that had passed. Then Nimshi suddenly appeared, running as hard as he could. "Abbi! Geber!" he shouted. "The Philistines are using the chariots to bring more men! And they've lined the bottom of the north slope with units of militia!"

Jonathan and Ethan glanced at each other. "And I was hoping for a rest during the heat of the day," the Habiru said in disgust.

Chapter 33

I sighed. Our plan had several inevitable weak points, but it couldn't be helped. I simply didn't have enough men. After explaining what we planned to do, I ordered everyone to get into position, reminding them we wouldn't attack until the heat of the day had passed, having learned our lesson on the trip down here.

Cautiously, my men started down the sides of the depression again, using as much cover as they could find. I had Zelek and Ithmah the Moabite with me. We were nearly halfway down when Ithmah pointed.

"Adoni, there's a tent that collapsed."

As I turned to look, an arrow hissed by, burying itself in the ground just above me.

"Archers! Take cover!" Jonathan ben Shagay yelled from off to the side, his warning echoed by someone on the other side of the depression. Frantically, we plunged down the hillside, arrows raining around us. Zelek cried out and fell. Ithmah and I both dived to the ground, dragging him with us to the shelter of a palm tree, where a tent a little way away blocked us from view.

We had barely settled ourselves when the tent swayed, and then slowly folded up, settling to the ground. Leaving Zelek behind the tree, Ithmah and I dived away to either side. Ithmah sheltered behind a rock, and I landed in a small depression barely large enough to hide my stretched-out body.

What view I had around a small rock revealed tent after tent settling to the ground, leaving a few strategically placed ones with clear fields of fire, the warriors in them shooting arrows through slits cut into the tent walls.

I knew that Zelek must not be the only one of my men wounded and also realized that we had just lost any advantage of mobility. The last glimpse I'd had around the depression had been of most of my men plunging down to the edge of camp. But two units on the east end of camp had gone up the hill again, not down, so they were the only men now able to move. The rest of us were securely pinned down by those archers.

What had happened? Then I sighed. Someone must have seen my men withdraw and investigated. There were enough dead men throughout the camp to tell the tale of what we'd been doing. And someone still alive was a highly intelligent fighter. He'd managed a very effective trap for us, allowing them to use the weapon they were most skilled with, while still remaining trapped themselves.

To my left, Asahel suddenly dashed from the shelter of a rock, his speed unexpected enough that he made it to the shelter of a tent at the edge of camp ahead of the arrows that followed him. "Are you all right, Dodi?" he asked loudly enough for me to hear.

"Yes, just disgusted!" I replied. "Do you know how they collapsed the tents?"

"Loosened some ropes and attached another to the appropriate tent pole. They strung that rope back to the one they were in so that it could be pulled when they wanted a tent to fall."

"Asahel," someone called from up above.

I twisted my body around to look behind me.

Ahiam stood above, signaling to us.

"What's he saying?" I asked unable to get a good view.

"Two units not pinned down. Six wounded. Half the units have adequate cover. What do we do?" my nephew interpreted.

Thinking, I eased back down. The sun beat against me, promising even more heat. "We wait," I decided. "Tend to the wounded as best we can. We'd be fools to attack in the face of those archers. When night comes, we'll have the advantage again."

Asahel signaled my decision, and I ducked my head again, knowing that I'd made a major mistake planning this attack. I'd done exactly what I'd warned Eleazar of earlier today. I'd gone into battle without an open line of retreat. And even though the coming of night would give us the advantage again, thirst would drain us during the long hours of waiting, and my men were already exhausted from the exertion and lack of sleep during the past two days. By the time dusk arrived, we'd be in as bad a shape as the Amalekites. And there were more of them. "Yah, cover my error," I whispered. "Give us strength when we need it. Bring Your word to pass."

Scooping sand from the depression I had taken refuge in, I made it deeper and found a cooler layer of soil beneath. Then I got as comfortable as I could to wait out the heat of the hours just after noon.

"And Yah, may I never meet up with this man when he's not sick!" I muttered to myself.

¥ ¥ ¥ ¥ ¥ ¥

Holding the twisted brass earring, Hassar Jonathan glanced around. Dara was resting while he could in the shade from the hot noon sun, with Nimshi not far away. Ethan was examining his bowstring and counting arrows. They were halfway up the gentler south slope of a hill cut into a triangle by watercourses. The north side at their backs was much steeper, and enough trees covered the slope ahead of them to provide adequate cover and, at the same time, give them a good field of fire. Their battle line stretched about a thousand feet, and they barely had the men to cover it.

Jonathan, with the king behind him, was at the east end, deliberately so, since east was still the best way for Shaul to escape. Ishvi was farther down, and a little below, with Malchi on the west again, the first and second units gathered around him. The hassar's heart ached at the losses they had sustained out on the plain. The battle line had been too far from the hills, and the units were only remnants of what they had been, with only Ram, Libni, and Pasach remaining to command them. Natan had fallen somewhere back there, as had too many others. The Habiru had lost three men, something they could ill afford.

Suddenly curious, Jonathan turned to Ethan. "What are you doing here?"

"Fighting Philistines," Ethan replied without looking up from his arrows.

The hassar smiled. "Other than that."

Ethan scooped the arrows up and put them into the quiver, laying it aside. "Oh, I don't know. I just thought you might need some help. I'm getting sentimental in my old age, I guess."

"Old age?"

"I'm in my fifties, like you, Hassar," Ethan reminded him. "Besides, the first battle against Philistines I fought, you were there. It just seemed right that I should fight my last battle against them with you also."

"What do you mean, your first battle?"

The Habiru leader looked over at him, that wry amused smile on his face. "I was there, at Michmash, Hassar. I saw you and Dara climb over the top of that cliff."

"But the Habiru there were hired by the Philistines!"

"Yes, we were, and I didn't like a minute of it, either. We were Yahweh's Arrows, and even though my abbi had hired us out, I kept arguing with him, trying to get him to leave. Then you showed up and started fighting. And after Yahweh joined in with the earthquake, I decided I'd waited long enough for Abbi, and I started after the nearest Philistine."

"That was you!" Dara exclaimed. "You were the one who turned the Habiru against the Philistines!"

"I guess," Ethan said, startled. "I never thought of it that way. I just attacked, and the next thing I knew, everyone else did also."

Jonathan shook his head. "Yahweh does indeed work in strange ways. It seems Michmash was the beginning of a great deal for both of us."

"It was, Hassar."

"You don't have to stay," Jonathan added after a short silence. "Dahveed needs all the help he can get."

Ethan's lips twitched. "Dahveed doesn't need me so much as he does Jamin and Nimshi. He's got Jamin. But do what you can to save Nimshi," he added softly, jerking his chin to where his youngest son rested with his eyes closed.

"I will," the hassar promised, stuffing the earring and chain into his girdle. "But I will not survive this day, Ethan."

The Habiru shrugged. "Neither will I, Hassar, and Hassarah Ruth knew it."

"She had some last words for you?"

"Not directly. She told Dahveed's brother Shammah that when all Five Cities gathered at Aphek, Yahweh would have need of us one last time on the south slopes of Gilboa's spur. Shammah told me what she'd said the day we buried her. We have been here since Shaul arrived at En-harod."

"You have certainly been useful today. But you don't have to die, Ethan."

The Habiru turned to look him in the eye. "You can't get rid of us that easily, Hassar. We are Yahweh's Arrows. We go where He sends us. It is our honor to die with Yahweh's Bowman."

Jonathan glanced down at the sleek, beautiful bow waiting for him to pick it up again. "No, Ethan. It is my honor to die beside his Arrows."

"They are coming, adoni," one of Natan's men called from the streambed below.

As the hassar picked up the bow and slung the quiver over his shoulder, the sound of the arrows rattling in it roused Dara. "Let's not give away our position by yelling," Jonathan said. "We don't want to attract reinforcements."

His orders quickly spread down the line as the men positioned themselves. The Habiru went down the hill, concealing themselves behind the oaks, sycamores, and pines dotting the hillside, some of them finding hollows and spiny broom to shield them, another crouching behind a clump of oleander. The column of Philistines advanced from the west, walking on both sides of the streambed, bows and swords at ready.

No one stirred as the column filled the area below.

Notch your arrow, My Bowman. Moving slowly to avoid drawing any attention, the hassar reached back, pulling an arrow from his quiver and notching it in the string. The invisible hands moved his upward a little, and his eye followed the arrow until he saw the now-familiar shine from a helmet. Behind him, he heard the king shift positions a little from the vantage point slightly above. Jonathan waited in the absolute stillness as the helmet came into view, a seren by the looks of him, attended by a young warrior who might be Nimshi's age.

At the last second, the young man hesitated, pulling the seren to the side as Jonathan's arrow left the bow. The seren screamed, clutching his shoulder, and every archer along the Israelite line let fly without a sound.

Nearly a quarter of the Philistine line fell. Jonathan shot again, at a commander directly below him, that arrow tumbling the man over twice before he lay still. More arrows rained down on the line, then followed up the opposite slope as the Philistines ran for the cover of the trees. The Habiru rose from their places, silently charging across the watercourse and up into the trees. The rest of them followed, Jonathan pausing now and then to loose another arrow, and then Dara had the shield on his left, and Shaul's spear flashed in the light on his other side as the king struck down man after man, that strange light shining in his eyes, his face triumphant.

Shouldering the bow, Jonathan pulled his sword, ignoring the black shadows that gathered around the tall man beside him as they fought side by side once again, advancing across the streambed, avoiding the dead as they pushed the Philistines left alive up the ridge. Then a shout rang out, and more Philistines appeared on the top of the ridge. Instantly, they charged down.

"Get the king back!" Jonathan shouted at Cheran.

The fresh swordsmen crashed into the Israelite line, and those that didn't fall were pushed back to the streambed, Israelite blood joining the flow of Philistine blood already there.

Out of the corner of his eye the hassar saw Cheran pulling Shaul up the slope, the Israelites still alive struggling to follow and take what advantage they could from the higher ground.

Then that shine flashed in Jonathan's eyes, and he reached back, his fingers finding one more arrow. Whipping it to the bow, he was guided upward, toward the top of the ridge, as still more archers and swordsmen topped it, sending a searching volley across the watercourse. Dara's shield blocked his view, and he stepped around it, giving himself into the hands that covered his on the bow. The gleam appeared again, and he let fly, the arrow streaking between the trees before finding its mark, the Philistine's scream fading as he fell down the opposite side of the ridge.

Jonathan whirled. "Nimshi!" he yelled.

"Here, geber," the young warrior cried, rushing to him, the case of the bow bound to his back.

Jonathan thrust the bow at him. "Take this. You will know what to do with it. Give this to Dahveed," he added, pulling the earring from his girdle and stuffing it into Nimshi's. "Tell him that I'm placing my death in his hands just as I placed my life!"

"Geber!" Nimshi gasped.

"Take the king east, Nimshi! Go south from the summit, or continue east across the Jordan!"

"But, Geber–"

"For the love you have for me, Nimshi, save Abbi if you can! Go!" He shoved his armor-bearer up the hill, then whirled again, jumping down to join Dara, his sword already in his hand, just in time to meet the crash of bronze against bronze as the Philistine swordsmen smashed their line.

"Ishvi! Ethan! Move them west!" he roared. Then there was time for nothing else but the myriad of swords that pressed around him, striking at him everywhere he turned. He gave ground, shuffling off to his right, drawing the Philistines after him, man after man falling to him and Dara. He connected with Ethan, and the three of them kept pushing west, cutting through anything in their path.

A Philistine backed away, and Jonathan looked down the hillside covered with fighting men, the Habiru warriors clearing off more than their share of Philistines. He couldn't see Ishvi, but Malchi was beyond, still surrounded by the second unit, all of them fighting like demons.

Then Dara was down, and up again, following him, holding the shield to block an arrow before he went down again. The hassar grabbed his belt knife, raising his arm to block the sword coming down on him, and a piercing pain stabbed under his left arm, making him stagger. "Yah, grant Abbi hesed!" he said, and those large, strong hands caught him as he fell.

¥ ¥ ¥ ¥ ¥ ¥

Cheran stood trembling as Shaul backed up, his face gray. The king stumbled east along the hillside until he could see the streambed again. Then he turned dazed eyes to his attendant. "They're dead. They've been killed! My sons are all dead!" His voice rose.

An arrow whistled by, thunking into a tree. With a start, Shaul turned around, looking frantically in every direction.

Cheran grabbed his arm and pulled him back to the little circle of rocks they had found close to the top of the hill. They had retreated here after seeing the hassar send that young warrior up to them, but he had never made it. In his scramble to get to them, he'd slipped on the hillside, and tumbled all the way to the rocks of the streambed and hadn't appeared again. Shortly after that, a unit of Philistines had come up that very streambed, and Cheran knew the young man was now dead. He looked around worriedly, having no idea where to go, or how. The only thing he could think of was to stay here until dark. Then they might be able to slip away.

Another arrow struck the rock, and they ducked down. "Archers," Shaul said, his eyes wild. "The archers have found me!" Shaking, he huddled by one of the small boulders. "They will come. I know they will."

"Maybe not, adoni. They might not get up here." But he didn't believe it, and knew that his voice didn't carry conviction.

"I've—I've been betrayed again," Shaul whispered. "They lied to me! She said they would protect my sons, but they didn't! I turned against Yahweh for nothing! The spirits didn't protect my sons! I cannot go back to Yahweh! I cannot!" He was sobbing now.

The words pierced Cheran's heart. Seeing the hopeless despair of the king, he finally understood what the hassar had said to him earlier. "You have taken all hope from my Abbi." Bitterness welled up in him. The Elohim had betrayed him, too. They were supposed to bring comfort to the king, and they had only led him into despair.

"If my sons are dead—if they didn't protect them—they won't protect me!" the king gasped, his face draining of all color. "I will be taken. There is no one left to help me!" He stared around in terror. "It's just as Shamuel said. It's always been as Shamuel said. And the archers will come!"

Trembling like a poplar leaf, the king hugged himself, twisting this way and that. "They will do terrible things to me," he moaned softly.

"You're not alone, adoni. I'm here," Cheran said, his heart devastated by the king's fear.

Shaul looked at him blankly. "You? Cheran?" Then he got to his knees, his hands pulling the man close. "Kill me. You have a sword. Kill me."

"Adoni, please don't speak so. I can't kill you! I'm no soldier."

Below them, a line of men started creeping up the hill.

"They are coming," Shaul gasped, turning frantically to Cheran. "You must take your sword and kill me! You know what they will do if they find me! They will torture me, and humiliate me, and drag me before their temples and their gods!"

"Cover the whole hillside," the command drifted up to them. "Be careful. There's movement up there!"

Shaul groaned, nearly pulling Cheran to the ground. "You must kill me," he begged. "I can't stand what they will do, how they will abuse me, like they did to Samson—or worse!"

The agony in the king's voice was too much. Tears streaming down his face, Cheran pulled his sword, wishing the feel of it was more familiar, that he knew where to strike to give the least pain. His hand shook so badly that he could hardly hold it.

"Yes, kill me!" Shaul ordered.

But the armor-bearer found himself unable to even lift the sword. "Adoni, I can't. You are the king, Yahweh's Mashiah. I dare not!"

Shaul slumped back, despair on his face.

"Over that way!" the voice called out.

Looking wildly around again, Shaul pulled his own sword. "They won't have me," he said feverishly, still on his knees. "There is nothing left for me anyway." He reversed the blade, fitted the point under the bronze bands of the cuirass and threw himself forward, driving the sword into his heart.

Cheran bent down in horror as Shaul rolled into his legs, blood dripping through the cuirass. "Adoni! Adoni," he sobbed, cradling the king in his arms as the man died. He eased the king's body to the ground. What should he do? Go back to Naphtali and his home with the knowledge that he had been the one to tell Shaul of En-dor, bringing his final fear on the adon he had tried to serve? Maybe if he hadn't told him of that medium, maybe the king would have turned to Yahweh at last, and this battle would have had a different ending. He sat a few moments longer. As the sun's slanting rays found the boulders, he picked up his sword and followed his adon's actions, joining him in death.

¥ ¥ ¥ ¥ ¥ ¥

"Dodi!" a voice said.

Groggily opening my eyes, I tried to pull away from the dream that clung to me of blood under the trees on a hillside, and dark shadows surrounding it.

"Dodi!"

A pebble hit my head, and I moved my hand.

"Stay down!" the voice reminded me.

That woke me up. I glanced around. In spite of everything, I must have slept. My mouth was thick with thirst, and I had to squint in the slanting rays of the sun.

"Elhanan says the Amalekites are moving about the camp," Asahel said from behind the tent he used as cover.

"Are our men ready?" I asked, trying to shift myself around to discover which of my stiff muscles would still respond.

My nephew glanced back up the hill. Elhanan was in view and signaling something. "He says everyone is ready."

"Tell him that if the Amalekites try to run, we attack," I said, barely able to get my voice to work since my throat was so dry. "Otherwise we wait for dark, and then we attack." I peered around the rock again toward the center of camp, just in time to see the tent flaps fly open, and the Amalekite warriors rush out, all of them headed east.

"Attack!" I yelled, lunging off the ground. "After them!"

I dived behind a standing tent as three archers turned toward me, loosing arrows. A battle cry surged from my men as they left their positions, charging after the enemy. But the flight had been so sudden that our response was ragged at best.

Ithmah appeared beside me, and we ran after the raiders, Zaavan urging his men on with hoarse shouts. Arrows whistled through the air, the Amalekites shooting them on the run, and I heard two more of my men cry out. The enemy made it to the east edge of camp, breaking through our circle at the exact spot we had no units waiting and where the hill was least steep. They fled up it, and Ithmah paused, taking aim, picking off one of the warriors climbing the slope.

"Archers! Men of Benjamin! Take them!" I roared.

Eleazar and Abiezer, with their men, charged from the Geshurite tents directly into the flank of the Amalekite line, cutting it in two. Ithmah and I plunged into the fight. I realized my sling was hanging from my hand, but had no memory of using it. Whipping it around my arm a couple times, I pulled my sword, and an Amalekite turned at bay. We sparred briefly, but there was no power in his blows, and he stumbled nearly every step he took. I closed with him, knocking his sword aside, and bringing my blade into the side of his neck.

When he fell, I darted on, stabbing into the back of another Amalekite, one of three pressing one of my men back. An arrow knocked the leg from under the next one, and I plunged my belt knife into him, silencing his scream of pain. The third fell to my man's sword, Joab, I realized with surprise. Then Naharai appeared on my nephew's other side.

"Go, Dahveed," the Gibeonite yelled, gesturing toward the rim of the hill.

Amalekites were disappearing over it, and I charged forward, collecting Hiddai and Eliphelet on my way. The thief was using a javelin he'd picked up, and I couldn't tell if he thought he had a sword or a spear, but he killed three Amalekites with it as I watched, acting as if he'd never been afraid of the sight of blood in his life!

"Come with me," I ordered, shouting in his ear.

His face was white and still as he followed. Hiddai grabbed Ben-Shimei, and we plunged through the fight and up the slope, Ithmah bringing up the rear, shooting a stream of arrows over our heads.

We burst over the rim to see Elhanan and Uzzia's units trying to stop the stream of Amalekites. I paused to assess the situation. Somehow, Zaavan had gotten a few of his men outside of camp, and they had saddled camels waiting!

"Pull back!" I yelled. "Let them go!" Once the raiders got on those camels, my men would be clear targets from their elevated positions. We would just have to leave the results of this battle to Yahweh. "Elhanan! Uzzia! Pull back! Let them go!" I repeated.

Reluctantly, my men obeyed, panting as they watched the Amalekites scramble onto the beasts and urge them to their feet. Zaavan turned back, and for a moment, I thought he would order a charge on us. Then the Benjamite archers appeared behind us, loosing a volley. Two of his men fell from that, and several camels bawled in pain.

With a cry of rage, the Amalekite turned his animal toward the desert, and all the camels strode away, enough arrows following them that they quickly broke into a lope, their heads down, riders leaning forward as they fled across the dry grass of the plain in the deepening dusk.

I turned back to Eliphelet, who held that javelin as if he still intended to use it. "I see you found that you could fight," I said impassively.

He stared balefully after the retreating warriors. "They touched the Gebirah," my personal thief said, his voice savage. "No one touches the Gebirah!"

Chapter 34

Day Seven

Akish cursed, staring at the bodies now touched by the morning sun and lining the streambed. "How many did you say were here?" he asked Ittai savagely, leaning heavily on a spear, his right arm bound to his side.

"Three full units, Dodi. Gadmilk's by the looks of them," his nephew replied calmly.

"And where is that cursed valley where I got wounded?"

"Farther east about a mile."

"Seren!" A courier came panting up to him. "We've found another ambush! Two units of archers and one of swordsmen."

The ruler of Gath looked bitterly down at the helmet the messenger gave him. It had his own crest on it. No wonder he couldn't find his archers last night. When he threw the helmet down in rage, pain exploded from his shoulder, making him gasp and sway.

"Dodi, you should be resting," Ittai said, his voice worried.

"Not yet," his uncle snarled. "There's too much to do. Take a unit, and strip the dead back there," he ordered the messenger. "Bury however many we can."

"Yes, Seren," the man said, jogging away.

Leaving another unit to attend to the watercourse, Ittai helped Akish back onto the mule, and they returned to the hill where the seren had been wounded. As they rounded the corner of the streambed, the scene of death opened before them. "Dagon, help us!" Akish exclaimed. "Did anyone survive?"

"Not many," Ittai replied, his face white.

A cry rose from above them, and they turned that way.

"Seren! It's Seren Baalyaton! He's dead!"

"How?"

"Arrow."

"All the way up there?" Akish asked, looking puzzled. "Bring it!" he ordered.

While they waited, the two units left with them spread out, turning over a body here or there, trying to see what had happened, drifting west down the streambed. Ittai led the mule toward the opposite slope, keeping a good hold on the bridle, for the animal did not like the smell of death one bit.

"Seren, here is the arrow," a soldier said, walking up to them and holding it out.

Akish took it and nearly dropped it. "It's exactly the same as the one that hit me," he spat. He turned to the soldier. "Spread the word, here and out on the plain. I want every arrow that looks like this, and I want to know where they were found."

"Yes, Seren," the man said, taking the arrow with him. Before he'd gone very far, he stopped, looking down. "Here's another one."

"Take it," Akish said, his face grim.

Ittai guided the mule a little farther, then Akish slid off to join him. Rolling a dead soldier over, his nephew paused a moment before kneeling down, his face white.

"What?" Akish asked.

"Just someone I knew," Ittai said softly. He unfastened something, rising with a black mantle in his hands that he folded carefully before moving on. He stopped again and bowed his head, tears coming from his eyes.

"You'd better hope the men with us think those tears are for our side," Akish warned in a low voice.

"I'm sorry, Dodi. But he was a good man. You would have liked him."

"Who?" Akish said, staring at the bodies around him.

"Hassar Israel," Ittai said, pointing.

"Liked him?" Akish said, walking forward to stare down bitterly at the dead man. "I'd rather kick him!" He drew back his foot, and then cried out, seizing his shoulder and nearly falling.

Once again Ittai supported him. "Do no despite to the dead, Dodi, and maybe Yahweh will let you live. You would have liked him," he repeated. "I did."

Akish said nothing more, watching his nephew go from body to body with a purpose now.

"What are you looking for?"

"If the hassar is here, so are the others."

"Shaul, too?"

"Most likely."

"Seren, you must come," another man said, his face white. "You have to see this."

Back on the mule again, Akish followed the soldier west.

"There," Ittai said. "That's probably Sar Ishvi." They stopped to move the body aside. The side of his helmet was caved in from a sling stone, and by his side lay a young man, still clutching a shield, a sword wound in his back.

Continuing on, they rounded the bend in the streambed and halted in disbelief. Everywhere they looked, the dead stared back. The men who had found the place simply stood, unwilling to disturb anything.

Sliding off the mule again, the seren followed Ittai as the young man respectfully picked his way along. His nephew paused to pull back another body. A quick sob shook him, and he moved on, coming at last to a rock protruding from the hillside ringed by the dead. He had to shift several bodies before he found the one underneath and stepped back.

"Who were these men?" Akish asked in awe.

"Shaul's son Malchi, and the Sar's Own Unit," Ittai said, his voice shaking.

Clutching his shoulder, Akish looked around again. "We must have lost four units just here! They were some of our best, too. Those crests are from Ashdod. And there's Ashkelon."

"Seren! Seren," another courier shouted.

"By the Elohim, what now?" Akish nearly groaned.

"The men went up the hill. They think they've found the Israelite king!"

"What do you mean 'think'?"

"There wasn't any headband or armband like you told us to watch for, but it looks as if he should have one on, and he's tall enough to be Shaul."

Ittai's eyes closed a moment, and he swayed. "Dodi, may we leave?"

"Yes," Akish said, gripping his shoulder. "We'll go now."

¥ ¥ ¥ ¥ ¥ ¥

The sun was low in the sky when Shagay jogged back to me. "We're at the Besor," he said, shaking his head in wonder. "Dahveed, I don't know how that Egyptian does it. He acts as though there's a boundary stone at every mile telling him exactly where he is. I can take you east, west, north, or south, but I think Khay could take you to any particular tamarisk tree you asked for!"

"Maybe he can. He's been in this desert for a long time, you know. How's his strength?"

"We finally got him to ride a donkey. But only because I threatened to get Uzzia to carry him again. He's terrified of losing your protection."

I looked back down the long line of people and laden animals following along behind me. I was very glad I had listened to Uriah back there at the oasis, for with the huge herd of animals and caravan of spoils, most of my men were working at their limit just keeping everything in line. We simply couldn't have guarded the women and children while trying to defeat the large number of raiders at the same time. The final portion of the trip back to Ziklag tomorrow would be easier, since I'd have the rest of my men to help. We'd need those we had left behind at Besor, for those with me were nearly dropping now in spite of the sleep we'd had last night.

As many warriors as I had with me had fled with Zaavan, and we had to let them go, too exhausted to do anything else. After we had returned to camp, I found my men going through everything, making sure the Amalekites were dead. Once that was done, we were too tired to properly appreciate the welcome we received from our families, and all of us simply lay down and slept.

Irad had set some of the captives as guards, and sent Casluh out with the other youth to collect any animals that had wandered off. Ahinoam and Abigail organized the women to tend our wounded and go through the camp, collecting and packing spoils. By the time we woke this morning, a meal had been waiting, and all the spoils had been packed and loaded on the animals. As before, we did not strip the slain, but folded them into the tents, dragged them into piles, and set them ablaze.

Even now, I could make out the thin column of smoke still rising on the horizon. Increasing my pace, I advanced up the line until I reached its head, where Khay rode, the darker green of the trees lining the Besor visible on our right.

"Will we be back at our previous camp tonight?" I asked, coming up beside the slave.

His head jerked around to see me, and his face paled. "Adoni! Do not be angry with me," he gasped. "They made me ride! I didn't want to! I wouldn't!" He tried to dismount, confusing the donkey so that it bobbed its head in protest.

I put my hand on Khay's arm, stopping him. The way he instantly stilled at my touch reminded me of the way Manani's slaves had acted when we first caught them. "Stay on," I ordered. "Your strength is too valuable to waste walking."

The donkey had gone several paces before Khay started to tremble. "Yes, adoni."

"How long has it been since you drank?"

"When we watered the animals, adoni," he said nervously.

"Why haven't you had something since then?"

The Egyptian slave looked at me, hunching his shoulders a little. "I wouldn't take water from you, adoni, or anyone else! Please, I know my place!"

The donkey carried a cruse of water, and I untied it, holding it out to Khay as I walked.

"What is your wish, adoni?" he asked without looking at it.

"Take the cruse."

He did, still keeping his eyes away.

"That's your cruse. I'm giving it to you now. It holds your water, which is there for you to drink whenever you want."

Khay said nothing for a while, but he trembled again. "Adoni, what am I to do with this?" he finally asked.

I shrugged. "That's for you to decide. If it were me, I'd probably tie it on my girdle so I wouldn't lose it, but if you prefer to hold it, that's your choice." Then I noticed that he still wore rags, and the rope he used for a girdle would probably break if he tied that cruse to it.

"Or, you could tie it back on the donkey. Right up there in front so you can get it easily. Will there be water in the Besor for the animals?"

"There's a large pool not far from here," he said, dazed. "The animals can drink there. The camp is just half a mile west of that. There should also be enough for the animals to drink before we leave tomorrow." While he talked, I noticed that he drew the cruse close to his side.

"Very good, Khay." I fell back again, keeping an eye on him, but it was some time before he drank.

¥ ¥ ¥ ¥ ¥ ¥

"That can't be right," Muwana of Ashkelon said, his face white. "Surely there's something wrong with those numbers."

"They are accurate," Akish said. "I checked them myself."

The sun had nearly set, and he stood by the bed where Muwana lay in the governor's palace at Beth-shean. Wounded in the left hip, the seren could hardly move for the pain. As soon as he'd walked into the room, Akish's eyes had riveted on the arrow lying on the table. But he had said nothing about it, however.

"Forty?" the man said. "That's, that's nearly every seren and sar we have!" When he tried to move, he groaned and clenched his teeth. "What does Baalyaton say?"

"He's dead. So are Gadmilk and Hanabaal. I have two serens left alive, and there are three of yours from Ashkelon that I've found so far. It wouldn't surprise me if all the others are dead. As far as sars go, two from Hanabaal have reported, three of yours, none from Ekron or Ashdod, and I've only heard from one of mine. I've heard a rumor that another may be alive, but I don't know."

Muwana looked so pale that Akish decided not to break the news that every one of the dead sars and serens had been killed with the same arrows, and he knew that meant the same bowman. Ittai had called him Yahweh's Bowman, and Akish privately agreed.

He could still see the fleeting streak of blinding light as his nephew had pulled him to one side, and then the overwhelming slash of burning pain that had seared into him, sending him spinning to the ground screaming as he never had in his life. Even now, the wound burned despite everything done for it.

"What about our professionals and militia?" Muwana asked.

"We lost all of our best archers and swordsmen, most of them on the south side of the spur. That's in addition to the numbers killed on the plain. The Israelites fought better than we expected there. As for militia, about what we expected. A quarter of them or so."

"By Dagon, any more victories like this, and the Israelites will occupy our cities," the seren from Ashkelon spat out.

Akish said nothing, remembering Ittai's prediction that the battle would end in unexpected ways.

"So the only good news is that we found the bodies of Shaul and his sons?"

"Shaul and three of them, Seren. Apparently the youngest was not here. And there is no sign of General Abner."

"If that snake got away, we can never rest easy! Well, at least we can teach the Israelites a lesson. Hang the bodies on the city wall by the gates! And take Shaul's armor to the temple of Dagon in Ashdod. His head, too. Finally we'll be avenged for Goliath's head," the seren added bitterly. "We have to have something to show for this battle!"

"Seren, is that wise?" Akish said slowly. "This may only stiffen the Israelite resolve to resist us, and we have little to control them with now."

"Precisely why we must make a show of strength," Muwana snapped, then ground his teeth together, going rigid with pain.

"Doing despite to Yahweh's dead may not be wise."

"Yahweh certainly left them to us yesterday. Let Dagon worry about Yahweh. I want those bodies on the wall by sundown!" Then his face went white, and he gasped again. "See to it," he ordered the guard.

"Yes, Seren."

Silently Akish withdrew, clutching his shoulder, barely making it back to the room he stayed in before collapsing.

¥ ¥ ¥ ¥ ¥ ¥

The sun had nearly set when I had time to leave camp, making my way to the three wells the desert tribes had dug not far away. Ahinoam had found some clothes for me to give to Khay.

The fact that he wasn't around puzzled me, for I knew he had come this way. Hearing some splashing sounds, I wandered behind some boulders sheltering a shrub or two. There I found Khay's rags first and then saw him washing himself off. He was about the same height as my nephew Joab, but more slender, and a few scars testified to previous abuse. I'd heard that Egyptians bathed frequently, and seeing him doing it now after all these years away from his home made me believe it.

When he was done, he reached for his rags.

"Don't bother," I said softly. "Use this." I handed him a cotton loincloth.

He jumped, whirling around to face me, then quickly averted his face, flushing.

"You need to take it," I added after a moment or two. "If I drop it on the ground, it will get dirty, and you've just washed."

After he accepted it, I turned my back, getting the other clothes while he put it on. Giving him the undergarment, I waited while he donned that. When I handed him a robe, he looked stunned. Once he was in that, I brought out the girdle, made from thin leather that Parai had tanned and sewn together. The supple material molded easily to his waist as I wrapped it around him and tied it on.

"Where's that cruse?" I asked.

He reached down and picked it up from underneath the rags. I tied it onto the girdle and stepped back. "Ahinoam has probably found sandals for you by now. Shall we return to camp?"

Khay didn't move, his hands slowly stroking the robe he wore. "Adoni, these are not clothes fit for a slave," he said, looking at me puzzled.

"They are not on a slave. If it were not for you, we would still be wandering around this land looking for our families. Given how much you have returned to us, the least I can do is give you back your freedom."

"What do I do for you in return?"

"You've already done your part. Now I'm doing mine," I replied patiently.

"Where do you want me to go?"

"It might be best if you returned to the camp with me and stayed for a while. Once you're used to things, you can decide what you want to do."

"Yes, adoni," he said absently, his hands feeling the girdle now.

"Khay?"

He looked up.

"We are grateful," I said, bowing slightly. Then I turned and left. Before not too long, I heard his footsteps behind me. "Adoni?"

I paused. "Yes?"

"What god do you worship?"

"Yahweh. What made you ask?"

He clutched the cruse nervously. "You are used to the wild places, adoni, the places where the gods dwell. I thought you might—" He stopped.

"Tell me, Khay," I said gently.

"I thought maybe you worshipped El Shaddai. He is of the desert. You could not worship Qas!" he added, shuddering.

"Yahweh is El Shaddai's personal name," I said, walking on again.

I didn't have long to wonder about Khay's questions, for I could hear voices raised in argument in the camp, and I hurried forward. I saw Hiddai and Ben-Shimei confronting Elika, Shammah, and Gareb, with others gathering around.

"You didn't fight so you don't deserve to have the rewards!" Hiddai snapped.

"That's right," Ben-Shimei added. "You didn't go running around the desert in the heat, and have to stay awake all night, then fight the next day after nearly getting killed by archers!"

"We did all the work, we deserve the spoils!" Ahimelek the Hittite put in. Several of the others around him spoke their agreement, and I realized Hiddai's usual crowd had gathered to back him up.

"And the only reason you could go running around was because we stayed behind, guarding all your possessions!" Elika replied angrily. "I lost everything I had in this raid. It should be returned!"

"Well, certainly your wife and family," Hiddai conceded. "But if Akish had rescued you, you wouldn't be asking him to divide up the spoils! They belong to the victor, and that's us!"

"Don't let your greed run away with you, Hiddai, or I'll consider the stuff you left in my care mine now," Igal said, his voice flinty. "And would you take the sheep and goats from the families that need them?"

"The animals are Dahveed's share," Abishai interjected.

"Who decided that?" Ben-Shimei demanded. "You stayed behind like the others! It's not for you to say!"

"The commanders who went decided that," my nephew replied.

"But that's what a ruler like Akish would claim!" Hiddai sputtered.

Abishai turned to him. "Isn't that what Dahveed is?"

"He is as far as I'm concerned," Shagay said, stepping forward.

"We don't call him 'adoni' for nothing," Ahiam added.

"He is the Mashiah, and that means he outranks Shaul," Josheb put in. "So if we treat him as melek, we have reason to. I suggest you remember that," he said, leaning his tall, elegant form on his spear while the Gaddites gathered behind him.

I walked into the firelight. "Dare I say 'Shalom' to you all? What seems to be the problem?"

Hiddai turned to me. "The men who stayed with the baggage are claiming part of the spoils! And they accuse *us* of greed! They can have their families back, but not any of the rest!"

"We fought and got wounded," one of the men behind him added. "That stuff belongs to us! The victory was ours!"

I stepped forward. "Ours?" I said, turning to Hiddai and the rest with him. "Would you take what *Yahweh* has given us and make it an object of contention? If Yah hadn't guided us, prepared the way before us, and fought with us, the victory would not have been ours. We were outnumbered and outmaneuvered, and only because He gave the raiders to us, did we win anything at all."

They averted their faces, shifting nervously.

"That being the case, don't expect anyone to listen to this, certainly not me. Once we have returned everyone's possessions, we will divide up what's left equally. I expect everyone to share alike whether they went into battle or stayed with the baggage."

Raising my voice a little, I faced the crowd that had continued to gather. "And in order that this incident will never be repeated, let me state now that this is the way spoils will be divided up from now on. Is my will clear on this?"

"Yes, adoni," everyone said.

¥ ¥ ¥ ¥ ¥ ¥

Rizpah stood perfectly still in the dark courtyard of the house she shared with Hassarah Ahinoam while the courier gasped out his news. "The battle yesterday went against Israel, Hassarah! There were so many Philistines! They drove the army back, and used the chariots to bring more men to follow them into the hills. The army is gone. There is no one left. And the king—the king is dead, Hassarah."

Ahinoam swayed a little, one hand holding her side. "What of the king's sons?" she asked in a low voice.

"They are dead, too," the messenger replied, his voice shaking.

"All of them?" Her voice was drained of all emotion.

"It is said that Sar Eshbaal and General Abner survived, Hassarah. At least their bodies were not found."

A few more questions brought out the totality of the defeat, and then Ahinoam dismissed the courier.

Seeing the stark pain on her face, Rizpah began to shake. Sixteen-year-old Armoni walked toward her, bringing 12-year-old Mephibosheth with him. Armoni was already taller than she was, and looked more like Shaul every day, while her second son resembled her side of the family.

"You must go," the hassarah said, looking up at Rizpah. "With this complete defeat, the Philistines may arrive here at any time. They must not find you and your sons, or Meribbaal either. You have to leave tonight!"

"Where should we go?" As Rizpah hung on to her sons, she could only imagine how Ahinoam's arms must ache now that her sons were dead.

Shaul's widow took a deep breath. "Go to Barzillai in Jabesh first. He can shelter and protect Meribbaal. Your abbi is still alive, right?"

"Yes, Sahrah."

"We must pack something," Ahinoam said, her voice trembling as she turned toward the house.

Rizpah straightened. "Armoni, get a mule and go to Hassar Jonathan's estate in Zelah. Tell Peleth and Judith what has happened, and that Judith should bring Meribbaal to the crossroads where the Gibeon road meets the Jebus highway up to Bethel. We will wait there for her. Be sure she understands that we must cross the Jordan tonight."

"Yes, Immi," her son said, hurrying away.

"Mephibosheth, go find the donkey cart and hitch the donkey. By the time you return, Ahinoam and I should have our things ready."

As her youngest ran off, Rizpah went to the house. She had to try to convince Ahinoam to come with her. But the hassarah never gave her the time to say anything, working feverishly to get together what they needed.

In very little time they had some food and changes of clothing packed and loaded on the cart. Armoni returned with the assurance that Judith would meet them. As her oldest son led the donkey out of the courtyard gate, Rizpah turned to Ahinoam. "Come with us. The king is dead."

The older woman's lips trembled. "Yes, the king is dead. And for that very reason, my place is here, with the people of Gibeah. Your responsibility is to save the king's seed."

With no further protest, Rizpah bowed. "As you wish, Hassarah. Yahweh keep you, and all here."

"Yahweh keep you, also, baalah."

As Rizpah turned down the street outside the house, she heard the hassarah's bitter sobbing as Shaul's widow mourned.

Once outside Gibeah's gates, Armoni kept the donkey at a trot, and they hurried south toward the crossroads two and a half miles away. Once there, they guided the donkey off the road and settled down to wait, knowing that Judith and Meribbaal had a mile further to travel than they did.

But sooner than Rizpah expected, they heard the clop of donkey hooves approaching through the darkness from the west, and Judith appeared, practically dragging a donkey behind her as she rushed toward them.

"Didn't you bring anything?" Rizpah asked, seeing only 5-year-old Meribbaal on the donkey.

"I didn't want to miss you," the servant gasped. "Peleth is packing some things and will follow after us, but we must get Meribbaal to safety. Since he's Jonathan's son, the Philistines will want him especially. They hate the hassar so!"

"Put him on the cart, then. You won't have to worry about balancing him on the donkey, and we can go faster."

Hastily Judith grabbed the bewildered child, lifting him off the donkey and turning to the cart. But he began to squirm in her arms, then slipped from her grip just as she was stretching toward the cart. He landed hard, feet first, and as they twisted underneath him, he tumbled sideways, screaming.

Judith instantly picked him up and held his face against her chest to muffle his cries.

"Hush, now, little one," she said anxiously, rocking him a little. But that only seemed to make him cry harder. No matter what they did, Meribbaal continued to wail, and Rizpah glanced up at the stars. They were losing too much time.

"Armoni, pack some of the bundles on the other donkey. Judith will have to ride and hold Meribbaal. But we must go."

Once the rearrangements were made, they helped Judith onto the cart, where she cradled Jonathan's son against her, and they started east, the road quickly descending into the steep defiles that led down to the Arabah and the Jericho fords.

It wasn't until daylight and they were across the Jordan, that they discovered both of Meribbaal's now swollen ankles had broken from the fall.

Chapter 35

Day Eight

We'd gotten an early start from Besor to avoid the heat and had covered the 15 miles north to Ziklag by noon. On the way, I finally had the time to talk with Ahinoam and Abigail and hear their story of what happened.

Hanan met us a mile from the town, stepping out onto the road as I passed. He started to greet me, then his head swivelled around, and he stared at Khay who walked not far behind me.

"He's called Khay," I said, smiling a little.

I expected that the Egyptian would be uncomfortable under Hanan's stare, but to my surprise, he returned it, his head coming up, and he smiled, the first one I'd seen from him.

Hanan cocked his head, then disappeared to take the news of our triumphant return to the men waiting with the ark. Gad and Beriah remained at the ruined gate, but Abiathar hurried anxiously down the road toward us.

"What's the matter with the hakkohen?" I asked.

Ahinoam watched him a moment. "I don't know."

He barely looked at me as he bowed briefly, his head swiveling around, trying to look every place at once. "Jotbah?" he called.

The Gebirah's handmaid stepped from the line. "Abiathar?"

The hakkohen walked toward her. "Thank, Yahweh! You are all right? Did anything happen?"

"No," she replied, looking down, her rather plain face lit with a smile. "Yahweh protected us all."

When Abiathar opened his arms, she threw herself into them, sobbing hysterically.

Shouts and cheers broke from everyone around, and people began asking when we would have the wedding. Both the hakkohen and the handmaid ignored them, walking away and clinging to each other.

I looked around at the ruined town, which suddenly looked very good to me. We were home. All of us, and there would soon be a wedding to rejoice at. Yahweh had given hesed to us all.

"What do we do now, Dodi?" Abishai asked, approaching me.

I glanced up at the sun. "It's noon. Get some food out, we'll eat a little, and rest. Then we will begin to rebuild."

I spent the afternoon answering questions. Ahinoam and Abigail assumed charge of everything connected with the spoils, taking Abishai away from me at the same time, and absolutely forbidding any other man to approach the many bundles spread out on the ground.

Taking the opportunity to put everyone else to work, I sent the married men from the town into it with Eleazar, telling them to see what repairs must be done for each house. All the other men accompanied me down the road toward Gerar. We must dispose of the bodies left by the Amalekites.

The sight was sickening enough as it was, and I was profoundly grateful that Shagay and Jonathan had prevented us from coming here when we thought the bodies were those of our loved ones. After we dug a large mass grave, we carefully placed the remains into it. The fire had been well started and had burned for some time, so most of what we moved were bones. Then we heaped dirt over it, placing a cairn of stones on the top.

Sending the men back to Ziklag, I took Josheb and Gad with me to the settlement a mile or two on. It was deserted, but many of the houses had hardly been damaged at all.

"What are you thinking?" my third retainer asked.

"The Cherethites and other captives. Their men are all fighting with Akish, so the women and children have no one to provide for them. From what Ahinoam and Abigail told me, their homes were destroyed in the raids. I thought they should stay here. They are close enough that we can protect them until the men return."

"We should send some guards with them," Gad suggested. "They'll need someone to keep Hiddai and his crowd away."

Smiling sourly, I headed back to Ziklag.

By the time I returned, families had reclaimed their possessions. The animals had been divided into those claimed by someone and those without any owner, which the people insisted would be set aside for me. I wasn't sure what to do with them all, but when I tried to refuse, Abigail shook her head, the look in her eye telling me she had an idea. So I said nothing more.

That evening, after Abiathar had offered a thank offering for all of us, and one for me personally, I got out the harp, which Ahinoam had found the night they re-packed the spoils and had kept close by her since. As I oiled it, I found the gouge on the bottom where it had probably hit a sharp rock or something. But the small hole hadn't gone all the way through the wood, so it did not affect the sound. I filled it with a bit of pitch, oiled it well, and smoothed it even with the bottom.

 I played, and we rejoiced and sang late into the night, thanking Yahweh for His care for us.

¥ ¥ ¥ ¥ ¥ ¥

 It was so late, and she was so tired, that Rizpah wasn't even certain she was knocking at the correct gate.
 "What is your business here?" a rough male voice asked.
 "We come seeking Adon Barzillai. Is this his house?"
 "It is," the voice replied cautiously.
 "Please, tell him that his cousin's son is here."
 Footsteps receded behind the gate, and Rizpah leaned against the cart. The donkey stood with its head down, and she suspected Mephibosheth was more asleep than awake as he hung onto the second donkey's pack. Meribbaal had finally fallen asleep in spite of his pain, and Rizpah doubted whether Judith would ever forgive herself for dropping the boy.
 At last the gate opened, and a torch shone in her face.
 "Adon Barzillai?" she asked, trying to straighten up.
 "Rizpah? Rizpah bat Aiah, what are you doing here?" the adon gasped, pulling the gate open all the way. "When the news came that Shaul had died in the battle, I wondered if you would come, but I didn't expect you until tomorrow at least!"
 "We left as soon as we could, adon. Meribbaal would be a prize much sought after by Jonathan's enemies. May we enter?"
 "Of course! Your sudden appearance has addled my wits. Come in at once! What a journey you must have had to get here so quickly!"
 "We need a healer, too," Rizpah added as they passed through the gate. "Meribbaal is injured. Please send for one right away. We must get everything unloaded, and—"
 "And you are going to rest," Barzillai said, looking at her keenly. "I've my wits about me again, baalah, so don't worry about anything."
 As the calm voice issued orders, she let herself be led to the side and seated on a cushion. Then she looked around. They were here,

and safe, and someone else would make the decisions for a while. And Shaul was dead. She put her hands over her face and started to cry.

Day Nine

Dawn had barely broken when Rizpah awakened. She stared around at the unfamiliar room for a moment before memory returned and the weight of sorrow for those lost crashed back onto her. She got stiffly up from the bedroll, her entire body aching from the strain of the hurried journey. The cool air outside welcomed her, and she got some water from the jar by the door, wiping off her face and trying to smooth back her hair.

Perhaps Peleth would arrive today with Judith's child and the things for Meribbaal. She hoped so. The servant needed her child right now, having sobbed herself to sleep after the healer left just a couple hours ago. The woman had straightened Meribbaal's ankles as best she could while the young child shrieked in agony, and then bound them up. But there was no way to disguise the fact that Meribbaal would never be able to walk normally on them again.

After dosing the young boy with poppy, the healer had slipped some of the soporific into Judith's wine, and it was only that, Rizpah knew, that had finally eased the woman's frantic remorse enough for her to sleep.

As the house woke up around her, Rizpah realized that Adriel and his five boys were here also. He brought her some of the bread and parched grain to break her fast, and she ate slowly, not certain yet that she really wanted to.

"Did Sahrah Michal come here also?" she asked after she'd eaten a little.

Adriel shook his head. "No. I tried to get her to. She had brought the boys back up here after the army left, you know, and planned on staying a while. But as soon as she heard the news, she left for Gibeah."

"Good. Ahinoam needs her."

"It's a good thing she left," Adriel said in a low voice. "I don't know what she would have done if she'd seen what they did at Beth-shean."

Rizpah stared at him. "What did they do?"

The man flushed. "Well, it need not concern you," he said, starting to rise.

"Adriel, what did they do at Beth-shean?" Rizpah repeated, catching and holding his gaze.

"I—really, I don't think I should say."

Rizpah just stared at him.

Shaul's son-in-law slowly sat down. "After they found the bodies of Shaul and the sars, they hung them on the wall," he said in a low voice.

Rizpah gripped her stomach hard, bending over, sick. "When?" she demanded. "When did they hang them?"

"Late in the afternoon, day before yesterday."

Shaul's concubine pushed herself off the ground and stumbled away.

¥ ¥ ¥ ¥ ¥ ¥

Leaning on Ittai, Akish slowly made his way through the governor's palace at Beth-shean to the room that Muwana still occupied. The Ashkelon seren was sitting up, but the paleness of his face told everyone that he'd rather be lying down.

"How's your shoulder?" the seren asked as Akish eased into a chair.

"Feels as if it's on fire again today. Nothing seems to help."

"The healer is beginning to wonder if there was poison of some kind on the arrow," Muwana grunted.

"There wasn't," Ittai said quietly.

"How would you know?" the seren snarled, irritated.

"Your wounds will burn until you pay respect to Yahweh's dead," the young man replied.

"Yahweh has nothing to do with it! Yahweh was defeated by Dagon!"

"Was he?"

Muwana looked as if he might explode, so Akish flicked his hand at Ittai, dismissing him. His nephew left the room.

"Insolent half-blood!" Muwana spat.

Akish caught his fellow seren's eye. "He is also my nephew, Muwana. Take care how you speak of him."

The man snorted, but he looked down. "Why do you keep him around?" he asked in frustration.

"Because he speaks the truth. Now, what are the Five Cities going to do with our victory?"

"Victory is hardly the word to describe the mess we're in," the ruler of Ashkelon fumed. "And since the other serens are not here, we can decide nothing!"

"The other cities do not have serens at the moment. That leaves just you and me. And given the circumstances we find ourselves in, I don't think we have time to wait until the news reaches the other cities and they select new serens."

Muwana leaned his head back, his eyes calculating. "You may be right, Akish. There are some crucial decisions that need to be dealt with now, and we're the only ones able to make them."

"My thoughts exactly. There has been so much confusion, and we've kept the units so busy with the aftermath of battle, no one has had time to realize just what happened to us. That will change by tonight, so I suggest that we implement any plans we make this morning."

"Sound thinking, Akish. What do we have to work with?"

"Next to nothing. The backbone of our armies is gone, and it will take years to rebuild and train competent sars to command. The same with the serens. All we're left with are minor, inexperienced men, who will need a great deal of direction if we are to remain the principal power in the land.

"On the good side—"

"There is a good side?" Muwana said sarcastically.

"On the good side," Akish repeated, undisturbed, "the backbone of the Israelite army is gone also. From the reports I've gotten, nearly all of Shaul's professionals died with him. So Abner is in exactly the same position we are, only he doesn't have nearly the resources we do, and he doesn't hold the loyalty of the people like the hassar did."

"So the tribes just may fracture again," Muwana mused. "That *is* good news. It means that we don't necessarily have to control them by military means. We may be able to sit back, mend our wounds, and let them fall apart on their own."

"Exactly. But we do need to make some claim to victory, enough to keep Abner wary of us."

"How are we to do that?"

"We'll move into the Jezreel. As soon as word got out that we'd routed Shaul, all the Israelites there fled. Most of them went north, into Issachar, Naphtali, and Zebulon, but many have also come here to cross the Jordan. I've had agents out, listening to what's being said. The general opinion is that we have thoroughly defeated Israel and can do what we want from now on."

"And moving settlers into the vacant homes and estates will underline that. I like the way your mind works, Akish. Now, as to internal politics, we're going to have to call a meeting of every seren who survived, and place them in charge of the troops from their cities . . ."

Akish leaned back, pleased, as Muwana continued on that subject. He'd accomplished what he wanted. The Ashkelon seren had bought into his plan to make them the only two serens who counted in the alliance. And he'd successfully distracted Muwana from any thoughts of what those Habiru south of Gath might be useful for in the future.

¥ ¥ ¥ ¥ ¥ ¥

The whole population of Ziklag was up early, everyone eager to get the debris cleared away and houses repaired as soon as we could. Families needed shelter before the fall rains, and the weeks of summer left to us would be barely enough to get everything rebuilt.

The Cherethite women were embarrassingly grateful for the solution I found for their comfort, and I sent the younger boys under Casluh's direction to help them move. We were so hard at work that none of us noticed the stranger until he reached the market square. His clothes were torn, and dust and dirt covered his hair. The sight of him gradually brought silence to the square.

My stomach in a knot, I approached him.
"Dahveed Israel?"
I nodded.
Dropping to his knees, he then stretched out on the ground in front of me.
My heart suddenly pounding, I stepped closer. "Where have you come from?"
"I escaped from the Israelite war camp," he answered, getting on his knees.

Suddenly everything that might have happened up north while I was chasing the Amalekites ran through my mind. "How did things go?" I asked instantly.

He didn't reply.

"Please, tell me," I added.

"The people fled from the battle, adoni. Many of them died." The man looked up at me. "Shaul and Jonathan died also."

My heart stopped beating. Then a chill went through me and my heart pounded again. He couldn't have said what I heard. It couldn't be true. Maybe he'd just heard that, and was reporting it as truth.

"How do you know?" I demanded roughly, angry already that he would do such a thing to us.

"I was at Gilboa and happened on Shaul. He couldn't stand without the help of his spear, and the Philistines and chariots were nearly to him again. He turned around and saw me, adoni, and called me over, asking who I was. I told him I was an Amalekite. He saw the Philistines coming, and he asked me to kill him since he was in such pain, but still alive."

I listened, unable to believe what I heard. His words didn't make sense somehow.

"He couldn't have lived anyway, so I did what he asked. Then I took the king's headband, and his armband, and I brought them here to you, adoni," he finished, taking the things from the pouch he carried and holding them out to me.

"Yahweh save us!" someone whispered.

I stared at what he held. I'd seen the openwork of that headband flashing from Shaul's forehead too many times to mistake it now. Shaul was dead.

"Jonathan?" I asked, my voice hoarse.

The Amalekite shrugged.

I reached down and wrenched the hem of the kilt I wore, ripping it all the way to the girdle, the sound echoing all around me as my men did the same. Dazed, I landed on my knees. "Yahweh, it can't be true," I whispered. "It can't be!"

But Israel's crown gleamed in the sunlight before my eyes, and the matching armband shone beside it. Suddenly I slammed my fists into the ground. "NOOOOO!" I screamed, sobs shaking my body. But even as I mourned for Shaul, I knew in my heart that Jonathan was not dead! Yahweh loved him! He would preserve him, protect him from any harm! That man hadn't seen him dead, so he was still alive.

¥ ¥ ¥ ¥ ¥ ¥

The noon rest was over before Rizpah returned to Barzillai's compound in Jabesh. She had put dust in her hair and ripped her robe in three places. Dry-eyed, she checked on Judith and Meribbaal, relieved to see that the poppy given to the young boy still had him sleeping, although a feverish flush had spread across his cheeks. Judith refused to leave the lad, and Peleth had not yet arrived.

The concubine drank a little, then wandered out of the courtyard and found her way to the market by the city gates. The stalls were open, and people were there, but talk was quiet, and no one seemed interested in purchasing anything. The conversation stilled to complete silence as she approached the elders.

"Baalah," they said, nodding respectfully.

"What are you going to do about it?" she said without preamble. "We gave him our loyalty. He saved everyone in this city from King Nahash of Ammon. I stand testimony to our gratitude. Does it end with his death?"

A couple elders looked at each other as if she was crazed, but Barzillai turned to her. "Yes, we owe Shaul ben Kish, and you have taken our gratitude to him faithfully, giving him two fine sons who are with us today. What else do you see that we can do for our adon?"

"His body, and the bodies of his sons, hang on the wall of Beth-shean," she said, her voice flat. "Should our loyalty to him allow this?"

No one spoke.

"What would you have us do, Rizpah?" Barzillai asked gently.

"Bring them here, so that they may be decently buried. If not for them, half of this town would have been buried long before this day."

"Take them from the wall?" someone gasped. "The Egyptian governor would have our heads!"

"The Egyptian governor will most likely do nothing," Rizpah said. "His concern is the trade routes."

"The Philistines then, they would catch us, and we'd all be decorating that wall!"

Rizpah's head went up. "Our gratitude runs so shallow?"

"No," Barzillai said thoughtfully. "But our gratitude does no good if we die."

Silence settled on the crowd again, and Rizpah simply stood there, her very presence unsettling everyone.

"I'd be willing to go," a man said at last, stepping forward. "I was just old enough to be included in Nahash's decree when Shaul saved us. The baalah is right. It shames us all that our adon should be treated in this manner."

"He was Yahweh's Mashiah," another man spoke up. "To treat him so should not be done."

"And from what I've heard," Armoni, who had followed his immi to the market, now spoke, "the Philistines may not be so eager to come after us. There have been whispers that most of their commanders and serens perished in the battle."

The tall youth, who so resembled Shaul, seemed to be the final spark needed.

"I'll go," another man volunteered.

"So will I," someone else said, and a general murmur of assent rose from the crowd.

Barzillai turned to Rizpah, bowing slightly. "Go and rest, daughter," he said gently. "You have shown us the last service we can do for the one to whom we owe so much. It shall be as you wish."

Shaul's concubine left the market.

As dusk descended on the city, every fighting man Jabesh possessed filed out of the gate and down the road to the Arabah, headed for Beth-shean, 13 miles away on the other side of the Jordan.

Chapter 36

Day Ten

I watched the sun come up over the hills to the east. Shaul's regalia sat on the three-legged table in my house, which still had no roof, and the Amalekite who'd brought the news slept with several others of my men around one of the fires in the market. Our grief had confused the man. He had thought he was bringing good news, not being the harbinger of disaster.

But I'd had all night now to take apart the story that man had told, and it didn't make sense. There was too much that needed explaining. Who was he? His face was certainly Amalekite, but his clothing and manners were of Israel. Why would he have to "escape" from the Israelite camp? And if he had done that, what had he been doing at Gilboa? With the Philistines chasing Israelites in the Gilboa hills, escaping meant you would go anywhere but there.

"He lied," I said to the sun. I began to pace. He just happened upon Shaul on Gilboa? And the king was alone? That didn't make sense, either. "Chariots!" I said in disgust. "There's not a chariot made that can chase a man to exhaustion in those hills! It would be in pieces before it had gone half a mile, and the horses lamed in the bargain. Out on the plain, maybe, but not on Gilboa."

So what had really happened? How did I know that anything at all he said was true? Had Israel really been defeated by the Philistines? The only thing I knew for certain was that he had the king's regalia. He could very well be an escaped slave who had stolen it and brought it to me with his story, thinking I'd reward him when he brought me the "good" news.

That was the most likely, I told myself. He'd lied about everything. Maybe there hadn't been a battle yet at all. Shaul wasn't dead, and neither was Jonathan. Until I knew otherwise, I'd work on that assumption. I'd have to deal with this Amalekite, and just coming back from the Negev as I had, I wasn't feeling all that charitable toward any of his people, especially one who lied to me. Then I'd have to find some way to return the headband and armband. I couldn't imagine Shaul was too pleased to be without them.

Everyone was stirring around by now.

"Zelek?" I called, "Would you bring the Amalekite here? I've got a couple questions."

"Yes, adoni," my half-cousin said, returning in a few moments with the man in tow.

He looked a bit hopeful, as if he was finally going to be rewarded for his deeds.

"Where are you from?" I began.

His eyes flickered a little. "I'm the son of an Amalekite who lives in Israel," he replied.

"Where?"

"In the north," he said vaguely, shifting his feet.

"Why did you have to escape from the Israelite camp?"

He eyed me warily. "I didn't want to fight, adoni."

"If that's true, why did you run right to the battle?"

"There was nowhere else to go, adoni," he said sullenly, looking down.

"I've been to Gilboa. The hills there will not permit chariots to navigate in them."

"The chariots were out on the plain." He began to squirm.

"Then how could they be pressing closely on the king?"

Silence.

"You lied. But I will believe you are a resident in Israel, for your clothes and your accent testify that you are. You know, then, Yahweh's commands, and you know that you are required to live by them."

"I have not lied," the man protested. "Shaul asked me to kill him, to save him from the Philistines. I did so."

"So be it," I said, realizing that we'd never be able to find out the truth from him. One fact still stood, however. He had taken the king's regalia. If Shaul was alive, he had stolen them and was worthy of death. And if Shaul was dead, they belonged to Jonathan, so he had still stolen them and deserved death. And if he had really somehow killed Shaul, that in itself was a capital crime. But since he claimed to have killed Shaul, I would sentence him for that. "Knowing you are bound by Yahweh's commands, why weren't you afraid of destroying Yahweh's Mashiah?"

Sudden fear leaped into the man's eyes.

"Kill him," I said to Zelek.

The Ammonite obeyed instantly.

"His blood is on his own head because he said he killed Shaul, Yahweh's Mashiah," I pronounced formally. "Take his body and leave it on the grave beside the road to Gerar."

In disgust I turned away, going back to the house.

"What happened?" Abigail asked, watching Zelek and Elhanan carry the Amalekite's body outside the gates.

"He lied," I said shortly.

"Dahveed," she said softly. "He brought Shaul's regalia. You know the most likely thing is that Shaul is dead."

I slumped down against the table. "I know," I whispered. "But that doesn't mean Jonathan is dead. He never claimed to have seen the hassar dead, just that he killed the king. And if the hassar is alive, the crown and the armband belong to him."

Abigail's arms circled my shoulders. "You won't give up hope, will you?"

"I can't," I admitted. "It hurts too much to bear if I do."

We didn't know what to do that day. Some of the men stayed in the market quietly talking, others openly mourned, and still others worked a little, clearing out more of the houses. I paced, unable to settle down to anything, my heart fighting to retain hope even while the fear crept up on me that the Amalekite was right after all. Hanan had vanished, as was his way, and I'd sent for Shagay's Jonathan, hoping to send him out to see if he could learn anything, but he hadn't shown up yet, though hours had passed.

Ahinoam and Abigail kept the women and children organized, and we'd had a noon meal, although I had no idea what I'd eaten, or even if I'd eaten.

"Adoni, somebody's coming," Pekah shouted, running through the gap where the gates had been. "Jonathan's bringing him."

I strode out to the road down the slope. Toward the east, I saw Jonathan holding someone on a mule that limped badly as they slowly approached down the road.

My heart froze in my chest. I knew that mule. "Hassar!" I whispered, then found myself racing down the slope, somehow dodging the obstacles in my way. By the time I got to the road, I knew the figure on that mule wasn't the hassar, but I couldn't stop running.

"Who?" I asked as I dashed up.

"Nimshi," Jonathan said shortly. "He's in bad shape, adoni. He's been like this since I found him this morning."

Ethan's youngest son slumped on the mule, his face white and eyes glassy, his breathing in great shuddering sobs.

"Get him into the town, quickly," I ordered, grabbing the mule's bridle.

"Adoni, the mule can't go any faster."

By now, Pekah had arrived. I threw the reins to him and pulled Nimshi off and over my shoulders, carrying him as quickly as I could to the town.

Asahel met me at the gate, took one look, and started snapping orders while I eased the young man down by a fire.

"Dahveed," he said hoarsely. "Where's the Habiru Dahveed?"

"I'm here, Nimshi!" I said, lifting his shoulders from the ground. "You found me. You made it, Nimshi!"

"Dod?" he asked, his eyes trying to find me.

"Here, Nimshi. Right here," I said, touching his face.

He looked into my eyes, and then his face crumpled up, and he grabbed my shirt, his whole body shaking. "He sent me," he said. "I tried, but I fell, and then the Philistines came, and I had to bring this to you." After fumbling at his girdle, he pulled out the twisted brass earring on its gold chain. "They're dead, Dahveed," he sobbed. "All dead. The king, and Abbi, and my geber, and everyone. They were all killed right there!"

Burying his face in my shirt, he sobbed so hard that he seemed to shake everything around him.

My hand closed around the earring, unable to speak as pain slashed through me. I stayed there holding Nimshi in my arms as he choked out the words to tell us the gist of what had happened after he fell, bruising his right shin so badly that he couldn't walk, and the swelling on it even now was close to the size of a sling stone. He'd hidden until the night after the battle, then crawled away. The hassar's mule, wandering the hills, had found him, and he'd managed to get on and make his way east toward Beth-shean. Passing the city the next day, he had seen the bodies on the wall. After that, he didn't remember much, just heat and thirst and urging the mule on toward the south somehow. He clung to me even after Asahel got him to drink something, and after he was asleep, my nephew pried his hands from my shirt.

Moving away in a daze, I strapped on the harp case without thought. At last I found myself outside the town under the stars, at the high place beside the still-ruined altar. The thought of Israel's beloved Hassar, along with his Abbi and brothers, stripped and dead, pinned as war trophies on the walls of Beth-shean, was more than I could handle. I sat down and stared at the twisted brass earring dangling under my hands, unable to cry as my heart slowly tore itself in two.

516 ~ Yahweh's Soldier

The glory, O Israel, on your heights is pierced!
How have they fallen, the mighty ones?
Do not tell it in Gath,
Do not make it known in the streets of Ashkelon,
Lest they rejoice, the daughters of the Philistines,
Lest they exult, the daughters of the uncircumcised.

O Mountains of Gilboa,
Let no dew and no rain be on you, or fields of offerings;
For there it was defiled, the shield of the mighty.
The shield of Shaul was not anointed with the oil.

From the blood of the pierced ones,
From the fat of the mighty,
The bow of Jonathan did not recoil.
The sword of Shaul did not return empty-handed.

Shaul and Jonathan were the ones worthy of love,
and the ones delightful in their lives.
Even in their death, they were not separated.
They were swifter than eagles,
They were mightier than lions.

O daughters of Israel, bewail Shaul,
The one who clothed you luxuriously in scarlet,
The one who lifted up ornaments of gold on your clothing.

How are they fallen, the mighty ones, in the midst of the battle?
O Jonathan, pierced on your heights!
I am distressed over you, my brother Jonathan!
You were very pleasant to me!
It was wonderful, your love to me,
More than the love of women.

How have they fallen, the mighty ones?
That they perished, the implements of war?

Epilogue

Tamar bat Dahveed

Rizpah sat under the stars, watching as the men piled on a few more pieces of firewood and then lit the blaze. They were outside of Jabesh, and the men had returned from Beth-shean late that afternoon with the bodies of Shaul and his sons wrapped up on a cart. Since they had been dead for four days now, it was thought best to burn them, cleansing the bones for burial.

As the flames leaped up, Rizpah could finally weep for them. The entire town had gathered and remained there through the night, keeping the fire going until only the bones remained. Then, as dawn lit the sky, they carefully gathered them and placed them in the grave dug for them under a tamarisk tree outside of the town. A tamarisk, the concubine thought, fresh tears coming from her eyes, just like the one Shaul sat under in Gibeah to hold court on hot days.

She was the last to leave. "Rest here in peace, all of you," she said softly.

Tamar bat Dahveed
Second year of Solomon
(968 B.C.)

Maps

519

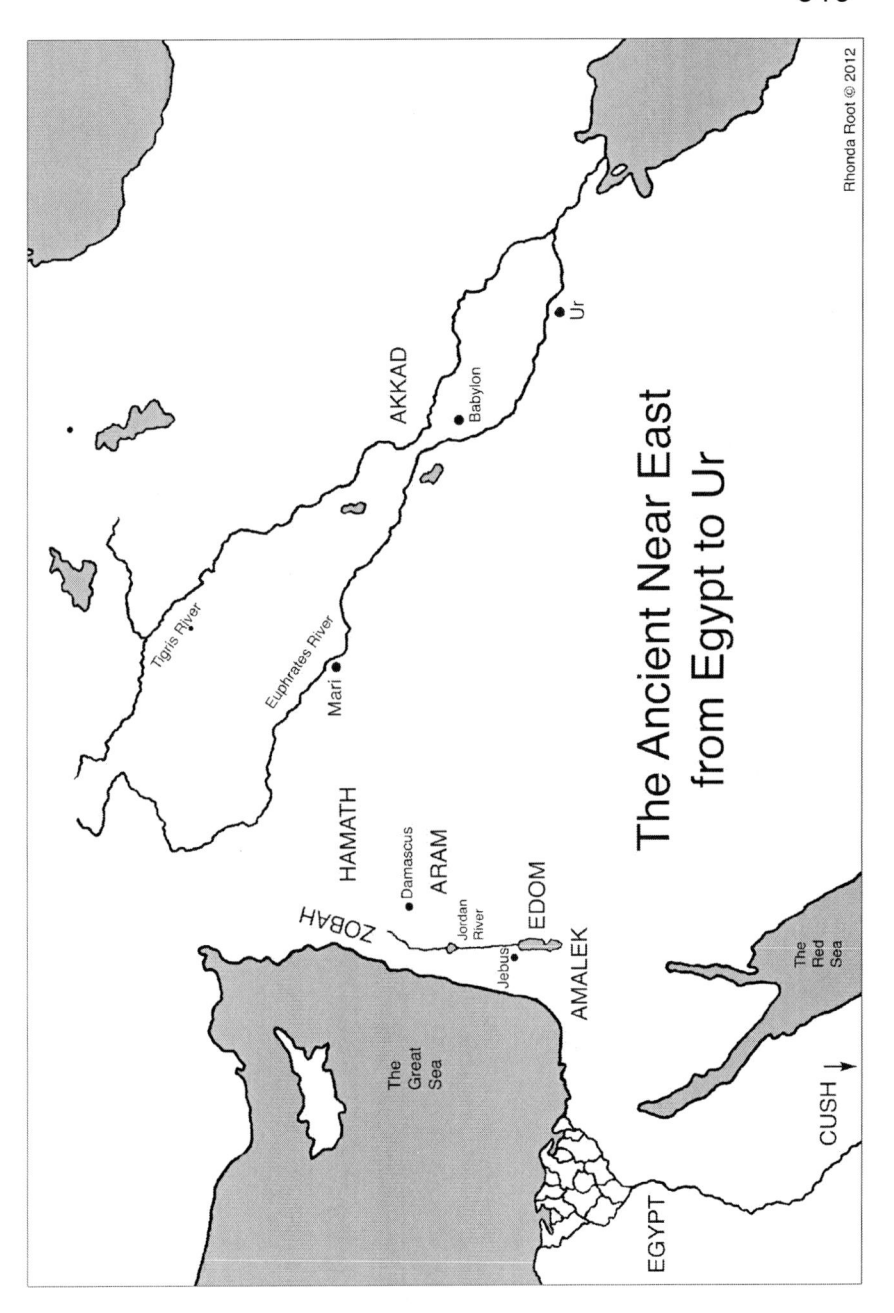

The Ancient Near East

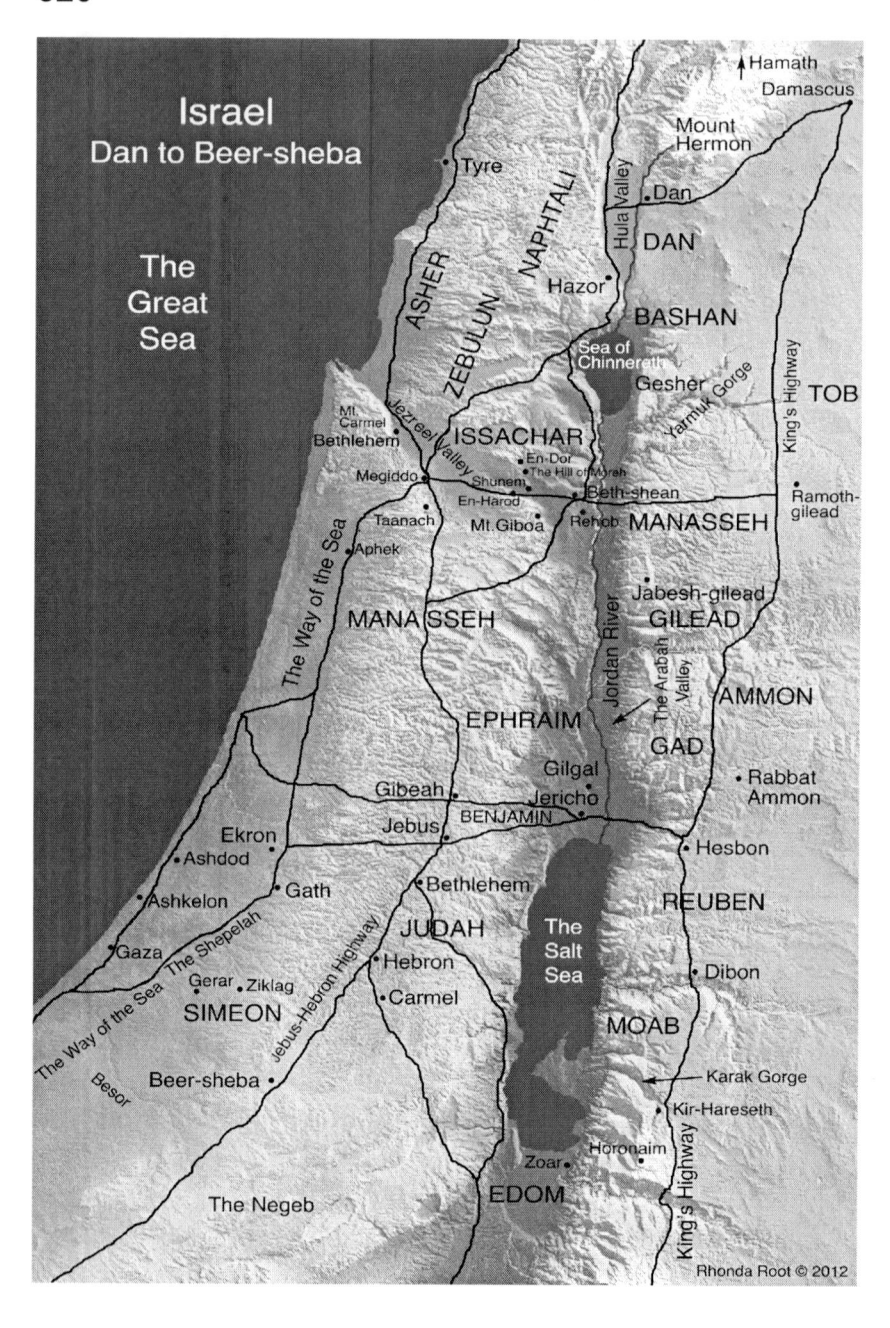

Israel

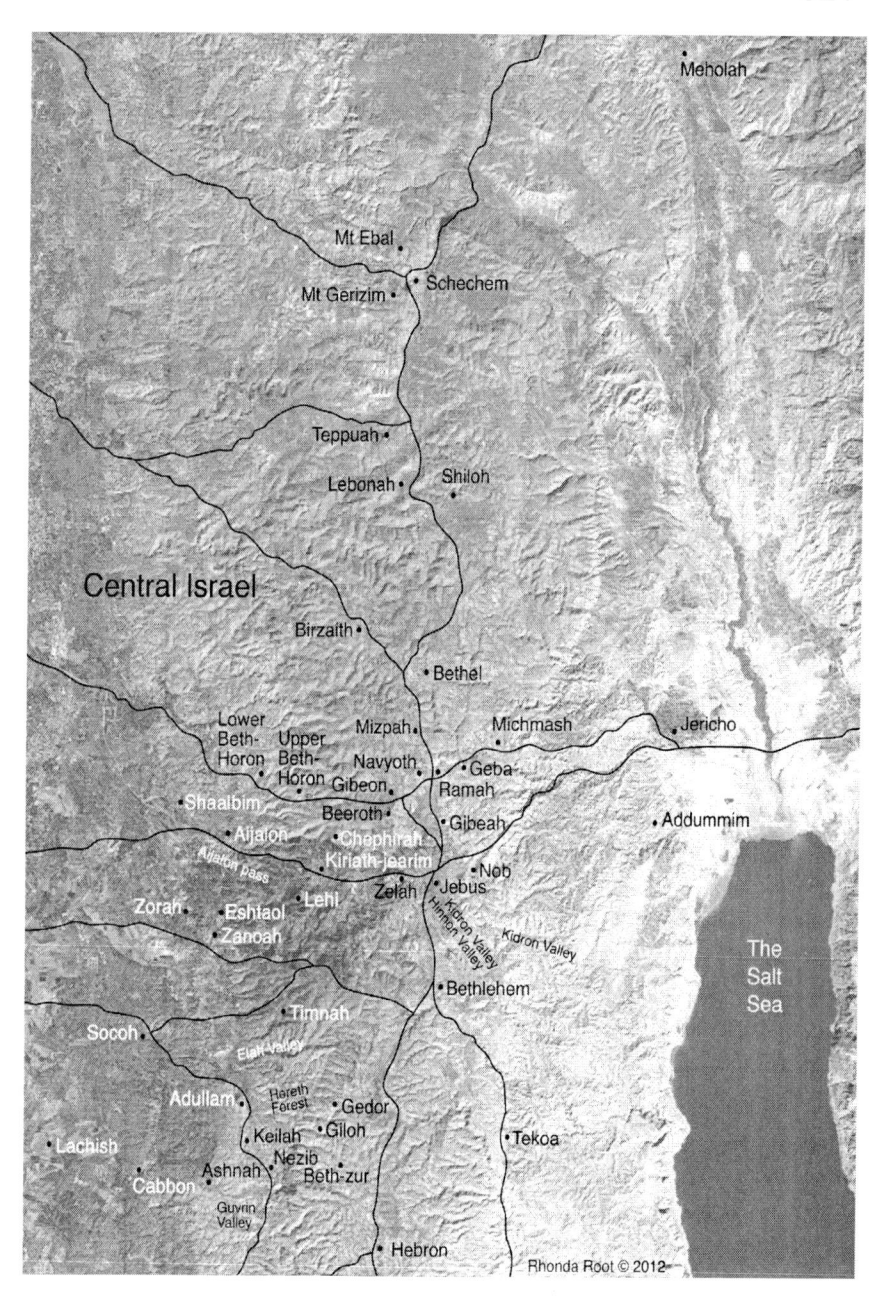

Central Israel